The
Disappearance
of
Alistair Ainsworth

Center Point
Large Print

Books are produced in the United States using U.S.-based materials

Books are printed using a revolutionary new process called THINKtech™ that lowers energy usage by 70% and increases overall quality

Books are durable and flexible because of Smyth-sewing

Paper is sourced using environmentally responsible foresting methods and the paper is acid-free

Also by Leonard Goldberg and available from Center Point Large Print:

The Daughter of Sherlock Holmes
A Study in Treason

**This Large Print Book carries the
Seal of Approval of N.A.V.H.**

THE
DISAPPEARANCE
of
ALISTAIR AINSWORTH

A DAUGHTER *of*
SHERLOCK HOLMES MYSTERY

Leonard Goldberg

CENTER POINT LARGE PRINT
THORNDIKE, MAINE

This Center Point Large Print edition
is published in the year 2019 by arrangement with
St. Martin's Publishing Group.

This is a work of fiction. All of the characters,
organizations, and events portrayed in this novel
are either products of the author's imagination
or are used fictitiously.

The text of this Large Print edition is unabridged.
In other aspects, this book may vary
from the original edition.
Printed in the United States of America
on permanent paper.
Set in 16-point Times New Roman type.

ISBN: 978-1-64358-391-4

The Library of Congress has cataloged this record under
Library of Congress Control Number: 2019946716

In memory of The Dink,
forever in our hearts

CONTENTS

Silence speaks when words cannot.
—ANONYMOUS

1

The Unannounced Visitor

November 1915

There are times when the forces of nature are so fierce they demand we seek immediate shelter and warmth. Such was the midwinter's night that found us ensconced in our rooms at 221b Baker Street. Outside, the wind howled in powerful gusts and the rain pelted our window so intensely it produced a sound reminiscent of fingers tapping on glass. My father and I sat around a cheery fire and tried to distract ourselves from the inclement weather by reviewing an old case of Sherlock Holmes's, which interestingly enough took place on a similar, dreadful night in London some twenty years ago.

"Holmes believed the wind and rain gave the criminal every advantage," my father remarked.

"It certainly made the investigator's task far more difficult," said I.

"Indeed it would, but in ways one might not anticipate."

"Such as?"

" 'Beyond the obvious,' Holmes had replied

when I asked him the very same question. Then he said no more." My father pondered the enigmatic answer briefly before glancing over to my wife. "Would you care to decipher that rather cryptic response, Joanna?"

She was standing by the window and staring out intently at the thoroughfare below, for something had caught and held her attention.

"What is it you see?" my father asked.

"Cover," Joanna replied.

"From what, pray tell?"

"From every crime you wish to mention," Joanna said, turning to us. "Which is also the answer to your first question. The obvious reason my father believed such weather favored the perpetrator is straightforward. It removes or distorts virtually every clue and track left behind. Give it a moment's thought and you can readily list the ways foul weather can throw the detective off."

"A strong wind and rain would certainly wash away any bloodstains or signs of a struggle," I proposed.

"But there would be other, less obvious advantages as well," Joanna went on. "The storm, along with its lightning and thunder, would drown out cries for help or screams of terror. And a heavy mist and rain would blind any eyewitnesses. You must also keep in mind that a lengthy gale, such as the one we are facing, would delay the arrival of Scotland Yard and give the criminals abundant time to escape and conceal their tracks."

I involuntarily raised my hand as a new thought came to mind. "Thus far, our discussion has been focused on crimes that occurred outdoors. Would not the dreadful weather be of less hindrance when the evil act is committed indoors?"

"The advantages, although somewhat diminished, would still hold for the criminal," said Joanna. "A clumsy investigator, along with a throng of constables, might well track mud and water onto the crime scene, and in the process muck up or eliminate any number of clues. Moreover, the thick walls of an enclosure would further dampen cries for help or screams of terror, which clearly work to the perpetrator's benefit."

"And Scotland Yard's response would remain less than prompt," my father noted.

"All of which explain why foul-weather crimes for the most part go unsolved," Joanna concluded.

Her attention was suddenly drawn back to the window. She moved in so close her nose seemed to be touching the glass pane. "I say! It seems we have a visitor coming our way."

My father and I hurried over and peered down at the hansom that had stopped at our doorstep. A hatless man, small and thin in figure, dashed toward the entrance of 221b Baker Street.

"Who would dare go out in this ungodly weather?" I asked.

"Someone with a most urgent need," Joanna replied.

"Which obviously cannot—" My voice was rendered inaudible by a loud crack of lightning, followed by a clap of thunder and an even heavier downpour of rain. Baker Street became little more than a blur through our window.

Moments later there was a soft rap on our door and our landlady, Miss Hudson, looked in. "Dr. Watson," she said to my father, "a Dr. Verner is downstairs and wishes to see you on a most pressing matter."

"Please show him up."

As the door closed, Joanna asked, "Do you know this Dr. Verner?"

"I do indeed," my father replied. "He bought my practice in Kensington just prior to my retirement."

"Have you remained in contact with him?"

"I happen upon him now and then at medical conferences I still manage to attend," said my father. "As a matter of fact, I chatted with him only last month at a symposium on malaria, at which time he informed me how well the practice was progressing. He also mentioned how superbly his son was performing at Eton, which of course is the same school your Johnny attends."

"Are they friends?"

"I asked, but Verner was unsure."

Joanna waved away that point of the conversation. "It is highly unlikely that he is here to talk of Eton or his son."

My father nodded. "Obviously it must concern a most serious medical dilemma."

"Do you believe he is here to consult on a former patient of yours?" I inquired.

"That would be most unusual, particularly at this time of night and in this weather, unless the patient was in great distress. If that was the case, such a patient would best be served in a hospital, like St. Bart's, where Verner has admitting privileges."

"Perhaps he wishes you to join him there," Joanna suggested.

My father pointed to the telephone. "That would not require an out-of-the-way journey to Baker Street. Bear in mind that when a patient is in dire straits, the smallest amount of time can be of the greatest consequence."

We heard a second rap on our door and Miss Hudson showed in the thin, rain-drenched visitor. Dr. Alexander Verner was even smaller than he appeared at a distance, with a height barely reaching five feet. His face had fine, gentle features, but there was distress in his eyes.

"Here," my father said, taking the doctor's soaked topcoat and scarf. "Warm yourself by the fire while I hang up your garments."

As Verner sat in a cushioned chair, I noticed a tremor in his hands that could not have come from a chill, for our sitting room was nicely warmed by a three-log fire.

"How long was your walk?" Joanna asked.

Verner looked at her quizzically. "From my hansom to your doorstep?"

"No, no. From the lengthy walk you took prior to entering your hansom."

"How could you possibly know this?"

"From your soaked outer garments and shoes, the latter of which produce a watery squish with each step you take and leave behind a wet footprint on the floor of our parlor. Your shoes could not be so affected by the short journey from your hansom to our doorstep. They have obviously been exposed to a long walk elsewhere through the rain, for the mud and grass clinging to their soles and heels are not to be found on the cobblestone streets of London. So I can deduce you were very recently about in the countryside or in some locale that was similar to it."

Verner's face brightened for a moment. "You must be the daughter of Sherlock Holmes I have read of and so admired."

"I am indeed."

Verner turned to me and said, "And your resemblance to your father tells me you are the son of the good Dr. Watson."

"Correct, sir," I said.

"If you wish, my husband and I can adjourn to our room and give you and Dr. Watson total privacy," Joanna offered.

"Oh, please stay," Verner implored. "For I am certain it will require all of your minds and wits to make sense of the harrowing adventure I have just experienced."

"Harrowing, you say!" my father exclaimed as he drew up a chair.

"I do not exaggerate, my dear Watson. When I give you the particulars, you will understand how unnerving my journey was and continues to be. It all began with a late-afternoon caller to my practice who had a most unexpected request. He introduced himself as the representative of a distinguished personage who had a seizure disorder and was now suffering with abdominal pain. The visitor had learned of my knowledge in gastrointestinal disorders and implored me to come with him and see the patient. I of course agreed and closed my practice for the day, believing there was nothing peculiar about the caller or his request. But this changed the moment I stepped into the carriage awaiting us. Its windows were covered with thick cloth that allowed in only streaks of the late-afternoon light, which was quite dim because of the approaching storm. It was therefore impossible to see out and determine our direction. The visitor explained that it was necessary to keep the whereabouts

17

of the ill patient a secret because neither his identity nor location were to be disclosed under any circumstances. Such measures, I was told, were required for high-profile, distinguished individuals for whom public disclosure of illness could have unwanted consequences. This suggested to me that the patient to be seen was either royalty or a governmental official of considerable standing. Despite these assurances I remained uneasy, for there was something foreboding about the caller. He projected an air of cruelty that indicated he was not a man to be trifled with."

Verner paused, as if to gather his thoughts. But the expression on his face turned more ominous. "I assumed the patient resided close by, but this was not the case. Our journey lasted at least thirty minutes, but it was not straightforward by any means. I had the distinct impression that at times we were traveling about in circles, followed by a series of sharp turns. It was impossible to tell where we were or our direction."

Joanna interrupted. "Were you moving over cobblestones or a paved road?"

"Both. While riding over cobblestones, the wheels produced noise that muffled the sounds outside our carriage. When we rode over smooth, paved streets, I occasionally heard motorcars passing by or the screech of brakes being applied."

"Were the brakes loud, such as those made by a bus or similar large transport vehicles?"

"I could not tell, for the rain was beginning to fall heavily and it muted other sounds. Is that important?"

"It could be, for we are dealing in darkness here and any glimmer of light might be most helpful."

"I did see streaks of light intermittently at the edge of the cloth curtains covering the carriage windows."

"For the entire journey?"

"For the first half or so."

"Which indicates you were on a major thoroughfare."

"But then it became quite dark."

"Which tells us you had most likely entered a residential neighborhood."

"And so we had," Verner concurred. "When the carriage came to a final stop, we were in a neighborhood that was quiet, with large, two-story houses belonging to the upper middle class. I should mention it was very dark indeed because the path leading up to the house was lined with trees and covered with shadows. I was hurried into a foyer that contained a small table with unopened mail stacked upon it. Unfortunately I was not near enough to read an address. As soon as my hat and coat were removed, I was led into a large, sparsely furnished bedroom. There was a single bed upon which rested a heavyset man, with a protuberant abdomen and the look of distress on his face. At this point I was told that the patient was a mute and could communicate only in sign language, with which I am unfamiliar. Thus, the patient had to write down his symptoms using chalk and a small blackboard."

"Did he have a good command of the English language?" Joanna asked.

"Quite."

"Did he write like an Englishman would or was there evidence of foreign influence?"

"Definitely an Englishman."

"Pray continue."

"And so my examination began. He complained of abdominal pain of a day's duration, with some nausea and lack of appetite. I next went to palpating his abdomen and it was at this point I felt something was amiss. He had motioned to the umbilical area as being the area of greatest pain, and when I pressed upon it he moaned loudly."

"Nothing unusual there," my father remarked.

"What was unusual," Verner continued on, "was that he made no hand sign to express his pain. I have seen a number of mutes in my practice over the years, and when you press on a tender spot they automatically make a hand sign, indicating pain and telling you to stop. And they do not groan, but cry out with a high-pitched utterance. The patient did neither and I began to wonder if his complaints were those of a feigned illness.

"Now, I realize my conclusion thus far is based on subjective findings, but what I am about to disclose is not. When I asked the patient to point to the exact location of greatest pain, he took my hand and placed it to the right of the umbilicus. Then I inquired if the pain radiated away from that site and he slowly moved my hand to the left and surreptitiously spelled out the word *HELP,* which was written in letters."

"Are you absolutely certain of this?" Joanna asked at once.

"At first I was not, but then I asked the patient to again demonstrate how the pain radiated. Once more he carefully guided my hand and wrote the word *HELP.* I next adjusted the position of my body so the other man in the room could not visualize my hand, and I spelled out the word *NAME* on the patient's abdomen. He responded with the letters *TU* and was adding a third but did not continue, for the other man moved in for a closer look. Thus, no further messages could be transmitted between us."

"Could you make any meaning of the interrupted third letter?"

"It seemed to be a straight vertical line, with a curvature at its top, but it was indecipherable."

Joanna furrowed her brow in thought and began to softly utter a string of letters to herself. She would nod at one, then shake her head at another.

"Any ideas, Joanna?" I asked.

"Too many," she replied. "A straight vertical line with the beginning of a curve at its top could be a *b, d, p,* or *r.* And we do not know if it is a complete three-letter word or simply the start of a longer one. The possibilities are too numerous."

"My thoughts exactly," Verner said.

Joanna waved away the problem for the moment. "I take it the other man in the room watched your every move from then on."

"Like a hawk. Something I had done had obviously aroused his suspicions."

"Perhaps it was your prolonged examination of the patient's abdomen," my father surmised. "Or your movement to obscure the man's view of your hands."

"It could have been either or both," Verner said. "In any event, I completed my examination and pronounced the diagnosis to be acute inflammation of the gallbladder that demanded immediate hospitalization. The other man stated this was not possible, for it would surely expose the patient's identity. Thus, all treatment would have to be done at home. I explained the risks if we followed that course of action, but it seemed to make no impression. Thus I had no choice but to prescribe laudanum for pain and asked to be notified if the patient's symptoms worsened."

My father asked, "Did you mention the

possibility of peritonitis, which could be a death knell in this instance?"

Verner nodded. "I did, but to no avail. It was made quite clear that hospitalization was out of the question. Despite my dire warning, I was ushered out of the house and into the carriage with all of its windows still covered. I was instructed not to mention my visit or the patient to anyone, for to do so could result in incalculable harm. I was further told that if I did not follow these instructions, the consequences could be very unpleasant for all concerned. As I noted earlier, his voice was cold and menacing, and left no doubt whatsoever to whom the threat was directed. Trust me when I say I could not wait to separate myself from that man and his carriage. We proceeded to ride in silence over cobblestone and paved roads, with no sounds to be heard or sights to be seen. After nearly twenty minutes the carriage stopped and I was let out without a single word, although I was paid two pounds for my services. So here I was in the midst of a storm, with the cold wind howling and a pounding rain soaking me to the marrow. I walked a good mile before I came to Hampstead Station where I was able to hire a hansom that brought me to 221b Baker Street. I know my story sounds strange and most peculiar and at times farfetched, but I swear to you it is true in every regard. And although no crime can be proven here, I fear a man's life may be in danger." Verner took a long, worrisome breath before adding, "Perhaps I should have gone to Scotland Yard."

Joanna flicked her wrist at the notion. "They would have paid little attention to your story. They would have demanded evidence that a crime had been committed or was in progress, and you had none."

"But the poor mate was crying out for help," I argued.

"Which breaks no law," Joanna countered. "Also, remember that the patient suffered from a seizure disorder. Had he experienced a recent attack, he may have been disoriented and unaware of the people around him. When introduced to the newly arrived Verner, he felt he could trust the kind doctor and thus issued a plea for help."

My father nodded in agreement. "When Joanna was a practicing nurse, she no doubt saw this strange transformation after a seizure. I too have seen the postictal phase of an attack last for half an hour or more, with disorientation a prominent feature."

"And this would be particularly pronounced in a dark room with no sound," Joanna added.

Verner stared at Joanna at length. "Are you telling me that no crime has been committed here?"

"No, Dr. Verner," Joanna said, reaching for a

cigarette and carefully lighting it. "I am telling you why Scotland Yard would give little attention to your story. I, on the other hand, find your adventure to be of considerable interest. But I require more details if we are to put this puzzle together. Let us begin with the prisoner. Can you describe him for us?"

"I must tell you that the bedroom was not well lighted, and his bed was against a far wall where the lighting was dimmest. Thus it was not possible to delineate all his features. Nevertheless, I could ascertain he was a short, heavyset man, in his middle years, with unkempt hair and an unshaven face. The odor of his body indicated he had not bathed for a number of days."

"Were there any distinguishing features, such as scars, blemishes, or evidence of foul play?"

"None that could be seen."

"What of the bedroom he occupied? How was it furnished?"

"It was quite sparse, with only a bed and several wooden chairs."

"Did it contain mirrors or paintings on the wall?"

"None."

"A dresser?"

"No."

"Curtains?"

"Tightly drawn."

Joanna stood and began pacing the floor,

leaving a trail of cigarette smoke behind. "Was the patient dressed in nightclothes?"

"He was not," Verner answered. "His shoes were removed, but he continued to wear trousers and shirt."

"Tell us of their quality."

"The trousers were well tailored and made of tightly woven wool. His shirt was opened so I could examine the patient's abdomen. It too was well made and had the feel of fine Egyptian cotton."

Joanna spun around. "Was there a monogram on the shirt?"

"None that could be seen."

"Most unfortunate," Joanna said, muttering to herself, as she went back to pacing. "When the mute patient answered your questions on the blackboard, are you quite certain he wrote as an Englishman would?"

"Very much so," Verner replied. "On my inquiring if he had gastric distress, he reported he had a *touch* of nausea. Not a little or small amount, but a *touch*, much like an Englishman would say."

"Well put," Joanna said, apparently pleased with the information. "Now be good enough to describe in detail the man who came to your office and guided you back to the patient."

"He was tall and broad shouldered, with a ramrod-straight posture, reminiscent of a military officer. His hair was blond and cut short, although I saw only its fringes because he wore a derby."

"And the color of his eyes?"

"Blue and cold as ice."

"Were there any distinguishing features about his face?"

"None that stood—" Verner stopped in mid-sentence and pointed to his cheek. "He had a noticeable tic about his left eye. The spasms around his orbit occurred with some frequency and involved both the face and eyelid."

"Was there any evidence of trauma around the affected eye?"

"None that I could see, which suggested it was a true nervous system disorder."

Joanna nodded at Verner's assessment and hummed softly to herself, indicating she was storing the presence of the facial tic in her memory bank. "Very good," she continued on. "Now please tell us about the man's voice."

"It was cold and menacing, and left no doubt that—"

"No, no," Joanna interrupted. "I am not interested in the emotions it elicited, but in its origin. Did the man speak English like it was his mother tongue?"

Verner gave the matter thought before answering. "His grammar was quite good, but at times he spoke as if he had learned the language in school."

"Let us have an example."

"When I completed my examination and was about to leave the bedroom, he said, 'Now we return to our carriage.' An Englishman would have never put it that way."

"Indeed," Joanna said, as a hint of a smile came to her face. "While you were in the house, did you come across any others, man or woman?"

"There was one other man whom I neither saw nor heard."

"Then how did you learn of his presence?"

"There was a bit of noise in an adjoining room that upset the man who brought me to the house. The man opened a side door and yelled out something that ended with the word *FENSTER*. It may well have been a person's name, of that I cannot be sure. Then I heard the sound of a drawer closing before the door was shut. Thus, I assumed there was another man present and that he had been given a command of some sort."

"I believe your assumptions are for the most part correct."

"And my assumption that the poor man is a prisoner being held against his will?"

"That too is correct."

"Then how will you proceed?"

"By making the necessary inquiries," Joanna said, and walked over to the rack that held Verner's topcoat and scarf. "And now the hour is late and you should be on your way. I take it your hansom awaits you?"

"It does," Verner said, being helped into his outer garments. "Is there any further assistance I can lend in this matter?"

"Not at the moment."

"What if the man returns for me to again examine the patient? I would have no choice but to accompany him back to the house that holds the prisoner. Indeed, I might be forced to do so."

Joanna considered the doctor's dilemma at length before asking, "Do you have chloroform in your office?"

"A goodly supply."

"Then somehow manage to spill some of it on your shoes prior to leaving with him."

"That is a rather odd request."

"Your life may depend on it."

Verner's eyes flew open. "Why would they do me harm?"

"Because you are the only link to the patient's true identity, and they will go to any lengths to ensure he remains nameless."

2

The Advertisement

As was my custom, I awoke early the next morning but found Joanna's side of the bed vacant. After dressing quickly, I entered our parlor and was greeted by a dense haze of cigarette smoke, through which Joanna was pacing back and forth. She rarely smoked except when involved in a difficult case, at which time she could easily consume two packs of cigarettes daily. And like her esteemed father before her, she could go sleepless for days until the problem was solved or she determined more data was needed before a solution could be reached. My father, attired in a maroon smoking jacket, was seated in a cushioned chair and puffing on his favorite cherrywood pipe, all the while watching Joanna pace.

"It appears my wife has a three-pipe problem before her," I remarked, referring to Sherlock Holmes's description of a perplexing case that required at least three pipes to bring to a successful conclusion.

"So it would appear," my father agreed. "Yet at the rate she is smoking, I fear the underlying reason for Verner's harrowing adventure continues to escape her."

"To the contrary, my dear Watson. The purpose is well in hand," Joanna said. "It is the solution that remains problematic."

"Please inform us of its purpose," I requested.

Our conversation was interrupted by a gentle rap on the door. Miss Hudson stepped in and was immediately aghast at the cloud of smoke that enveloped her. She hurried over to the window and opened it for fresh air to flow in.

"How can you possibly remain in this room under such foul conditions?" Miss Hudson asked.

"Because, Miss Hudson, the conditions lend themselves to solving a most urgent problem," Joanna replied.

Miss Hudson uttered a hopeless sigh and handed my father several morning newspapers. "Would now be a convenient time for breakfast, Dr. Watson?"

"If you would be so kind," my father said.

Upon Miss Hudson's departure, Joanna dashed over to close the window. "She means well, but is unaware of the high-stakes game that confronts us. You see, the captive that Verner described to us will shortly end up dead unless we intervene."

"What is this dreadful assumption based on?" I asked.

"Everything we have been told," Joanna replied.

"The entire story of the mute patient is a total fabrication. First, we are required to believe that the patient is a distinguished personage in whom disclosure of illness would cause public alarm. This would indicate the individual is well-known royalty or a high-ranking official in the British government who would be easily recognized. All of which is absolute nonsense. Officials at the highest level, as well as the royalty, have their own personal physicians who are always at their immediate disposal. Furthermore we are asked to believe this well-known, distinguished individual is a mute. Is there a member of the royal family who is so afflicted? Can you envision any politician, whose career depends on his ability to speak and convince, being unable to do so? And if by chance there was such a rare individual, he would be widely publicized and instantly recognized by Dr. Verner. Thus, we can conclude this person is neither royalty nor a politician at the highest level nor a mute. He was presented as a mute and made to write his words to ensure he could not reveal his identity or circumstances."

"And Verner was under the impression that the patient was feigning his illness," my father added.

"Precisely," Joanna went on. "The prisoner feigned an illness so that his captors would have no recourse other than to call in a physician. This of course could provide him with an opportunity

33

to inform the doctor of his situation. It may have represented his only chance of escape."

"The prisoner seems to be quite clever," I remarked.

"Even more clever than you believe," Joanna said. "His brain thinks several moves ahead, much like a chess master outmaneuvering his opponent. He could have chosen a variety of illnesses that required the presence of a doctor, yet he selected abdominal pain. Why? Because he knew the doctor would ask him the exact location of the pain and, since he could not speak, he could guide the doctor's hand to the right side of the abdomen. From there, he might be able to surreptitiously spell out his cry for help. So, taking into account the cut of his clothes, we have a very astute, upper-class Englishman who is being held captive."

"To what end?" I asked at once.

"For classified information, I would think."

My father and I exchanged puzzled glances before I asked, "Upon which evidence do you base this?"

"The identity of his captors," Joanna replied. "You see, he is being held by Germans, which makes me believe they are holding him for information he has and they desperately want."

"How can you possibly know that the man's captors are German?"

"By their use of the word *FENSTER*, which

Verner thought was the name of a man who was being called upon," Joanna answered. "Recall that Verner heard a sentence with the word *FENSTER* in it, and this was followed by the sound of a drawer being closed. He overheard correctly, but drew the wrong conclusion. *FENSTER* in German means window, and the man was ordering another to close a window. That was the sound Verner misinterpreted as being a drawer being shut."

My father bolted upright suddenly. "Are you saying the Englishman was taken captive by German agents?"

"Since we are currently at war with Germany, that would be a logical assumption," Joanna said. "But everything revolves around the man whose name begins with the letters *TU*. Until we know his identity, I fear we remain in the dark."

"With the prisoner's life at stake."

"That too."

"Scotland Yard must be notified," my father urged.

"So they shall be shortly," Joanna said, crushing out her cigarette in an overflowing ashtray. "But for now, Watson, I will leave you to your newspapers while I change into clothes more suitable for one of Miss Hudson's sumptuous breakfasts. I suggest you begin with the *Daily Telegraph*, which tends to report the more current London news."

"Is there anything in particular that I should search for?"

"Look for unusual happenings in the upper-class neighborhoods of Belgravia, Mayfair, and the like."

"Do you believe our man is an aristocrat?"

"Perhaps. Or with his sharp mind, he might have associates in these neighborhoods and his absence would be noted and reported."

My father scanned the *Daily Telegraph* while I busied myself with the *Standard*. We saw nothing of interest on their fronts but, as we turned to the inner pages, my father abruptly jerked his head forward. He read hurriedly, moving his lips but making no sound until he cried out, "I think we have our man!"

Joanna rushed out of our bedroom and, sitting on the arm of his chair, peered over my father's shoulder as he read from the notice.

> "Anyone supplying information on the whereabouts of Alistair Ainsworth, who also responds to the name Tubby, will be rewarded. Because of injury, he may not be aware of his identity. To gain the above reward, please reply to X2810."

Joanna jumped to her feet and asked my father, "Do you have Verner's phone number?"

My father reached for the nearby phone and

quickly dialed the doctor's number by memory. Holding the phone close to his ear, he waited only a moment before dialing the number once more. "The line is busy," he announced.

Joanna raced for the bedroom as she called over her shoulder, "We must hurry!"

"To Scotland Yard?" my father asked.

Joanna shook her head. "To Verner's office, for his life is now in real and immediate danger."

"But he did not write the notice," I argued mildly. "He had no knowledge of the prisoner's name."

"It does not matter whether he wrote it or not, for the Germans will believe he did and thus want him silenced permanently," Joanna elucidated. "It is the time sequence that is so important here. Alistair Ainsworth has been missing, for days on end, as evidenced by his unkempt appearance, which Verner duly noted. Yet concern for his disappearance suddenly shows up in print only now, shortly after Verner's visit. The Germans may have no proof that Verner had the notice published, but they will suspect he did and take no chances."

We grabbed our coats and hats and dashed down the stairs, passing a startled Miss Hudson carrying up our breakfast tray.

"Will you be returning shortly?" she called out.

We did not bother to answer, for our minds were totally occupied with the terrible fate awaiting Alexander Verner.

3

Dr. Verner's Office

We did not make good time, for traffic was heavy and sections of the streets remained flooded with last evening's torrential downpour. Nevertheless, Joanna used my father's walking stick to repeatedly rap on the roof of our carriage, urging the driver to go faster and faster.

"Perhaps the Germans did not read the morning newspaper," I hoped.

"I can assure you they have," Joanna said. "They will scour over every page, searching for information about the missing man and whether there is any mention of an ongoing investigation. You see, the Germans are aware they have a valued prize on their hands and will wish to know if there are any clues indicating the authorities are closing in on them."

"But it is unlikely such information would find its way into the newspapers," I argued.

"To the contrary, Scotland Yard takes great delight in publicizing their pursuits and accomplishments, real or imagined. They do this to project an image of sharpness that is all too often lacking."

My father nodded at Joanna's assessment. "Holmes would tell you that, with few exceptions, they are a collection of bunglers who depend on informants to solve most of their cases. It is not that they don't have brains; it is that they refuse to use them."

"Then our last, best hope is that Verner read the morning papers and, realizing the danger, has fled," I said.

"That is wishful thinking," said Joanna. "Had Verner read the notice, he would have certainly called to inform us of the new information and to seek further instructions."

My father sighed dispiritedly. "Everything seems to be going against poor Verner."

"Let us pray we are not too late," said Joanna.

But it appeared we were. Stationed at the doorstep to Verner's practice were two police constables. Because of our past association with Scotland Yard, we were recognized and allowed immediate entrance. Expecting the worst, we hurried into Verner's surgery but found only Inspector Lestrade standing amidst evidence that indicated a struggle had taken place. A metal stool and instrument table were overturned, with scalpels and forceps strewn about the floor. Off to the side was a medicine cabinet, with its glass door shattered and blood smeared across its handle. The strong odor of chloroform filled the air.

Our presence seemed to catch Lestrade by surprise. He tipped his hat to us and, skipping the usual amenities, asked, "Are you friends with Dr. Verner?"

"He is a former colleague who bought my practice some years ago," my father replied.

"I take it this is not a social call."

"It is not."

"May I then inquire as to the purpose of your visit this morning?"

"We hoped to prevent harm from coming to Verner."

"And pray tell, how did you know this harm might occur?"

"Because my daughter-in-law predicted it."

Lestrade gave us a long quizzical look. "How did she arrive at this conclusion?"

"From a meeting we had with Verner late last night."

"Here?"

"In our rooms at 221b Baker Street."

"Might I know the reason for this late-night meeting?"

"Perhaps the most unusual tale you will ever hear," my father responded. "Please allow my daughter-in-law to describe the frightful journey Verner was compelled to take."

"Compelled, you say?" Lestrade asked at once.

"*Persuaded* may be a better word," Joanna said, and began a detailed narrative, often using

41

Verner's own words to describe the major features.

Lestrade listened intently, but his interest was obviously piqued by the mention of a carriage, with its windows covered, that traveled a most circuitous route. He tapped a finger against his chin before asking, "The doctor had no idea of his destination?"

"None whatsoever," Joanna replied. "He was told the patient was a personage of high standing whose identity and location were not to be disclosed under any circumstances."

"Strange," Lestrade commented.

"Stranger yet was the fact that the patient was supposedly a mute who could only converse with chalk and blackboard, since Verner was not familiar with sign language. I will not go into detail at this point, but suffice it to say Verner was under the distinct impression that the patient was feigning his symptoms of abdominal discomfort."

"Why would the patient conjure up such an illness?"

"As a clever way to communicate. When asked where his pain was most severe, the patient took Verner's hand and pressed it to his abdomen. When asked if the pain moved about, the patient surreptitiously guided the doctor's hand and spelled out the word *HELP* on his abdomen."

Lestrade's eyes widened. "Was Dr. Verner convinced of this?"

"Beyond any doubt, for Verner repeated the question and once more the patient wrote the word *HELP*. In that a secret method of communication was now established, Verner inquired as to the patient's name. The supposed mute was only able to spell the letters *TU* before he was compelled to stop because his captor had become suspicious and moved in for a closer look. Verner quick-wittedly made the diagnosis of acute inflammation of the gallbladder and advised immediate hospitalization in an effort to remove the patient from his captivity. But the captors refused to follow the advice and only asked for pain medication before sending Verner on his way."

Lestrade shook his head in wonderment. "In all my years I have never heard such a tale."

"Nor I," Joanna said. "And now allow me to explain why we feel Dr. Verner is in such danger. After departing the patient's house, he was driven some twenty minutes away and unceremoniously let out in the midst of a storm, with a most menacing warning not to mention the patient or his illness to anyone. He was told the consequences of such action would be very unpleasant for all involved. We of course advised Verner to follow those instructions while we devised a plan of action."

"I take it he did not and this is the reason for your alarm."

"Oh, but he did. Unfortunately his captors thought otherwise. You see, in the morning newspaper, there was a notice offering a reward for information on the whereabouts of Alistair Ainsworth who also responds to the name Tubby. Thus it seems clear that our supposedly mute patient was attempting to spell out his nickname."

Lestrade's jaw dropped. In an instant he dashed to the door of the surgery and closed it securely. When he rejoined us, he spoke in a voice so low it resembled a whisper. "Have you spoken to anyone of this?"

"Only you," Joanna replied.

"See that it stays that way," Lestrade said. "For you have entered dangerous waters."

"Please be so kind as to—"

Lestrade held up his hand. "At this point, you must allow me to ask the questions, with you supplying the most detailed of answers. It is the location of the house the doctor visited that is of obvious importance. Although the windows of his carriage were covered, did he give you any information on the neighborhood they eventually reached?"

"Only that it was residential and of the upper class. It was quite dark, but he could discern the house was two storied and well built."

"And its interior?"

"Unremarkable, except there were indications the home was rented."

"Why rented?"

"A number of features, which included a lack of furniture and no mirrors or paintings on the walls. In addition, there was unopened mail stacked up on a table in the foyer. Obviously the captors had little interest in the mail. Long-term occupants would, short-term renters would not."

"Did Dr. Verner give a description of these captors?"

Joanna thought for a moment before saying, "He came in contact with only one. The man was tall and broad shouldered, with close-cut blond hair and a noticeable facial tic."

"His accent?" Lestrade asked pointedly.

"Neutral, but he was in all likelihood a German."

"Based on his physical characteristics?"

"Based on his use of the word *FENSTER*," Joanna said, and explained its German meaning and the context in which the term *window* was used. "There is no doubt that German was his native tongue."

An expression of deep concern came to Lestrade's face and this was attested to by the gravity of his next words. "We must locate this house at all costs. There is not a moment to lose."

"Unfortunately we have so little to go on," my father said unhappily. "There are dozens of upper-class residential neighborhoods in London, all of which have well-built houses too numerous to count."

"But the house was in all likelihood leased," Lestrade noted. "Perhaps we could narrow down our search somewhat by inquiring about recent rentals from leasing agents."

"That would take far too long," Joanna pointed out. "Moreover, we do not know if the house was in fact let by an agent and, if it was, how long ago the transaction took place."

"The owner could have simply posted a to-let advertisement in various bulletins or newspapers," I added.

Lestrade sighed resignedly. "I am open to any other courses of action we might pursue."

"There is one that may prove worthwhile," Joanna said, and motioned to a small broken bottle on the floor next to the bloodstained cabinet. "You will note the strong odor of chloroform that emanates from that broken vial. A fierce struggle took place here during which the cabinet door was smashed and a small bottle of chloroform fell to the tile floor and shattered. Dr. Verner and his captors may have stepped upon the damp areas of chloroform and thus they carry its scent on the soles and heels of their shoes."

"So?" Lestrade asked impatiently.

"It can be followed."

"By whom, may I ask?"

"By a hound named Toby Two who has the keenest nose in all London."

"Where do we find this hound?"

"At number three Pinchin Lane in the lower quarter of Lambeth," Joanna replied by memory. "Tell the kennel owner that only Toby Two will do and that the request is made by Dr. Watson, the longtime associate of Sherlock Holmes."

"Are you convinced the dog can perform such a feat?"

Joanna nodded firmly. "She once tracked the faint odor of French perfume from Victoria Station to the northern reaches of Edgware Road without missing a beat."

Lestrade raced for the door. "I must call Lieutenant Dunn and request that he join us at once."

"From Naval Intelligence?" I asked. "Is he the same officer who was a member of our team that solved the case of *A Study in Treason*?"

"The very same."

"So we are dealing here with espionage."

"I can say no more," Lestrade said. "Now I must ask that you remain in this room and speak to no one until Lieutenant Dunn arrives. A constable will be posted at the door to make certain no unauthorized person can enter this surgery."

"Please instruct the lieutenant to make haste, for we are faced with a most urgent matter,"

Joanna implored. "Dr. Verner's life is very much at stake here."

"As is the fate of all England," Lestrade said darkly, and closed the door behind him.

4

The Chase

Lieutenant Dunn arrived before Toby Two. On entering, he gave us a perfunctory nod, then led the way into a vacant, windowless office where, upon closing the door, he briefed us on the Official Secrets Act, to which we were about to be sworn. As he uttered the solemn oath that bound us to keep secret all matters revealed and committed to us, the gravity of the situation grew even greater. Lestrade's warning that "the fate of all England" may be at stake continued to ring in our ears.

"Now let us begin," Dunn said in an emotionless voice. "I would like you to again recount the entire story told to you by Dr. Verner. Give me only facts and avoid assumptions."

"Any assumptions I render will be based on fact and should not be so readily discarded," Joanna countered. "With so little to guide us, both could prove to be quite useful."

"Agreed, but you must distinguish between the two," Dunn said. "Please start with the moment Dr. Verner arrived at your rooms on Baker Street."

Joanna repeated the strange tale, providing the same details given to Inspector Lestrade. The only additions were the reasons why Verner believed the patient was not mute, but was instructed by his captors to act as if he were. "I assumed Verner was correct in believing Alistair Ainsworth was not mute."

Dunn did not reply to the assumption. "Was he restrained?"

"Not that Verner mentioned."

"Or evidence of torture?"

"Again none was mentioned, but I feel certain that, if any were present, Verner would have been impressed and brought them to our attention."

"Torture is not uncommon in these situations," Dunn remarked. He was a tall man, well built, with a resolute expression and deep-set, piercing eyes. "The Germans are quite expert at inflicting pain when it serves their purpose."

"It may have been used here, but the evidence was hidden from sight," Joanna replied. "When Vernon performed his examination, Ainsworth was fully clothed, with only his shirt opened to allow for inspection of the abdomen. Thus, torture applied to the captive's back and extremities would go unnoticed."

"Your point is well taken," Dunn said, with the briefest of nods, then tapped a finger against his chin while muttering something indecipherable under his breath. "Well, at the least he remains alive, which indicates they have not yet broken him."

"Perhaps they won't," Lestrade said, injecting a note of optimism.

"Every man has his breaking point," Dunn said stonily. "Even the toughest of them. And once broken, they spill everything."

"Exactly what is it that Mr. Ainsworth will be spilling?" Joanna asked. "And why is it so valuable to the Germans?"

Dunn's face closed. "You and your associates are on a need-to-know basis. The questions you ask are well beyond your purview."

"Do you wish our assistance?" Joanna asked.

"Indeed we do."

"Then you must remove our blindfolds, for if we remain in the dark, no solution will be reached."

"I can only state that Mr. Ainsworth was involved at the highest level of national security."

We returned to the examining room and carefully avoided stepping on the scattered glass and instruments strewn on the floor near the medicine cabinet. Joanna stressed the need to avoid anything that carried the aroma of chloroform, which was the scent to be followed.

"It will require the keenest of noses to track that evanescent odor across London," said Dunn.

"One is on the way," Joanna assured.

"Can the hound do it from a moving carriage?"

"That is where she performs best."

"So you have been told?"

"So I have witnessed."

The door to the examining room opened and Toby Two romped in, sliding across the slippery tile floor. She came to a stop at Joanna's feet and looked up, as if awaiting instructions. The hound appeared to ignore everyone else in the room.

Joanna reached down to scratch the dog's head, then grasped her leash before addressing the group. "Toby Two, Watson, my husband, and I will be in the lead carriage. Inspector Lestrade and Lieutenant Dunn should follow in a second carriage, accompanied by two constables. I would advise you have your weapons at the ready."

"How will you determine we are on the correct track?" Dunn asked.

"By observing Toby Two's tail," Joanna replied.

She went to the medicine cabinet to obtain an empty glass vial with a screw top. After opening it, she secured a small piece of glass from the shattered chloroform bottle and placed it into the vial before resealing it tightly.

"If we travel by motorcar, it will save a great deal of time," Dunn suggested.

"It might also confuse Toby Two," Joanna said. "Motor fumes carrying the strong smell of burned petrol will accumulate within the car and could throw Toby Two off her mark."

We hurried to our carriage and headed away from the heavily populated, commercial district of Kensington. Joanna waited until we were two blocks west of Verner's practice before opening the glass vial and placing it under Toby Two's nose. She waited only a few seconds for the hound to familiarize herself with the odor of chloroform, then resealed it and gave out instructions, "Go, girl! Go!"

In an instant Toby Two had her head out the carriage window, yelping happily, with her tail wagging at a rapid pace. There could be no doubt we were on track, which stirred excitement among us all. But the most vexing questions remained foremost in our minds. Who was Alistair Ainsworth and what was his governmental function that was so vital to England?

"Could Ainsworth be a spy?" I wondered aloud.

"That is unlikely," Joanna replied. "British spies for the most part operate in foreign countries, not in London."

"Perhaps he is a high-ranking officer in the Admiralty," my father suggested.

"Who was out of uniform when captured?" Joanna countered. "You may recall that Alistair Ainsworth was dressed in civilian attire when he was examined by Verner."

After a prolonged pause, I offered another possibility. "Perhaps he was a diplomat or courier of some sort."

Joanna flicked her wrist. "Guesses! All guesses, none of which advances our cause. All we can say with certainty is that Alistair Ainsworth was privy to very sensitive information that the Germans desperately wish to lay their hands on."

Suddenly Toby Two became overly excited. She yelped and, with her paws on the bottom of the window, extended her head out into the morning air. The strength of the scent had obviously intensified. All eyes went to the neighborhood we were passing through. It was not residential, but rather a street lined with fashionable stores and quaint shops. Toby Two was now leaning so far out the window I feared she would fall onto the cobblestones below. I grabbed her leash and tried to pull her back, but with little success.

Joanna rapped forcefully on the roof of our carriage and shouted up to the driver, "Stop immediately!"

Our carriage came to an abrupt halt and we hurriedly alighted onto a slate-covered footpath. Joanna took hold of the leash as Toby Two barked joyfully and led the way into a well-appointed tobacco shop. Behind a splendid display of cigars was a portly man, with thinning, dark hair and a well-trimmed goatee. He quickly straightened his posture at our entrance, his gaze going to the two uniformed constables now posted at the door.

"May I be of service?" he asked nervously.

"You are the owner, I presume?" Joanna said, bypassing the introductions.

"I am indeed."

"When did your shop open?"

"Just over an hour ago."

"How many customers have stepped through your door since opening?"

"Two."

"Describe them."

"The first was Mr. James, an elderly gentleman who favors Dutch Masters—"

"And the other?" Joanna interrupted.

"A large, broad-shouldered man who purchased a package of Pall Mall cigarettes."

"Was this his first visit to your shop?"

"To the best of my recollection."

"Could he have phoned in for a delivery?"

The owner shook his head. "We only deliver to known customers with accounts."

"Did he linger while in your fine shop?"

"No, madam. He seemed a bit hurried."

"And one final question," Joanna requested. "Did this particular customer have any unusual features about his face? A scar or blemish perhaps?"

The owner gave the matter thought before he nodded slowly. "He had a nervous tic that seemed to come and go."

"Thank you for your assistance," Joanna said

and, pulling on Toby Two's leash, dashed out of the shop.

"We have our man!" Lestrade cried out.

"We also have a very ominous sign," Joanna said darkly.

Our carriages continued on their way, with all eyes now on the residential area we were entering. It appeared every house was white in color, at least two stories high, and shaded by tall trees. A passing dog on a leash barked at our carriage, but Toby Two ignored it, her nose ever to the wind. As we approached the corner, Toby Two let out the loudest of howls and pointed at a two-story, white house well back from the street. Her tail was now fixed and straight as an arrow.

"Here!" Joanna bellowed out.

The carriages screeched to a halt and all occupants bolted out, except for Toby Two who was tied to a seat and left behind. Lestrade and Dunn raced across the lawn, weapons drawn and at the ready. Every window in the house was closed, with their drapes tightly drawn.

Lestrade signaled the constables to cover the rear of the house, then pounded on the front door and called out, "We are here from Scotland Yard! You are to open the door immediately!"

A full thirty seconds passed without response. Our ears were tuned in to any sound emanating from within this stately house, but all remained silent. A constable's whistle sounded, indicating they were in place at the rear of the house.

Lestrade banged on the door once more and issued a final warning. "You have one minute before we resort to forced entry!"

Dunn waited only ten seconds to kick the front door off its hinges. He and Lestrade rushed in, but no shots were fired and we heard no sounds of a struggle. The two constables raced around from the rear of the house and entered the foyer at full speed. We could see them sprinting up a flight of stairs. The silence returned and continued until Lestrade appeared at the entrance and waved us in.

"The Germans have fled," he said gloomily.

"And Verner?" Joanna asked.

"Dead."

We hurried through the foyer and passed a small table covered with unopened mail. On entering a large bedroom that held an unmade bed, we were taken aback by the gruesome sight of Alexander Verner. He was seated in a wooden chair, with his wrists and ankles restrained by thick rope. But it was his facial expression that was so disturbing. It showed absolute terror. There was no sign of Alistair Ainsworth.

"They tortured the poor doctor," Dunn reported grimly. "They burned his palms and soles, which are the most sensitive parts of the body."

"Using lighted cigarettes, I presume," Joanna said.

"That appears to be the case," Dunn agreed. "But how could you discern that from across the room?"

"Because the German agent bought a single packet of Pall Mall cigarettes on his way back to the house," Joanna explained. "Here they were, racing against time in a mad dash to determine how much the doctor had divulged, yet they stopped for cigarettes. It was an utter waste of time, which they had little of."

"Perhaps he was strongly addicted to tobacco," Lestrade advanced. "The nicotine drive can be quite overpowering, as Dr. Watson can attest to."

"The evidence is twofold against a strong addiction," Joanna said, glancing down at the burn marks. "First, despite living close by, he had visited the tobacco shop only once. And secondly, a man heavily addicted to cigarettes would have bought several packets, not simply one. Thus I concluded the agent must have had another use for lighted cigarettes, such as torture."

"And Verner made no mention of a strong odor of tobacco smoke during his description of the house, which would have been present if any of the occupants were heavily addicted," my father noted.

"All well and good," Dunn said impatiently. "But unfortunately, this does not bring us any closer to Ainsworth's captors."

"Perhaps there is evidence on Verner that will

tell us more," Joanna said as she briefly examined the doctor's outer garments. "Were his pockets searched?"

Dunn pointed to the belongings on the bed. There was a gold timepiece, a leather billfold containing seven pounds, a mechanical pen, and a set of keys. "They left nothing of value to us behind."

"Or so it would seem," Joanna said. "But we should allow my husband, who is an experienced pathologist, to examine the corpse and make certain there are no hidden clues."

Lestrade gestured his approval.

The smell of burned flesh, with which I was familiar, told me what to expect. On Verner's palms and soles were small, deep, blackened circles, some crusted over, others not. The burns penetrated well beneath the dermis of the skin and must have caused unbearable pain. There was dried blood on the right palm as well as rope indentations on both wrists, which were produced by Verner as he tried desperately to free himself. But his neck and eyes held the most unexpected findings.

"There is even more cruelty here that goes beyond words," I commented.

"How so?" Joanna asked.

"They not only restrained his neck, they throttled the poor man when they were done with him," I replied, and pointed to the rope around the victim's throat. "The rope marks are deep enough to compress Verner's trachea and thus prevent him from crying out while being tortured. But in addition, there are small hemorrhages, called petechiae, in his conjunctivae, which are clear evidence of strangulation. The forces closing off a person's airway also impede the return of blood from the head, which increases the venous pressure in the eyes and causes the small blood vessels within to rupture. I am confident a postmortem examination will reveal a fractured hyoid bone as well, and that is conclusive evidence he was strangled. Verner was no doubt aware this was happening and that accounts for the look of absolute terror on his face. He knew his end was near."

"Bloody Huns!" my father cried out, his face now red with rage. "Is there no end to their savagery?"

"Not in war," Dunn replied.

"But to do this to such a fine and gentle man who did only good while on this earth," my father said, taking a deep breath to control his anger. "There was no need for such cruelty."

Joanna leaned in for a closer inspection, seemingly unaffected by the viciousness of the crime. "Is the rope they used in any way remarkable?"

"I am afraid not," I replied. "It is made of common hemp and can be purchased at numerous stores throughout London."

Joanna sniffed the air. "The odor of chloroform still emanates from his shoes."

"I am surprised the Germans did not detect it."

"I'm certain they did, which gave them yet another reason to kill Verner." Joanna turned to Lestrade and Dunn and asked, "Was there any evidence upstairs that indicated the Germans' next move?"

"Nothing," Lestrade answered. "All of the rooms were bare, with no articles or written documents other than old newspapers."

"How old?" Joanna asked at once.

"Some dated back ten days."

"During which time they no doubt planned the details of the kidnapping. Which tells us this was no spur-of-the-moment event, but one that was carefully devised. They laid their trap and had this house waiting well in advance." Joanna thought for a moment, then returned to Lestrade. "Are you certain there were no receipts or delivery packages? After all, they were here for at least ten days and must have required food and drink and other essentials."

"Other than an unmade bed, there was nothing to indicate the house was lived in."

"What of the unopened mail in the foyer?"

"All notices and advertisements addressed to Occupant."

"These are very experienced agents," Joanna

remarked. "The Germans have obviously sent their best on this mission, which highlights its importance. They swept the entire house clean in a most professional manner."

"Surely they could not have been that perfect," said I. "Not in a house this large."

"Do not underestimate German obsessiveness when it comes to order," Joanna reminded. "Nonetheless, with their hurried departure, they may well have overlooked some small, secluded item."

"That very thought crossed my mind," said Lestrade. "For that reason, I have instructed the constables to perform yet another foot-by-foot search of each and every room."

"Any clue would be most welcome at this point," I remarked.

"Perhaps the nearby neighbors should be questioned," my father suggested.

"And so they shall," Dunn said. "But I have my doubts they will be of help. Keep in mind that foreign agents are for the most part very skilled at concealing themselves. They also know how to instantly disappear into thin air."

"So it would seem we have reached yet another dead end," Lestrade said dismally. "And all the while, Mr. Ainsworth's chances of survival are slipping away before our very eyes."

"And they will slip away altogether unless we quickly intervene," Joanna warned. "Once the

Germans have the information they wish, Alistair Ainsworth is a dead man."

Our conversation was abruptly interrupted by a constable who dashed into the bedroom at full speed. He held up a dripping-wet wallet and announced, "Sir, we discovered this in the water tank of a nearby lavatory."

"Was it floating or had it sunk?" Joanna asked quickly.

"Floating, ma'am," the constable replied.

"Excellent," Joanna said, more to herself than to the others.

Lestrade took the wallet and, after dismissing the constable, asked, "Why is it so important that the wallet remained afloat?"

"Because it tells us the wallet was recently placed in the tank," Joanna elucidated. "Had it been deposited some time ago, it would have become waterlogged and sunk."

"Why is that of significance?"

"Because the scrupulously neat Germans most assuredly did not deposit it there," Joanna replied. "Thus, in all likelihood, the wallet belonged to Alistair Ainsworth, and since it recently found its way into the water tank, we can deduce he placed it there and was leaving us a trail to follow."

"Perhaps he was simply leaving us a sign to indicate he had indeed been here," Lestrade proposed.

Outside, there was a loud roar of thunder

followed by a sudden, heavy downpour. The rain appeared to beat against the window, much as it had done the night before.

"Bad," Joanna said, staring at the streaked windowpane.

"The rain?" I asked.

Joanna nodded. "It will wash away any trace of chloroform that might have rubbed off on the German agents and their carriage."

"Rubbed off, you say?" Lestrade asked as he carefully opened the soaked wallet.

Joanna nodded again. "Verner's shoes would have left behind the evaporating scent of chloroform on the floor of the carriage, and vapors of that aroma may have seeped into the agents' shoes as well. Unfortunately now, with the rain pounding down, that scent will either disappear or become so faint that even Toby Two will be unable to track it."

"So we have obviously lost that advantage," Lestrade groused.

"I am afraid so, but we will give Toby Two an opportunity to pick up the scent, remote as it may be." Joanna moved in nearer to Lestrade who was emptying the contents of the wet wallet. There were two five-pound notes, several identification cards, and a soggy photograph of a middle-aged woman. He held the photo up to the light for a better view.

"Do you recognize her?" Joanna asked.

"She is Ainsworth's invalid sister who must be looked after," Lestrade replied. "They are very close."

"Have you questioned her?"

"At length and on two occasions. She only knew that he did not return home from his office and has been missing since. He had not called or made any contact with her, which was most unusual. Thus, she obviously feared for his safety."

"I presume it was she who posted the notification in the newspaper?"

"She did so without consulting us first," Lestrade grumbled.

"Which may have cost Verner his life," my father said.

"And might have encouraged the Germans to move along more quickly, for they will wonder whether Verner shared this information with the authorities," Joanna noted. "All of which places Ainsworth's life in even greater peril."

Lestrade nodded gloomily at the assessment.

"May I?" Joanna reached for the photograph and examined it carefully, then extracted a magnifying glass from her purse and focused in on something of obvious interest. "Her hands," she said to my father. "Look at her hands, Watson, and tell me what you see."

My father studied the photograph intently as he moved the magnifying glass back and forth in a slow, deliberate fashion. "Her fingers are deformed from a severe form of inflammatory rheumatism."

"Would it be generalized?"

"In all likelihood."

"I take it she would require assistance in her basic daily activities?"

"Beyond any question."

Joanna turned her attention to Dunn. "Did you question her as well, Lieutenant?"

"I did," Dunn replied.

"Were there others attending her?"

Dunn shook his head. "The housekeeper and cook were in the kitchen at the time. They too were interrogated, but could offer nothing that was helpful."

"So no one else was present?"

"No one."

Joanna gave Dunn a lengthy look, then reached in her purse for a cigarette and lighted it, all the while keeping her eyes fixed on the lieutenant. "There are too many missing pieces here."

"You have the information we have," Dunn said.

"To the contrary," Joanna countered. "I know little about Alistair Ainsworth and you know all."

Dunn stared at her in silence.

Joanna began pacing the floor, puffing absently on her Turkish cigarette. Back and forth she went, intermittently mumbling to herself or shaking her head at some notion that did not fit. A stream of blue smoke seemed to follow her across the room. Abruptly Joanna crushed out her cigarette in an ashtray and turned to Dunn. "I require detailed information on Ainsworth's secretive position."

"I can only tell you that his duties involve national security at the highest level," Dunn said carefully.

"That will not do," Joanna pressed.

"I regret I cannot divulge more."

"Without the information I requested, you make it impossible for me to reach a resolution. You are asking me to make bricks, yet you are unwilling to afford me the clay necessary to do so, which renders the task hopeless. I fear it would only be a waste of our time and yours for my colleagues and me to participate further in this investigation. And at this point, time is something we have precious little of. Surely you must realize that Alistair Ainsworth's life hangs in the balance and that chances of a rescue fade away with each passing hour." Joanna waited for a reply, but when none was forthcoming, she turned to my father and said, "Perhaps we should have Watson call the First Sea Lord and ask that he intervene."

"The First Sea Lord is not so easily reached," Dunn challenged.

"He is when you are a personal friend."

An uneasy silence hung in the air as Joanna and the lieutenant locked eyes, neither giving ground. Seconds slowly ticked by in the stillness.

"I believe I have his number," my father said, reaching into his coat pocket for a card that Sir Harold Whitlock had given him last year while visiting us at 221b Baker Street on a sensitive matter. "It is a direct line, as I recall."

"Allow me a moment," Dunn urged, and hurried over to a telephone on a desk in the far corner. We were to later learn that the Germans had insisted the homeowner's phone remain in place as part of the rental agreement, and had paid a handsome fee for this service. Dunn dialed a number, then turned his back to us and spoke in a low, indistinguishable voice. Apparently he was seeking permission from those in high position. But the request was no simple matter, for he was forced to wait several minutes before an answer was given. Finally Dunn replaced the receiver and turned to us.

"Keep in mind you are sworn to the Official Secrets Act," Dunn reminded.

"We are aware," Joanna said.

Dunn went to the door and ensured that it was tightly closed, then came back to us. Despite the total privacy, he spoke in a low voice. "What I am about to disclose to you is so sensitive it is known by only five people in the entire British Empire. These include the Prime Minister, the

First Sea Lord, the director of Naval Intelligence, the assistant director, and myself. Not a word of what you hear is to be breathed outside this room. Am I clearly understood?"

The three of us nodded in unison.

"Alistair Ainsworth is the highest-ranking member in a clandestine, top-secret cryptanalysis unit. His primary function is to make certain all of our naval codes are fail-safe and cannot be deciphered by the enemy. Thus, coded messages of the greatest priority pass before his eyes on a daily basis. He and his colleagues study the code and once broken they then instruct us on how best to alter it to one that is indecipherable."

"I take it they have a high rate of success," Joanna ventured.

"Remarkably so. They seem to do it with such ease that we often ask them to assist in deciphering some of our enemy's most convoluted coded messages. And Ainsworth is the most talented of the lot." Dunn paused to take a long, heavy breath. "If he worked for the Germans, I fear we would have lost this war long ago. And now he may be doing exactly that."

Joanna asked, "You mentioned he worked within a group. How many are there?"

"Four, among which are some of the most unusual characters you will ever encounter. You see, they are creative thinkers, with remarkable intellects, whose greatest joy in life is unraveling complex riddles. They are nonmilitary personnel, with a variety of backgrounds; they include linguists, chess masters, and crossword experts. They can solve a difficult crossword puzzle in minutes, and untangle an anagram as soon as the letters are written down. Play charades with them and they not only produce the correct answer, but five others that are equally as good. They are multilingual and can speak German, French, and Spanish in the same paragraph. Yet they have no overwhelming ambition in life and are at their happiest when faced with a seemingly unsolvable problem. These features make them the perfect fit for our cryptanalysis unit. They break codes in an indirect and creative fashion, using reasoning that is not obvious and has no relation to step-by-step logic. Needless to say, their value is so great it cannot be measured."

"Ainsworth will no doubt be missed," my father said. "But you still have three members of this group to continue their important work."

"I am afraid our problem goes much deeper than that," Dunn explained. "You must keep in mind that German intelligence has no doubt intercepted most of the messages we have sent and, although undeciphered, have them on file. If Ainsworth is broken, they will read those coded messages as easily as they read their newspapers, and have access to the most vital information including our war plans, naval strategies, and clandestine operations. It would give Germany an advantage from which we might never recover."

"You are facing yet another dilemma that is equally serious," Joanna warned. "There is a spy in your midst. Someone had to know of Ainsworth's position and that someone pointed him out to the Germans."

"We are quite aware of that," Dunn said. "I can assure you that individual is not the Prime Minister, the First Sea Lord, the director of Intelligence, or the assistant director. That leaves Ainsworth, whom we can exclude, and his three colleagues whom we cannot."

"But if one of the three is involved, why bother to have Ainsworth kidnapped?" Joanna asked. "The Germans have their man planted in the group and capable of feeding them information on a continuing basis. Why would they even hint that they have a reliable, well-concealed operative in the unit?"

"Exactly, madam," said Dunn. "So you can see our quandary. We are faced with the crime of espionage and have no credible suspects."

"Every one of those mentioned is a suspect until proven otherwise," Joanna insisted.

"But certainly not the Prime Minister or First Sea Lord or—"

"They all have secretaries and undersecretaries close at hand," Joanna interrupted. "All that is required to set the wheels of espionage in motion is a simple eavesdrop or careless utterance or discarded document that should have been destroyed but wasn't. One misstep by those privy to this cryptanalysis unit and your wall of absolute security disappears."

"I remain convinced that those at the highest echelon are not involved," Dunn persisted. "It must be one of the three in the unit."

"Well then, you should pursue your avenue of investigation while we pursue ours."

"Which is?"

"Oh, there is no need to go into that now. It is best you take your route and we ours. Along the way we can compare findings, which may very well complement each other."

On that note we returned to our carriage where Toby Two, although happy to see us, showed no interest in tracking further. As Joanna had predicted, the heavy rain that was now coming to an end had blotted out any further traces of a chloroform trail.

"Where to now?" I asked.

"The single source most likely to lead us to Alistair Ainsworth."

Joanna held up an identification card taken from Alistair Ainsworth's wallet. Although the card was soaked, Ainsworth's home address remained clearly visible.

5

The Sister

As our carriage traveled south to Knightsbridge, Joanna peered out at the fashionable stores on Brompton Road and appeared to be preoccupied with her own thoughts. Her silence was unusual in that she believed nothing cleared up a puzzling case like stating it to another person. On occasion she would even wake me and my father in the middle of the night to serve as sounding boards for her conclusions. Thus, her lack of words during our journey made me wonder if Joanna already had a solution at hand. We rode on for several more blocks before she nodded to herself and turned her attention to us.

"At times," Joanna noted, "there is nothing more deceptive than an obvious fact."

"I recall Sherlock Holmes making a similar statement," my father said.

"And for good reason," Joanna continued on. "When a fact is taken for granted, it often loses its importance. Such as the instance of the wallet in the water tank."

I shrugged. "It is obvious that Alistair

Ainsworth left it behind to alert us to his presence in the house."

"So it would appear on the surface."

"Do you believe Ainsworth had another purpose in mind?"

"Beyond any doubt. You see, he was convinced we would find the house where he was held captive."

"How could he possibly know that?"

"His major clue was the odor of chloroform Verner carried with him," Joanna elucidated. "When Verner was brought into the house, he was in all likelihood tortured in front of Ainsworth in an effort to frighten the intelligence agent and thus break him. Ainsworth detected the scent of chloroform on Verner's clothes and knew it had been placed there to serve as a trail to be followed."

"He could not have been aware of that," I argued. "Verner was a doctor and might have accidentally spilled a bit of chloroform on himself while opening a bottle of the anesthetic."

"No, no, John," Joanna said, shaking her head at me. "You are thinking like Lestrade and Dunn. Rather, you should place yourself in the position of Alistair Ainsworth who is a master when it comes to creating and solving puzzles. Let us go through the deductions, step by step, just as Ainsworth would have. First, Verner was taken captive early in the morning, prior to opening his practice. So the question must be asked—what was he doing with a bottle of chloroform at that moment, much less somehow managing to douse himself with it? Secondly, if that occurred, Verner had more than enough time to change clothes and remove the unpleasant odor from his examining room. Thus, with these points in mind, Ainsworth would have correctly deduced that Verner spilled chloroform on himself for the sole purpose of leaving a trail, just as I had instructed the doctor earlier. All of these facts, when taken together, allow for only one conclusion. Ainsworth knew the authorities would not be far behind."

"And closing in," my father added. "For there was the very real possibility that Verner had alerted Scotland Yard about the house and its captive."

"That too," Joanna said with a firm nod. "The German agents, who we know are very skilled, would have surely detected the odor of chloroform on Verner. Which of course was another reason for them to kill him. The last thing they wanted was to leave a strong scent for us to follow."

I said quickly, "But if Ainsworth was aware the authorities would arrive shortly to rescue him, why did he bother to leave his wallet in the water tank?"

"Because if the attempt was delayed or failed,

he wanted to inform us how to go about finding him," Joanna replied.

My father gave her a puzzled look. "I am not sure I follow here. The wallet only contained two five-pound notes, several identification cards, and a picture of his frail sister."

"It was the sister's picture that was so revealing," Joanna told us. "He obviously loves her and cares for her very much, and that is why he carries her picture. We know she is crippled with severe rheumatism and is for the most part confined to her home. Thus, it is fair to assume that Alistair Ainsworth shares the stories of his life in London with her. It would be her major contact with the outside world."

"But Ainsworth's work with Naval Intelligence is so secret, he would never speak of this with her," I said.

"It is not his work, but his life away from the agency that is so vital here," Joanna explained. "Remember, Alistair Ainsworth was not taken prisoner in his workplace, but somewhere outside the agency, preferably in a secluded location where no one could see the capture or hear his cry for help."

"A wooded area? A forest perhaps?" my father suggested.

"Not necessarily," Joanna said. "There are more than a few tucked-away places in London where capture could have occurred."

"Such as?"

"A pub on a dark street late at night, a female companion who lives on the outskirts of the city, and so on. The list is quite long."

"How do we go about narrowing it down?"

"Like most of us, Alistair Ainsworth is a creature of habit, and that will dictate his whereabouts. Thus, our best course of action is to learn of his daily habits and follow them."

"Which of course his invalid sister could provide."

"Spot on, Watson, for it is with her that he shares the details of his life away from home."

"And you believe this will lead us to Ainsworth's captors?"

Joanna nodded as we turned onto a street lined with stately, handsome homes. "Think of it as the first piece of the puzzle. Solve it and the other pieces will begin to fall into place."

Our carriage drew up to the curb in front of a two-story, sandstone house on Cadogan Square. It had an imposing mahogany door, with brass fittings that shone in the late-morning light. Another carriage was waiting outside.

"We must be delicate with our questioning," Joanna cautioned. "Make no comments or inquiries that might disparage the man, for his sister will be very protective of him."

"But surely we will have to ask about possible vices," I said.

"If the subject arises, pry gently."

As we alighted from our carriage, the drapes covering a first-floor window opened briefly, then closed. I thought I saw a fleeting shadow behind them, but could not be sure. It required a full minute before our rap on the mahogany door was answered.

"May I help you?" asked a rotund housekeeper with her gray hair held tightly in place by a bun.

"We are here to see Miss Ainsworth," Joanna replied.

"She is not receiving visitors today, madam."

"Oh, I am certain she will see us," Joanna said. "Tell her that the daughter of Sherlock Holmes wishes to speak with her."

"Y-yes, ma'am," the housekeeper stammered, obviously in awe of Joanna and her lineage. "Please come in and wait while I announce your presence."

The name of Sherlock Holmes was still like magic in all of London and this aura carried over to Joanna, in large measure because of the stories I chronicled about her remarkable crime-solving skills. Indeed, her public esteem was now approaching the same level as that of her father before her. Yet Joanna for the most part appeared unimpressed by her fame. To her, it was just a by-product of her deductive abilities.

We stepped into an eye-catching foyer that spoke of both wealth and taste. It was done in white marble, with a fresco of angelic figures painted on the ceiling that were reminiscent of those in Michelangelo's Sistine Chapel. The air around us was still and very, very warm and held the aroma of burned wood.

Joanna whispered, "I take it those with chronic illnesses are quite sensitive to the cold."

My father nodded. "Particularly those with painful rheumatism."

"If the conversation turns to her rheumatic condition, I should like you to do the questioning."

"Are there areas I should avoid?"

"Use your own discretion."

The housekeeper returned and, with a half bow, led us into a large drawing room. The temperature of the air was now even higher, due in part to a large fireplace with its logs burning brightly. The furniture was French antique, the walls adorned with Italian tapestries and paintings of aristocratic personages. Near the fireplace sat a tiny, frail woman in a cushioned wheelchair. Despite the deformities of her hands, she was well groomed, with her hair neatly cut and dyed and her makeup carefully applied. By contrast, next to her was a tall, large-boned woman, with a most attractive face and long, brown hair that cascaded down to her shoulders.

"Thank you for seeing us on such short notice," Joanna began after introducing us and stating the purpose of our visit.

"It is I who should thank you," Emma Ainsworth replied. "I believe you know my dear friend Lady Jane Hamilton."

"Indeed I do, for my late husband, John Blalock, was best man at her wedding," Joanna said, and turned to the visitor. "It is always good to see you, Jane, but of course not under these dreadful circumstances."

"I too wish it was otherwise," said Lady Jane. "We so hope you can solve this terrible mystery and help locate our Tubby."

"I shall do my best."

"If you wish, I can leave and give you complete privacy," Lady Jane offered.

"Please stay, for you may be able to provide information that could assist our search."

After we were all seated, Joanna asked, "May I inquire as to how your brother acquired the nickname Tubby?"

A faint smile came to Emma Ainsworth's face. "As a child my brother loved to play with his toy boats while bathing in a tub. Our parents had to literally pull him from the water, against his pleas and demands to remain. He would cry out, 'The battle is not done!'"

"The battle?" Joanna queried.

Emma nodded. "Yes, the battle. You see, Tubby did not simply play with the ships, as one might expect. He would set up harbors and fortifications, then move the fleet around so he could devise various strategies for naval warfare. He could recite the tonnage and speeds of the ships, from destroyers to battleships, and how well they could maneuver and what their strengths and weaknesses were. My brother has always been remarkably bright, and this was evident even as a child."

"I suspect it was this obvious intellect that led to his current position in the government," Joanna pried gently.

Emma shrugged. "He never spoke of it, except to say it was part of the war effort."

Lady Jane volunteered, "He once confided that his assignment was top secret, but would say no more. He would not speak of where he worked and with whom."

"As would be expected," Joanna said, and leaned in closer to the fire to warm her hands before turning to Emma Ainsworth. "On the day of your brother's disappearance, please recall every step that you knew he took."

"It was his habit to awaken early, usually at six, dress and have breakfast by seven, then read the newspaper prior to departing. He did precisely this on the last day I saw him. He called at three to inform me not to wait for dinner, for he would be dining out with a friend."

"Did he mention which friend?" Joanna asked.

"He did not, although I assumed it would be Roger Marlowe, who is a lifelong chum and works alongside Tubby at the government office."

"Could you give me a bit more information on Roger Marlowe?" Joanna requested.

"It might be best to let Jane answer," Emma replied. "She and Roger and Tubby grew up together, and she was once engaged to Roger."

"Briefly engaged," Lady Jane said with no bitterness. "But in response to your question, Tubby and Roger are much the same. Both are exceptionally bright, both educated at Eton, then Cambridge where they received honors degrees in archaeology. Shortly thereafter they traveled to Germany to study ancient Greek at the University of Heidelberg. They were both very keen on interpreting some recently discovered papyrus sheets that dated back thousands of years."

"What year were they at Heidelberg?" Joanna asked at once.

"Just before the turn of the century," Lady Jane recalled.

"Eighteen ninety-seven, to be exact," Emma answered.

"Did they stay on longer?" Joanna asked.

"Oh yes, but in a roundabout way," Emma replied. "They mastered ancient Greek in short order and went on numerous archaeological expeditions that were sponsored by the university. I believe those were the best years of Tubby's life, but they were interrupted when I came down with severe rheumatism and he had to return home to look after me. I always felt very guilty about that."

"He was simply doing what would be expected of a good brother," my father commented.

"True," Emma said. "But that did not lessen my guilt. To be near me, Tubby took a position at Imperial College where he remained until being called into government service."

"Did Roger Marlowe return as well?" Joanna asked.

Emma shook her head, which brought about neck pain and caused her to wince. "Not for several years. He continued to excel at Heidelberg and became so fluent in German that he was given the opportunity to join their faculty. But he chose to return to Cambridge where he delved into mathematics. It was during this time that Roger's family suffered painful financial reverses that forced him to return to London where a more gainful position awaited him."

"His mathematical equations were so astute that several were adopted by the London School of Economics," Lady Jane noted. "He was eventually offered a professorship there, but it held little interest for him."

Joanna's brow went up. "But surely such an advancement would have been far more remunerative and aided his family who were in need at the time."

"It would have kept them afloat, but little more," Lady Jane said. "However, with the sale of country land, the family straightened out their affairs, but never to the level they once enjoyed."

"So you have kept up with Roger over the years," Joanna concluded.

"We would run into each other on occasion," Lady Jane said evasively.

"At Cambridge?"

"At social gatherings here in London," Lady Jane replied. "He left Cambridge for his current position several years ago."

"I take it that Alistair and Roger Marlowe have remained close friends," Joanna said.

"The best of friends," Emma emphasized. "In addition to their remarkable intellects, they share a good many other qualities. Both are what one would call delightful rogues. They enjoy life to the fullest in every way."

"Such as?" Joanna probed.

"They enjoy their drink and can often be found at the Admiralty where they are well-known."

Joanna's brow went up again, but this time it stayed up. "The Admiralty? Are you referring to His Majesty's Navy?"

A brief smile crossed Emma's face. "It is a pub located near Trafalgar Square. They frequent the Admiralty prior to gaming at various casinos."

"Do they gamble often?"

"Quite."

"Is there a single casino they favor?"

"Laurent's is the one Tubby usually speaks of."

"Do you know if they bet heavily?"

I could readily see the reasoning behind Joanna's line of questioning. Betting large sums could lead to large debts that could lead to blackmail.

Emma gave the matter thought. "I do not believe they bet heavily, but they do win with great frequency. You see, both Tubby and Roger are wonderful at mathematics and have thought up a method for counting cards in play and predicting those that remain in the deck."

"The casinos must be aware of this."

Emma nodded. "So much so that Tubby and Roger have reached an agreement with the casino, in which they are allowed to play but must limit their winnings to twenty pounds or less. Again you can see that it is not the money but the challenge of defeating a skilled opponent that is so important to my brother."

"But their constant winning must have drawn the attention of other gamblers," Joanna said. "I would expect the casinos to somehow limit your brother's access to the gaming tables."

"Oh, I can assure you they try. Since the owners cannot lawfully deny my brother and Roger entrance to their establishment, they have devised a method to keep them away from the tables. As soon as the casino operators see the faces of

Tubby and Roger, they signal for employees who are mingling about to quickly take all the open seats at the table. Thus, none are available for the new arrivals. I forget the names by which these employees are called, but Tubby assures me they are present and perform their tasks on a moment's notice."

"They are referred to as *bonnets*," Joanna informed.

"Yes! Exactly! How did you come by this information?"

"I read it in a magazine," Joanna said. "Their usual role is to play at the table and bet heavily, using the casino's money. They either win or lose large sums and act out their feigned emotions while doing so. These acts are said to draw crowds to the table and encourage others to bet."

"That is word for word what Tubby once told me," Emma said, and gave Joanna an admiring look. "It is extraordinary that you would know this."

Joanna waved away the compliment and asked directly, "Does your brother drink a great deal at home or at the Admiralty?"

Emma shook her head, but this time slowly and carefully. "He never imbibes more than a glass or two of Scotch, and I have never seen him intoxicated."

"Does he have any vices you disapprove of?"

"Only his occasional visits to the opium dens," Emma said frankly.

"How often were these visits?"

"Quite infrequent, I believe," Emma answered. "It only came up because I once noticed the peculiar aroma of burned maple on his jacket. He explained it was the smell of opium that resulted from a visit to the opium den. He apologized for the aroma, and since I never encountered it again, I assumed he did not revisit the opium den."

"A reasonable assumption," Joanna said, and leaned back in her chair. I could sense there was another question she wished to ask about the use of opium, but decided against it. "Tell me, Miss Ainsworth, has your brother in the past ever spent the night away?"

"Only on the rarest of occasions. When he does, he always calls to inform me and make certain the housekeeper will stay the night to look after my needs."

"And to make certain you take your medicines," my father added.

"Indeed, Dr. Watson," Emma said, and held up her gnarled fingers. "Even with medication, these poor fingers can barely grasp the aspirin tablets I require on a continuing basis."

"I know they give you some comfort."

"They ease the pain, but unfortunately do little to prevent the unsightly deformities." Emma attempted to make a pinching motion with her fingers, but was unable to do so. "I can no longer hold a chess piece, not even a king or queen, and am thus prevented from playing my favorite game with my brother, who is a chess master. I am convinced it is the heaviest toll this awful disease has taken from me."

"Are you as talented at chess as your brother?" Joanna asked.

"Oh, heavens no! As a matter of fact, Tubby would have been promoted to grandmaster if he so desired," Emma replied. "A number of England's grandmasters will attest to Tubby's remarkable ability at chess. They will tell you that my brother does not concern himself with titles, but only with the challenge of the game."

"Has he actually defeated grandmasters?"

"I believe so from the reports of others, but Tubby would never make mention of it," Emma said, then sighed regretfully and gazed down at her deformed fingers. "I only wish these hands would allow me to play once again with my dear brother."

"There are now several glovelike devices that could help you in that regard," my father suggested.

"I was unaware," Emma said, and seemed to perk up at the helpful advice. "I shall inform Tubby when he—" She stopped in mid-sentence and sadly corrected herself. "If he returns home."

Joanna rose and said, "You have provided information that may well be of assistance."

"So you believe there is hope yet?" Emma asked.

"Only a glimmer," Joanna replied honestly. "But rest assured we shall do our best to bring your brother home safely."

We walked out into a gray, gloomy day and spoke no further until we were seated in our carriage. Joanna stared out at the dense fog that was gathering around us, as if the answer to our problem might lie within.

"I fail to see the glimmer of hope you mentioned," my father said.

"Do not focus on the end, but concern yourself with the beginning," Joanna told him. "There are links here, each of which has to be carefully examined and placed in its appropriate position."

"Like pieces of a game puzzle?"

"Precisely. You see, an observer who has thoroughly understood one link in a series of events should be able to connect all the others, before and after."

"But which is the one link that will lead to the others?"

"That is what we must determine."

Our carriage rode away just as another sudden downpour began. The dour weather so matched my mood that I could not help but comment, "I am afraid time is very much against us. We have so little to go on and soon Ainsworth will be broken, and all will be lost."

"And once they break him, he is a dead man," my father said.

"Do not be so certain of that," Joanna advised.

"Surely once they have the codes in their possession, they will have no further use for him."

"Oh, I suspect that might not be the case."

"Based on what?"

"The fact that Alistair Ainsworth is a chess master and the Germans are not."

6

The Trail

We dined early at 221b Baker Street because Joanna had a surprise journey in store for us later that evening. After a superb dinner of roast beef and Yorkshire pudding, my father and I settled in front of a glowing fire while Joanna paced back and forth across the parlor, oblivious to my presence. The speed of her pacing seemed to correlate with the rate of her deductions, as she nodded at one conclusion and grumbled at another. She continued on for several minutes before reaching for another Turkish cigarette. But then she changed her mind and abruptly turned to us.

"There are three major links that point to the disappearance of Alistair Ainsworth," Joanna proclaimed. "These are . . . the Admiralty pub, Laurent's casino, and an opium den. Which do you consider the most promising?"

My father and I exchanged puzzled looks before I said, "But you stated earlier that Ainsworth was taken prisoner in a secluded location. None of the sites you mentioned measure up. In fact, they are often crowded with people who know one another."

"That is so during the early hours of the evening, but the crowds thin later on. At that time the streets will be deserted, with only a straggler or two about. It is then that the moment is ideal for kidnapping."

"I favor a casino, for they stay open until the wee hours of the morning," my father proposed.

"They do indeed," Joanna agreed. "But keep in mind the players in these gambling halls are for the most part well-to-do and would have their carriages waiting at the doorstep."

"But the same would hold true for the Admiralty pub and most certainly for the opium dens, for the latter are located in the very worst section of London," I argued. "Ainsworth's carriage would be within shouting distance."

"True," Joanna said. "So we can conclude that the location does not seem to favor one establishment over the other. Nevertheless, I favor the pub or the opium den, for after drinks or drugs one's defenses would be impaired and thus make the taking easier."

"But that alone would not exclude the casino," I countered.

"Of course not, and that is why we must visit all three tonight."

I gave the plan thought and a difficulty came immediately to mind. "We know the location of the Admiralty pub and Laurent's casino, but finding the opium den Ainsworth visited is another matter. There are dozens of those establishments in East London, some of which are hidden from sight."

"There is a way to narrow down the number," Joanna said, unconcerned.

My father asked, "Would it not be easier to simply call Roger Marlowe, with whom Ainsworth presumably spent the evening, and inquire about the places they visited?"

"You are assuming Roger Marlowe is not involved in the kidnapping," Joanna said.

"But he works for the intelligence unit," my father asserted. "I am certain he was carefully vetted before being allowed in. In addition, he and Ainsworth are the closest of friends."

"That does not exclude him," Joanna said. "Recall that Marlowe spent years at the University of Heidelberg and was so well thought of he was offered a faculty position. Moreover, he speaks the language fluently and no doubt still has friends and contacts there."

"Are you contending that he may have an allegiance to Germany?" my father cried out.

"I am saying that everyone is a suspect until proven otherwise," Joanna said. "With of course the exception of Emma Ainsworth."

"And Lady Jane Hamilton," I opined.

"Do not be so quick there," Joanna cautioned. "There is a history behind this woman that you may not be aware of."

My father and I leaned forward to catch every word.

"Some is gossip, some is fact," Joanna said carefully.

"How are we to distinguish between the two?" I asked.

"In this case it is the opinion of most that the truth outweighed the rumor," Joanna said, then continued on with the story. "It was widely believed that Lady Jane had an affair with a handsome German diplomat some years ago while her husband was at sea in command of one of His Majesty's warships. The affair ended with the return of her husband and the transfer of her lover to another part of the Continent."

"Are you saying the affair continues?" I asked in a low voice.

"I am saying no one knows," Joanna replied. "But the connection was there and may still exist."

"And there was her involvement with Roger Marlowe who may have also come under German influence," I noted.

"*Was* involved, you say?" Joanna asked in a questioning tone. "What makes you believe it has ended?"

"She stated their engagement was brief," I recalled.

"That does not exclude a secret, ongoing romance," Joanna said. "A married woman who has strayed once may well do so again, particularly with a former lover."

"For which we have no proof," I remarked.

"But the suspicion remains," Joanna said. "And it thus should be kept in mind."

"Which brings yet another unknown piece to the puzzle," I grumbled. "We seem to be going off on tangents."

"I too am not certain these confusing details bring us any closer to Alistair Ainsworth," my father agreed. "If anything, they seem to be clouding the picture even more."

"To the contrary, Watson," Joanna said. "I believe a solution will shortly be at hand."

"And how do you propose coming to such a resolution?"

"By employing my father's deductive reasoning," Joanna replied. "I shall take note of all the details and circumstances relating to a single event—namely the disappearance of Alistair Ainsworth—and put them together in their proper order. Once this is done, we shall be able to explain how the event occurred."

"But where do we begin?"

"By discovering the major link that holds the key to our mystery," Joanna responded. "Everything revolves around the site where the kidnapping occurred. That is where the link lies."

"Pray tell, Joanna, why do you place such

emphasis on the locale from which Ainsworth disappeared?"

"Because, if my assumptions are correct, it will lead us to the person who betrayed him."

Before leaving our rooms, Joanna called Inspector Lestrade and asked that he join us at Laurent's casino. The request was most unusual, for Joanna much preferred to follow her own line of investigation while Scotland Yard went about theirs. From experience she felt Lestrade, although tough and tenacious, could all too often be led astray and pursue avenues that were unproductive.

"Lestrade is so unimaginative," Joanna said as our carriage passed the Marble Arch and turned onto Park Lane. "He searches for hidden clues when the most important ones lie before his very eyes."

"Why then invite him to join us at Laurent's?" I asked.

"Keep in mind, John, that Lestrade has police powers and we do not," Joanna replied. "We could be denied entrance to the casino, but not with the inspector at our side. He can enter, investigate, and even obtain search warrants, all under the law. In addition, my questions will be answered more truthfully in Lestrade's presence, for not to do so could be considered obstruction of justice. Thus at times Lestrade can be a most helpful ally. The powers he has also explain why he is so intimately associated with Lieutenant Dunn's search for Alistair Ainsworth. Dunn's Naval Intelligence unit is a division of His Majesty's Secret Service, which has immense authority but no police powers. For this reason Dunn requires the inspector's presence."

"Do you believe Lestrade will bring Dunn along to the casino?" my father asked.

"I would think not," Joanna replied. "A uniformed naval officer would be of no help at this point and might well serve as an unwanted distraction."

Our carriage came to a stop at the elegant entrance to Laurent's casino, whereupon a uniformed doorman rushed up to open our door. As we stepped out, Inspector Lestrade hurried over to us.

He tipped his derby and, after the amenities, asked, "Is there reason to believe the casino is involved?"

"That is to be determined," Joanna said.

We entered a large front room that was brilliantly lighted. On one side stood a buffet covered with wine and liquors and behind that a smaller room given up to cold chicken, salads, and other dishes. Directly before us were long gaming tables covered with green cloth that were surrounded by players and governed by croupiers and dealers. Toward the rear were round card tables above which arose a cloud of tobacco smoke. The noise of loud conversations filled the air.

A short, rotund man wearing a well-fitted tuxedo rushed over to us. Behind the casino manager were two large, formidable men who blocked our view of the gaming room. They positioned themselves so that we could not see the throng of gamblers, nor could the gamblers see us. Their purpose, I assume, was to keep the well-known Inspector Lestrade out of sight, so as not to upset those at the tables. For obvious reasons, the presence of police was not welcomed at casinos.

"May I be of service, Inspector?" the casino manager asked.

"There are questions my associates believe you can answer," Lestrade replied. "Please do so and keep in mind this is an official investigation."

"Is this regarding activities of an employee within our casino?" the manager asked worriedly.

"It is regarding one of your players," Joanna said, stepping forward. "We are told he frequents your establishment. His name is Alistair Ainsworth."

"We are very much aware of Mr. Ainsworth, but have not seen him this week."

"Is that unusual?"

"Quite so, madam. We count on him visiting the casino every Monday night, for that is his custom."

"As is his custom of winning."

"He does well."

"Not to exceed twenty pounds."

"He has set limits," the manager said, now alerted that Joanna already knew a great deal about Alistair Ainsworth, for this information would only be shared by those closest to the gambler. "This is mutually agreed upon."

"But I suspect this agreement did not extend to his losses."

The casino manager nodded ever so briefly, as if not willing to acknowledge the fact.

"Was Mr. Ainsworth accompanied by others while gambling?"

"Sometimes he was alone, but on most occasions Mr. Marlowe sat across from him."

"Was the limit to include Mr. Marlowe's winnings as well?"

"It was and for good reason," the manager answered. "They had a method, we believe, in which they could mentally count cards and know which remained in the deck."

"Cheating, were they?" Lestrade interrupted.

"They claimed it was simply luck, but we thought otherwise," the manager said. "Is that the purpose of your visit tonight?"

Joanna ignored the question. "Was Mr. Ainsworth accompanied by anyone other than Mr. Marlowe?"

The manager thought for a moment. "On a

number of occasions, a rather striking woman was with them."

"Describe her in detail," Joanna said at once.

"She was a large woman, not in girth, but about the upper torso, with a most attractive face and long, brown hair that flowed down to her shoulders. It was her hair that immediately grabbed one's attention."

Lady Jane Hamilton! My father and I exchanged knowing glances, for the manager had described the woman perfectly.

"Did she gamble?" Joanna asked.

"Never."

"Did they leave together?"

"Always, and usually quite late."

"To the best of your recollection, did Mr. Ainsworth associate with any others in the casino?"

"Not that I was aware."

Joanna let the new information sink in, then looked over to my father and me. "Do either of you have questions?"

"Just one or two," my father said. "Tell me, manager, has anyone else inquired about Mr. Ainsworth?"

"Not to my knowledge," the manager answered promptly. "But if one did, it would prove fruitless. We scrupulously guard any and all information about our clientele."

"Did you ever see Mr. Ainsworth intoxicated?"

"Never."

My father gestured to me but I hesitated, for I had no further questions regarding Ainsworth. Yet Lady Jane Hamilton remained on my mind. "You mentioned a female companion a moment ago. Do you know her name?"

"I did not inquire."

"Did it appear there was a special relationship between the woman and either man?"

"None was apparent."

Joanna nodded at my question, obviously pleased I had asked it. Seeing we had no further inquiries, she thanked the manager for his time and led the way out into a clear, brisk evening. The traffic on Park Lane was heavy and loud, so there was little chance we would be overheard as we strolled toward our carriage.

"Not very informative," Lestrade pronounced.

"At least we can say with certainty that Ainsworth was not taken at the casino," Joanna noted.

"Which I would have thought unlikely, even before our visit," Lestrade said.

"True," Joanna said. "But now it is entirely out of the question, for Ainsworth was frequently accompanied by friends and that would have surely dissuaded the Germans."

Lestrade shrugged his shoulders, unimpressed with Joanna's conclusions. "In your phone call you mentioned a second place you wished to visit. Perhaps that will prove more rewarding."

"We shall see. Please be good enough to follow us to the Admiralty, a pub frequented by Alistair Ainsworth."

We remained silent as our carriage traveled down Park Lane and turned left at the statue of the Duke of Wellington. But our collective minds were centered on Lady Jane Hamilton. Why had she lied to us? Why had she told us she occasionally ran into Roger Marlowe while in fact she was a frequent companion at Laurent's casino? Was she still close and romantically involved with Marlowe, and was either or both still connected to the Germans? There was one certainty, however. Both knew of Alistair Ainsworth's habits and could have betrayed him to the enemy.

"Perhaps we should requestion Lady Jane," I suggested, breaking the silence.

"To what end?" Joanna asked. "She would simply say she had forgotten about the visits to the casino and considered them unimportant. She might insist they were spur-of-the-moment invitations."

"While we believe otherwise."

"But cannot prove."

I was surprised by Joanna's response. "Are you saying we should ignore it?"

"I am saying we should docket the information, for it may become important later on," Joanna advised. "We should do nothing to alienate or alarm Lady Jane, for I believe there is much more to her than meets the eye."

"Such as a romantic assignation with Roger Marlowe?"

"At this point that is a guess and guesses will not help our cause," Joanna said. "For the present, let us be aware that Lady Jane is being less than honest, and thus she is hiding something."

"But what?"

"A secret that she guards closely."

Our carriage continued on, and reached Piccadilly Circus with its fashionable shops and restaurants. Couples were leisurely strolling about on a pleasant evening, seemingly oblivious to the depressing news from the war front. The Second Champagne Offensive was not going well and our losses were said to be dreadful. It was fortunate indeed that the public was unaware of the disappearance of Alistair Ainsworth and the disaster that awaited England were he not rescued promptly. As Dunn had stated, every man had his breaking point and it was only a matter of time before Ainsworth reached his.

We came to a halt in front of the Admiralty, which was located on Trafalgar Square, just across from Lord Nelson's monument. Lestrade led our way into the large, well-appointed pub that had a long, polished bar with throngs of people crowded around it. A curved flight of stairs ascended gracefully to a noisy second tier.

Lestrade was familiar with the Admiralty and explained that such crowds were not unusual at this hour, for it was a favorite of theatergoers and government officials who worked nearby. From my vantage point, all those in attendance appeared to be well dressed and upper middle class.

At the bar Lestrade showed his credentials to the barkeep and said, "We require information on one of your patrons. Any and all details may prove to be helpful, and thus nothing should be withheld."

The tone of Lestrade's voice placed the barkeep instantly on guard. "Is—is this individual said to be a regular here?"

"That is to be determined," Lestrade went on, without answering the question. "The gentleman we are interested in is Mr. Alistair Ainsworth."

"Oh, of course," the barkeep said, now at ease. "We see Mr. Ainsworth virtually every evening at six or so."

"Was he in attendance this past Monday evening?"

The barkeep thought back before answering with a firm nod. "He stopped in, with his colleague, Mr. Marlowe, at the usual time."

"How long did they stay?"

"No more than a half hour, during which they both enjoyed a glass of single-malt Scotch before going on their way."

"Did they chat with others?"

"Of that I can't be sure."

"Yet you seemed to remember their presence without hesitation."

"That is because they always order *Old Vatted Glenlivet*, a most expensive Scotch that very few can afford."

"Were there any foreigners about that evening?"

The barkeep shrugged. "Inspector, we see a good many tourists in our establishment."

"Any of German extraction?"

The barkeep's face hardened. "They would not dare."

Lestrade motioned to Joanna to indicate his line of questioning was finished.

"I assume that Mr. Ainsworth and Mr. Marlowe are employed nearby, like many of your patrons," Joanna began.

"Indeed they are, ma'am," the barkeep replied promptly. "They labor with the Admiralty Club."

"The Admiralty Club, you say!" Joanna exclaimed, feigning real interest. "Are they associated with His Majesty's Royal Navy?"

"Oh no, ma'am," the barkeep replied. "I believe they took that name because the rooms they occupy are located on the uppermost floor above us."

I smiled inwardly, admiring Joanna's clever interrogation technique. She was well aware of how the club had gained its name, but pretended ignorance to gauge the accuracy and depth of the barkeep's knowledge.

"Did you ever inquire about their work?" Joanna asked.

"I did, and they were quite eager to speak of it. They spend all their time devising word games and puzzles for newspapers and magazines. Since they were so finely dressed and drank the most expensive of Scotches, I could only assume they were well paid for their services."

"Are they the only members of the Admiralty Club?"

"I can't be sure of that, ma'am. You see, they do not go through the pub to reach the third floor. There are stairs at the rear of the building that allow them to enter."

"I take it you never hear voices through your ceiling."

The barkeep shook his head. "They are quiet as church mice."

"Do the pair ever stay late into the evening?"

"Never."

"Are they ever accompanied by a woman?"

"Not to my knowledge."

"I have one final question that I would like you to consider carefully," Joanna said. "Is it possible that Mr. Ainsworth, without your knowledge, returned later this past evening for a nightcap?"

The barkeep rubbed his forehead while he concentrated. "I think that is most unlikely.

As I mentioned, the gentlemen insisted on *Old Vatted Glenlivet*. When I served them Monday evening, I noted the bottle was nearly depleted and had enough remaining for only two or so more drinks. Because of this, I placed an order for an additional bottle." He turned and reached for an elegantly crafted bottle on a shelf behind him, then held it up for us to see. "The amount remaining is the same as when I poured the pair their drinks earlier Monday evening."

"An astute observation," Joanna praised. "Thank you for your assistance."

Outside, a thick mist was forming and the air was once again filled with moisture. Joanna looked about before gazing up to the windows on the third floor. I followed her line of vision and saw that the rooms were dimly lighted. There were no shadows or figures moving about.

"I believe you have dug another dry well," Lestrade remarked.

"So it would seem," Joanna said.

"I trust there are no other stops required of me this evening."

"None that cannot wait."

"Well and good, then," Lestrade said and, tipping his derby, bade us a pleasant good-night.

We entered our carriage and remained silent until Lestrade was far out of earshot. Only then did Joanna rap on the ceiling and give the driver an East London address.

She sighed to herself and commented, "Lestrade detects the important clues, but in this instance fails to see their significance."

"Which clues in particular?" I asked.

"The ones that make it clear that Ainsworth was not taken captive in the early evening at the pub, which indicates the capture took place elsewhere."

"But there are no clues to indicate where."

"Those will not be handed down to you on a platter, John. They must be sought and placed in order to learn where Ainsworth and Marlowe traveled to after leaving the pub."

"How can one go about gaining that information?"

"By a number of avenues," Joanna said, as we left Trafalgar Square behind. "First, as you no doubt noticed, there is a line of taxis outside the pub that drop people off and take them away. It would not be difficult to question the drivers and learn if one picked up the pair and where they were let off."

"That seems a long shot," my father mused aloud.

"Well then, here is one that is not so long," Joanna went on. "It is now close to eight, yet the lights are still on in the rooms occupied by the Admiralty Club."

"So?" I questioned.

"Which indicates they work into the late hours.

It would have taken only a moment to go to those rooms and ask the members if Ainsworth or Marlowe mentioned where they were headed that evening. It is the trail that is so important here and following it has allowed us to exclude the casino and pub as the site of Ainsworth's disappearance."

"If your assumption on the three possible locations is correct, then the opium den is our last and best hope."

"It is, and I believed that to be the case from the very start," Joanna said. "There would be no better place for kidnapping than an opium den that is dimly lighted and open until the late, late hours when the streets are empty and taxis in short supply. In addition, the victim would be groggy and under the influence of the drug, thus rendering him defenseless and easy to capture."

"But there are dozens of these dens in East London, many of which are well hidden."

"True," Joanna said. "But there is only one major player who will know all. His name is Ah Sing and he owns a string of opium dens, which are said to be among the more exclusive in that community. I have read that this particular Chinaman is reputed to know the secret of mixing the best of opium that affords the most pleasant of effects. Our Alistair Ainsworth is accustomed to only the highest quality, as witnessed by his selection of twenty-five-year-old *Old Vatted*

Glenlivet at the Admiralty. I therefore believe it is fair to say he would frequent an opium den of the highest quality, such as Ah Sing's."

We rode on in silence until we reached the dark district of Limehouse in East London. Our carriage turned onto Narrow Street and continued on for another block before coming to a stop at a storefront that had Chinese characters written upon its window. Lurking about in a nearby alley I could see shadowy figures in the dimness. The entire setting was ominous, to say the least.

"Perhaps we should have brought Lestrade along, if only for protection," I thought aloud.

Joanna waved away the suggestion. "With the presence of police, everyone within the den would have instantly clammed up or taken cover and our journey would have been wasted."

I motioned with my head toward the alleyway. "Nevertheless, I sense real danger here."

"They are here to protect the clientele," Joanna said without concern. "Should anyone cause a disturbance, those in the shadows would see to it that person disappeared. You must remember that Ah Sing is a businessman, first and foremost, and he will not allow anything or anybody to interfere with his income."

"May I inquire how you came upon this knowledge?"

"I asked," Joanna said, and left it at that.

She rapped on the thick door, which opened

immediately. A young, sharp-featured Chinese woman led us into a smoke-hazed den, where beds and mats took up most of the space. Upon them rested Englishmen, upper and lower class, all puffing on long pipes that were being held over lamps. The patrons were reclining in order to hold their lengthy opium pipes over oil lamps that heated the drug until it evaporated, thus allowing the smoker to inhale the vapor.

We were approached by a stout Chinaman in his middle years, wearing Oriental garb and slippers. His jacket was made of blue silk, as was his simple hat that covered all of his hair except for a tightly braided pigtail that extended halfway down his back.

"May I be of service?" he asked in perfect English.

"Are you Ah Sing?" Joanna returned the question.

"I am."

"Excellent. Do you have an office where we can speak?"

"This is my office."

"Then we shall conduct our business here," Joanna said, but moved the conversation nearer to the door, putting some distance between us and the opium smokers. "I have come for information that I believe you can provide. If you are unwilling to do so, I can return later with Inspector Lestrade of Scotland Yard."

Ah Sing seemed unmoved by the mention of Scotland Yard. "May I ask who you are?"

"I am the daughter of Sherlock Holmes."

A hint of a smile came to Ah Sing's inscrutable face. "Are you truly as keen and clever a detective as your father before you?"

"There are those who believe so, Mr. John Johnson," Joanna replied. "Or do you prefer to be called Ah Sing?"

"In here, the name Ah Sing suits me best."

For the hundredth time or more, I was amazed at the depth of Joanna's knowledge of such a wide variety of subjects—which included the mean streets of East London. She seemed to know so much about opium and opium dens, and even more about Ah Sing who had apparently taken on an English name.

"Well then, Ah Sing, tell us if you can recall a frequent visitor to your establishment whose name is Alistair Ainsworth."

Without hesitation, Ah Sing said, "He, along with his friend, preferred the mats in the corner."

"His friend's name?"

"Mr. Marlowe. He never gave us his first name."

"Were they frequent users?"

"They were not addicted, if that is your question. Their custom was to arrive just before nine every Monday night, smoke a pipeful or two and then be on their way."

"Always at that time?"

"Always," Ah Sing reaffirmed. "They insisted on having mats in the far corner, which I reserved for them at an additional fee, I should add."

"Am I to assume Mr. Ainsworth was here this past Monday night?"

"Correct. He arrived at nine and smoked two pipefuls."

"Did Mr. Marlowe do the same?"

Ah Sing considered the question briefly. "I believe he left early, after a single pipeful." He snapped his fingers to a small Chinese woman sitting at a nearby table and uttered a command in their language. In an instant she hurried over and handed him a thick notebook. Ah Sing quickly thumbed through its pages, which recorded the patron's name and amount of opium he used. "Yes. One pipeful for Mr. Marlowe, two for Mr. Ainsworth."

"Was that their usual consumption?"

"On most occasions they each smoked two, but as I said Mr. Marlowe left early, which accounts for his single pipeful."

"So I take it Mr. Ainsworth remained alone to enjoy his second purchase."

"But only briefly, for another customer appeared and took the mat Mr. Marlowe had vacated."

Joanna's brow went up. "Was this new arrival a friend?"

"I could not be certain, but they did talk at length."

"Had you seen this man before?" Joanna asked quickly.

"On occasion," Ah Sing answered. "But he was not a user of any significance. He never had more than one pipeful and rarely finished that."

"I would like you to describe this man in detail," Joanna urged.

Ah Sing thought back, as if trying to picture the man. "He was Caucasian and quite tall, with broad shoulders."

"His hair color?"

"I cannot recall."

"Did you yourself serve him?"

"I did."

"Can you remember any feature of his face that may have stood out? I am thinking in terms of blemishes or scars."

"He had none of those, although I did wonder if he had some ailment affecting his eye," Ah Sing replied. "He continued to blink, as if something was caught up in it."

The German agent with a facial tic! the three of us thought simultaneously. The description was a perfect match.

"Do you have a name recorded for this man?" Joanna asked without inflection.

Ah Sing shook his head. "There was no need, for his visits were so infrequent."

"Did the two of them leave together?"

"Of that I cannot be certain."

Joanna gazed over to my father. "Do you have any questions, Watson?"

"Ah, the inestimable associate of the late Sherlock Holmes," Ah Sing said, obviously pleased with my father's presence.

"I am indeed," my father said, with an acknowledging bow of his head.

"And beside you is your son who so resembles you and has taken over the role of chronicler of the daughter's detective skills."

"I take it you have read his accounts of our mysteries."

"As has every Londoner," Ah Sing said. "It would be my honor to answer any of your questions."

"I have only a few," my father began. "Did you speak with the man?"

"I did."

"Could you detect a foreign accent?"

"Not that I recall."

"From your description of the man, I would think he was a novice at opium smoking."

"Quite. Why a man would spend for a pipeful and use only half is beyond me."

"If there was a fight or struggle or cry for help, would your men stationed in the alley intervene?"

"Instantly," Ah Sing replied. "And the person

causing such a disturbance would leave with a reminder never to return."

"Finally, was the duo of Mr. Ainsworth and Mr. Marlowe ever accompanied by a woman?"

"Never in my presence."

A group of Chinese sailors appeared at the door, obviously in a cheerful mood. Ah Sing waved to them and, turning back to us, asked to be excused.

"Of course," Joanna said. "And thank you for your assistance. You have been most helpful."

"So there will be no need for Inspector Lestrade to visit?"

"None whatsoever."

We walked out into a light drizzle and hurried to our carriage. Again I saw lurking shadows in the dark, nearby alley, but now they seemed comforting rather than menacing. And more importantly, it was clear that were Alistair Ainsworth to cry out for help, his attacker would have no doubt been brutally punished, for Ainsworth was obviously a favored patron at the opium den.

"You have concluded that Alistair Ainsworth could not have been taken captive here," Joanna said matter-of-factly.

"How do you manage to read my mind so?" I asked in bewilderment.

"You stared at the shadows in the alleyway and your expression, rather than tightening, became relaxed," Joanna elucidated. "Thus, you no longer see them as a threat, but as protectors who would instantly come to Ainsworth's aid if he cried for assistance. The Germans would have been aware of this as well and planned their attack to take place some distance away from Ah Sing's. With all these facts in mind, you reached the correct conclusion."

"Kudos to both of you," my father chimed in. "Although I must admit that I too was reaching the very same conclusion, based primarily on the shadowy figures lurking nearby."

Joanna nodded. "That was the defining feature."

"And you knew beforehand that the abduction of Alistair Ainsworth would take place in the vicinity of the opium den," I continued on.

"It was the most likely scenario, but needed to be proven."

"So it seems that question has been answered with certainty," I said. "But does that bring us any closer to finding Alistair Ainsworth?"

"I believe so," Joanna replied. "For it now asks the most important question. Namely, how did the Germans know Ainsworth visited Ah Sing's with such regularity every Monday night at nine o'clock promptly?"

"Because the Germans had to have seen him in the opium den," I answered. "The agent's presence was observed by Ah Sing on several occasions."

"Do you believe the German agent, who was clearly unaccustomed to using opium, just happened to stop in to Ah Sing's and spot Ainsworth in a smoke-filled corner?"

"He had to be informed," I said at once.

"Of course he was. The agent was tipped off by someone who knew exactly every step of Ainsworth's routine."

"It had to be someone in the Admiralty Club," my father concluded.

"Such as Roger Marlowe who departed the den early that evening and left Ainsworth alone," I added.

"His departure was most convenient," Joanna noted.

"But Marlowe's early departure does not prove him guilty of treason," my father said.

"It does not prove him innocent either," said Joanna, and stared out into the rain now pounding down on the dark streets of East London. "We are moving into murky waters here."

"But surely the list of guilty candidates has been narrowed down," my father asserted.

"Do not be so certain of that, Watson," Joanna said as she leaned back and closed her eyes.

It was her way of ending a conversation. It was also her method of concentrating on every clue and detail of a difficult case, and arranging them in an order that led to resolution.

We continued on in silence, with the only

sound being made by the wheels of our carriage clocking against the cobblestone road. But my mind remained fixed on who had betrayed Alistair Ainsworth. Certainly Roger Marlowe stood high on the list, with his *convenient* absence from Ah Sing's the night Ainsworth disappeared. Yet there were a number of unnamed suspects to be considered as well, such as anyone who had access to Ainsworth's file at the Admiralty's Office of Naval Intelligence. Or, as Joanna had suggested earlier, perhaps it was a careless word or a document that should have been destroyed but wasn't that led to Ainsworth's identity being uncovered. The possibilities seemed endless.

Turning onto Edgware Road I became acutely aware of the eerie blackness that surrounded us. There was hardly a light to be seen, for even the streetlights had been turned off. All of London was now under a blackout, so as not to guide Germany's zeppelin fleet to its bombing target. Blackouts were only instituted when there was a warning that the hydrogen-filled zeppelins were silently approaching, but these events were happening all too often, bringing terror to London and its nearby cities. In the distance I heard the muffled sound of exploding bombs and could only hope they would not draw closer.

Our carriage came to a stop outside our rooms

at 221b Baker Street and we hurried up the stairs to dim the light that remained on in our parlor. At the door we heard the sound of a loudly ringing telephone and dashed in, the three of us wondering who would be calling at this late hour and for what reason. From our collective experience in medicine and crime, we knew such calls often brought the worst of news.

Joanna reached the phone first, with my father and I only a step behind, our ears pricked to catch every word.

"Yes?" Joanna answered, then, after a brief pause, responded, "Ah, Johnny! How are you, my dear son?"

She listened intently for a moment before the worry left her face. Only then did she place a hand over the receiver and whisper to us, "He is well."

My father and I nevertheless remained concerned, for the lad rarely called home and never after the ten o'clock hour. There had to be a problem of some magnitude. But what?

Pressing the phone to her ear, Joanna seemed to be concentrating on each word, yet her face remained expressionless. After a long interval, she spoke again. "How very kind of you . . . Of course. We shall meet you at Paddington Station tomorrow morning . . . Yes, yes. Until then, my dear son."

Placing the phone down, Joanna explained the

nature of the call. "What a strange set of events Verner's death has brought into play."

"Pray tell, what?" I asked anxiously.

"It seems that Johnny and Verner's son, Thomas, are friends," Joanna replied. "Poor Thomas is grief-stricken by his father's passing, and the headmaster at Eton thought it best he be accompanied home by a friend. Our Johnny volunteered without hesitation."

"Good show!" my father pronounced proudly.

"As would be expected of the lad," I added. "But I am somewhat surprised they are such close friends, for the good Dr. Verner appeared to be well into his middle years and thus his son should be considerably older than Johnny."

"One might think so," said my father. "But Verner married late in life to a lovely nurse from St. Bartholomew's Hospital, and his son's age is in all likelihood close to Johnny's."

Joanna asked, "Would I have been familiar with his wife during my stay at St. Bart's?"

"Perhaps," my father replied. "Her maiden name was Mary Todd, as I recall. She was a head nurse on the medical ward, while you spent your days in the surgery section. Still, your paths may have crossed."

"I do believe I remember her," Joanna said, thinking back in time. "She was somewhat delicate, with a kind face and prematurely graying hair."

"That is her."

"How sad for such a tragic circumstance to bring us together again."

"A tragic circumstance indeed," my father concurred. "But I must admit that I am relieved that the phone call did not tell of any misgivings for our Johnny."

"Of that, I am not certain," Joanna said.

"Why so? Was there something amiss in his tone of voice or in the words he spoke?"

"Nothing that one could detect."

"Then what is the basis for your worry?"

"Maternal instinct," Joanna said, and without further comment, she drew the curtains and retired for the night.

7

Paddington Station

An early morning rain was beginning to fall as our four-wheeler turned sharply off Edgware Road and onto Praed Street, where Paddington Station was located. We were making good time and well ahead of schedule when traffic came to an abrupt halt, for before us was a line of ambulances offloading patients into St. Mary's Hospital, which was situated next to the train station.

"Are these casualties from the war?" I inquired.

"I think not," my father replied. "Most likely they are the injured from last night's bombing raid that took its toll on Surrey." He pointed to an arriving vehicle that had the county's name printed on it before adding, "According to the morning newspapers, a nursing home suffered a direct hit, with dozens killed and wounded."

"Bombs have no conscience," said I.

"Nor do the pilots of the zeppelins," my father remarked.

Joanna asked, "Will St. Mary's be prepared to deal with so many badly wounded patients?"

"Not all will come here, for there is a mass

casualty plan in place that distributes the patients to the major hospitals throughout the greater London area," my father responded. "But those who are admitted to St. Mary's will receive the best of care, for it has an excellent staff in both surgery and medicine."

"Did you have admitting privileges here?"

My father nodded. "I held that privilege for many years, as did Alexander Verner. As a matter of fact, it was there that I first met him and became aware of his remarkable diagnostic skills. He could solve the most difficult of cases, as the royal family can attest to."

"The royal family, you say?" Joanna asked, leaning forward with interest.

"Close to the king himself," my father replied. "A royal, who shall remain nameless, had a dreadful fever of unknown origin. Despite being seen by numerous specialists and undergoing countless tests, no one could come up with a diagnosis. Verner was called in and made the diagnosis of a hidden abscess that was treated surgically and cured. For his efforts, Verner was invited to tea at Buckingham Palace."

"That must have been the talk of the hospital," I ventured.

"It was, but not because Verner spoke of it, for he never did," my father reminisced warmly.

"Doctor-patient confidentiality, I would think," said Joanna.

"That and the fact that Alexander Verner was a most humble man who never considered himself extraordinary, although he obviously was."

Traffic began moving again and we quickly reached the front entrance to Paddington Station. Hurrying in, I was immediately impressed with the major upgrades the station had undergone, while preserving its basic architecture as much as possible. A number of additional platforms had been built and service kiosks installed, all housed beneath a glazed, curved ceiling that rose to a height of over a hundred feet. For reasons known only to God, the station had been spared damage from the multiple bombing raids. Glancing about, we had no difficulty locating the correct arrival platform, for my father recognized Alexander Verner's widow standing near a giant, elevated clock. She was a thin, small woman, in her middle years, with snow-white hair and dressed entirely in black. By her side on a short leash was a huge, brown mastiff that had a black snout and a gaping mouth. The massive hound sat on its haunches and carefully eyed anyone who approached.

"It is unfortunate the mastiff was not with Verner the morning the Germans barged into his office," I remarked in a low voice.

"Indeed," Joanna agreed.

No introductions were necessary, for Mary Verner seemed to remember us from our time together at St. Bartholomew's. Despite her very white hair, she had aged well, with her delicate features for the most part unchanged. But the signs of sorrow were obvious, as evidenced by her reddened eyes and the corners of her lips being slightly pulled down. It was with effort that she managed a weak smile.

"Allow me to offer our deepest sympathy on the passing of your husband," my father consoled. "He was such a fine doctor and an even finer gentleman."

"He thought the world of you as well, John," Mary responded in a soft voice. "He often told me that if he were to become ill, you would be the doctor he would choose."

"That is high praise indeed," my father said, with a half bow before turning to us. "I take it that you remember my son and his wife, Joanna, from your nursing days at St. Bart's."

"I do indeed," Mary replied. "I particularly recall Joanna for her skills in the operating room. We were all quite envious of you back then."

"Thank you for such a kind remembrance," said Joanna.

"Not at all," Mary went on. "And now you have made quite a name for yourself as a most capable private detective. I was more than pleased to learn from Inspector Lestrade that you are now involved in this detestable crime. I can only hope you will bring those responsible to justice."

"I shall do my very best," Joanna promised as her brow furrowed briefly. "May I ask why the inspector contacted you?"

"It was I who contacted him," Mary replied. "I called because I remembered something my husband had told me the evening before his death. While relaxing from his ordeal over brandy, he recalled hearing one of those dreadful people shout the word *rot* from an upper floor. This occurred as my husband was departing from the patient's residence. He did not know if the word had significance nor did I, but I thought it best to bring it to the inspector's attention."

"Most wise," Joanna agreed. "But was it simply *rot* he overheard or was there a word before or after it?"

"Just *rot* as he recalled," Mary answered. "Is that important?"

"Perhaps," Joanna said. "We shall see."

Our conversation was interrupted by the approaching train from Eton. We stepped back to allow Mary Verner room to embrace her grieving son. It was the worst of all situations, I thought, as I envisioned a grief-stricken son coming home to a grief-stricken mother, with each trying to somehow comfort the other. A son returning from school was usually a most joyous event. Today it would be sad beyond words.

Moments later the two lads disembarked and, after waving, hurried over to us. Thomas Verner was small and quite thin, much like his father, except his hair was long and tousled, with a lock hanging over his forehead. By contrast, Johnny Blalock was tall for a boy of twelve, with a handsome, narrow face and a jutting jaw. Yet it was his eyes that caught your attention. They were half lidded and gave him a serious, studious look. For those familiar with a photograph of a young Sherlock Holmes, Johnny could have passed as Sherlock's twin.

Thomas raced to his mother and tightly embraced her, with tears now flowing freely across his cheeks. The boy continued to sob uncontrollably, pausing only to say, "Oh, Mother! Oh, Mother!"

We decided to take our leave, for there was little we could do to comfort the heartbroken family. But before our departure, Mary asked my father if he would be good enough to serve as a pallbearer at her husband's funeral. My father was greatly moved and responded that it would be his honor to do so.

It was only after passing through the station's front entrance that Johnny and his mother exchanged warm cheek kisses. Joanna then took a moment to straighten Johnny's tie that had gone a bit askew.

"Thank you, Mother."

"You are welcome," Joanna said. "Now tell us, how was your trip?"

"Dreadful," Johnny replied. "Poor Thomas was inconsolable."

"Which is understandable, for he has lost a dear father, much as you did," Joanna reminded him.

"The sadness and grief are to be expected, but I see no need for it to be publicly displayed."

"Some are not as strong and resolute as you are," my father remarked. "Nevertheless, it was fortunate he had a close friend to lean upon."

"We are not close, but simply acquaintances," Johnny said candidly. "Since no one else volunteered for the journey, I decided I should, for it was obvious that Thomas would have difficulty traveling alone."

"It was still good of you to do so," my father commended.

"Yes, it was," Johnny said and left it at that.

My father and I exchanged knowing glances, with both of us no doubt thinking the same thought. Not only was Johnny's appearance remarkably similar to Sherlock Holmes, so was his emotional control. Statement of fact and deductive reasoning took precedence over feelings, which were either pushed aside or absent.

As we took our seats in a waiting carriage, Johnny asked, "May I know the details of Dr. Verner's death?"

"He was tortured and murdered," replied Joanna.

"Tortured? How?"

"With a burning cigarette."

"Most painful," Johnny said, seemingly unmoved by the suffering Verner must have endured. "But why?"

"To obtain information."

"What sort?"

"That is undetermined."

"But what has been determined is a proper hanging for those responsible." My father bristled, his anger showing briefly.

Johnny noted my father's change in temper and remarked, "Thomas mentioned that you and Dr. Verner were colleagues."

"And good friends," my father said, then added firmly, "I will not rest until those responsible are apprehended and punished."

Johnny pondered the matter before asking, "Are there any clues as to who carried out such a heinous act?"

My father looked at Joanna who answered, "We believe foreign agents."

Johnny's half-lidded eyes abruptly widened. "Was Dr. Verner somehow involved with foreign agents?"

"So it would seem."

The information Joanna gave was now public knowledge, with all newspapers reporting the details of the crime, but without mention of Alistair Ainsworth or his abduction. My attention returned to Johnny who was gazing intently at his mother. It was as if he were trying to read her mind without success.

"Mother," he said finally, "I do believe you are withholding important clues."

"For now, I am afraid I must," Joanna said, then flicked her wrist to dismiss the subject. "So tell me, dear son, how go your studies at Eton?"

"Well enough, but I am bored."

"Your grades say otherwise."

Johnny shrugged indifferently. "But the subjects have little appeal. I am expected to memorize facts that have no bearing on the profession I have chosen to pursue. You see, Mother, I plan to follow in your footsteps and become a private detective. I truly believe that is my calling."

"That calling must await your completing your studies," said Joanna. "You will soon learn that the seemingly irrelevant facts you commit to memory now will become most useful in the future."

"Oh, I wish to continue my studies, but not at Eton."

"Where then?"

"At home, here in London at 221b Baker Street," Johnny continued on eagerly. "We shall choose the subjects that provide the information that is paramount in criminal investigation. We can hire a tutor to guide me, much as we did when living with Grandfather Blalock."

"A formal education is much preferred, for it

will greatly increase the scope of your knowledge, far more than will tutorial learning," Joanna explained patiently. "And life experiences away from home will sharpen your instincts and insights in ways that books cannot."

"You really should finish up your studies at Eton, for you may decide on yet another profession later on," my father chimed in.

"And an honors degree from Eton will pave the road to success, no matter the field you choose to pursue," I added.

"My mind will not change," Johnny said stubbornly. "I carry the genes of Sherlock Holmes and they will dictate what I do in life."

Joanna sighed resignedly. "I take it you have given this decision considerable thought."

"I have, Mother."

"Then I will ask that you give the matter even more careful consideration, for such changes often do not work out well."

"This will be for the better," Johnny persisted. "Of that, I am certain."

"It may be so," Joanna agreed halfheartedly. "Only time will tell."

Johnny brightened. "Does that mean I have your permission to withdraw from Eton?"

"It means the matter is not entirely settled," Joanna said in a measured voice. She seemed to think further before asking, "When are you expected to return to Eton?"

"Within the week."

"That is time enough for you to reconsider, for I wish you to do so," Joanna urged. "You will give the matter careful thought, paying particular attention to the advantages and disadvantages of leaving a distinguished school like Eton, in favor of a private, tutored education at home. At the end of the week, you will let me know of your decision and the reasons behind it."

"You make it sound like a formal presentation."

"It is, for you must convince both yourself and your mother that such a move is to your advantage."

"I can do that."

"I suspect you can."

As our carriage continued on, Johnny sat back with a confident smile on his face. He was beyond a doubt certain he would prevail. I gazed over to Joanna, expecting her to be disheartened or, at a minimum, concerned over her son's plans, which were so clearly to his disadvantage. Instead, she gave me the subtlest of smiles that told me that young Johnny Blalock was destined to return to Eton and complete his studies there.

8

The Admiralty Club

Having left Johnny in our rooms to enjoy a well-deserved nap, we hurried to Trafalgar Square where a most important meeting awaited us. With Lieutenant Dunn's permission and under his supervision, we visited the Admiralty Club just as Big Ben struck the noon hour. The third floor was designed most peculiarly and was not what we expected. Illuminated by a skylight, it contained a large, circular center that opened to four separate offices, three of which were currently occupied by the three remaining members of the secret organization. Off to the side near the entrance was an armed guard wearing the uniform of His Majesty's Navy.

Joanna carefully studied him before turning to Dunn. "Is it not odd to have such an important unit housed above a pub? Surely a more secure location would be in order."

"It is odd indeed, but please keep in mind the type of individuals we are dealing with. They are free thinkers to the greatest extent and will not accept military discipline or regimentation of any sort. They do as they wish when they wish and will ignore any restrictions you place on them. So it was not surprising that they refused to be housed at the Admiralty in Whitehall where they would be forced to sign in and out and be subjected to repeated interruptions. They demanded a comfortable situation that was distant and separate from the Royal Navy. In their minds, these rooms provided the ideal location to perform their vital work."

"It sounds as if the Royal Navy bent to the group's every command."

"We had little choice. Under ordinary circumstances, they would have been conscripted and ordered to commence with their duties, but you can easily imagine where this would have taken us with this independent group. So we reached a compromise. The rooms above the Admiralty pub were selected, but only after the group's approval, of course. With reluctance, they accepted the presence of an armed guard at the door to deny entrance to unwanted visitors or intruders."

"Does the guard remain on duty into the night?"

Dunn shook his head. "He departs promptly at six, with me, after the messages and communiqués have been collected."

"I take it the armed guard is at your side when you arrive in the morning."

"He is. As a matter of fact, the attaché case holding the coded messages is never out of his sight."

"Be so good as to describe how the messages are gathered at Whitehall and then distributed to the individual members of the group."

"The coded messages are placed in an attaché case under the eyes of the assistant director of Naval Intelligence, then brought to these rooms at eight a.m. promptly. Here, the case is opened and the documents disseminated to the group by Alistair Ainsworth. Each document is numbered so they can be easily tracked if necessary. I return at six p.m. sharp and the decoded messages are placed in the attaché case, after which the case is locked. The lock is such that it cannot be opened except by special key that is only available at Whitehall."

"Are all documents retrieved?"

"Without fail. We carefully check the numbers on all of the coded messages and their translated counterparts, and only then are they placed in the attaché case and locked away."

"What of the scattered notes and reminders that the members may have jotted down?"

"All are collected."

"So none are allowed to leave these rooms?"

"That is an absolute restriction."

"Are the members searched as they depart for the evening?"

"They would not stand for that."

"Then you have an obvious breach in your security."

"It is possible," Dunn conceded. "But I doubt anyone could make much from their scribbled notes."

"That depends entirely on who is reading the scribble." Joanna gazed around the room once more until her eyes came to rest on the entry door. "I assume the door is securely locked after hours."

"When the last person leaves, the door is to be locked shut."

Joanna nodded, but the furrowing of her brow told us she was not satisfied with Dunn's answers. Something about the door caught her interest, for she continued to stare at it and the guard beside it.

"Are there other questions?" Dunn asked impatiently.

"None at the moment."

"Then let us proceed."

We began our questioning with Mrs. Mary Ellington who we were told had recently lost her son on a battlefield in Belgium. She was a small woman, slight of frame, with a kind face and gray-brown hair pulled back tightly into a bun. If she was intimidated by our presence, she showed no signs of it.

"I do hope Tubby is all right," Mary said, leaning back in a swivel chair, with her hands clasped together behind her head.

"As do we," Joanna said.

"But I fear the worst."

"Why?"

"Because Tubby is a man of strict habits," Mary replied. "Only the direst of circumstances would cause him to deviate."

"Did you know him well?"

"You make it sound as if he is already dead."

"Do you know him well?" Joanna corrected.

"Well enough, but only at work in these rooms," Mary replied. "Yet his routine is so precise and predictable, one could set a clock by his actions."

"Was this the case the Monday of his disappearance?"

"In every way. He arrived at eight sharp, stayed in his office until teatime at ten thirty, left for lunch at one, returned at two, used the loo at three, and worked until six on the dot, at which time he departed for the pub downstairs."

"Did you speak with him that day?"

"We chatted only briefly, for we tend to work alone in our offices, where we can produce the best results. On occasion, however, we do collaborate, particularly when we require another's skill set."

"Could you give us an example?"

Dunn quickly intervened. "I do not think we should go there."

"Oh, come now, Lieutenant," Mary said briskly. "Do you consider the daughter of Sherlock Holmes and the Watsons untrustworthy?"

Lieutenant Dunn stared at her, tight-lipped, but gave no response.

"My particular skill deals with codes that consist of numbers and symbols," Mary continued on. "If I come across anything that has overtones of German history or geography, I would consult with Roger Marlowe who is very familiar with that dreadful country. Tubby, on the other hand, is a wizard with word games, such as puzzles and anagrams."

"Both are also very good at mathematics as well, I was told."

"So am I," Mary interjected. "Which is attested to by my honors degree from Oxford. I consider mathematics my strong point."

Here was a woman not to be trifled with, I thought. She would easily be a match for either Ainsworth or Marlowe, and her forthright manner indicated she would not tolerate a pecking order in the group. At that moment, I noticed her black armband and recalled she had recently lost her son in the war.

"I know you are quite occupied with your work, so I shan't take up more of your time," Joanna said. "However, I do need to know if Alistair Ainsworth ever mentioned he was being followed."

"Never," Mary answered promptly. "And were that the case, it would have been brought to the attention of our intelligence liaison officer."

"Lieutenant Dunn?"

"Lieutenant Dunn."

"Did you see or chat with Ainsworth on the day of his disappearance?"

"I only saw him briefly and that was at a small, nearby café where I passed his table at lunch. He was seated with Roger Marlowe and a rather attractive woman who was introduced as Lady Jane something or other. From their seating arrangement, I would guess she was there with Roger rather than Tubby."

"Close, were they?"

"Quite."

"Thank you for your time and service to England," Joanna said, then added, "and we should like to offer our condolences on the loss of your son in defense of our country."

Mary Ellington nodded ever so solemnly. "He was such a good boy."

"I am certain he was."

We returned to the central area where we waited while Lieutenant Dunn took a phone call in Alistair Ainsworth's vacant office. The other doors were closed and we could hear no sounds coming from within.

"Mary Ellington seems to be holding up well from her loss," I commented.

"Some women are better than others at hiding broken hearts," Joanna said, then turned to Lieutenant Dunn as he returned. "Let us move on to the next member of the group."

"His name is Geoffrey Montclair, a genius at design engineering," said Dunn. "In addition, he has a photographic memory and can memorize a chapter from a book or a long conversation and repeat it verbatim a week later. You can see his value when dealing with a multitude of codes that may have similarities."

We entered Geoffrey Montclair's office and found him feeding and talking to a caged parakeet. The bird responded with a series of pleasant chirps.

"I do wish you would leave the parakeet at home," Dunn admonished.

"He becomes lonely," Montclair said, and ignored Dunn as he dusted off his hands and introduced himself. He was a tall, lean man, with rosy cheeks and curly blond hair. His graceful, exaggerated motions, together with his high-pitched voice, gave him a somewhat feminine flair. "It is so unlike Tubby to go missing."

"How well did you know him?" Joanna asked.

"We did not socialize together, but crossed paths often enough at chess matches."

"Were both of you masters?"

"Yes, although I considered my game superior to Tubby's."

"Did Ainsworth share this opinion?"

"Quite the opposite," Montclair said, with a smile. "We didn't take each other too seriously. It was all in good fun."

"When was the last chess tournament?"

"A month or so ago."

"I would assume that most of the players were Englishmen?"

"Oh, there were some from the Continent as well, primarily Poles and Russians."

"Was that the last time you saw Ainsworth outside the office?"

"It was."

"On the day of his disappearance, did you converse with him at all?"

The parakeet began tweeting loudly from its cage. It was not a single chirp, but seemed to go on and on. Montclair turned to the bird and hissed, "Hush! You silly bird!"

The bird obeyed and went about pruning its feathers quietly.

"Tubby and I spoke briefly." Montclair came back to Joanna's question. "He mentioned that he and Marlowe would be dining at Simpson's-in-the-Strand, which is a restaurant we both favor."

"I take it that was late in the afternoon."

Montclair nodded. "On his way out."

"Thank you for your time and assistance."

Once we were in the central area and the door to Montclair's office closed, Joanna turned to Dunn and asked, "How thoroughly was Geoffrey Montclair vetted?"

"Most thoroughly, top to bottom," Dunn said. "His record and résumé were spotless."

"Is he or was he ever married?"

"No," Dunn replied. "Nor was he known to be involved in any long-term relationships. His social life was investigated vigorously and there was nothing unusual discovered."

"I see," Joanna said, but the tone of her voice indicated she was not convinced. "Were there any particular women in his life?"

"Some years ago he was involved with a secretary at a prominent law firm."

"Was she looked into?"

"In detail," Dunn reported. "She spoke of him as being charming and witty, and liked by all."

"It sounds as if their relationship was never serious on a romantic scale."

"That was our impression as well, but I can see what your questions are leading to. And the answer is there was no evidence of sexual deviation."

"Yet for a man Montclair's age to have had only a single, lukewarm relationship over the years would surely strike one as being unusual."

Dunn shrugged indifferently. "Some men are simply put together that way."

"So I have been told," Joanna said as we strode toward Roger Marlowe's office.

But I could tell the matter of Montclair's sexuality was of real concern to her, for homosexuality could be used as a tool for blackmail. In several well-publicized cases, personages in high places were forced to resign and leave office because of their sexual orientation and the vulnerability that accompanied it. With this in mind, I concluded that while Dunn's investigation of Geoffrey Montclair may have ended, Joanna's most assuredly had not.

"Allow me to provide you with the details on Roger Marlowe whom you will interview next," Dunn said.

We listened with feigned interest to the lieutenant's description of Marlowe's background, which was not nearly as complete as the information we had received from Emma Ainsworth and Lady Jane Hamilton. Dunn appeared to believe that Roger Marlowe's time and contacts during his years at the University of Heidelberg were a major asset rather than a dangerous liability.

"I doubt that he will be able to add much to your investigation," Dunn stated, ending his summary.

"We shall see," Joanna said.

Following Dunn into an office larger than the others, we had to step around a chair that held a carelessly placed cashmere topcoat. I paid little attention to the ruffled coat whilst Joanna gave it a quick, yet studied glance. Standing behind an orderly desk was an imposing man wearing a dark, expensively tailored suit and red silk tie. Roger Marlowe was both dashing and handsome, with aristocratic features and dark hair that was beginning to gray at the temples. He was clearly forthright and accustomed to taking control of a given situation.

"Allow me to summarize," he said, obviously aware of who we were. "Tubby Ainsworth and I are lifelong friends. We grew up together, went to Eton, Cambridge, and Heidelberg as a pair, and stayed close after our return to England. We dated the same girls, fell in love with the same woman, and never married because the single life was so enjoyable. Our lives remain intertwined, for we delight in the best of food and drink, as well as in the thrill of gambling and the pleasure of an occasional pipeful of opium. We are more like brothers than friends, and I am with the Admiralty Club at his urging, although I must admit I find the challenge of codebreaking irresistible."

"Thank you for your concise summary," Joanna said. "It is most helpful, but it is the details of your last evening with Alistair Ainsworth that we need to hear. We know of your visit to the Admiralty pub where you ordered your usual *Old Vatted Glenlivet*, and of your final stop at Ah Sing's."

"You neglected our fine dinner at Simpson's."

"Only because it has no importance, unless you believe otherwise."

"I do not."

"Excellent. Then let us stay on course and learn

the particulars of your early departure from Ah Sing's."

Marlowe reached for an engraved silver cigarette case and slowly extracted a cigarette, his eyes never leaving Joanna. One could almost sense the man's brain at work. "I see the circle you are drawing. We smoke a pipeful of opium and drift off into a haze-filled dream, at which point I depart, leaving Tubby alone and defenseless. Then he disappears, which happens to coincide with my disappearance."

"That is the sequence," Joanna agreed.

"But you have ignored the reason for my departure. I left early because of a blinding head-ache that the drug can sometimes induce. The doctors Watson can attest to this side effect."

My father and I nodded simultaneously, for although opium was a painkiller, it at times induced headaches similar to a migraine.

"Tubby wished to leave with me, but I insisted he stay and enjoy the remainder of the evening," Marlowe went on. "To ensure his safety, I arranged for a taxi to be at his disposal."

"Do you know if Ainsworth actually took the taxi?"

"I assume he did, for I paid the driver his fee well in advance."

Joanna dug into her purse for a Turkish ciga-rette and lighted it carefully, then blew smoke in the direction of Roger Marlowe. I had the distinct impression that a war of wits was about to begin.

"I can assure you I had no part in Tubby's disappearance," Marlowe said earnestly. "He is the dearest of friends and I now fear for his life."

"From whom?"

"Let us not waste time with the obvious."

"Which brings us to my next line of inquiry," Joanna said, taking another deep draw on her cigarette but keeping her focus directed at Marlowe. "I am referring to the individual who befriended Ainsworth after your departure."

Marlowe's eyes narrowed noticeably. "That would be most unlike Tubby. He did not stray outside his social circle, and went to great lengths to avoid others who frequented Ah Sing's."

"That being the reason he insisted on occupying mats in the far corner away from the other customers."

"Exactly. He and I paid an extra fee for that consideration."

"The man who appeared to befriend Ainsworth was said by Ah Sing to be large and broad shouldered."

"There are no doubt dozens who would fit that description."

"But this one had a distinctive facial tic."

Marlowe nodded at once. "I remember the fellow, but he was hardly a friend. We chatted with him briefly on occasion, and nothing more."

"Was he an Englishman?"

Marlowe shrugged. "I do not recall an accent, if that is what you are referring to."

"Did he give his name?"

"I have no such recollection. But you may wish to ask Ah Sing, for he keeps a careful record on all his clientele."

"So we shall," Joanna said, and crushed out her cigarette.

Marlowe was reaching for the ashtray when the phone on his desk rang. He quickly brought the receiver to his ear and said only, "Yes?" which was followed by a terse "Who?"

Marlowe listened intently as a most serious expression crossed his face. He handed the phone to Dunn, saying, "For your ears only."

We were ushered out to the central circular area and told to remain there, with instructions not to continue further interviews without Dunn being present. Once Marlowe closed the door to his office behind him, Joanna hurriedly turned to us.

"We must delve deeply into Marlowe's finances," she said in a whisper.

"Because of his excellent tastes?" I whispered back.

"Because his tastes are far too expensive for a man of his apparent income."

"Dinner at Simpson's and a nightly glass of *Old Vatted Glenlivet* would surely be within his means," my father said.

Joanna shook her head firmly. "Did you not notice his cashmere topcoat, with a label stating it was made by Gieves and Hawkes, the most expensive tailor on Savile Row? Were you not impressed by his bespoke suit and his sterling silver cigarette case that had its engravings filled with semiprecious stones? I can assure you these items greatly exceed his level of pay. There must be an outside source of income to account for these expenditures."

"Such as?"

"There is a foreign country that would pay handsomely for his knowledge," Joanna said.

The door to Marlowe's office opened and we were permitted to enter once again. If the two men standing beside the desk had encountered a reversal of some sort, they showed no evidence of it. Nevertheless, the tone of Dunn's voice indicated the amount of time allotted to us was now limited.

"You may continue with your questions," Dunn said tersely. "But please be concise."

"We shall be as concise as the answers we receive," Joanna retorted, then turned to Marlowe. "We were speaking of the man whom Ainsworth happened to meet at Ah Sing's. Did you by chance ever see this fellow at Laurent's casino?"

"Never."

"Might he have chatted briefly with Ainsworth

or the lady who often accompanied you there?"

"That would have been most unlikely, for our attention was focused entirely on the cards that had been played. We would not have tolerated interruption from anyone."

"Including the rather attractive woman who was always at your shoulder?"

"Jane?" Marlowe said, with a forced laugh. "Her only concern was attempting to learn the method we employed to win so frequently."

"Did she?"

"We did not disclose our method to her, or to anyone else for that matter," Marlowe lied easily.

"Could you be so good as to tell us about this woman Jane?"

"Her full name is Lady Jane Hamilton, a good and close friend to both Tubby and me through the years. It was Tubby who was closest growing up, for they lived only houses apart."

"Did this association continue after she married?"

"With Tubby it did. For he shared with her a talent I do not possess. Tubby is a gourmet cook whose dishes and delicacies can rival any restaurant in London. He loves to prepare dishes for her and his invalid sister Emma, and does so at least once a week."

"I take it Lady Jane supplies the essentials since the sister cannot."

"She does indeed," Marlowe replied. "And she

is very good at that, but does so under Tubby's supervision."

"She actually shops with him?"

"Hardly," Marlowe said, with another forced laugh. "She sends her grossly overweight cook to the Covent Garden market every Thursday where she meets with Tubby at the poulterer's stall. There, Tubby selects the finest goose, duck, or pheasant, which will serve as the entrée. My friend has amazing knowledge about these fowl and has no difficulty selecting the finest for the oven."

"I am surprised that Ainsworth takes such time away from his important work with the Admiralty Club."

Marlowe flicked his wrist at the perception. "He only goes on Thursday and meets with the cook promptly at noon in front of Hoover's stall. Tubby skips lunch that day, I might add, so the king still obtains a full day's work from him."

"This poulterer Hoover must be rather exceptional."

"He is among the best of the lot."

"My father-in-law is virtually addicted to the taste of fine pheasant," Joanna remarked. "But the birds our fine landlady has brought home lately are somewhat lacking in quality."

"Then Hoover is the poulterer you must see."

"H-O-O-V-E-R?"

"Yes. It is so spelled over his stall."

"Have you actually been there?"

Marlowe shook his head. "Tubby showed it to me in a photograph that was taken of him standing beside the poulterer."

"So I should have no difficulty finding the stall."

"None whatsoever."

Lieutenant Dunn was more than anxious to usher us out, but not before reminding us that we remained sworn under the Official Secrets Act. We carefully descended the wet stairs at the rear of the building, then circled back to Trafalgar Square, which was now heavily populated with tourists and pigeons waiting to be fed.

Using his umbrella, my father hailed an empty four-wheeler that promptly pulled up in front of us. As we climbed in, my father asked, "What say you, Joanna?"

"I say we go to Covent Garden on Thursday."

"To what end?"

"To see the poulterer Hoover."

"Why is he of such interest to you?"

"His name."

"What of it?"

"Hoover is the anglicized version of the German surname Huber."

9

Blood Smears

Our plans for the following day included a visit with Sir David Shaw, an old friend of my father's, who was currently a curator in charge of Mesopotamian script and languages at the British Museum. Johnny showed scant interest in such a trip, believing that museums were little more than storehouses for ancient relics and various remains from the long-ago past. But he became quite excited when he learned that Inspector Lestrade had called and asked us to return to the crime scene, for something curious had been discovered in the late Dr. Verner's office.

After calling Sir David to inform him that our arrival would be delayed, we hurried over to the Kensington address and found a constable standing guard at the front steps of the practice. With a knowing nod, the officer allowed us immediate entrance, although his eyes narrowed somewhat at the presence of young Johnny.

In a low voice, I asked Joanna, "Did Lestrade give any clues as to this new finding?"

"Only that it was noticed by a cleaning crew brought in by Mrs. Verner to scrub the office,"

Joanna replied. "Apparently the practice will soon be placed on the market, and thus all traces of a murder must be removed."

"But, Mother," Johnny argued mildly, "the dreadful death of Dr. Verner will have been reported in all the newspapers, so all the public will surely be aware."

"Reading about a murder and viewing the evidence of one are two entirely different matters," Joanna explained, bringing a finger to her lips as we approached the office. "Now, Johnny, you must not ask questions or in any way involve yourself, for this is an official police investigation. And if the inspector asks you to leave, you must do so without delay, regardless of any keen interest you may have."

"I understand, Mother."

On entering the office one could still detect the faint aroma of chloroform in the air. It emanated from a towel beneath the bloodied cabinet, which had apparently become doused during the course of the crime. Even with the passage of time, some dampness remained and accounted for the characteristic odor.

"What is that smell?" Johnny asked, unable to control his curiosity.

"No questions," Joanna said, and gave her son a stern look. "But in this instance, I will permit it and answer your inquiry. It is the singular aroma of chloroform, which a student in an advanced chemistry class would instantly recognize."

My father and I exchanged subtle smiles, for Johnny was now being educated in more ways than one. Yes, I thought, the aroma of chloroform would certainly be experienced in a chemistry laboratory at Eton, but never during a tutor's lesson. I glanced over to Joanna's son to determine if the point had been made, but his expression remained unchanged.

Standing by the broken medicine cabinet, Inspector Lestrade greeted us with a tip of his derby. "It was good of you to come so promptly," he said, with his eyes fixed on Johnny.

"Not at all," Joanna replied before introducing her son. "We were about to depart for the British Museum when your call came. I trust you will not be bothered by the presence of my son, but if so, I can have him wait in our carriage. I hope the latter will not be necessary, for the morning air is unseasonably cold."

"Under the vast majority of circumstances, this would not be allowed," Lestrade said. "However, since virtually all of the evidence has been removed, I see no harm in it, as long as the lad is not upset by the sight of dried blood. Of course details of the case must not be discussed in his presence, nor should he later speak of what he sees in this office, for it is best kept from the public eye."

"But, sir," Johnny interrupted politely, "it is

already being spoken of by the cleaners who could barely wait to tell their friends and fellow laborers."

Lestrade was caught off guard by the lad's keen insight, but recovered rapidly. "Nevertheless, I prefer you make no mention of it."

"Then I shan't," Johnny promised, and quickly began glancing around the office. "Where is this dried blood you referred to?"

Joanna gave her son another sharp stare of displeasure.

"Sorry," Johnny murmured, his face coloring at the silent reprimand.

"Which you should be," said Joanna. "Now, Inspector, please proceed."

"The stain is on the cabinet itself, which was the last standing item the cleaners were to tidy up," Lestrade told us. "Here, I will show you."

As we walked over, my father stepped on a large shred of brown glass that, despite his weight, remained intact. He used the toe of his shoe to move the shred aside.

"The cleaners were to do the floor as they departed," Lestrade explained.

Johnny stared down at the piece of glass and asked, "Why did it not splinter when stepped upon so firmly?"

Joanna sighed resignedly, understanding there was no way to suppress the lad's curiosity. She picked up the fragment and held it under Johnny's nose. "What do you detect?"

"The aroma of chloroform!"

"Precisely," said Joanna. "And in what type of bottle would you find chloroform?"

Johnny shrugged, saying, "I am unsure."

"Perhaps we should ask Watson, who has experienced chloroform in both a chemistry laboratory and in the practice of medicine."

"It is always contained in a thick, brown glass bottle that prevents the container from breaking were it to fall accidentally," my father elucidated.

"Then why did it shatter here?" Lestrade inquired.

"Because Verner meant it to," Joanna replied. "He must have thrown it to the floor with some force, so that its contents would spill out and leave a trail to follow."

"A most clever deduction," Lestrade said admiringly.

"Based on my wife's experience with chloroform as a surgical nurse," I surmised.

"Actually I first learned about its properties in a class at nursing school," Joanna said, in a comment clearly made for her son.

Lestrade brought our attention to the far side of the medicine cabinet. Written on its white wall was a streak of blood that was shaped like the letter *h*. There was a large, nondescript smudge of blood directly above it.

Joanna moved in with her magnifying glass and carefully examined the streak and the smudge. She performed this maneuver twice, paying particular scrutiny to the smudge, before turning to me and asking, "Did you notice any lacerations on Verner's hands when you examined them at the murder scene?"

I thought back and shook my head. "There were none. His hands were tightly bound to the arms of the chair, but I detected neither cuts nor gashes, which would have been quite evident."

"Did you examine both the palms as well as the dorsal surfaces of the hands?"

"Both were clear except for the cigarette burns and a broad bloodstain on the right palm."

"Then, in all likelihood, the blood belonged to the German," Joanna concluded.

"Does it matter whose blood it is?" Lestrade asked.

"A great deal," Joanna replied, and studied the stains yet again with her magnifying glass. "For it informs us what transpired during the struggle and who his captors were."

"Why, the Germans."

"Where is your proof?"

"There is circumstantial evidence."

"Not good enough."

Lestrade blinked repeatedly as he tried to come up with a more convincing answer.

"It is here in the stain, for everything points to

Dr. Verner cutting his captor's hand and using the blood to write a message," Joanna elucidated.

Johnny stepped in closer to see what his mother saw, but the expression on his face told us he did not. Yet the lad's inquisitive mind and brightness were more than obvious, as was his maturity that was far beyond his twelve years. "Mother, could you please explain the bloodstain to me?"

"And to me," Lestrade added.

Joanna handed her son the magnifying glass and said, "Examine the smudge and look for a pattern within, then tell me what produced it."

Johnny studied the smudge at length before noting, "I see the impression of lines, many of which are slanted, although a few are vertical."

"What would make such an imprint?" Joanna asked.

"I am at a loss."

Joanna reached for a gooseneck lamp and turned it on prior to placing it by the bloodstains. "Now tell me what you see."

Johnny closely reexamined the smudge for a full half minute, then jerked his head up and exclaimed, "It is a palm print!"

"But whose?"

"It is impossible to tell."

"Gaze carefully at the top of the narrow streak and determine if there is yet another imprint."

After a quick study, Johnny cried out, "A fingerprint!"

"Excellent!" Joanna lauded. "So would it not be a reasonable assumption to say that the fingerprint and the palm print were made by the same individual?"

"Almost certainly."

"Thus, we appear to have an uncut hand making a bloodied palm print and, in all likelihood, a finger on this very hand dropping down to leave its print before forming the letter *h*."

Johnny looked at his mother quizzically. "I am having difficulty following your line of thought."

"All of the evidence points to the fact that the blood on the palm print and fingerprint did not come from Dr. Verner."

"So Dr. Verner did not make the prints."

"I did not say that," Joanna corrected. "I distinctly said that the blood on the prints did not come from him."

"But how then—"

"It is blood from a German," Joanna pronounced. "The sequence of events occurred in this order. Verner sees the Germans coming for him, so he dashes to the medicine cabinet for the bottle of chloroform. As he reaches in, the German grabs Verner's hand, but the doctor resists, and in the process manages to push the German's hand against the broken glass in the cabinet door."

"But Verner was a small man and could not have possibly overpowered the German," Lestrade argued.

"Small, but with a powerful grip," my father informed us. "Alfred Verner had incredibly strong arms that could restrain a highly agitated patient without great effort. I myself witnessed this feat at St. Mary's Hospital."

"Thank you for that helpful information, Watson," said Joanna. "So Verner's hidden power allows him to push the captor's hand into the broken glass, which causes a deep laceration that bled heavily. The blood soaks the surface of Verner's hand and eventually produced a bloodied palm print. Verner then uses the blood to leave us a message as to the identity of his abductors."

"How can you know this?" Lestrade asked.

"Because at the very top of the bloodied streak is a fingerprint, no doubt belonging to Verner, which will descend and form the letter *h,* for us to see."

"And what do you believe the *h* stands for?"

"Hun," Joanna replied. "Verner was telling us he was taken prisoner by the Huns."

"As in Attila the Hun?" Johnny inquired.

Joanna nodded. *"Hun* is a derogatory term for the Germans, who are known for their viciousness in battle."

"Of course Verner could not have used the *G,* for the Germans would have noticed it and had it removed," Lestrade surmised.

"Nor could he have scripted a *D,* which his

captors would have known stood for *Deutschland*, the German word for their fatherland."

"It does all seem to fit, yet you must admit your evidence remains circumstantial," Lestrade challenged.

"But can be proven beyond a doubt," Joanna countered. "Have a fingerprint taken from Verner's remains and matched against the bloodied print on the cabinet. I am certain the Fingerprint Branch of Scotland Yard would be up to the task."

"Indeed they would," Lestrade concurred, and quickly jotted down a note to himself. He paused for a moment as he tapped his finger against the notepad, obviously lost in thought. "I am still not convinced that a small man like Verner could struggle against a larger foe and inflict such damage, at least not with the evidence we have on hand."

"There is more," Joanna went on. "For embedded in the top of the bloodied smudge is a fragment of human tissue, which in all likelihood was gouged from the German's hand."

"Pray tell, how do you know it is human tissue?"

"Because it has several hairs protruding from it, and one of those hairs appears to be blond, which Verner was not," Joanna affirmed. "This tissue comes from a German, who now has a gouged-out wound on his hand that bled excessively."

Johnny asked, "Did he place a bandage over it, Mother?"

"He may have, but it was a very serious laceration that would continue to bleed."

Johnny considered the matter further before saying, "Perhaps he persuaded Dr. Verner to care for it."

Joanna's eyes suddenly widened as a smile came to her face. She reached over to affectionately ruffle her son's hair. "A most excellent thought, and one that had not crossed my mind."

"Is it helpful?"

"Very," Joanna said, and turned to the group. "With a large, deep wound that continued to bleed, the German may well have required medical attention and would certainly not depend on Verner, who was to be tortured and killed as quickly as possible. He would have most likely gone to a clinic or private physician for treatment. You see, such a wound would undoubtedly require sutures. This being the case, he would not have sought treatment nearby, for they would have hurried to depart the area."

Lestrade nodded his agreement. "They were aware of the trail left by chloroform, which could be followed."

"They were not fools," Joanna went on. "So they would have visited a doctor or clinic away from the crime scene and nearer their next residence. With this in mind, a bulletin should be sent out to every physician in the metropolitan London area, seeking information on a Teutonic-appearing patient, perhaps with a facial tic, who was treated for a serious laceration of the hand."

"But the event would have occurred days ago," Lestrade countered. "The patient is in all likelihood long gone by now, and may have even relocated to yet another neighborhood."

"True," said Joanna. "But keep in mind, sutures had to be used to close the wound and must remain in place for at least a week to allow for complete healing. Once that has occurred, the sutures must be removed. And the physician who inserted the sutures will be the one to remove them."

"A bulletin will be sent out to *all* physicians in London as well as to those in its remote suburbs," Lestrade said, with a firm nod. Turning to Johnny, he added, "That was a fine observation on your part."

Johnny showed no response, other than to say, "It was obvious the wound would require care."

Again my father and I exchanged knowing glances. The lad was so much like his mother and grandfather before him, in that praise meant little, the significance of an observation every-thing.

"Mother, what determines how much time will be needed for a wound to heal?"

"It might be best for Dr. Watson to answer your

question, for he has extensive knowledge on the subject, both in war and peace."

"Healing time is largely measured by the size and depth of the wound," my father informed. "A superficial laceration caused by a knife or razor would heal nicely in a week after suturing. By contrast, a jagged, wide wound caused by a shell fragment would require weeks. If it was too wide to suture together, it would heal from the bottom up by the process of granulation, which could take a month or more."

"Can you determine beforehand the time needed for a terrible wound to heal?" Johnny asked thoughtfully.

"Not precisely," my father replied. "That requires repeated examinations of the wound, which allows one to estimate the rate of healing."

"So, here it depends on the doctor's experience."

My father shook his head gently. "Here it depends on what one has learned in the class-room about the signs of healing, which can then be applied to the examiner's careful observations, which in turn will lead to an accurate assessment. You see, without facts, observations have little merit or even less depth."

Johnny nodded ever so slightly, then mused to himself, "Facts together with observation is the key."

"Facts together with observation is the key," my father reiterated.

Another lesson learned, I thought, watching the subtlest of smiles cross Joanna's face.

As we headed for the door, Johnny stopped to stomp down on a large piece of brown glass from the chloroform bottle. He then leaned over to pick up and study the piece, which had remained intact. Satisfied, he tossed the shard aside. Like the best of investigators, he was unwilling to accept the observations of others, but would depend only on those he himself made.

10

The British Museum

We hurried into the British Museum, for we were already twenty minutes late for our meeting with Sir David Shaw. As was frequently the case, the first floor was crowded with tourists, many of whom seemed to congregate around the Rosetta Stone, which was considered a most prized possession of the museum.

"Why do people find that large stone so interesting, Mother?" Johnny asked.

"Because the writings on it provided the key to unlocking the mystery of Egyptian hieroglyphs," Joanna replied.

"Why was that so important?"

"For many reasons, but mainly because it was a script that mystified the world for thousands of years," Joanna explained. "It also told the history of ancient Egypt in great detail."

"Did they not have books back then?"

"Apparently not."

"So these peculiar figures carved into stone were like a secret language?"

"One might very well say that," said Joanna, as we strode by the Rosetta Stone. "But you should

169

save your questions for Sir David Shaw who is a true expert on the subject."

"How do you come to know him?"

"Through Dr. Watson, for they are friends dating back to the Second Afghan War."

Johnny quickly turned to my father, his curiosity aroused. "I had no idea you fought in that war."

"It was a very long time ago," my father said, downplaying his soldiering days.

"Were you wounded?"

My father nodded. "A jezail bullet found its mark in my shoulder."

"How long did it take to heal?"

"Over a month, for although the wound was sutured, its edges did not hold well."

"Thus, it had to heal from the bottom up."

"So it did in large measure."

"I believe you called the process granulation."

"That is the correct term."

How remarkable, I thought. The lad had a mind like a steel trap, for once a fact entered it, it did not escape.

"And now," called out a guide leading a group of tourists, "we shall visit the Elgin Marbles."

The announcement was greeted with loud and obvious approval. En masse the group moved away from the Rosetta Stone, but Johnny kept his eyes on them as they walked on.

Joanna smiled at her son. "And now you no

doubt wish to know what these Elgin Marbles are."

"I do indeed, for they seemed to generate a lot of interest."

"I am afraid my knowledge on this matter is somewhat limited," said Joanna. "I was told these huge slabs of marble, with their intricate carvings, were taken from the Acropolis in Greece by Lord Elgin during the last century, and eventually found their way into the British Museum."

"Were they stolen?" Johnny asked, searching for a possible crime.

"That is another question we might ask Sir David," Joanna replied. "Or perhaps we should purchase a monograph on the subject that will provide even more detailed information."

"I favor the monograph, which I can discuss with the tutor we shall choose."

We took the stairs to a quiet, upper floor, with my father and Johnny leading the way. The corridor itself was vacant, but we could hear muted conversations coming from behind closed doors. A stale, musty odor filled the air.

"Pray tell, Joanna, what brings us to see Sir David?" my father asked quietly.

"He is a multilingual codebreaker, is he not?" Joanna replied.

"Of the first order."

"Then we shall present him with the German

word *rot,*" Joanna went on. "You may recall that the good Dr. Verner heard that word being shouted from the house where the prisoner was held."

"It was from the second story."

"Precisely," said Joanna. "What do you make of it?"

My father shrugged. "I am afraid French is my only foreign language."

Joanna turned to her son. "And what about you, Johnny?"

"We are just beginning the class in German at Eton and have not yet come to *rot.*"

"It means red."

Johnny gave the matter thought. "I trust the word has some significance here."

"It does indeed."

"Well, I am certain my tutor here in London will inform me of the German term for red and its variations."

"I am certain he would," Joanna said. "But he would teach you grammatical German, which will give you a fine vocabulary, but will not give you the fluency you require as an investigator," Joanna cautioned. "To that end, Eton will serve your purpose far better. In your classes and clubs you will have no choice but to speak German, and thus learn all of its subtleties and nuances. If you are not entirely fluent in a language, it will be of little help in your investigation, for you will only be aware of the obvious. You do wish to be a cut above the others, do you not?"

"I do, Mother."

"Then carefully consider my words."

"Nuances and subtleties," Johnny uttered to himself.

Upon turning a sharp corner, my hand touched Joanna's and I allowed my cheek to brush up against her hair. We exchanged secret smiles as a warm, wonderful feeling flowed through both of us. My mind went back to our first journey together at the British Museum when our hands had touched and brought about the very same captivating sensation. Then as now, I was certain I would never grow accustomed to the wondrous affection that such simple contact brought with it. For the hundredth time I was reminded how fortunate I was to have married the most stunningly unique woman I had ever encountered.

Approaching Sir David's office, Joanna reached into her purse for a folded slip of paper and gave it to Johnny, with the following instructions. "You are to open it once we leave the museum."

"Is it a puzzle?" Johnny asked.

"More like a solution," Joanna replied.

Sir David Shaw met us at the door to his office, and I was again struck by how odd the man looked. He was tall and stoop shouldered, with reddish-gray hair and a hawklike nose upon which rested the thickest spectacles I had ever seen. But behind those heavy lenses was a brilliant mind, the owner of which had been knighted by Queen Victoria for his wartime skills in deciphering top secret, coded messages, some of which were so sensitive they would never be allowed to see the light of day.

"Ah, Watson!" Sir David greeted, and cordially extended his hand to my father. "What a pleasure to see you again."

"The pleasure is mine," said my father, with a most vigorous handshake. "I believe you recall my son and his wife, Joanna, from our earlier visit."

"I do indeed."

"And with them is Joanna's son, Johnny, who has a number of questions for you."

Sir David gave the lad a half bow. "Are these questions of yours difficult to answer?"

"So it would seem, sir."

"Good," Sir David approved. "For those are the only questions worth asking." He gestured to the chairs in front of his cluttered desk and waited for us to be seated before sitting and continuing on. "Now, my good fellow, tell me of your questions. Do they have a unifying topic?"

"They concern the Egyptian hieroglyphs, sir."

"Ah, the mystery of all mysteries," Sir David cooed, obviously warming to the subject. "Let us begin with the Rosetta Stone. Are you aware of its significance?"

"Only that it is said to be the key."

"Oh yes! But a marvelous key to a script so complex it baffled us for thousands of years." Sir David reached for a clay tablet that had hieroglyphs written upon it and handed it to Johnny for examination. "Tell us what you can make out."

Johnny studied the tablet at length before noting, "I see rows of small figures that have no meaning."

"Ah, but to the Egyptian scribes who devised the script they had every meaning," Sir David said. "Believe it or not, the hieroglyph system contains over seven hundred basic symbols, pictures, and signs that represent objects, activities, sounds, and ideas. All of it was indecipherable until Napoleon's soldiers discovered the Rosetta Stone in the Egyptian desert. The stone had three distinct scripts carved into it. The upper text was Egyptian hieroglyphs, the middle written in demotic Egyptian, and the lower in ancient Greek. Because all three read essentially the same, it unlocked the mystery of the Egyptian hieroglyphs. The tablet you are holding contains one of the simpler hieroglyphs."

Johnny restudied the tablet at length in an attempt to decipher the hieroglyphs. "I clearly see a drawing of a bird in profile."

"Which translates to weak or small," Sir David said.

"And a feather."

"That signifies justice or balance."

"What of the reclining lion?"

"It designates a temple or tomb."

"Then I note a circle with a dot in its center."

"Which indicates the sun or strong light."

Johnny furrowed his brow in concentration before a faint smile crossed his face. "The circle with the dot precedes the reclining lion and that tells us the sun was shining on a temple."

"A born cryptographer!" Sir David praised.

"But I chose the simplest of the hieroglyphs to interpret," Johnny said candidly.

"An important first step nonetheless."

"Do you function as a tutor in hieroglyphic script?"

"I cannot spare the time, but there is an informal class that meets here at eleven each morning, if you are interested."

"I most certainly am, sir," Johnny said eagerly, and turned to Joanna who nodded her approval.

"But will this not interfere with your formal education?" Sir David queried.

Johnny hesitated before answering. "Well, sir, I am currently enrolled at Eton—"

"Excellent!" Sir David broke in. "There is a Museum of Antiquities at Eton that has a superb Egyptian section, the director of which is a personal friend. I shall arrange for you to continue your study of hieroglyphics under his tutelage." After jotting down a note to himself, he looked to Joanna and said, "Now let us turn to the puzzle you wish to bring to my attention."

Johnny quickly raised his hand. "Sir, may I be permitted one last question?"

"Of course," Sir David replied patiently.

"Could there be a hidden code within the hieroglyphs that we have yet to decipher?"

"It is a possibility."

"But what do you believe?"

"I am very careful in my beliefs, for in my world things are often not what they appear to be."

"So too is it in the world of crime, which brings us to the purpose of our visit," said Joanna. "Watson mentioned that you were fluent in many languages, including German."

"Seven to be exact. English, French, German, Spanish, Arabic, Dari, and Pashto."

"It is German I am most interested in," Joanna went on. "Because of the sensitivity of the case, I can give you only limited background information."

Sir David tilted back in his chair, but his eyes never left Joanna. "The words *German* and *sensitivity* are usually not found in adjoining sentences at this moment in history—unless of course one is speaking of espionage or war plans."

Joanna ignored the conclusion and continued on. "An Englishman was abducted by people unknown. Someone overheard the word *rot* being shouted from the second floor of the house in which the Englishman was being held captive. What do you make of it?"

"What do you?"

"*Rot* is the German word for red."

"Yes."

"But is there more to it?"

"Perhaps," Sir David said. "But I require more information. To begin with, was the word cried out *rot* or *rotes*?"

"*Rot* as far as we know."

"Good. For *rotes* is the adjective form of *rot,* so in all likelihood we are dealing with the noun—*rot* or red. This would tend to exclude the possibility that the crier was referring to an object, such as *rotes Hausen* or red house."

Johnny raised his hand. "Could it not be a red bandage covering a cut, Mother?"

I could not help but be astonished at the lad's quick mind. He was connecting a red bandage to the deep gash in the German agent's hand. He was unaware that the shout of *rot* had occurred prior to the struggle in Verner's office.

"I am afraid that would still involve the use of the adjective *rotes*," Sir David said. "A red bandage would be *ein rotes Verband.*"

"More importantly, the Germans would never use that term for a bloody bandage," Joanna informed. "They would say *blutig Verband.*"

178

Sir David nodded. "I see you too are well versed in German."

"I have some grasp of the language," Joanna told him. "I accompanied my late husband, John Blalock, on a sabbatical to Berlin where he learned new techniques for tendon and ligament repair. For six months I worked beside him as a surgical nurse."

"Where you no doubt saw more than your share of *blutig Verbanden*," Sir David said.

"I did indeed."

"This must have occurred when relations between the two countries were far more cordial."

"A lifetime ago," Joanna said with a hint of melancholy, then flicked her wrist to dismiss the subject. "But let us redirect our attention back to the word *rot,* which we believe was not used to denote an object. So it must be a person."

"Most likely," Sir David agreed. "But what kind of person? A red can refer to a communist or socialist, which of course is the antithesis of the German mind-set. Or could red be part of an address where a given man lives?"

"There is a Red Lion Street in Holborn," my father recalled. "And a Red Lion Square."

"I would still favor it being the name of a person," Sir David said. "But to my knowledge, there is no German name such as Red."

"A nickname, perhaps," I suggested.

"Very unlikely in German," Sir David answered

at once. "First, in contrast to England, nicknames are seldom used in public for adults. They are primarily employed as terms of endearments. Secondly, five to ten percent of the German population, depending on the region, is redheaded, so the name Red would not be very distinguishing."

"Are you excluding *Rot* as a name?" Joanna asked.

"I am excluding it as a nickname," Sir David corrected. "You must allow me to put all of your clues together in a neat little package. You initially told me we are dealing with an individual shouting out the word *rot,* which indicates that person possesses a German vocabulary. You also informed me that this matter is very sensitive and cannot be spoken of in detail, and that indicates this German should not be in England. And since we are at war with Germany, I think it fair to conclude this German is here secretly and is up to no good. It all smells of espionage, and I therefore believe *rot* in fact refers to *Rot,* the code name of an agent."

"You have been very helpful," Joanna said as she pushed her chair back. "I trust you will not speak further of this matter."

"Most assuredly." Sir David rose and said a final word to Johnny. "We shall see you tomorrow morning."

"Indeed you shall, sir."

Hurrying down the corridor, we remained

silent, for there were others strolling about. We passed a group of chattering children in their school uniforms on the stairs, then went by a throng of tourists clustered around the Rosetta Stone. Only once we were outside did we speak of our meeting with Sir David.

"It would appear we have a nest of Huns amongst us," my father grumbled. "Heaven knows how many."

"Four at a minimum," Joanna estimated, then counted them off on her fingers. "Number one has a facial tic. Number two is the agent who closed the window in the adjoining room, and number three is the just-mentioned Rot."

"Who is number four?" I asked.

"The driver of the carriage who delivered Verner to the house," Joanna replied. "They would not dare assign that role to an outsider."

"Your knowledge of German has served you well yet again," my father remarked. "Nevertheless, even with your fluency in the language, we required Sir David's assistance to come up with the notion that Rot was in fact the name of one of their agents. But then again, he was knighted for seeing things others did not."

"But Mother helped him along," Johnny asserted.

Joanna turned to her son and gave him a warm smile. "You may now read the slip of paper I gave you."

As Johnny unfolded the slip, my father and I glanced over his shoulder at Joanna's writing. It read:

CODE NAME FOR GERMAN SPY

Johnny nodded slowly to himself. "One has to be aware of the nuances of the language."

"Quite so," Joanna agreed. "But it is always wise to seek a second opinion from a renowned expert, eh, Watson?"

"It is the smart move and an important one, for now we can place a name on a member of the spy ring," my father replied. "Perhaps Scotland Yard or Naval Intelligence can put a face to the name."

"If so, they may have the names and descriptions of Rot's usual associates," I added.

"You both are making a number of assumptions that for the most part are highly unlikely," Joanna said. "What are the chances our agencies would have photographs of Rot or know of his associates?" She paused a moment before answering her question. "Very small indeed."

"But surely there is no harm in asking," I ventured.

"Oh, but there is," Joanna cautioned. "Keep in mind we have a traitor amongst us, and one loose tongue will alert Rot we are aware of his presence, which would send him into deeper cover or cause him to flee England altogether.

And that, dear John, is what we must avoid, for it will remove any advantage we now have."

"But how then are we to delve into the identity of Rot and his associates?" my father asked.

"There are a number of avenues, including a phone call to Sir Harold Whitlock, the First Sea Lord, who knows us well," Joanna responded. "He could surely make a quiet inquiry into the matter."

"Lestrade and Dunn will be most unhappy with your decision."

"I am not concerned with their happiness, but only with the rescue of Alistair Ainsworth," said Joanna, as she gestured to a nearby carriage. "And if we ruffle some feathers along the way, so be it."

11

Covent Garden

Joanna awoke the next morning with a dreadful cold, yet still managed to see Johnny off for his hieroglyphics class at the museum. Coughing and hoarse, she had no choice but to remain home in bed. But she stressed the importance of investigating Hoover the poulterer, and bade us to take her place at the Covent Garden market.

"You must be very careful," Joanna implored, with a raspy voice. "Do not speak condescendingly to Hoover, but rather engage him, like someone interested in sharing information about geese. He will know vastly more than you, but you will have enough knowledge to indicate you are not novices on the topic and only wish to learn more from an experienced hand. He will then speak freely and take delight in conversing with gentlemen of your obvious standing."

"But neither of us has the knowledge you speak of," my father said.

"You will shortly," Joanna said, and paused to loudly sniff and swallow. "Follow my instructions and this will play out the way we wish it to. First, do not make idle conversation when you approach the poulterer's stall. Go directly to a goose and examine the bird with your hands. Smell it and comment on the aroma in one fashion or the other. An unpleasant odor tells you of poor quality, you see. Pick the bird up and determine if the skin is smooth and free of bruises or blemishes, for these are always absent in the best of geese. When you finally decide on which to purchase, make certain it is plump and well formed, since this will cook best. Make a point to ask if the goose you select is country or city bred."

"Does this matter a great deal?" I interrupted.

"It does to those who know their way around geese," Joanna replied. "Those raised in the country feed only on grass, which gives their meat a richer, tastier flavor. In addition, the country bred are reputed to be quite tender, and for all these reasons are far more desirable."

"What about size?" my father asked. "Should we select a larger bird?"

"You must be careful here," Joanna cautioned. "Have the poulterer weigh the bird, for you must stay below ten pounds. Those that are larger often yield the tougher meat."

My father and I had to smile at one another, both of us dazzled by Joanna's command of such a peculiar subject. We were aware she could talk exceedingly well on a broad variety of topics, but usually chose not to show her brilliance unless it could be readily applied to a criminal investigation. Yet how she became so informed about geese was a wonderment. In our year of marriage I'd never seen her once go near Miss Hudson's kitchen or inquire about recipes or makings of a dish.

"How did you come by all this information on geese?" I asked. "And please do not tell us you simply read about it."

"I had no such books to consult," Joanna said.

"Then how?"

"By asking Miss Hudson the name of her poulterer and spending an hour with him yesterday afternoon. He was most helpful." Joanna arose from her chair by the fireplace as she suppressed a weak cough. "Now you should be on your way, for we are only an hour from noon at which time Lady Jane's cook will arrive at Hoover's stall. You must remain unnoticed, but close enough to observe the interchange between the cook and the poulterer. Only approach Hoover's stall when it is clear of customers."

"It is difficult to believe a simple poulterer is involved," my father said. "What purpose could he possibly serve?"

"Keep in mind the Germans never forget the Fatherland," Joanna replied. "It runs in their blood."

"I am still not following you."

"He could be a go-between," Joanna explained.

"The traitor and his German masters will stay as far apart as possible to avoid raising suspicion. Nevertheless, they must have a method to communicate and exchange messages. If Lady Jane is the guilty party, what better liaison than an inconspicuous poulterer who is available every day and on a moment's notice."

"The messages might even be concealed within a plump goose," I ventured.

"Which could be purchased on site and delivered to a given address," my father added.

"Precisely," Joanna said. "That is why I inquired whether there was evidence of food being delivered to the empty house the Germans once occupied. If wrappings containing goose feathers had been found, it would have represented a most compelling clue. But unfortunately, that was not the case." She coughed weakly again and cursed at her illness. "In any event you must shortly be on your way. I suggest you take a very slow stroll over to Covent Garden, which is just over a mile south. By my estimation you should arrive shortly before noon. Remember to stand well back from the stall and watch the cook's hands as well as those of the poulterer. Stroll over to the stall only after the purchase is made and the cook departed."

"Should we mention Alistair Ainsworth to the poulterer?" I asked.

"Yes, but only casually and in the course of your

conversation," Joanna replied. "For example, if Hoover were to inquire how you came upon his stall, say that you were referred by Alistair Ainsworth and watch for the poulterer's reaction. See if his face loses color or his mannerisms become abrupt. But appear not to notice."

"Your keen eye would be most helpful here," my father said.

"But alas, my keen eye will have to remain in bed with my miserable cold," Joanna said, and headed for her bedroom. "Now be on your way."

We took my wife's advice and set out on a slow stroll to Covent Garden, timing our walk so we would arrive at the appropriate time. All the while we wondered if Lady Jane Hamilton, her cook, and the poulterer could all be intertwined in a most traitorous affair. It seemed so unlikely that Lady Jane, a woman of such high standing, would be involved in this sordid matter, and even less likely that a simple poulterer would be by her side. But, as my father reminded, we should never underestimate Joanna's keen instincts. She often saw what others failed to see.

As we approached Covent Garden, one could not help but be impressed by the size of the marketplace and the huge crowds mingling through it. Carts and wagons and lorries rumbled into three acres of profusion, bringing with them the produce of nearby farms that were in such abundance they dazzled the eye. It was a world of vegetables and fruits in all their splendor, which included oranges, tangerines, festoons of grapes, Canadian apples, and grapefruit from Cuba. And to this assemblage, add the colors of masses of glorious flowers. Making our way through the crowd we came upon a line of stalls, some large, others small and barely a yard wide. One of the more prominent ones had a sign that read Hoover & Son, Poulterers.

At the stall's counter was the heaviest woman I had ever encountered. At five feet in height, she weighed in excess of two hundred pounds, with rolls of fat stretching her garments to the breaking point. But she seemed nimble enough as she began her examination of a snow-white goose. Lifting the bird's wings, she gave the underneath skin a most careful study. Satisfied, she next went to the goose's head and neck. All the while the poulterer remained well back from the counter, his hands clasped together upon his apron.

"I believe she is unaccompanied," I said from the side of my mouth.

"Which is to be expected," my father said. "If Lady Jane is implicated, she would wish to keep her distance from the poulterer."

I gestured with my head toward the stall. "Ah! She has made her purchase. See how well the goose is being wrapped."

"I noticed nothing untoward with the poulterer's or cook's hands," my father remarked.

"Nor did I."

We concentrated further on the happenings at the poulterer's stall, but our line of vision was abruptly interrupted by a rather tall flower girl, with long blond hair that was covered with a tattered bonnet. She was more woman than girl, with a sad face and a smudge of dirt on her chin. Her sadness seemed to be exaggerated by her spectacles, which had a cracked lens. The white blouse and floral skirt she wore were so threadbare that light could go through them.

"Please, guv'nor, please buy me flowers," she begged, holding up a packed basket. Her Cockney accent was so deep it was difficult to understand. "Two bundles a penny, primroses!"

"Be on your way," my father ordered, making a sweeping motion with his hand. "We have important business here."

The flower girl stood her ground, undeterred. "Sweet violets, penny for the whole bunch!"

"Later perhaps," my father offered. "You must move on at once!"

The flower girl hung her head in defeat and, approaching the next prospective customer, called out, "Buy me violets, oh do, please!"

We returned our gaze to the poulterer's stall and watched the massively overweight cook waddle away, with the wrapped goose under her arm. She apparently was well-known in the market, for she waved to more than a few and stopped to chat with a man of middle years, who was likewise considerably overweight.

"The cook is distracted, so let us commence," my father said. "I shall do the talking, but feel free to enter the conversation at any time. And remember, be pleasant and be interested."

The poulterer saw us approaching and, sizing up our fine attire, hurriedly swept the counter clean of goose feathers and other debris. Involuntarily he rubbed his hands over his soiled apron, then straightened his tie.

"May I be of service, gentlemen?" the poulterer offered.

"We are searching for a fine goose as a present to a friend," my father replied.

"Then you have come to the right place."

My father reached for a large goose at the end of the counter and mimicked the cook's method of examination. With a careful eye, he studied the bird's entire skin, beak to tail, then raised its wings for a close inspection of what lay beneath. Turning the bird, my father pointed to a small bruise on the lower belly.

"This will not do," he said with the tone of authority.

"A minor blemish," the poulterer attempted to excuse.

"But our friend is quite special, and so must our gift goose be," my father insisted.

"Then I shall show you my very finest," the poulterer said, and reached for a large bird whose neck hung over a side counter. "You will not find a blemish or bruise on this one, mark my words."

As my father began another examination, I gazed about at the assortment of people passing by. They were laborers and merchants, along with the rich and penniless, and a scattering of individuals from foreign lands, with their distinctive features and attire. It was a splendid cross-section of modern-day London. In my peripheral vision, I saw the obese cook some ten yards away, now engaged in a lively conversation with the flower girl we had encountered earlier. They seemed to be having a cheerful, animated talk. The cook appeared oblivious to our presence.

"Country bird, was it?" my father inquired.

"Every day of its life," the poulterer replied. "It fed only on sweet grass and never saw a speck of grain."

"Which renders the meat tender and gives it a much richer taste."

"Indeed it does, sir," the poulterer said. "Which of course makes it a shilling or two dearer than those that are city bred."

My father flicked his wrist dismissively at the added expense. "How much does this bird weigh?"

"Eight pounds and an ounce over."

"Which assures its tenderness."

The poulterer nodded in a most pleasing manner. "You know your way around geese, sir."

"As does my friend Mr. Alistair Ainsworth, who referred us here."

"Ah, Mr. Ainsworth!" The poulterer's face lighted up. "Now there is a gentleman who is an expert on geese, by anyone's measure. But I see in the newspapers that he has gone missing."

"So it would appear."

"Let us pray no harm has come to him."

"We shall."

"And now, sir, if I may, could I ask for your name? I should very much like to list you among my special customers."

"Of course." My father obliged and handed the poulterer his personal card.

We purchased the goose and set off for Baker Street, with the wrapped bird tucked securely under my arm. Along the way we stopped at a small café for tea, over which we discussed our adventure in the Covent Garden market. The café was crowded, with noisy conversations filling the air, but we still kept our voices low so as not to be overheard.

"That was a fine performance, Father," I praised.

"I did a bit of acting at Cambridge," he commented, with some pride.

"It certainly came in quite handy today."

"As it did in the past with Sherlock," my father reminisced, and took a deep sip of Earl Grey tea. "But I'm afraid my acting served no purpose, for nothing of value was uncovered at the poulterer's stall. There was no evidence of an exchange of messages between the poulterer and the cook."

"None whatsoever," I agreed. "I kept my eyes on their hands throughout their meeting and saw nothing out of the ordinary."

"And my mention of Alistair Ainsworth elicited a most pleased reaction," my father noted. "I had the impression the poulterer genuinely missed seeing him alongside the cook."

"As did I. Thus, it would appear we have not advanced our cause one iota."

"Nor shall we, it would seem, as long as Joanna is confined to her bed."

We enjoyed a second cup of tea, during which we recounted every detail of our visit to Covent Garden, but could discover nothing that would have been of interest to Joanna. Nevertheless we both had the uneasy feeling that we had overlooked something Joanna would have seen and docketed. She had often remarked that it was the trivial that at times led to the significant. Yet using the best of our minds, we could not come up with even a minor happening worthy of note.

A half hour later we arrived at 221b Baker Street and were met at the door by Miss Hudson.

With her keen olfactory sense she sniffed at the wrapped package I held, and a look of displeasure crossed her face.

"I smell goose," she pronounced.

"It is," I said.

"Has something been amiss with the goose dishes I have prepared?"

"They have been outstanding, and that is why my father and I journeyed to Covent Garden to find the perfect goose as a present to you."

"In gratitude for your most excellent food," my father added. "Which we always look forward to."

Miss Hudson blushed and brought a hand up to cover it. "Why, thank you! That is ever so thoughtful."

"Not at all."

"Would you like it for dinner tonight?"

"Under ordinary circumstances we would be delighted, but unfortunately Joanna has come down with a rather nasty cold and would have little appetite for a tasty goose."

"Poor thing," Miss Hudson remarked. "She sounded awful when I saw her by the stairs as she was seeing her son off. I offered her tea and honey, which I thought might soothe her throat."

"Did she partake?" I asked.

Miss Hudson shook her head. "She only wished to climb back into bed and not be disturbed."

We adjourned to our rooms and, after lighting

a cheery fire, sat in front of it to enjoy our pipefuls. Outside, the sky was rapidly darkening, bringing with it the promise of yet more rain. With the wind beginning to gust, we felt great comfort being in the pleasant warmth of our drawing room. Our quiet peace, however, was soon interrupted by a rap on the door. It was Miss Hudson and we feared something was amiss with the goose.

"I am sorry to bother you, Dr. Watson, but there is a flower girl downstairs who insists on seeing you," she announced. "The girl claims you dropped something at Covent Garden market and wishes to return it."

My father and I rapidly checked our pockets and found nothing missing. Wallets, timepieces, keys, and coinage were accounted for. "Did she mention what item we had lost?"

"She did not," Miss Hudson replied. "But she demanded to return it in person, for a reward I would guess."

"Please show her up," my father said, rechecking his pockets as the door closed.

"I wonder how the flower girl learned of our address," I queried.

"Probably from the card I gave the poulterer," my father said.

Moments later the flower girl entered our drawing room and did a brief curtsy. Her white blouse was now damp from the rain that was beginning to fall. She had both hands around her basket of flowers.

"I'll wager a shilling you'll buy me flowers now," she said.

"What exactly have you found?" I asked.

"Information that could prove most useful," Joanna said, removing her bonnet, blond wig, and broken spectacles.

To say that my father and I were stunned by the sudden transformation would be an understatement. Her disguise was so ingenious that there was not a single inkling to indicate Joanna Blalock Watson was beneath it. Even the sharp-eyed Miss Hudson who viewed all visitors with suspicion had been fooled.

"I have many questions," my father said finally. "But first off, how did you manage this clever charade with such a terrible cold?"

"Because there was no cold," Joanna answered. "All that is required to imitate one is a sniff of black pepper. Inhale a healthy dose and you will repeatedly sneeze as your nose runs rampant. Another dose will irritate your throat and produce a raspy voice and cough."

"But why?" I asked. "Why not include us in your carefully constructed masquerade?"

"For several very good reasons. First, I had to make certain my disguise and accent were spot on and not easily seen through. You and Watson would not have been the best of judges, for your opinions could be clouded by emotion and thus cause you to hesitate to point out any defects in my disguise. I needed an independent judge, so I returned to the poulterer whom I visited for an hour yesterday and begged for some scraps. He promptly escorted me out of his shop." Joanna paused and chuckled to herself. "He also bluntly suggested I go back to East London and take my Cockney accent with me.

"The second reason for my secrecy was to keep you in the dark at the Covent Garden market," she went on. "Despite your best efforts you would have no doubt continued to steal glances my way and the workers about the stalls would have noticed this behavior. In their minds, they would see two finely dressed gentlemen eyeing a poor flower girl and think the worst of it. They would have watched my every move and yours as well, so as to serve as my protectors. This would have in all likelihood disrupted my plans to arrange an encounter with Lady Jane's cook. So, all in all, it was best I remained unknown to you. I trust you will forgive my deception."

"You are forgiven," my father said, with a warm smile. "And I must say that Sherlock Holmes would have been most delighted with your disguise."

"From the stories I have read, my father was quite good at improvising disguises."

"He was a master at it and took great pleasure

in surprising me, just as you have," my father reminisced. "And he took even greater pleasure in explaining why such a disguise was necessary. Perhaps you will now tell us the main reason you went to such extraordinary lengths to conjure up such a magnificent disguise. It had to be more than just to keep John and me in the dark."

"It was indeed," Joanna said. "I needed the disguise in order to go places that a lady of standing would never gain entrance to."

"Such as?"

"The world of Lady Jane's cook."

"Exactly what in the cook's world merited so much of your attention?"

"Why, Lady Jane's secrets, of course."

My father and I drew in closer to Joanna, so as not to miss a word.

"You see, everyone has their dark, deep secrets that they guard zealously. This holds true particularly for the aristocracy, who would not divulge their secrets, even if questioned a thousand times. After poverty, disgrace is the very worst affliction they could ever suffer. But such secrets are often known by the household who keep it to themselves and their peers for obvious reasons."

"How could you hope to pry such information from the cook?" I asked. "After all, you were neither friend nor peer."

"That took a bit of doing," Joanna replied.

"But my task was made easier once I learned the cook also spoke Cockney. With my rather pronounced Cockney accent, we immediately became sisters in arms who would delight in trading juicy gossip. I provided her the story of a royal couple who had a rather odd sexual fetish involving the great toe. Good manners prohibited me from mentioning the family name, to which the cook nodded her approval. This tale set the stage for her to return the favor by revealing romantic encounters—real or imagined—that circulated amongst Lady Jane's household."

"Really, Joanna!" my father protested mildly. "This all seems so beneath you."

"When dealing with sordid matters, one has to be prepared to sink to a lower level," Joanna said, with an indifferent shrug. "In any event, by all accounts Lady Jane goes shopping at Harrods several times a week on a regular schedule. She steps off her carriage at the front entrance, enters the store, and promptly exits via a side door. You see, although her carriage remains in front, a close friend of her driver parks his carriage on a side street, and it is he who witnesses Lady Jane's rather hurried departure. She moves quickly in a direction away from Brompton Road and returns an hour or so later, again using the side entrance. Now, considering Lady Jane's past, what do you make of this?"

"She has strayed again," I answered at once. "She is meeting up with a secret lover."

"Or with a German agent," my father suggested.

"Or both," I ventured, but then I had second thoughts. "On the other hand, we may be making too much of her adventure. It could be quite innocent."

A mischievous smile came to Joanna's face as she asked, "Suppose I told you these disappearances cease when her husband, Lord Oliver Hamilton, returns home from sea duty."

"She is straying," I said resolutely.

"But why and with whom?" Joanna pondered. "Those are the important questions that need to be answered."

"How do you propose we go about this task?"

"By following her," Joanna replied.

"I am afraid your flower girl outfit will not serve as well in that regard," said I. "You would stand out like a sore thumb in the fashionable Knightsbridge area."

"I would indeed," Joanna agreed. "It is for that reason we must hire someone inconspicuous to do the following for us."

My father nodded. "They would have to melt perfectly into the background."

"And have an air of innocence about them," Joanna said, and reached for a bell to summon Miss Hudson. "By the way, was there any exchange of notes between the poulterer and the cook?"

"Absolutely not," my father replied.

"I too had my eyes on the pair the entire time and saw no such exchange," I agreed.

"Did you notice the cook offered no payment for the goose?" Joanna asked, and waited for a reply that was not forthcoming. "The goose was certainly not free, which would indicate an invoice was placed within the wrapping. Such a sealed invoice would then be promptly handed to Lady Jane. Could there be a more innocent way for the Germans to send instructions?"

My father and I exchanged glances, both of us with the same thought. Joanna was so much like her father, Sherlock Holmes, for whom a single trivial clue could lead to a significant conclusion.

"One would never have guessed at Lady Jane's involvement," my father said, shaking his head dolefully.

"It is best not to guess," Joanna cautioned. "It is a habit of the worst sort. One should wait for the clues that will remove all guessing."

With a rap on the door, Miss Hudson called, "Yes?"

"I have a note to be delivered," Joanna said. "Please send for a messenger straightaway."

12

The Baker Street Irregulars

They sounded like a herd coming up the stairs, stomping on each step as if to make their presence known. Unlike our earlier encounter with the Baker Street Irregulars, there were three of them rather than two, and each was clad in their Sunday best, clean and smart, head to toe. Closing the door behind them, they stood silently and awaited Joanna's inspection. One could not help but be impressed with their transformation to the middle class, for they all had started out and still dwelled in some of London's poorest neighborhoods.

According to my father, there was an extraordinary history behind the Baker Street Irregulars. Holmes had somehow gathered up a gang of street urchins that he often employed to aid his causes. They consisted of a dozen or so members, all streetwise, who could go anywhere, see everything, and overhear everyone without being noticed. For their efforts each was paid a shilling a day, with a guinea to whoever found the most prized clue. Since Sherlock Holmes's death, more than a few of the original guttersnipes had drifted away or become ill, but Wiggins, their leader, remained and took in new recruits to replace those who had departed.

Standing before us, Wiggins appeared even thinner than when last seen. There was a look of hardness about him, with his hollowed-out cheeks and dark eyes, which made him seem older than his twenty years. By contrast, the two members beside him had angelic faces. Little Alfie, whom I recalled from our last adventure, was small for his fifteen years, with tousled brown hair and an air of innocence that made him look even younger. Next to him was a thin, dark-complected girl of no more than ten whom I did not recognize.

"Here we are, ma'am," Wiggins said. "Dressed to the nines and dapper as can be. The clothes for Little Alfie and Sarah the Gypsy come to a pound extra for each."

"Well spent," Joanna said, and peered down at the young girl. "And what role will Sarah the Gypsy play?"

"She and Little Alfie will be the team that follows your fine lady," Wiggins replied. "In addition, Sarah has a sixth sense that tells her when she is being watched or if there is a copper nearby. More importantly, when people see her they feel sorry for her rather than threatened. This is doubly necessary when a snatch is about to occur or is in progress."

"She puts people at ease, I would imagine," my father said.

"That she does, guv'nor."

Sarah remained quiet, but watched every move with her doelike eyes. She seemed to be assessing some characteristic we possessed. Beneath her innocence there was cunning, I suspected.

"Now, ma'am, please give us the particulars on this lady we are to follow," Wiggins requested.

"She is an elegant lady who resides on Curzon Street in a quite splendid house, the address of which you will have shortly. You are to go there by yourself and keep your eye on the door in a most inconspicuous manner. An exceedingly attractive woman, tall with flowing brown hair, will depart from the house and stroll to her waiting carriage. You are to memorize her face, but do not follow her."

"I take it you know where the lady's carriage is headed," Wiggins surmised.

"To Harrods where she will enter via the front entrance. Minutes later she will leave the store, using a side door that opens onto Hans Road. From there she will travel southward away from Brompton Road, and it is at this point she is to be followed."

"Will she be accompanied?"

"No."

"Or carry packages?"

"None."

"Will a carriage follow her?"

"If it does, you have picked the wrong woman."

Wiggins carefully considered the matter before inquiring, "That neighborhood is quite fancy, yet it is not usual for ladies to stroll alone down a side street. Are you certain she will not have a protector watching over her?"

"She is being very secretive, so I would think not."

"To be sure, Sarah will be on her toes, won't you, ducky?"

Sarah nodded, her expression unchanged. "I'll pick him out faster than you can sneeze."

"Now, I will need the exact address to which she goes," Joanna instructed them. "Make certain to survey the entire building to determine if there is a rear or side door from which she could depart. Once you are certain the lady is remaining in the house, learn who she is visiting. A crown for his description, a pound for his name."

"And if we overhear their conversation?"

"Another pound."

"And actually witness the goings-on between the two?"

"A fiver."

Wiggins's jaw dropped at the offer. Five pounds was a great sum to the lower class, equivalent to a hundred shillings, which translated into the pay for three months' labor. Wiggins exchanged pleased glances with the other Irregulars, all eager to pocket the enticing reward. Their expressions indicated they would go to any length to learn every detail of Lady Jane's visit.

"There will be some added expenses," Wiggins said.

"Such as?" Joanna asked.

"We will require jackets of different colors for Little Alfie and Sarah," Wiggins explained. "Changes of color make for a different appearance. A little girl in blue looks different from one in red. Then we'll need packages for them to carry that can hide their faces. And books would come in handy as well."

"To what end?"

"Children carrying books are seen as middle class or better straightaway. You see, Little Alfie and Sarah must fit well into the neighborhood."

"All well and good then," Joanna agreed, and motioned to the door. "Now, be on your way. Keep in mind, the quicker you return with the information, the better."

As soon as the Irregulars departed, Joanna lighted a Turkish cigarette and began pacing back and forth across the drawing room. It appeared her conversation with Wiggins had brought some important matter to her mind, and she was now dwelling on it.

"Something is of concern to you," I said, as she stopped by the window and peered out to Baker Street.

"It is the five pounds I offered as a reward," Joanna replied. "It may be too great of an enticement and cause the Irregulars to take unwarranted chances."

"They are in a risky business," I reminded.

"Nevertheless," my father joined in, "five pounds seems an extraordinary amount."

"Not if it saves the life of Alistair Ainsworth," Joanna said, and went back to pacing the floor.

13

St. John's Wood

We waited impatiently for news from the Baker
Street Irregulars, although we knew it could
be days before their service bore fruit. Our
stalemate, however, came to an end with a phone
call from Inspector Lestrade. An important
clue had surfaced regarding the location of the
German agents, and the inspector wished us to
join him on his way to the site.

"I am surprised at his generosity," Joanna
remarked. "In dramatic instances such as this,
Lestrade prefers the limelight to be on Scotland
Yard alone, for it greatly enhances their reputation."

"I suspect it is not his generosity that beckons
us, but his need for an investigator who is
fluent in German," my father said. "Moreover,
it sounded as if the idea was as much Dunn's as
his."

"You may wish to bring along your service
revolver, Watson."

"But surely Dunn and the inspector will be
armed."

"But your aim is quite excellent, and at this

point a wounded German agent would be of far greater use than a dead one."

Fifteen minutes later we were seated in Lestrade's four-wheeler, racing for St. John's Wood. We moved along at a good speed until we departed Baker Street and turned onto a wider avenue where we were slowed by an accident involving two large transport lorries. With the additional time, Lestrade reviewed the details of the fortuitous encounter that might well lead to the rescue of Alistair Ainsworth.

"A gardener overheard a conversation that was going on at a nearby house that he knew had been recently leased," Lestrade told us. "Now, with the war on everybody's mind, anti-German sentiments are running high. So, when the gardener heard what sounded like German being spoken, he moved in for a closer look. In the back, hidden garden of the leased house, a pair of Teutonic-appearing fellows were having an animated chat. One was pointing to his stomach and saying the word *smearhar* over and over. He could make no sense of it, but it sounded very suspicious to him, so he promptly called Scotland Yard. And we of course notified Lieutenant Dunn at once. We both recalled from the case of *A Study in Treason* that you are quite fluent in German, which would come in most handy at the moment. Indeed, we are wondering if the gardener had misheard, for we could find no word resembling *smearhar* in the German dictionary."

Joanna thought for a moment before asking, "And the gardener stated the man was pointing to his stomach when the word was spoken?"

"So I was told," Lestrade said. "But then again, there is a question whether he heard the word correctly."

"He heard it correctly," Joanna said as our carriage came to a halt.

We alighted to find the area swarming with the forces of Scotland Yard. Near a stand of oak trees were a dozen uniformed constables, along with armed sergeants who had their holstered weapons on display. At the rear was Lieutenant Dunn surrounded by several naval officers. Upon seeing our arrival, Dunn broke away from the other officers and hurried over to us.

"Thank you for coming so promptly," he said. "Allow me to give you the latest details. The furnished house was recently leased for six months, all paid in advance. The neighbors saw nothing out of the ordinary, other than the new-comers kept entirely to themselves. There were no noises, disturbances, or unusual visitors. It is the gardener's report that the new occupants spoke German that brings us here."

"I should like to speak with the gardener," Joanna requested.

"This way." Dunn led us to a nearby fence, beside which stood a portly man with a ruddy complexion and protuberant abdomen. The gardener seemed to be enjoying the attention he was receiving.

Joanna approached him directly and said, "You stated the neighbor was motioning to his stomach when he spoke the strange German word."

"Yes, ma'am. He most certainly did," the gardener replied. "He did it several times to make his point."

"Can you remember his words exactly?"

"Only one, and I heard it clear. It was *smearhar*."

"Could it have been *Schmerz hier*?"

"That's it! Like I said, *smearhar*."

"Thank you for your keen observation," Joanna said and walked away, with the rest of us hurrying to catch up.

"Well?" Dunn asked.

"*Schmerz hier* translates to *pain here*," Joanna responded. "So, with the German gesturing to his abdomen, he was stating where the pain was located. And this of course was the location of Alistair Ainsworth's discomfort that forced the German agents to summon Dr. Verner."

"It would appear Ainsworth was gesturing that his pain persisted or may now be even more intense," I concluded.

"Or so he wished the Germans to believe," Joanna said.

A uniformed constable sprinted up to Lestrade

and, after catching his breath, said, "Sir, the house is completely surrounded, front and back, with no means of escape."

"Inform the sergeants they should have their weapons drawn," Lestrade ordered, then turned to Dunn. "Would you care to do the honors?"

Dunn reached for a megaphone and strode to the front gate of the stately house on Wellington Road. In a stern voice he called out, "You in the house at seven-two-five. You are surrounded by Scotland Yard and have exactly one minute to show yourselves. If you choose not to surrender, you will be taken by force."

We waited anxiously and hopefully, but there was no movement in the house or the surrounding garden. As the seconds slowly ticked by, Lestrade and Dunn checked their weapons, as did my father. He was a true marksman from his soldiering days in the Second Afghan War and had kept his aim sharp by practicing at an enclosed firing range. Despite his age, my father's distant vision was excellent.

"Try not to kill," Joanna said quietly. "A wounded agent can provide information that a dead one can't."

"Your point is well taken," Dunn said, and glanced at his watch. "Their minute is up. I favor the front entrance."

"As do I," Lestrade said, and called over to a group of well-proportioned constables. "We shall

all rush the front entrance, with the lieutenant and I a step behind. You are to quickly kick the front door open, then move aside."

The constables tightened their chin straps and readied themselves while awaiting the inspector's command.

Ten more seconds passed before Lestrade cried out, "Now!"

A force of five sprinted for the front door, with Lestrade and Dunn keeping their weapons trained on the curtained windows. My father had his Webley No. 2 pistol aimed at the upper floor should shots be fired from there. With powerful kicks, the front door was made to fly off its hinges and land inside the house with a crash. Lestrade and Dunn dashed in, followed by the constables. There was no sound coming from within.

More police rushed into the house while others tightened the circle surrounding the garden. The sergeants beside us had their revolvers pointed at the front entrance. Another minute passed before the call of "All clear!" rang out.

We entered the stately house and were guided into a large drawing room that was handsomely appointed. The furnishings were Victorian in style except for two sturdy, leather-upholstered chairs near a brick fireplace. There were opened pages of a newspaper strewn about the floor next to the chairs. An overturned cup of tea had badly stained the front page of the *Standard*.

"Rather messy," I commented.

"Obviously," Joanna said, and strolled over to the fireplace. Using an iron poker, she stirred the still-hot ashes and watched scattered cinders turn bright red. Next she leaned over and touched the tea stain on the newspaper. She used her handkerchief to remove the wetness from her fingertips.

Dunn came into the drawing room, shaking his head angrily. "They have gotten away and left no clue behind."

"Clever devils," Lestrade groused. "They have somehow managed to outwit us again."

"They were warned," Joanna said. "They knew we were coming and would be here shortly."

"Perhaps the gardener inadvertently tipped them off," Dunn surmised. "He may have been foolish enough to snoop around."

"But he was told in no uncertain terms to stay away from the house when he called Scotland Yard," Lestrade said.

"When were these instructions given?" Joanna asked.

"An hour or so ago," Lestrade answered, then rubbed at his chin pensively. "He could have gone back for yet a second look and that would have most certainly alerted the Germans."

"Well, whatever the reason, they are gone," Dunn said unhappily. "And they've taken Alistair Ainsworth with them."

Joanna went back to the fireplace and, using a poker, pushed a well-burned log aside. Beneath it were more ashes and cinders, but nothing recognizable. At the rear of the fireplace, tucked under a protruding brick, however, was a partially scorched slip of paper. Joanna plucked it out and, with her magnifying glass, studied it carefully.

Dunn moved in quickly and asked, "Are you able to make out the writing?"

"It appears to be a receipt from a restaurant called François," she replied.

"I know it," my father said at once. "François is a quite pricey restaurant located on Portobello Road. It is frequented by tourists, so the Germans would not seem out of place."

"They are burning every trace of their trail, being ever so cunning to leave nothing behind," Lestrade grumbled.

Joanna restudied the receipt, front and back and against the light, before placing it on a nearby table. Using the iron poker, she again stirred through the ashes and cinders, without finding anything of value. With Lestrade's assistance, she pulled out the single, remaining log and rolled it out onto the wet newspaper. There were no clues attached to it.

"Another dead end," Lestrade growled.

A uniformed constable dashed into the room and held up a map of London's train stations.

"Sir, we found this item glued by the toothpaste to the rear of a bathroom mirror."

Lestrade quickly reached for the thin map that appeared to be relatively new, yet had torn edges. He took a moment to remove flakes of toothpaste from his fingertips before opening the guide and spreading it onto a nearby table. The only remarkable sign was a circle drawn in black around Waterloo Station. "This map must have come from Ainsworth."

"But why did he circle Waterloo?" Dunn asked promptly. "Certainly the Germans would know that it, like all major train stations, is under close surveillance."

"Perhaps there are other clues on the map that might only be uncovered by experts," Lestrade said, then appeared to second-guess himself. "Assuming of course that Ainsworth drew the circle and hid the map."

"Who else would?" I asked.

"Any number of people," Lestrade replied. "But particularly the Germans themselves who wish to lead us on an errant chase."

The remainder of the house was searched top to bottom, without anything of value being discovered. Lestrade and Dunn remained behind to requestion the nearby neighbors, which Joanna assured us would be unproductive. The Germans were simply too skilled to let themselves be seen close up and would avoid any contact with the neighbors. As we approached our carriage, Joanna spotted the gardener who had called Scotland Yard, and strolled over.

"Thank you for your assistance," she said. "Your sharp eyes and ears have proven to be quite useful."

"I hope they catch those bloody bast—" he said angrily before catching himself. "I mean those bloody Germans."

"As do I," Joanna went on. "Allow me to ask one final question. After calling Scotland Yard and being instructed to stay away from the house, did you do so?"

"Oh yes, ma'am," the gardener replied without hesitation. "I walked to the corner garden and worked there until the police arrived. I didn't want to give the Germans even a hint I was on to them."

"Well done," Joanna praised, and strolled away. Then abruptly she turned and asked the gardener, "Where did you find a phone to call Scotland Yard?"

"At the pub down the way, ma'am."

"Very good."

As we rode back to Baker Street, Joanna closed her eyes and leaned back, oblivious to everyone and everything around her. This was her posture when assembling clues and placing them in an order that allowed her to reach a conclusion. She nodded at one notion, then at another, before opening her eyes.

"We have a true, well-hidden traitor in our midst," Joanna said at length. "This traitor warned the Germans we were on our way, and they made haste to escape."

"It still might have been the gardener," my father countered. "He could have been too obvious in his first sighting and thus alerted the Germans."

"The timing does not fit that line of reasoning, Watson," Joanna said. "Permit me to give you the sequence of events as the evidence so informs us. First, the gardener called Scotland Yard an hour ago, but he initially saw the Germans at least a half hour in front of that. You must take into account that prior to making the call he had to carefully observe the Germans, then find a phone to use. The closest phone available to him was the pub we passed on our ride in. That pub is a good twenty minutes' walking distance away. Thus, an hour and a half had transpired since the initial contact between the gardener and the Germans."

"It is still possible the gardener's presence made the Germans suspicious," I said.

"But that would not have caused such a hasty exit that occurred only thirty minutes before our arrival," Joanna elucidated. "The Germans are such orderly people, yet we found newspapers strewn about the floor and an overturned teacup atop a front page. These skilled agents were obviously so surprised by the warning that they jumped up from their chairs, with the newspaper flying and their cups of tea overturning."

"But what evidence indicates their exit occurred only thirty minutes before our arrival?" I asked.

"The hot ashes and sparks in the fireplace suggest this to be the case," Joanna answered. "In addition, the tea stain on the newspaper was still quite wet and showed no signs of drying. Over the course of an hour and a half, the tea would have surely begun to dissipate and dry, particularly in front of a warm fireplace."

"But to where does this sequence lead us?" my father asked.

"To the traitor," Joanna replied, as a Mona Lisa smile crossed her face. "And our search may well be facilitated by the receipt found in the fireplace."

My father shrugged. "It simply stated that a meal was enjoyed at François."

"Oh, it revealed much more than that," Joanna went on. "Had you the opportunity to study the receipt closely, you would have noted that it was dated the exact same day that Alistair Ainsworth disappeared."

My father stared at Joanna quizzically. "Are you saying that the receipt may somehow be connected to the cryptographer's disappearance?"

"Only if my assumption is correct."

"Which is what, pray tell?"

"That the receipt belonged to Alistair Ainsworth and not to the Germans."

14

The Secret Companion

We arrived at François at the latest possible hour, having wished to be amongst the last to dine and thus the last to leave. Our intention was succeeding nicely, for as the clock struck ten there were only two other tables occupied in the upscale restaurant. Near the window was a young couple signaling for more coffee, while an elderly gentleman at an adjacent table studied his bill.

"How shall we determine which of the waiters served Alistair Ainsworth?" I asked quietly.

"It is not the waiters but the maître d' we should concern ourselves with," Joanna whispered back. "He will know the most."

My father asked, "And what will be the topic of your conversation? Obviously you must be somewhat circumspect for the maître d' will be reluctant to share information on an aristocratic patron."

"We shall talk of the excellent food at François," Joanna replied.

"Which requires no exaggeration," I interjected.

The dishes we had ordered—both the chicken cordon bleu and the coq au vin—were truly superb in every aspect, particularly when topped off by a delicious but far too expensive Chablis. The restaurant itself had a definite French feel to it, with its quaint tables upon which rested long, elegant candles that gave off gentle illumination. The low lighting seemed perfect for the engravings by Renoir and Monet that decorated the walls. Despite the charming atmosphere, our collective minds remained focused on Alistair Ainsworth and the fate that awaited him.

I asked Joanna in a whisper, "Why are you so convinced that it was Ainsworth and not the Germans who visited François on the day of his disappearance?"

"Because foreign agents do not dine at expensive, popular restaurants," she replied. "Nor do they hold on to receipts for days and days. They immediately destroy all items that might leave a trail behind."

"But Ainsworth may have dined here for lunch, long before he vanished," I argued mildly.

Joanna shook her head at the notion. "Recall that Mary Ellington saw him at lunch with Roger Marlowe and Lady Jane Hamilton on that very day."

"The same Roger Marlowe who was said to have had dinner with Ainsworth at Simpson's-in-the-Strand that evening," I commented.

"The very same."

"Strange business here," my father remarked.

"Or quite revealing, if we can determine who Ainsworth had dinner with on that fateful night," said Joanna.

"What is the evidence that he had company?"

"The scorched receipt, which listed two separate entrées."

Over by the window, the elderly gentleman had paid his bill and was preparing to leave, while the young couple watched their coffee cups being replenished before returning to their deep conversation. The waiters began dousing the candles on unoccupied tables.

"Now," Joanna said in an undertone and signaled to the maître d'. The tall, thin man, with a perfectly trimmed moustache, hurried to our table.

"Yes, madam," said he.

"I must tell you that your food far exceeded our expectations," Joanna lauded.

"Thank you, madam."

"The chicken cordon bleu was superb."

"As was the coq au vin," I interjected.

With a half bow, the maître d' stated, "Those are the two dishes most favored by our patrons."

"Our good friend Alistair Ainsworth did not overstate when he called François the best French restaurant in all London," Joanna remarked.

"Oh, Mr. Ainsworth is a true connoisseur, whom

I had the pleasure of serving this past week."

"Was he accompanied by our mutual friend Mr. Roger Marlowe, who also happens to be a connoisseur of French cuisine?"

"Oh no, madam. He brought along the same charming woman he always dines with."

"Then the rumors are true."

"Rumors?"

"Indeed. As you may know, Alistair Ainsworth is a lifelong bachelor and his family has feared he will remain so. But, as of late, some say he is attached to a most charming lady, which gives the family hope."

"They did seem to enjoy one another's company," the maître d' said, then lowering his voice, added, "as evidenced by their gaiety and touching of the hands."

Joanna nodded, with a smile. "So they appeared to be romantically involved."

The maître d' nodded back. "They made no effort to hide their affection for each other."

"Good show!" Joanna said approvingly. "Perhaps there is a wedding in the offing after all."

"Perhaps, madam," the maître d' agreed, but hesitatingly so. "You should know that there is an obvious age difference, with Mr. Ainsworth being her senior by a good twenty years."

Joanna shrugged indifferently. "In these days and times, that does not matter as much as it once did."

"Happily so."

"Well, enough of such talk, let us now turn to dessert and indulge ourselves with your crème brûlée."

"An excellent choice."

"And please ask your chef to stop by our table, so we can praise his delicious dishes."

"With pleasure, madam."

My father waited until the maître d' was out of earshot, but still spoke in a quiet voice. "Well done, Joanna!"

"But we require more information on the woman, which I hope to gain from the chef," said Joanna. "She is the key here."

"How can the chef who spends all of his time in the kitchen be of assistance?" my father asked.

"Keep in mind that Alistair Ainsworth is a gourmet cook and a connoisseur of fine foods," Joanna replied. "I can assure you he had more than a few conversations with the chef that almost certainly took place in the presence of the woman."

"But, for the most part, they would have spoken of food."

"As did I with the maître d'," said Joanna, before uttering in a whisper, "Shhh! The chef approaches."

The middle-aged man looked the part. Short and stout, he had a round, pleasant face that was accentuated by a traditional chef's hat that rested low on his forehead.

"You wished to see me, madam?" he greeted.

"What I wish to do is inform you that your chicken cordon bleu was quite simply the best I have ever eaten. It was beyond superb."

"*Merci beaucoup, madame*," the chef said, with a half bow.

"Now as I have some knowledge of the makings of a chicken cordon bleu, one must ask if it is the type of cheese you use that allows for such a distinctive taste?"

"You are correct, madam," the chef answered, with another half bow. "In most kitchens, the chicken is wrapped around Swiss cheese. We use a tasty, complex cheese that gives the bird a richer flavor."

"But I would think one has to be careful here, for according to Alistair Ainsworth, if the cheese is too strong, it may dampen the flavor of the ham."

"Not to worry, madam. If one uses a salty prosciutto, it will hold its own against any of the cheeses."

"As I recall, I believe Alistair preferred a nicely smoked Polish ham."

"Many gourmet cooks do, in that it blends so well with the cheese."

"Particularly when a touch of Dijon mustard is added."

"Aha! So Alistair shared the secret ingredient with you," the chef said happily. "He is truly a gourmet cook, with whom I am delighted to trade recipes."

"I am told that his female companion is also a connoisseur of French food."

The chef uttered a dismissive sound. "She is not so well informed, madam. She dared to compare my veal cordon bleu to that of a restaurant in Heidelberg. Heidelberg, mind you!"

Joanna's brow went up. "Is she German?"

"I do not think so," the chef said, after a moment's thought. "Her English is very good, and the restaurant in Heidelberg was one she had visited as a student some years ago. Perhaps it was there she acquired the bad habit of ordering a Riesling to go with the veal cordon bleu."

"A poor match," said Joanna.

"Indeed. A hearty Bordeaux Sauvignon is much preferred by most."

"When we return then, we shall have the veal, with a fine Bordeaux that I trust you will help us select."

"It would be my pleasure, madam," the chef said, stepping away as the crème brûlée arrived.

We rode back to Baker Street in a motor taxi, for another storm was under way, with strong winds and a heavy downpour that threatened to flood the streets. No mention was made of our journey to François and our new but tantalizing

231

clues, for we wished not to be overheard by our driver. Upon reaching our rooms, we changed into more comfortable attire and settled in front of a blazing fire to enjoy snifters of Napoleon brandy.

"I had no idea you were so familiar with French recipes," my father remarked to Joanna.

"I had little such knowledge until this afternoon when I read several texts on the subject," she replied. "When in a foreign land, you do well to speak their language. And in an upscale French restaurant, food is the singular, sacred language spoken."

"But how did you determine they would be so familiar with Alistair Ainsworth?" I asked.

"That was fairly simple," Joanna answered. "We learned from several sources that he is a gourmet cook, who even went to the bother of selecting his own birds for the oven. When such an individual visits a fine restaurant, you can bank on him visiting with the chef. You see, they both feel they belong to a rather select group, and are more than happy to chat with one another."

"So you had to walk the fine line of knowing some but not too much about French recipes."

"Everyone loves to converse about their particular area of expertise, and the chef at François was no exception. Of course he readily recognized his knowledge was superior to mine, which made him even more eager to discuss his dishes."

Joanna swirled the brandy in her snifter before taking another silent swallow. "But one must be careful and always cloak your questions with inquiries about food. Thus, when asked about Ainsworth's companion's knowledge of various French dishes, the chef was only too happy to tell us of her lack thereof, and the apparent German influence on her choice of wines."

"Do you believe her to be German?" I asked at once.

"It was not possible to tell with certainty," Joanna replied. "But I doubt very much that she was a visiting student who spent only a brief time in Germany. Such students have a limited income and do not frequent expensive restaurants in Heidelberg, nor do they order veal cordon bleu, which is always a high-priced item on the menu. And preferring a Riesling to go with the veal is a German taste and not an English one."

"If she is German, how do we connect her to Ainsworth's disappearance?" my father queried. "Could she in fact be a German spy?"

"Why not?" Joanna asked in return. "Spies come in all shapes, sizes, and genders. Moreover, I am always a bit suspicious when I see a match between a man and woman with a wide difference in their ages. Of course she could be attracted to older men or to his wealth and social status. But this does not explain his reluctance to introduce her to his sister and friends. He lies to his sister and informs her that he will be having dinner with Roger Marlowe, all the while sharing a clandestine dinner with the woman at François. Even Roger Marlowe lies for him."

"Could it be that Ainsworth is ashamed of the age difference between the woman and himself?" I wondered.

"Unlikely," Joanna said. "Most middle-aged men are delighted to be seen with much younger women. They consider it a sign of virility and charm."

"Let us return to the premise that she may be a German spy," I proposed. "What role could she play?"

"A guide as to what Ainsworth was doing at a given time," Joanna answered. "Allow me to give you an example. On the evening of his disappearance, there was no certainty he would be visiting Ah Sing's. Since they were dining together, one might assume they would be spending the entire evening together. But if the woman learned he was to later visit Ah Sing's, she could have well notified the Germans once she left Ainsworth and the restaurant."

"The agents could have been in a carriage a block away and never be seen."

"Indeed."

"But does that role not seem somewhat unlikely, with the obvious feelings of affection they had for one another?"

"I suspect their relationship was quite platonic."

"Why so?"

"Because Alistair Ainsworth came home to his sister at night without fail."

"So we are faced with yet another riddle within a riddle."

"Which can only be unraveled if we know who the woman truly is," my father remarked.

"And how do we accomplish that feat?" asked I.

"By learning why Alistair Ainsworth went to such lengths to hide their attachment," Joanna said and, after finishing her brandy, retired for the evening.

15

A Coded Message

There was a mood of gloom at the Admiralty Club the following morning. It was now evident that Alistair Ainsworth had been broken and at least one of the deciphering mechanisms revealed.

"We must redouble our efforts," Dunn beseeched all those gathered. "For it appears that our decoding system will shortly be entirely compromised, and at that point Ainsworth's life will be ended and the fate of England put at great risk. The former would be unfortunate, the latter a disaster."

"May I ask how you came to know that a deciphering mechanism had been broken?" Joanna asked.

Dunn hesitated at length before saying, "We intercepted a wire from German Naval Intelligence instructing their submarines to vacate their positions immediately. I shall leave it at that."

"You must give me the details, Lieutenant," Joanna insisted. "I need to know what the Germans know."

"That information is so sensitive I cannot—"

"Oh, Bloody Christ!" Marlowe interrupted. "Tubby's life is at stake here, and we have no time for your silly games. Either you provide her with the information or I shall."

Dunn gave Marlowe a stern look as his face closed. It took a moment for him to regain his composure, and only then did he turn to Joanna. "You should keep in mind that what I am about to reveal is highly classified."

"Get on with it," Marlowe demanded.

"Last month," Dunn began, "a coded message was sent to our fleet, warning that a number of German U-boats were spotted in the waters off Scotland's Orkney Islands. We have a major naval installation in that area, and ships moving in and out would be prime targets for submerged U-boats."

"I require the entire message," Joanna said.

"Oh, I remember that one," Montclair recalled. "There was a group of U-boats roaming about the innermost of the islands, which placed them near one of our critical harbors."

"Was the particular island named?" Joanna asked.

Montclair closed his eyes, as if thinking back. "That was not mentioned. However, that would not be unusual since the Orkneys are an archipelago consisting of seventy islands, most of which are uninhabited and unnamed."

"So now," Dunn concluded, "our destroyers,

which have been endlessly scouring these waters to hunt down the U-boats, will have been sent out on a meaningless mission. And those same U-boats are no doubt currently at an undisclosed location, waiting to inflict damage and death on us."

"But no harm has been done yet," Joanna said. "There were no ships sunk and no lives lost. Furthermore, the communiqué caused the Germans to withdraw their U-boats and now your critical harbor is safe."

"Are you suggesting Ainsworth did us a favor?" Dunn asked sharply.

"I am suggesting that Alistair Ainsworth purposely selected this message for us to decipher," Joanna replied.

"To what end?"

"The message was not of great strategic importance, but it gave the German agents a taste of things to come, thus ensuring that Ainsworth will be kept alive. In essence, I believe Ainsworth is simply buying time and hoping we will eventually come to his rescue."

"That is a possibility," Dunn agreed.

"Allow me to present another possibility," Joanna continued. "Remember, Ainsworth is an accomplished chess master who thinks two or three steps ahead of his opponent. With this in mind, perhaps he is doing much more than simply buying time."

A smile came to Mary Ellington's face. "Tubby may be sending us a message within a message!"

"Precisely," Joanna said. "That is why the exact wordage of the intercepted dispatch is so important."

Dunn reached into his attaché case for a thick file and opened it. "The German communiqué reads as follows: 'Three U-boats off innermost Orkney Islands discovered. Vacate area immediately.' "

All in the room went silent as we gave the matter long, concentrated thought and tried to decipher a code within a code. Marlowe and Mary Ellington jotted down the message, while Montclair closed his eyes and appeared to be summoning his memory bank. I wondered if we should consult with Sir David Shaw, the renowned codebreaker who might be of assistance here. But it was a certainty Dunn would not allow any further outsiders into the group.

"If it's there, it is well hidden." Mary Ellington broke the silence.

"Tubby would have it no other way," Marlowe said. "He had to design a code that was impossible for the Germans to notice, which in turn makes it difficult for us to decipher."

Mary counted aloud up to ten. "There are only ten words in the message, with one number and no symbols or apostrophes to provide a hint."

Montclair opened his eyes. "Something is a

bit off in Tubby's message. I can't put my finger on it, but there is something that feels out of order."

"With a single word or the message itself?" Joanna pressed.

"I am not certain," Montclair said, with a shrug. "Perhaps I am confusing it with another communiqué."

Joanna asked, "Did you work with Ainsworth on this particular message?"

"Only to a limited extent," Montclair replied. "As I recall, our original coded message to the fleet was based on a biblical passage of some sort."

"Which passage?" Joanna asked quickly.

"Tubby never mentioned it because he was too consumed recoding the dispatch so the Germans could not decipher it. To that end he used a nursery rhyme."

"Do you remember the rhyme?"

Montclair shrugged again. "Only that it included a lot of numbers, with each number representing a letter in the alphabet."

"That does not appear to be the case here," Joanna said.

"It can't be that complicated," Montclair opined. "Most likely there is only a single word or two that is the key to the message."

"We need to come up with answers here," Dunn urged. "Please keep in mind that your colleague's life is on the line, and that line grows shorter with each passing minute."

"We were so close yesterday," Marlowe groused. "If the troops had arrived at the home in St. John's Wood just a bit sooner, Tubby would be sitting with us this moment."

"I am surprised you were not invited to join in yesterday's pursuit," Joanna said to Marlowe. "Your knowledge of German and Germany might have been quite useful."

"I tried to convince Lieutenant Dunn of that, but he insisted I stand back," Marlowe explained. "He uttered some sort of nonsense about me being too valuable to put in harm's way."

"I can assure you my superiors would have never allowed it," Dunn said firmly. "Now let us move on." He walked over to a nearby desk and pointed to the opened map of London's train stations that had been glued behind the bathroom mirror at the last house the Germans inhabited. "Have you had any luck with the map?"

There was no response from the group.

"Can you attach any meaning to the circle drawn around Waterloo Station?"

"There are at least a dozen interpretations," Marlowe replied. "None of which brings us any closer to Tubby."

"List the two or three you believe most promising."

Marlowe reached for his sterling silver cigarette

case and lighted a Player's Navy Cut. "Each of us shall give you our best choice and the reasoning behind it. But please keep in mind that at this point we are only stating our best guesses."

"Yes, yes," Dunn said impatiently. "But nevertheless, let's have them."

"First, we have to assume that Tubby did the circling to leave us a message," Marlowe began. "Secondly, we must believe that he had overheard or otherwise come by information that indicated the Germans' next move. This would be the critical message he wished to transmit to us. That being the case, I suspect Tubby was not referring to the train station, which would be far too obvious, but to Waterloo where the historic battle between the French and British troops took place. Now we all know that Tubby was multilingual, but his weakest language was French. Because of this, he kept a French-to-German dictionary in his desk and actually penned important notes in it. I believe some notation in that dictionary will tell us where the Germans are headed next."

I could not help but be impressed by Marlowe's creative and lateral thinking. How could one possibly go from a train station in London to a French-to-German dictionary was far beyond me. But then again, that was his skill and that was what made him so valuable to His Majesty's intelligence service.

Montclair squinted an eye, then added, "As I

recall, Tubby kept a copy of the Old Testament in his desk as well."

"Is he of the Jewish faith?" Joanna asked.

"Tubby is of no faith," Montclair replied. "His interest in the Old Testament involved a peculiar code we solved together. There was a passage in which God polluted the Nile River with blood, thus turning it red, to punish the Egyptians. But I doubt the Old Testament is in any way related to our current puzzle. I think we should concentrate on Tubby's French dictionary, for it is clearly linked to the word *Waterloo*."

"Agreed," Dunn said. "What say you, Mrs. Ellington?"

"I too am under the impression Tubby was pointing to the Battle of Waterloo," Mary said. "But from there, I traveled in a different direction. The French were of course commanded by Napoleon who was married to the enchanting Josephine. On a whim I investigated to see if there is a Josephine Street in London, and there is one located in Reigate. We are currently determining if any houses in the district were leased over the past year, with all rents paid in advance."

"If such leases are uncovered, it would be important to learn if the lessees had Teutonic features," my father advised.

"That would be the second question asked," Mary assured.

"And you, Montclair, have other ideas crossed your mind?" Dunn asked.

"We should not overlook the British side at the Battle of Waterloo, where our troops were under the command of the Duke of Wellington. Tubby may be directing us to the monuments that were built in honor of this celebrated hero. As you know, there are two of these. The first being the statue at the southeast corner of Hyde Park where all is very busy and wide open, and, for the most part, commercial. That would not be a locale the Germans would select. The second monument is much more likely. The duke is entombed in a crypt at St. Paul's Cathedral, and the residential neighborhood could readily meet the Germans' requirements. We are at this moment scanning the entire area for recently leased houses." Montclair rocked back and forth in his chair, then added, "I am also considering the possibility there is a connection between the message Tubby decoded and the one he left for us behind the mirror. Now, wouldn't that be clever of old Tubby?"

"I do not see how the two could be connected," Dunn said. "One is attempting to tell us his location, the other simply buying Ainsworth more time."

"So it would seem, but that does not exclude their linkage," Montclair argued. "You might be interested to know that in chess there is a strategy called the combination, in which a planned series of moves gives you the advantage and leaves your opponent in a weakened position. Tubby knows this gambit all too well, Lieutenant. Do not underestimate his ability to outwit the Germans."

"Then you had best work your hardest on both coded messages," Dunn implored. "If even the barest of clues suggests where the Germans are located, please bring it to my attention immediately. We have the manpower to cover all possibilities, no matter how remote."

The phone on Roger Marlowe's desk rang. Dunn picked up the receiver and quickly brought it to his ear.

"Dunn," he said curtly, followed by, "When?"

Dunn listened carefully, then replaced the receiver and reached for his attaché case. "It would appear you have all been off the mark on the last message Ainsworth left us. A suspected German agent was just taken into custody at Waterloo Station."

16

Waterloo Station

Led by Lieutenant Dunn, we hurried up the metal steps and entered the train where the German spy awaited us. The car itself was vacant except for two constables and a solitary figure seated by the window and shrouded in a wool blanket.

"The spy?" Dunn asked, pointing to the figure.

"Yes, sir," replied a constable.

"Why is he covered?"

"Because he is dead, sir."

Dunn was taken aback for a moment, then quickly recovered. "How did this happen?"

The constable shrugged. "I do not know, sir. We had placed him in handcuffs when he smiled at us, then took a last gasp and was gone."

"Did you harm him in any way?"

"We arrested him without a struggle and applied the handcuffs. Nothing more was done, sir."

"Remove the blanket," Dunn ordered.

The figure was uncovered and revealed a heavyset man, in his middle years, with a strong jawline and bright red hair. His suit was well made and unsoiled, as were his shoes and the hat on his lap.

"The bomb planner himself," Dunn murmured to himself and moved in for a closer inspection of the corpse's hands and face. "There are no signs of violence to explain his sudden death."

"Perhaps he had a fatal heart attack," Lestrade suggested.

"Individuals do not smile while experiencing a myocardial infarction," my father rebutted.

"Nor do men such as this one die unexpectedly, even when placed in the most challenging of situations," Dunn said, and came back to the lead constable. "I need to know every detail, from the moment he was spotted until his capture. Leave out nothing, for the smallest happening may be of consequence."

The second police officer stepped forward and introduced himself. "I am Constable Harrison, sir. It was I who first noticed the suspicious man and gave chase. Officer Bates actually followed him into the train and made the arrest."

"What made you suspicious of him?" Dunn asked.

"His red hair, but only after he tripped over a pram," Harrison replied. "I was mingling amongst a group of departing passengers when I saw a man hurry by and trip over a moving pram. He lost his balance and, in the process, his hat became dislodged and revealed his very red hair. As he readjusted the position of his hat, I heard him utter a German-sounding word."

"Do you recall the word?" Joanna interrupted.

"It was *achtgeben* or something quite close to that."

Joanna nodded. "It is German and it means to be careful or watch your step."

"That would fit, madam," Harrison agreed.

"Get on with the chase," Dunn implored.

"I shouted for him to stop immediately, but he fled and I sounded my whistle to alert the other constables. The exits were quickly secured and, having no other recourse, the suspect ran across the tracks and into a train from which passengers were alighting. At this juncture, it was Constable Bates who was close on the suspect's heels and followed him into the train. I raced to the exit at the other end of the car and thus blocked any chance of his escaping. He gave up without a struggle. He had no identification papers and this of course made him even more suspicious—that together with his shocking red hair, sir. It was only moments after his arrest and having been placed in handcuffs that he smiled at us and promptly died."

Joanna addressed both constables. "Did either of you see the suspect reach into his pockets after he was obviously cornered, with no hope of escape?"

They shook their heads simultaneously, but it was Harrison who spoke. "Because of fear that he was armed, we kept our attention focused on his hands while he was in the process of being captured. His hands were visible at all times and he made no attempt to go for his pockets."

"One last question," said Joanna. "You mentioned that it was the suspect's red hair that alerted you initially. Why was that so?"

Constable Harrison looked to Inspector Lestrade, who nodded his permission to answer. "We were given a bulletin instructing us to keep a sharp eye out for a redheaded German agent who was most dangerous."

"When was this bulletin issued?"

"Weeks ago, ma'am."

"Thank you for the helpful information," Joanna said, and gave my father and me a knowing look, for the agent was most certainly Rot, whose name Verner had heard shouted out at the Germans' residence.

Lestrade stepped forward to praise the constables. "Both of you are to be commended for your fine work, which will be duly noted in your records. Now, I should like you to arrange for a gurney and transport to carry the corpse to the morgue at St. Bartholomew's. You are both to stand by the remains at all times and make certain it is not touched or in any way disturbed until I give further instructions."

"Very good, sir," Harrison said.

"And finally, there are no doubt many onlookers outside the train at the moment. Please disperse them and have a constable posted to keep the curious clear of this car."

The constables gave Lestrade a brief salute and hurried to their tasks. Once they had departed, Lestrade quickly searched the suspect's clothes. As expected, the spy had no wallet or identification papers, nor were there any labels to indicate where his suit was made. There were two five-pound notes in a pants pocket, but no foreign currency. The heels of his shoes were worn and showed no markings that might have revealed their country of origin.

"Please see if the heels contain a secret compartment," Joanna requested.

"To what end?" Lestrade asked while determining no such secret space existed.

"For the poison he used to kill himself."

"May I inquire what brings you to that conclusion?"

"There is no other explanation," Joanna answered. "When a man dies with a smile on his face, he is expecting death or may even be relieved that it is coming. Thus, I believe it is fair to say he somehow brought about his own demise."

"There are ways to inflict sudden death other than poison," Dunn countered.

"Such as what, pray tell?"

"Swallowing an object that would completely occlude one's airway."

"But that would have induced an involuntary choking seizure, which did not occur here," Joanna refuted. "Nor would it have brought a smile to his face."

"And where would he obtain such an object?" I interjected. "Keep in mind the constables watched his every move and saw no such act committed."

"Well put, John," Joanna said with a nod. "We can also exclude blows to the head and neck because there is no evidence any were administered and, unless repeatedly applied, would not induce death."

"Nor would a concealed, self-inflicted knife wound," my father chimed in. "Which, in any event, would have been quite impossible with his hands handcuffed behind him."

"All of which leaves us with poison," Joanna concluded.

"But how was it given?" Dunn asked.

"That is what we must determine," replied Joanna and turned to me. "We should have my husband examine the corpse to see if there are any telling signs. John, please be good enough to look for injection sites on the arms and parts of tablets in the corpse's oral cavity."

"But the constables kept their eyes focused on every move of his hands," Lestrade argued. "Surely they would have seen him inject himself or reach for a tablet to swallow."

"I am afraid you give them too much credit, Inspector," Joanna responded. "You must remember that the spy fled into this car ahead of the constables and for a brief moment was alone and unobserved. That is when he could have swallowed a tablet or injected himself."

"If he injected himself, where then would the needle be?"

"He could have discarded it so that it is currently out of sight, or hidden it in his clothes, which were only examined in a cursory fashion."

"All reasonable possibilities," Lestrade said before gesturing to me. "If you would be so good as to lend us your expertise, Dr. Watson."

I began my examination with a careful inspection of the corpse's fingertips. A hidden needle, dipped in a curarelike poison, could easily pierce the skin of his fingers or palms, but no such injection site was to be seen. Nor were any pinprick marks present on the forearms or in the antecubital fossa where a rich supply of veins would rapidly carry the poison into the bloodstream. The oral cavity revealed good dental hygiene and again no injection sites. I lifted the tongue to search for particles of a tablet that had been administered sublingually, but found none. Moving in closer to examine the back of the pharynx, I detected a familiar scent.

"Cyanide!" I announced to the group. "His mouth has the aroma of bitter almonds."

Lestrade stepped in for a deep sniff. "Blimey! It is cyanide. But how did he manage to do it?"

I reexamined the oral cavity and saw no mucosed pockets where the poison might have been hidden. The gingival tissues were clear as well, and the tongue revealed no tears. But one of the molars at the very rear appeared to be cracked open. The other teeth were in fine condition and showed no such abnormality. Then I saw the telltale sign. Wedged into the cracked tooth was a particle of a capsule that solved the problem. "We are looking at remarkable German ingenuity."

"How so?" asked Lestrade.

"They hollowed out one of his molars," I described. "Then they placed a capsule of poison within it before capping the tooth. All the spy had to do was grind his teeth together, which would disrupt the cap and release the poison. Which in this case was cyanide that produced instant death."

"No hands required," my father added.

Joanna moved in near to the corpse and studied its face at length before asking, "What was so unique about this spy that he had to avoid capture at all costs?"

"He was a master spy who sat at the very top of our most wanted list," Dunn replied. "In a recently decoded message, we learned that Rot's primary mission was to plot and select the major sites in London to be bombed by the Germans' zeppelin fleet. These dirigible airships were responsible for hundreds upon hundreds of British deaths. Should he have been taken prisoner, I can assure you he would have been treated quite harshly and beyond a doubt executed."

"But why was Rot at Waterloo Station, which he would have known was under close surveillance?'

"Perhaps it was a site he was selecting," Lestrade suggested.

"That would be most unlikely," Joanna said. "Please recall that the zeppelin raids always occur at night when the station would be virtually empty. To bomb a vacant station would go against the airship's main purpose, which is to terrorize the civilian population."

"Then why was he here?" Lestrade wondered.

Joanna shrugged. "All we can say for certain is that he was here and Alistair Ainsworth circled Waterloo Station on the map."

"Are you connecting the two?" Dunn asked at once.

"I have not excluded that possibility, nor should you. Keep in mind that Ainsworth may have known of Rot, in that both occupied the house that Verner had been taken to." Joanna stepped away from the corpse and gestured to Lestrade. "You may wish to carefully reexamine the corpse's clothes to see if there are hidden clues that could help us in this regard."

Lestrade emptied each of Rot's pockets one by one, turning them inside out. All the search uncovered was a soiled handkerchief, a half-crown coin, and a broken toothpick enmeshed in lint. The buckle on his belt had no secret compartment.

"Nothing," Lestrade announced.

"Perhaps the postmortem examination will be more revealing," said I.

"He may have swallowed a note or some item he wished to conceal," I replied. "Thus, the contents of his esophagus and stomach will be carefully scrutinized."

"Also please determine if his shoes show any traces of chloroform," Joanna requested.

"But certainly any aroma that may have been on his shoes would have disappeared by now," Dunn argued mildly. "As I recall, the odor of chloroform is quite evanescent."

"Ah, but the chemists at St. Bart's may well have a test that can detect the barest traces of chloroform," Joanna rebutted. "And chloroform on Rot's shoes would place him in Verner's office and connects him beyond any doubt to the disappearance of Alistair Ainsworth."

The four of us carefully inspected the train car, searching under the seats and in the compartments above for items the master spy might have discarded. Nothing of value was discovered. Dunn remembered a case in which an important clue on a train was hidden beneath the ashes at the bottom of an ashtray. Thus, each of the ashtrays was emptied and inspected, but to no avail.

The two constables returned to inform us that a transport for the corpse would arrive shortly and that the authorities at St. Bart's had been notified and instructed on how the body was to be kept. To make certain the instructions were adhered to, Lestrade directed the constables to accompany the corpse to the morgue and stand guard over it until the postmortem examination was under way. After a final glance around the car, he ordered the corpse to be re-covered and the shades on all windows drawn. We waited for the commands to be followed before departing.

The large crowd that had earlier gathered outside the train had been dispersed, and uni-formed constables were stationed to assure it remained so. It was now near noon and the station appeared filled with passengers, arriving and leaving, all of whom seemed to be talking at once. The loud hum of combined conversations drowned out any attempt for us to speak further about the strange events surrounding this most unusual case. But in an instant, everything went silent.

Down the platform and approaching us was a small funeral procession. It consisted of an expensive, polished casket being pushed along on wheels by porters on each side of the carriage. At the front was the funeral director, dressed entirely in black, with a most solemn expression on his face. To the rear was a rather tall woman, likewise attired in black, with a matching veil that hid her face. As the cortège neared us, I took note of the small bell atop the casket, to which was attached a cord that dropped into the casket itself. This arrangement was instigated by the widespread fear of being buried alive, for a few such cases had been publicized during last year's cholera epidemic. The ringing of the bell would alert all that the person within was alive.

But Joanna's attention was fixed on the veiled woman at the rear of the procession. I saw nothing unusual about the woman or the polished coffin, with its brass fittings, that she accompanied. I doffed my hat out of respect for the departed, as did the others around me, including the officers from Scotland Yard.

Joanna quickly turned to Lestrade and said, "Please stop the procession, Inspector."

Lestrade gazed at her oddly before asking, "For what purpose?"

"To prevent Alistair Ainsworth from slipping away under our very noses."

In an instant Lestrade spun around and moved the onlookers in front of him aside. He dashed over to the funeral director and brought the cortège to a halt. Interested onlookers moved in for a closer view and to possibly overhear any conversation that might explain the odd interruption.

"Is there something amiss?" asked the funeral director.

"Perhaps," Lestrade replied. "I should like you to answer all questions asked by my associate."

"Of course, sir."

Joanna stepped forward, but her gaze was focused on a narrow rubber tube that exited the casket an inch beneath the edge of its lid. Like the bell, this apparatus was based on fear of being buried alive. It provided a supply of fresh air should the presumed-dead individual within the casket suddenly awaken.

Joanna asked the funeral director, "When did the departed die? And please be exact."

"Just over three days ago."

"And the destination of the remains?"

"To Shoreham."

"Did you yourself place the body in the casket?"

"No, madam. His family performed the task, and it was done in total privacy."

"Most unusual."

"Quite," the director agreed. "But I was informed it was a strict family custom that only close relatives were allowed to touch the deceased."

"And I take it they secured the lid in total privacy as well?"

"That too was insisted upon, madam."

Joanna leaned forward and brought the rubber tube exiting the casket to her nose. She quickly dropped the tubing in disgust. "Open the casket at once!"

"But, madam, I—"

"It is a sham funeral!"

The woman at the rear of the procession suddenly bolted.

"Stop him!" Joanna cried out.

"Who?" Lestrade shouted back.

"The mourner dressed as a woman!"

The tall mourner fled into the gathered crowd to seek concealment, but his head was clearly above those around him. Thus we could follow him as he shoved onlookers aside and trampled over the ones who remained in his way. He appeared to take a circuitous route before suddenly veering off and dashing into the ladies' water closet where he was met with a chorus of screams and shrieks. But these sounds were soon muted by gunshots and the noise of shattering glass.

"Outside!" Joanna called out above the commotion. "He is escaping through the window!"

Uniformed constables and Lieutenant Dunn sprinted for the entrance to the station while Joanna raced into the ladies' water closet, with Lestrade, my father, and I only a step behind her. Pale, frightened women were huddled together off to the side, well away from the shattered glass window. On the floor near the window was a torn black dress, and atop it a wig and dark veil.

"With his head start, we will never catch him," Lestrade said disheartedly.

"I should have discovered him earlier," Joanna grumbled. "The clues were there, staring at me and waiting to be discerned."

"Pray tell, what were these signs that the rest of us overlooked?" asked Lestrade.

"First, the mourner's body size," Joanna elucidated. "Did you not notice the tall height and broad shoulders, which would be most unusual in a woman? Then there was the thick veil that hid the face completely. The vast majority of mourning veils will hide a woman's tearstained cheeks, but not her most prominent features, as this one did. You could see nothing behind it, which would effectively conceal any masculine characteristics. And the final clue was the noxious odor emanating from the rubber tube that originated from within the casket. The deceased had only been dead for three days and it requires eight to ten days for putrefaction to occur. Thus, the malodor could not have come from the corpse."

"So what then caused the awful smell?" Lestrade asked.

"Oh, there are a number of ways to accomplish that," Joanna replied.

"But it still could have been a woman,"

Lestrade insisted. "There are ladies who are tall and broad shouldered, and the mourner may have used the dress, wig, and veil to disguise her true identity."

"All true," Joanna agreed. "Except when he bolted, I noticed that his shoes and heels were those seen only on men. A woman would never wear them."

We hurried out of the ladies' water closet and returned to the casket, which Lestrade ordered to be opened at once. The gathering of onlookers, which had increased to twice its original size, was urged to step away, but few did. Most stood on their tiptoes for a better view.

When the last screw was removed and the lid opened, a terrible stench arose from within the casket. Lying atop sacks of sand was a long-dead cat, with its insides gutted. The lid was hurriedly closed.

"A trial run." I stated the obvious.

"A dress rehearsal in full regalia to iron out any flaws in their plan," said Joanna. "If there were defects, better to find them now rather than later, when a drugged Alistair Ainsworth would be inside the casket."

"But why the dead cat?" asked Lestrade.

"That was a nice touch," Joanna explained. "Had anyone demanded the casket be opened, simply cracking the lid open would have released a most putrid odor and, in most instances, necessitated immediate closure. I can assure you a cargo inspector would not have wished to look further."

I had to admire the ingenuity of the foreign agents. Like the true Germans they were, they rehearsed every step of the funeral down to the smallest detail. And except for a redheaded spy tripping over a pram, they might well have gotten away with it. I nodded to myself as yet another part of their clever plan came to mind. Thinking aloud, I said, "In all likelihood the train's destination to Shoreham was not some random choice. Shoreham-by-Sea is a small port where a German U-boat could easily slip in unnoticed during the dark of night and transport a most valuable cargo back to Germany."

"So cunning," my father remarked.

"Oh, they are beyond cunning, Watson," said Joanna, as a thin smile crossed her face. "A foreign agent of such clever thought is one I would be eager to do business with."

Dunn, with a pair of constables at his side, ran up to us and grimly announced, "He has gotten away scot-free. Of course, the entire surrounding area will be thoroughly canvassed and searched, but the chances of finding him are virtually nil."

"So we are back to square one and the Germans remain one step ahead of us," Lestrade said unhappily. "We have gained nothing despite our cleverness."

"Oh, I believe we have gained some much-needed information," Joanna informed.

"Pray tell, what?" Lestrade asked.

"The Germans now know we will closely surveil every train station within a fifty-mile radius, so they can no longer move their cargo by train," Joanna replied. "They are thus forced to travel by motorcar or carriage to reach their desired destination."

"That gives us no advantage," Lestrade argued. "It is quite impossible to block all roads leading out of London, and we most certainly cannot search every vehicle that wishes to pass."

"We must think moves ahead if we are to counter their next step," Joanna advised. "It is not their way out of London that we should be concerned with, but rather their destination."

"How can we possibly determine that?"

"By deduction, Inspector, which goes as follows," Joanna went on. "John is correct in his reasoning that their ticket to Shoreham was not a random choice, but one that takes them to a small port where, in all likelihood, a German U-boat will await them."

"But surely they will not return to Shoreham now," said Lestrade. "Particularly since they know we are aware of their train's destination."

"I would not rush to that conclusion," my father cautioned. "Perhaps the Germans in their cleverness now believe we will pay little attention to Shoreham and thus proceed with their original plan."

"Very good, Watson, for you are now beginning to think as the spies would," said Joanna. "Of course, another very real possibility is that Shoreham-by-Sea was never their intended port of departure. It, like the funeral procession, may have been false. For obvious reasons they would keep their final destination secret until the very last moment."

Lestrade pondered the dilemma at length before asking, "Are you suggesting we must cover hundreds of small ports on the east coast of England?"

"It can't be done," Dunn said firmly. "We do not have the manpower to undertake such a task, and the local police are not clever enough to measure up. If these foreign agents can outwit us so easily, it would be no problem for them to outmatch a small district constabulary."

"There are ways to narrow down the list of ports from which the Germans might depart," Joanna told us. "We now know they cannot transport their cargo by train, which restricts their movement to roads. In all likelihood they will have a bound, drugged Alistair Ainsworth in their motorcar or carriage, which necessitates them traveling in the dark of night to avoid curious eyes. They cannot stop at an inn or hotel, and thus would be obliged to ride straight to their destination. By car or carriage, a single night's journey would be limited to seventy-five miles or less. We can further reason that they will not travel south to the Southampton area, which is England's major port and whose waters are closely guarded by His Majesty's warships. No U-boat would dare come near. When all is said and done, I think it fair to say that the Germans plan to depart at a port seventy-five miles or less north of London."

"There are dozens of such ports, some of which are mere villages with hidden docks and wharfs," Dunn countered. "Moreover, we must consider the possibility that the Germans have a safe house along the way outside of London. Here, they could rest and delay their departure for a more suitable date."

"I think your latter point is unlikely," Joanna responded. "The Germans must be very exact in their escape, which no doubt was planned in advance. They would be on a strict schedule—as would the U-boat—that dictates how and when the transfer of Alistair Ainsworth would occur. To be successful, these types of maneuvers must be carried out on a precise timetable. We can therefore assume that, on leaving their current location, the next move is to go directly to their port of departure. Nevertheless, your description of the small villages with their secluded docks and wharfs is well taken and could present a surveillance problem. Yet, with the forces of Scotland Yard and Naval Intelligence, you should be able to find a way to cover them."

"We shall give your suggestion our closest attention," Dunn said. "But we should realize that, even with our best efforts, surveillance of all the inlets and estuaries would be next to impossible."

"Nonetheless we should try," Joanna persisted.

"And we shall."

We paused briefly as hospital personnel entered the train car to retrieve the body of the German spy. Moments later the covered corpse was wheeled away, with strands of his bright red hair protruding out for all to see.

"Perhaps we should concentrate on the dead spy," my father proposed, as the door to the car closed. "Does his presence here give us any clues that could lead to the whereabouts of the other German agents?"

"You assume that he is connected to the sham funeral," Dunn said. "There is no evidence to associate the two. One must consider the possibility that it was a random, unplanned encounter."

"Spies do not do *random*," Joanna said. "There is a purpose behind every action they take, and that was certainly the case here."

"But where is your proof to back up such an assertion?"

"Let us begin with the premise that two of

Germany's most skilled foreign agents show up at the same place at the exact same time," Joanna elucidated. "And this takes place during the rehearsal of a plan to smuggle Alistair Ainsworth out of London. What is the chance of these events simply being coincidental?"

"None," I replied at once. "Absolutely none."

"Exactly."

Lestrade asked, "But what was Rot's purpose?"

"A number of possibilities come to mind," Joanna answered. "He might have been an uninvolved observer who was there to oversee the plan in action and determine if there were any flaws. Or he could have been here as a protector for the actors in this play. And then there is a third, more likely reason that could tie Rot to the other German agents. Perhaps he was at Waterloo Station to conduct business that required a face-to-face encounter with the others."

"But would he have taken such a risk, knowing the station was under close surveillance?" Dunn challenged.

"The risk was not as great as one might think," Joanna replied. "Rot would have melted into the crowd without notice had he not tripped and exposed his red hair. And no one would have ever considered the woman in mourning to be the recipient of a spy message."

"But all eyes would have been on the funeral procession," Dunn persisted.

"Not initially," Joanna responded. "Arrangements for moving the casket would have been carried out in a private room where Rot could have stopped in to pay his condolences. I can assure you no one would have paid his visit the least bit of attention."

"But why take the risk at all?" Lestrade asked. "Why not send the information by wireless?"

"They would have been concerned the vital message might have been intercepted and decoded," Joanna told him. "The safest and most secure method would be a hand-to-hand transfer, and this indicates how very important the message was."

I inquired, "Do you have any idea what was in the message that made it so vital?"

"Here we must depend on logic and ask ourselves the following question. What was Rot's singular mission while stationed in London?"

"To select the sites to be bombed by the zeppelin fleet!" I cried out.

"Precisely," said Joanna. "That is what made the message so important. And I suspect the information was meant to be transferred to a U-boat, along with Alistair Ainsworth, and sent on its way to Germany."

"If we assume the list was in his possession at the station, the possibility exists that he chewed and swallowed it prior to his apprehension," I surmised. "That being the case, parts of the message may yet be in his esophagus and gastric juice."

"And his clothes must be torn apart thread by thread to search for additional notes that could lead to the operatives holding Ainsworth," my father proposed.

"This is all supposition," Dunn warned. "And if no such notes are found, we might justifiably conclude that no such transfer was ever intended."

"Or it might indicate that the transfer had taken place prior to Rot's apprehension," said Joanna.

On that unhappy note we hurried out of Waterloo Station and into our carriages, all headed for St. Bart's, where we hoped the post-mortem examination on Rot would reveal hidden clues that could help us unravel this most perplexing case that so threatened England.

17

Lady Jane

Later that afternoon my father and I settled in front of a warming fire to search the evening newspapers for any happening that might apply to the disappearance of Alistair Ainsworth. Periodically I glanced up to watch Joanna pace back and forth across our parlor, smoking one cigarette after another as she attempted to assemble the available clues into a recognizable order. She would nod at one piece of evidence and flick her wrist at another, all the while muttering to herself, which further indicated the degree of difficulty in solving the problem. To add to our predicament, the postmortem examination of Rot turned up nothing of consequence. Carefully sewn into the shoulder pads of his suit were two hundred dollars in American currency and a false Portuguese passport, as one might expect of a spy. He was also quite ill, with prostatic cancer that had painfully spread to his pelvic bone, which might have accounted for his readiness to take his own life. No chewed items or notes were found in his esophagus and gastric juice nor any clues uncovered that might lead to the whereabouts of the other German agents. It would seem we had reached a dead end in our search for Alistair Ainsworth, but the Admiralty Club believed otherwise. They were of the opinion that Waterloo Station circled on the train map held a second meaning that indicated where Ainsworth and his German captors were located.

"Do you also think that Ainsworth had a double entendre in mind when he circled Waterloo?" I asked, breaking the silence.

"That is the most likely case, for that is how the brain of a cryptographer would work," Joanna replied. "It is the best of hidden messages, with one being obvious and the other obscure."

"So it is the obscure you are searching for."

"I will leave that to the Admiralty Club," Joanna said, as she crushed out her cigarette. "It is the second message Ainsworth sent that draws my attention."

"The one that tells us of the U-boats off the Orkney Islands," I recalled. "Do you believe it points to the method by which the Germans will move Ainsworth to Germany?"

"I think not," Joanna replied. "Allow me to take you through my line of reasoning, and if by chance you detect any flaws, please do not hesitate to interrupt. Let us begin with the well-founded premise that the first message—the circling of Waterloo on the map—was meant to inform us of Ainsworth's location, either in the train station or at a street address."

"But how could he possibly predict we would see through the funeral ruse at the station?" I questioned.

"It might not have been a ruse to Ainsworth," Joanna answered. "The plan he overheard may not have mentioned a rehearsal."

"And that was how Ainsworth learned he was soon to be smuggled out in a casket and transported to Germany by U-boat," I thought aloud.

"Which was the obvious reason for him to circle Waterloo Station on the train map," Joanna went on. "But there was always the chance that his initial message would not be interpreted correctly or perhaps interpreted too late. With this in mind, he had to devise a second coded message that would lead to his rescue."

I attempted to think through the meaning of the second message without success. "How could the position of U-boats off the coast of Scotland possibly reveal Ainsworth's location?"

"That is the point, dear John," Joanna said, and began pacing again. "It may well be that the second message does not refer to location, but rather to information of another sort that will lead to Ainsworth's captors. I further suspect that the critical information is contained in a single word, for—as Geoffrey Montclair mentioned—the code is just a little off from one sent earlier. And that is what so draws my interest to the second message."

"Perhaps the answer is more straightforward than you believe," I opined. "Could it be that the last message is simply telling us that he will shortly be spirited out of the country on a German U-boat and that the Royal Navy should be put on immediate alert?"

"Oh, it runs deeper than that," Joanna said. "I believe there is a hidden message here that is meant for our eyes only."

"Another puzzle within a puzzle," my father remarked.

"So it would seem."

Our conversation was interrupted by the return of the Baker Street Irregulars who, after a brief rap on the door, entered unannounced. They were all dressed every bit as smartly as before. The only difference was that Little Alfie now carried a large, gift-wrapped package, whilst Sarah the Gypsy clutched a pair of new books.

"The lady came and went just as you said she would," Wiggins reported.

"I take it she was not in any way protected?" Joanna queried.

"All alone, she was. But she walked a bit uneasy, not like she was on a Sunday stroll, you see. Every half block or so she glanced around, but tried to cover it."

"How so?"

"She would look like she was sneezing into a handkerchief or shading her eyes from the sun, but all the while she was peering about and behind her."

"But Little Alfie and Sarah remained unnoticed. Correct?"

"The fine lady never knew we were there," Little Alfie replied. "She was more interested in keeping her head down as carriages passed by."

"Was she recognized by anyone?"

"She gave no sign of that."

"Good," Joanna approved. "Which of you followed her initially?"

"I did, ma'am," Sarah the Gypsy said, and stepped forward. "Like Wiggins told you, she kept to herself and tried not to be seen. She walked on the inside of the footpath and pulled her bonnet down when anyone approached."

Sarah's vocabulary was not that of a ten-year-old, but more on a level with Little Alfie, who had some education as I recalled. She was probably near his age as well, but her growth and maturation had been stunted by a harsh upbringing.

"Did the lady make any stops along the way?" Joanna asked.

"No, ma'am," Sarah replied. "Not until she reached her destination."

"So you followed her the entire time?"

Sarah shook her head. "We played the now-you-see-me, now-you-don't game. I would follow her for a block, then move off to put on a different coat brought along by Wiggins. All that while, Little Alfie was trailing her from the footpath on the other side of the street."

"How far did the lady travel?" Joanna inquired.

"Just over five blocks, ma'am. She continued straight on until she came to number twenty-five Ovington Street where she entered."

"Describe the house."

"Two stories, made of brick, and opened onto the street."

"I need to know every step she took from the moment she arrived at the Ovington address."

"At that point, ma'am, Little Alfie was closer than I."

"I take it you were on the other side of the street when she entered."

"Yes, ma'am. But Little Alfie wasn't."

"Held my package up high, I did, like a proper carrier on the rush." Little Alfie picked up the story. "But I slowed to catch ongoings. She rapped on the knocker twice and the door opened quicker than a hiccough. She hurried in, without so much as a hello, and the door closed."

"Did you have a look at the person who greeted her?" Joanna asked at once.

"Not even a glimpse, ma'am," Little Alfie

answered. "It happened too fast, like in a half second."

"We must learn who the lady visited in that house," Joanna urged.

"She was with a gent," Little Alfie said without hesitation. "Appeared upper class, he did, with his black frock coat and pearly-gray trousers."

"But you told us you could not see him because the door closed too quickly," Joanna contended.

"That is a fact, ma'am. But I had a better look when I slinked down the alleyway and peeked into a side window."

"Excellent!" Joanna lauded. "I would like you to describe every feature of the man, down to the finest detail."

"Mind you, I was looking through a dirty window and the couple was a good ten feet away."

"The couple, you say!"

"They were embracing, ma'am."

"A close embrace?"

"About as tight as you can make it, and still have room to kiss."

"Tell us about this man."

"I saw him only in profile, but he appeared handsome enough, with moustache and neatly trimmed beard. No spectacles or monocle that I could see."

"Was he taller than her?"

"By a good six inches."

Joanna turned and nodded to us, as the same thought went through our collective minds. It was a certainty that Lady Jane Hamilton was not meeting Roger Marlowe. "Well done!" she said, returning to Little Alfie. "After the kiss, were you able to notice anything else of interest?"

"No, ma'am. I had to move on down the alleyway, for fear of being seen. However, on my trip back to the street, I took one more peek into the room. The couple seemed to be studying papers of some sort. I then returned to Ovington to continue our watch, for you told us the lady would stay for an hour."

"How was this watch accomplished?"

"From a distance, with me and Sarah taking turns parading up and down on the opposite side of the street. Wiggins made sure we were wearing coats of different colors on each pass-by."

"Did the lady stay the entire hour?"

"Just about," Wiggins replied. "Then Little Alfie and Sarah followed her back to the side entrance of Harrods. I stayed in place in case the gentleman made a move, and he did. Shortly after the lady left, the gentleman came out, smoking a cigarette in a holder. He opened an umbrella, although there was hardly a drop of rain falling. By my reckoning, he was using the umbrella to cover his face. Did a good job of it, I might add. He then strolled to a nearby tobacco shop and walked out clutching two packages of cigarettes.

The gentleman lighted up yet another cigarette on his return to twenty-five Ovington."

"Could you determine what brand he smoked?" Joanna asked.

"Player's Navy Cut," Wiggins replied. "On his way to the shop, he stamped out the one he was smoking. I picked up the stub and read its label."

"Did you note the time at that moment?"

"Just after three."

Joanna nodded, obviously pleased with Wiggins's observations for reasons that were beyond me. "Tell me," she went on, "were there any features about the gentleman that Little Alfie did not mention?"

Wiggins pondered the question briefly. "Nothing in particular, except for his military posture. Ramrod straight, it was."

"Very good," Joanna said. "Now, I have further work for you, if you feel up to it."

"Involving the lady?"

"Involving the lady."

"Day or night?"

"Both."

"Then we must increase our fee to two shillings each."

"Done," Joanna agreed. "I need you to keep a watch on twenty-five Ovington around the clock as well. See who comes and goes, and if on foot, follow them."

"There will be added expenses, ma'am, for food and drink and other clothing."

With a nod, Joanna said, "Be off with you then, and report back with the very first sighting."

Once the Irregulars had departed, Joanna rubbed her hands together gleefully. "The chase now becomes even more interesting. There is nothing more tantalizing than a case in which everything goes against you."

"Were you not disappointed the man was not Roger Marlowe?" I queried.

Joanna waved away the notion. "That was never a serious consideration. They are close friends and need not steal away to some pricey Knightsbridge house to conduct their romantic affair. They could have easily used Marlowe's home or the home of confidants or a dozen less conspicuous places."

"Do you believe the man is a German agent, then?"

"That is a possibility," Joanna said.

"Particularly since Little Alfie saw them reading or exchanging papers," I added. "That would not be the first thing on the minds of secret lovers."

"Your point is well taken," Joanna said, with a mischievous smile that quickly faded. "But until we know who the gentleman is and what papers were of such interest to the couple, I am afraid we are guessing, which does not help our cause. It is a capital mistake to theorize before one has the data, for it tempts one to twist the facts to fit the theory."

"So what steps do you propose we take next?" I asked.

"Why, the obvious. We must identify the man who holds the key to the mystery surrounding Lady Jane."

"Which the Baker Street Irregulars will provide for us."

"No, John. They will see, but cannot identify. That is a task we alone must accomplish."

"And how do we go about that?"

"By visiting Knightsbridge."

"Shall I arrange for a carriage?"

"A motorcar will suit our purposes better."

From outside came the distinct sound of hammers breaking stone that was shortly followed by several dull thuds. Joanna hurried to the window overlooking 221b Baker Street and stared out as the hammering grew even louder. Slowly her head began to move up and down, as if tracking some moving object.

"What so holds your attention?" my father asked.

"Danger," Joanna replied.

"Imminent?"

"Quite."

The door to a bedroom opened and Johnny, holding a small blackboard with hieroglyphics written in chalk upon it, dashed out and over to his mother's side. My father and I were only a step behind. Across the street in a light rain, workers were busily removing the stone parapet from a sturdy brick building that rose up three stories. We watched as large pieces of stone were dismantled, a few of which fell off the roof and toppled to the footpath below.

"Should they not close off the footpath, Mother?" Johnny asked.

"They have," Joanna replied, and pointed to the wooden barricades a half block away that people ignored and walked around.

"Flying stones can cause terrible injuries," my father remarked. "Such blows to the head can be fatal."

"Particularly when they are descending at a rate of thirty-two feet per second per second," Joanna noted.

"How do you know they fall at that speed?" asked Johnny.

"It is a law of physics and one worth remembering."

Johnny gave the matter momentary thought and shrugged. "If it falls rapidly, it falls rapidly."

"No, no," Joanna rebuked mildly. "The rate of descent is most important, for it once determined whether a witness was in fact telling the truth."

"How so?" Johnny asked, now keenly interested.

"A witness, who was a gardener, claimed that he saw a man leap to his death from a three-story building, with his arms flailing wildly in the air. The problem with his account was that the witness was nearsighted and needed spectacles for distant vision. At the moment the victim supposedly leaped from the window, the gardener was not wearing his spectacles."

"But surely he put them on to view the fall," Johnny said at once.

"It required five seconds for him to reach into a coat pocket for his spectacles, place them on, and look up," Joanna delineated. "The Watsons and I actually timed how many seconds the act would have consumed. Now, recalling that a three-story building is thirty-two feet tall, the poor man who fell would have struck the ground in one second. Thus, there is no way the gardener could have witnessed the event."

"Why would he lie?"

"That is not the point," Joanna went on. "The point is the gardener could not possibly have seen the fall and therefore his story was false. And it is all based on a law of physics that states that an object falls through space at a rate of thirty-two feet per second per second. You would have certainly learned this in your physics class."

"But, Mother, I am not scheduled to enter physics until next year."

"Then should you return to Eton, you must take

a seat at the very front of that particular class."

"Do you truly believe the study of physics will be to my advantage in the profession I have chosen for myself?"

"You should ask Dr. Christopher Moran."

"Who is he?"

"The man who murdered his friend and pushed the body off a three-story building."

Johnny allowed the new information to set in before asking, "Was the crime uncovered because of a gardener who could not possibly have seen a body fall thirty-two feet to the ground?"

"It was a major clue that eventually led to the arrest and conviction of Dr. Moran."

"And where is this doctor now?"

"He is awaiting hanging at Pentonville."

"Thirty-two feet per second per second," Johnny uttered solemnly and, with his black-board in hand, returned to his room to continue the study of Egyptian hieroglyphics.

18

The Mysterious Gentleman

We were seated in the rear compartment of a hired motorcar half a block up from 25 Ovington Street. Outside, our driver had the bonnet of the vehicle opened and appeared to be inspecting its engine. It was all theatrics designed by Joanna to give us a clear view of the entrance to the brick house Lady Jane Hamilton had visited the day before.

"What makes you confident our unnamed gentleman will visit the tobacconist today?" I asked.

"Two reasons," Joanna said. "First, he is a heavy smoker, quite addicted to cigarettes. During his short stroll to and from the tobacconist, he consumed two cigarettes. At that rate, he will easily go through two packages a day, which is the number of packages he bought at the shop yesterday. Thus, he will be driven to replenish his supply this afternoon."

"But he might have taken the walk much earlier or do so much later in the day. Yet you are somehow convinced he will make his move at three o'clock. How could you possibly predict that?"

"Because like most of us, he is a creature of habit," Joanna replied, her eyes fixed on the house down the street. "In addition, according to Wiggins, our man has a ramrod posture that suggests a military background. Those individuals are the most regimented of all. You may recall that Wiggins recounted the time of the gentleman's stroll. He did so yesterday at three; he will do the same today."

My father glanced at his timepiece. "It is ten after three, Joanna."

"His nicotine urge will prompt his departure momentarily."

Despite Joanna's confidence, I feared we were in for a prolonged wait that would take up precious time of which we had so little. The investigation into the disappearance of Alistair Ainsworth had come to a stalemate in every sense of the word. Lestrade had informed us that to date no progress had been made by Scotland Yard in tracking down addresses that could have been related to the Waterloo Station circled on the train map. All possible locations that might be linked to the Battle of Waterloo were being carefully looked into, without success. Inspectors and constables were scouring Josephine Street in Reigate and the neighborhood surrounding St. Paul's, but to no avail. There was nothing to suggest a German presence or influence. Moreover, the mystery of the second U-boats message remained unsolved. The only bit of good news came from an intercepted note from the German high command that stated their zeppelin fleet was awaiting further orders before taking to the air again. We all wondered if the agent Rot had handed the list of selected bombing sites to Ainsworth's captors and whether the German command was waiting for it, along with Ainsworth, to be delivered. And then the bombing would be resumed.

"There he is!" Joanna cried out, and rapped on the side window of the motorcar.

Our eyes went to the doorstep of 25 Ovington Street from which a tall, well-dressed man was departing. He was attired in a tweed suit and derby, but had no umbrella as the weather was cloudless. In his left hand was a walking stick, in his right a cigarette in a holder. He kept a hand on the holder as he smoked, thus obscuring most of his face.

Our driver hurriedly closed the bonnet of our hired motorcar and drove us toward a tobacco shop two blocks down. We stared straight ahead, not daring to even steal a glance at the walking man as we passed by. Our driver was instructed not to wait outside the storefront, but rather to circle the neighborhood and return every few minutes.

From the outside, the tobacco shop of Thomas Duvane and Sons appeared well appointed, and the interior did not disappoint. The air held the sweet aroma of cut tobacco, with all the shelves and paneling done in polished wood. There were elegant displays of fine pipes, cigars, and cigarettes that were obviously meant for the well-to-do.

Joanna immediately went to the nearest section where a most excellent variety of pipes were on exhibit. Her focus was directed to a long-stemmed cherrywood that was beautifully shaped.

"Look, Watson! Here is a type of pipe my father so enjoyed," Joanna noted.

"Indeed it is," my father said. "That, along with a blackened clay, were his favorites."

"I read he gravitated to the clay pipe when in a disputatious mood."

"Which occurred with uncommon frequency. Because of this, I often referred to that particular pipe as Holmes's disputable clay."

"Which of course was the one he favored when involved with a three-pipe problem."

A short man, slight in figure, with neatly combed gray hair and a gentle face, came over to greet us. "What type tobacco did your father favor, may I ask?"

"Common black shag, coarsely cut," Joanna replied.

"He enjoyed a most vigorous smoke."

"And one that left a dense, blue cloud behind."

"Quite," the tobacconist said. "I am Thomas Duvane and would be happy to be of service to you. Is it the long-stemmed cherrywood that is of interest?"

"Not at present," Joanna said. "But come next Christmas I shall return, for there are people close to me who would be delighted to receive such a gift."

"I would think so. The best of the cherrywood are now a seven-shilling pipe."

"And well worth it," Joanna went on. "The person I have in mind is happiest when smoking his cherrywood while reading the newspaper. We know that the cherrywood pipe has a flat bottom that allows it to stand on its own when placed down. This of course allows the reader to rest his pipe and keep both hands on his newspaper."

"I have more than a few customers who purchase the cherrywood for that very reason."

Joanna reached for a briar pipe and examined it carefully. "But I am told that those of briar absorb the moisture from the tobacco better than the cherrywood, which gives the former a more flavorful smoke."

"I have heard that as well, but in my opinion the cherrywood holds its own in that regard."

"I value that opinion and will keep it in mind."

Duvane gave Joanna a half bow. "It is a pleasure speaking with someone so informed about pipes. May I ask where you acquired this knowledge?"

"From my father," Joanna replied.

"Does he enjoy cigars as well?"

"Havanas on occasion."

"A man of excellent taste."

"Who unfortunately is no longer with us."

"My condolences," Duvane said sympathetically.

"Thank you," Joanna said. "I should also like to thank you for the new information, which I will find most useful. And now I would very much like to purchase three packages of Player's Navy Cut."

"Of course, madam," he said, and walked to the shelves that held the cigarettes.

"Why have you asked for Player's when you have always smoked nothing but Turkish cigarettes?" I asked quietly, following Joanna to the cigarette section.

"How many packages of Player's do you see on the nearby shelf?" Joanna replied in a whisper, motioning with her head.

"Three."

"There is your answer."

"Why are you buying the last?"

"To empty the shelf when the approaching gentleman comes in for his two packages. If there are no more in stock, I will generously offer to share and thus strike up a conversation with the unnamed man."

"Clever," I remarked.

"I try to stay ahead of the game," Joanna said with a smile.

But the smile quickly left her face when the door to the shop opened and the tall, well-dressed gentleman entered. Joanna hurriedly turned away and moved back to the pipe section. In a low whisper she said, "John, stand between me and the new arrival. Position yourself so that his view of me is blocked. Watson, step to my right and hide my profile, which I do not wish him to notice on his way out."

My father and I rapidly followed Joanna's instructions and appeared to be focusing on the display of fine pipes, but our ears were concentrated on the conversation taking place on the counter behind us.

"Your two packages of Player's, sir?" Duvane proffered.

"If you would be so good," the man replied in clipped English.

"The Dutch Masters you ordered should arrive tomorrow morning."

"Quite popular, are they?"

"The blunts are in constant demand, sir." Duvane reached for two packages of Player's Navy Cut. "As are the Player's that are by far our most preferred brand."

The transaction was completed without further conversation and the well-dressed gentleman departed. The tobacconist hurried behind a curtain at the rear of the shop and returned with a fresh supply of Player's Navy Cut. As he placed them on a mid-level shelf, Joanna strolled over and asked, "Would it be too much of a bother to change my order to Turkish cigarettes?"

"No problem at all, madam."

"Thank you."

"Three packages, then?"

"I think two for now, for they are a stronger smoke."

"With more intense flavor, I might add."

"Quite so," Joanna said. "Would you also be good enough to replenish my father-in-law's supply of Arcadia mixture? I think three ounces would suffice."

"Very good, madam," the tobacconist said and once again disappeared behind the curtain at the rear.

My father said quickly, "But, Joanna, I have an adequate supply of Arcadia mixture at home."

"We need time to make certain the gentleman is well away, for I recognized him and he may recognize me."

"How do you know him?"

"Through his wife."

"Who is?"

"Lady Jane Hamilton."

19

The Unexpected Death

We did not retire until the late hour that evening, all the while trying to unravel the mystery of the strange meeting between Lady Jane Hamilton and her husband. My father and I finally went to our bedrooms at midnight, and left Joanna pacing the floor and smoking one cigarette after another as she grappled with the unsolvable problem. When I entered the drawing room the next morning, Joanna was still pacing through a dense haze of cigarette smoke.

Opening a window for fresh air, I said, "I take it the mystery remains."

"I have the knot partially untied," Joanna said. "It is the end equation that continues to elude me. But it too will come into view when I acquire the singular, most important piece of the puzzle."

"Which is?"

"The papers that Little Alfie saw Lady Jane and her husband studying. Show me their contents and everything immediately falls into place. Nothing else begins to approach their relevance."

"But I would think that Lady Jane and her motive are the key."

293

Joanna flicked her wrist at the suggestion. "She is but a carrier or go-between. She either brought the papers to her husband or he had them waiting for her arrival."

"Where would she have gotten the papers you speak of?" I queried.

"A dozen places or more," Joanna replied. "They could have been handed to her by Roger Marlowe at their luncheon meeting, or delivered during her walk through Harrods where we had no eyes on her, or even placed in the wrapped goose from the poulterer. But then again, it is equally possible that her husband provided the papers. After all, Sir Oliver Hamilton is a high-ranking officer in His Majesty's Navy and has access to the most sensitive documents."

"Surely you don't suspect him of treason."

"I suspect everyone until they are proven innocent."

My father entered the drawing room, neatly dressed and already smoking his first pipeful of Arcadia mixture. "Through my opened door I heard your conversation and wondered if all three of those you mentioned were somehow involved. In particular, could Lady Jane be a go-between for both her husband and dear friend Roger Marlowe?"

"Capital, Watson!" Joanna exclaimed. "That very thought crossed my mind as well and cannot be easily discarded. It is a most convenient triangle in which Roger Marlowe decodes the message, hands it to Lady Jane who then rushes it to her husband, and who in turn decides if it is important enough to transmit to the Germans."

"But why would a titled, distinguished naval officer resort to treason?" I asked.

"Uncover the perpetrator and I will give you the motive," Joanna responded. "Nevertheless, there are difficulties with this line of reasoning. In particular, it does not explain why husband and wife must meet in a secret location and avoid being seen together. Such a transaction could have taken place in their home and no one would have been the least bit suspicious. Also, recall that Lady Jane's disappearance for an hour only occurred when her husband was supposedly at sea. Why the need to make him absent when it serves no apparent purpose here?"

"Yet, as you just mentioned, we cannot totally disregard their involvement," I opined.

"Nor do I plan to," Joanna said. "But we must keep our focus on the Admiralty Club where most of the naval codes are broken and devised. That is where the traitor is. All the others, if implicated, are simply coconspirators. Bear in mind, our traitor knew Alistair Ainsworth well, was aware of his work and unique skill as a decoder, and was cognizant of his habits. Only those belonging to the Admiralty Club meet all these requirements. Thus, the traitor must reside within this group."

"That being the case, I would favor Roger Marlowe," my father said. "As Joanna has pointed out, his earnings can't begin to cover his lavish tastes. There must be an outside source of income."

"The years he spent in Germany at the University of Heidelberg would also cast a shadow," I added.

"Indeed," my father agreed. "And his closeness to Lady Jane makes her the perfect go-between for Roger Marlowe."

"Should we then not concern ourselves with Geoffrey Montclair and Mary Ellington?" Joanna asked.

"Not at all," I said. "I am still concerned with Montclair's somewhat feminine features. If he does have sexual peculiarities, it would make him a most tempting target for blackmail."

"I am certain his past was carefully scrutinized before he was allowed into the Admiralty Club," my father argued mildly. "Surely they would have discovered any such doings."

"Even if they did, perhaps they were willing to overlook them," I countered. "Remember that talents like Montclair's are not easy to come by."

"Particularly his photographic memory," Joanna recalled. "That unique characteristic makes him invaluable when deciphering multiple codes."

"Thus, both Roger Marlowe and Geoffrey Montclair are suspects, but certainly we can exclude Mary Ellington," I concluded. "After all, she has lost a son in the war and must hate the Germans for that reason alone."

"Or perhaps she holds a similar grudge against England for sending her son off to a war she disapproves of," Joanna said.

"How do you know she disapproves of the war?" I asked.

Joanna shrugged. "I don't. I was simply raising the possibility."

"You must admit that is highly unlikely," I said.

"Do not overlook the unlikely, John," Joanna cautioned. "For at times, it is the unlikely that shines a light on the likely."

"The other side of the same coin," my father noted.

"Precisely," Joanna said. "Recall the case of *A Study in Treason* in which a most expensive Havana cigar was reportedly purchased by a stable boy who had a salary of far less than a pound a month."

"So then, all things considered," my father concluded, "we now have three suspects and at least two coconspirators. But alas, that does not bring us any closer to Alistair Ainsworth."

The telephone on our desk rang and my father picked up the receiver, saying, "Watson here."

He listened intently, then slowly replaced the

receiver. A grim expression came to his face. "It seems our list of suspects at the Admiralty Club has been narrowed to two. Geoffrey Montclair has been found stabbed to death."

We arrived at the Admiralty Club just as a homicide team from Scotland Yard was departing. Fortunately, the body of Geoffrey Montclair had not been moved and was in the exact position when first discovered. According to Inspector Lestrade, the body was discovered by Lieutenant Dunn on his arrival at 7:45 a.m.

Montclair's corpse was slumped over his desk, his bloodied right hand extended and resting on the keyboard of a typewriter. There was a large, pearl-handled dagger plunged so deep into his back its blade was not visible. The blood spread over his back and shoulders was well clotted and blackish maroon in color, indicating the stabbing had taken place hours earlier.

"He never saw it coming," Lestrade proclaimed. "All evidence strongly suggests he was sitting at his desk, working away on his typewriter, when he was attacked from behind. You will note he made no effort to turn or resist, which I believe tells us the murderer crept up silently on his victim. Death must have come quite quickly."

"There is obviously no sign of a struggle," Joanna said.

"None whatsoever," Lestrade agreed. "But there is clear evidence the motive was robbery. You will note that the drawers in the victim's desk are opened and have been rummaged through. More importantly, Montclair's wallet and gold timepiece are missing."

"Were the desks in the other offices rummaged through as well?" Joanna asked.

"Not that we could see," Lestrade replied. "We believe the thief was in too big a hurry to depart. After all, he had just committed murder and had no idea if other coworkers might be returning shortly."

"Was the main door locked?"

"There was no sign of forced entry, if that is your question."

Dunn stepped forward and said, "I am afraid that the members of the Admiralty Club all too often leave the door unlocked in the late evening, although repeatedly warned not to do so."

Joanna moved over to the desk and motioned to the items atop it. There was a leather card case, a silver fountain pen, and some loose coinage. "And these?"

"They were found in the victim's pockets," Lestrade replied.

"Strange."

"How so?"

"That they were left behind," Joanna said, and turned to the group who was gathered just outside

299

the door. "Who was the last to see Montclair alive?"

"I was," Roger Marlowe answered. "It was almost seven when I said good night to Geoffrey and traveled down to the pub for a quiet drink."

"Did you lock the door after you?"

"I do not recall, but it is my usual custom to do so."

"At the time of your departure was Geoffrey Montclair working on the message in his typewriter?"

Marlowe nodded. "As he had been for most of the day. He felt certain there was something amiss within Tubby's last message that was of critical importance."

"Are you referring to the one he decoded for the Germans?"

"Yes."

"Did Montclair give any hint as to what he was searching for?"

"He continued to state that something was off," Marlowe answered. "Apparently some fact tucked away in his photographic memory seemed to contradict the current message."

"Was it common for Montclair to remain after the others departed?"

"That was most unusual, for he always seemed to have other engagements for the evening," Marlowe said. "But in this instance, he thought he was very close to the answer and wished to pursue it, rather than break his line of concentration."

"So death could have occurred any time between then and now," Joanna concluded.

"Unfortunately that is so, for we have no way to time the event with precision," Lestrade said. "Nevertheless, the coldness of the corpse would suggest death happened some hours ago."

"Perhaps my husband could be of assistance here," Joanna suggested.

"We would be most grateful for his expertise in this matter."

I began my examination from a distance and purposely avoided the fatal wound, for not to do so can distract the examiner from other less obvious clues that may be equally important. The slumped position of the corpse over his typewriter and the failure to see blood elsewhere indicated the death blow was administered while Montclair sat at his desk. There were no defensive wounds about his hands and wrists, which was additional proof that Montclair was caught totally unawares. I glanced down at the corpse's groin and saw no blood or evidence of sexual mutilation which at times occurs when the victim is killed in a bout of homosexual rage. The muscles of the arms and face were only beginning to show signs of rigor mortis. Finally I inspected the knife wound that penetrated so deeply into the thorax it would have caused injury to or perhaps severed a great artery. Grasping the knife's handle, I attempted to move it side to side in order to gauge the knife's depth, but found it quite fixed in place. My gaze went back to the victim's bloodied hand, and I wondered how the blood arrived there. There were no wrist or arm wounds to account for this.

Joanna asked, "Tell me, John, what so draws your attention to the victim's hand?"

"I was trying to determine how the blood reached it."

A Mona Lisa smile came to Joanna's face. "Curious, isn't it?"

Lestrade stepped in for a closer look and said, "He was probably reaching back in an attempt to extract the knife."

"The wound would have been quite painful," my father interjected.

"My reasoning as well, Dr. Watson," Lestrade said. "The thief steals up on Mr. Montclair, stabs him in the back, and allows him to briefly struggle against the wound before removing the victim's possessions and fleeing."

"Such a waste," Mary Ellington declared. "He had such a fine mind. And he seemed so close to solving the coded message now in his typewriter. As a matter of fact, he called me last evening just before nine to confirm the exact number of Orkney Islands. He seemed to think that might be an important clue."

"Were you able to give him the answer?" Joanna asked.

"I confirmed there are seventy islands in the archipelago," Mary responded. "He said he would add the number into his equation, whatever that meant."

"Well then, we can now state with certainty that the victim was murdered some time after nine in the evening," Lestrade said.

"Can you be more precise than that, John?" Joanna asked.

"Death occurred approximately five hours ago," I answered. "Rigor mortis is now setting in more completely and involves the muscles of the jaw, neck, and upper extremities. In that the body was discovered at seven forty-five this morning and rigor mortis requires five hours to show itself, we can estimate he was murdered at two forty-five."

"At which time the pub below was closed," Joanna said unhappily.

"Of what significance is that?" Lestrade asked.

"Possible witnesses," Joanna replied. "Of which we currently have none."

"We are now scouring the neighborhood in that regard," Lestrade said. "Although I must admit that I am not optimistic."

Joanna went over to the window and attempted to open it, but it was securely fastened. Next she gazed at the door and the transom over it. "Tell me, Lieutenant Dunn, is this facility not kept under some sort of surveillance late at night? After all, important, sensitive documents pass through these rooms."

"There is no need," Dunn said. "As I mentioned earlier, the documents you refer to are secure in Whitehall at that hour. No personal items are left behind either."

"And that is why our common thief found nothing of value in Montclair's desk," Lestrade noted. "But his mistake may have been in taking Mr. Montclair's gold timepiece. He will no doubt attempt to pawn it, and we will alert all pawnshops to be on the lookout for the timepiece, which, by the way, we are informed has Montclair's initials engraved on its back surface."

"Do you believe the thief is that stupid?" Joanna asked.

"Most of them are, madam."

"Well then, we shall leave you to your investigation," Joanna said, taking a final glance at the typewriter and the bloodied hand that rested upon it. Something about the message within the typewriter seemed of particular interest.

Lestrade followed her line of vision before saying, "I trust you will inform us if any further clues come to light."

"Rest assured I will."

As we stepped into the central area of the

Admiralty Club's rooms, Mary Ellington raced after us. She was holding up a folded slip of paper. "Mrs. Watson, I believe this just dropped from your purse."

Joanna took the slip and, without looking at it, returned it to her purse. "Thank you," she said warmly. "I sometimes make little notes to myself."

"As do I," Mary said, and retreated back into her office.

Once we had carefully climbed down the wet back stairs and were seated in our carriage, Joanna sighed deeply to herself. "This is obviously not the work of a common thief."

"Surely you do not think the German agents performed this dastardly deed," I said.

"Of course not," Joanna said. "Such an adventure would have been far too risky for them. If they wanted him silenced, why would they endanger themselves by coming to these rooms? There are a dozen other places they could have dispatched him without raising suspicion."

"Who then?"

"The traitor."

My father and I leaned forward, both of us wondering what signs we had missed.

"There is no other explanation, and all clues point to that singular conclusion," Joanna elucidated. "Let us begin with the supposed common thief. He is tall and no doubt powerfully built, yet he enters Montclair's office unnoticed. With Montclair's desk facing the door, surely the thief would have been seen."

"How did you determine the thief was both tall and powerful?" my father asked.

"From the angle of the knife, which was at forty-five degrees," Joanna explained. "Thus, it had to be delivered by someone who loomed above Montclair's upper thorax. A short man could have never performed such a feat."

"Is your observation that the murderer was powerfully built based on the depth of the knife wound?"

"That and John's inability to move the position of the blade," Joanna replied, and turned to me. "It was rather fixed in place, was it not?"

"Indeed," I said, then recited the obvious. "It was either embedded between the ribs or jammed into the vertebrae of the spine. Only a powerful man could have delivered such a blow."

"So we have a tall, well-built thief who passes within touching distance of Montclair, yet his presence goes undetected," Joanna continued on. "This would have been highly unlikely, and even more unlikely is the conclusion that a common thief would kill Montclair. There was no need for murder. The thief could have easily overcome Montclair with a single blow to the head. Also, keep in mind that even stupid thieves will avoid murder at all costs, for if caught, robbery lands them in prison for five years, while murder assures them the gallows."

"You raise good points," my father said. "But they are hardly conclusive."

"Ah, but the list goes on. What sort of thief takes a gold timepiece and wallet, yet leaves behind a leather card case and fountain pen that can easily be pawned? And there were four shillings in Montclair's pocket that our thief overlooked or ignored. It is also striking that he didn't bother with the ring on Montclair's finger that would have brought a pretty price on the black market."

"I too saw the ring, but did not place great significance to it," I admitted. "Pray tell what made it so valuable?"

"Its Freemason symbol, which consists of a Masonic square and compasses, with the letter *G* in its center," Joanna described. "No thief worth his salt would ever leave it behind. You see, after money, thieves search meticulously for the next most valuable item, which is jewelry. Finally, your attention should be drawn to the position of the corpse's hands. Do you observe anything in that regard, Watson?"

My father took several puffs on his cherrywood pipe as he considered the question. "There was a bloodied hand resting on the typewriter."

"A *single* hand," Joanna emphasized. "Now, I ask you, who sits at a typewriter with only one hand on the keyboard? The answer is no one. He had a hand on the typewriter in a final effort to point to the sheet of paper it possessed. He even smeared his blood on the sheet so we could not help but notice it."

"Perhaps it was simply a random motion of a dying man," my father suggested.

Joanna shook her head at once. "Highly skilled codebreakers, like Montclair, do not make random moves. Every act they take has a purpose. Thus allow me, if you will, to reconstruct the last moments of Geoffrey Montclair's life. Someone he knows enters his office, causing no alarm. That person gazes over Montclair's shoulder at the sheet in the typewriter and becomes aware that Montclair is close to uncovering the traitor's identity. The person then stabs Montclair in the back and attempts to make the scene appear that of a common robbery. He leaves the office, believing Montclair is dead, but the codebreaker still has a breath of life in him. With his last move on the face of the earth, Montclair dips his finger in his own blood, which is pouring out from the wound just below the neckline, and points to the sheet in the typewriter. You may recall that people facing such a death often try to leave a message behind that names the murderer. Thus, the message on that sheet will tell us who murdered Geoffrey Montclair and who the traitor is, for they are one and the same."

"Which narrows the list of suspects to Roger Marlowe and Mary Ellington," I concluded.

"With Marlowe being the most likely by far," my father asserted.

"So it would appear," Joanna said as she reached in her purse for the folded slip Mary Ellington had retrieved.

"I was unaware that you wrote notes to yourself," I remarked.

"I don't," Joanna said.

"But you accidentally dropped a slip of paper from your purse."

"I lost nothing from my purse," Joanna said. "I was simply covering for her."

"Covering what?"

"Her rather clever way of sending me a message."

Joanna unfolded the slip. It read:

The Poets' Corner at noon

20

Westminster Abbey

At noon, Westminster Abbey was overflowing with tourists, many of whom were congregated in the Poets' Corner to pay homage to England's greatest poets and writers. We found Mary Ellington standing over the tablet in the floor bearing the name Alfred Lord Tennyson.

"Is Tennyson your favorite poet?" Joanna asked quietly.

"My very favorite," Mary answered. "His haunting lines in 'The Charge of the Light Brigade' continue to resonate in my mind. You may recall how they read: 'Theirs not to reason why, theirs but to do and die'. Those few words remind us of the futility of war in a most powerful manner."

I did remember the famous lines that commemorated the tragic loss of life in the Battle of Balaclava during the Crimean War. It brought to mind that Mary Ellington had also paid the terrible price of war, having lost her only son in battle just months ago.

Mary sighed sadly and strode over to the William Shakespeare memorial. She waited for a group of tourists to depart before saying in a low voice, "What do you think of the message in the typewriter?"

"It needs to be deciphered," Joanna replied.

"Oh, you think more than that. I could not help but notice how intently you studied it. Be good enough to inform me what so drew your attention."

"Notes left behind by the deceased can be quite revealing," Joanna said. "When an individual commits suicide, the note will speak of despair and an occasional good-bye. Those in a case of murder are often an attempt to identify the person who perpetrated the crime."

"This is certainly not suicide, is it?"

"Not unless you can describe the mechanism by which one plunges a dagger into one's back."

"So we can conclude that Geoffrey Montclair was trying to name his murderer."

"That is a reasonable assumption."

"It is also reasonable to assume I remain high on your list of suspects."

"Why do you think so?"

"Because you considered the possibility that my invitation might be a trap of some sort," Mary said tonelessly, then gestured with her head at the entrance to Poets' Corner where my father was stationed. "Is he armed?"

"Of course."

"Better safe than sorry."

"But I must say you are not very high up on the list of likely suspects."

"I should hope not, for time is now of the essence," Mary said in a voice meant only for us. "With that in mind, let us return to the heart of the matter, which is the coded message within the message. I am your only chance to decipher it and that is why you are here."

"Roger Marlowe could be of assistance," I suggested. "Particularly since he was quite close to Alistair Ainsworth."

Mary shook her head at once. "Roger is far too high on your list of suspects for obvious reasons. So you must either trust me or walk away now."

Joanna and I remained in place.

"Let us begin with Geoffrey Montclair," Mary continued. "He knew something was amiss with the message in the typewriter and wondered if the critical clue was the number three or some variation of it. For example, could it refer to every third letter in the message or such? Or to the square root of three or a multiple of it? Now, with Roger Marlowe being the mathematical wizard, Montclair went to him for ideas. Roger tried a variety of equations, but could not apply the number three to the remainder of the message. They both began to believe that the number was not the key and had little relevance in deciphering the code. I believed otherwise and still do, but find myself at a stalemate. Which brings us to the purpose of this meeting. At this point I require outside assistance to unravel the code. I need to know everything the police know about the life of Alistair Ainsworth outside the Admiralty Club. In particular, please focus on the number three, as in Tubby's address, phone number, passport, appointment times unrelated to work, and the like. I am certain therein lies our answer."

"Might I inquire how a street address could be useful?" I asked.

"Permit me to give you a simple example," Mary replied. "Let us say the number in question is twenty-five and the person lives at twenty-five or two-five Iron Road. The two or second letter in the address is *r,* which is followed by an *o.* The five or fifth letter in the address is also an *r,* followed by an *o.* Thus, we have *ro* mentioned twice, and we recall that the first name of the prime suspect is Robert, and so the finger of guilt points directly at him."

"Or the *ro* could signify the name Roger," I thought aloud. "As in Roger Marlowe."

"Good," Mary approved. "Now you begin to see the light."

"Do you consider him a prime suspect?"

"Don't you?"

"There is one consideration we have not yet discussed," Joanna said, then paused as a well-dressed couple strolled by in front of us. "That being the message itself. Are we certain the line—'Three U-boats off the innermost Orkneys'—is correct in every regard?"

"To the best of my knowledge."

"Is there more written in the original message sent out to the Royal Navy?"

Mary furrowed her brow in concentration, obviously thinking back. "Of that I cannot be certain. But the line you quoted is the essential one."

"We must have the entire message," Joanna beseeched. "The number three or a variation thereof may point to other letters in less important lines. It would also be helpful to have all messages that relate to U-boats off the Orkney Islands."

"I very much doubt Lieutenant Dunn will let us pry into those," I said. "Obtaining the complete first lines from him earlier was akin to pulling teeth."

"But I may have some of that information in my notes at home," Mary volunteered. "Assuming I have not tossed them into the fireplace as is my habit when done."

"But Dunn specifically told us that members of the Admiralty Club were not allowed to take documents and notes from their offices," I recalled.

"When in heated pursuit of a code, we do not concern ourselves with Lieutenant Dunn's instructions," Mary said. "Nevertheless, I am not optimistic I have the entire message in my possession."

"But you must search," Joanna implored. "We should keep in mind that Alistair Ainsworth is a master cryptographer, and he would be aware that most people would expect the key to the code to be located in the first line. That of course may not be the case."

Mary nodded at the notion. "That would be very much like Tubby. That is, let your opponent concentrate on the first line, while you orchestrate your move on the second."

"Or the third," Joanna suggested. "As in the number three."

"Indeed."

I could not help but be impressed with Joanna as she matched wits with one of England's finest codebreakers. But then again, I recalled her deciphering a most confusing code that consisted of only slanted lines. It was of such complexity that it even baffled Sir David Shaw who was knighted for his codebreaking accomplishments.

"In addition, it would be most useful if you could obtain the sheet of paper that was secured in Geoffrey Montclair's typewriter," Joanna requested.

"That might be quite impossible, for I am certain Scotland Yard will wish to hold on to it as evidence," Mary said. "But I can copy it word for word if you like."

"No, no. It is the original I require, and it must be gotten at all costs."

"What makes the sheet itself so important?" Mary asked.

"The blood upon it," Joanna said and, taking my arm, strolled away from the Poets' Corner.

.

21

A Strange Meeting

We spent the entire afternoon trying to decipher
Alistair Ainsworth's message, but to no avail.
The singular significance of the number 3 in
the coded communiqué continued to elude us. It
did not refer to the third letter of the alphabet,
c, nor to the ninth letter, *i,* 9 being the number 3
squared. Neither the combination of the *c* and the
i nor the reverse revealed any hidden meaning.
There were no symbols or apostrophes, the latter
being of great importance since they are always
followed by the letters *s, t, d, m, ll,* or *re.* We even
employed the Caesar shift using the number 3. In
this sophisticated code, you shift the alphabet a
certain number of spaces in one direction. For
example, using 3 as a guide, *a* becomes *d, b*
becomes *e,* and so on. Thus, the word *boat* would
be decoded as *erdw,* which made no sense. As
darkness fell and our fatigue set in, we decided to
adjourn for dinner and start afresh in the morning.

Taking our seats in front of a nicely burning
fire, we enjoyed a richly flavored amontillado
while Joanna gave us the detailed history of this
fine sherry.

"It is named after the town of Montilla in Andalusia, the region of Spain where its grapes are grown," she told us. "The grapes are often dried up to twenty days prior to fermentation, which is known as the *soleo* process. The actual aging in casks can vary for different varieties, but all must be stored away in oak casks. The sherries are naturally sweet for the most part, but in some instances the winemaker adds ingredients to make it so."

"Is all sherry from Spain?" my father asked.

"Without exception."

"But how did it become so popular in Great Britain?"

"There is a merry history behind that," Joanna said as she replenished our glasses. "It became quite popular after Sir Francis Drake sacked the city of Cadiz in 1587. At the time, Cadiz was a major port, and Spain was preparing an armada there to invade England. Among the spoils brought back by Drake after destroying their fleet were two thousand nine hundred barrels of sherry that had been waiting to be loaded onto Spanish ships. This event popularized sherry throughout the British Isles."

I was aware that Joanna was well versed in any number of subjects that were related to crime and criminal investigation, but on occasion she surprised me with her considerable knowledge of other, unconnected topics. Nevertheless, I wondered if perhaps her enlightenment on sherry served some investigational purpose. "Why this insight into sherry?" I asked. "Was there something that spurred your interest?"

"I delved into the subject after reading Edgar Allan Poe's short story, 'The Cask of Amontillado.' It was not so much a mystery as a tale of horrific murder."

"Was the cask of sherry the murder weapon?"

Joanna shook her head with a smile. "It was the enticement."

There was a brief rap on the door and Miss Hudson peeked in. "I am sorry to disturb you, Dr. Watson, but the street urchins have returned and insist on being seen, even at this late hour."

"Please show them up," my father said. "We shall not take long."

"I should hope not, for the goose you brought me is nearly done."

"Which we so look forward to."

As the door closed, Joanna said, "Something of the utmost importance must have transpired."

"New and unexpected visitors?" I wondered.

"Most likely," Joanna replied. "And they must have some unusual features that could not wait until morning to be reported. Keep in mind that, although the Baker Street Irregulars are young, they are streetwise and not easily moved. It is either the individual or an event instigated by that individual that has brought the Irregulars here at this unusual hour."

We heard racing feet coming up the stairs and quickly finished the last of our sherries. The trio of Irregulars sprinted into our drawing room, with Wiggins leading the way. He was dressed in workman's clothes, while Little Alfie and Sarah the Gypsy were still in their Sunday finest.

"What a tale we have for you, ma'am!" Wiggins exclaimed, catching his breath.

"I want every detail," Joanna said. "Start from the very beginning and leave not a syllable out."

"Well now, we took our positions early on, we did," Wiggins began. "Little Alfie and Sarah paraded the street, while I pretended to be a laborer seeking a day's wages."

Joanna asked, "Did that not make your presence obvious?"

"No, ma'am. There was plenty of workers about the neighborhood—roofers, plasterers, painters, and the like. It was not easy to find a nearby position, but luck struck as the sun began to fall, for a crew appeared to repair the cracks in the cobblestones. I landed a job pushing a wheelbarrow and that gave me a good view of the house. And it was then that a carriage arrived at the house and the lady stepped out."

"What lady?"

"Why, the fine lady you had us follow a few days back. Got right off, she did, without so much as a glance around, and entered the house."

"Did she make any effort to conceal her arrival?"

"None that I could see. Pranced right in, like she had no concerns."

"Did Little Alfie manage to peek into the house once again?"

"I did, ma'am," Little Alfie said, stepping forward. "They met in the parlor as before, but this time there was no embrace or kissing. It was all business, it was, with serious talk. Then the phone rang, which I could hear through the glass window. And they just stared at it a bit, before picking up. It was most solemn, I would say. I did not stay longer, for fear of being seen."

"We thought that was the end of it." Wiggins continued the story. "But we could not have been more wrong. For fifteen or so minutes later, a mighty military man arrived in a bloody big limousine."

"Mighty, you say!" I exclaimed.

"And then some, with his uniform all covered with ribbons and decorations. He also had one of those gold strands across his shoulder, indicating he was of high rank. I would guess the couple inside the house knew he was coming because the door opened for him without a knock."

"I need an accurate description of the naval officer," Joanna implored.

"He was a big man, with broad shoulders, and he carried himself very well indeed. His face looked royal, with high cheekbones and the like. I am guessing he was in his fifties because he had gray hair and thick, gray sideburns but no moustache."

"Was his head covered?"

Wiggins nodded. "With one of those strange, peaked navy hats that sit high."

Joanna turned to Little Alfie. "Were you able to sneak a peek after the officer entered?"

"That was a bit tricky, ma'am, for the officer's driver remained standing by the limousine, like a man keeping a careful eye out. But I got around him with Sarah's help. She walked by him, with a painful limp, which took his attention away from the alleyway, so in I went. It was quite dark by then, so I felt I could stay a bit longer without being seen. And there was this small crate in the alleyway that I could stand on, and this gave me an even better look."

"How many people were in the drawing room?"

"Three," Little Alfie reported. "The gentleman and the fine lady from earlier, and the new man in uniform who Wiggins just described for you. Now the talk continued to be quite serious. There were no smiles or handshakes nor any sort of refreshments. Then the old man in the uniform pulls out a map, and they all gather around it."

"Could you make out the details on the map?" Joanna asked quickly.

"I was too far away for that, ma'am. But I can

tell you it was a bloody big map, for he had to open and hold it with both hands."

"I take it that it was impossible to overhear any of the conversation."

"Only two words, ma'am, and that was because the old gent shouted it out."

"And the words?"

"Damned spy!"

Joanna's eyes narrowed abruptly. "Are you certain?"

"Loud and clear it was, through the glass," Little Alfie replied. "And the old gent was bloody mad too. He had a tightly clenched fist to go along with his raised voice. Then, in a huff, the lady and old gent left. They were most unhappy, I can tell you that."

"The lady went directly to her carriage, and the naval officer to his limousine," Wiggins continued. "There was no exchange of words that I could see."

"Was anything said or done to identify the naval officer?" Joanna asked.

The three Irregulars shook their head simultaneously.

Joanna thought for a moment before asking, "Wiggins, you mentioned the officer had ribbons and decorations on his coat. Could you make any of them out?"

"No, ma'am. I was across the street at the time and the light wasn't all that good."

"I did see some sort of scroll on his sleeve," Little Alfie recalled. "When the gentleman was holding up the map, I had a clear view of his black sleeve. Near the cuff was a thick band of gold, with a circle atop it."

"Was the gold circle part of the band?"

A puzzled look came to Little Alfie's face. "I am not sure what you mean, ma'am."

"Now think back," Joanna urged. "Was the circle partially buried into the top of the gold band or was it placed separately atop it?"

"It was a bit buried," Little Alfie replied.

"Very good," Joanna said. "You must now return to the house on Ovington Street and report all comings and goings without delay."

Once the Irregulars had departed, Joanna lighted a Turkish cigarette and began pacing the floor, obviously lost in thought. For some reason, she concentrated best while on the move, much like Sherlock Holmes according to my father. From outside came a loud clap of thunder, followed by cracks of lightning, which Joanna paid no attention to as she continued to pace back and forth. Finally she stopped and, on tossing her cigarette into the fireplace, said, "This goes to the very highest level of government."

"Is this based on the appearance of a naval officer in a limousine?" my father asked.

"It is based on his rank," Joanna said. "The insignia on his sleeve denotes a rear admiral in the Royal Navy, and such a man does not make clandestine meetings in the dark of night unless the need is urgent."

"That is obvious from the words *damned spy* being shouted by the officer," my father noted.

"Oh, it goes much deeper than that, Watson. We have Lady Jane Hamilton sneaking away to visit her husband who is supposedly at sea, yet resides on Ovington Street in Knightsbridge and remains out of uniform so as not to be noticed. Does that not strike you as being odd?"

"But she made no effort to conceal herself this evening," my father argued mildly.

"That is because it was already dark and there was little chance she would be recognized. In addition, she was apparently in a rush and had no time to bother with unnecessary concealments. So we have Lady Jane Hamilton hurrying in the night to visit a hidden-away husband who should be at sea. Now, if that is not strange enough, add to the mix a rear admiral dashing in, carrying a large map and shouting 'Damned spy!' What a most odd confluence of events that needs to be explained."

"Apparently they are all involved in uncovering a spy," I surmised.

"Why would that require a rear admiral racing over to share such secretive information with Lady Jane?"

"Because she is close to Roger Marlowe," I replied at once.

"And who is Roger Marlowe close to?"

"Alistair Ainsworth!"

"And so the circle tightens," Joanna pronounced. "There is a common link among all these individuals and the events they are tied into."

"But what is the link?" I asked.

"That remains to be uncovered, John. For therein lies the answer to the disappearance of Alistair Ainsworth."

"But everything seems so disconnected."

"It is not as disconnected as you believe," Joanna said, reaching for a poker to stir the fire. "I only require one more piece of the puzzle and all will fall into place."

"Where is this piece to be found?"

"In Geoffrey Montclair's typewriter."

22

Hyde Park

My father awoke the following morning with his arthritic knee acutely inflamed, so he required assistance as we climbed into the carriage and traveled to see a rheumatic specialist whose office was located just off Park Lane. The specialist had devised a new topical treatment for such flare-ups, using heat and a cream that contained a high concentration of aspirin. This treatment was well suited to my father, for the increasing doses of aspirin he had been taking orally was causing him gastric distress. Rather than wait in the specialist's office for my father to be seen, Joanna, Johnny, and I chose to cross Park Lane and take a leisurely stroll through Hyde Park.

It was a surprisingly warm winter's day, with a clear sky and a gentle breeze coming off the Serpentine Lake. Dozens of people were out and about in the park, enjoying the glorious weather that we knew would be all too brief. Ahead of us, Johnny seemed to be in constant motion, glancing from side to side as if in search of something.

"Why does your son gaze around so?" I asked.

"It is a game we have played since he was a little boy," Joanna replied. "He searches for a scene at a distance and attempts to discern what is transpiring. We then compare our observations and match wits."

"With you winning, I would imagine."

"Yes, but the day will come when he is my equal."

"I truly doubt that."

"Watch," Joanna said, and gestured for her son to come join us. "What in this park so interests you, Johnny?"

"The two men by the lake who appear to be having a heated discussion."

"Do you envision it leading to fisticuffs?"

"That is unlikely, Mother, for there is a woman standing close by."

"Perhaps she is attempting to intercede."

"Perhaps, but there is a dog near the woman and it does not seem concerned," Johnny noted. "Dogs are very keen at anticipating trouble and would not simply sit back on their haunches and watch such an event."

"Pay attention to the dog and why it is not concerned with the obvious goings-on."

Johnny studied the scene once again before sighing under his breath. "I see a small hand feeding the dog. There is a child behind the woman, and were there the slightest hint of trouble the mother would quickly depart with her child in hand. Yet she stands in place, for the argument is apparently a friendly one."

"Well done, Johnny."

"I must learn to observe more carefully."

"You shall."

I asked, "Precisely how does one learn to observe more carefully?"

"By seeing the obvious, but not concentrating on it," Joanna replied. "You must then direct your study to the periphery where more clues await, which will allow you to see the whole picture rather than only a portion of it. Using this practice, you may well be able to connect all the clues and reach a sought-after resolution."

We walked across the expansive lawn until we came to the magnificent equestrian statue of the Duke of Wellington. It rested upon a tall stone pedestal, with only the name WELLINGTON engraved into it. Joanna slowly strolled around the statue and studied its every aspect, paying particular attention to the engraving.

"Do you note anything of consequence?" I asked.

"Nothing that will tell us why Waterloo was circled on the map."

Johnny inquired innocently, "Was it a map of Belgium that indicated where the battle was fought?"

"Are you familiar with the battle?" Joanna

queried, evading the reason for her interest in Waterloo.

"Quite," Johnny replied. "And even more familiar with the Duke of Wellington who stands as one of England's greatest heroes."

"Which every English schoolboy will proudly state," said I.

"Yet with all their knowledge about the duke, not one in ten can tell you his given name."

"Which is?"

"Arthur Wellesley."

Joanna smiled at her son. "I was unaware."

"And not one in a hundred can name the horse the Duke of Wellington rode into battle," Johnny went on.

"Which is?"

"Copenhagen."

Joanna and I exchanged knowing glances, for the names Arthur Wellesley and Copenhagen should be brought to the attention of the Admiralty Club. It was indeed possible that Alistair Ainsworth had those names in mind when he circled Waterloo on the train station map. What a stroke of luck that would be for all concerned!

Joanna asked, "May I inquire how you came about all this knowledge?"

"I learned of it from my tutor at Eton," Johnny answered. "He is considered to be a recognized authority on the subject, having written his thesis on the Duke of Wellington."

"Would you have ever learned these hidden facts from a private tutor we might have to hire?"

"No, Mother, for that information is not known by most."

"So we can conclude there is something rather special about your tutors at Eton."

"Oh yes, they are in every way special."

"Do you believe we can easily find their equal here in London?"

Johnny stared out at length and watched the ripples crossing the Serpentine Lake, for the wind was now picking up. Birds flew overhead, but made no sound. "Mother," he said finally, "I think it is in my best interest to return to Eton."

"A wise decision."

We turned as the group Johnny had studied was gaily strolling toward us. The adults were smiling and laughing, while the little girl led her dog on a merry chase. It was clear that the observations made by Joanna and her son were correct, yet they showed no delight in their achievement. Indeed, Johnny paid only scant attention to the approaching group before dashing off in search of more challenging scenes to be considered and discerned. I could not help but wonder if I was witnessing yet another reincarnation of Sherlock Holmes.

23

Exodus

That afternoon, with my father's knee much improved, we were summoned to the Admiralty Club where the news was dire. Alistair Ainsworth had been broken completely. The Germans were now aware of Exodus, a plan to blockade Kaiser Wilhelm's navy and all the shipping lanes into Germany's major ports. It was a disastrous blow to Great Britain's war effort.

Dunn's face was haggard as he spoke to us in a most grim voice. "The plan was to shortly deploy a squadron of ten ships from His Majesty's Navy to the North Sea where they would patrol the waters off the mouth of the Baltic Sea. From this position, they could hinder German warships entering the Atlantic and stop all the merchant vessels heading for German ports. Thus, Germany would not only have been deprived of a strong naval presence in the North Sea, it would have also been denied vital raw materials they need so desperately. Now that the Germans *have been informed of our war plans,* they will put their ships into the North Sea at once, have their U-boats swarm the area, and of course stockpile critical raw materials."

"We know that Germany has learned of our plan because of a communiqué that was intercepted by Naval Intelligence," Dunn continued on. "It read simply 'Exodus broken.' Needless to say, it is a devastating hit and we fear the worst is yet to come. As I mentioned earlier to you, the Germans have been keeping on file all of our messages and communiqués, much like we do with theirs. Up to the present, our messages have for the most part been undecipherable, but all that changes now. With Ainsworth broken, the German intelligence unit will provide their navy with information of the greatest value. They will have detailed knowledge of our fleet, including the number and whereabouts of our ships, our naval strategies, and our alliance with other navies. It will put us at the greatest of disadvantages. With this in mind, I must ask you to redouble your efforts to locate Alistair Ainsworth before even more damage is done."

"Are we certain that Tubby gave them accurate information on Exodus?" Marlowe asked. "Perhaps he only gave them the name of the plan, with otherwise false information."

"That is wishful thinking," Dunn said. "Naval Intelligence has confirmed that a squadron of German warships has departed from their home ports and is currently passing through the Kattegat Strait, heading for the Atlantic Ocean.

Yet additional warships are being prepared to make sail. These moves indicate they know the details of *our naval strategy*. There is no question that Ainsworth has been broken, and at this point we must attempt to salvage whatever we can. Thus, our first and only order of business is to find Ainsworth and learn what other information he might have shared with the Germans."

Dunn took a long, worrisome breath before gathering himself. "That is my directive and I mean to carry it out. So let us return to Ainsworth's first message, which was the Waterloo train station circled on a map. I need to know if any of your ideas have offered even a glimpse of a clue. Now, what about the French dictionary in Ainsworth's desk? Anything there, Marlowe?"

"Nothing of value," Roger Marlowe reported. "It contained numerous notes scribbled in the margins that dealt with nouns of no relevance. I could not find numbers or symbols that might lead to a cryptic message or location."

"Did you examine his copy of the Old Testament?"

"In detail, but I could find no hidden messages or clues. I of course concentrated on the book of Exodus this morning, but saw no inscribed markings, arrows, or symbols. I could see nothing to indicate Tubby had employed that section of the Old Testament to break or construct codes."

"Was there no writing at all?"

"Not on those pages."

"You must continue your search of the two books unless you uncover a better avenue to investigate," Dunn ordered, then turned to Mary Ellington. "As I recall, you also believed that the circled Waterloo somehow referred to our epic battle with France. In particular, you thought Ainsworth could be pointing to the emperor Napoleon who led the French forces."

"Tubby would have never been that direct," Mary said. "As I mentioned earlier, it was far more likely he was referring to another feature of Napoleon, namely his lovely wife Josephine. There is a Josephine Street in Reigate that Scotland Yard is currently investigating."

"With little success," Lestrade interjected. "No Germans or individuals with German-sounding names live there, nor have any houses been leased recently. We are now extending our search to other limits of the Reigate district."

"And what of Geoffrey Montclair's notion that the word *Waterloo* was intended to direct us to monuments built in honor of the Duke of Wellington?"

At this point Joanna raised the possibility that Ainsworth's coded message was referring to Arthur Wellesley or Copenhagen, and told of their connection to the Duke of Wellington. The Admiralty Club knew of the duke's family name, but were unaware that his horse was called Copenhagen and deemed it worth studying.

"Nevertheless, we are continuing to investigate both monuments," Lestrade said, consulting his notepad. "It is our belief that the St. Paul's area is the more likely since it contains several large residential pockets, in contrast to the neighborhoods surrounding Hyde Park. We have had no success to date, but our investigation is not nearly completed."

"You may wish to double the manpower to that area," Dunn recommended. "If need be, draw on the police forces from outlying districts. When asking about recent leases, how far back in time did you go?"

"Six months."

"Extend it to a year," Dunn said. "These types of operations by foreign agents require great planning that takes far more time than one might think."

"Then more men will definitely be required."

"Draw as many as you deem necessary. Better too many than too few," Dunn said, then waited for others to speak. When none did, he added, "I am open to further suggestions."

Joanna asked, "Does it not surprise you that Ainsworth gave away such a valuable plan, when he could have chosen one of lesser importance?"

"Perhaps they threatened him with death should he not do so," Dunn surmised. "With a knife at one's throat, one's resistance tends to disappear rather quickly."

"That is a possibility," Joanna agreed. "But allow me to raise another. Perhaps he chose the plan called Exodus to provide an additional clue to his whereabouts. After all, the Germans would not have known of the plan's name unless Alistair Ainsworth so informed them."

"That is correct," Mary said at once. "Only we knew the name of the plan, yet the Germans mentioned it in their communiqué. Thus, Tubby must have purposely given it away."

"But what would its significance be?" Dunn asked impatiently.

"Exodus is the first book in the Old Testament," Joanna replied. "The answer may lie therein."

"The Old Testament!" Marlowe cried out. "Exodus could have a religious connotation, which might tie into the St. Paul's neighborhood. St. Paul's, of course, is Christian, while the Old Testament is the Jewish Bible. Is Tubby telling us there is a Jewish temple or synagogue near St. Paul's, and his location is between the two?"

"Quite possibly," Dunn said, and gestured quickly to Lestrade. "Please look into that, Inspector."

"Done!" Lestrade said.

"There is yet another possibility that needs to be raised," Joanna went on. "Perhaps there is a passage in the book of Exodus itself that holds Ainsworth's message."

"Are you familiar with that particular book?" Dunn asked promptly.

"I am about to be," Joanna answered.

"Perhaps we should bring in a theologian," Lestrade suggested.

Dunn shook his head dismissively. "We require a codebreaker, not a worshipper."

"Tell me, Joanna, what sort of passage in Exodus would you look for?" Mary asked.

"Any phrase or word that could relate to modern London," Joanna replied. "For example, if Pharaoh had a tower where prisoners or hostages were held, it could point to the Tower of London, which is located on the north bank of the Thames in central London."

"Or to Moses's journey up Mount Sinai," Mary added. "We should see if there are any synagogues or temples near St. Paul's that bear the name Mount Sinai."

Lestrade hurriedly copied down notes in his small notepad, writing on one page after another. "It might be wise to look into all Mount Sinai and Sinai synagogues, and not only those near St. Paul's. After all, the Germans may have moved yet again."

"Indeed," Dunn approved. "You should focus on those situated in residential neighborhoods."

"And those located on streets that have French-

or German-sounding names," Joanna advised.

"Quite right," Lestrade said, and jotted down another reminder.

"Are there other ideas?" Dunn asked and, when none were forthcoming, he walked over to a large window and peered out at the tourists gathering in Trafalgar Square. He appeared lost in his thoughts for a long moment before turning back to the group. "Let us redouble our efforts, for so much is at stake here."

As we strolled through the central area of the Admiralty Club, Joanna motioned with her head to the now vacant office of Geoffrey Montclair. On his desktop was the typewriter containing the bloodied message.

"We need that typewriter," Joanna muttered under her breath.

"Perhaps the bloodied sheet can be retrieved," I hoped.

"But I require it to be in the typewriter," Joanna whispered. "That is of the utmost importance."

Outside, the day was clear and brisk, so we strolled over to Nelson's towering monument and found a space free of tourists. Nevertheless Joanna glanced around to make certain no one was within hearing distance.

"We are running out of time," she said in a concerned voice. "I fear that Alistair Ainsworth will shortly be out of reach."

"Surely they will not attempt to move him to Germany so quickly now," my father asserted. "Not with the English ports under such close surveillance."

"At this juncture a rapid move would be the smart move," said Joanna. "The Germans have already had several close encounters with us, and will not wish to push their luck further. They are very much aware that the longer they remain on British soil, the greater the chance they will be apprehended."

"It would still be a dicey maneuver," my father noted.

"But worth the risk," Joanna insisted. "Imagine the immense value of having Alistair Ainsworth imprisoned in Germany. Not only could he decipher all the coded messages they have on file, he could decode all future communiqués as well. Ainsworth would become a never-ending font of information."

"It would be a nightmare for the Royal Navy."

"From which they might never awaken."

"But even if this transfer were to happen, you assume that Ainsworth would continue to cooperate with the Germans."

"Once a man is broken, he stays broken."

"Your point is well taken, but I continue to believe the German agents will bide their time and await a more opportune moment to carry their catch to Germany."

"To the contrary, they will now move with haste."

My father gave Joanna a most serious look and asked, "What indication is there to show this will occur?"

"The word *exodus,* which means to go out or go forth," Joanna said. "Alistair Ainsworth is telling us that the Germans are about to depart, with him in tow."

24

The Deciphering

On returning to our rooms at 221b Baker Street, we immediately retrieved Sherlock Holmes's copy of the Old Testament and gathered around the fireplace as Joanna read from the book of Exodus. The initial reading revealed no clues, but the second was more productive.

"Perhaps the number ten is important here," Joanna ventured. "Ten is mentioned twice in this passage. The first being the tenth plague in which God threatened to kill all the Egyptian firstborn. The second refers to the ten commandments that Moses received on Mount Sinai. Thus, we have two tens, which may or may not be relevant."

My mind went back to the instructions given to us some time ago by Sir David Shaw, the curator at the British Museum who was a master codebreaker. He had stressed the importance of a particular number in deciphering coded messages. "Sir David would tell us that ten could represent *j,* the tenth letter in the alphabet, or the number ten could be one-aught, with the one being the letter *a* in the alphabet, followed by aught or the letter *o*." I shrugged my shoulders at the possible variations of *j* or *ao*. "But neither makes sense here."

"Do not discard the relevance of the number ten so quickly," my father advised. "For there is yet another ten to add to the equation. Recall that in the coded naval message a squadron of ten British ships was to be deployed to the projected battle area."

"Can you somehow relate that to the message sent by Alistair Ainsworth?" I asked.

"Sadly, I cannot," my father said. "Perhaps Joanna can help us in that regard."

Joanna shook her head. "The permutations are endless. Furthermore, now that I give the matter second thought, if the number ten is so important, Ainsworth would have inserted it in the original message he decoded for the Germans. He could have said that there were ten rather than three U-boats off the Orkney Islands. This would not have raised suspicions with the Germans, in that their major concern would have been the submarines themselves being detected, not their exact number. They might have even enjoyed the British exaggeration of their strength."

"So we have reached yet another dead end," I said.

"When it comes to numbers we have," Joanna concurred, then furrowed her brow in thought. After a long pause, she said, "Perhaps we should not be searching for some deeply hidden passage, but for a key that is rather obvious."

"But Alistair Ainsworth is a master of codes," I challenged.

"That is my point, dear John. Because he is such a master, we have assumed he would use this unique skill to send his message. But that may not be the case. You must consider the dire situation in which Ainsworth finds himself, with time being of the essence. He had to communicate quickly, using a code that could be obvious to his colleagues, but not to the Germans. The key word here is *obvious*. He would not transmit a message that would require days and days, if not weeks, to decipher."

"How can you be certain your assumption is correct?" my father asked.

"By putting myself in his place," Joanna replied. "It is the avenue I would have taken under the circumstances."

"But we know every word in the message Ainsworth sent," I argued. "Yet we remain in a quandary."

"That is because we do not have the complete original message to compare with the one in Montclair's typewriter."

"I am having difficulty finding your line of reasoning."

"Allow me to explain," Joanna went on. "We have an individual who studied the original message and the one sent by Alistair Ainsworth, and that individual is now dead. And it was Montclair who insisted there was a difference between the two messages, but could not recall it. His exact words were 'Something was amiss, something was off.' Now please be good enough to place all these indisputable facts in order and tell me what conclusion you draw."

My father and I tried to connect all the facts, but to no avail. We gave each other puzzled glances.

"Come now!" Joanna urged. "Concentrate on the difference that Montclair was pursuing."

My father's cherrywood pipe dropped from his grip as the answer came to him. "Montclair was murdered because he remembered the difference!"

"Spot on, Watson! Somehow the traitor learned of it and had no choice but to dispatch Montclair." Joanna reached down for my father's pipe and handed it back to him. "And I will go a step further. The message itself was no longer of value to us or the Germans. Dwell on it for a moment. The message stated there were U-boats off the innermost Orkney Islands. The secret was out. We knew, the enemy knew. So why kill Montclair over an already decoded message?"

"As we discussed earlier, the message must be pointing to the traitor," my father replied.

"And now you see the importance of us having both the original message and the one in

Montclair's typewriter," Joanna continued. "It is the difference between the two that is of paramount importance, for it will disclose who the traitor is."

"We should ask Lieutenant Dunn for the original message in its entirety," I urged.

"Which may or may not be forthcoming," Joanna said. "There might well be other sections of the message that are not meant for our eyes. Even our sworn oath to the Official Secrets Act will not prevail if the document was classified as top secret."

"In which case it would be heavily redacted before being shown to us," my father noted.

"And thus would be of little use to us," Joanna agreed.

"But we should still ask for it," I insisted.

"So we shall, but we should be prepared for disappointment," Joanna said, reaching for a Turkish cigarette, which she studied at length. "And we face another problem in that obtaining the sheet from Montclair's typewriter will be no simple matter."

"Surely Lieutenant Dunn will allow us to examine it," I said.

"It will not be in his hands, but Lestrade's," Joanna reminded us. "Montclair's death is now a murder case, and Scotland Yard will have complete jurisdiction and consider the sheet prime evidence."

"Then Lestrade will have no objection to our reviewing the bloodied sheet."

"But it will in all likelihood have been removed from the typewriter."

"Is that of such great importance?"

"Any move that alters or distorts the crime scene is important." Joanna rose to light her cigarette and began pacing the floor. She continued to do so for several minutes, all the while ignoring us. Then she abruptly turned and, with a firm nod, said, "I still believe the word *exodus* has the most relevance here. Why else would Ainsworth go to such lengths in order to bring it to our attention?"

"Should we again read that particular section of the Old Testament?" I asked.

"The answer is not in a single passage or line," Joanna replied. "Ainsworth is directing our attention to the word *exodus* or something closely attached to it. Using that scheme, it would have to be relatively obvious, yet still hidden."

"Such as?"

"Blood," Joanna replied. "Therein must lie the answer, for Montclair used his own blood to point to something on the sheet in the typewriter."

"Perhaps his blood was the only inklike material available," I suggested.

"That is not the case," Joanna said. "Remember that among Montclair's personal possessions was a fountain pen. It would have been far easier for him to use it, rather than reaching to the stab wound in his back for blood. That, my dear John, was done on purpose. Montclair is literally screaming 'Blood!' from his grave."

"Blood is mentioned several times in the book of Exodus," my father recollected.

"Actually twice," Joanna said. "It was used in the first and tenth plagues."

I rapidly turned the pages to the section in the Old Testament that described the ten plagues. "I shall begin with the part that deals with the first plague, and read it word for word."

Joanna waved away the idea. "It would be best if you simply summarized it for us. The answer is not in a given word, but in the underlying meaning of a particular passage."

After reading about the first plague that was entitled Blood, I encapsulated the story as follows. "It seems that when Pharaoh refused to set the Israelites free, he was threatened with the plague of blood, in which the waters of the Nile River would turn red with blood and thus be unusable for human consumption. Pharaoh ignored the threat and God polluted the river with blood in full view of the Egyptian leader."

"Does it speak of how the feat was performed?" Joanna asked.

"It only states that God did it."

"No subterfuge, eh?"

"None that was mentioned," I replied. "I suspect there was a reason God performed this mighty act in the presence of Pharaoh. In that fashion, there could be no magic or trickery to explain away the incredible feat."

"A wise move," Joanna said, more to herself than to us. "Let us now turn to the second mention of blood. I believe it occurred just prior to God's threat to kill all Egyptian firstborn."

I quickly went to the tenth plague. "Here," I told them, "God sent the Angel of Death to kill the firstborn, with instructions to spare those of the Israelites. In order to assure that the Jewish firstborn were left unharmed, the head of each such household was ordered to paint the sides and tops of their door frames with lamb's blood. The Angel of Death, on seeing these signs, would pass over the houses of the Israelites, and thus their children would be saved. And this is the origin of the Jewish religious holiday of Passover, which commemorates this miraculous event," I concluded.

"I can make nothing of it," my father grumbled. "And lamb's blood certainly does not equate to human blood."

"It is not the source of the blood that is important here, but the fact that it was used as a signal," Joanna said, as she continued to pace. "That is the common denominator. In both the tenth plague and in Montclair's message, *blood* was used to reveal identities."

"Yet it remains a puzzle within a puzzle," I said

unhappily. "And we have only the word *blood* to go on."

"The answer is in the tenth plague," Joanna reaffirmed. "Ainsworth's message led us to the book of Exodus, and Montclair's message was signaling us with blood, just as the Israelites signaled the Angel of Death with blood."

"Are you suggesting we read of the tenth plague yet again?" I asked.

"We have no other recourse."

My father sighed with fatigue. "Perhaps we should have Miss Hudson prepare an early dinner, for we are certain to be working late into the night."

"A nice glass of sherry would also offer a most welcome respite," I added. "Perhaps two glasses would serve that purpose even better."

Joanna shook her head vigorously. "Every moment we waste brings England closer to disaster. We have no choice but to persevere. Refreshments can wait."

"Does it not strike you as odd that the messages left by the two dead men, Verner and Montclair, were both written in blood?" I queried. "Could there be a revealing connection?"

"The only connection here is that both men used blood as ink to identify their murderers," Joanna replied. "With this in mind, we should focus on the last plague, for therein is the answer to Montclair's coded message."

I wearily turned my attention to the description of the tenth plague. "Shall I begin with the Angel of Death?"

Before she could answer, the phone rang out and Joanna quickly picked up the receiver.

"Yes?" she said in a most curt manner, then listened and responded more gently. "Of course I recognize your voice."

Joanna's brow went up. "You have both?

"Fifteen minutes would be very convenient," she said, and placed the receiver down.

"The tide of fortune is changing," Joanna announced. "The caller was Mary Ellington, and she has found her notes on the original document that she helped Ainsworth decode."

"Hooray!" I shouted.

"Most importantly the message mentions the word *exodus,*" Joanna went on. "So in essence, Alistair Ainsworth has pointed to the very word twice."

"Which tells us we are on the correct track," my father concluded. "Yet we still require Mont-clair's bloodied sheet to solve the puzzle."

"Not to worry," Joanna said, and gleefully rubbed her hands together. "You see, Mary Ellington has that sheet in hand as well."

"But it should be in Scotland Yard's possession, should it not?" my father asked.

"Yes, it should," Joanna said, with a mischievous smile.

"Then how did she come by it?"

"I did not ask, for it is a crime to remove prime evidence from a crime scene," Joanna said, and hurried over to the large table on the far side of the room. "Let us clear the surface, for Mary Ellington will arrive shortly."

The long rectangular table was brimming with materials used by Joanna in her investigations. There were bottles of various reagents, a Bunsen burner, glass flasks, test tubes, and the very same microscope that her father, Sherlock Holmes, once peered through. We closed and pushed aside texts and manuals that dealt with the principles of codebreaking. Despite our careful study, the books had proved to be of no help in deciphering the coded message that lay before us.

Time seemed to drag by as we anxiously awaited the arrival of Mary Ellington. My father checked his timepiece every minute or so, but its hands refused to move faster. Joanna began pacing again, no doubt arranging and rearranging the facts surrounding the coded message. Yet even she periodically glanced at the window, anticipating the arrival of a most important visitor. Finally there came a rap on the door. But it was not Mary Ellington.

"There is a lady downstairs carrying a large package who wishes to see you, Mrs. Watson," Miss Hudson said.

"Be good enough to show her in," Joanna said. "And please see to it we remain undisturbed."

As the door closed, Joanna again happily rubbed her hands together. "Pray tell, what do you think of the large package Mary has in her possession?"

"It could be anything," I replied.

"Oh, you can do better than that, John," Joanna coaxed. "Why would a small lady like Mary Ellington bother to lug around a large package to visit us at this time of evening?"

I had no answer.

"It is the typewriter," Joanna said joyfully. "This Mary Ellington knows the value of evidence that must be taken as a whole. She would make a fine detective, for she realizes the typewriter itself may provide important clues."

With a rap on the door, Mary Ellington entered, holding on to a quite large package with both hands. "Where shall I place it?"

Joanna motioned to the large table against the wall. "There will do nicely."

Mary carefully put the package down next to Sherlock Holmes's microscope and went about unwrapping it. The typewriter, with the bloodied sheet it contained, appeared exactly as it did in Montclair's office. "Aren't you going to ask how I obtained it?"

"I suspect you simply walked out with it," said Joanna.

"Right you are," Mary said. "Scotland Yard left the crime scene as it was, so they could return tomorrow and complete their investigation. I, shall we say, ah, borrowed it for now and will return it before the detectives revisit in the morning. Since there is a slim possibility they will come back sooner, we should move along quickly."

"Let us begin with your notes on the original message, and then compare them to the message in Montclair's typewriter."

"Not only do I have the notes, I have a complete copy of the document itself that I had taken home."

"I thought that was strictly prohibited," my father remarked. "According to Lieutenant Dunn, that was an absolute rule not to be violated."

Mary smiled slyly. "It was and is, but we often do so when struggling with a particularly difficult code. Lieutenant Dunn's mind works eight to six, while ours must remain powered on twenty-four hours a day."

"Which is much to our benefit at the moment," I thought aloud.

Mary nodded and reached for a folded sheet in her handbag. Unfolding it, she placed it on the table and stepped back for us to see. It read:

4 U-boats off innermost Orkney Islands
Exodus must be delayed

357

"What the communiqué in fact states is there are four German submarines close to a major naval installation," Mary interpreted. "Thus, the plan to send our warships from this port to the Baltic Sea entrance had to be put on hold for the present. You will also note the obvious discrepancy between the two messages. In the original message, four U-boats are mentioned, while the sheet in Montclair's typewriter speaks of only three. I believe this was Tubby's method of telling us to concentrate on the original message."

"Which contains the word *exodus,* and which he again used in the second message," Joanna emphasized.

"Precisely my point," Mary continued. "Tubby is informing us that is the key to the code or some passage contained therein."

"We reached the very same conclusion and searched through the book of Exodus with diligence, but could uncover no clues," Joanna said. "We are of the opinion that Montclair used his own blood to signal something of utmost importance in the message, much as the Israelites employed the blood of a lamb to signal the Angel of Death to pass over their homes and thus spare their firstborn."

"Ah yes," Mary said, nodding. "The tenth plague, which was inflicted when Pharaoh refused to free the Israelites."

"The horror of killing the Egyptian firstborn,"

Joanna murmured, leaning in to concentrate on the bloodied sheet in the typewriter.

"It is most unwise to upset the Heavenly Father," Mary remarked.

Joanna carefully removed the sheet from the typewriter and placed it upon the table, which allowed all of us a clear view of the stained message.

3 U-BOATS OFF INNERMOST ORKNEY ISLANDS

"On examining the blood-smeared sheet, I see where the number three is underlined by a streak of blood," Joanna noted, now using her magnifying glass for a more detailed inspection. "Thus, we can conclude he wanted us to concentrate on the three. Then he left the *u* intact, but smeared out *boats* with blood. Since we know the correct number should be four, let us substitute that for the three. This interpretation of the code reveals the number four, followed by a large *U,* which reads '4 U.' "

"Perhaps the discrepancy in the numbers is simply a signal to draw our attention to a hidden message within," Mary suggested.

"I believe otherwise," Joanna contended, and returned the sheet to its original position in the typewriter. "The discrepancy in numbers must be of greater significance than to simply draw our attention, for the presence of blood alone would accomplish that. There is a deeper reason Montclair went to such obvious lengths to emphasize the number four. He actually underlined it. You must remember he was breathing his last. He had to make every second and every word count. We must therefore concentrate on the number four and what it represents."

"Perhaps it refers to the fourth word in the message," Mary surmised, and counted words on the sheet. "Which is *innermost,* and that is of no help."

"Or it might represent the fourth letter of the alphabet, which is *d,*" Joanna said. "That letter placed next to U-boats spells *duboats.* There is no such word in the German language."

"Nor in French," my father noted.

"Nor in Spanish, Italian, or Russian," Mary said.

Joanna studied the bloodstained sheet once more at length. "Perhaps Ainsworth meant for us to see only the *d* and the *u,* which combines to form the German word *du,* which translates to *you.* But then, it was followed by *boats. Youboats off* is nonsensical, as would be the German *duboats off.*"

"For some reason, I feel we are on the wrong path here," Mary said. "Tubby would have made it more sophisticated than just moving a few words around. You see, the Germans might have detected that, for their experts no doubt studied Tubby's decoded message with that in mind."

"He would not hide it so deeply," Joanna asserted. "That would take far too long to decipher, and Ainsworth knew time was short."

"Sometimes the most clever codes are the most obvious ones," Mary stated. "The answer can be directly in front of your eyes, yet difficult to see."

Joanna stared at the typewriter and studied its keyboard at length, then the letter itself. Her line of vision went back to the keyboard, upon which was drawn the figure of a hand in chalk. "Who drew the outline?"

"Scotland Yard," Mary replied. "Inspector Lestrade made the drawing just before the body was removed."

"Well done," Joanna said, and placed her right hand over the outline, extending her index finger so that it touched the bloodied sheet. "As I recall, Montclair's index finger was the only one extended. Correct?"

"Correct."

"And he was right-handed. Correct?"

"Correct."

"So we can conclude it would be his writing finger that pointed to the word *innermost* on the sheet."

"And?" Mary queried.

"Perhaps he purposely stopped there."

"To what end? The word *innermost* by itself has no real significance."

My father said, "Perhaps Montclair's finger stopped because death came at that moment."

"Or shortly thereafter," Joanna agreed. "You will note that the blood smear drops off acutely after the *inner* in the word *innermost*."

Mary leaned in for a closer inspection of the letter. "For some reason Montclair underlined the number three that should be a four, and smeared through *boats off*. He then died as he reached the word *innermost,* and at that point the blood-stain stopped and dropped off. So, following this schematic, we have the letters *d* and *u,* and the word *innermost,* which together spell *duinnermost*. It has no recognizable meaning."

Joanna's eyes narrowed noticeably as she read the sheet yet again. Then, using her finger, she began pointing to each individual letter. She performed this act twice before announcing, "All becomes clear."

"But I see only garbled words," Mary said.

"To the contrary, it is a complete message," Joanna asserted.

"Based on what?"

"Passover," Joanna replied. "How clever! How very clever!"

"Please explain," Mary requested. "For you see what I do not."

"Montclair had obviously worked with

362

Ainsworth on the original message and knew it involved the Exodus plan. That was the key Ainsworth was now passing to Montclair and the others in the Admiralty Club, knowing that they alone could decipher the secret message. He did it as follows. First, Ainsworth substituted the number three for the number four, so that the group would be aware that the number four was of critical importance. In this instance, the number four stood for the fourth letter in the alphabet, which is *d*."

"How can you be certain of this?" Mary asked.

"Because I know the remainder of the message," Joanna answered, then continued on. "Thus, we have the letter *d* at the beginning. Following that, the *u* in *U-boats* was left untouched while *boats* was blotted out with blood, which leaves us with *du*."

Mary nodded hurriedly. "Montclair was telling us to pass over the words covered with blood, just as the Angel of Death passed over the Israelite homes marked with lamb's blood."

Joanna nodded back in agreement before saying, "Now, follow the smear as it continues on through *boats* and *off*, and note that it blurs the letter *i* in *innermost* before dropping off. And there you have Ainsworth's coded message."

<u>3</u> U-BOATS OFF INNERMOST
ORKNEY ISLANDS

"And remember the three is a four, representing *d,* which is the fourth letter in the alphabet," Joanna prompted.

Mary Ellington's eyes flew open. "That bloody traitor! Who would have ever guessed it was him?"

"Who?" I asked aloud. "Who is it?"

"Follow my finger, John," Joanna said and pointed to the number 3. "The three is really a four and thus is a *d,* after which comes *u* in that the *boats* portion of *U-boats* has been blotted with blood. So now we have *du.* Then the smear continues through the word *off,* and partially smears the letter *i* from the word *innermost,* leaving *nn.* Now, combine *du* with the letters *nn,* and tell me the result."

"Dunn!" I cried out.

"Our murderer," Joanna said without inflection. "And our traitor."

"We should contact the First Sea Lord immediately," my father demanded.

"I am afraid that may not be possible," Mary said. "The First Sea Lord is currently attending a meeting in Paris."

"How do you come by this information?" Joanna asked.

"My brother told me at dinner last night."

"And he is?"

"The director of Naval Intelligence," Mary replied. "His name is Admiral Lewis Beaumont,

Beaumont of course being my maiden name."

"Then you must contact him now."

"At this late hour?" Mary asked. "Would it not be best to wait until morning when we have the full resources of Scotland—"

"Now!" Joanna insisted. "We have not a second to waste, for I fear the word *exodus* represents a double entendre. Ainsworth may also be telling us that the Germans will depart shortly, with our man in tow. This being the case, we shall lose all hope of ever finding them."

Mary Ellington reached for the phone, again muttering "Bloody traitor!" under her breath.

25

A Traitor

There was excitement in the air at the Admiralty Club the following morning. We gathered around Inspector Lestrade and listened intently as he brought the new developments to our attention. A concerned citizen had called Scotland Yard only hours earlier with information that could lead directly to Alistair Ainsworth and the German agents who had taken him prisoner.

"A man walking his dog early this morning noticed some strange activities in a house next door that had been leased to individuals who kept to themselves," Lestrade told us. "The drapes were always drawn and it was difficult to see any activities within, for the lights were rarely turned on. But this morning the man's dog broke from his leash and chased a squirrel into the adjoining garden. It was then that he looked into the house, for there was a narrow opening in the closed drapes. He clearly saw a motionless man in bed who was being shouted at by others. The neighbor is of the belief that the language being spoken was foreign."

"Was he able to describe the men in the bed-room?" Joanna asked at once.

"The one doing the shouting was said to be a large man with broad shoulders, but his face was not clearly visible," Lestrade replied. "However, the neighbor's wife was in her garden a few days earlier and saw one of the household in broad daylight. She could no doubt give us a better description, but unfortunately she was admitted to hospital yesterday with an infection of some sort. She is now being questioned by Scotland Yard and I shall join them shortly. If their story is accurate, we should have both Alistair Ainsworth and the Germans within our sights before noon."

"Was the neighbor able to see the man in bed?" my father asked.

"He was not, Dr. Watson, for the lighting was not good and the men standing around the bed partially obscured the view of its occupant. Thus, at this point we should focus our attention on the man in the garden, and for this I shall ask your assistance. As I recall, you and your colleagues were given a rather detailed description of the lead German agent by Dr. Verner. Are there any particular features other than his facial tic that we should be aware of?"

"Certainly the aroma of chloroform on him is long gone," Joanna remarked.

"Nevertheless we shall ask about it," Lestrade said, and turned to Roger Marlowe. "You and

Mr. Ainsworth are lifelong friends, so I was told. Is that correct?"

"From our childhood days."

"Then you should be able to provide essential information we may require. In the event our informant leads us to the whereabouts of Mr. Ainsworth, we shall insist on proof of life. You see, the Germans when surrounded might decide to use him as a bargaining chip. His life for their freedom, that sort of thing. In other words, they threaten to kill him if we do not acquiesce to their demands. Thus, we have to firmly establish that he is alive."

"Speak with him on the phone," Mary suggested. "Tubby has a most distinctive voice."

"But his voice may be altered in his weakened state," Lestrade said. "Furthermore, the Germans may not have installed a phone since they are rapidly moving from one house to another."

"Then have them show Tubby standing before a window," Marlowe said.

Lestrade shook his head. "He could be quite dead and they could have him propped up."

"Could we have an unarmed mediator enter the house and verify?" Mary asked.

Lestrade shook his head once more. "If Ainsworth is dead, the mediator becomes a hostage and the Germans yet have a bargaining chip. The very best way to establish that Ainsworth remains alive is to ask a question he can answer but the Germans cannot. With that in mind, Mr. Marlowe, what information might you and Mr. Ainsworth share that the Germans could not possibly be aware of?"

Marlowe rubbed his chin pensively before saying, "We both enjoy a most expensive Scotch called *Old Vatted Glenlivet,* which is seldom ordered by others."

"The Germans might well know this," Lestrade rejected. "All that would be required is for the Germans to have followed him into a pub."

"It cannot be anything from Alistair Ainsworth's recent history," Joanna added. "It must go back to his childhood days."

"Such as?" Lestrade asked.

"The name of a pet would work nicely," Joanna replied. "Did Ainsworth have a dog when he was a boy?"

"A collie called Ollie," Marlowe recalled. "They were inseparable, even sleeping together in the same bed."

"There is your answer, Inspector," Joanna said. "The Germans could not possibly know this."

Lestrade nodded slowly. "I believe you are correct, but the Germans are very clever. They may have asked Mr. Ainsworth about the names of past pets, with this in mind."

"Would they have inquired where the dog slept?" Joanna asked.

"Most unlikely."

"Then use that as well."

"So we shall," Lestrade said, and quickly glanced at his timepiece. "Now I must hurry to St. Bart's and join in the questioning of the neighbor's wife. She may provide us with even more helpful information."

Joanna cleared her throat audibly. "Inspector, may I make one last suggestion?"

"Of course."

"I think it would be wise—" Joanna stopped in mid-sentence to sneeze. "Ah-choo!"

Immediately she dashed to the coatrack where her purse hung and reached for a handkerchief. She seemed about to sneeze again, but suppressed it and apologized. "I shall rejoin you in just a minute."

"Do not rush, madam," Lestrade said, and used the time to ask Marlowe if Alistair Ainsworth had other pets he was attached to as a child. He was told that there was another dog later on that Ainsworth looked after with care.

As Marlowe spoke of a spaniel with a bad leg, I watched Joanna turn away from the group and face the topcoats hanging on a wall rack. She blew her nose softly and walked over to us while closing her handbag.

"What was the spaniel called?" Lestrade was asking.

"Bella," Marlowe replied.

Lestrade jotted down the name, then came back

to Joanna. "Madam, I believe you had one last suggestion before I leave."

"It may not be necessary, but I think it wise to have a sharpshooter with us, in the event a gun battle were to erupt. He could be well hidden and take down the German agents from afar."

"A capital idea, madam," Lestrade agreed wholeheartedly and looked over to Lieutenant Dunn. "Lieutenant, does the navy have sharp-shooters in their ranks?"

"Not to my knowledge, but the marines do," Dunn responded. "We are of course speaking of long rifles."

"Of course."

"And the distance for their marksmanship?"

"Fifty to a hundred yards."

"That will present no problem."

"Said and done," Lestrade concluded. "I shall return shortly with all the incriminating information in hand, for I am confident our suspicions will be confirmed. Let us meet here again at eleven o'clock to finalize our plans."

Lestrade and Dunn reached for their topcoats and hurried from the room, closing the door behind them. The group waited for a full minute in silence before speaking in low voices.

"I still cannot believe it is Dunn," Marlowe said quietly.

"Oh, but it is so," Joanna assured.

"Your decoding was a fine piece of work,"

Marlowe went on. "But it will never hold up in a court of law. If I wished, I could have rearranged the words and letters in the book of Exodus and made Pharaoh the traitor."

"But Pharaoh is not here, and Dunn is," Joanna said.

"There is no doubt Dunn is the traitor," Mary said. "I stayed awake half the night wondering how Geoffrey Montclair had deciphered Tubby's message. After all, he did not have blood smears to guide him. Then I recalled a code he and Ainsworth were devising in which the key word was *off,* meaning to remove as in *hats off.* They inserted the word *off* to inform the reader to blank out the *off,* then proceed to remove letters and/or words next to it until one reached a meaningful message. Thus, in Tubby's message, which included the word *off,* if one removes *boats* from U-boats and the *i* from innermost, you end up with *Dunn.* It is a clever but simple code and Tubby knew that Montclair, with his photographic memory, would remember it."

"Extraordinary," my father said in awe.

"That is still not good enough," Marlowe rebutted. "You must have absolute proof in order to convict him of treason."

"Which I will have shortly," Joanna said.

"And who will provide the evidence?"

"Why, Lieutenant Dunn himself."

"Do you care to share this plan with us?"

"It is best that I do not," Joanna said. "For the smallest slip can ruin the most excellent of plans. Thus, the fewer people who know of it, the better."

"It is as if you do not trust us," Marlowe persisted.

"I assure you that is not the case," Joanna said. "My concern is that you might unintentionally give away our knowledge that Dunn is the traitor."

"Surely we would not speak a word of it to him."

"It is not your speech but your expressions that would give rise to Dunn's suspicions. I could not help but notice the stern, harsh look you gave Dunn when he took the floor to tell us of marine sharpshooters. There was a definite change in your usual expression toward him. He did not detect your animosity, but had he, all could have been lost. So for now, I must ask you to trust me on this matter. You might also soften your expression in his presence."

"And so we shall," Mary said. "But it still escapes me why a trusted naval officer would betray his country."

"I am afraid only Dunn can answer that question," Joanna said.

"Money, perhaps? They say that every man has his price."

"But the price is not always money," Joanna

told her. "Blackmail, lust, and revenge can also bring forth the most evil of behaviors."

"But one would expect more from a naval officer."

"Those motives fit all," Joanna said, then walked over to the window and peered out. "I see our good lieutenant is having a rather animated conversation with Lestrade while the inspector's carriage waits."

I came to Joanna's side and followed her line of vision. "It would appear that Dunn is in no rush to arrange for the sharpshooters."

"A worthy observation," Joanna noted.

"But should he not be hurrying? I would think that sharpshooters are not readily available on such short notice."

"He is in no rush, for he is certain the house that holds Alistair Ainsworth will be vacant when we arrive."

"How can he be so confident?"

"Because he plans carefully," Joanna replied. "You must keep in mind that Dunn is most clever to have gotten away with his traitorous acts thus far."

"But he is about to be undone."

"Only if he remains unaware," Joanna cautioned, then pointed to the street below. "Ah! Lestrade departs and Dunn hails a taxi."

"And now he appears to be hurrying somewhat."

Joanna smiled humorously. "Does it not strike you as strange that Dunn does not have his own carriage?"

"That is a bit unusual. What do you make of it?"

"The most likely explanation is that he does not wish his customary driver to know where he is about to be taken."

"Should he not be followed?"

"Not at the moment."

Mary asked, "What if Dunn suddenly becomes suspicious and returns here?"

"Then he will find Watson, my husband, and me absent, for we have other duties to attend to."

"But we shall have to explain your absence."

"Be inventive and give him a reason to hurry back to his well-thought-out plans."

"Such as?"

"Inform Dunn that we remembered yet another important feature of the German agent that could be most helpful, and we are racing to St. Bart's to supply Lestrade with the information."

"That will surely spur him on."

"In the event this occurs, do your very best acting. Appear to be worried, but hopeful. Give him no reason to become even more suspicious." Joanna gave Dunn's departing carriage a final glance, then hurried to the coatrack. "And now, we must be off!"

As Joanna put on her topcoat, Mary asked her

a last question. "I still cannot fathom how Tubby discovered that Dunn was the traitor."

"The answer to that will have to await our rescue of Ainsworth. But it obviously occurred while he was being held captive."

"Surely Dunn would not expose himself to Tubby."

"That would be foolish and someone as clever as Dunn does not make foolish mistakes. More likely, Ainsworth either recognized Dunn's voice in an adjoining room or overheard the agents speaking of their spy. I suspect it was the latter since Ainsworth is quite fluent in German." Joanna buttoned her coat and called over to me, "John, please be good enough to open the window and signal our carriage with a wave of your hand."

"Do bring Tubby back alive," Mary implored.

"That is my intent."

We raced down the back stairs and, just as we reached the street, our carriage pulled up to the curb. On entering I was surprised to find an admiral in the Royal Navy, who was dressed in full regalia, seated by the window. He had a distinguished appearance, with chiseled, aristocratic features and silver-gray hair that extended into his muttonchop sideburns.

"Allow me to present Admiral Lewis Beaumont, the director of Naval Intelligence," Joanna introduced. "The gentlemen with me are my husband, John, and his father, Dr. John Watson."

"I am honored, sir," my father said.

"As am I," said I.

Beaumont greeted us with a brief nod, then turned to Joanna. "This is most irregular and were it not for my sister, Mary, I would not be here."

"What is more irregular, Admiral, is that you have a traitor in your ranks."

"You will require more than a weirdly decoded message to prove that assertion."

"Oh, I will prove it to your satisfaction and to the satisfaction of any hard-nosed military tribunal," Joanna assured.

"May I ask what this evidence is?"

"I will show it to you shortly."

At that moment I heard the friendly bark of a dog and looked out to see Toby Two happily wagging her tail. On the other end of her leash was Wiggins, the leader of the Baker Street Irregulars.

"Here you are, ma'am," Wiggins said, handing the leash over to Joanna and watching the spaniel jump into the carriage. "She is all excited to see you again."

"She and I are old friends," Joanna said, and gave the lad a half crown. "You have two more services to perform. The first is to take this glass container and walk quickly down the Mall for a mile, then dispose of it."

I watched Joanna dig into her handbag for a

small, cylindrical vial with its top screwed on securely. Toby Two suddenly yelped with joy and wagged her tail furiously. Joanna brought her attention back to Wiggins and said in a firm voice, "Under no circumstances are you to open the container or loosen its top. Understood?"

"Yes, ma'am," Wiggins said obediently. "Shall I toss it into the pond at St. James?"

"No need. Simply place it in a rubbish bin."

"Done, ma'am. And your second request?"

"You are to return here to this very spot and await my return with Toby Two."

"Here I will be."

Joanna held the vial under Toby Two's nose for only a few seconds, which caused the dog's excitement to increase even more. Then, in a quick movement, she gave the vial to Wiggins, saying, "Now be off!"

Toby Two extended her head out of the carriage window and watched Wiggins trot away. Only after the lad had disappeared beyond the Admiralty Arch did she lose interest. Joanna gently pulled the half spaniel, half bloodhound back into the carriage, then patiently allowed for more time to pass.

"Why do we wait?" Beaumont asked.

"For the scent Wiggins carries to completely dissipate," Joanna replied, then held her hand out of the window. "Ah, good! The wind is against us."

"Which means?"

"A great deal to Toby Two," Joanna said, then permitted Toby Two to again sample the air outside the carriage, but away from the Admiralty Arch. Suddenly the dog stiffened, her nose rapidly sniffing the cool air. Then her tail went straight as an arrow and remained perfectly still.

"What does she point to?" Beaumont asked.

"Alistair Ainsworth," Joanna replied.

26

The Trap

With the help of Toby Two's nose, we caught up with Dunn's hansom that had been slowed by heavy traffic. A moment later the hansom did the unexpected. Rather than head north, it turned southward and entered Whitehall before stopping in front of the building that housed the Office of Naval Intelligence. Without so much as a glance about, Dunn hurried up the steps and disappeared behind a set of imposing doors.

"Surely you do not believe Alistair Ainsworth is situated within the Office of Naval Intelligence," Beaumont grumbled.

"You are correct in that assumption," Joanna said.

"But Dunn's hansom has stopped here and your dog continues to point keenly in the direction the lieutenant has taken."

"It is not his direction that so attracts Toby Two, but the scent that Dunn carries with him."

"Which scent?"

"That of a carcass, which all dogs find irresistible."

While we waited for the traitor to make his

next move, Joanna told us of the trap she had set for Dunn. During the group's meeting with Lestrade, she had pretended to sneeze and require a handkerchief, which gave her an excuse to visit the coatrack where her handbag hung. Unnoticed by us, she reached into her handbag and, after opening the glass vial containing the smell of carcass, allowed its vapor to seep into the hem of Lieutenant Dunn's naval topcoat. Thus, wherever Dunn went, the scent went with him and so did Toby Two's nose.

"Will Dunn not detect the malodor?" Beaumont asked.

"He will not notice the faint odor, but Toby Two, whose nose is a thousand times more sensitive than Dunn's, will follow it with ease."

"Curious behavior, that," Beaumont said, obviously interested. "Why does the smell of carcass attract dogs so powerfully?"

"No one is certain of the cause, but there are two likely answers," Joanna replied. "First, it may represent a source of food. Secondly, it may well be a clever way to disguise their own aroma. You see, when dogs find the source of the smell, they will often roll about in it. This behavior is believed to be a holdover from primitive dogs that had to hunt for food and wished to hide their scent, so as not to alert their prey."

"Must it be a rotting carcass?"

"That seems to work best."

"Might I inquire as to the source of your carcass?"

"I journeyed to our local poulterer whose shop had a goose that had hung too long and ripened too much. He was happy to oblige me."

Beaumont stared out at the closed doors to the ministry building and said, "Dunn remains inside too long for this simply to be a hasty visit. And the longer he stays in the building, the more my doubt grows that he is the traitor. It may be that he is innocent or, if guilty, has outfoxed us."

"He is not and has not."

"But the passing minutes say otherwise."

"Be patient, for he will shortly appear."

"What makes you so confident?"

"He has ordered his hansom to wait for him," Joanna said, and pointed to the taxi a half block ahead.

We continued to wait somewhat uneasily, but Joanna showed no concern whatsoever. She rested her head back and closed her eyes as she seemed to drift off into one of her pensive moods. Toby Two suddenly yelped as her tail began to wag.

"He comes!" Joanna cried out as Dunn appeared. Quickly she rapped on the ceiling of our carriage to alert the driver. "You must follow at a discreet distance and remain a block or so behind at all times. Do not be concerned if you lose sight of the hansom, for I shall be able to guide you."

My father asked, "Why do you believe he bothered to visit the Office of Naval Intelligence?"

"To arrange for the marine sharpshooters that he knows will not be needed," Joanna replied. "He is a very clever man who is covering his tracks. He performs his duty for all to see, then, like a chameleon, turns to a different color."

With a sudden thrust our carriage began its journey through the crowded streets of central London. As ordered, our carriage stayed well back of Dunn's hansom in the distance. But the wagging of Toby Two's tail told us we were on the correct track. I gazed out at the motorcars passing our carriage and wondered if the odor of burning petrol would interfere with the dog's keen sense of smell. But the same concern had crossed my mind earlier and Joanna had assured me that Toby Two would have no difficulty distinguishing between the two odors. As a matter of fact, scientific studies had shown that dogs could easily differentiate between a hundred different aromas when all were presented simultaneously, thus proving that the nose of a dog was one of nature's most sensitive instruments.

"I am having difficulty believing a British naval officer would be a traitor," Beaumont said, breaking the silence.

"Come now, Admiral," said Joanna. "I am aware you suspected a spy long before Alistair Ainsworth went missing."

"Why do you think that?"

"Because I know of your clandestine meeting with Lady Jane Hamilton and her husband, who was supposedly at sea but wasn't."

Beaumont raised his brow. "Who informed you?"

"I have my sources," Joanna replied evasively. "In the dark corners of our mind, we wondered if Lady Jane and Roger Marlowe had become romantically linked, while her husband was away. Marlowe's close association with the Germans in the past would make him a prime suspect in the disappearance of Alistair Ainsworth, and perhaps he had persuaded Lady Jane to join him. But we learned it was not Marlowe whom Lady Jane was visiting secretly, but her own husband who was residing in Knightsbridge while he was supposedly out at sea. Then, to our surprise, you show up unhappily at the residence late one evening. Putting everything together, Admiral, you were searching for a spy, using Lady Jane as a conduit and her husband as the source of information. You see, with her husband supposedly away, Lady Jane would be free to associate often with Roger Marlowe who, if the traitor, might confide in her or perhaps make a mistake that would confirm your suspicions."

Beaumont breathed heavily. "You would do well in our Office of Naval Intelligence."

"I already have a position, thank you," Joanna

said. "Allow me to continue, but do not hesitate to interrupt if my conclusions are in any way incorrect. You too suspected Marlowe and had Lady Jane feed him naval intelligence that of course was given to Lady Jane by her husband, all under your supervision. Whether Lady Jane and Roger Marlowe were romantically involved I do not know and do not care, but she was the perfect conduit and could lure Roger Marlowe while he believed her husband was at sea. Am I correct thus far?"

"Quite."

"Your visit was occasioned when you learned that the secret information being gathered by the Germans was not coming from Marlowe, but from another source. Thus, the traitor was still concealed within the Admiralty and continued to give away sensitive information."

"It was the damned Exodus plan on which so much depended," Beaumont groused. "Of course, Ainsworth could not be the spy and our suspicion of Marlowe had diminished considerably, but not disappeared altogether. With Mary being as innocent as the driven snow and Montclair dead, we had run out of suspects. We never suspected Dunn in the least. He himself was not privy to the coded messages, you see."

"Oh, but he was," Joanna refuted. "He must have had the opportunity to see many of the messages in the late afternoon as they were being placed in the attaché case at the Admiralty Club. And those were the messages that were given over to the German agents."

"All he needed to do was look over Ainsworth's shoulder," Beaumont grumbled.

"Exactly," Joanna said. "Certainly with that in mind, you did not exclude him altogether."

"I am afraid we did, even after reviewing his dossier," Beaumont admitted. "However, in retrospect, there were subtle hints on when and how he might have been turned."

"A woman," Joanna said without inflection.

"How could you possibly know that?"

"The most rigid are usually the most vulnerable to feminine charm," Joanna replied. "But do go on."

"For four years Lieutenant Dunn served as a naval attaché at our Berlin embassy. He became deeply involved with an actress who happened to be the daughter of a high-ranking German naval officer. This occurred in the early nineteen hundreds when relations between our countries were far more cordial."

"Were there any signs that Dunn's relationship with this actress continued after he left his post in Berlin?"

"None that we were aware of, although he made quite a number of official visits to the Continent since returning to England."

"To Germany?"

Beaumont shook his head. "To France and Belgium."

"From where he could have journeyed unnoticed to Germany."

"Ma'am!" the driver called down. "The hansom has come to a stop!"

"Drive by at a steady speed and pay no attention to the hansom or its occupant," Joanna called back. "Once past them, tell us the activity that caused them to stop, then turn right at the next intersection."

"Toby Two will bark," I warned.

"No, she will not," Joanna said, reaching in her handbag for a large dog biscuit that she gave to me. "Feed her this as we approach Dunn's hansom. And now, Admiral, I must ask you to crouch quite low, as shall I, so that our traitor cannot see us."

"Are you certain the biscuit will distract her?" I asked.

"Oh yes, for to a dog nothing supersedes filling its stomach."

My father buried his face in a newspaper while I pretended to light my pipe and paid no attention to the stopped hansom. Toby Two's eyes and nose were fixed on the dog biscuit, her tail barely wagging.

"Now, John!" Joanna instructed.

Toby Two quickly grasped the biscuit between her teeth and chewed on it vigorously. The part of her that was bloodhound caused her to drool excessively and this appeared to only heighten her appetite. The odor of a dozen carcasses could not have drawn her attention away.

"The empty hansom is stopped in front of a tobacco shop, ma'am," the driver reported.

"But Dunn does not smoke," Beaumont said worriedly. "Has he stopped to have a look about?"

"Most likely," Joanna replied.

"Then he knows us."

Joanna shook her head. "I believe he is simply being careful."

"I am afraid he is on to us."

Joanna shook her head once more. "If he were, he would have immediately turned his hansom around and headed back to the ministry. Clever scoundrels like Dunn take no chances."

"Perhaps he will still do so, after leaving the tobacconist," I wondered aloud.

"I think not," Joanna said. "He will have another look around and, seeing nothing suspicious, will move on to his destination."

As our carriage turned right, Joanna and the admiral sat upright and my father put down his newspaper. Toby Two had finished off her dog biscuit and was eyeing me for another.

"Out the window your nose goes," Joanna said, and reached over for Toby Two.

At first, the dog demonstrated no particular

interest, but then her tail began to wag again. Gradually the speed of the wag increased and, with her head now fully extended into the wind, Toby Two yelped happily.

"Onward!" Joanna cried out. "With a right turn at the intersection!"

"Why right?" I asked.

"Because straight ahead narrows and takes a circuitous route before ending in an open park area," Joanna explained. "Moreover, it is a strictly commercial area."

Joanna's prediction proved accurate. We continued on course, using Toby Two's nose and tail to guide us. Dunn's hansom took only one evasive action, in which a complete block was circled before it again headed in a northward direction. Once past the theater district, we drove through Covent Garden and approached Great Russell Street where the British Museum was located.

"Do you believe he will turn for the museum and attempt to lose himself amidst the heavy traffic and swarms of tourists?" I asked.

"Not at this point," Joanna replied. "He cannot afford to waste any more time, for he now has precious little at his disposal."

"But, being the clever person he is, Dunn will certainly try one more evasive maneuver," my father surmised.

"It may not be necessary," Joanna said. "The

German house is in all likelihood in a residential area where traffic is light and views up and down the street unobstructed. He would have no difficulty spotting us or anyone else that chose to follow him."

"You seem to know his moves," Beaumont said.

Joanna shrugged. "I am simply putting myself in his place and how I would go about this sordid business."

"And what will his next move be?"

"To alert his German friends so they can make a hasty exit and thus escape our grasp. Then he will hurry back to the Office of Naval Intelligence to firm up the arrangement for the marine sharpshooters before returning to the Admiralty Club."

"He is a very clever fellow who knows how to hide his tracks."

"Not quite as clever as you might think, for along the way there were clues that pointed to his guilt and that I ignored but should not have."

"What clues, may I ask?"

"A surprising number that I will list for you," Joanna replied. "First, how do we explain the Germans always being ahead of us by just a fraction of time? This occurred both at the house where they tortured Verner and at their next home in St. John's Wood from which they were forced to depart in great haste. Obviously someone from within had to inform them that Scotland Yard would shortly be on their doorstep."

"That individual could have been any member of the Admiralty Club," Beaumont argued.

"Not so," Joanna said. "No one in the group knew of our visit to the first house. But Dunn did. With that in mind, let us go to the next, overlooked clue. With the group now excluded as suspects, another insider had to point out Alistair Ainsworth as the master decoder to the Germans so they could follow him and learn of his habits in order to pick the most opportune time to kidnap him. In this regard, Dunn would have been most helpful. He would be aware that Ainsworth's past had been thoroughly scrutinized before being allowed to join the Admiralty Club. Dunn could have reviewed Ainsworth's dossier and learned of his visits to Ah Sing's in the dark streets of East London. It was the ideal place to take a semidrugged Ainsworth captive."

Beaumont nodded grimly. "Dunn was in charge of vetting the prospective candidates."

"Which indicates he was perfectly positioned," Joanna said. "And this brings us to the third clue that should have drawn our attention. I am referring to the strange death of Geoffrey Montclair. Only an individual known to him could have entered his office late at night without arousing suspicion. That person had to find his way behind Montclair's desk with ease, then stab the poor fellow to death. And that person had discovered that Montclair was about to reveal the traitor."

I raised a hand and interrupted. "But wouldn't Montclair's discovery make him very suspicious of Dunn to say the least?"

"I do not think Montclair knew the answer yet," Joanna replied. "I suspect he was pointing out something in the message to Dunn that caused the lieutenant to believe he would shortly be revealed as the traitor. Thus, Dunn murdered Montclair to prevent him from deciphering the entire content of Alistair Ainsworth's message."

"But how did Dunn manage to see this particular message?" Beaumont asked. "We had strict procedures in place that permitted only members of the Admiralty Club to read the classified material."

"I do not think that presented a problem to Dunn," Joanna replied. "The lieutenant was trusted by all, you see, and could enter the various offices without suspicion and glance over the member's shoulder at what was being deciphered. I suspect that was what Dunn was doing when he realized Geoffrey Montclair was about to expose him."

"It all seems so clear now," Beaumont said.

"It should have been clear earlier," Joanna admonished herself. "I have been blind to the obvious, but it is better to learn late than never learn at all."

Our carriage was now entering the outskirts of St. John's Wood, with its stately houses and lovely gardens. My jaw must have dropped as I realized we were approaching the area in which was situated the last known residence of the German agents. I quickly glanced over to Toby Two. She was still on scent, with her tail wagging happily.

"St. John's Wood," I breathed excitedly. "The Germans never left the area."

We passed through an intersection and continued on, but Toby Two became clearly unhappy. She made a whining sound as the tail dropped and its wagging diminished.

Joanna rapped on the roof of our carriage and called up to the driver. "Return to the intersection and wait for further instructions!"

Our carriage did a slow turnabout and came to a halt at a wide intersection. Toby Two immediately jumped to the opposite window and yelped in a most pleasing manner.

"Turn left!" Joanna ordered the driver.

"Left, you are, ma'am, and onto Wellington Road," the driver called down.

"They are on this street," Joanna said to us without inflection.

"How can you be so certain?" Beaumont asked.

"Because of the map that Ainsworth left for us,

on which he circled Waterloo Station," Joanna replied.

A confused look crossed Beaumont's face. "I am at a loss here."

"Ainsworth was also telling us to concentrate on the battle at Waterloo where the Duke of Wellington was the victor," Joanna explained. "He was drawing our attention to Wellington Road where the Germans decided to reside yet again, but in a different house a good distance away."

"Very clever," Beaumont said.

"Very," said Joanna, and called out for the driver to stop, thus giving the carriages carrying Lestrade and his men the opportunity to catch up.

27

Alistair Ainsworth

From a distance and using a handheld telescope, Joanna watched Dunn enter a fashionable two-story house that had an expansive lawn in its front. With the address that housed the Germans and Alistair Ainsworth having been located, Wellington Road was closed off for several blocks in both directions. A few carriages were allowed through, for they carried innocent-appearing Scotland Yard sergeants in civilian attire, who would surround the house to ensure that escape was not possible. The homes on each side of the Germans' abode had been commandeered so that constables could be placed on their second stories to serve as lookouts. The quiet neighborhood was as peaceful as one might find in all England. But this was soon to change.

A sergeant sprinted up to us and reported to Lestrade, "Sir, the men are now in place and await further orders."

"Make certain the drapes are tightly drawn, with only the narrowest of openings," Lestrade said.

"Done, sir."

"I trust you instructed them in the proper use of their whistles."

"They are to sound off loud and clear at the earliest sign the Germans are attempting to escape."

"Well done."

"There is one other precaution I took upon myself, Inspector," the sergeant added. "At the first shot, if there are any, the occupants of the adjacent homes are to retreat to their innermost rooms and lie flat on the floor. I thought this wise in the event of a fierce gun battle, in which shots might go astray."

"A most excellent idea," Lestrade praised. "You may return to your post and keep the sharpest eye out."

"Very good, sir."

I could not help but be impressed with Lestrade's command of the dangerous situation. Whether he had been involved in similar activities in the past, I could not say, but he behaved as though he had. Admiral Beaumont stood by patiently, but had no official capacity, for the intelligence service did not possess the power or authority of police. Nevertheless, Beaumont's presence could be of value should an exchange of prisoners be proposed. As director of Naval Intelligence he knew what could and could not be offered to the Germans.

"However," Lestrade was predicting, "I feel they will fight to the very end, like good German soldiers."

"They may," Beaumont said. "But when given the chance to live and perhaps fight another day, they often change their minds."

"Who would be involved in this exchange?" Lestrade asked.

"Their spies for ours," Beaumont replied tonelessly. "This rather unpleasant task is done under civilian guise in a neutral country such as Portugal."

"I take it they have one of our agents whom we would very much like to bring home," Lestrade surmised.

Beaumont nodded. "A fine young lad from Winchester who was providing us with information on the movement of German warships."

"I trust that Dunn will not be part of any such exchange."

"Dunn will be marched up to the gallows and hanged."

"In total secrecy, I would think."

"It is best not to advertise there is a traitor within your ranks."

Lestrade turned to the street as a carriage slowly passed by. The occupant closest to us doffed his derby twice.

"The house is surrounded," Lestrade announced. "We shall shortly begin our move."

"May I suggest offering them the opportunity to surrender?" Beaumont advised.

"I think it would be of no use and only serve to warn them," Lestrade said.

"But it could work and thus save Ainsworth's life."

"I too would vote for the warning," Joanna said. "For if the battle goes against them and they are down to the last man, he will surely kill Ainsworth."

Lestrade contemplated the matter at length before reaching for a megaphone.

"*Achtung*! *Achtung*!" he bellowed out in German, which was certain to arouse the agents' attention and further unnerve them in the process. "You are surrounded on all sides by Scotland Yard, with no hope of escape. You must surrender immediately or you will be taken by force. We will allow you one minute to reach a decision."

I concentrated my attention on the windows of the Germans' house, watching for any movement behind them. But I could see none, for their drapes were tightly closed. The roof appeared to be gently sloped, with scattered brick chimneys, but there was no motion there either. Joanna's eyes were on the back garden where there were tall willow trees and flowering bushes.

"What in the garden so grabs your attention?" I asked quietly.

"The most likely escape route," Joanna replied.

"I doubt the Germans would be so bold."

"They may have no choice."

"You have thirty seconds remaining!" Lestrade called out.

To my right I saw a group of sergeants carefully checking the rounds in their service revolvers. Behind them was a smaller group of police constables, holding on to a long, thick spar that was unadorned and resembled a utility pole. There was no nervousness about them, only the steely resolve of brave men about to do their duty.

Lestrade signaled over to the group. In quick order the armed sergeants formed a phalanx around the men now holding the sturdy beam in a horizontal position. The last seconds dragged by in a silence so eerie that even the birds above stopped chirping.

"The Germans will open fire from the second floor," Joanna said in a whisper.

"Why so?" I asked.

"It is the point of greatest advantage."

"But certainly our side will return fire, will they not?"

"It is a well-known fact that it is easier and more accurate to shoot down rather than up," Joanna said.

"Which I can attest to," my father agreed. "For it is so cited in the *Military Manual of Arms*. I can also vouch for this fact from personal experience."

Joanna beckoned over to Lestrade. "Inspector, it might be wise to have your men focus their attention on the windows of the second floor."

"I see no activity there," Lestrade said, after taking a studied look.

"You will once the attack begins," Joanna said. "Have your men train their weapons on the glass panes themselves and be prepared to open fire immediately. Shattering glass, you see, will throw off the aim of even the best of marksmen."

Lestrade quickly passed on the instructions, then brought his arm up and abruptly dropped it as he called out, "Now!"

The constables manning the battering ram charged forward, with a phalanx of sergeants rushing alongside them, weapons drawn. A volley of shots rang out from the second-floor windows of the surrounded house. Two of the advancing sergeants fell, one clutching a bleeding shoulder, the other shouting in pain from a leg wound. Those left standing returned fire with round after round, many of which found their mark. Windowpanes were blasted apart, sending down a shower of shattered glass. For a brief moment there was a halt to the German fire, which gave the men with the battering ram an opportunity to charge once again. On the second try the fortified door crashed with a loud bang. The constables hurriedly stepped aside as a barrage of shots came from within the house. The sergeants, now in shooting positions, gave as good as they got and then some, firing round after round and reloading to fire even more. Suddenly all went quiet. Ever so cautiously the Scotland Yard operatives advanced, with their weapons cocked and at the ready. The sergeants closest to us kept their service revolvers aimed on the blasted-out second-story windows. Those too were now quiet.

Our attention was abruptly drawn to the rear of the house from where we heard a window being smashed apart. A heavyset man, clothed only in underwear, rolled out onto the grass and crawled on his hands and knees to the nearby shrubbery. The sergeants rapidly trained their weapons on the partially clothed man.

"Hold your fire!" Beaumont shouted loudly. "It is Ainsworth!"

Sergeants and constables from all sides converged on the Germans' house, all crouched low and expecting a fight-to-the-death struggle. But it did not occur, for there was neither a shot nor sound coming from within.

It required a full ten minutes for the house to be searched and deemed safe for us to enter. In the foyer, where they decided to make their last stand, lay three German agents. Two were dead with head wounds, the third was gasping and exhaling a bloody froth. As my father examined him to determine if any treatment could be applied, the German agent, with the broad shoulders and facial tic, breathed his last.

"All clear of Germans," a sergeant reported to Lestrade.

"What of Dunn?" Lestrade asked at once.

"Not to be found, sir."

"I want every square inch of this house gone over, cellar to attic," Lestrade ordered, and watched as the officer raced away.

"How could he have possibly escaped?" I wondered.

"The cleverest always have a way out," Joanna said.

"But the house was being watched from all sides at every moment," I argued. "How could he have executed such an escape?"

"There are two possibilities, and I suspect Mr. Alistair Ainsworth will tell us which one is true."

"I will indeed, madam," Ainsworth said, strolling up to us. He was now covered with a blanket and bleeding from dozens of small cuts on his face and arms. "Although I perceive from your tone of voice that you already know the answer."

Joanna gave him a humorless smile. "Dunn presented you with the opportunity to escape."

"Oh, he did much more than that," Ainsworth said. "The German agents had tied me to a chair when they became aware of your presence. They wanted to be certain I could not bolt and make a run for it. When the firing started and the others were preoccupied, Dunn untied me and pointed to the rear window, which was obviously my only avenue of departure. At first, I thought he'd had a change of heart."

Joanna shook her head. "Evil men do not change their hearts; they adapt."

"So I was to learn."

"Were you able to discern the direction Dunn took after freeing you?" Joanna asked.

"He dashed for the stairs while the Germans provided covering fire."

"Did you in fact see him go up?"

"I did not, but I heard him call out to the German agents that he was going upstairs where he could keep Scotland Yard at bay."

"He escaped through the attic," Joanna said, and led the way up to the top of the stairs where a group of sergeants stood. "Where is the opening to the attic?"

"At the end of the corridor, ma'am," the lead sergeant replied. "You will find the opening there, with its ladder down. But the attic is clear, ma'am."

"It is not the attic you should be concerned with, but the roof."

Joanna hurried over to the hinged ladder and ascended it, with Lestrade, my father, Beaumont, and I only steps behind. The attic was dark and cluttered, and had the stale odor that was characteristic of an enclosed space with poor ventilation. Two sergeants followed us in and lighted the attic with powerful torches. Most of the articles were stored in boxes and bins, whilst used pieces of dust-covered furniture were heaped up one upon another in tall columns.

"There!" Joanna pointed to a large couch upon which rested a desk and atop the desk was a wooden stool. She waited for the sergeants to shine the light of their torches to the column of stacked furniture. Behind it was a stepladder of considerable length that went up to a closed trapdoor. Narrow streaks of sunlight clearly illustrated its outline.

"Do you believe the scoundrel is up there, having found a hiding place?" Lestrade asked.

"That is unlikely, for the longer he remains on the roof, the greater the chance he will be discovered," Joanna replied. "The smart move is to keep moving."

"But to where?"

"That is to be determined."

"Let us be certain," Lestrade said, and gestured to the two armed sergeants. "Inspect the roof with the greatest of care. If Dunn is found and resists, do not hesitate to shoot."

As he watched the sergeants scale the ladder, Beaumont suggested, "Perhaps Dunn is attempting to throw us off the track."

"That being the case, he would not have gone to the trouble of hiding it so well," Joanna countered, and began to search the area surrounding the stepladder. Finding nothing of interest, she went to a large wooden crate that was nearby and had its top incompletely closed. She opened it and extracted an officer's coat of the Royal Navy, with its lieutenant insignia clearly visible. "And there is your proof. Of course he would change into civilian attire, for his naval officer's uniform would surely attract attention."

"He was a most careful planner indeed," Beaumont said.

"The best of them always are." Joanna dug deeper into the crate and found an oversized hammer, with a large, squared head. The metal section of the hammer was coated with white dust. "What do we have here?"

"An old hammer that has been sitting there for quite some time," Lestrade answered, moving in for a closer look.

"Why do you believe it has been in this position for such a long while?" Joanna asked.

"Because it is covered with dust," Lestrade replied.

"The head is, but the handle is not," Joanna observed. "The wooden handle is clean and spotless, which indicates it was used recently."

"But how do you explain the dust?" Lestrade argued.

Joanna reached for her magnifying glass and studied the head of the hammer. "It is not dust, but a powdery substance filled with small particles. Thus, it would seem this hammer was used to strike stone or plaster."

"To what end?"

"I believe the answer to that question lies on the roof."

"All clear!" a sergeant shouted down from the open trapdoor.

We followed Joanna up the stepladder and onto a broad slate roof that was bordered by a stone parapet approximately three feet in height. The roof itself was somewhat sloped, with a multitude of brick chimneys, so we walked with care.

The two sergeants rushed over to us, with their weapons holstered. "Nothing," one of them reported. "There is no place to hide nor any stairs or steps leading to the ground."

"I would not have expected to find those, for he would have been visible to the constables while climbing down," Joanna said.

"But during his stay on the roof, he had to conceal himself from the lookouts," Lestrade opined.

Joanna studied the slate roof at length before turning to me. "John, please be so good as to stroll over to the easternmost edge of the roof that overlooks the adjacent house and tell me what you see."

I walked over to the eastern parapet and gazed out at the nearby house and the activities in its front courtyard. "There is nothing remarkable about the house itself, but in the courtyard I can see the wounded sergeants being attended to."

"Excellent!" Joanna cried out. "Now wait a moment, then turn around and describe my whereabouts."

I did as instructed and saw the entire group of men—Lestrade, his two sergeants, the admiral, and my father—but Joanna had disappeared. "Has she gone back downstairs?"

"No, I have not," Joanna answered, and stepped out from a pair of brick chimneys. "I simply slouched low where Dunn must have, and was thus hidden from the view of Lestrade's lookouts."

"But where did he go from this point?" Lestrade asked. "He was trapped unless you believe he was capable of flying away."

"That is a talent he does not possess," Joanna said, and once again studied the entire roof until her eyes came to a halt on a large willow tree whose slender limbs were touching the rear section of the parapet. She hurried over and stopped abruptly in front of a leaf-covered limb. "Here!" she called to us and gestured downward.

We dashed over to the area of the parapet that acted as a barrier to the smoke discharged from the close-by chimney. The slate roof adjacent to the parapet was covered with a thick layer of soot and ashes, in which resided two handprints and two round smudges made by Dunn's knees.

"He crouched down on his hands and knees at this position, and waited for his chance," Joanna said. "As soon as Alistair Ainsworth crashed through the window, all of our eyes went to him, and that was the moment Dunn escaped."

"But this is a willow tree and its fragile branches could not begin to support a man of Dunn's weight," Lestrade contended. "And its trunk is well away from the roof and would require an exceptional jump to be reached."

Joanna inspected the tree and its nearby limbs at length, then moved in closer to the parapet and examined its inner surface and top. Finding nothing of consequence, she leaned over the stone parapet to view its outer face. "Hello!"

"What do you see?" Lestrade asked at once.

"The answer," Joanna said, and stepped back to give us a clearer view. Driven into the top, outer surface of the parapet was a thick metal spike, from which extended a long rope that reached down to the garden.

"Which explains the powdery grit on the head of the hammer," I thought aloud.

"Precisely, John," Joanna agreed. "The metal spike was driven in with the hammer and a sturdy rope tied around it, which gave Dunn his escape route. The heavily leafed willow tree camouflaged his descent into the garden. This lieutenant of ours is very clever indeed, for he had earlier planned this last route of escape, in case others were not available."

Lestrade turned quickly to a sergeant. "We had an officer stationed in the rear garden, did we not?"

"Yes, sir," the sergeant said. "I called down to him from the roof and he had seen nothing unusual. All was quiet after Mr. Ainsworth crashed through the window, except for a dog nearby that was barking at the disturbance."

"I suspect the dog was not barking at the disturbance, but at a disturber," Joanna discerned. "When you examine the area around the base of the willow tree, you will in all likelihood find broken plants and shrubbery that Dunn stepped on while running for his life."

"And so he is gone," Lestrade said sourly.

"I am afraid he has given us the slip," Joanna concurred.

"I shall order an all-points warning immediately," Lestrade asserted.

"A good idea, Inspector, but one unlikely to bear fruit," Joanna said. "A clever planner such as Dunn will disappear into thin air."

We returned to the foyer where Ainsworth, still wrapped in a blanket, was now seated and shivering against the late morning chill. The scrapes and cuts on his face and arms, which

411

had stopped bleeding, would yet require medical attention.

"No luck, eh?" Ainsworth asked.

"None," Joanna replied.

"As I expected," Ainsworth said, and asked around for a cigarette, which a sergeant provided, along with a light. Inhaling the smoke deeply, Ainsworth continued on, "You see, Dunn only partially untied the ropes binding me, and for obvious reasons. He wanted to delay my escape until he was prepared to take his. So I was the distraction, was I not?"

"So it would seem," Joanna said.

"But at least it kept me alive, although I am sure that was not Dunn's intended consequence," Ainsworth said. "That was no doubt the critical event in saving my life, along with someone decoding the messages I sent. Who was responsible? Marlowe?"

"No," Beaumont answered.

"Mary?"

"She neither."

"Then it must have been good old Montclair."

"You are half correct," Beaumont told him. "Montclair was about to decipher the message that pointed to the traitor, but Dunn learned of it and murdered him."

"Bloody bastard!" Ainsworth cursed aloud.

"Of the worst order," Beaumont said. "But he too left behind a message and it was decoded by the lady who is with us and happens to be the daughter of Sherlock Holmes."

"I have read of you and your talents," Ainsworth praised. "It was you who untangled the most difficult code of the slanted lines, was it not?"

"It was."

"With of course Dr. Watson's help," Ainsworth added.

"I would be lost without my Watson," Joanna exaggerated, yet it still made my father smile. "But I should mention that I could not have deciphered your Exodus message without the assistance of Mary Ellington."

"That does not lessen my debt of gratitude," Ainsworth went on. "To you I owe my life and I would very much like to reward you and the Watsons in some small way by inviting you to join me at Simpson's-in-the-Strand for dinner, which of course will have to await my recovery."

"With pleasure," Joanna accepted. "Will your daughter be accompanying you?"

"She will indeed," Ainsworth said. "But may I inquire how you know of my daughter?"

"The maître d' at François informed us of your frequent visits," Joanna replied. "He also mentioned that she for the most part was schooled on the Continent."

"She was until her mother passed away five years ago," said Ainsworth. "I was of course delighted to arrange for her admission to the University of Manchester, from which she graduated with honors. She now attends University College London where she is pursuing a doctorate in archaeology."

"Like her father."

"Very much so, with a decided passion for Egyptian hieroglyphics."

I feigned an interest in their talk of hieroglyphics, all the while wondering how Joanna had discovered that Ainsworth had a daughter. But then I thought back to our visit to the French restaurant, and all the clues behind her line of reasoning came to mind. They seemed so obvious now. Ainsworth's companion at François was twenty or so years his junior, which would be the correct time frame for his daughter being conceived while he was a student studying at the University of Heidelberg. Moreover, their display of affection at the restaurant could well have been that exhibited by a loving father to his daughter, rather than one of romance. And in all likelihood the daughter was born out of wedlock, which accounted for Ainsworth keeping her existence a secret from his family. Upon the mother's death, however, Ainsworth felt an obligation to look after the girl, as any decent father would. Of course Roger Marlowe knew of the daughter and lied about dinner with Ainsworth to cover for his dear friend.

"Well then, I suspect our dinner together will be a most interesting one," Joanna was saying, "but before you leave I have a last question that I hope you will be permitted to answer."

"Let us hear it."

"You are a chess master and, from what I have read, there is a stratagem called the combination, in which one sacrifices something seemingly small in order to gain something great. It is a form of distraction. Did you employ this maneuver while being held by the Germans?"

"I did indeed," Ainsworth said, with a mischievous grin before turning to Beaumont. "With your permission, Admiral."

"Is it an event done and finished with?" Beaumont asked.

"It is."

"With no consequence were it now revealed?"

"It might well embarrass the Germans."

"Then, by all means, proceed."

"As you well know, Admiral, the British and German fleets were believed to be evenly matched, with the Royal Navy having only a slight advantage. Furthermore, several of our ships were known to be in port undergoing repairs, while others were busy protecting cargo ships coming and leaving British ports. Thus, if ever the Germans were to attack our navy and gain control of the North Sea, this would be the opportune moment. I thought I took care of this danger rather well. The message I saw stated the Germans had eighteen battleships while we had twenty. So I simply changed the number and told the Germans we had twenty-five battleships; that of course caused them to reconsider any attack plan they may have been considering."

"Good show," Beaumont said.

Joanna asked, "But what was the distraction?"

"The sacrifice of merchant ships."

"Not one of ours?" Beaumont asked anxiously.

Ainsworth shook his head. "A convoy had been spotted off the coast of Portugal who we know will shortly side with Germany in this war. I invented the story that these merchant ships were carrying raw materials and headed for England. I had hoped the Germans would dispatch a group of warships to intercept these merchant vessels, and thus diminish the size of their fleet in the North Sea. They did, but by then the convoy had mysteriously disappeared. They still may be searching for these ships."

"Well done," Beaumont lauded.

"I considered it one of my better moves," said Ainsworth, then unsteadily arose from his chair. "And now I must take my leave and go home, for my dear sister is no doubt terribly worried about me."

"Might I impose on you for one final question to satisfy my curiosity?" Joanna asked.

"Of course."

"How did you learn that Dunn was the traitor? Did you overhear the Germans speaking of him?"

"In a way I did, but they never mentioned him by name. During their conversation they boasted that Germany had knowledge of the Exodus plan prior to the outbreak of war. At that moment in history, the Admiralty Club had not yet been founded and none of the members had worked in Naval Intelligence. Thus the traitor could not be Roger, Mary, or Geoffrey, and that left Dunn, who was aware of the plan before the war and one of the few who knew it was the Admiralty Club who gave the plan the name Exodus. This of course was by no means conclusive evidence, but all this changed when I overheard the Germans debating how accurate my deciphering truly was. They decided to check my reliability by having me decode a message that they had already decoded. They chose the Exodus plan, but were uncertain which of the messages should be used. It was agreed the selection would best be made by the man who carried the communiqués back and forth to the Admiralty Club."

"Which could be none other than Lieutenant Dunn."

"Checkmate," Ainsworth said with a pleased smile.

Joanna watched Ainsworth walk away, now aided by two powerfully built sergeants. "And we are done here."

"It has been my honor to work with you," Beaumont said sincerely.

"And mine as well," Lestrade said, doffing his derby.

As Joanna strolled away, arm in arm with my father and me, she had a second thought and turned back to the admiral and inspector. "Gentlemen, there is an important lesson we should all learn from this case."

"Which is?" Lestrade asked.

"Do not attempt to match wits with a chess master," Joanna instructed. "For if you do, you will surely lose."

"But as I recall, you are not a chess master, yet it was you who deciphered Ainsworth's code and thus clearly matched his wits."

"That is because I had a chess master to guide me."

"Who, may I ask?"

"Geoffrey Montclair, who used his own blood to not only decipher the message, but lead us to the biblical tale of Passover."

"Absolutely mind-bending," Beaumont said, and shook his head in wonderment. "He performed magic by using his own blood."

"Quite."

"Clever beyond clever."

"And he was yet more ingenious, for in his very last breath Montclair employed a combination stratagem to defeat his opponent."

"How so?"

A Mona Lisa smile came to Joanna's face as we stepped toward bright sunlight. "On his return to supposedly discover the body, Dunn must have seen the bloodstained message in the typewriter. He beyond a doubt paid attention to it, but its relevance escaped him. This then was the move that distracted Dunn, so that he could be conquered by the next."

Beaumont called after us, "But the blood on the message was both distracting and the conquering move."

"And that, my dear Admiral, is the pure genius of a chess master."

CLOSURE

Some ten months later Admiral Beaumont visited us at 221b Baker Street unannounced, bringing with him the fate of Lieutenant Richard Dunn. He accepted a glass of Madeira as we gathered around the fireplace and waited for the thunder and lightning outside to abate.

"First, we were correct in believing the German actress played an important role in turning Dunn," Beaumont began. "Our best intelligence has confirmed he married her secretly during his stay as a naval attaché at our embassy in Berlin. His wife and young son have a home in Bremerhaven that he had managed to visit on his diplomatic trips to France, presumably traveling through the neutral Netherlands. But there was a second key factor in Dunn's becoming a turncoat. He had always desired to have command of a warship and his dossier is filled with requests that he be allowed to do so. However, we did not feel he possessed the seamanship qualities necessary for such a promotion, and thus his requests were denied. He must have become quite embittered and disappointed by this decision, and eagerly leaped at the opportunity to eventually command a German warship. We believe this offer was made in nineteen fourteen, just before the war started. That was when Dunn turned and became a highly valued German agent. His position within the Admiralty Club was an absolute godsend to the enemy, which continued until the day he was uncovered. After Dunn escaped and fled to Germany, he was no doubt greeted with open arms."

"Was he, being a foreigner, actually given such an important station?" Joanna asked.

"He was," Beaumont replied. "He was promoted to lieutenant commander and assigned to a destroyer that had several decisive victories, for which he would shortly be elevated to the rank of captain. However, on his last voyage he had the misfortune to encounter one of the Royal Navy's most powerful warships. A fierce battle ensued and Dunn's ship was sunk, with all hands lost."

"Good riddance," I murmured under my breath.

"So Dunn and his traitorous acts now sit at the bottom of the sea," my father concluded. "Which unfortunately spares him from a well-deserved hanging."

"Quite true," Beaumont said. "But I think you would find it most fitting to learn more about the British warship that sent Dunn to his watery grave. It is His Majesty's newest and most powerful battleship, and carries the proud name *Revenge*."

Poetic justice, everyone sitting in the room thought at once. Poetic justice indeed!

Acknowledgments

Special thanks to Peter Wolverton and Jennifer Donovan, splendid editors, who make my novels ever so much better.

Center Point Large Print
600 Brooks Road / PO Box 1
Thorndike, ME 04986-0001 USA

(207) 568-3717

US & Canada:
1 800 929-9108
www.centerpointlargeprint.com

BY

Erna Fergusson

NEW MEXICO
A PAGEANT OF THREE PEOPLES (*1951, 1964*)

MEXICO REVISITED (*1955*)

CUBA (*1946*)

CHILE (*1943*)

OUR SOUTHWEST (*1940*)

VENEZUELA (*1939*)

GUATEMALA (*1937*)

_____

These are Borzoi Books
Published in New York by ALFRED A. KNOPF

New Mexico

SAN JUAN RIVER
FARMINGTON
DULCE
TIERRA
AMARILLA
RATON
El Vado Dam
ELVADO
CIMARRON
RIO CHAMA
TAOS
Chaco Canyon
Ruins
CUBA
ESPANOLA
WAGON
MOUND
CANADIAN
GALLUP
Jemez
SANTA FE
Santo
Domingo
Conchas Dam
RIVER
Zuni
RIO GRANDE
ALBUQUERQUE
PECOS RIVER
TUCUMCARI
Quarai Ruins
Alamogordo Dam
Abo Ruins
FT. SUMNER
Gran Quivera
Ruins
MOGOLLON
SOCORRO
GILA RIVER
ROSWELL
Elephant Butte
Dam
MESCALERO
SILVER
CITY
ALAMOGORDO
HOBBS
LAS CRUCES
CARLSBAD
MESILLA

U.S. FOREST SERVICE AND THE SOIL CONSERVATION SERVICE,
ALBUQUERQUE, NEW MEXICO

New Mexico

A PAGEANT
OF THREE PEOPLES

Erna Fergusson

SECOND EDITION

NEW YORK: ALFRED·A·KNOPF

1 9 6 4

L. C. catalog card number: 64-19099

THIS IS A BORZOI BOOK,
PUBLISHED BY ALFRED A. KNOPF, INC.

PUBLISHED NOVEMBER 12, 1951.
REPRINTED ONCE.

Chapter V includes a portion of "Our Modern Indians," originally published in *New Mexico Quarterly*, Spring 1959

For LINDA MUSSER,

who helped me to know my own state,

not only because she saw it freshly as a newcomer,

but because her sympathetic appreciation of its people

has always been spiced with lively humor.

Foreword

NEW MEXICO *is the scene of the longest span of human development in the Western Hemisphere. Traces of earliest man have been found in a mountain cave; on a high plateau the atomic bomb was made. Much of the long drama of human development has been only faintly reflected in New Mexico, but the acts that have been played here have left to the modern state vestiges of a pageant of three peoples. The rites of prehistoric Indians and of Europeans of the Middle Ages are still practiced here. The two frontiers—Spanish and United States—met and fused in New Mexico. This is important for the record. It is of greater value, now that our country has been forced into world leadership, that in New Mexico the peoples of three cultures have successfully worked out a life together.*

Acknowledgments

Many people—too many to name—have helped me, in conversation and in correspondence, to gather and to evaluate the material used in this book. I will only name certain authorities who have been kind enough to read chapters and to check them for factual errors. They are: archæologist Erik K. Reed of the National Park Service; anthropologists Dr. Clyde Kluckhohn, Harvard, and Dr. Anne M. Smith; William A. Brophy, former Commissioner of Indian Affairs; historians Dr. France V. Scholes and Dr. Dorothy Woodward, University of New Mexico, and Fray Angelico Chavez; sociologists Dr. Lyle Saunders and Dr. Paul A. F. Walter, Jr., University of New Mexico, and Dr. Florence Kluckhohn, Harvard; Dr. Lloyd S. Tireman, Professor of Education, University of New Mexico; Richard L. Strong, District Conservationist, and Harold B. Elmendorf, Water Division, Soil Conservation Service; Eastburn Smith, Regional Administrator, Bureau of Land Management; Frank Pooler, former Regional Director, U.S. Forest Service; Dr.

William Long, Professor, New Mexico School of Mines; Walter Connell, sheepman; and Kenneth Adams, Professor of Art, University of New Mexico.

Portions of this book appeared, in earlier and different form, in the following periodicals, whose editors I wish to thank: *Américas* (Pan American Union); *New Mexico Quarterly* (University of New Mexico Press); *Think* (International Business Machines Corporation); and *The American Indian* (Association on American Indian Affairs, Inc.).

Contents

xii   Contents

Illustrations

PART ONE

Indian

New Mexico, showing county lines and names, larger cities and towns, and principal roads.

New Mexico

❧ ⊂⊒ ❧

I

FIRST DISCOVERERS

⊂⊒   So FAR as we know—though archæologists are forever digging, cowboys forever riding around, Boy Scouts
forever exploring, and anything can show up any day—the
first discoverer of New Mexico was Sandia Cave Man, so
called because all we know of him was found in a cave in
the Sandia Mountains east of Albuquerque. The first trace
of him was a claw uncovered by Boy Scouts in 1927. Any
archæologist would have recognized that claw as belonging
to the giant sloth, an animal extinct for ten thousand years
or so. But no archæologist saw it then. It was not until 1936
that an archæology student from the University of New
Mexico happened upon the same cave. He reported his discovery to his professor, Dr. Frank Hibben, and several seasons of careful excavation followed.

In a fascinating small book, *The Lost Americans*, Dr. Hibben has described how his students uncovered layer below
layer of rock and earth laid down by nature, and layers of
debris that only man could have made. Man, with his unvarying gift for leaving a mess, always bequeaths to his
heirs evidence beyond price. In this case, sure proof of
man's presence was found in two strata separated by a deposit of yellow ocher that had taken thousands of years to
accumulate. It was this irritating, powdery dust that had
discouraged the Boy Scouts; and that was fortunate because
it carried real danger of silicosis and because the boys' desertion saved the cave for investigation by trained observers.

In the layer under the yellow ocher scientists have found

3

evidences of human occupancy: scrapers and flint points, crudely worked but deadly when hurled by a strong arm. Unquestionably they were the work of man; only men make things. Sandia Man also knew how to use fire. Even before man reached America the race had produced a genius comparable to an atomic scientist, who had put fire to use. The first cooking may have resulted from clumsy fumbling, but the intelligent use of a natural force for man's good implies thinking. We know that Sandia Man cooked, for he left two hearths, as archæologists call burnt-over places. He must have been wrapped up in skins. Why else would he need scrapers? So here had been a man, skin-clad and fed on meat. This is all we know of him or of his family. No human bones were found. It was a very annoying habit of New Mexico's first discoverers that they did not leave even one tiny bone on which scientists could erect a complete and probably quite accurate skeleton.

In the stratum above that yellow ocher, and therefore indicating later occupancy of Sandia Cave, were found flint points such as had been seen before in northeastern New Mexico.

In 1925, before the Boy Scouts found Sandia Cave, a Negro cowboy, George McJunkin, riding along an arroyo near Folsom, pulled some queer-looking bones out of the cut. Along with them came flint points that looked strange to him, and he had seen many Indian arrowheads. Report of his find reached the University of Denver and started a rush of archæologists toward Folsom. For that observant cowboy had unearthed the earliest evidence then known of man in this hemisphere.

These flint points were exquisitely made. From one to three inches long, they were evenly flaked and smoothly grooved to fit a spear or dart. And with them were found the bones of mammals that had been extinct for ten thousand years. So men were here when these plains were dotted with great lakes and lush with vegetation that fed a type of bison long gone, mammoths, elephants, mastodons, four-toed horses, and giant ground sloths. With his chipped stone weapons man killed them all; and when he butchered the wide-horned bison he took the tail with the hide, as later butchers do. Many skeletons have been found, but no tail bones. Folsom Man also chased animals that we know: deer, antelope, and smaller species. He was a mighty hunter indeed, and he ranged from northeastern Colorado to the southeastern corner of New Mexico. And, like roaming men of all ages, he brought things home. In a few places odd articles have been found, things not made there. So trade had begun.

These were the ancestors of our modern Indians. But they too had ancestors. Archæologists agree that man came into the Western Hemisphere as man. This country was settled by immigrants from the start. And—if one wishes to strut a bit—by real men. It is also agreed that human beings came from Asia across Bering Strait. Maybe they crossed on the ice; maybe it was dry then and they walked across on sand. Through eons, then, they drifted southward, a slow trickle of shivering, shelterless nomads, for it was bitter cold and life was full of terrors. Man's food depended on his hand-hacked stone weapons and his skill at hurling them; he had to kill the beast or be killed by him. Archæologists will hazard no guess as to how long that slow dispersal took; certainly it was millennia before the first Americans had made their way the length of the land mass and spread over South America, where they were to attain their highest prehistoric development. We do know that they crossed New Mexico and that some of them stayed.

Sandia Cave has been studied by the late Dr. Kirk Bryan, professor of geology at Harvard. In an appendix to Frank Hibben's *Lost Americans*, Dr. Bryan maintains that the layer of yellow ocher was laid down some twenty-five

thousand years ago and that Sandia Man laired there just
before that era, Folsom Man just after. Some geologists
think that Kirk Bryan erects too heavy a conclusion on so
thin a layer of yellow ocher. Dr. Bryan was one of the
world's outstanding geologists and his conclusions deserve
deep respect; but the layman willingly leaves the scientists
to argue about the difference between ten thousand and
twenty-five thousand years.

What concerns us is that men, with a suitable complement of women, lived in New Mexico at least ten thousand
years ago. And that the New Mexico we know is, in large
outline, very like the land the first inhabitant knew. Dr.
Eliot Blackwelder, in *The Great Basin,* writes: "The mountains and basins remain as they were in late Pleistocene
times." Sandia Man, from the crest above his cave, got the
view we get gazing high across the valley that seems un-
naturally foreshortened from that height. Mount Taylor,
then as now, rose palely blue against a bluer sky; that dead
volcano would long before have spewed forth the lava that
we call the *malpais* between Grants and Laguna. Perhaps
plants had even then begun to break the lava apart, as the
fluffy Apache plume still does. Sandia Man would have
seen the azure Ladron and the purple Socorro Mountains
to the southwest, and to the northwest the deep blue, cor-
rugated Jemez range. That confused conglomeration of
mountains was formed by volcanic action when several cra-
ters, still discernible, overflowed the Valle Grande with hot
streams of lava. Travelers between Albuquerque and Santa
Fe and farther north along the Rio Grande gorge below
Taos may still trace those lava flows where they congealed.

In such places one sees how New Mexico was made;
many processes of its making go on still. An occasional
earth tremor suggests the vast upheavals that brought the
mountains up or tilted them to form slanting cliffs like the
sun-drenched face of the Sandia range above Albuquerque.

Boiling springs still bubble out of furnace-hot underground rocks. Sulphur Springs, above Jemez, with its white and yellow crusts that steam stinkingly, suggests the anteroom of Hades. The Mimbres Mountains are dotted with hot springs of undetermined therapeutic value, but prolific of legend. More immediately impressive is erosion, the dusting away of topsoil by wind and the flash floods that bring the good brown earth down arroyos while long lines of automobiles wait and drivers rage. These are minor changes; the big job of forming the land was completed before man appeared here.

Beyond Sandia Man's indifferent vision lay the pattern of the state as we know it. Trisected by two confused series of north-and-south mountain ranges, it has the Rio Grande for its lowest point and is set off east and west by the High Plains and the Colorado Plateau. New Mexico's sierras form the south end of the Rocky Mountains. Their tallest peak is Wheeler, near Taos, with an altitude of 13,151 feet. Farther south, Lake Peak and Pecos Baldy dominate the sierra that shelters Santa Fe from east winds and supplies its water from snow-fed lakes. This range divides the headwaters of New Mexico's two most useful streams, the Rio Grande and the Pecos. Doubtless magnificent brimming rivers ten thousand years ago, both now quite regularly dry up in rainless summers. But they and their tributaries have provided irrigation for many centuries of farming, and they have had long and dramatic histories in interstate and international affairs.

South of Santa Fe the mighty Rockies peter out, as indicated by the name Cerrillos, Little Hills; the Sandias come on like an afterthought. But there are elevations on southward to keep the Rio Grande and the Rio Pecos quite distinct, even above-timberline peaks, not so tall as Wheeler Peak, but quite as impressive, especially under snow. The sierras of Manzano, Los Pinos, Oscura, and San Andres show quite well who named them. Only the Organs, rising like serried pipes east of Las Cruces, have adopted a newer speech. All these mountains now start hopeful streams eastward toward the Pecos, making its absent-minded way to join the Rio Grande and thus go on to the Gulf of Mexico. Some of these little hopefuls get lost in sand before reaching the river, but they all offer incontrovertible evidence that this was once a well-watered land.

East of the Pecos there are no mountains, just the high plains that break down in steep escarpments, known for a hundred miles or more as Cap Rock. Men marked their trails across those grasslands with stakes, which gave them the name of Llano Estacado (Staked Plains). Buffalo, and later cattle, grazed there. Deep under the high plains the slow seepage of ages had been storing water in vast beds of sand long before Sandia Man. Those sands held petroleum too, in deep dark pools where water sometimes floated on the oil. Both oil and water are making history now. In the Pecos valley, underground water had chiseled out those miraculous caves we know as the Carlsbad Caverns, and doubtless others still undiscovered but made manifest by the Bottomless Lakes near Roswell, the Blue Hole near Santa Rosa, and other unnamed holes reported by cowboys who always just save themselves from falling in.

Northeastern New Mexico is drained by the Canadian River, which rises not far from the Rio Grande's headwaters under Colorado's peaks. It collects lesser streams whose names appear and reappear in our history: the Cimarron, the Mora, Ute Creek, the Tucumcari, and the Conchas. Where they rise, near the Sangre de Cristo Mountains, these creeks have for many ages irrigated soft green valleys. But the Canadian's longest course is through cattle country, and its most dramatic history belongs to the Staked Plains and even to Oklahoma and to Arkansas, where it flows into the Mississippi.

Between the headwaters of the Canadian and Rio Grande and those of the San Juan runs the Continental Divide, that wavering ridge which divides waters between the Gulf of Mexico and the Gulf of California. The Pacific drainage in New Mexico begins with the San Juan River, which rises in Colorado but swings so wide and generous a loop into New Mexico that it brings in more water than all the state's other streams. Its bright green course is weirdly vivid in the Navajo's rolling desert, where the only peaks are as lordly remote and unscalable as Shiprock, and sand colors are even more startling than the river's green. Heading north again, the San Juan almost touches Four Corners, the only spot in the United States where four states meet. In Utah it joins the Colorado above the Grand Canyon. Fed by the streams of seven states, the Colorado now supplies southern California with water from Hoover Dam and causes more inter-state and international disputes than the Rio Grande and the Pecos combined.

Near the border between Colorado and New Mexico the Continental Divide swings slightly west of south, crosses the highway near Thoreau, and follows the crest of the Zuni range to pass over the Lava Fields and meet the tourist again at Pie Town in the Datils. Tipping New Mexico definitely eastward, the Divide runs west along the ridges of the Tularosa, the Black, and the Mogollon ranges, and on to the Mexican border through the Burro and the Pyramid mountains. All these sierras send what water they have to the Colorado, but north of the Lava Fields it is very little. The southern ranges do better, pouring down hundreds of tiny rills that unite in ever larger streams to form the San Francisco and the Gila rivers, which join before they enter the Colorado.

Dr. Ross Calvin has given the Gila its best name in the title of his book, *River of the Sun*. Knowing its every foot and all that lives there, Dr. Calvin has described from personal intimacy the entire valley's flora and fauna, from the springs where icy driblets water subarctic lichens to the splendid blossoming desert where the Gila enters the Colorado. Prehistoric man, with his Stone Age weapons, fished and hunted in so many of those canyons that the Mogollon and the Mimbres mountains are among the archæologists' most fertile fields.

The river that most fully exemplifies New Mexico and all the peoples who have made it is the fabled, historic, and forever undependable Rio Grande. Coming too from that mother of rivers, Colorado, the Rio Grande flows almost due south through the very heart of New Mexico. A strong, clear current in its upper section, the stream has cut through layers of basalt and sandstone to make the Cañon del Norte. The new road to Taos avoids that splendid gorge, leaving it to fishermen who flip big speckled trout out of pools under foaming rapids. Geologists think that the entire prehistoric stream was of this character, clear and swift in its graveled channel before man-made erosion filled it with silt. Now it is never clear again after its confluence with the muddy Chama River.

Starting limpidly up under the snowy peaks of southern Colorado, the Chama, reinforced by rushing mountain brooks, has soon cut through red sandstone in Apache Canyon and become heavy with reddish silt. Below the village of Abiquiu, sitting aloof on its hill, the Chama is roiled with mud that it dumps into the main stream at Española.

The Rio Grande then flows along a meandering channel through a widening valley cut by numberless arroyos that are either desert dry or running in flash floods from the mountains. The principal silt-bearers are the Galisteo from the east and the Jemez and Rio Puerco from the west. The Jemez comes sparkling from the center of the Jemez range and slices its way through strata of sandstone and volcanic deposits colored like the rainbow. But when it enters the

Rio Grande it is foul with mud. In its middle course the Rio Grande lives up to the name the Spanish gave it: Rio Bravo (Fierce River). Although it is reduced to a trickle in dry weather, melting snows or heavy rains may swell it into a raging torrent that inundates farms and towns. Even Albuquerque has seen cloudbursts that reduced shining real estate developments to soggy ruin. Run-off is slow because silt has aggraded the river bed and waterlogged it for a hundred miles. Towns in the lower valley have their own enemy in the Rio Puerco, Dirty River, whose name pictures well the load of silt it brings from the western slopes of the Jemez range.

A distinctive feature of New Mexico's landscape is the *bolson*. This Spanish word means money-bag, and geologists have adopted it to describe an enclosed valley, dead as the Dead Sea, with no tributary streams and no outlet. In some cases, as on the San Augustine Plains south of the Datil Mountains, there is a fine stand of grass in good years. In others, the drying waters have left basins of salt or gypsum where nothing will grow. There are salt lakes east of the Manzano range. And farther south lies the Jornada del Muerto, Journey of the Dead, where many Spaniards perished. Another bolson, the Tularosa Basin, cradles the White Sands, gypsum beds whose deadly glitter, snow-white but bone-dry, was a fitting background for the first atomic explosion.

Such basins have been true wastelands. But New Mexico, newly eager to turn her liabilities into assets as tourist attractions, advertises the White Sands widely. Dr. Calvin has suggested that the entire Tularosa Basin might be set aside as an outdoor museum for the study of the panorama of Southwestern flora and fauna with a bit of archæology thrown in.

Many of these features of the New Mexico landscape may be traced to an age-long drought after Sandia Man's

time. The climate may have cooled off then. Geologists estimate that snow and timberlines were a thousand feet or so
lower then than now. Pine and cedar then grew on the
mountain's lower slopes, and many of our bare mesas were
wooded. It is likely that the line, now near Socorro, where
the typical northern piñon and juniper yield to mesquite
and creosote bush was farther south. And when precipitation was heavier the rivers were certainly longer and
deeper. Creeks that now run only in flood or disappear in
sand were then permanent rivers. Only so could the land
have supported the huge herds of herbivorous beasts that
Sandia Man and Folsom Man killed with their flint points.

Then everything changed. Over the ages rainfall lessened; rivers narrowed, shortened, or dried up altogether.
The prehistoric beasts disappeared. It has been suggested
that man, always a greedy hunter, slaughtered so many tender calves that he eliminated whole breeds. But any New
Mexican knows that a prolonged drought can kill off anything. The only large animal to survive was the bison, but
he persisted only as a smaller type and with less hornspread. The horse, that long-haired, four-toed racer, was
seen no more until the Spaniards brought in his distant relative, also an Asiatic original. Some Navajos say their people
knew the prehistoric horse, but this myth finds no scientific
endorsement.

Through those long ages of drought, man, always
tougher than animals, survived. Such earlier types as archæologists guess Sandia Man and Folsom Man to have been had
interbred with later arrivals from the north, and so evolved
a human being not unlike the modern Pueblo. These people
lived all over New Mexico as the Spaniards knew it in their
most grandiose period. From northern Colorado and Utah
south into Chihuahua and Sonora, from the Gulf of Mexico
to the Gulf of California, we find traces of people who
were learning to make things. Everything they left, show-

ing steady improvement from good to better to best, indicates people of intelligence, inventiveness, and adaptability. Above all, they had phenomenal endurance. The land they roamed did not make for an easy life.

Their New Mexico was the semi-arid mountain and desert country we know. Below timberline the mountains bear a fine stand of conifers, dark and ever green, set off by patches of evanescent quaking aspens whose color follows the seasons from the spring's pale green to the golden yellow of autumn and winter's silver gray. Where water is scarce, piñon and juniper grow sturdy though not tall. These are New Mexico's colors: dark and light green, varied by gray in chamiso and cactus and set against rocks more vivid than the plants. And over-all, of course, and unforgettably, the unexcelled blueness of the sky.

In all the sierras some canyons carry water. Most of them are dry except in flood time, when they bring down rocks that the waters deposit as waterworn stones, coarse gravel, and fine, soft sands. Broken slopes that roll down to the rivers are commonly called mesas in New Mexico, though the true mesa, as its name implies, is flat on top and has steep sides.

Where the streams form permanent rivers, the valleys have fed many tribes of men fairly well on native plants; have fed them even better when men learned to irrigate. Wherever the soil accumulates, it is rich. Mountain canyons are leafy with alder, willow, and mountain cottonwood, and are starred with exquisite flowers and ferns. Deer disappear into thickets, squirrels chatter, bluebirds flash. On the lower terraces quail whirr in the aromatic chamiso and take on all the colors of the land. The river bottoms are shaded by stately cottonwoods and come alive, twice a year, with migrating water fowl. In the hottest areas mesquite grows into a tree giving a lacelike shade, and yucca holds up its tall candlelike white blooms. Such soil produces everything that a temperate climate can, but only where water can be put upon the land.

Altogether, New Mexico was to prove a land where men could live well if they learned to respect water and to use it sparingly, to deal fairly with good soil, and to lay by for the inevitable years of drought. How succeeding peoples have worked out these problems over two thousand years is our story.

FIRST SETTLERS

For ages impossible to calculate accurately, men roamed the wide Southwest, living on roots and berries, seeds and nuts. They were hunters too, but their flint points were cruder than those made by their progenitor, Folsom Man. In time some genius thought of grinding seeds on rough stones. Perhaps a man invented the metate and mano, grinders that have kept the Indian woman in stooping servitude ever since. But more likely a woman thought of saving seeds for next year's planting: only dauntless women could have held off hungry mates and squalling brats from edible hoards. Stone-lined storage cists have been found, especially in the Cochise Mountains of southeastern Arizona, and their builders have been called Seed Gatherers.

The most important seed was maize. It was long believed that corn came north from Mexico about A.D. 700. But in 1949 two Harvard students excavating in the Bat Cave near the San Augustine Plains in New Mexico came upon tiny cobs. No thicker than a pencil and less than two inches long, they were unmistakably corn; up to 1950, 766 examples had been studied and dated. It is now believed that the Indian's sacred plant was known in New Mexico as early as 2000 B.C., by when it was probably being planted, tended, and garnered.

When they had corn to hoe, men began to build permanent homes. The prehistoric farmers, like many today, built a granary before they built a house, but by the time the Southwesterner was really settled he had dug and roofed another circular pit and had a home. The mounds that have grown up over these pit houses are found all over the area from south of Utah's Great Salt Lake, across southern Colorado, in the San Juan and Rio Grande drainages in New Mexico, along Arizona's Gila and Little Colorado and their tributaries, as far as the Colorado to the west, and southward into Chihuahua.

The growth of pines varies so much between wet and dry years that cut trees may be dated by their rings, and beams have been found that were cut as early as A.D. 217. The dry air of the Southwest has preserved other evidences of man's slow but sure conquest of his environment. The ancients provided well for their dead, and burials reveal and help to date developing techniques. Basketry led to pottery; the first pots were mud-daubed baskets; then pots were built up of coils of mud; and finally they were refined into polished, painted bowls and ladles. Weapons changed and grew tougher and more accurate through the years; and ornaments of stone and bone were enhanced by the turquoise so typical of New Mexico and so like the sky's blue.

Dr. Marie Wormington, whose *Prehistoric Indians of the Southwest* gives many fascinating data, believes that the men wore the jewels. She draws a depressing picture of the women, who went unadorned and cut off their hair to weave with while the men kept theirs long and well-combed —we see the comb beside male skeletons. Dr. Wormington also suggests that the greatest advance was owing not to corn, but to the humbler though more exacting bean. You cannot go off and leave a bean patch as you can a corn field. And beans yield even more than corn of the protein on which civilizations are built. The bean ranks as one of the sacred plants along with corn, squash, and tobacco. But it is ceremonially celebrated only by the Hopis, in an archaic rite of extraordinary beauty.

Archæologists have studied and dated every find and

1 *The White Sands are gypsum dunes.*

CAPLIN AND THOMPSON, OLD ALBUQUERQUE

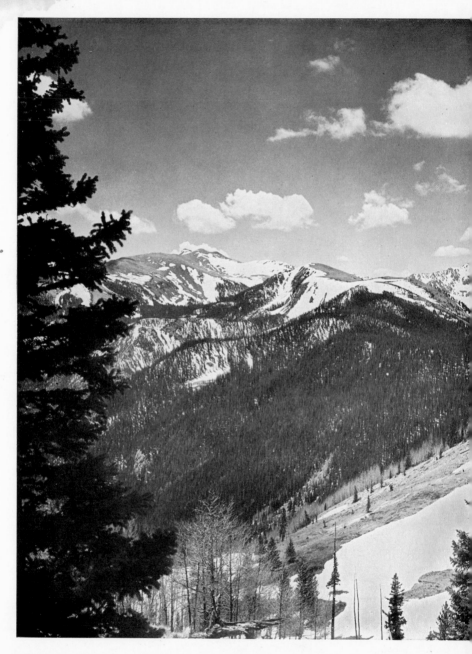

2 *Wheeler Peak rises regally above Taos pueblo.*

written a whole library on the details of pre-Pueblo life. For the casual observer, the arresting fact is that more than one thousand years of human development have been preserved in artifacts buried in the dry dust of New Mexico's ruins, but most miraculously in the customs of twentieth-century Indians who, in scores of ways, live and think and worship as their remote ancestors did.

The forebears of the Pueblo farmer of today scratched the ground with a stick and planted. Some prehistoric Indians dug little ditches near the streams, but the first remarkable irrigation systems were those of the Hohokam, a Pima word meaning Those Who Have Vanished. In the Salt River valley of Arizona, students have uncovered 150 miles of well-platted canals indicating superior intelligence and stability. Dating the work of the Hohokam is difficult because they built with mesquite and cottonwood, whose rings are not reliable guides as are pine rings. But their pottery seems contemporary with pre-Pueblo work of about A.D. 700.

The Hohokam made an interesting fusion with a people from the north, called Salado because they lived by that river whose name means salty. They had moved out of cliff houses and into the valley because of a dire drought between 1277 and 1299; niggardly growth of tree rings proves this clearly. There the two peoples lived side by side for centuries, keeping their customs distinct. The Hohokam cremated their dead; the Salado buried theirs. Hohokam pots are not large; a Salado jar has been found with a capacity of thirty gallons.

The Salado built with adobe poured in layers and then plastered with caliche, a hard native lime. This technique produced the magnificent structure first described by Father Eusebio Kino, a seventeenth-century Jesuit, who called it La Casa Grande, The Big House. Even in ruins its four-storied bulk looms out of the desert so grandly that it should have been spared the hideous wooden shed the Park Service has built to protect it. Some archæologists venture to guess that the Casa Grande may have been the center of an autocracy such as ruled the Aztecs, Toltecs, and Maya of Mexico. If so, it is the only indication of dictatorship uncovered in Southwestern archæology. All other evidences indicate a life in which no man was better fed than another and in which superiority was an individual attainment and never hereditary.

It has been guessed that a Salado group may have wandered far enough from the Salt River valley to settle on the Galisteo in New Mexico. For this there is no material evidence, but excavations in the Mogollon Mountains have uncovered a kiva that may link the Arizona folk with pre-Pueblo people developing farther north.

It would be hard to imagine a more delightful place to seek a missing link than a University of Chicago site at Pine Lawn, near Reserve, New Mexico, where the digs are shaded by aromatic conifers and one can catch a trout for supper. The few roads across the Mogollon range are snowbound in winter and subject to summer washouts. But between times a well-graded highway offers stupendous vistas as a car swoops around hairpin turns revealing wide green slopes, craggy primeval canyons, and sky-high blue peaks. This is the mountain wilderness whose streams drain finally into the Gila, Ross Calvin's "River of the Sun."

On one of the Gila's tributaries, the Mimbres, lived a mysterious people whose pottery—thin, balanced, and exquisitely colored and decorated—is so fine that it has been compared to the best Greek work. Douglas and d'Harnoncourt, in *Indian Art of the United States*, find it individual enough to be the work of one man. Archæologists say it is too widespread for that, but certainly Mimbres pottery is the work of one school. Its conventionalized bugs, birds, animals, and imaginative monsters show not only perfection of craft but also very sophisticated humor. Mary Jane Colter of the Harvey System has copied them on dishes where all may see them.

Peoples easier to trace into the modern world were called the Anasazi (The Ancient Ones) by the Navajos, who knew their ruins well and speculated about them. At Mesa Verde, Aztec, and Chaco Canyon archæologists have traced their whole course from pit houses to great apartment dwellings, from nomadic clans to urban dwellers. By A.D. 1000 these pre-Pueblo peoples were living in true cities.

With city life came civilization. Agriculture produced enough for all and winter leisure gave time for artistic expression. The best work of the great prehistoric period is equal to that of any Stone Age people. As populations grew, government became more centralized and priesthoods may have forced an almost theocratic state. But life was basically democratic, as may be deduced from the modern pueblos, where customs still observed and rites still practiced indicate an unbroken line of descent from the ancients. This unique situation makes New Mexico a paradise for both archæologist and ethnologist and provides material for the accurate dioramas that are so helpful a feature of the Park Service museums at Mesa Verde, Aztec, and Chaco Canyon.

These three great centers of pre-Pueblo living were occupied concurrently and abandoned, in the order given, during the thirteenth century. Chaco Canyon was the last to be deserted. Its people apparently drifted westward onto the Pajarito (Little Bird) Plateau, and on into the Rio Grande valley. Visitors may readily visit these splendid ruins in the order of their desertion.

Mesa Verde, as its name states, is a green tableland forested with piñon and juniper varied by the taller ponderosa pine and Douglas fir. Good cover for mule deer, foxes, coyotes, and bobcats. During the tourist season few wild creatures appear near the roads, but the traveler may glimpse a deer and can always see the flicker of sun and shadow and patches of brilliance in Indian paintbrush, pentstemon, and lupine. The mesa is slashed deep by numberless canyons, some with water, more without, all of the soft sandstone and limestone that wind has eroded into caves. Here are the dwellings, pale ghosts of cities four stories high with watchtowers, retaining walls, and many round kivas. Seen across a green canyon, Balcony House, Spruce Tree House, and the noblest, Cliff Palace, seem lived in or only just deserted.

Thousands of people lived here, farming in the canyons, lugging food and water up the cliffs in baskets or jars slung on tumplines; the men weaving, the women making pottery; all invoking good and fending off evil by kiva ceremonies. Their best pottery, with black designs on gray, is excellent; they used dyes in their weaving, and they left a profusion of jewelry. People with so much time for adornment were living well.

In 1276, as tree rings have proved, drought began. For twenty-four years each year's rings are tighter and narrower. Even a modern farmer would be put out of business by such a drought. People dependent upon flash floods and underground water were starved out. So they left Mesa Verde. Probably a few at a time, carrying burdens and babies, they moved off seeking water. Some may have become the ancestors of the modern Hopi. Others—judging by pottery remains—joined related Anasazi in the San Juan valley of New Mexico.

There they built a city that was miscalled Aztec by some reader of Prescott's *Conquest of Mexico* who did not know that these were a different people. The misnomer has stuck. These ruins center in an apartment house of five hundred rooms, largely excavated. Its solid outer wall and inner rooms, arranged in steplike tiers, are built of stone that had been carried fifteen or twenty miles; beams came from farther away. But the workers were not only burden-bearers; they were also architects who planned well, first-rate stonemasons, and decorators with a sense of form and design. Some walls still show colored stones laid in decorative courses, and some inner doors are fitted with reed curtains like split-bamboo shades.

Aztec's most impressive building is a kiva so huge that it must have been a center of elaborate ceremonialism. It is unique in having small rooms around the main chamber, which has a platform at its north end. Altogether that big kiva inspired a young archæologist to an unfortunate job of remodeling it into something resembling an Elks Lodge room. But aside from this monstrosity the ruin is vivid with a sense of lives lived there. These people, too, cultivated the soil, and they had a good water supply from the San Juan River. They were good craftsmen and traders. Their jewelry includes California shell, Utah and New Mexico turquoise, and even bronze bells from Mexico. But like Mesa Verde, this center was abandoned because of drought.

Early in the thirteenth century, Aztec's inhabitants began to drift westward; they may have joined related clans in Chaco Canyon. These centers had been in contact: Chaco Canyon types of material underlie Mesa Verde ware at Aztec. So Chaco Canyon was the first site to be settled as well as the last to be deserted; rings in the beams indicate that the last inhabitants moved away about 1300. Because they turned up finally in the Rio Grande valley there is a clear connection between the Anasazi culture and that of the modern Pueblos.

The first drifters into Chaco Canyon saw, as we see today, a wide shallow valley cut into the polychrome desert. In spots it is streaked with rose and ocher and with green too pale to be quite real; in others it is marked by left-over cones of darker, harder stuff. The Chaco was then, as it is now, a river flowing only with windblown sand, but under hard rains it can roar with a rush of waters that have dug deep tributary canyons. Before the white man's flocks and herds overgrazed and eroded the land, many underground pools were retained for the corn to reach. As the Hopis still do, those prehistoric farmers twirled holes in the sand with pointed sticks, dropped in the corn, and held the moisture by constant hoeing, using hoes with stone blades.

The Chaco Canyon people lived in small houses strung along the canyon for thirty miles, as well as in the splendid communal dwellings in the canyon. These could have housed ten thousand people; probably no more than five or six thousand lived there at any one time. The safest method of computing population fails at Chaco Canyon, where few burials and no evidence of cremation have been found. What the Southwestern ancients did with their dead remains an unsolved mystery, though Dr. Gerhardt von Bonin, professor of anatomy at the University of Illinois, suggests that bones of people as ill-fed as the pre-Pueblos would have disintegrated completely. Dr. Bonin bases this tentative theory on one summer's work at Pine Lawn.

Chaco Canyon's largest ruin is Pueblo Bonito, with eight-hundred rooms and thirty kivas, the largest apartment house constructed up to then or until New York arrived independently at the same idea in 1882. D-shaped Pueblo Bonito offers a blank outer face and is terraced down to the inner court. This fortresslike style is still hinted at by modern pueblos.

The overwhelming wonder of Chaco Canyon is its stonework, comparable at its best to the work of modern masons with stone tools. It shows artistry, too, as though the builder had stepped back to consider what would look best as well as be most durable. Most provocative in every way is Chetro Ketl, a super kiva like the one at Aztec and as inexplicable. The University of New Mexico, in excavating, has happily left it unrestored. Kivas and living rooms have yielded a mass of material now on view at the University in

Albuquerque and the State Museum in Santa Fe. This includes cotton blankets colored with vegetable dyes, pottery, basketry, and jewelry. Some of the finest bits have been found in wall crypts so cleverly plastered over that only chance has uncovered them. Among them are ceremonial objects like those in use today, notably *tablitas*, headdresses worn by women in the dances.

All the finds at Chaco Canyon reflect a life probably as good as men of any age could have achieved without metal. It is easy to think of prehistoric Indians as primitive, but they created a centralized government that did not preclude democracy and that lasted more than twice as long as the United States has endured to date.

The likeliest reason for the evacuation of Chaco Canyon is, as usual, drought, though imaginative theorizers have guessed at boredom or a mass scare induced by a plague of witches. The people left their homes in the broad Chaco Canyon, and after many years and many settlements came onto a forested plateau on the east flank of the Jemez Mountains, which Dr. Edgar L. Hewitt, who directed the first excavations there, called the Pajarito Plateau.

Driving along the wide highway from Santa Fe to the atomic city of Los Alamos, one can see how the plateau lies. In sublime quietude the peaks lift their deeper blue against the sky's clarity. The patches of bright green, like lawns, are aspen groves, and those rough, rocky knuckles thrusting toward the Rio Grande divide leafy canyons wherein tiny streams live as long as they can before they are buried in sand. Between peaks and valley the plateau of eight-thousand-foot altitude is studded with lime and sandstone mesas. It offered excellent living: water for irrigation in the canyons, conifers and aspens for building, and many caves already hollowed out in the friable volcanic tuff, which could be readily shaped and dressed to build rooms in front of the caves.

All around the Jemez range's roughly circular perimeter are such cliffs, stratified in terra cotta red, sulphur yellow, and dusty white often topped by dark basalt. It is the archæologists' exhaustless laboratory, and they have located hundreds of ruins ranging in style from the simplest single-room houses to the apartment dwellings at Puyé and Rito de los Frjioles (Creek of the Beans).

The Puyé ruins are owned by the Pueblo of Santa Clara, whose people speak Tewa, probably the tongue their ancestors spoke at Puyé. Santa Clara Indians often recognize artifacts discovered at those ruins, but dislike to talk about things that may have been sacred to their ancestors. South of Puyé are other towns with musical Tewa names: Tsankowí, Otowí, Tsheregé. Then the mesa is rent by a deep canyon wherein lie the most famous and most studied cliff dwellings of the Pajarito Plateau. The Rito de los Frijoles flows in the canyon. The ruins—guarded and expounded by the National Park Service—are called the Bandelier National Monument after their first student, Adolph Bandelier, a Swiss archæologist who visited them in the 1880's.

This canyon, not more than half a mile wide, never less than two hundred feet deep, and only six miles long, was a perfect homesite. The stream, fed by springs near the Jemez crest, sparkles in sunny spots, quiets itself in pools where trout glint against shining pebbles, and carries an ample flow for small-scale irrigation. Tall dark pines stand stately above thickets of willow, alder, and chokecherry. Raspberry and gooseberry bushes grow underneath, and strawberry plants carpet the ground. Deer and rabbits like such thickets, and birds nest there. The ancient people overlooked no useful plant or animal. They knew all the edible leaves and roots, as well as mint and watercress for flavor and many plants for conjuring or curing.

The canyon's south wall is a steep slope on which trees

grow. The north wall is as sheer as though a knife had cut through the yellow and white tuff, and as smooth as finished masonry. In places tuff cones, like tents, stand away from the cliff; in others the wall has fallen in a long talus slope. The cliff itself is potted with caves that the people had dug out and walled in to make homes. The whole settlement, strung along the cliff, was called Tyounyi. Petroglyphs scratched into the stone indicate the homes of clans, many of which persist in the modern pueblos—Bear, Sun, Water, Snake. On the canyon's floor is the ruin of an unfinished three-story circular dwelling. Many kivas indicate an elaborate ceremonial life. The largest and most interesting kiva is set into a wide arched recess, the Ceremonial Cave, two hundred feet above the canyon's floor. It can be reached only by modern pole-ladders and steps cut in the rock. The aboriginal approach has been lost.

Many other trails are known. Shallow hand and foot holes in the sheer cliff, barely negotiable by a shod modern, lead to the mesa above. The mesa itself it crossed by miles of trails—sometimes worn hip-deep by padding moccasins—that connected this tribe with the rest of the Indian world. From Colorado to Mexico and east and west, these trade routes can be traced one thousand miles or more.

We know well the ancient life of the Rito de los Frijoles from Bandelier's novel, *The Delight Makers*. First published in 1890, this is an absorbing romance accounting for the pueblo's desertion by a combination of feuds and witches at home and enemies without. Frijoles Canyon, like the other great prehistoric centers, was abandoned before historic times; but here, drought does not seem a likely cause.

The migration from the Pajarito Plateau into the Rio Grande valley was marked by a general decline. Building became poorer, pottery more careless in form and design; all standards appear to have been lowered. No reasons for this decline have been established. Perhaps old women or jittery leaders were fleeing haunted spots; the people may have had rows, as modern pueblos do, and split up in a huff. The occupied area was gradually narrowed to the Rio Grande drainage, with offshoots—by way of Laguna, Acoma, and Zuni—to the Hopi villages. These were the pueblos the Spaniards found inhabited in 1540.

All Pueblo people are of common ancestry, but they speak different languages or dialects that seem oddly related. The Hopis, that most peaceful folk, speak the Shoshonean language, as do the warlike Comanches; the Zunis' speech is theirs alone. In the Rio Grande area a basic tongue was diversified into several languages and dialects, much as Latin into the Romance languages. Tewa is spoken by the pueblos north of Santa Fe; Keres by those south of it along the Jemez River and—by a curious leap—in distant Acoma and Laguna. Taos and Isleta, separated by Keres and Tewa, speak a different tongue, Tiwa. People the Spanish knew as Tanos, living on the Santa Fe and Galisteo rivers, and the Piros of the Manzanos and the Socorro area have disappeared. So have the inhabitants of Pecos, except as their descendants are found among their relatives at Jemez.

Pecos—or Cicuyé, its native name—is a dull red adobe ruin set on the dull red banks of an arroyo that empties into the Pecos River. To the traveler along the highway, it looms up like a ruined castle among shrubbery. The valley is well watered; the mountains and plains offer good hunting. But anciently Pecos was easily accessible to the Pueblos' most feared enemies, the Comanches of the plains. This fact caused its final abandonment within the historic period.

Cicuyé offers the archæologist a key to the whole pre-Pueblo period. In 1916, when Alfred Vincent Kidder was excavating there for Phillips Academy at Andover, he realized that he could date all pueblo pottery by comparing it with Pecos ceramics. The harried pueblo had fallen and been rebuilt so many times that its trash heaps and crumbled rooms preserved layer under layer of potsherds in perfect order. They also yielded an unusually large number of skulls and skeletons buried in the trash heaps where digging was easiest. This custom is a boon to archæologists because pots, broken to let the spirit out, were buried with the bodies, and dating was thus made doubly sure.

Among villages, now lost, which the Spaniards knew were the Tiguez pueblos near modern Bernalillo. Of twelve named by the conquerors, one—Kuaua—has been unearthed and restored as the Coronado State Monument. Like Cicuyé, it marks a spot where archæology and history meet, but here the interest centers in certain frescoes.

In 1935, Gordon Vivian, a University of New Mexico student, was digging out a kiva. Suddenly he uncovered the painted fingers of an upraised hand and part of a ceremonial mask! It was an archæological thriller. After slow and painstaking work, excavators found that the four walls of a room eighteen feet square had been painted in earth colors: black, white, red, yellow, brown, and green. Only the east wall was too eroded to save. The other frescoes, though damaged, could be peeled off in sheets of plaster no thicker than wrapping-paper. Wesley Bliss worked out the technique that removed thirty-five layers, seventeen of them painted. These were remounted on fresh plaster, glue, and burlap. One set has been reproduced on the walls of the Hall of Ethnology in the State Museum at Santa Fe, where many Indians see it and silently nod their recognition of masks and symbols.

Even more provocative are reports of a lost fresco. In 1582, the Spaniard Espejo recorded that he had seen in one of the Tiguez pueblos a picture of the martyrdom of two Franciscans he had been searching for. In 1598, Oñate saw the same paintings and described their horrors fully. But there has been no further record. Perhaps Christianized Indians destroyed them; perhaps some still-buried ruin in the area will give up that unique painting.

More interesting as ruins are three pueblos on the slopes of the Manzano range. Officially called the Saline Pueblos because of the nearby salt lakes, they were more picturesquely named by Charles F. Lummis about 1890 as The Cities that Were Forgotten. The ruins that so impressed him were not prehistoric buildings, but seventeenth-century missions. The church towers at Quarai, rising solidly above the piñon wood, were lookouts too, from which sentinels could command the wide Estancia plain, where raiding bands of Comanches or Apaches might appear. Lummis, fresh from the green East, wrote: "Mid-ocean is not more lonesome than the plains, nor night so gloomy as that dumb sunlight." The Western eye, inured to the way that midday sunlight washes all color out, can distinguish many tones in those palely golden grasslands where in the hollows blue shadows deepen into plum-color.

Abó, in a sheltered canyon on the Manzano Mountains' south flank, may prove the most interesting as excavations go on. The mission is of handsome proportions, and its former size is attested by the numbers of cut stones that have been used to build small homes and sheep corrals in the vicinity.

Tabirá, out on the plain, is not only a ruined pueblo and a mission, but a legendary treasure-house as well. This place somehow became confused in popular imagination with the Gran Quivira that lured the Spanish conquerors off on a fruitless gold hunt. The legend has never died. Even today the Park Service superintendent at Tabirá is pestered by treasure-seekers who come with maps and deathbed confessions and—most lately—Geiger counters.

Paul A. F. Walter, in a report for the Museum of New Mexico, gave these pueblos another unforgettable name, that of his book, *The Cities that Died of Fear*. This phrase summarizes more than the fate of the Saline Pueblos. The whole pueblo world was declining; fear of the nomads was certainly one cause of their shrinking closer together. There may have been other reasons. Perhaps we shall never know. We can only guess that the last prehistoric period had prepared the way for an easy Spanish conquest; the conquered were subdued before the conquerors arrived.

III

THE WAY OF THE KACHINAS

THE PREHISTORIC Pueblos, like all peoples, based their religious beliefs on what they saw about them. According to their myths, they came not from the sea like the Greeks, nor from vast forests like the Norsemen. They imagined themselves as coming from an underworld, dark, damp, unlovely. Many Pueblos know the spot where their ancestors emerged. The tales are varied, but the Pueblos all came from below and suffered many vicissitudes on their long climb to the light. In some cases they lost children, who became the supernatural beings, *kachinas;* in others, the people's own evil led to such deformities as the Mud-Heads, masked figures who appear in the Shalako dance at Zuni, and who typify the offspring of incest. Always, after long wanderings, they reached the "middle." Many pueblos have such centers. At Zuni the Shalako begin their superb dance drama every year at the earth's very center.

As the people emerged blinking into light, they were guided by the kachinas, who taught them the true way. They were divided into clans related through the mother, or into moieties, divisions of the people known as North and South People among the Tewa; Turquoise and Squash People among the Keres. Each person had his appointed place in the scheme, and all relationships were so clearly defined that to this day relatives are greeted by special kinship terms.

The kachinas gave practical advice too: how to plant and harvest according to the moon and stars, how best to trap animals. Societies were formed for all purposes: war, hunting, growth, production, and healing. All life needed the help of everyone. The least child knew that he must keep his heart right for the people's good. Some men—and women too—who had special powers, became priests to direct the ceremonies and pray in secret.

The people's religion was founded in their origin myths and in what they had to cope with in their sunny, arid land. The best summary of the subject is Elsie Clews Parsons's *Pueblo Indian Religion.* She disproves the old idea that Indians were sun-worshippers. The sun was no deity, but it was watched and kept in its appointed track by ceremonies. The beautiful relay races at Taos in the early morning of May 3, and again on September 30, have to do with the sun's course. Visitors note how little the racers care to win as they speed back and forth from the aspen bower—delicate green in May, golden yellow in September. Stern competition is a white man's notion; Indians work together for the good of all. Stick-kick races at Taos and Zuni have a similar intent.

All Pueblos named the directions: sometimes five, counting the middle; sometimes six, including up and down. Zenith and nadir are personified in the Zuni Shalako and other dances, making six, but the number four figures importantly in the tales. As the heroes of our fairy tales fail twice and win on the third try, the Pueblo has four to go. Each direction has a special color, but these differ from pueblo to pueblo.

In a country of such impressive mountains and mesas, it was inevitable that the tribes should build legends around them as the Greeks did around Olympus, and the Jews around Ararat.

Pueblo Peak, rising so regally robed in purple above Taos, has been fiercely guarded by the people through the ages and even into the United States courts. The little Fire God of the Shalako comes from Zuni's sacred Corn Mountain. The Hopis go to San Francisco Peaks, where their kachinas live. The Tewas look toward Lake Peak in the Sangre de Cristo range, or toward summits in the Jemez Mountains; and the Keres are drawn—as who is not who lives in the Rio Grande valley?—to the oblique profile of the ever changing blue Sandias. As water is prayed for, it is held sacred too. Pueblo Peak guards the mystical waters of Blue Lake, and every August all of Indian Taos goes there for rites few white men have ever seen. Many Pueblos revere crystal springs that bubble out of rocks and run away to hide in sand. The Hopis' Shaded Water does that; and the Zunis' Shalako Spring moves so softly that it is called the Lake of Whispering Water. Indians never lack the poetic word or descriptive phrase.

Every winter certain kachinas come down from the San Francisco Peaks to dance in the Hopi villages. In midsummer they return to the sacred peaks. They are costumed with great beauty, and their symbolical appearance and withdrawal give point and significance to all life. Equally spectacular and complicated is the masked ceremony of the Shalako at Zuni. Its date, mystically determined by certain chiefs, is generally between Thanksgiving and Christmas. Houses are newly built or renovated to receive the kachinas, who vary from the slim, almost naked little Fire God to the four or five Shalakos whose eagle-feather crowns and monumental masks tower fifteen feet above their dancing feet. These, the pueblo's best dancers, have prepared themselves by prayer, fasting, ceremonial cleansing, and continence. They bear the responsibility of assuring good for all by their correct performance. Children certainly accept them as supernaturals; doubtless adults take them symbolically as Christians take many of their observances. But of reverent attention and careful observance of every detail there is no lack.

All kachina masks are sacred. Made of deerskin, buffalo hide, or cowhide, they are shaped and decorated under rigid conditions, guarded in certain homes, and "fed" with smoke, sacred meal, or the scent of food. Their number is legion. Dr. Parsons counted sixty-seven in Zuni. Doubtless there are as many in the eastern pueblos, where no outsider sees the masked dances. When a polite Indian turns back a car outside a Rio Grande pueblo or miles away from the rock of Acoma, the visitor may be sure that a masked ceremony is going on. This exclusion is due to the ban put upon all Indian ceremonies by the sixteenth-century missionaries. The Pueblos conformed outwardly, but continued the ceremonies in secret. In some cases masks are used in public dances. Buffalo- and deer-heads are worn like masks; eagle dancers are masked, as is the amusing Pecos Bull, at Jemez on August 2. The dancer with bobbing horse's head and tailed rump represents the mounted Santiago, the patron saint of medieval Spain. He, of course, appears freely anywhere. But this was miming the monks could understand. Those monstrous forms with massive beaks, horns, and fearsome rolling eyes smacked too much of devilishness.

Masked dances were not suppressed among the Hopis and Zunis because the Spaniards did not conquer them in any lasting way. When overcome, the peoples soon ejected their conquerors and went back to their heathen ways. Or to the ways of the kachinas, according to the point of view. The happy result is that we may see these marvelous masked dances, the finest in our hemisphere, perhaps the finest anywhere, in choreography, costume, steps, and especially in ritual significance.

These ceremonies are based on the legends, and their exact meanings are often obscure even to the Indians. But in general the Pueblos think of all life as interrelated and good, and of all forms of worship as right. Proselyting is inconceivable to the Pueblo, who accepts every man's faith as best for him; he will even adopt and add to his own what he likes of the proselyter's offering. Perhaps the Corn Mother, who figures in many myths, comes closest to our Jewish-Christian conception of an individualized creator.

Corn is the most sacred plant; even stripped cobs are handled reverently, and dried husks tied to the Koshare's head add their color of death to his skeletonlike ensemble. Corn, as pollen or as once-ground coarse meal, is used as Catholics use holy water. It is strewn over prayer sticks and feathers, tossed toward the sun at dawn, dropped on dead faces, rubbed on the newborn.

Birds and animals have their sacred as well as their practical uses. Buffalo- and deer-dances are prayers for good hunting, but they also explain to the game the need for their sacrifice that the people may have food. Needless slaughter is foreign to the Pueblos: they kill only for food or for ceremonial use. In such cases the killing is a rite, as when the deer is smothered with sacred meal.

The lowly, ubiquitous coyote was a legendary clown, the kind who always wins with a grin, and his swishing tail is worn in many dances. So is the tail of his cousin, the fox. The turtle's shell makes rattles, and the turtle, who likes water, is entrusted with prayers for water as in the Turtle Dance at Zia and other pueblos. The snake plays many roles, though never as a tempting devil. Its sinuous movements suggest water, and the most striking prayer for rain is the Hopi Snake Dance in August. Snake symbols are easy to identify on pottery and in decoration generally.

Birds, who fly skyward and are so beautiful and gay, give their names to many clans and provide feathers. Every dance costume includes feathers for both color and meaning. Many feathers used ceremonially are easy to identify. Turkey and eagle tails ray stiffly out; bluebird, duck, and hawk are familiar. Much of the cloudy white is the down of eagles kept in cages. Many a tiny tip set in a headdress or tied to a prayer stick may be understood only by the shaman who uses it. The value of feathers may be linked with the little-known habits of certain birds or their part in legend; but it must be obvious that they lend fleetness to a runner or waft a prayer to the home of the gods.

Throughout the pueblo world prayer sticks are used, except at Taos where only loose feathers appear in ritual. Three or four inches long and only a bit thicker than a pencil, the prayer stick must be made from the prescribed wood taken in the right way, often only by the shaman. Each quill or downy tuft tied to the stick or floating from it on a cord, every bit of paint, even the twisting of the yucca string, must be meticulously right, just as the kachina taught. Prayer sticks have many uses. They may represent pleas for future good, appreciation for good received, or an out-and-out bargain. "I plant the prayer stick; you bring on the rain." Perhaps they serve all these purposes. Like sacred meal and pollen, prayer sticks are found in sacred spots, are thrown into holy springs, hidden in house rafters, planted in the corn field, buried with the dead.

Prayer sticks adorn the altars, and altars are of infinite variety. The most elaborate are set up for ceremonies, usually in kivas or society rooms where the outsider may not go. But correct altars are sometimes shown in the Harvey hotels at Albuquerque, Santa Fe, or the Grand Canyon. One easily recognizes the medicine bowl filled with water for asperging, the painted kachinas, the sun, lightning, cloud, or rain symbols. Often there is a sand-painting on the floor and a path of sacred meal to lead or lure the kachina to the place. Indians making paths of sacred meal and sprinkling it may be noted by any watchful visitor. Shalako are sprinkled as they pass the rows of spectators; paths are clearly marked at the Snake Dance; the game killed in the Deer Dance is sprinkled. Often fetiches stand by the altar: little clay or stone figurines of birds or beasts tied up with feathers and turquoise and shell beads. The stone lions of Cochiti, now almost worn away by weather, still serve as fetiches for the hunt. In the Hopi and Zuni villages, known as the West, fetiches are generally considered most potent. They are worn as charms and are placed on the altars, which are also adorned with kachina dolls made to represent the gods as the masked dancers do. These dolls are carved by men from waterborne cottonwood roots, and they serve as children's toys as well as altar ornaments. All these things are highly conventionalized and must be made precisely as the kachina taught. Only so can they bring the good.

A Jemez Indian told Dr. Parsons: "If our customs and medicine are good, they have power. If we have power we bring rains, good crops, and health." All is postulated on good: having a good heart with no ugly thought, as well as a body cleansed both inside and out. The medicine may be medication, but it is also the form, the correctness. The power comes—as in other highly developed faiths—from making and keeping contact with supernatural good. The ancient Pueblo had no sense of sin; the Catholic missionaries labored valiantly to give him that. Modern psychologists are more inclined to approve the effect of his ancient beliefs.

The making of the altar and other preliminary cere-monies may take days; they are secretly performed in the kiva or the society chamber. They include ceremonial smoking, relating of suitable legends, chanting, and the asperging and dressing of dancers for their public appear-ance. This is the dance to which visitors flock. When it is due, the correct standard is raised above the kiva: a tall pole topped with a ball painted white, black, and turquoise, and adorned with parrot and eagle feathers, embroidered sash, or coyote skin.

With the dancers comes their chorus; men who chant to drum accompaniment and make gestures suggestive of falling rain. The music seems simple, though it is often complicated with three or even four rhythms carried at once by chanters, drummers, dancers, and in gesture. Trained musicians faint before this feat. Different dances require different music, often mimetic. Bull-roarers swung by a strong man make the sound of wind; thunder-stones struck together should start a rolling in the clouds; lightning-frames shoot in and out in colored zigzags; bone whistles, flutes, and rattles produce suggestive sounds. Instead of beating on drums, the musician may beat on a rolled sheepskin or inverted basket or rub one notched stick over another. Everything is to inform the supernaturals that rain is wanted. Most rituals include prayers for rain, from which all good comes: food, health, and the tribe's increase.

The ancient Pueblos' calendar was worked out by the shamans and adjusted at need. Most ceremonials are still dated thus, to the utter confusion of tourists. Each season had its appointed ritual. Between times, or when war, disease, or other evil threatened, shamans or societies made retreats to pray and fast. The societies varied from pueblo to pueblo, but there were few men who did not belong to one. Many belonged to several, and in some places women were society members.

The Pueblo's personal life was standardized as rigidly as the year. No room for individual vagary, none for genius or revolt. This way of thinking is breaking down, but so slowly that use of the present tense is still correct in discussing it.

The child is born into his mother's clan or becomes a member of his father's moiety. In the West, where clan predominates, he is named by his mother's sister, and her brothers are more important to him than his own father. This system weakens toward the East, where European customs have strengthened the father's position and the boy takes his

father's name. In every pueblo the baby learns songs and
dance rhythms as grandfather jounces him and tells stories
to explain why the crow is black, how the rabbit turned
white, and how the old coyote fooled everybody. These
tales are infused with Pueblo humor, ranging from subtle
allusion to vulgar slapstick.

At puberty, boys go into the kiva for training. All boys
must learn ritual: only so will they be able to do their share
in society or moiety. They must also prove their manhood.
Girls learn from their mothers, especially corn-grinding,
which is a ceremonial as well as practical accomplishment.
Beautiful songs accompany the swing of the woman's body
over the metate. Women may serve in societies, especially
in the West; they take part in most dances, their slow
shuffle, without raising the feet, symbolizing woman's contact with mother earth. This makes a fine contrast to the
man's insistent pounding. Children learn to dance by dancing. Tiny ones, fresh from modern schools, but correctly
accoutered and serious, keep the perfect rhythm all day, un-
tiring.

As they grow, children take part in old rites of exorcism
before planting, in ceremonial rabbit drives, and in kick-
stick races. They learn dances to bring success in the hunt
or in war.

In all Pueblo life and thought the most pervasive and persistent conception is that of group good. Morality consists
in conformity to custom and correctness in performance.
Neglect or error will bring evil to the people. The idea of
individual sin or reward for individual good does not enter
into Pueblo thought. A man's worth is computed not by
what he has amassed for himself, but by what good he has
done his group.

These customs and beliefs—the ways of the ancients—
have survived into the middle of the twentieth century to
give the individual Pueblo personal integration and security

within his group. Certainly all have not been true to their best ethic, any more than all Christians have. But the Pueblo's confidence in what the kachinas taught has given him notable dignity, spiced with humor, and the strength to adjust to many changes without losing his inner verities.

IV

CHANGING PUEBLO LIFE

⊂ꓱ AT FIRST glance, the fascination of pueblo life lies in its seeming changelessness. In a sense, of course, this is true. But the oldest ruins show that life was in a state of flux even when they were occupied. Elsie Clews Parsons takes two hundred pages of text to describe interpueblo borrowings owing to travel, trade, intermarriage, and imitation. The Pueblos are a flexible people; they often show themselves more realistic about inevitable change than their white friends do.

One young student, determined that pottery types must be kept pure, scolded a Santa Clara potter for using a design that belonged to another pueblo. She answered: "This is too my design. My sister-in-law from over there in Zia, she gave it to me." John Adair, collecting data for his excellent study, *Navajo and Pueblo Silversmiths*, traced designs and methods from whites to Pueblo to Navajo and back again.

Even religious rites, the least alterable element in any culture, have been freely exchanged. Zunis perform a Navajo Yeibechai dance better, many think, than the Navajos do it. Pueblos exposed to Comanche raids learned the Comanche War Dance as the best medicine against their enemies. Dr. Parsons relates that Taos once sold its Elk Dance to a Nambe chief for ten turquoise, five red beads, twelve dance-blankets, twelve deerskins, and the promise that the dance would always be correctly performed. But even correct performance has been subject to modifications, most noticeably in dance costumes. Originally garments of daily wear, these naturally were a mélange of many tribes' dress; and now they are heavy with manufactured bells, buckles, and beads taken over from whites during four hundred years.

In the westernmost pueblos Hopi and Zuni remain much alike; they have influenced the Keres pueblos of Acoma and Laguna, and to a lesser degree Tiwa Isleta. Taos, farthest north, shows so many Apache, Comanche, and Ute traits that Taoseños have been called Plains Indians living in a pueblo. They show, however, the influence of the Tewas to the south, and Tewas and Keres have affected each other. The best example of this interinfluence is in the curing societies and the priestly functions. Curing, everywhere important, is a group function in the West and pretty well into the Keres pueblos. But in Taos the shaman may cure through his individual dreams and powers, as the Plains Indians cured. The intervening Keres and Tewas partake of both systems.

The extreme test of Pueblo adaptability came with the Spanish conquerors, who brought a new government, a new religion, and a whole set of new superstitions. A less pliant people might have been overwhelmed. But not the supple, subtle Pueblos. They accepted what fitted into their preconceptions and sidestepped what did not. With essential and mystical practices they retreated into the kivas, to undisclosed shrines, and especially into a secretiveness that persists to this day. The youngest Pueblo child has learned not to tell a white person anything. A supervisor, visiting a schoolroom in Santo Domingo, inquired gaily: "And what did you children have for breakfast this morning?" The class leader, a bright-eyed imp, hissed a swift incomprehensible phrase, undoubtedly the Keres for "Clam up!" Not one word could be got out of any of them. What would have been merely an adult's stupid condescension to white children was inexcusable prying to the little Pueblos. Eth-

nologists report that many intelligent informers, even college graduates, show fear of divulging sacred matters. Talk
lessens power; revealing a rite may destroy its force. It is
not surprising that lacunæ exist in our knowledge; what is
amazing is that we know so much.

The Spanish thought they had converted the Pueblos;
they got them to build churches, attend services, and bring
their children for baptism and even confirmation. But the
Pueblos were accepting the new faith with discrimination.
They rejected the conception of a personalized, omnipotent
God; the idea of sin punishable by torment in an after life;
and especially belief in vicarious atonement. Christ the Re-
deemer does not enter strongly into Catholicism as practiced in the pueblos. Few gory crucifixes appear in their
churches. And such self-torture as they saw Spanish flagel-
lantes inflict struck them as silly. Saints, however, offered
no jolt to the Pueblo mind. Like kachinas, saints had been
human and were now transfigured into supernaturals with
special powers. Carrying the saint's statue out to bless the
fields was in the kachina tradition.

The ancient Pueblo calendar was easily adjusted to that
of the Christians, which was based, after all, on the same
seasonal changes. Solstice ceremonies and hunting dances
belong to midwinter, just as Christmas does: they turn the
solar system back toward light and life. At Taos, after
Christmas Eve vespers in the pueblo, the priest returns to
town and the pueblo to its old ways. Tall bonfires, flaming
skyward from the terraced roofs, redden the snow where
brown bodies stamp and shake their bells in the dance. In
the Keres pueblos and at Isleta, wise Catholic priests permit
buffalo- and deer-dances in the churches. Nothing in New
Mexico is more dramatic than the painted figures wrapping
themselves in blankets and approaching the crèche with
bowed heads and offerings ready. Twelfth Night is in-
auguration day for the newly elected pueblo governors, and

the people observe the ancient custom of throwing gifts from the housetops to the dancers below. Easter, Christian season of rebirth, is celebrated by many pueblos with their corn dances which also honor the patron saint on his holy day. This tolerance of pagan rites is one of the most gracious of Spanish concessions to an alien expression of the religious spirit.

In practical matters the Pueblos accepted Spanish ways without much difficulty. After a few battles they were allowed to stay in their towns, theirs now by the mercy of His Most Catholic Majesty of Spain. They built churches, as they had built their homes, with stone and adobe; but they painted pictures and carved wood as the padres directed. They cut doors in their house walls and learned to make chimneys. And they gratefully accepted domestic animals. Moccasins were more durable with cowhide soles, sheep pelts were soft to sleep on, and wool was easy to weave. The black wool dresses Pueblo women still wear in the dances replaced deerskin or cotton slips, and wool blankets were quite as warm as, and easier to make than, the old robes of twisted rabbit skin. Here enters the "blanket Indian" in the white man's blanket! Above all, the Pueblo found glass beads and shiny bells much gaudier and noisier than the old wampum, turquoise, and bones.

To facilitate gathering tribute and enlisting workers from the pueblos, Governor Castaño de Sosa ordered each pueblo to elect a governor. We like to think that manhood suffrage is an Anglo-Saxon gift to the Americas. But here it was, thirty years before the Pilgrims landed, and from imperial Spain. The Pueblos accepted the new officer as a link with the white man's government, and added ex-governors to their governing council. The Spaniards, recognizing the ancient religious leaders, called them caciques, an Arawakan word meaning chief which is still generally used.

Problems were discussed and rules made in council.

There was never any hurry; every man was given time to express his opinion fully while every other man listened respectfully. Unanimity was the desideratum; the concern of all was to avoid a sharp division or an open break. However acrimonious the feeling, no decision was final until all were convinced that a right solution had been reached. White people are always irked by these interminable council meetings and the way they leave an important matter unresolved for the moment—or the year. But this was the way of the ancients.

The Spanish governor presented each pueblo governor with a silver-headed cane. This was an acceptable badge of office because it was similar to the ritual wands of society chiefs. In 1863, when twenty pueblo governors called upon President Lincoln he gave them each another cane with his name and the date inscribed on it. These two canes are now the required badge of office; no governor is considered properly installed or empowered to act unless he has them in his possession.

So the Spaniards brought much that was good and not too hard to take. But they also brought diseases devastating to people who had no inherited immunity against them. Smallpox, which killed off five thousand Indians in the epidemic of 1780, receded only after the Indian Service enforced vaccination. Tuberculosis is still far too prevalent, as are trachoma and syphilis. Children die from measles and whooping cough, and—lacking still enough screens, sanitary privies, and clean water—dysentery kills babies every summer. Many of these afflictions are still blamed on witchcraft, not yet eradicated.

When it came to witches, the Pueblos and the Spanish understood each other well. Indians had long blamed sickness on ghosts or wrong thoughts; as a shaman could cure evil, he could cause it. The notion that any person might be a witch was European, but the Pueblos were ready to agree that evil thoughts might come from a malicious neighbor. Sticking dolls full of cactus spines in order to hurt an enemy, heeding the owl's hoot, and covering the baby's head to ward off the evil eye were quickly adopted. The monks and their converts differed only when the Inquisition tried as witches shamans who were performing ancestral rites for the general good.

So with all their changes in Pueblo living, the Spanish did not change Pueblo thinking much. The monks did their best. They established some schools. The priest at Jemez won special commendation for teaching a few of the boys to read. But the monks taught mostly doctrine; a boy knew enough if he could serve Mass and grow up to be a fiscal and collect the tithes. The Pueblos went on living as the kachinas had taught. The deep currents of life were unaffected. Group solidarity was maintained, and in it the individual found his strength.

It took the United States, with its Nordic rigidity, to begin to break down this power-giving integration. The United States, for over half a century, tried deliberately to eradicate the old customs and ways of thinking. It was an unsuccessful undertaking as planned, but it has resulted in some curious confusions and paradoxes and has made life harder for many Pueblo people.

The United States, taking over in 1846, declared the Indians citizens, confirmed them in the communal ownership of their lands, and put the Army in charge of them. The Army used Pueblos in wars against Navajos and Apaches, but did nothing to educate them. Then, in the eighties, a new policy assigned all Indians in the United States to various religious bodies, and Protestant missionaries appeared in New Mexico.

Protestants were no less convinced than Catholics that their faith, and only theirs, was God's, but they were less experienced with Indian converts and less patient with slow or partial conversions. Precipitately they invaded every phase of Indian life and demanded conformity in every particular. Thus they broke up families, divided village groups, and caused many personal problems not primarily religious. Dr. Parsons relates that a Baptist missionary, who settled in Laguna in 1851, caused a split that has never healed. Elected governor by his converts, the Reverend Samuel Gorman so alienated the unconverted that they left their village. What he left undone was finished off by a Presbyterian who arrived in 1875. Between them these pious gentlemen stirred up such dissension that the Lagunas now live in six pueblos, and many Laguna families are found in Isleta. Dr. Parsons also quotes a Hopi on missionaries. "Why," he asked, "do they come into our plazas? The plazas are for kachinas. The chapel is for Jesus." Granting that there is more than one way, the Hopi asked to be allowed to follow his way in peace. But freedom of religion had not then been construed as applying to the Indians, who were offered only the freedom to choose among Christian faiths.

This widespread invasion of privacies had consequences that might seem funny if one did not know how hurtful may be a tug of war between respected mentors. White administrators insisted upon cutting the boys' hair and required all children to wear white man's clothes. As a cropped Pueblo was not allowed to appear in certain ceremonies, this barbering might deprive a man of his right and his duty to serve his people. Most pueblos have been forced to yield on this point of hair. But in Taos, where G-string, leggings, and moccasins are orthodox male attire, dress poses a problem to this day. In his sensitive novel, *The Man Who Killed the Deer*, Frank Waters shows how trousers and heeled shoes may symbolize the struggle between old and new in Taos.

Long before the Pueblo baby can talk, he is subjected to contradictory pulls. Born into clan or moiety, he is named according to tribal custom and sprinkled with holy meal; he may then be baptized and sprinkled with holy water. As late as 1949, an infant was buried with Christian rites, but clothes, food, and toys were cast into the grave. The growing child acquires manners, learns to be quiet, uncomplaining, respectful to the old, and is taught his duty to the group. He is seldom punished, but may be shamed or ridiculed into doing right. But in the government-run Indian School he learns new myths, other morals, and a new series of shames. White teachers are often appalled at sexual knowledge shown by Pueblo children, to whom the facts of nature and the forms of the body may be interesting but are never evil. Such teachers are doubly shocked when Indian parents, appealed to, find the protest funny.

Very small children are faced with decisions that would test an adult. At the Christmas dance in Jemez in 1948, Santa Claus appeared along with the masked buffalo, deer, and antelope dancers. This was in the tradition of adding a new figure to the pantheon. But something was troubling a fourteen-year-old girl from the Catholic school. Watching her younger brother she was nervous, biting her fingers.

"I do hope," she kept saying, "he won't take a feather."

"Take a feather? Why?"

"Yes. See the old men giving the boys feathers? If a boy takes one he has to go to the kiva with the old man and join his healing society. . . . But we don't want any more of that! That's old savage stuff!"

Not many old men did well with their feathers. Three or four, stately in their blankets, left the plaza with one little boy tagging behind, but most of them, six or seven, left alone. Another day, in another pueblo, the tale might be different.

Kiva training for boys continues in the face of government schools and truant officers. Some Pueblos, like the British, believe that at adolescence a boy should be trained for a man's life by men. This means months out of school, longer for those selected for priestly discipline. Up to now most boys submit willingly. Even their mothers do not complain at having to prepare orthodox food for their sons in kiva instead of the canned meals they serve at home. Protests come from white teachers, who invoke attendance rules. But federal courts have held that the Pueblo is entitled to religious training without interference. At last the Indian is allowed freedom to choose his own ancient religion.

This attitude, long advocated by individuals and by associations for protection of Indians, became official policy when President Hoover, himself a Friend, appointed two Friends, Charles J. Rhoads and Henry Scattergood, as Commissioner and Assistant Commissioner of Indian Affairs. Military discipline was replaced by modern educational methods, uniforms were abandoned, girls were issued bright ginghams and taught to make their own dresses in any style they chose. Jails were turned into workshops or wash-houses; children were allowed to speak their own languages; and their religion was not scorned. Owing to pressure from the New Mexico Association on Indian Affairs and the Association on American Indian Affairs, Indian arts and crafts were introduced in the schools. Pottery-making was not a success; Pueblo women did not wish other pueblos to learn their techniques. Weaving, silversmithing, and woodcarving have remained regular courses and are generally taught by Indians.

Then came John Collier. Appointed Commissioner in 1932, he came from years of work for Indians and as a scathing critic of government policy. A student of anthropology, he undertook sweeping reforms. Inevitably they encountered opposition from white people who did not understand, and from Indians who always distrusted Uncle Sam's

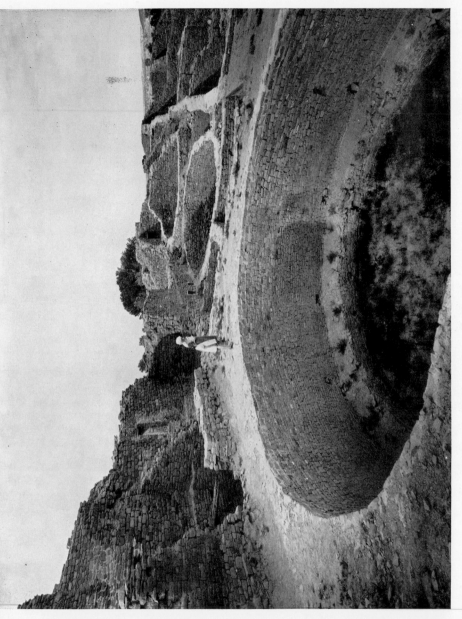

3 *The ruins at Aztec are vivid reminders of the life of the ancients.*

NEW MEXICO
STATE TOURIST
BUREAU

4 *Modern Pueblos still make good drums.*

erratic caprices and who thought that these reforms might soon pass away.

A successful policy has been that of raising boarding schools to the status of high schools and of keeping small children in schools near home, where motherly Pueblo housekeepers can help with the new language. A few textbooks were prepared for Pueblo children, and pamphlets such as *Respect for Indian Culture and Religious Freedom* were issued and presumably read. But teachers firmly rooted in our folkways are not too capable of helping children across a gap between cultures, often being unaware that such a gap exists. A modern teacher said: "Oh, well, if you're going into their *psychology!*"

Indian Service teachers' salaries are too low to attract many people willing or able to understand the Pueblo child. Many complain that their pupils are dull, sullen, unco-operative. They refuse to enter into the spirit of a game or to compete for high grades. Most baffling of all, they never jeer at a lagger; they are more likely to wait for him or to offer help. The Pueblo child has learned long before school age that the individual must act for the group. The will to win, with our traditional "and the devil take the hindmost," is hard to inculcate.

Most Pueblos finish only the six grades offered in the day school. They do as well as other children with a language handicap. Attendance sometimes as high as ninety per cent suggests that even conservative Pueblos value education, if only as protection against the outer world.

But the outer world has been winning steadily. What teachers and missionaries, backed by the full force of the United States, could not do is being gradually done by gadgets, jobs, and youthful desire to conform. Children, home from school, prefer shoes, pants, and dresses. Girls who have learned to open cans buy store goods. Kerosene lamps light the whitewashed rooms, and buckets replace *ollas*. It has got so a photographer has to bring his own moccasins and painted jar to get a picturesque shot of an Acoma woman reflected in the water hole or of a Taoseña dipping water from Taos Creek. Farmers have bought wagons and then automobiles.

The individual is taking on comforts and conveniences at a great rate. But communal ways change by slower transition. A century ago the War Chief's duties were implicit in his title. When the Spaniards gave the Pueblos horses, his function was readily extended to their care. That led to control of grazing lands and of all flocks and herds. Without a bobble, the War Chief has now taken over irrigation ditches, and it is his musical yodel that calls men out to clean them in the spring. Only his duties have changed, not the War Chief's title or dignity.

Changes are of the outer life that all can see. But there is no lack of evidence of a hidden constancy that lies deep. Taos Creek, from which young women dip their water in tin pails, flows from the sacred lake. Jemez, dominated by a shining metal watertower, keeps captive eagles on its roofs. Acomas live near their fields at Acomita, leaving only old people on their rocky mesa as guards, but on holy days they all go home. So do the progressive Santa Anas. Only an aged sentinel lives in their old pueblo; young men operate a tractor co-operatively on their rich valley lands. And all pueblos bar visitors on the days of their most sacred dances.

Any pueblo on a dance day presents a panorama of this changing pueblo life, especially in the Rio Grande pueblos, where the Catholic church is strongest. The many corn dances, held to celebrate the day of the patron saint, are typical. Mass in the mission church is conducted by friars in the habit of a medieval order, though their ways, like the Indians', are affected by modern life. Franciscans come in motor cars and wear well-shined shoes. The sermon may be in English followed by a Spanish translation. The congregation's garb reflects every prehistoric and modern age, from shell ornaments to Army issue and the permanent wave stylish in the nearest railroad town.

The day of the Indian begins when the saint has been reverently borne by a chanting procession from the church to a shrine in the plaza. Then the priests retire and interest shifts to the kivas. Above each one rises the feathered standard, brilliantly outlined against the sky. And there a man sits, immobile, patiently biding the end of the Catholic stir below. When the dancers emerge it is clear that they are the day's real meaning. Even the saint's leafy shrine, guarded by men with guns and visited at intervals by worshippers, becomes only a background for rites hallowed for the Pueblo by observance much longer than that of any Christian ceremony.

The Pueblo, humanly wise and often with a mystic wisdom too, is not overly impressed with the white man's religion as he practices it. And he suffers to see how the white man violates nature. The Pueblo has lived long in this difficult country. Deep down he knows that this spring's warm brown water depends upon rainfall and that rainfall depends upon certain rites. Young men must learn those ritual observances lest both land and people perish. He loves his land and he believes in the kachinas who have taught him to use it harmoniously. Should he, then, give up the ways of the ancients for untried ways that do not seem to work as well for their practitioners? On the whole, he thinks not.

So the Pueblo, while tolerantly practicing alien ceremonies, continues to perform the rites the kachinas taught. Not only the rain and hunting dances that outsiders are welcome to see, but many others of even deeper power. His images and myths are as vital to his thinking as the Biblical myths are to ours. We accept facts established by geologists without losing the story of Adam and Eve in the Garden. So to this mid-twentieth century the Pueblo brings old beliefs that may light his life with beauty or shadow it with fear, but that surely pervade his daily thinking. His problem is to reconcile "the ways of the ancients" with the concepts and needs of today: rain dances with farm machinery, innoculations with curing societies, old moralities with modern taboos—or old taboos with modern moralities. The dance that may impress the white onlooker as a triumph of art in step, costume, music, and choreography is to the Indian—observer as well as performer—the renewal of an ancient faith and the bulwark of his security.

THE MODERN PUEBLO

THE PUEBLO INDIAN won the right to vote in 1948, a belated recognition of the citizen status granted him by the United States a century ago. In theory he has been as free as any American to speak his mind, worship as he prefers, go where he likes, and learn what he can. But problems that have bedeviled these village Indians for centuries have been intensified, at midcentury, by the increasing need for speedier adjustment and have been complicated by the returned veteran with his rights, needs, and desires.

Pueblo Indians have served in all our wars since they were recruited about 1850 to fight Navajos and Apaches. In World War I Indians were not drafted, but a few Pueblos volunteered and brought home excited tales of the world beyond the great water. In World War II Indians were subject to the draft, and most Pueblos accepted it readily. The United States was their country; they were willing to fight for it. A few individuals tried to get exemption; some claimed religious obligations. This pleased and amused aging caciques who had feared the loss of old rites for lack of learners, and who now had novices under vow. But such cases were few. The Pueblo record, on the whole, was as good as any.

The villages sent their young men off with what protection they could, probably a dance. In Isleta such a dance could be called only by the full council, and the draft board had precipitately removed one councilman to boot camp thousands of miles away. The Indian Service, informed of the case, presented it to the proper commanding officer, who allowed the young councilman to return. The dance was held, and we won the war.

Meanwhile old men had been praying and seeing visions. A very dependable Isleta, whose son was fighting in the South Pacific, remembered that a clan headman had called on him in May 1945. The old man said nothing for a long time. Then he spoke. "I know how troubled you are. We are all troubled. For your son. For all our sons. It is bad over there, very bad. But it will soon be over. Something will come from the clouds. Maybe our old thunder gods. I don't know. But from the clouds it will come, and the fighting will end. This I know." And so it came. From the clouds.

In World War II, 1,065 Pueblo men and women served in all theaters and in all services. Twenty-five were lost; many were wounded. Those at home did well in buying bonds and in factories where their dexterity, quick eyes, and ability to learn were invaluable. A few have stayed on in factories and in cities. Most of them returned to the pueblo with its securities, practical as well as mystical.

Most of these young Indians had finished the pueblo day school before the war. A few had gone on to high school; fewer to college. But there has been a notable lack of trained technicians and professional people. The Indian Service's answer to such criticisms is that funds are inadequate.

But young Indians are being forced into modern life by the same pressures that affect young white people. Their lands are inadequate to support a growing population; they can earn more in industry than as farmers; they long to better their living conditions and to see their children advance. But they also feel the pull of their inherited traditions and tribal customs.

This paradox is sharply evident among Pueblos whose

young men are working in Albuquerque and Santa Fe as mechanics, at Los Alamos as trained technicians in many lines; quite a few have gone into selling Indian artifacts and even making a business of Indian songs and dances. But a majority retain their status in the pueblo, where they enjoy the advantages of inalienable landownership of tax-free lands, a situation not wholly enviable.

There are nineteen pueblos in New Mexico and naturally they differ in many ways, as people always differ even in fairly homogeneous groups. But they have enough similarities to allow us to consider the Pueblo people as a whole. Traditionally their governments are sacerdotal in character, dominated by shamans, generally old men who understand the ways of men and of nature and the importance of keeping men and nature in harmony. This idea underlies the Pueblo saying: "If our hearts are right, the rain will come." Such leaders are naturally influential even in the selection of elected officials as well as in every detail of daily life. The extent of this priestly control and of the younger people's struggle against it largely determines whether a pueblo is considered conservative or progressive.

Pueblo youngsters who go to college maintain a fair average. A few do notably well; several have gone on to advanced degrees and professional or technical training. But the government has been woefully slow to help the Indian of superior capabilities. Great as is the need for trained people to work with their own groups, the Pueblos have produced no doctors, dentists, or lawyers, though a few surveyors, engineers, and agronomists have graduated from agricultural colleges. In 1959 the Indian Service invested $145,000 in Indian scholarships. The tribes in New Mexico have done much better since the discovery of oil, gas, and uranium on their reservations; Navajos, Apaches, and some Pueblos have established really handsome scholarships for their young people.

Pueblo Indians, with few exceptions, are not happy in town. Though they are invited to municipal and church activities, few really throw themselves into YM or YWCA's, Scouts, Epworth Leagues, or the Youth Center. On their evenings off, they are more likely to be found strolling the streets, eating at the hamburger joints, attending the movies, dancing—always with Indians. Perhaps the other ways are too alien. Perhaps it is because few Pueblos have yet entered the white-collar jobs that lead to their being enough at ease for social acceptance. It is sadly true that Pueblos living in Albuquerque or in Santa Fe can meet the rents only in slum or near-slum areas. Naturally they prefer life in the pueblo and on their tax-free lands.

To most of us freedom from a land tax would seem wholly enviable. But both New Mexico and Arizona long denied the vote to "Indians not taxed." In fact the Indians pay all taxes except those on the communally owned lands granted them by the King of Spain and confirmed to them by the United States in 1846. This anomalous situation of U.S. citizens and inalienable lands lies at the root of the Pueblo's dilemma.

Few pueblos ever owned enough land to support the people in what we consider decency, and for generations white settlers continually encroached on both land and water rights without hindrance. Indians had no vote; nobody cared. Then New Mexico's Senator Bursum introduced into the Congress in 1922 a bill that would have confirmed the intruders in their holdings. That stirred up a public furor led by Santa Fe's artists and writers, who foresaw the doom of much beauty in craft, dance, and living, as well as a people's starvation. Ten years of struggle brought two results: the pueblo lands were saved or just compensation paid for those not deemed recoverable; and associations for the protection of Indians became unremittingly vigilant.

Plenty in the Pueblo's situation still taxes the ingenuity

and patience of his wisest and most sympathetic friends. Pueblo lands are still inadequate to meet rising standards of living or increasing populations. The Pueblo farmer has to seek seasonal work on ranches or a job in town and permit his women and children to sell pottery and turquoise along the highways. But it is never just a question of finding outside jobs. What has baffled generations of lawyers is the Pueblo's position as landowner.

Pueblo lands are inalienable, but the federal government reserves the right to supervise their management, to lease them to outsiders, and to buy or lease additional acreage for the pueblo. Each pueblo is an autonomy within New Mexico, but not subject to the state's laws. It is self-governing through a council chosen by varied forms of manhood suffrage, and with ex-governors as members. The individual Pueblo man is subject to council rulings unless he breaks a federal law. This does not make him a ward of the government, but, like any citizen who uses the federal domain, he must obey regulations governing land use. Through the years the adaptable Pueblo has managed well enough between pueblo council and federal government. But his quandary is deepened by the vote and the veteran. Politicians have come into the peaceful pueblo scene. And some veterans have acquired the white man's desire for a sharp division and a quick decision. It would be a paradox indeed if the Indian's way of long talk ending in general agreement were to be lost just as the United Nations are trying to learn the method.

In several cases Pueblos egged on by white advisers have gone into the federal courts to protest what they considered violations of their rights as citizens. The courts have held that with Indians as with whites the local government's authority must be recognized. Disgruntled Pueblo's, Judge Colin Neblett reminded them in deciding a Taos case in 1949, have the same right to change their government as have citizens anywhere—in New Jersey, say, or Louisiana, or Boston.

Pueblo people, as a rule, bow without demur to council authority. Even veterans have submitted to whipping for drunkenness (the lash in such cases may be laid onto a man's blanket rather than his backside). Pueblo law, like our common law, has its presumptions: courts have ruled that a Pueblo council is as entitled to whip a drunk as the State of Delaware is to flog a wife-beater.

Drink has caused many a conflict between pueblo elders and the returned veteran. According to a federal law passed when all our frontiers were harried by savages inflamed with firewater, it is a penitentiary offense to give or sell liquor to Indians. This law has never been repealed, but in 1953 New Mexico and in 1954 Arizona legalized the sale of liquor to Indians. Since then the Navajo Tribal Council has prohibited the sale of liquor on the reservation; arrests for drunkenness had markedly declined, though it is still a problem.

The liquor problem may underlie council opposition to on-the-job training. Veterans of one pueblo had signed up for work in a garage in town when councilmen, in blanketed dignity, called on the garage owner and declared the deal off. In that case the veterans slipped away to the garage at night; technical training became an underground activity. Pueblo veterans, applying for on-the-farm training, encountered a triple difficulty. Bankers, ready to treat all GI's alike, found that the Pueblo could not mortgage his house, though he had built it, owned it unquestionably, and was a good credit risk. Nor could he show title to the land he tilled. And councilmen feared that veterans might claim ownership to pueblo lands to which they had only the right of use. Such objections were overcome finally by special written agreements with pueblo councils. In Zuni, where old men feared that the old societies would be disrupted by on-the-farm training, a wise administrator suggested organizing classes along the lines of the ancient pueblo societies, and the old men agreed. Deeper fears were that modern farming methods might interfere with the ancient ceremonial calendar. But as the kachinas seem to have been good farmers with sound ideas about planting and harvesting, these difficulties too were surmounted— after long discussion.

Over two hundred veterans have taken technical training and as many more have studied agriculture. The matter-of-fact men who train Indians find that they are just like anybody else: they range from poor to good to super. Not a few have been called first-rate, and several have gone on to technical and agricultural colleges. All this should lead to more productive farms and, in time, to men who can qualify as supervisors and directors not in the pueblos only, but in state and county in general. This will provide a true bridge between cultures.

The real tug for the trained Pueblo comes when he must decide between two standards of value. As a good Pueblo he should take part in certain kiva rites and respond when called to serve as a pueblo official. As a worker in town he should not leave his job. Adjustments are made on all sides. A substitute may be hired to perform the appointed task in the pueblo. Many employers in town grant time off, accepting the Pueblo's religious obligations as they do those of the Catholic or the Jew. Sometimes practical considerations are baffling, as in Taos, where nobody may stay out of the pueblo overnight. Reconciling this rule with the demands of a waitress's job in town would tax a diplomat.

The extreme test is that of a man earning twenty dollars a day at Los Alamos who is summoned to an unpaid honor in San Ildefonso or Santa Clara. Years ago no cash consideration would have outweighed the Pueblo's obligation to serve or the prestige his service would bring him. But our money standards are affecting the Pueblo even at religious depths. Some Pueblos give up a good job for the unpaid dignity; a few deliberately begin to live like white men, though one who stays away too long may lose the right to land. This situation may mark the beginning of capitalism in the ancient pueblo communes. The man who stays at home farms more land than his share; he is using the city worker's portion. So the rich grow richer and the poor poorer. The class consciousness that often follows such a trend has not yet invaded the pueblos. But some day a matron whose husband runs large herds is going to hire a neighbor to help in the house. Then the democratic pueblo will begin to go the way New England went.

Pueblo people do not like to see the beginning of inequalities. An Isleta man, himself running more stock on pueblo land than he thinks fair, is studying a plan to protect the town workers by some system of rental payments for land use. The Pueblo still thinks first of the general good. And many of the most modern, preferring life with family, friends, and the old ways, are making smooth personal adjustments.

An Isleta veteran, who is a draftsman with the Army Engineers in Albuquerque, commutes thirteen miles daily in order to live at home and bring his child up as a good Pueblo. His wife, a nurse, agrees fully. Their adobe house has a screened porch, an electrical kitchen, and a neon-lighted workbench for the man. Such young men and women may manage a workable fusion of modern conveniences and ancient values. This would be a triumph of true civilization; but the hazards are many, for while pueblo life is being assailed from without, its internal affairs are often in confusion because old customs do not meet modern conditions. This Isleta veteran is typical of many now employed at atomic centers.

An Acoma who had been living with his Laguna wife in

her pueblo got the Acoma cacique's permission to move his 250 sheep back home. When he arrived with family and goods in a truck and his teen-age son driving the sheep, the governor stopped him. The Grazing Service had ruled that the Acoma lands could not support additional sheep; moreover, the cacique had no right to act in a civil matter. At a conference suggested by the Indian Service, the old cacique yielded gracefully and the claimant returned to his wife's pueblo, where land was available. This ruling, incidentally, drew the line between religious and civil authority within the pueblo. It is more difficult to define pueblo jurisdiction when it conflicts with that of the state or nation.

Marriage and divorce, long considered the pueblo's own affairs, produce both comedy and tragedy. A Laguna pair had been married according to Laguna custom for thirty years. Then the husband, an employee of the Santa Fe railroad, reached retirement age. As his pension would be figured on the number of his dependents, the Santa Fe asked to see his marriage certificate. The Laguna couple had no proof of marriage; just the children. Not acceptable. So the long-wed couple, highly amused, had a wedding with license, children, grandchildren, and a party.

It does not always work out so pleasantly. In another pueblo, a man married by tribal rites went to war, leaving a wife and three children. On his return he was married to another woman by a justice of the peace and went to a priest for the religious ceremony. The padre, making a routine check, learned of the former marriage and refused to officiate. The Indian Service attorney, William Brophy, held that the pueblo marriage was valid. The wife filed suit for divorce in the state court, thus marking a break with old custom.

Any individual Pueblo is free to employ counsel and bring suit. But the pueblo as a unit must be represented by the Indian Service attorney or one approved by him. This rule was designed to protect Indians from shysters; but the people have not forgotten that the Indian Service failed to guard their land and water rights. Even today they complain that the government closes deals in their interest without consulting them. Men of the caliber of councilmen naturally resent such tutelage and often consult private attorneys, though any lawyer who advises them must act as a friend, without fee or other emolument.

Some pueblos have large business deals with outsiders. Santa Clara and San Ildefonso have contracts with Los Alamos for sand and gravel sales and for land rents that run into five figures annually. And Isleta, given a small herd of cattle during the depression, did not butcher it but bred up the stock and used the income for the general good. This income has put in a water system and a sewer is proposed. In 1949 the pueblo herd brought in about ninety thousand dollars, which was used for electrification of the pueblo.

In such matters the council acts. In 1849 New Mexico's first legislature ruled that each pueblo was a body corporate. Isleta is organized as a corporation. But in operation most councils proceed by the old Indian way of long talk, no matter how long it takes to reach a decision. Isleta once suffered a split in the council that tied up business important to white men, who urged forcing the issue. But the majority leader demurred. "Give me time and I'll get an agreement." In time he did. The minority leader resigned in order to make the decision unanimous, saying: "God has forgiven us all. Let us forgive each other."

In affairs of wider concern the pueblos are united in the All Pueblo Council, organized in 1922 to fight the Bursum Bill. It meets on call, preferably with no non-Indian observers. Even if white advisers are invited, they are bowed politely out at the end of the matter in hand. Santo Domingo has been the traditional meeting place since Spanish days. Once a council officer, a Baptist and an Indian Service employee, called a meeting at a Baptist church in Albuquerque. Not a pueblo representative appeared. Many Indians dislike seeing an "agency Indian" in a position of power; others did not wish to convene in a church.

Unhappily, missionaries, devoted preachers of the religion of peace, produce divisiveness and bad feeling among the Pueblos. They not only oppose the ancient beliefs, but also, lacking the Indian's tolerance, often openly combat one another. Missionaries of eight or ten churches proselyte among the Pueblos, furnishing that humorous folk with amusement, but also with concern. When the children of a Holiness Pilgrim complained that Catholic children had stoned them, the people were aroused; children should not be taught to hate. But when a couple of Latter-day Saints were ordered out by elders who thought they were preaching polygamy, laughter ran through the Pueblo world. "What sort of a religion is that?" snorted the anciently monogamous Pueblos.

Among the faiths that the Pueblos know is the peyote cult, which involves the taking of peyote, a stimulant drug from mescal buttons. It has been taken since time immemorial by Mexican Indians, but it entered New Mexico from the Plains tribes. John Collier, when he was Indian Commissioner, welcomed it as a possible means of uniting the Indian population; Indians often call it "the Indian Church." In New Mexico the peyote cult has taken root only among the Navajos and in Taos pueblo, where the conservatives opposed it because it emphasized the individual rather than any group. Some whites have opposed it as immoral: a New Mexico statute makes the possession of peyote a crime. But by federal ruling peyote is not a narcotic. This confusion needs further court action. The question remains: is the taking of peyote a silly custom, a vicious habit, nobody's business, or the Indians' true religion?

Despite all outside pressures, the Pueblos seem most at ease with the Catholic Church. But they are capable of taking issue with it. When an archbishop asked Santo Domingo for land on which to build a convent, the council politely refused, explaining that on certain days no outsider might enter the pueblo. No defiance was intended; they were all Catholics, but no land would be given. His Grace, unaccustomed to opposition, reminded the council that, as Catholics, they could be excommunicated; denied the Church's sacraments they might go to hell. Here he was on the caciques' own ground. "Tell him," one directed the interpreter, "that God does not care how we express our reverence, with holy water or holy meal. And if it comes to a future life, we know as much as he does about that. . . . You talk a lot about heaven," he concluded, "but you can't produce one single angel, not even a little one." This exchange was delightedly quoted by a visitor from another pueblo.

The Church withdrew its clergy, and for some years Santo Domingo was without Catholic Mass. Then, urged by a white friend, the council recanted in a public statement: ". . . fully realizing that the Catholic religion is the true one . . . the only faith practiced among its people since the time of the Spanish Franciscians, [the council] do hereby pledge themselves to keep their people practicing the said religion." This, as the Indian Service attorney, himself a Catholic, was quick to point out, was contrary to the Constitution. Even the council could not deny religious freedom to any person who might prefer a faith not Catholic. So, though the Catholic mission was reopened, other faiths were not barred.

There remained the question of the caciques' right to require certain duties of Christian Indians. Where does civic duty end and enforced support of religion begin? A federal court has ruled that "no tax . . . may be levied to support any religious activities . . . whatever they may be called." How does this affect the Pueblo required to sweep out the plaza before a dance? Such services have been construed as civic duties and, for refusing them, men have been deprived of their land rights. The United States Supreme Court has not yet ruled on any specific case.

The Pueblos, as usual, make their own adjustments. A baby baptized by the Catholic priest was presented to the cacique for the clan naming. Lifting it toward the sun, the old man said: "May this child grow into a man who will learn the white man's ways and use what is good; may he also learn the Pueblo way, respect it, and cherish its best too."

A veteran home from the European theater described his solution. "When I was little," he said, "I used to worry because my teachers told me my people would go to hell because they were pagans. That was hard for a little boy of ten. I used to look at my family and wonder. They looked so nice; they laughed so much at home. I really suffered. . . . Now, of course, I know better. I go to Mass, but I don't worry about my family any more."

Thus the Pueblo's age-old sublety still finds ways to hold fast the traditional verities, often so quietly that the outsider suspects nothing. The traditional September fiesta in the progressive pueblo of Laguna seemed to have become a county fair where the most blatant modernity had smothered both the pueblo dance and the Catholic saint's day observance. Mass was said in the pale old adobe church and a shrine for San Jose was set up in the dance plaza. But the day's big event was the baseball game.

On a diamond ringed with cars and trucks, the Winslow Redskins and the Lagunas were playing off the final of an eighteen-pueblo series. The Laguna governor and the president of the All Pueblo Council, both Protestants and "agency Indians," were there. Indian rooters from two states yelled defiance at the umpire and swarmed among booths where cones, Cokes, and hot dogs were sold. Across the din of the merry-go-round came the sound of Indian music; Manuel Archuleta of San Juan and his Laguna wife were doing a brisk business selling records of Indian songs.

The dancing, when it came, was a sorry travesty of the ancient ceremonies. Two young dancers attired in black velvet Eton jackets and knee-breeches cut to show their fine musculature performed the Hoop Dance with professional skill and aplomb. But it had no meaning whatever: it was a vaudeville turn, no more. The old dance, correct for the day, came on raggedly with a few old men and women shuffling aimlessly, untrained, poorly costumed, the dying remnant of a vigorous religious expression.

On such a day Laguna seems to offer sad proof that the splendid old ceremonies with their deep meaning are forever gone. But in many pueblos they exist in gorgeous correctness. Even World War II and Korean veterans with their squared military shoulders appear stripped and painted, conventionally accoutered for the dance. One, between figures at Zia, came to greet a friend. "Yes," he said, "we dance. While we were gone the old folks kept these things going for our protection. Now we must do our part."

Even the fiesta at Laguna is not the proof of degeneration that it seems. It is rather evidence that the Pueblo has again found his way to evade the intruder. A Laguna woman said: "Don't you worry about the Lagunas. Our private dances, the ones white people never see, are still the most beautiful anywhere. Everything is perfect, everybody watches and is absolutely quiet. Nobody cares about what white people see."

So the Pueblo, having absorbed Catholicism, American education, and a cash economy, may be able to preserve his ancient ceremonies in secret societies, as other esoteric rites have been preserved. If these fine ceremonies are hidden from the outsider, it will be our loss, not the Indian's.

THE TRADITIONAL NAVAJO

THE NAVAJOS, known to themselves as Diné (the People), have been the most widely and seriously studied of all our tribes. Volumes have been written about their ceremonies. More volumes are in the making as students continue to delve into this curious culture, which seems ever more mature in the light of modern thinking. The best examples of Navajo handiwork win respect everywhere. Musicians and choreographers record their songs and study their dance techniques. Literary critics consider Navajo legends equal to the world's most poetic mythologies. And students of comparative religion find in Navajo ceremonies "splendid symbols of abstract ideas." The Diné may not be dismissed as a primitive tribe; they are a highly developed people worthy of respectful study.

The related Navajo and Apache tribes were latecomers into New Mexico, appearing from the north about one thousand years ago. Both brought many Plains Indian traits, some of which persist as proof of their common origin. The Spanish, more correctly than they knew, lumped the two groups as Apaches de Navajo or Navajo-Apache. The word *Navajo* has been translated as "planted fields," and also as "knife." Both translations have applicability.

Long before the Spanish came, Navajo and Apache cultures had begun to differ as the people drifted apart and borrowed from others. The Navajo developed further and more elaborately because he could always improve on what he learned. As a trader he roamed widely, swapping buckskin, buffalo hides, and baskets for Ute beadwork and elk skins in the north, for Hopi cotton mantles and ceremonial articles in the west, and for fruits and maize and the sacred turquoise along the Rio Grande. Always he learned the ceremony that went with the article he bought, or the story that explained it.

A Navajo trade trip, like all their life, proceeded with ceremony. A smart trader—one who had performed the rites correctly or who had supernatural powers—was chosen leader. During the journey prayers were chanted at every stop. In his *Ancient Navajo,* Dr. Willard Williams Hill quotes an invocation. "The beautiful thing is starting to-ward me, I being the son of the sun." That song ends: "The beautiful one is come to me, I being the son of the sun." Riding to trade with the Pueblos, the song might be: "Dwellers in the earth, may I have success in dealing with them." Utes they called Dwellers in the Cedar-bark, and with them the approach was quite different. Each Navajo had a Ute friend with whom he exchanged gifts; no price was mentioned. But with the Pueblos hard commercialism was the rule. Clyde Kluckhohn quotes a modern Navajo as saying that you must watch the Pueblos: "They may give you only food." There were rites on the return journey too, and back at home every trader was purified of alien contact by the Blessing Chant. Trade articles also must be freed of malignancy: turquoise was "cooked" in a heated yucca root, a treatment that had the added advantage of deepening the prized sky color.

According to scattered Spanish records, the Navajos ranged over the northern and eastern portions of their present reservation. Dr. Hill has found a report dated 1744 that estimates their numbers at from two to four thousand. Many lived in stone huts such as are still found, and raised corn, beans, squash, and melons. By that time they had a few sheep and goats—got by trade or theft—and even a few horses. Plains Indians valued horses more highly than the sturdy boys and likely girls they also carried off. They cared little for saddles, but bid high for bridles, iron tools, and the brass and copper they hammered into jewelry before they acquired silver. They also swapped for *bayeta*, the bright scarlet English baize that lined Spanish officers' capes. Navajo women raveled this out and used it in their blankets, adding a rich red note to the natural colors of their wool. Navajo blankets soon became the most highly prized article of trade from the plains to Mexico.

The great annual fairs at Taos and Pecos brought together throngs of Indians of all tribes to barter their wares among themselves and to exchange them for Spanish manufactured goods. In spite of Spain's just laws and severe penalties for the protection of Indians, cheating was as general as trade, and bad feeling grew. Plains Indians, having made much peace talk at the fair, might stop on the way home to raid a pueblo or a Spanish hamlet. The Spanish could neither conquer nor convert them.

Henry Kelly, in a published thesis entitled *Franciscan Missions of New Mexico*, honors several intrepid and hopeful friars who tried to establish missions among the Navajos. One, who had settled a group of converts at Cebolleta, found on his next visit that they had all abjured the faith. They had, he was told, allowed "water to be thrown on their children" because of the presents. But presents were not enough to keep them, "who had been raised like the deer," in one place. They offered to be friends, but not Christians.

So the haughty Navajo did not even pretend conversion as the smoother and more easily subdued Pueblo did. The Navajo, mounted and armed and with a wide wilderness to roam, needed no faith other than his own, which was deeply integrated with his life and thought. Even his adopted Pueblo customs were Navajo now. He had fully incorporated the clan system, based on matrilineal descent, which came from the Hopi and the Zuni—as did the kachina cults. As with the Pueblo kachina, the Yei is both the dancer masked to represent a supernatural being and a carved doll. With the kachinas came the painted altar, the sacred meal, the prayer sticks, rattles, and fetiches, and the bull-roarer to chase evil away. Though these religious objects are as a rule more elaborately and more skillfully made by the Pueblos, the Navajos excelled in the imaginative development of the Pueblo myths and in the lofty spiritual content they gave them.

The Navajo twin heroes were born of Changing Woman at the behest of Begodchiddy, who comes close to the Jewish-Christian idea of God as Creator. Christianized Navajos sometimes use the words interchangeably. Changing Woman, also called Turquoise Woman, is the only altogether beneficent force in the Navajo cosmogony—a hint perhaps of woman's power and importance in Navajo life. All the tales of the wanderings, trials, and triumphs of the twins are infused with the beauty of color and light, of mountain and canyon forms, of cloud shapes and of the marvel of storms, as well as of the spiritual beauty of growth through meeting adversity strongly.

Like the Pueblo's mythical ancestors, the Navajo's climbed laboriously upward through successive worlds of greater light and understanding. Haniel Long, the poet, finds here the all-human "not-yet-finished emergence." This is the matter of the Navajo creation myth, one version of which has been translated into English of classic simplicity by Mary Cabot Wheelwright with the aid of the Navajo chanter Hasteen Klah. This myth may be traced from Mexico to the Great Lakes region; it may have wider connections. To the Navajo it is the basis of legends that explain his colored desert, gashed canyons, and towering peaks that became sacred to the supernaturals. On these tales are based the Navajo's ethic and his religious ceremonies.

Knowledge of the ceremonies is the vocation of the medicine man or chanter, who, like his Athapascan ancestor, may be and often is a mystic guided by visions. His priestly function and prescribed offices stem from the Pueblo culture and require rigid training. Learning even one ceremony may take years of extraordinary concentration. The chanter must know every word of hundreds of songs, each with its correct gestures, and must memorize every line and color of the sand paintings that illustrate the rite. A chant is as intricate as the Catholic Mass, and its symbolism dramatizes the myth as the Mass does the Passion, and no more obviously. Every "sing" is also a healing ceremony. Not only are physical ailments cured, but fears are eradicated and psychic disturbances resolved. The Navajo believes that every evil is the result of disharmony with spiritual forces; curing is bringing the patient back into right relationship with all life.

Right relationship is basic to the Navajo ethic. Even today the child learns how to enter the hogan (the Navajo house), where to sit, how to address each person, and how to manage his personal needs and to care for his belongings. Even small children own things, and their ownership is respected as they respect the right of others. Once beyond babyhood, they begin to share in the work. As most Navajos still live in the octagonal wattled log hogans, with a fire in the center, tasks have changed little through the ages. The floor must be kept clean, clothes and gear neatly hung around the walls, firewood and water fetched, and ashes carried out.

From infancy the child drops to sleep to the telling of his clan myth and many other myths. So when he goes out with his sheep he knows a legend for every mountain and

curious red sandstone formation, for every plant and animal. He knows the why of the bushy tail, the stripe, the
chatter, the quick flirt of a wing. And he can sing.

> Lo, the light brown one!
> Truly in the distant glade
> Below, through the opening
> In the far, green trees
> Wanders the antelope.

Or watching a ground squirrel scolding, he may chant:

> Slender and striped
> Slender and striped
> Look at him standing up there!
> He stands up there
> So slender in his stripes,
> The squirrel in his little, white shirt!

These translations are from Margaret Erwin Schevill's
Beautiful on the Earth, a sympathetic appreciation of Navajo mysticism in the light of Jung's psychology.

For the Navajo child, every act has its simple ritual. Each
day he greets the sunrise. Seasonally he helps with planting
and harvesting, lambing and shearing. All life is rhythmic;
for every important event there is a prescribed observance,
as for the baby's naming and in the puberty ceremony,
when boys and girls sit hooded under blankets and shivering
to hear the Yei's eerie hoot. Boys are then lightly struck
with yucca, and girls are touched with corn cobs. Un-
blinded, the children see that the Yei are men in masks;
achieving adulthood consists in learning that masked figures
are only symbols of the supernaturals. There are marriage
rites and cleansing ceremonies, the most important having
to do with curing and the eradication of sickness.

Although Navajo myths do not emphasize fear, and hell
is not taught, Navajos have an obsessive dread of the dead.

Even modern Navajos shrink from touching a corpse; men in military service devised cleansing rites for themselves. They have a related fear of ghosts, and few Navajos will walk alone at night when the dark unquiet dead may pull the living into their shadowy dwelling-place. Witches, who may be anybody, deal with such spirits and cause ills and evils. Dr. Kluckhohn's studies of individuals reveal that fear of being called a witch holds many a Navajo in the paths of rectitude. It also militates against our get-ahead ethic. A Diné who prospers may be doing so with unsanctified aid. Some students believe that work on the irrigated farms under the Fruitland Dam on the San Juan River lagged because men were afraid of being accused of witchcraft.

The individual Navajo protects himself against the spells of witches by observing taboos and by interpreting his dreams, if he can. If he cannot, he seeks a medicine man. Dreams are never meaningless. Some psychiatrists believe that unlettered shamans often use great wisdom in freeing their patients from conflicts reflected in dreams.

The Navajo's religion is individual. Like the Christian rather than the group-minded Pueblo, he is concerned with his personal relationship to the supernatural. But unlike Christian prayers, his chants are not supplications; they are invocations of universal power which even the supernaturals must obey. It is only necessary to do everything correctly; right thoughts, acts, and syllables bring good by inevitable law. Illness, a symptom of failure to do right, may be cured by a ceremony properly performed. Navajo sings—those marvelous combinations of prayer, chant, sand-painting, and dance—are held for the benefit of an individual.

The patient's family, which bears all the expenses, selects the medicine man and erects a large new hogan on a spot uncontaminated by human life, but near water and firewood. The chanter and his assistants come first, bringing their ceremonial bundles of sacred articles: long eagle-feathers, holy plants, pollen, and materials for the sand-paintings. The family meanwhile is building its camp and readying piles of fragrant piñon and juniper for the fires.

Word has spread by mysterious channels, and a great concourse gathers, often from many miles away. By wagon and horseback they come, women carrying babies on cradleboards, small children with bright quick eyes peering over a wagon's side. There are trucks, too, and cars of every type. Everybody is in his best velvet jacket to display his wealth in turquoise, silver, jet, and shell. Hundreds, even thousands, of Navajos come to help the cure by their good thoughts. But they gather also for gossip, trade, racing, and gambling. Often tribal business is transacted; old men stand to intone long speeches in their guttural phrases. A Navajo sing, like a Christian camp-meeting, is not religion undefiled.

Throughout the day people drift into the medicine hogan, where the chanter sits with his patient. The medicine man is usually past middle age; few young men have either memory or patience to learn the ritual; many chants have been lost for lack of neophytes. Others seem doomed to extinction. Oliver La Farge's sensitive novel, *Enemy Gods*, presents well the confusion of the young Navajo astray between faiths. For these reasons five-day sings are more common now than the nine-day ceremonies. The procedure is similar. The patient and all participants undergo bodily cleansing through light diet and daily emetics, and by continence; mental cleansing by right thoughts. Sometimes the patient is given a sweat bath or massage. Mostly the healing is through ritual touching of the body and by prayer and suggestion. The earlier parts of the ceremony free the patient from evil; then the powers are called upon to flood him with good.

On the last days, the medicine man directs the so-called sand-painting, which Dr. Kluckhohn prefers to call "dry painting" because many other materials are used with the sand. Sometimes a bowl of water is sunk in the painting's center. Charcoal mixed with white sand makes blue; ground rocks provide red and yellow; pollen and petals may be used, even twigs and cones. Beginning at the center of the area to be covered, the medicine man lets his color flow in a thin trickle through thumb and finger, making lines as accurately and as fast as an artist could make them with pencil or brush. As the painting grows, other painters join, to work under the quick eye of the medicine man, who corrects every error. No variation is permitted except in the decoration of the Yei's kirtle or bag.

The completed painting illustrates the myth. Begodchiddy is never pictured, and Changing Woman appears only in the most used Blessing Chant. Yei frequently appear as elongated full-faced figures; mountains, clouds, streams, and many animals are drawn symbolically, but recognizably too. Often the rainbow surrounds all as a protection. The finished work is exquisite in its soft clarity of color, its balanced composition. Other peoples in many parts of the world have made such dry paintings; none has ever equaled the Navajo for sheer beauty and high artistry.

Before sunset every painting must be destroyed; the hallowed sand is applied to the patient's body for healing. What then remains is carried reverently away.

To the average onlooker the night's dancing may be even more memorable than the day's quiet observances. As night comes, the rich red of sandstone cliffs has merged into purplish black, and the sharp sun and shadow of mesa and canyon have dulled into looming shapes and bottomless gulfs. Hard bright stars come out, or a frosty moon spreads silveriness over gray-green sage and green juniper. Then fires glow for supper and tall bonfires pierce the night. Always it is cold, for the great Navajo sings occur only in winter.

Unlike the Pueblo ceremonies, most Navajo dances are not accompanied by chorus or drummer. Dancers chant their own accompaniment in the harsh syllables and jerky rhythms so difficult for the white ear to catch. But by the time one has sat muffled in blankets through a long cold night, the falsetto wailing has created a spell in which the high-stepping masked figures making their angular gestures seem as natural as the wheeling planets in a starry sky. By the coming of the blue dawn in the white east the hypnosis is complete and no translation of the Blue Bird Song is needed to make the onlooker feel the beauty and the glory of the Navajo world.

Such a religion is a true contribution to universal culture. Wherever the Navajo got his legends and forms, his genuis has made of them a humanly wise and highly spiritual religion. One is impressed with the maturity of certain concepts. The hero must wander far and alone, facing dangers that test his integrity as well as his courage; he must even be brave enough to violate certain taboos. In one tale, when the hero's steadiness had dissolved the fearful whirlwind, its spirit says: "It was not so bad when you faced it. Was it?" The result of the typical hero's ordeal is a person fully in command of himself, spiritually mature. That all Navajos are not spiritually mature is no more remarkable than that all Christians are not Christlike. Many medicine men do seem to incarnate their ideals and to be philosophical, steadfast, and wise guides.

The first comprehending student of Navajo ceremonies was Dr. Washington Matthews, a U.S. Army surgeon who was also a musician and sensitive to beauty in any form. His *Mountain Chant* (1887) and his *Night Chant* (1902) were long the only source books for students of Navajo religion. There were not many students. Soldiers, missionaries, and Indian Service people, like the Spanish before them, had no preparation for understanding alien beliefs; they were never students, just critics. Only some traders accepted Navajo ways as valid. They learned enough Navajo to do business easily; some of them married Navajo women and adopted many traditions and customs. But few achieved real understanding of the culture they shared.

A few traders became legends in their own right. Lorenzo Hubbell, son of a Spanish New Mexican and a Connecticut Yankee, established the first trading-post at Ganado, Arizona, where life was baronial and patriarchal. His sons grew up speaking English, Spanish, and Navajo interchangeably and lived long fruitful lives among people never alien to them. Louisa Wade, born among the Utes in Colorado, spoke both Ute and Navajo as a child, and when she married John Wetherill and went to live at Kayenta, Arizona, she became trusted adviser to that part of the Navajo reservation. She collected vast lore; much of it was used by Frances Gilmor in *Traders to the Navajo*. The Day family of St. Michaels, like the Wetherills, lived close to their Navajo neighbors as friends and married partners. Such people accepted Navajo ways as children accept the familiar. Often they sang and danced and were healed, initiated, and included in tribal councils. Most of them neither made records of what they knew nor tried to evaluate it.

In 1912 there appeared *An Ethnologic Vocabulary of the Navajo Language*. Credited to the Franciscan Fathers of St. Michaels, this was the work of Father Berard Haile, a person so sympathetic that he could not serve people without studying them or teach them his faith without understanding theirs. So he learned to speak Navajo fluently and studied the ceremonies. He has published a translation of the *Star Chant* and a study of the war ceremony, *Enemy Way*.

The dance that ends this ceremony is known to many visitors as the Squaw Dance, a misnomer, as the Algonquin word "squaw" is never used by western Indians. It is properly called the Girl Dance. Each maiden chooses a man and dances him around until he buys her off. Originally the couple did not touch, but nowadays they link right arms and circle stolidly. The watching white is entertained to see how long they swing before the man pays. The watching Navajo knows that this ancient rite, borrowed from the Utes, is part of a war dance. But it is far from the frenzied rousing of the fighting spirit associated with Indian war dances. It is indeed never held before men go to war, but on their return; and it is a promise that the earth, blood-soaked from fighting, will again produce vegetation and that maidens will control the rain.

Naturally, Enemy Way was not held for recruits going off to World War II; for them a medicine man chanted the Blessing Way "that all might be beautiful before them." On their return, Enemy Way was necessary to purify the fighters of blood shed and death witnessed. Part of this cere-mony is "killing the ghost of the scalp." A real scalp is de-sirable. Old men used to cherish a dusty one buried some-where in a tin can; nowadays "the equivalent" will serve. It has been noted that even nowadays a Navajo murder gen-erally involves a crushed head that might have yielded enough skin and hair to serve as a scalp. In any case, the re-turned warrior, with face blackened to conceal him from the enemy, must shoot the scalp to kill it; thus its evil power becomes beneficent and is transferred to him. This ancient Navajo rite may be as sound a way as any to rid a battle-shocked veteran of the horrors he has seen. In modern life, Enemy Way is sometimes performed to cleanse a man of contact with such civilian enemies as policemen or prosti-tutes in town.

Every penetrating study of Navajo ritual attracted more students to the reservation, many of them for an initiatory talk with Father Berard in his austere study at St. Michaels. Among these was Clyde Kluckhohn, who, in his teens, went to visit relatives near Ramah, New Mexico, and was soon on a horse and away with the Navajos. That summer gave him command of their language and resulted in a book of youthful vim, *To the Foot of the Rainbow*. It has led to years of detailed and intimate study of Navajo life, and has brought many students to the reservation.

The Navajo reservation has thus become one of the most popular laboratories for the study of a fully developed culture. Out of numerous scholarly treatises some books of general interest have come. Gladys Reichard, who learned one summer the techniques of living in a hogan and weaving a blanket, wrote *Spider Woman*. As her knowledge widened and deepened, she produced *Compulsive Prayer*, the best short statement of the Navajo's sense of oneness with the universe and of his belief that good must come from right acts and thoughts. It paints a telling portrait of the dignified Navajo, standing erect and calling on universal law.

Then came Mary Cabot Wheelwright, a proper Bostonian, whose interest was aroused and her life work determined when she saw her first Yeibechai, the splendid nineday ceremony in which the Yei appear in masked dance. Distressed because nobody could tell her in detail what underlay such refined and elaborate ritual, Miss Wheelwright began to study, to seek.

Soon she met Arthur and Frances Newcomb at Nava near Two Grey Hills, New Mexico. Arthur was a trader who spoke Navajo. Franc was that rare Indian Service teacher who did not pity herself as marooned on a desolate desert, but congratulated herself on the discovery of a new art. Enthralled with the sand-paintings, she saw as many as she could. As she was not permitted to draw inside the medicine hogan, Franc Newcomb began to memorize the paintings; in time she developed a visual memory of amazing accuracy. Watching the medicine man, following each line as the sand dribbled, she soon mastered the basic conven-

5. The mission church at Santo Domingo stands apart from the village.

CAPLIN AND THOMPSON, OLD ALBUQUERQUE

6 *An Isleta
veteran of
World War II
prefers pueblo
life.*

CAPLIN AND
THOMPSON, OLD
ALBUQUERQUE

tions of the art: the placing of the sacred plants—corn, beans, tobacco, and squash; that black is north, white east, blue south, and yellow west. Also how the colors sometimes varied. Many things. Finally when she saw a new painting, Franc Newcomb had only to memorize its distinctive features.

The chanter who was Mrs. Newcomb's teacher was Hasteen Klah, whom she was to introduce to Miss Wheelwright. He had chosen the Newcombs' home for his after his friend Dick Wetherill was killed at Pueblo Bonito and Mrs. Wetherill had moved her children to town. At Nava, Klah lived alone in a hogan, using his gifts as requested, and weaving. A wise man in mundane as well as in spiritual things, Klah knew that his knowledge was doomed to disappear; every year he saw fewer singers trained, more chants lost. So he began to weave his paintings into blankets with sand-colored backgrounds and other colors of soft vegetable dyes. Weaving was woman's work, but it was the only way he had to preserve his paintings. But when he saw Franc Newcomb's work, Klah knew that there was another way. He began to correct her drawings and to tell her the legends they illustrated. It was the beginning of a remarkable collection, part of which has been published. In 1937, working with Gladys Reichard, Mrs. Newcomb produced *The Navajo Shooting Chant;* later she published *The Mountain Chant* and *Navajo Omens and Taboos.*

It is difficult and expensive to get such work published or properly displayed. Miss Wheelwright, gratefully appreciative of what the trader's wife and the shaman were doing, undertook that task. She had a broad knowledge of comparative religions, especially oriental mysticisms, and she constantly added to that lore while she collected Navajo chants. Working with Hasteen Klah and an interpreter, Miss Wheelwright published several important chants with text and sand-paintings. She has, besides, twelve ceremonies "more or less complete" with both myths and sand-paintings. It is pitifully few. Nobody knows how many there may have been; as each ceremony requires possibly fifty chants and at least four sand-paintings, and as only thirty-five complete chants are now known, the loss has already been great.

To house her collections and to provide a repository where the work of others might be preserved and studied, Miss Wheelwright endowed the Museum of Navajo Ceremonial Art. Built with Klah's approval and blessed by him, this is a hogan-like structure among the piñons near Santa Fe. Klah died in 1937, but Miss Wheelwright, until her death in 1958, continued to work with the few remaining chanters on the reservation; her peerless collections continue to grow. In 1950, the Bollingen Foundation of New York presented the Museum with fifty-two sand-paintings meticulously copied by Maude Oakes.

These are the records of a dying art, a vanishing faith. Many important sings have already disappeared. Students agree that few chanters know more than one complete ceremony; as each old medicine man dies, his knowledge dies with him. This is a loss to universal culture. Our civilization has destroyed most, if not all, of the ancient mystical world in which the Navajo lived, the ancient ethic he practiced. Only time will tell how well he is compensated for this loss by industrial and scientific wonders and assorted faiths.

❦ ⊂❦ ❦

VII

THE MODERN NAVAJO

⊂❧ THE NAVAJO tribe, the largest and now the richest
in the United States, has grown in less than a century from
15,000 to over 90,000 people living on a reservation about
the size of West Virginia. The largest part of the reservation is in Arizona, but there are small areas in Utah and
Colorado, and a larger area in New Mexico, which counts
about 30,000 people. Most of the Navajos live outside the
reservation in an area west of Albuquerque, which has its
own problems because it is policed by county sheriffs,
States Highway patrolmen, and Navajo police, known as
Law and Order men. A lawbreaker has only to slip from
one jurisdiction to another to escape arrest; bootleggers
have flourished and drunkenness remains a major problem
in this area.

The Navajo diet still averages about 1,200 calories daily,
as contrasted with our national minimum of 2,500. Infant
deaths from diarrhea and enteritis are many times the national percentage, and epidemics of children's diseases are
frequent and devastating. In 1950 infant mortality was
318 per 100,000; but by 1959 it had decreased to 236 per
100,000. The spreading of information about birth control,
the humane way to limit children to the number that might
survive, is impossible because of certain minority beliefs.
The Navajo death rate is 74.7 per cent, as compared with
a 26.3 per cent national death rate. That this is a national
problem became apparent in 1942, when draft boards rejected 65 per cent of Navajo draftees as physically unfit.

Tuberculosis was the most frequent ailment; then followed venereal disease, undernourishment, and congenital diseases. So few Navajo recruits could write or even speak English that a special training center was established for them. There they learned with alacrity. Over two thousand Navajos served in all the services and many others worked in war plants. But these were a minority of the tribe, and few of them really mastered English.

The United States has dealt with the Navajo since 1846, when the Navajos, having refused to make peace with Mexico, welcomed the American occupation of New Mexico. So an expedition under Colonel Doniphan was dispatched to the Navajo country to "require of the Navajos security for their future conduct."

Colonel Doniphan's Missourians were appalled to see Isleta Indians dancing around a pole topped by "the scalps of three warriors, the long straight black hair sweeping the wind."

Going on over "craggy mountains of stupendous height . . . steep and rugged acclivities, precipices and yawning chasms," the lowlanders finally came upon Navajos. At first they made friends. But at Ojo del Oso (Bear Spring) Doniphan heard a young chief state the Navajo position. Sarcillo Largo said: "You have a strange cause of war against the Diné. We have waged war against the Mexicans for years. You have lately . . . conquered them. . . . Now you turn upon us for attempting what you have done yourselves."

But they signed a treaty, the first of many that were violated by the Indians. Navajos who signed treaties said that Navajos who broke them were not of their people. Maybe they were not; the tribe was, as it still is, loosely knit.

In 1848, President Taylor appointed James S. Calhoun Indian Agent in New Mexico. Calhoun sent another expedition against the Navajos under Lt. Colonel John M. Washington, whose unlikely name adorns a pass in the Chuska Mountains. Out of this foray came a New Mexico classic. *Journal of a Military Reconnaisance*, by James H. Simpson, contains some of the best descriptions ever written of the stupendous Navajo country, and his illustrator Kern's drawings are more accurate than any photograph. Both young men were much taken with the peaceful domestic life of the Navajos. In Canyon de Chelly's wide valley of golden sands with the mysterious White House set like a cameo in the pinkish canyon wall, they found women weaving under the piñon trees while men coaxed corn and peaches to grow. Canyon de Chelly was to be the last refuge of the Diné in their final despair.

Colonel Washington's treaties fared no better than earlier ones or those which followed. Navajo bands continued to raid peaceful settlements while the white man's rage mounted. The Army built forts. In the very heart of the Navajo country they erected Fort Defiance, whose remaining stone buildings are eloquent of its name.

Then came the Civil War, and Indians got out of hand. In 1862, Brigadier General James H. Carleton, new Commander of the Department of New Mexico, declared an end to treating with Navajos. They must be defeated. As colonel, the general named Christopher Carson, the redoubtable Kit, who could not write but whose dictated autobiography bristles with the phrase "Done it."

Carson's orders were to round up all Navajos, peaceably if possible, and move them to the Bosque Redondo (Round Wood) near Fort Sumner. The Navajos refused to budge. So on the deadline date, July 20, 1863, Colonel Carson moved against them with a regiment of New Mexico volunteers, men with generations of depredations to avenge. Fighting like Indians—hard-riding, light-eating, unresting— Carson's troop flushed Navajos out of canyons, pursued them across deserts in sandy heat and over mountains in snowy cold, killed three hundred of them in 1863, and finally, in February of 1864, trapped the last of them in lovely Canyon de Chelly. Then started what the Navajos called their "long walk," which brought them to Fort Sumner, where they were to be held in exile. Carson could report "Done it."

History knows no more tragic displaced persons than the Navajos at Bosque Redondo, where three thousand of them were penned in with a band of Apaches who were their bitter foes. General Carleton installed a few brush dams along the Pecos, dug a ditch six or seven miles long, issued seeds to his captives, and asked Archbishop Lamy to send over some padres to open a school. But the general failed to count upon human nature, Indian nature, and nature.

Worms ate acres of corn, drought caused three crop failures in succession, smallpox decimated the people. Meanwhile unprincipled storekeepers were selling liquor and firearms to Indians and supplying them with tainted and even maggoty beef. One agent was indicted for fraud.

The tribe made one break for freedom, but was rounded up by Apache Scouts, a new and trusted arm of the Army. By this time the Diné were defeated, sullen, embittered, and ready to agree to anything if only they might go back to their homeland, where the four sacred mountains stood guard and the supernaturals could hear them. In 1868 their chiefs signed a treaty agreeing to keep the peace. The United States agreed to restore the people to their ancient range and to supply each family with a few animals, tools, seeds, and cash for a couple of years. This was done, and the pattern of modern Navajo life emerged. The people became good sheep-folk, with children herding and women shearing, washing, carding, and weaving. Men remained the hunters and chanters. They had brought home from their dire exile the new art of silversmithing, and Navajo jewelry became an article of trade, first with Indians and later with white traders. None of this altered the old life much. The Diné continued to live in groups scattered over their vast domain, looking to medicine men for spiritual guidance and to headmen for practical advice.

The one possible way to bring such a people into the current of our country's life—by education—the government bungled badly. In 1868 the United States had promised schooling for every Navajo child between six and sixteen, with compulsory attendance and a teacher for every thirty pupils. This promise has never been kept. Even at the middle of the twentieth century, Congressional appropriations for Indian education would leave some nine thousand Navajo children without schooling. Apologists for the Indian Service state that Navajos fought against education. As indeed they did.

Those old-time Indian schools were even more terrifying to Navajos than to Pueblos. Naturally people hid their children from the government man who came to take them to some dreadful place. Those who were taken often did not return for years; by that time they had forgotten their language and certainly had missed training in the ways taught by the supernaturals. Life in those schools was grim; success seemed to be measured by clothing. Get an Indian into trousers and you were civilizing him. The best Indian was the one who did not "go back to the blanket." There was no idea of helping the Indian to live better at home or to reconcile his ancient ways with the needs of his status as a citizen.

To a tragic extent this thinking still prevails. Mission schools naturally set out first to destroy the ancient religion regardless of its importance as an integrating force in the personality. And many Indian Service people show little understanding of the new teaching methods, though they promised even more for Navajos than for Pueblos. On the reservation, day schools could minimize the barbarous disruption of family life caused by snatching six-year-olds away from home; and each might serve as a community center where adults could use such equipment as lathes, sewing-machines, and washtubs. Such a program's success would depend upon teachers capable of understanding it.

A few understanding teachers appeared; some continue to serve out of pure devotion. Salaries which in 1950 began at $2,498.28 per year have risen to $4,345 per year with annual increments of $165. For this honorarium a college degree is required, with courses in "education," but no special preparation for dealing with people of an alien culture.

A manual training instructor proudly exhibited flowerpots from the dime store that his pupils had turned upside down and hung with cords—as birdcages. "Do Navajos keep birds?" "Oh no, these go to Indian Service people." Primary arithmetic charts showed pictures of Scottie dogs, elephants, and oranges. Granting that future voters should be able to count elephants, sheep would seem a more suitable symbol for little herders who have learned to tally their flocks long before reaching school age. A primer is illustrated with pink-cheeked children running out of clapboard houses onto green lawns, or indoors at properly laid tables. The end story presents Mother's pink ruffled dressing-table with powderbox! Navajo children are brown. Their homes are hogans, and lawns are unknown. Tables are rare; the dressing-table seems the ultimate insult to the Navajo way of life.

Some teachers pitch out all such books and charts and make their own. Margot Astrov, an anthropologist, increased the attendance at a day school some children rode forty miles to attend. Her pupils learned words needed daily and made their own charts. Recognizing the traditional mobility of the Navajo, Mrs. Astrov took her classes out to gather edible and medicinal plants and to fetch shrubs and bright stones to beautify the school yard. Talking and writing about their finds and illustrating them with crayon and clay made the children eager to learn. When the class found good potter's clay, a boy brought in his grandmother, who had almost forgotten the potter's art, but was willing to teach. As an interpreter was needed, Mrs. Astrov proposed barter: for every Navajo word she learned she offered two English words, written as well as spoken.

Clyde Kluckhohn has suggested a study of the mental habits of white people associated with Navajos, an idea that merits serious consideration. Their training might well begin with *The Navaho Door*, by Alexander and Dorothea Leighton, whose basic idea seems too sensible to need stating. "In helping people adjust themselves one must be sure he is not attacking beliefs and practices vital to their welfare." As physicians primarily concerned with health, the Leightons enlisted the interest of medicine men. "You burn down a hogan in which a death has occurred? So do we use fire or boiling water to destroy the evil of disease."

If every Indian Service employee had understood such ideas, much dull covert opposition might have been avoided. Teachers resisted what they did not understand; traders backed them up; and missionaries decried any respect for the Navajo's ancient beliefs. Among them they incited some old Navajos to demand a return to the hickory-stick education that had beaten some English into them.

Despite its critics, the new education might have succeeded if it had not suffered collapse along with the rest of Collier's well-conceived program. The cornerstone of that program was stock-reduction, and here speed was most essential. An illiterate generation may be succeeded by literate children. People as recuperative as the Navajos might improve their health in a decade of sanitation and decent care. But land once rendered desert does not come back.

While the tribe increased, its land steadily deteriorated.

Photographs taken in the 1870's show knee-high grass, clear pools, and permanent streams where now there is only desolation. Then eight thousand Navajos ran thirty-four thousand sheep. Through the years the government expanded the reservation and issued more sheep; Indian agents as well as Indians believed that the more stock a man had the richer he was. But flocks were not improved. "Navajo sheep" were long-legged scrubs. By 1933, one and a half million superannuated ewes, rams long past their vigor, and puny lambs were vying for the scant grass with thousands of bony horses and a few scrawny cows. Their hoofs had so loosened the topsoil that every storm was flushing tons of silt down the Colorado River; when it threatened to choke Hoover Dam Californians began to take notice. A stock-reduction program won Congressional approval, and the Soil Conservation Service took charge. They decided what animals must be sacrificed, beginning with nonproductive stock. And they decreed how many animals a family might graze, and where.

This new policy, a complete reversal of former ideas, was accepted by the Navajos in council. But many a man changed his mind when he reported to his wife: Navajo women own the sheep. Overlooking them was a major error. Another was failing to propitiate the traders, who damned stock-reduction almost to a man. Some feared a lessening of profits in wool. All knew of families left without enough sheep to live on, or whose only saddlehorse or wagon team was taken. Navajos asked them: "What shall we leave our children?"

The administration's program, which included the building of roads, dams, and schoolhouses, would have employed many men at good wages and compensated them for the loss of their sheep. But the outbreak of war put an end to that, and the Navajo's failure to understand the whole situation left a residue of bad feeling and distrust of government.

When Navajos and their mentors are observed in meeting, the wonder grows that anything is ever understood. Government directives phrased in Washington's legalistic language are presented to the Navajo council in bureaucratese. "In setting up this machinery we plan to tie it in with your experience. . . . We must iron out some problematical points . . . before testing the reactions of your people." How incomprehensible is such talk—quoted from the transcript of an actual meeting—is proved by the hours of elucidation that follow it. "I meant to say. . . . Let me clarify." But "in the event that," is still not "if"; and "testing the reactions of" has not become "ask." The Leightons have drawn up some suggested speeches-to-Navajos which might well serve as models for administrators.

The Navajo Council, where such deliberations occur, was set up in 1923 as an elective, representative body. It has worked fairly well; experienced students of the Navajos, including Father Berard Haile, believe it would work better if it recognized the Navajo's natural leaders. Headmen are still powerful. Many of them belong to the forty or fifty thousand "long hairs" who speak no English and may live one hundred miles from a highway. But council action often waits on their judgment.

Headmen from distant places ride days to attend such a gathering as the annual fair at Shiprock. On one such occasion, where hamburgers tainted the air and cars and trucks lighted the circle where the Yeibechai would dance, thousands of Navajos had gathered to hear their problems discussed in their own tongue. Man after man spoke, long speeches in the harsh gutturals, with dramatic pauses; few gestures. None of the audience wearied; even young people in modern dress attended closely, grunting approval or laughing at a humorous sally. How shrewd are the judgments of such leaders appears when Washington's best ideas come back tattered by the Navajo's criticism.

To reach these leaders who had no English, a linguist on the Superintendent's staff, aided by bilingual Navajos, issued a Navajo-language paper. It was discontinued in 1958 because it was no longer needed. Schoolchildren learned to read it aloud, older people were eager listeners; the little sheets were worn out by handling. It was a good bridge to the many Diné still living in lonely hogans, miles beyond communication.

Stop where a motor can go no farther. Sky-piercing peaks inclose a silent land, sage- or piñon-scented, scarred into deep red gashes by seasonal storms. Not a house. No road, but just a wagon track discernible only to the accustomed eyes. Then a moving mass colored like the plain. A band of sheep followed by a little girl shy as a squirrel and with shining, inquisitive black eyes. Or a distant puff of dust approaches slowly to reveal a creaking wagon. A man sitting leanly erect. A woman in a fringed shawl bunched beside him. The box swarming with children and the aged. The family is going to the trading-post.

For many Diné the trading-post remains almost the only contact with the outside world. Traders believe that they are the Navajo's best and only realistic friends. Good men or bad, sensible or erratic, stayers for generations or flitters-by who make a trading-post the scene of a picturesque interlude, they have always been useful. Shirtsleeved and suspendered, with sweater frayed at the elbows, the trader stands all day behind his counter. Day begins at dawn and ends when he pushes the last Navajo out at dark. He may have a helper or two, often his wife or son. There is little light, and the air is pungent with the odor of unwashed Navajo, laced with the scents of piñon and tobacco smoke, an unforgettable smell. A fat stove stands in a sand-box that serves as spittoon. No chairs; sometimes a bench. Mostly the customers stand, saying nothing, moving little. Trading is done by gestures. A woman will point with her chin at what she wants. Coffee, sugar, and lard. Canned goods, especially tomatoes and green chile. Beans. Plush for blouses, and for skirts the transparent velvet in luscious fruit-colors which has replaced the old-fashioned calico. Levis. Sturdy high shoes for the sheep-herder; otherwise oxfords. Candy for the child who has stood patiently with begging eyes but no coaxing. When all is in a pile the woman points to the pelts she has dumped on the floor or unwraps her latest blanket from a flour sack.

Then the dickering begins. It ends when the Navajo says: "Put it on the paper." This means more credit from the trader, who takes in pawn silver belts, bracelets, and rings or strings of turquoise and shell. That pawned jewelry, hung in picturesque masses above the groceries, is not a tourist lure; it is sound security.

Progressive Indian Service people advocate "giving the Indian responsibility, letting him make his own mistakes, but helping him to adjust to the modern world." The trader, if he condescends so far, reminds us that this is precisely what traders do. For seventy years they have done business with the Navajo, giving him credit. They issue silver and turquoise to the smiths and guarantee to take the women's blankets. And long before Indian associations were formed, the trader was demanding the Navajo's best work and marketing it.

Lorenzo Hubbell at Ganado urged Navajo women to copy the best old designs and accepted only their finest work. C. N. Cotton, a wholesaler in Gallup, first put Navajo blankets on the eastern market and suggested their use as rugs. At that time, about 1890, there were nine licensed traders to the Navajos; their numbers increased as eastern markets were developed. Mike Kirk at Manuelito and Bertram Staples at Coolidge made heavy old Navajo silver a jewelry fad, and Staples developed flat table-silver in true Navajo feeling. Rugs became known by the names of traders who insisted upon old designs and vegetable dyes. J. B. Moore's rugs from Crystal and Two Grey Hills; Cozy McSparron's Chin Lee rug with its soft yellow stripes; and a similar one developed by the Lippincotts at Wide Ruins. By 1940 there was a Navajo Traders Association of dealers who exacted good work and who were paying some $1,865,000 annually for Navajo products.

Traders tend to regard government doings as unrealistic, at worst even vicious, at best a damned nuisance. Paper promises pile up, but the trader still prescribes patent medicines off the shelf, aids the woman in labor or the child strangling with diphtheria, and makes bone-breaking drives to doctor or hospital. Education is promised, but the trader must still speak Navajo all day. Irrigation is discussed, but young men still have no lands to till. Worst of all, the returned veteran faced a future of disillusionment and frustration.

He had stormed ashore at Anzio, marched across Germany, sailed the Pacific as a pharmacist's mate, or been one of the Navajo Marines who outwitted Japanese intelligence by inventing a Navajo vocabulary to convey military information over walkie-talkies. The war over, he, like all soldiers, wanted to go home. Stepping off the train at Winslow or Gallup, he was welcomed by a patriotic committee. But his chances of achieving the American way of life he had been fighting for were meager indeed.

Back on the reservation, he found that the stock-reduction program had proved itself; even the most recalcitrant traders had stopped their grousing. Grass was beginning to come back along the draws; in fenced demonstration-areas it now stood as tall as it did in the eighties. And fewer sheep were producing more wool and meat. Fleeces now average six and seven pounds instead of four and a half; lambs weigh in at sixty-five instead of forty pounds. Navajo stockmen—and women—take pride in breeding up their herds; the canniest of them are buying up nonreservation lands and competing with their white neighbors. Navajo women in bright plush blouses appear at wool-growers' conventions, fingering the prize fleeces and nodding their chignons over a speaker's points.

But for the returned veteran there are no sheep; there is no way that he can get any. Under the stock-reduction program only stockowners were awarded grazing permits; no provision was made for young people growing up. This has tended to establish a moneyed aristocracy and to leave a majority of the tribe in poverty. A man who is a silversmith may make a living, but only some three hundred families work at the ancient crafts of smithing and weaving. Markets fall off as factory goods supplant handwork and ruin the taste for it.

Farming, then? But land under the Fruitland Dam on the San Juan River had been allotted while the soldier was away. At best, five acres will not support a family, and the veteran was not a good farmer. On-the-farm and on-the-job training lagged, and the Navajo veteran, like the Pueblo, found loans hard to get. The tribe's revolving credit fund has done better: in 1949 such loans set up thirty families in trading-posts, coal mines, log-hauling, trucking. Qualified veterans found jobs with the missions, the traders, and at the superintendency at Window Rock. Several supervisors and a score of range riders are Navajos. But few GI's had the necessary qualifications for such work. Like the rest of the tribe, they had to seek manual labor.

The individual Navajo remained poor and ill equipped to better himself until oil and uranium came along to change his life and orientation. The Navajo reservation, assigned to the Indians as hopelessly arid land, began to spout oil about a generation ago, and in 1953 the discovery of uranium by the Navajo Paddy Martinez on Santa Fe Railway land was followed by the discovery of vast amounts of uranium on the reservation. In 1948 the average family income was $400.00 a year; but by 1958 it had increased to $2,335.00. The tribe received in 1958 approximately $16,000,000 from leases for uranium, oil, and gas and also from forests.

Some advanced ideas have been put into effect at Window Rock, a great red-sandstone-windowed butte which is the Navajo capital. There the Navajo Tribal Council meets, and the Chairman of the Council, presently Raymond Nakai, has his office. The Remington Rand Company was hired to set up the tribal offices with all the necessary equipment, and there trained Navajo stenographers, filing clerks, and bookkeepers handle banks of filing cases and card catalogues. A record is kept of every Navajo who has applied for any service in health, education, welfare, employment, recreation, or management in marketing his herds, flocks, or handicrafts. An annual fair is held at Window Rock which brings together not only thousands of Navajos but almost as many whites and Indians of other tribes. They come to do business with this tribe which now owns and operates lumber mills and a coal mine. The tribe is encouraging industry to settle on the edge of Navajo country.

Before the great uranium development, programs of industrial development were begun with money borrowed from the federal government, but now the tribe is affluent enough to finance its own industries, which include several trading posts, tribal motels, and several housing developments that have survived a period of experimentation. Generally more successful have been the efforts to cooperate with industry in towns that can hire Navajo labor and the programs to train and place Navajo workers.

Such people naturally have a broad and well-financed educational plan with the ultimate goal of producing Navajos fully adapted to modern life, including their own professionals to lead and direct the tribal business. The tribal budget for fiscal 1958 called for the expenditure of twelve million dollars, of which five million was for education. The purpose is to keep every Navajo child in school, well fed, well clothed, and fully supplied with all he needs in order to absorb all the education he can. For those who can progress beyond grade school the tribe offers a series of high school, college, and professional scholarships. Navajo children average well in school; their only handicap —lack of English—is being overcome by the special language training being offered in the public schools.

Health, so closely tied in with education, is being rapidly improved on the reservation, where modern medicine is reducing the incidence of tuberculosis and trachoma.

An important factor in the improvement of health conditions is a Navajo woman, Anna Wauneka, a Council member who heads the Health Committee and serves on the U.S. Public Health Advisory Committee. She goes on the radio to spread useful information in both Navajo and English. Many Navajos have radios—if not in the hogan, then in the pickup truck—and those who do not can easily get to listen to one in the nearest trading post or clinic. People who once distrusted white doctors and were terrified of hospitals as places where people died, are now quite willing to go to a clinic for examination or treatment and to a hospital to have their babies delivered or even for surgery.

The Navajo's readiness to go along with whatever seems good became evident when Salk anti-polio vaccine was suddenly available in sufficient quantities to protect most of the population. Doctors all over the United States found it difficult to get people to bring their children in for inoculation. But on the Navajo reservation it was different. Anna Wauneka, as chairman of the Health Committee, got on the radio and in both English and Navajo explained that here was real protection against a hideous and crippling disease. She urged the people to take their children at once to the nearest center, at a trading post or a clinic. The Navajos, even those who did not understand English, responded promptly and in such numbers that the doctors ran out of vaccine. They consider the outlook for continuing immunization very good indeed.

Part of this happy result is due also to the government's policy of inviting medicine men to participate in the health program. Most medicine men now refer patients to hospitals and clinics.

The reservation's resources, including the human, could stand a lot of developing. Though only some twenty thousand acres of land are deemed irrigable, better farming could make them more productive. A fine stand of ponderosa pine, handled by the Forest Service, is an inexhaustible resource. But the tribal sawmill, employing 350 Navajos, is managed by white men; Navajos do not qualify for technical or managerial jobs. This is true also of a flour mill at Round Rock. Small coal-mines employ about two hundred men, owners and their families. Other minerals include oil, gas, and such more precious substances as uranium. The tribe get about $445,500 in royalties and leases, but the vast potential wealth from such sources remains untapped.

The Indian Service hopes to inaugurate a processing economy. Navajos did well in war factories. Why should they not manufacture their own raw materials: wood, leather, wool, and metals? Here one runs into outside hostility. Capitalists hesitate to invest where government supervision may be implied, especially where government policies change as rapidly as they do in the Indian Service. But chambers of commerce in towns like Gallup, Winslow, and Farmington are beginning to take an interest.

To develop that prime resource, the people, the government has established agricultural and vocational schools, and likely youngsters who have missed schooling are being taught English in special classes. Their progress is phenomenal. The Navajos' opposition to education is no more—now they demand it. But until a generation has been trained, most Diné must move away from their reservation and the sacred mountains that guard it.

The Indian Service's vigorous employment service has placed as many as 15,000 men in one summer. They find all-year work on railroads and sawmills, seasonal jobs in the sugar-beet fields of Colorado, the orange groves of California, the carrot farms of New Mexico. Such workers are hired in groups of twenty men including one who speaks English. The Indian Service insists upon the minimum decency of houses with roofs that do not leak, water spigots not too far away, and sanitary privies.

Such measures, and the fact that a man can have his family with him, are lessening the employer's plaint that Navajos are undependable. The sawmill manager complained: "Come word of a Squaw Dance or let a man get worrying about his wife and off he goes. Navajos have no sense of responsibility." This carping manager has a home at the mill where his family lives with him; Navajo workers have not.

The rare English-speaking Navajo who tries to make his way outside often meets conditions too hard to take. Men who met no discrimination in service find lack of protection and even vicious mistreatment in town. At best, they encounter indifference. It must appear that the only white men concerned with Navajos are the operators of speakeasies and brothels. Police in the towns that ring the reservation readily pick up any Navajo as a vagrant or a drunk; many have been denied legal advice or medical care; a few have been beaten; at least one died unattended in jail. Town police and county sheriffs complain that they have too few officers to handle the Navajo problem; the reservation police number only a dozen. All around the reservation lies a no man's land of lawlessness comparable with the West at its wildest.

Drunkenness is rife among young Navajos, a symptom

of personal dislocations and social evils. The few Diné who could return to the faith of their fathers have done best. Many families held an Enemy Way for the returned soldier, to cleanse him of the touch of death. One who had been bombarded in an abandoned tomb on a Pacific Island talked it out with the medicine man and was at ease. But those who could not accept the old ways have suffered grievously. One, a WAVE, tried to escape by expressing scorn for the old ways, and then through drink; finally her fine mind gave way.

To relieve the reservation's overpopulation, Navajos must be induced to migrate. In 1943 a resettlement project was undertaken to establish more than one thousand Navajos, Hopis, and Mojaves under the Parker Dam on the Colorado River in Arizona. Starting with forty acres and a government loan, many of these new farmers paid out within three or four years and were living nicely in screened homes with water piped in and electricity. Veterans are quick to unite in buying machinery, in making cement, and in farming cooperatively.

Yet this project, well conceived and administered, has encountered the same difficulties as the Bosque Redondo scheme in 1863. Mojaves resent seeing Navajos and Hopis on lands that were theirs. Hopis traditionally distrust Navajos. Navajos react normally, with both dislike and distrust. And missionaries of various faiths add religious tensions to those already existing among the tribes.

Many veterans, more articulate or freer than their elders, express bitter resentment against the missionaries. The reservation is a mission field where eleven churches maintain 134 missionaries, 69 missionary teachers, and 1 unaffiliated missionary. At St. Michaels the Catholics support a school in which children are taught, indoctrinated with the faith, directed in scrubbing and window-washing by exacting nuns, and proudly turned out quite unable to readjust to family or home. A Methodist school at Farmington is similarly successful and boastful. Indian Service people remind us that mission schools choose their pupils, skipping the backward children and the obstructionist parents. It seems true that these schools will be more successful in training Navajos to leave the reservation than in teaching them to cope with life at home.

What Navajos make of this varied religious experience is indicated by the rapid growth of the peyote cult. Navajos first adopted it from Taos, but it has also entered the reservation from other tribes, especially the Colorado Utes. Unlike some earlier students of peyote-taking, students of the Navajos find no evidence that it is habit-forming or that it breaks down the moral fiber or leads to sexual orgies. They find a peyote ceremony marked by reverence, and unadorned to bareness. In an ordinary hogan men and women sit solemnly around an earth mound that bears crescent marks, but not the colors of a sand-painting. A fire burns, and drums accompany songs that go on all night or are stilled for reports of experiences. Peyote buttons may be eaten or taken in smoke; two, three, or four, are the usual dose. The effect varies. Sometimes the drug blocks the motor nerves, and the eater or smoker cannot walk. Others see greatly enhanced visions in color. The sorriest result seems to be nausea. The meeting ends at daybreak with a ceremonial taking of food. Later there is a large meal including the four "goods": meat, water, corn, and fruit.

No ill effects follow a peyote session. In contrast to a cocktail party or some camp-meetings, its evil sequelæ are nil. Among peyote's good effects is an aversion to alcohol. Abstention from liquor is required of peyotists; this odd cult seems to be the best, if not the only hope of curing the tribe of increasing alcoholism.

Students watch hopefully for evidence that the Navajos will deepen and enrich this faith as they did the Pueblo myths so long ago. But so far peyote rites are kept unified by supervisors who travel from tribe to tribe. Songs are sung in many languages—Ute, Kiowa, Comanche. Navajos have begun to make songs. Observances are based on the Mexican myth of a sufferer who journeys, seeks, and finally finds surcease in peyote. But, like all new religions, peyotism has been deeply marked by what it supplants. The influence of Christianity is especially strong. Jesus is invoked in many songs; one begins "J, E, S, U, S." Catholic derivation is clear in a song that calls on "God, Jesus, Mary, and the Heavenly Angels." But among Navajo peyotists the mark of Christianity is deepest in their attitude toward prayer. The ancient Navajo compulsive prayer has been supplanted by the Christian prayer of humble supplication.

Christian exclusiveness has not yet prevailed over the ancient Indian tolerance. Both peyotists and adherents of the old religion hope to keep them separate. But conversions to the peyote cult are on the increase. Even a few chanters have been converted, producing confusion rather than modification. One chanter carries a peyote button in his medicine bag; a peyote priest also puts on sings as a medicine man. So far only one trivial innovation has appeared on the reservation. Near Shiprock peyotists practice the *V-Way* that they invented to protect their soldiers going to war in 1942. The usual peyote rite is called the *Moon-Way*. The *V-Way* includes speech as well as song, and speech that suggests the soul-cleansing of the prayer-meeting sinner who confesses all.

The hold of peyotism on the Navajo is probably best explained by one of them. "The old Navajo religion," he said, "gave us curing and religion. Christianity gave us religion and salvation, but no curing. The white doctor gives us curing, but no religion and no salvation. Only peyotism gives us everything."

⊕⍥⊕

VIII

THE WARLIKE APACHE

⊂⋕ APACHES have long been thought of as the most fe-
rocious of savages, viciously cruel and unconquerable because they were treacherous and untrustworthy: they broke
treaties. It is worth remembering that this reputation comes
from their enemies, Spanish and American officers whom
they outsmarted or settlers who suffered hideously at their
hands. Later writers parrot the phrases. A modern Christian
gentleman writes: "to the red man's untutored sense the distinction between *meum* and *tuum* is nowhere important,"
and "Kindness was for them not even weakness. To their
benighted intelligence it was an unexperienced emotion
hardly to be comprehended." But soldiers who fought him
respected the Apache as a fighting man and for the skill of
his leaders. When paratroopers sought a war cry expressive
of invincible defiance they chose *Geronimo!* That they
hit upon the least admirable of Apache chiefs is only another proof of the white man's lack of perspicuity about
Apaches.

Fortunately for the final record, some white men got on
well with Apaches. They did this by treating them like human beings, not like untamable savages, and by distinguishing between good and bad Apaches. Such men might have
accomplished without warfare our national purpose of de-
spoiling the Indian of his lands. But their advice was consistently disregarded by an Army bent on war and by a
distant government guided by the counsel of officers in the

field. This resulted in thirty years of warfare and unnumbered horrors perpetrated by both sides. Not all the atrocities were Apaches'.

The Apache has been little studied, probably because the culture of the related Navajo developed so much more richly. Both spoke an Athapascan tongue, but the Apache culture shows more traits of the Plains Indians and fewer of the Pueblos. They packed their goods on travois, hauled by dogs or women; lived in pointed tepees or flattened them down into the thatched wickiups still used in Arizona. The best account of Apache mores is in the studies of Edward Morris Opler, especially *The Apache Life Way*. Here we get the impartial view of the anthropologist, whose concern is to know rather than to decry or to change other people's ways.

When white men first knew them, the Apaches were emerging from the seed-gathering era, though men hunted and women scratched the ground and raised what corn they could between moves. The most useful wild plant was the maguey, whose fibers served as strong thread, its thorns as needles, its broad leaves as waterproof thatch, and its crown as a succulent roasted dish. The women cooked, fermented corn into the potent tiswin, wove baskets, and tanned buckskin and the tougher buffalo-hides into silky suppleness. They made the men's long-sleeved buckskin shirts and knee-high boots, and their own modest garments. These straight slips of buckskin, elaborately adorned with beaded yokes, may still be seen at the girls' puberty rites. Girls were trained in all these crafts, as well as in racing. An Apache woman might have to make a long run with her baby hung on its cradleboard from her brow. And she had to be brave and enduring. Britton Davis, in *The Truth About Geronimo*, tells of a young mother whose leg had been shattered by a shot. The surgeon, busy with soldiers, left her for hours and finally amputated the leg without anæsthetic or even a drink of whisky. The Apache girl uttered no cry.

Girls worked and played apart from boys, but premarital unions were not unusual. Two caught in the sex act were made to marry. Rape was considered bad, but might be settled by the gift of a couple of horses. Incest was unforgivable because it partook of sorcery. An unfaithful wife might be punished by having her nose cut off. An Apache chief was highly indignant when asked by a U.S. Army officer to forego this husbandly prerogative.

Chastity was esteemed, largely because a virgin might have mystical experiences valuable to the tribe. A modern Jicarilla girl was told by a prairie dog that the drought was caused by poisoning its kind. Another Jicarilla girl, walking among flowers, heard a voice warning her that evil impended because medicine men were neglecting the use of flower pollen. Both girls warned the old men, who mended their ways. People were expected to have such experiences; men or women who developed unusual powers became shamans.

Power might be used for either good or evil. Witchcraft is still widely accepted among Apaches, and the uneasy dead, wandering as dark ghosts, are feared. Shamans were called upon to make cures by removing spells and exorcising spirits. Moral training came from the family. Opler quotes some precepts. "Do not use a bad word you wouldn't like used to you. Do not feel that you are anyone's enemy. Do not take anything from another child, just because you are bigger. [If the United States had heard this one, the Apache Wars might have been avoided.] Don't steal from your friends. [Stealing from enemies was approved. Ask any hero of World War II.] Don't fight a girl; girls are weaker. Don't laugh at feeble old men and women." Before such axioms the notion of the benighted savage is hard to maintain.

Boys were trained as hunters and fighters. They were tossed into cold water to toughen them, made to run to a mountain top to improve their wind, punished by smothering if they cried, taught to fight other boys. The child was loved and knew it; so he accepted training, however severe, as necessary to make the tough, resilient, self-reliant man he wished to be. His arms were good; the Apache bow was the strongest ever made, his flint-tipped arrows could pierce a man to the heart; his sling, lance, and clubs were balanced and true. When he acquired the white man's gun the Apache became a fair shot. Mounted, he became one with the horse, which he trained to follow his voice and to respond to the lightest pressure of his bare thigh against its flank.

In their mountains these trained fighters were all but invincible. Where the Apache had cover and could reach water or carry it in an animal's entrails, he could live for days without food. When he had food he gorged; provision for the future was impossible. Critics of the modern Apache's improvidence might think of this.

Family groups, related through the mother, united at need into bands, but there was no tribal solidarity. White men came to call Apaches by the names of territories they ranged—Chiricahua, Mimbreño, White Mountain; by the names of their leaders—Cochise, Geronimo, Mangas Coloradas; or by some peculiarity. Mescaleros were addicted to mescal; Jicarillas wove *jicaras*, watertight little baskets.

These were the people the Spanish explorers met. Coronado found them friendly in 1540 when he crossed those widely magnificent borderlands between present-day Mexico and the United States. And he spoke well of buffalo-hunting people on the plains, who may have been Apaches. This word the Spanish adopted from the Zunis; it meant *enemy*.

Like the Navajos, the Apaches came to the fairs at Taos

and Pecos, where they exchanged their buffalo jerky, tanned skins, and captured slaves for white man's goods, especially metal. Here also they rested between raids and got a big feed and perhaps tips for the next raid. Often they detoured on the way home to strip some helpless *paisano's* harvest or to carry off his children as slaves.

Opler suggests that Apaches were not primarily warriors, but fought when they thought they had to. Men were expected to volunteer as proof of manliness; Opler quotes one who refused to go because he had nothing against the enemy. He was scorned as a pacifist is in our society. War fever was worked up in a big circle dance, and each man was provided with amulet and powder. During his absence his wife had to be true to him and to keep the woodpile tidy: if sticks got scattered her man might be lost. On the return, the warrior who had killed must pause outside the camp for purification. Booty was distributed among the poor.

The Spanish never succeeded in "reducing" the Apaches by either warfare or conversion. After the Mexican Republic had been established, Apache warfare became too hideous to contemplate; both sides committed horrors. Mexican governors tricked Apache bands into towns and slaughtered them; scalps were all but legal tender. When the U.S. Army marched in, in 1846, Apaches welcomed the Americans as allies against the common enemy, the Mexicans. They may have thought too that the bluecoats could control United States citizens. Apaches had known two kinds of men from the States. In 1826 Sylvester Pattie, leasing the Santa Rita mines, recognized Apaches as interested and held a council with them. All smoked, spat into a hole, filled it with earth and danced on the spot in token of burying all hatred. This treaty was scrupulously observed by both parties.

The other kind of United States citizen was James Johnson, a trader and friend of Juan José, an honorable and influential Apache chief. In 1835, when a captured Mexican spy told Juan José that the governor of Sonora had agreed to give Johnson one hundred pesos for every warrior of his band, the Apache did not believe it: his friend would not betray him. So Johnson found his work easy. He came as a friend into the camp where Juan José's three wives, many children, and others were going about their peaceful pursuits. As he dickered with Juan José for a mule, Johnson touched a lighted cigar to a powder keg and blew the whole place into a shambles, the while he shot his friend in the back. Johnson got away on a fast horse.

In no time two hundred Apaches were on the warpath, led by Mangas Coloradas, Red Sleeves, recognized chief of the eastern Chiricahuas, as Cochise was of the western. Mangas's first act was to fall on an innocent party of fur trappers and massacre them all. It was the first of half a century of "Apache atrocities." United States citizens were not told, of course, what had brought it about.

Mangas Coloradas had a huge head that held a good brain. He had attended Father Font's mission school at Santa Rita, and he knew that the United States could outnumber if not outfight Apaches. So when the Army came along he was ready to make treaties and to keep them, taking revenge only for evil committed. The Apache could distinguish between good and bad men, even under an alien skin.

In 1851 John Russel Bartlett surveyed the boundary between Mexico and the United States. Like the clumsiest tenderfeet, his men went advertising their whereabouts by large clouds of dust by day and huge campfires at night. Yet Bartlett, believing his party alone in unpeopled wilderness, was startled when an enormous, red-sleeved Apache silently appeared in his camp. Mangas Coloradas had come to warn him against "bad Apaches." Bartlett described this episode in his *Personal Narrative* and told how Mangas continued to protect the party's horses from marauders.

The two gentlemen, Apache and white, misunderstood each other only in relation to two captured Mexican boys whom Bartlett wished to restore to their families. Their Apache owner protested that he had made good Apaches of them, loved them as his own. Besides they were property worth money. Perhaps this point appealed to Bartlett, whose entourage included several Negro slaves. The affair was settled by cash.

U.S. Army officers, like the Spanish, ran into touble when they tried to protect their new citizens. The Apache saw no reason for ending his centuries-old warfare with Mexicans; nor did he grant Mexico's right to cede to the United States lands that had always been his. In formal parleys between bluecoated West Pointers and their bargaining peers in G-strings, the Apache always reserved the right to do as he pleased about Mexicans. Nor did he recognize any international boundary; his domain still included northern Mexico as well as much that was now United States territory. The stage was set for the Apache wars.

Kit Carson, who had been Indian Agent at Ute Park and at Abiquiu, had an Indian policy of his own. He wrote: "This country will always remain in its impoverished state as long as them [sic] mountain Indians are allowed to run at large; and the only remedy is to compel them to live in settlements, cultivate the soil, and learn to gain their maintenance independent of the general government." He disapproved of rations because the usual issue of a blanket, a knife or hatchet, some vermilion, and a length of cloth was less than the Indian could earn in one day's hunt and because bringing Indians into the towns was bad.

When it came to fighting Indians, Carson put his trust in experienced New Mexicans and in their leader, Colonel Ceran St. Vrain. "If," he wrote, "the volunteers had been under the . . . sole direction of Colonel St. Vrain there would have been no need for troops in this country."

An example of what he meant was "the White massacre" near Wagon Mound. Called from his home on the Rayado, Carson swiftly led a detachment of soldiers to the still-smoking camp where the men of Mr. White's party had been killed. Mrs. White and their six-year-old daughter had been carried off. Carson set off in hot pursuit, but the commanding officer, who outranked him, ordered him back. The next day, following the trail, Carson kept coming on bits of Mrs. White's clothing; perhaps she was trying to guide her rescuers. But they were too late. Her body, when they found it, was in such condition that Carson thought her better dead. The Indians were gone, and so was the child.

Years later there lived among the Jicarillas a woman named Inez in whose dark face bright blue eyes burned. She was all Apache, refused to speak English, told of no childish memories. Her son was called *Huero* (Blond); such a name might have been given the son of a blonde mother.

Between 1862 and 1871, the United States spent thirty-eight million dollars in its Apache wars, but it exterminated less than one hundred Apaches, including women, children, and men too old to fight. That made Apaches come pretty high.

Much of this fighting was in New Mexico, especially in its southwestern Grant County, whose widely scattered ranches and mines were easy targets for Apaches who knew every peak and crevice, every hidden vale, every box canyon. They struck like lightning, faded away like smoke, each man for himself, to gather again in a prearranged spot. Settlers grew alert to the owl's hoot, often the Apache's signal for attack, and to the thin line of smoke on a mountain top. The Army improved on this method with one using mirrors, flashing the sun's rays in readable dots and dashes.

The United States was learning that the Apaches were

not one people with a responsible leader. The lot you caught was never the one that had committed the outrage. It became routine to avenge every attack on a lonely ranch house or unprotected wagon train on the next Apache sighted. Silver City citizens offered $250 for every Apache scalp. Neither the Army nor civil authorities tried to find and punish the guilty individual Apache; nor did they proceed against white men who committed crimes against Apaches. Men were getting rich by selling arms, ammunition, and whisky to Indians, to say nothing of scalp bounties. The Army was good business too. Some men wanted no end to the wars. This was the wild west at its worst, when bad men dominated and decency had not arrived.

Fortunately for our national self-respect, there were always a few men, both military and civilian, who dealt honorably with Apaches, and whose neglected records prove that honorable dealing brought results. Notable among these forgotten men was John P. Clum, whose name does not appear in military accounts, perhaps because his methods might have made the military quite unnecessary.

Clum was twenty-two in 1871 when he was appointed Civilian Agent of the San Carlos Indian Reservation in Arizona. His qualifications were that he was already in Santa Fe, operating the first meteorological station in the Southwest, and that he was a member of the Dutch Reformed Church. The government had inaugurated its policy of making Indians the charge of churches.

Of the last two agents one had been killed and the other had escaped just in time. But Clum decided to accept the appointment. He spent some time in Washington, where he may have learned how not to handle Apaches. In any case, he reversed all previous policies, declined military protection, and established himself at San Carlos with one physician and one clerk as his sole support. By 1874, forty-five hundred Apaches had moved onto the reservation, which was just their kind of country: lofty, timbered, with bracing air, streams that swelled each spring with melting snows, plenty of game, and tiny flats where crops could be raised.

The amazing tale of what Clum did and how he did it may be read in *Apache Agent*, written from John Clum's notes by his son. It is a book to be read with reverence for the man's courage and decency and with sadness because we had so few John Clums.

Clum was sensible and no weakling, and he believed in the American system. He proposed to make his charges self-supporting and respectful of the law. He soon had four stout Apache policemen bringing in malefactors, who were tried in a court of Apaches sitting with Clum. And he put men to work as fast as he could, laying stone foundations and making adobes for agency buildings. By 1875 he was issuing scrip for work and making the Apaches buy their own supplies. Agriculture was flourishing, with 200 acres under cultivation, and the tribe had 4,200 sheep, 200 cows, and 200 goats and burros combined. Clum reported: "The troops were gone, consequently morale was excellent."

The soldiers were gone, but certain officers were finding it intolerable that this civilian stripling in fringed shirt and sombrero should be making them superfluous. Clum's efforts were repeatedly nullified by unprovoked attacks on peaceful Apaches. Many reports to Washington were doubtless designed to undermine his authority. But Clum's Apaches stuck to him. They trusted his fairness, feared his toughness, knew that his courage never failed. Clum, for his part, had perfect confidence in his Apache police, who served not only to arrest transgressors, but also to propagandize newcomers to the reservation. Many Apaches came voluntarily seeking peace; other bands were sent there as they were conquered. This was the measure of Clum's success; that the government was always giving him more and more difficult assignments. But his policy of punishing crim-

7 a) Geronimo: This tough Apache chief's name was used as the paratroopers' battle cry.

NEW MEXICO
STATE MUSEUM

b) An Apache Scout, who fought loyally with the United States troops.

NEW MEXICO
STATE MUSEUM

8 *Apache Crown dancers' costumes retain only a few ancient items.*

CAPLIN AND THOMPSON, OLD ALBUQUERQUE

inal Apaches as criminals was never adopted: over and over again, evil individual Indians were given a chance to rest a while at U.S. expense and then go on the rampage again.

The highlight of Clum's career was his capture of the most vicious of these unconquerables, Geronimo. The only time that slippery savage was captured was by Clum and his Apache police.

Geronimo was a master of guerrilla warfare and a shrewd negotiator. He was also a medicine man with mystical knowledge of his enemy's whereabouts, strength, and plans. Opler quotes an Apache: "On the warpath Geronimo fixed it so . . . morning would break after we had climbed a mountain. So Geronimo sang, and the night remained for two or three hours longer. I saw this myself." To make his medicine, Geronimo smoked in the four directions, using a downy feather, an abalone shell, and a bag of pollen. Then he sang about his "power," which was most appropriately the coyote, a wily trickster, sly, and with the gift of disappearance. Geronimo too could make himself invisible, and he had a gun ceremony that made him invulnerable. He was never wounded. Singing, Geronimo accompanied himself on a drum; at the end he howled like a coyote. This was the supernatural power the U.S. Army faced, all unknowing.

Geronimo liked to bathe at Ojo Caliente in Monticello Canyon, where there had been an Indian agency. Learning that Geronimo and his band would be there, the Indian Commissioner in Washington wired Clum at San Carlos: "If practicable, take your Indian police and arrest renegades at Ojo Caliente, New Mexico. Seize stolen horses in their possession; restore property to rightful owners. Remove renegades to San Carlos and hold them in confinement for murder and robbery. Call on military for aid, if needed. (signed) Smith, Commissioner."

Clum got this order on March 20, 1877. By this time

Clum's Apache police force consisted of fifty-four men
who had been drilled by his assistant, ex-Army sergeant
Sweeney, into a body of men who could take orders like
white men, as well as see, hear, endure, and disappear like
Apaches. This was the nucleus of the famous Apache
Scouts, without whose special gifts the Army might still be
chasing Apaches. And this was their first military assignment.

As soon as possible, Clum started, on foot, the four-hun-
dred-mile march across those cactus-maguey deserts which
so appall the motorist even with his thermos bottles, his air-
conditioning, and his speed. John Clum set twenty-five
miles as the day's march, though the Indians, saying that
they could easily do forty, put on a dance one night to show
how unwearied they were. Clum wrote: "If some of you
white he-men challenge my judgment, I suggest you try it
for yourself. The route is still there. . . . The trail distance
still remains four hundred miles; the sand storms still blow,
and the sun still broils." His challenge remains unanswered.

Clum, with his footsoldiers, crossed the Black Range
much as the motor road now crosses it. It is superb country,
with thick timber, tall grass studded with brilliant wild-
flowers, and glimpses of wild creatures in the thickets. They
dropped into Ojo Caliente knowing that Geronimo had
seen them come. But Geronimo did not know that eighty
reserves, commanded by Lieutenant Beauford, had slipped
in the night before. Apache scouts had outwitted Apache
renegades. Major Wade, ordered by General Hatch to meet
Clum on April 21, had not appeared. So Clum proceeded
without benefit of the military.

On the morning of April 21 the slight and boyish Clum
stood on the agency porch to face sour-visaged Geronimo
and his most scowling chiefs. Clum, who could be stern and
autocratic at need, gave the Apache no chance to parley. He
did the talking, charging Geronimo with breaking treaties,

with violating agreements, with many specific robberies and murders. He promised peace to the people who would come peacefully to San Carlos. He must have looked the innocent, easy to handle. But Clum had arranged a series of signals. When he put his hand to his hat, Beauford and his eighty trained Apaches ran out of the agency building. In a trice they had surrounded Geronimo's band. In another they had disarmed the mighty Geronimo and placed his band under guard.

Geronimo, who had outwitted the U.S. Army for years, had been captured by one young man with a steady eye, a cool nerve, and one hundred Apaches he could trust. The Army, represented by three troops of cavalry under Major Wade, arrived the next morning just in time to see Victorio, the other unconquerable, make his surrender.

Clum made his victory secure. He humiliated Geronimo by putting him and other chiefs in irons and by hauling them in wagons to San Carlos, where he put them in the guardhouse. He then notified the sheriff that he held prisoners charged with murder. He had reduced the doughty warrior, enemy of the United States, to the status of a sordid criminal answerable to a county sheriff. He wired the Commissioner of Indian Affairs that his instructions had been carried out to the letter.

But the Army could not let Clum alone. General Kautz, commanding the department of Arizona, ordered Lieutenant Abbott to take over as military inspector at San Carlos. Geronimo was released.

Clum informed the officer that any show of military would send hundreds of Apaches out on the warpath again. At the same time he wired the Commissioner: "If your department will increase my salary sufficiently and equip two more companies of Indian police for me, I will volunteer to take care of all Apaches in Arizona—and the troops can be removed. (Signed) John P. Clum, U.S. Indian Agent."

The result might have been expected. Newspapers throughout the country excoriated the young upstart who would boast that he could do better than the Army. Arizona citizens especially demanded that the Army stay. One said to Clum: "What are you trying to do? Ruin my business? . . . Most of our profit comes from feeding soldiers and army mules."

So Clum resigned; he had repeatedly proffered his resignation.

Not until 1886 did General Nelson A. Miles take Geronimo, and then he did it by a bit of double-dealing. Geronimo, needing a change of scene and a rest from constant fighting, sent a courier to General Miles at San Carlos with an offer to come in and surrender. General Miles accepted, but instead of giving the renegades the freedom of the reservation, as usual, he imprisoned them. Within one week he had some 350 Apaches on a train rolling off toward Florida.

The hideous feature of this affair is that neither Miles nor his officers discriminated between men who had been hostile and men who had been scouts; many of Clum's police, who had really made possible the captures, were shipped off with the real enemies, imprisoned like them, and, like them, separated from their families.

Clum was not alone in believing that the Army was often ruthlessly and stupidly wrong in dealing with Apaches. Britton Davis, a United States Army officer, wrote: "We have heard much talk of the treachery of the Indian. In treachery, broken pledges on the part of high officials, lies, thievery, slaughter of defenseless women and children, and every crime in the catalogue of man's inhumanity to man, the Indian was a mere amateur compared to the 'noble white man.' His crimes were retail, ours wholesale." Sergeant Neil Erickson, Swedish-born, quoted by Colonel C. B. Benton in *The Westerners Brand Book*, said: "I can tell you now though that if I had known as much about Indians then as I do today . . . I think I would have deserted the U.S. Army and gone with the Apaches. Those Indians got a raw deal."

So the Apache wars came to an end with most of the Apaches, good and bad alike, imprisoned in muggy Florida, where, being mountain people, they suffered extremely. The protests of Herbert Welsh, secretary of the Indian Rights Association, got them moved to Fort Sill in the Indian Territory, where some of their descendants are today. But most of them, given a chance to choose, made their final trek by train back to the mountains of New Mexico. Geronimo died in Oklahoma in 1909, his wife on the Mescalero reservation in 1950.

Modern Apaches know their history, but scouts and the sons of scouts seem to have forgotten the painful injustice of their removal to Florida. A few wizened old men still appear at G.A.R. meetings, some wearing the close-fitting cap that only a medicine man may wear and that may be the only Apache item in a heterogeneous uniform. Younger men are proud of descent from U.S. Apache Scouts. Nor have they reason not to be proud of descent from other Apaches who fought as brave men have done in all times and places for their own homes and way of life. It may be that time will teach us that these fearful Apaches were more warred against than warring.

THE MODERN APACHE

Mescalero

In 1949 Albuquerque suffered what may have been the last Apache raid—or the first one indicating the completeness of this aborigine's adjustment to modern methods. The Mescaleros, sponsored by the Chamber of Commerce and an American Legion Post, were presenting their Devil Dance in the baseball park to raise funds for a community center on their reservation.

These Mescaleros are descendants of Lipans from Texas and the last of Geronimo's eastern Chiricahuas. Their reservation contains some of the best land in New Mexico, with fine grazing on the slope toward the Tularosa Basin and superb forested uplands in the White Mountains. It supports one thousand people fairly well; properly developed, it could do better. Some Mescaleros boast of ancestors who were Apache Scouts; others take pride in their descent from Geronimo. A bad enough forebear is a good ancestor.

These commercially-minded Mescaleros are cashing in on their good location as a stopover for tourists traveling between the Carlsbad Caverns and Santa Fe. They engaged the Stanford Research Institute, and on their advice have set up a civic center to accommodate tourists as well as for conducting tribal affairs. Handsome buildings house administrative offices, along with a motel, a restaurant, and a shop for the sale of traditional bead- and leatherwork.

The Mescaleros are cattlemen with a thriving lumber business too. Their forests have been well managed and produce an average annual income of about twenty-five thousand dollars. But lumbering is secondary to the cattle business, for which the reservation is singularly well fitted. Rising from plain to peak, its wide meadows permit grazing in the upper levels during the summer; the lower pastures grow heavy grass for winter feeding. Cattle sales have grossed some fifty thousand dollars annually. Of an average ten thosuand head, ninety per cent are owned by individuals, some of whom live well and hire Texas "hands" to work their herds.

Non-Indian cattlemen complain that the Mescaleros, who pay no taxes, offer unfair competition with those who do. But the average Mescalero family income is less than two thousand dollars a year, and many of the people are poor. None lives so well as the complaining stockman. These Mescaleros are one of the few tribes in the country whose conditions are improving.

That life is not better for the Mescaleros is partly their "own fault"—or the fault of human aversion to change. Few men flex their muscles to chop trees, raise ridgepoles, build good houses. After the Reorganization Act of 1934, in the first fervor of self-government, the tribal council borrowed $350,000 to build homes. These loans, plus interest, were promptly paid off from sale of the tribal timber; the tribe still owns the houses, which are occupied on a perpetual-use assignment. But the excellent plan went no farther. Most people live contentedly in wickiups, tents, or half-roofed shelters, and drink from the clear ditch that gurgles by. In that salubrious climate and for people generally unacquainted with modern conveniences, such homes are comfortable enough. Typhoid is rare. Home-building and water development would be logical and practicable next steps, as would be windmills and spreader dams for watering cattle, diversion dams for irrigation, and wells for domestic use. But eager superintendents have so far been unable to stir the council out of its age-old lethargy.

This is a prime example of the real Indian trouble. How long should Indians be protected while they learn to govern themselves and to manage their own affairs? Mescalero also has enlightening political implications.

The council, discovering a surplus in 1949, figured out that funds in hand could give each individual, infants and all, fifty dollars in cash. The Superintendent forwarded their proposal to Washington with his recommendation against it. It came to the attention of a Congressional committee. An election was due, the first at which New Mexico Indians could vote. Certain lawmakers, doubtless inspired by the truest American principles, supported the Indians. Here is a true test of the expressed determination of Indian Service administrators to "let the Indians make their own mistakes," as the only way to true self-reliance and self-control. Fifty dollars in the pocket of each Mescalero would be gone within the month; fifty thousand dollars invested in water development would put the reservation into practically perfect shape and result in more cash and better living for all. Such are the problems of Indian Service administrators. How it looks to the Indian was wryly expressed by an old Apache. "When the Reorganization Act came we were proud to be like other Americans; to be elected to serve our people. We had always sat in the back of the wagon like children while a white man drove. Now we thought we could take the reins, while the Superintendent went ahead pointing the way. But now we see the Superintendent in the driver's seat while we still sit in the back. Sometimes we can't even see where our wagon is going."

Even a passing visit to the reservation demonstrates that Mescaleros are fast adopting our customs, if not our cannier virtues. Women no longer flounce about in the long ruffled skirts and loose overblouses that supplanted their ancient buckskin dresses; only smart town shops now make Apache skirts and pleat them wet on broomsticks. Mescalero women wear clean prints and saddle shoes. Few men still wear the long pigtails under tall black hats; they affect Hawaiian shirts and blue jeans. Many Apaches drive cars, even if they live in huts and drink ditch water. They attend Mass in the Catholic church or the service of the Reformed Church in America. A few heed the itinerant Latter-day Saints who visit them occasionally. That medicine men still operate is, of course, no incongruity to Indians. Ghosts still walk, bad people still conjure up evil spells. But these are the things that white people know nothing about.

Sadly, the old ways pass; too often what is forgotten would fit well into the new life or carry the old moralities onto the modern scene. Crafts are practically lost. Youngsters will not learn the old songs; they will dance all night in a cheap place in town, but are reluctant to enter the circle dance that old people still find important. Only the dark underside of life remains Apache, kept alive by silly fears and hatreds.

Even young men who served in World War II have not wrought notable changes on their people or in their own lives. More than one hundred served with credit to the United States and to their tribal reputation for courage. But only ten have taken any training under the GI Bill. Most of them live at home as before.

One notable exception is a descendant of Geronimo who replaced his progenitor's faith in his medicine with trust in instruments. As a navigator in the Air Force it was the young Apache's responsibility to take a plane from a point in Florida to a certain spot in England. "They guyed me a good deal. A poor ignorant Indian! I had to prove my race as well as hit that spot. So I checked and checked again. I was nervous, all right. But when we landed I had hit it right on the nose!"

Most Mescaleros move along together, adopting what they see, fending off what they do not comprehend, appear-

ing in public as Apaches only on the Fourth of July when
the ancient puberty ceremony for girls is held. The general
scene is like a camp-meeting. Cars stir the heavy dust that
makes noses painfully sensitive to the acrid smell of frying
fat. El Paso, Roswell, and Alamogordo have sent ice cream
trucks and every sort of legal bottled drink. Every stand has
a radio. Happily, Manuel Archuleta's Indian records compete with be-bop. Illegal drink is also available; its traces
are clear in wavering foot-trails and mad driving on moun-
tainsides.

The Apache policeman said: "It is not Indian, it is a white
man problem, this drinking. If white men would control
their sales we could control our young men." A sage older
man thought beer halls with music and dancing on the reservation would help to cut down dangerous drinking.

Only at dead center of the whirling, noisy, dusty show
was there a hint of old Apache. It was a canvas tent, not a
skin tepee, but it was cooled with leafy boughs. Within, old
women sat on their heels chanting hour after hour. It was
as though their wailing and their persistence might keep
alive some old flame as well as prepare these maidens for
maturity. The little girls stood shuffling in the dance, soft
faces serious, eyes downcast, their costumes the fine buckskin dresses newly made for the ceremony, with deep fringe
and wide yokes trimmed with beads.

Outdoors the long hot day wore slowly on. Steaming
people went from the rodeo to the food, perched talking on
woodpiles, bought silly gewgaws. No Apache baskets were
offered for sale, but only bits of beadwork made for the
cheapest white taste. A photographer from El Paso had
been commissioned by the Council to take pictures for post-
cards. He caught a girl on her way to the tepee with an aged
aunt in attendance; an old scout lifted his hat to show his
twisted pigtails; a careful young matron removed the mos-
quito netting from the cradleboard that held her flat-faced

baby. But it was hard to find anything typically Apache. The cameraman hoped for some night scenes with fires.

At evening cool there was a shift in the audience. Tourists were on their way. The games had ended and the grandstand crowd had left. Old Indian Service people and townfolk who come every year drove up to see the dance. They were quieter; knew what they would see. First there was the circle dance that everyone should have joined, but from which young Apaches held aloof, leaving its mystic generation of power to old folk and a few loyal Indian Service employees who helped to enlarge the ring. Finally a score of old Apache women, soberly stamping, and more and more younger folk joined in, in self-conscious groups. At the end girls ran giggling and young men pursued, but it was all done in the light of the neon glows from food stands. No real capture nowadays, so far as anybody knows or will say.

Very late, when the moon had sunk lopsidedly over the divide, leaving the sky to a thick misty coating of stars, the dying fire was rebuilt and the Crown Dancers appeared. Scents came from burning piñon and night dampness; radios were muted; the ignorant and irreverent had gone; drunks and babies had toppled over asleep. To rattle and chant, to tiny beaten drum, the weird figures came in their squatting pose, seeming quite properly attired in shawls instead of skins. The crowns, which give the dance its name, are tall painted structures made of thin withes and adorned with feathers. Each one jerks with the dancer's movement. There was seriousness now. Apache had replaced white man. But it was the disappearing Indian moving in a rhythm remembered mostly for show purposes in support of a faith all but outgrown.

Jicarilla

Life on New Mexico's other Apache reservation is

harsher. A reservation that straddles the continental divide between the Colorado-New Mexico boundary and the Albuquerque-Farmington highway, it is cold; often its winter temperatures are the lowest in the nation. Its tallest peaks rise above timberline, but lower down fine forests are slowly recovering from years of bad lumbering practices. In 1949 its timber brought the tribe ten thousand dollars. The reservation also supports eleven thousand cow units (an estimate based on the amount one cow eats), including sheep and goats as well as cattle, owned by the tribe and by individuals. No increase seems presently possible here; the range is stocked to capacity. Nor does farming seem a likely way out. There are few streams fit for irrigation; here and there tiny plots of dry farming give a dubious yield, but the growing season is too short for profitable agriculture. The Jicarillas must be stockmen, and are considered fairly good at it. But as the tribe increased between 1944 and 1950 from 799 to over 900 people, these Apaches were soon in as bad a fix as the Navajos, but their position is gradually improving.

Headquarters is at Dulce, a white clapboard town with well-built modern houses for Civil Service people, a store, post office, and government offices. Few Indians except government employees live here. Up the hill is the Dutch Reformed Mission: church, clubhouse, and homes for missionaries. And over the hill are the school buildings, with homes for the doctor and teachers.

The Apaches live in widely scattered, weathered frame shacks and dusty tents. The picturesque pointed tepees of their ancestors appear now only on ceremonial occasions; civilization seems to have brought ugliness with no greater comfort except that supplied by sheet-iron cookstoves. Other furniture consists of piles of dirty sheepskins and a few pots and pans. Flies, filth, and unwashed children abound. Water is scarce; often it must be hauled miles from the nearest lake. Dulce Lake, Horse Lake, Stinking Lake are set in grassy hollows like ultramarine jewels in plush, but their waters are often brackish and alkaline. Most homes are not permanent; sheep people drift with the flocks.

Teachers and missionaries, laboring devotedly for what they consider good for Apaches, seem doubtful of their success. A gentle mission worker carries a bunch of keys heavy enough to brain an ox, and unlocks and relocks every door as she shows the clubhouse for Indians. "They all steal; they even bring us their things to lock up." Missionaries find immorality on the increase: more illegitimate babies, more drunkenness. "They have lost the old taboos that kept boys and girls apart; they have not yet learned morality."

Teachers express the conviction that little Apaches are better off in the boarding school than in their homes. "Immorality and filth! Bickering and broken marriages!" They admit that most youngsters return home as soon as they can. Each year a few more enter the Indian High School at Santa Fe, but even those return home after graduation.

An Apache, middle-aged and learned in tribal lore, said: "The legends can only be told in winter. But the children are in school in winter, so they cannot learn what is right to do. They have no morals now." This is the measure and perhaps the reason for what fifty years of civilized training has done to an Indian tribe.

That training has not been long, and the best of it has been highly irregular and personal. A dictatorial triumvirate, representing business, government, and religion, wrought the greatest changes in the Jicarillas' ways. One thoughtful Apache, admitting its beneficence, blames this dictatorship for the self-distrust and lack of initiative of today's Jicarillas.

Emmet Wirt represented business. Coming west in the 1890's he had a butcher shop in which he sold the Army meat for Indians. Then he became a licensed trader at

Dulce. The Jicarillas were miserably poor. They earned only a pittance with basket and beadwork. Years of the dole had reduced strong fighting men and mighty hunters to dirty outcasts huddled in filthy hovels. They still hunted sporadically: mule deer, turkey, quail, and grouse for food; muskrat, beaver, mink, and weasel for hats and for fur to weave into their long braids. Wirt found markets for them; gave them credit at his store, even in defiance of the Indian Service; fed those who could not pay, but taught fair dealing his own way. Once he rode twenty miles after an Apache who tried to cash a government check off the reservation instead of paying a bit on Emmet's bill. When the man refused to stop, Wirt lassoed his horse, brought him down, and got the endorsed check. Such forthrightness, combined with fairness and friendliness, won the Apaches so completely that Wirt was the most powerful man on the reservation until his death in 1938. He was a man of his era: tough, just literate, but a reader; profane to a legendary degree; a shrewd trader; and an honest man whose morals were his own.

When the Jicarillas returned from a sojourn among the Mescaleros, a little girl came with them, riding behind her sister. She was extraordinarily lovely, with long-lashed eyes, delicate brown skin, and grace in every motion. Her beauty grew with her, and when she was still very young, tiny Tonita became a member of Wirt's household. She had several children by him. One son still living on the reservation talks quite unaffectedly of her, of his father, Wirt, and of his "Apache father" (his mother's Apache husband) and full-Apache half brothers and sisters. As a father, Emmet Wirt recognized and educated his illegitimate children equally with his legitimate daughter; as a friend, he willed his store to the tribe; it is still their main dependence.

Government was best represented by two men—an agent and a doctor. Chester Faris, as agent, believed in building manhood. He persuaded the government to issue sheep to the Apaches in 1921. Emmet Wirt heartily approved; the two men worked together to improve the breed. Four years later the average family still had only twelve sheep, but the Apache was regaining a measure of his manhood. He was killing predatory bears, bobcats, and coyotes instead of being a predator himself, and outdoor life with the flocks was arresting the tuberculosis that had reduced the tribe from 1100 in 1900 to 580 by 1921.

Children still died like flies, and parents feared and dreaded the school. Once, in 1921, after the bathing and delousing which was the preliminary scholastic exercise, two youngsters died in the school. Nobody remembers why; there was no doctor there. But the Apaches came, several hundred strong, to rescue their children; they were ready to burn down the school. While the principal escaped, hidden in a load of hay, Wirt held the mob. Speaking Apache with ease, he flailed his coatless arms, bullied, threatened, promised, persuaded them to wait on a council meeting to be held the next day. There Chester Faris presented to the six councilmen Dr. Howard M. Cornell, then serving as physician to a lumber company near by. With Emmet Wirt as interpreter, the doctor explained how those deaths might have occurred, how modern medicine might help the children. After the Council had sent the rioting parents home, Dr. Cornell was inclined to preen a bit. "Hell," said Wirt, "I had that all done before they ever met."

Dr. Cornell was persuaded to give up his lucrative post for the poor salary of a reservation doctor. On first examination, he found eighty per cent of the children tuberculous. So the triumvirate, Faris, Wirt, and Cornell, turned the school house into a sanitarium and sent the handful of healthy children to the mission school.

Dr. Cornell built up a staff of seven nurses, mostly from the Dutch Reformed Mission. One of them, Miss Hendrina Hospers, as visiting nurse, found a family of five down with flu. She stayed for three days, chopping wood, carrying water, sleeping on sheepskins alive with lice, and saved the family. Dr. Cornell, finding a woman in labor in the midst of a big fair, could persuade her to go to the hospital only if her Apache midwife went along. "Sure," said Dr. Cornell, "she can help me." He wrapped the midwife in a large white gown, showed her how to scrub her hands, explained the techniques as he delivered the baby. "Now," said the midwife to the doctor, "I know how. You get up on that table and I'll take down your big tummy."

The third influence, religion, is largely represented by the Dutch Reformed Mission manned by Hollanders. Spreading missionary ideas is a disappointing labor. Even the Jicarilla convert, mouthing the taught phrases—"Of course I don't believe any of that; Jesus is my Saviour"— seem to be dangling between beliefs, uprooted and convictionless. Perhaps only a student of comparative religions and of how myths grow could make the Christian faith comprehensible to an Apache. As it is, the pagan, not the Christian, seems to find harmony between the faiths. One Apache, having listened all afternoon to an exposition of redemption through the blood of Christ, said: "Yes, that's all true. There are many trails to the mountain."

Not surprisingly, the Jicarillas have lost their more elevated trails to the mountain while retaining many old-time phobias and exorcisms. One still hears of the burning of houses in which someone has died. Young people dread the dark where black ghosts roam and believe that if a child cries out in its sleep it is beset by bad spirits. Only painting an intended victim's face with red ochre will prevent the witch from recognizing him. Bobby-soxers from the school may be so adorned.

Even veterans of World War II cling to the old beliefs. One who broke his leg falling off a truck went as soon as he could to Taos. A medicine man there guaranteed to show the face of the guilty witch for ten dollars. The young GI sat enthralled while the shaman chanted and gesticulated over a black bowl of water. When the veil was withdrawn, sure enough he saw a face reflected. Satisfied that he knew who his tormentor was, he returned home and doubtless spent another ten dollars to counteract the spell.

The far-away doctor is often most revered. A Jicarilla who enjoyed no great fame at home made a good living among the Navajos, who found his invocations most effective in relieving pain. An inquirer learned that the storekeeper in Cuba had been wondering why that old Apache bought so much aspirin.

Even English-speaking Apaches who have been to school have curious experiences. One of them explained why some Apaches hesitate to kill coyotes; a typical white sheep-man's complaint is that their Indian neighbors will not co-operate in exterminating the lamb's most vicious enemy. Once, the Apache said, two of his nephews who were herding his sheep did not come home when expected. He went to investigate and found their bodies in La Jara Lake. "But my sheep, they weren't scattered like would be natural. They were just grazing, like with a good sheep-herder. Then I saw who was herding them. A coyote was there, just at the edge of the piñon wood, with his tail out all fluffy. When he saw me, I said: 'Thank you for taking care of my sheep.' Then he went away. . . . Yes, they were all right. Maybe he ate one or two, but that was for pay." He paused. "I belong to the coyote people."

The new culture's roots are not yet firm enough to displace the old culture. And distrust of the white man takes many forms. Once Emmet Wirt, who as Deputy U.S. Marshal had made enemies, saw an ex-convict coming at him with a knife. Just in time Wirt shot and the man fell dead. Wirt sent for the sheriff and was quietly awaiting arrest in a saloon when horses were heard outdoors. In no time the place was full of Apaches, who in those days still wore the tall black hats, pigtails wrapped in fur, and blankets. "Come," said the leader, "let's go. We brought you a good horse." Wirt's determination to stay, to stand trial, filled them with amazed distress. "Don't trust those white men, they'll hang you sure." Perhaps Wirt's acquittal on a well-sustained plea of self-defense had more educational value than many precepts.

The Jicarillas, like the Mescaleros, wonder how much self-government they really enjoy. Tribal funds are controlled by the Council, but their hired clerk, a Civil Service white employee approved by the Indian Service, disburses sums to maintain fences, windmills, and roads. The store Emmet Wirt left them is managed by a white man. More than once the Superintendent has overruled the Council to dismiss a man they liked or to appoint one they did not.

Like the Mescaleros', the Jicarillas' council wants to distribute a part of the tribal fund, in this case some third of a million dollars. People, they say, need wagons and horses to haul timber for better houses; cash to buy improvements; windmills to water vegetable gardens "so we can feed our children better." They name individuals whose tribal dole is inadequate for a minimum diet. "A good sheep-herder," said one councilman, "looks after the weak lambs. The government will not let us do that. They put in a storekeeper who will not give credit. What is a poor man to do until he sells his lambs? All stock business is done on credit."

Indian Service people aver that the Apaches have no money sense, their acquaintance with money being very recent. They doubt the Apaches' sincere desire for the better living they prate of. They name eight or ten families with annual incomes of ten thousand dollars or better. A few live in well-built houses with screened windows and porches, weatherproof barns, and a water supply. Others in that income bracket live like their poorer neighbors. Even those with access to piped water at Dulce make no gardens. A mature Apache, half white and the product of white schools, said: "I work for a good government salary; yet I owe $3,800 at the store. I ought to have that much in the bank. I could pay that off tomorrow; I have enough assets. But I won't. I'm just too Apache. No Jicarilla ever has a bank account."

Something must be wrong with educational and Christianizing methods that show no better results after forty years of school, church, government tutelage. The answer may lie in the present situation.

All Jicarilla children attend a boarding school at Dulce. The younger ones and some teachers are housed in a rickety old frame building; it is contrary to government policy to repair a condemned building. One only hopes that appropriations for a new structure will come before somebody drops a match. The older children occupy a newer and more solid building. Those who finish the eighth grade must go to the Indian School at Santa Fe for further training. There the Apache child has no chance to associate with white children, to learn their ways, or to adopt their standards. Naturally they return to the reservation—an island dominated by aliens, but home. Only three have ventured on to college; two half-whites, one adopted by whites. One has stayed away in a Civil Service job in Washington.

Back on the reservation the young Apache who has learned about movies and liquor finds both in the squalid villages that surround him. Police control is nil. One Apache policeman patrols the entire reservation and deplores the free selling of liquor to Indians. But the Apache may not arrest a white man, the U.S. marshal is far away, the state police are uninterested. If a deputy sheriff were reached, his brother-in-law, cousin, or his very self might turn out to be the liquor dealer. Drinking is increasing. One hears of young men, even high school graduates, veterans, even young women, who drink. The accent is on youth. For youth has lost the old taboos without taking on the missionaries' morals.

Perhaps these Apaches are the most instructive example of what our government has done with, or to, its conquered dependents.

PART TWO

Spanish

X

SPANISH DISCOVERERS

⟡ NEW MEXICO's second discoverers were soldiers. Although Europeans with white skins, they often had the flashing black eyes and blue-black hair and beard of their Moorish ancestors. Some showed traces of aboriginal American heritage, for Spaniards entered New Mexico fifty years after Columbus had first set foot on a Caribbean island; early enough so that sons of Indian women could have grown into Spanish soldiers. They were conquerors, just out of the age of knighthood, infused with the conviction that the world was theirs, that their right and mission was to take and hold it for the glory of the vast Spanish empire rapidly expanding throughout the Americas and across the Pacific. Clanking in armor, superbly mounted, these men represented the highest civilization of their time, and they brought unquestioning belief in their civilization and their religion.

With the soldiers came their men of religion. Franciscan friars walked in sandaled feet, meek and unarmed, but as determined as any soldier to conquer in the name of the cross they bore. They too brought mediæval ways of thinking. The Spanish discoverers had begun to leave Europe before the Protestant Revolt. They came from a unified, rigidly controlled world believing that only one way was acceptable to a just, a beneficent deity—an idea inconceivable to the tolerant Indian then, as it is now.

The conqueror was Francisco Vásquez de Coronado, whose conquest was celebrated in a Cuarto Centennial in

135

1940, and whose history has been many times retold. Its definitive telling may be in *Coronado and the Turquoise Trail* by Herbert E. Bolton, though Dr. Bolton modestly admits that more material may come to light. Archives in Mexico and in Seville are a bottomless mine of reports, letters, depositions, and trial records.

Coronado was not the first white man to know the vast stretches of mountain and desert that soon became known as Nuevo Mexico. Alvar Núñez Cabeza de Vaca, shipwrecked in 1528 at an unidentified spot in the Gulf of Mexico, and washed ashore at a place thought by some to be near the present site of Galveston, Texas, had walked across the continent with three companions. They were sometimes the slaves of Indians; sometimes they were revered for an unaccountable gift for healing. Historians think that they crossed the Rio Grande a few miles north of El Paso, and so touched New Mexico. There they saw Indians living in permanent houses and raising corn, beans, and squash. When they finally reached Mexico City after eight years of toilsome wandering, Cabeza de Vaca's tale roused that capital to a furor. Perhaps those towns farther north were the Seven Cities of ancient legend; they might be the center of an empire more splendid than that of Moctezuma, richer than that of the Incas.

Antonio de Mendoza, then Viceroy of New Spain, decided on further exploration. He needed a stupendous achievement to outclass Cortés; moreover, Mexico was filling up with roistering younger sons from Spain, trained as soldiers, but otherwise a nuisance. An impressive and profitable enterprise would enhance Mendoza's prestige and incidentally relieve his domestic problem.

Neither Cabeza de Vaca nor his two white companions cared for further faring into that fabulous northland. There remained only the fourth, a Moorish Negro slave named Estevan, who could be "acquired" without consulting his wishes. But Estevan probably welcomed the opportunity to go along. He had proved his ability to deal with Indians, he knew several of their dialects, and he had a feathered gourd given him somewhere north of the Rio Grande. Estevan was the man for guide.

The responsibility was given Fray Marcos de Niza, described by his Franciscan superior as "skilled in cosmography and the arts of the sea, as well as in theology." He was an experienced explorer who had been with Pizarro in Peru. His orders were to check on Cabeza de Vaca's tales, to report on the land and peoples he saw, to win converts, and by peaceful means to take possession of everything for His Most Christian Majesty, the Emperor Charles V. The good gray friar and the Negro went on alone, attended by Indians from the north as servants and burden-bearers.

The route they took seems roundabout to us, but they were retracing Cabeza de Vaca's trail west to Culiacán and north across modern Sinaloa and Sonora, hoping always for sight of the "South Sea." On his return, Friar Marcos reported a triumphant advance among Indians who welcomed him, received the faith, and told of other people up ahead who had gold. Gold was already the retreating mirage.

In northern Sinaloa, the friar sent Estevan ahead with orders to send back a cross one palm long if he had good news, larger if he had better news, very large if it were something grand. Estevan, pushing ahead with his Indian escort and shaking his gourd rattle as token of authority, soon sent back a cross as big as a man. Estevan had heard of Seven Cities of Cíbola (the first use of that name), but he had not seen them. Estevan's messenger said the Cíbolans lived in turquoise-studded houses and had much gold. This tale was enough to enable Friar Marcos, remembering Peru, to build up quite a gorgeous empire. So he kept on following the Negro, who left larger and larger crosses along the way, but kept elusively ahead.

As the friar came toiling along he heard more and more about the fabulous Seven Cities of Cíbola and saw natives wearing turquoise, cotton *mantas*, and well-tanned hides. The feeblest signs seemed proof of what he wanted to believe. His route was taking him down the Sonora River and over a divide near the present international boundary. There he touched the San Pedro River and swung northeastward across El Gran Despoblado, still a great unpeopled area of magnificent pine forest. Across the Gila River the friar's Indian guides angled sharply eastward, promising sight very soon of the Seven Cities.

Exact routes are hard to trace, but Agnes Morley Cleaveland points out, on her ranch in the Datil Mountains, three old oak trees that may prove that the expedition passed that way. Perhaps the crosses carved on the trees record the dramatic end of Estevan. That dashing Negro had been killed by the Cíbolan Indians. The tale long accepted is that he had been too free with women, but Elsie Clews Parsons suggests that the famous feathered gourd was bad medicine in Zuni, and that Estevan was killed as a witch, not as a philanderer.

When this sad news reached Friar Marcos, he soon turned back toward Mexico. Whether he had gone far enough to see Háwikuh, the first of the seven cities, is disputed. Even the friar reported seeing it only from a hilltop. Only distance could have invested those adobe walls with the shining glory they came to have in the telling. Certainly the friar's account lost nothing in the versions of it that sped through Mexico.

Viceroy Mendoza was overwhelmed by aspirants to lead an expedition to the new land of gold and glory, among them the richest, most experienced, most powerful officers in the Americas. He chose Francisco Vásquez de Coronado, who stands up well as the ideal Spanish conqueror. Son of a good family of Salamanca, he was a gallant officer.

We hope he was both fair-haired and handsome, though no portraits remain. He had married Beatriz, daughter of a wealthy noble family, had made a friend of the viceroy, and had been successful in various civil posts, including the governorship of Sinaloa. His capital, Culiacán, was well along on Friar Marcos's route.

Coronado was appointed commander of the expedition and captain-general of all the places mentioned by Friar Marcos, as well as of any others he might discover. In Mexico unattached young men rushed to volunteer; over three hundred men were quickly recruited, many of them on horseback; many were rich enough to equip themselves magnificently and to invest in the undertaking. The Spanish empire was enlarged at the expense of the explorers.

So the great expedition was as we like to think of it. Dr. Bolton estimates its cost, in today's figures, at one million dollars. It had officers in glittering armor with floating plumes and brilliant capes, mounted on fine horses, and followed by well-trained men, to say nothing of the hundreds of burden-bearing, working Indians. Spain's great gift for organization had, within twenty years, brought enormous Indian populations into servitude, though the fiction was that they entered it voluntarily.

The army rendezvoused at Compostela, five hundred miles northwest of Mexico City, where Mendoza came to see them off. Students have dug out detailed information of men, horses—stallions and mares—equipment, and arms; of coats of mail, buckskin jackets, and the padded cotton armor of the Mexican Indians. Arms varied from the Indian's clubs, javelins, and slings to European crossbows, lances, arquebuses, and even a few cannons. The muster roll reveals how this Spanish army came not from peninsular Spain alone, but also from Charles V's empire. There were five Portuguese, two Italians, one Frenchman, one Scotsman, and one German. Among them were three women, not high-born ladies, but the first of the stout pioneer women who were to have so much to do with New Mexico's long history. One of them has character for us: Francisca de Hozes, wife of Alonso Sánchez, was a good nurse, a great gossip, and a loquacious witness in Mexico years later.

This was a young man's army. Coronado was only thirty years old; most of his officers were younger. They were adventurous, daring, full of fun and horseplay, deeply religious, medievally superstitious, and hard to discipline. Above all, they were articulate and they revealed themselves and each other fully in their accounts and letters, and in testimony taken in investigations after they got back. Perhaps the best, certainly the most dramatic, firsthand story is Pedro Castañeda de Nájera's *Account of the Journey to Cíbola*. Of the start from Compostela he wrote: "Such a noble body was never assembled in the Indies, nor so many men of quality in so small a body." With them went Fray Marcos, heading a band of missionaries, just how many is not known.

Coronado was also supported by a naval arm. Hernando de Alarcón had sailed from Acapulco with two ships loaded with provisions for the army and gewgaws for Indians. Fray Marcos had implied that the sea was not far from his line of march. Alarcón also had orders to explore the island of California, already known and named.

Mendoza formally reviewed the troops, accepted each officer's oath of allegiance, and gave an inspiring address. All were confessed; Mass was said. On February 22, 1540, Coronado's army rode splendidly off, led by Fray Marcos along the route he had traveled.

This magnificent army had much to learn. Caballeros found that packsaddles slip, horses founder, and men eat unwisely and get sick. But they learned. Gentlemen on horseback were toughening into pioneers. The story is a marvelous one, full of amusing and thrilling adventure. Its significance for us today is not in what happened on the trail, but in what Coronado's men did in New Mexico.

It was to be many weary months before they reached Cíbola. Long before that, Coronado had begun to doubt Friar Marcos's geography. He did not get in touch with Alarcón as expected, and Indians told him that the sea was very far away. Crossing the Despoblado, he lost horses. Food became scarce. Curiously, these armed Spaniards did not kill game. Two men died from eating poisonous plants. The mountains were difficult; pack animals slipped and fell. But in time they descended to a stream they called the *Río Bermejo* (Red River), later called the Colorado, and followed it to its junction with the Zuñi River. An advance guard under García López de Cárdenas had a brush with some Cíbolans, who scared off the horses. But Coronado, hoping for a peaceful conquest, disregarded this inhospitable greeting. So he came within sight of the famed and fabulous city of Cíbola.

This was probably Háwikuh. It was not a shining city with turquoise set in the doorways, but an adobe pueblo "all crumpled together." Cárdenas wrote that the soldiers hurled such curses at Fray Marcos "that I prayed God to protect him from them." Coronado had met his first disappointment. And here he fought Spain's first battle against New Mexico's Pueblos.

The Cíbolans had no idea of surrendering to King and Church despite Coronado's most mellifluous promises of the King's pardon and the Church's grace. Smoke signals had brought up fighting men. Women and children had been removed to the sacred mountain. Zunis' characteristic intransigence was making its first appearance. Even Coronado's best suit of armor and plumed helmet did not impress them. Their terraced mud houses became a fortress; their stones and arrows made it impossible for horsemen to approach. But Spaniards on foot were equal to embattled Indians, and within an hour the pueblo surrendered. Coronado had been wounded, but not seriously. He was able to treat with the chiefs. He was not a bloodthirsty man, and he agreed to leave them in their homes. Food for his starving and bedraggled men was most important; at the moment, maize, turkeys, and good salt were more important than fine gold.

In a letter to Mendoza dated August 3, 1540, Coronado described the pueblo, noting exactly what strikes modern travelers—terraced houses, flat dry country, wind, and strong, sudden rains. He thought the Indians worshipped water, not a bad guess. He mentioned wild animals, including the cattle (buffalo) whose well-tanned hides he had seen. Coronado sent back a Zuni painting of these buffalo, along with some cotton cloth, bows and arrows, and a few turquoises. No wealth of the Indies here.

This episode followed the over-all pattern of the Spanish conquest of the Americas. Indians were called upon to submit to Emperor and God on promise of peace in this world, eternal bliss in the world to come. If they yielded they were baptized, introduced to tithes and taxes, and counted as Christianized and civilized. If they demurred, they were fought until they capitulated.

Coronado, recovering from his wounds at Zuñi, had heard of other "kingdoms." Any one of them might have gold; certainly all had souls to save. So he despatched Hernando de Alvarado eastward and Pedro de Tovar to the west, where lay the province of Tusayán, and where he might come upon the South Sea and meet Alarcón. Tovar had several footsoldiers and seventeen mounted men who slowed him down; the Zunis, even loaded, could out-trot the horses. With Tovar went Fray Juan de Padilla, a veteran of Cortés's conquest of southern Mexico. It was he who shouted for the advance when the Hopis drew a line of

sacred meal to indicate "thus far and no farther." They, like
the Zunis, would have none of King and Church. Like the
Zunis, they were forced to give in. They supplied a few
cotton mantas, some maize and piñones. Tovar had no
orders to go farther, so he returned to Cíbola. He had heard
of a great river, though no mention was made, it seems, of
the canyon it had dug. But he heard that there were giants
there. So Coronado sent off another detachment under
García López de Cárdenas, a dashing soldier and already so
adept in the Indian sign language that he refused to take an
interpreter with him. The people of Tusayán, whom we
know as Hopis, gave him food and guides, and he went on.
So Cárdenas was the first white man to see the Grand Canyon of the Colorado. Dr. Bolton thinks he stood near the
Grand View, the point from which tourists usually get their
first view of that stupendous gorge.

Naturally those adventurous youngsters wanted to get to
the bottom of the canyon, and three of the lightest and
most daring tried it. They did not get to the river, but they
slid, dropped, and helped each other down far enough to
report that the river was as wide as the Indians had said, and
that rocks that appeared man-size were "taller than the tallest towers of Castile." These were Castañeda's words. He
had been left behind with the main army in Sonora, but his
second-hand reports always enriched the style of any tale.

Here was no South Sea, no word of Alarcón—above all,
no gold. Coronado had written Mendoza: "It does not appear to me there is any hope of finding either gold or silver,
but I trust in God that if there is any to be had we shall get
our share of it." This pious hope he sent with Juan Gallego,
a horseman sturdy enough for a three-thousand-mile journey, and Melchior Díaz, one of his most dependable aides.
With them went Fray Marcos, New Mexico's first promoter, by then discredited, old, and perhaps ill.

Díaz went south as far as San Gerónimo and then struck

westward toward the sea, seeking Alarcón. All he found of him was a wooden cross at the junction of two rivers, the Gila and the Colorado. Alarcón had buried letters stating that he had turned back there. His cruise as far up the Colorado as Yuma had established that California was a peninsula and not an island, but he and Coronado never joined forces.

Coronado now turned his hopes eastward. He had heard of Acús, Acoma, and "other small kingdoms . . . on a river." This information came from two visitors from Cicuyé—Cacique and "a tall young man, well-built and robust," whom he called *Bigotes* because of his fine mustache. The visit was marked by a formal exchange of gifts—dressed skins, shields, and headpieces from the Indians; glassware, beads, and bells from the Spanish. Coronado then named the brilliant young captain Alvarado to take a score of soldiers and the bellicose Fray Juan Padilla and follow the visitors toward that river on the east.

Alvarado traveled an Indian trail across the malpais to Acoma, seventy-five miles east of Háwikuh, thus missing El Morro, the famous Inscription Rock, and hurting his horses' hooves very badly. One of his soldiers described Acoma as "the greatest stronghold ever seen," adding that if the Indians had not come hospitably down "we would not have been able to disturb them in the least." Alvarado and his men noted the peaceful lake that has given its name to Laguna, and in three days' travel reached a river they named Nuestra Señora because the date was September 7, eve of the Feast of Our Lady. It was probably near Isleta that white men first looked across our Rio Grande valley's maize fields and cottonwood groves and to the deep blue of the Manzanos. At that season they surely noted how silvery white the clouds were, with shadows not dark but blue.

9 Taos pueblo looks much as it did when the Spaniards first saw it in 1540.

CAPLIN AND
THOMPSON, OLD
ALBUQUERQUE

10 The older Marquez sons and daughters have attended college.

C. E. REDMAN, ALBUQUERQUE

The first pueblos Alvarado mentions were those of Tiguex, near Bernalillo, where he camped for a few days.

Alvarado was traveling fast with his guide Bigotes and with Fray Juan de Padilla, who was making converts at a great rate. Indians "even climbed on the backs of others to reach the arms of crosses and decorate them with feathers and roses." Alvarado visited all the pueblos along the river at the foot of the purply-black buttes that mark the end of the Jemez lava flow. He even made his way through the Cañon del Norte and across the plain fragrant with sage to Taos, which he called Braba. From Tiguex he wrote Coronado, advising him to winter there; this valley was much better than Cíbola. Then he set out for Cicuyé and the plains where the big cattle were.

Bigotes led the Spaniards along a trail he knew well: from the Rio Grande up the Galisteo, skirting the Cerrillos range where the turquoise mines were, through Lamy Pass and Glorieta Canyon, the route the railroad follows now. At Cicuyé, now so noble as the Pecos ruins, Alvarado found the people friendly, though they guarded their women as was their custom. Bigotes now declined to go farther, offering as guides two plains Indians, his slaves: Ysopete and another called El Turco because he looked like a Turk. This may have been intended as a trick to lead off and lose the intruders, but it resulted in greatly enlarging the Spanish empire.

From Cicuyé the trail went south along the Pecos, purling sweetly along between alders and willows, perhaps as far as modern Anton Chico, and then struck eastward and so down the Canadian to the plains. There white man first met the buffalo; herds of animals so multitudinous that they could only be compared with the fish in the sea. When angered, the bulls were fierce "with wicked horns," the meat was good, the hunt thrilling.

El Turco now tried to lead them on to Quivira, a land where there was much gold and where Bigotes had acquired a gold bracelet. That did it. Alvarado decided to go back to get that bracelet and some honest information out of the tricky Bigotes. But back in Cicuyé both Cacique and Bigotes denied all knowledge of any gold or any bracelet. Maybe El Turco was the liar. The Spaniard, gold-hungry and impatient, put both in chains and started back to Tiguex.

There he found Cárdenas, who had come on as an advance guard for Coronado and was already making his men comfortable in a pueblo that the Indians had evacuated for them. Alvarado and Cárdenas—young, high-handed, and impetuous—were preparing not only winter quarters, but also trouble aplenty for their more diplomatic and humane commander.

When Coronado arrived, he approved Cárdenas's arrangements, but more supplies were needed and soldiers were sent in all directions to requisition food, blankets, living space.

Coronado's own mind was preoccupied with El Turco's ever gaudier tales of Quivira's opulence. Bigotes's bracelet would have offered final proof of their truth, but that obdurate Indian persistently denied knowledge of it, even when Tovar's dogs were set on him. Perhaps Coronado knew nothing of this or of the reported rape of an Indian woman. His lust for gold was aroused, and he had to see this Quivira for himself. But first he had a battle to fight.

The Indians had been getting restive, especially because the hasty Spaniards allowed no time for the democratic Pueblos to consult everybody. Even their pious hospitality wore thin as these demanding guests became more grasping. Many Indians had been robbed of their winter supplies, others had seen the baiting of Bigotes. Runners sped from pueblo to pueblo. Finally a Spanish soldier, snatching a blanket, was struck. A savage had laid hand on an inviolable white man! The battle was joined at Arenal, where Alameda now stands.

By the end of December 1541 the Indians in all the Tiguex pueblos had been fought to a standstill. Those taken in battle were burned at the stake. These two atrocities—the baiting of Bigotes and the burning of captives—were of great importance in the later trials because Spain's humane Laws of the Indies had already been promulgated. Coronado, whom Bolton rates as one of the most humane of the conquerors, was cleared of guilt at his trial, and the impetuous Cárdenas held guilty.

By spring Coronado was ready to set out for Quivira with El Turco as guide. Following Alvarado's trail, he went farther onto the plains, where the Spaniards were overwhelmed by the vast flatness of those grasslands, trackless as the sea. The Indians they met were friendly, probably Apaches. The soldiers were amused at the funny prairie dog and its villages, and learned to relish its meat. They hunted buffalo. They were held up by the great Barrancas, those deep gorges that redly slash the Texas Panhandle.

Thence Coronado sent the main army back. He was beginning to distrust El Turco, but he pushed on with thirty men picked for courage, stamina, and good mounts. This party followed El Turco along the Red and Arkansas rivers, and came at last upon a huddle of Indian lodges. Tabás, they called it; it was probably near present-day Lyons, Kansas. There El Turco was finally proved an arrant liar; even he could think of no more promises to make. Pushed by his enraged officers, Coronado reluctantly consented to have the man garroted. Then he prepared to return to Mexico.

However disappointing to him personally, Coronado's quest had immense historical importance. For at the very time he reached that point in Kansas, De Soto had touched the Mississippi. Those two Spaniards had spanned the continent in 1541, and Spain could claim about one third of the present United States. Curiously, the final link in that human chain was supplied by an Indian woman, a slave of one of Coronado's captains, who ran away at the Barrancas and was seen by one of De Soto's men near the Mississippi.

Coronado knew nothing of this. When he was on trial in Mexico later, charged with having defrauded the Crown of incalculable wealth by going no farther, he could only admit that he had found no splendid cities, no gold or silver mines, but only vast lands that seemed poor, sterile, worthless. Coronado was cleared, but he died a few years later, probably about 1549. Others might try again for the riches of what they were calling La Tierra Nueva.

When Coronado had left Tiguex, three friars in his command had elected to stay on in that New Land; the wealth they sought was there in plenty: souls to be saved. But no word of them had come back from the mysterious north.

Fray Luis de Escalona, a saintly man, had settled with his Negro slave boy, Cristóbal, in Cicuyé, where he hoped for success with children. Later writers presumed that he was killed there. Of Fray Juan de la Cruz even less is known, though a later Franciscan chronicler listed him as a martyr too. The third was that intrepid Fray Juan de Padilla, as fierce in the faith as he was in battle. He made the long trek back to Quivira attended by two Indian lay brothers from Mexico; a Negro, Sebastián, with his family; and a Portuguese, Andrés do Campo, a gardener who had three horses and a buckskin coat. This was the man who came back after five years to report that Fray Juan had got on well with the Indians of Quivira, but had been killed by enemies of theirs farther east.

These martyrdoms naturally aroused the Franciscan Order throughout the Spanish world. But for forty years

La Tierra Nueva was not again invaded. Then Fray Agustín Rodríguez got permission to go north with two companions, Fray Francisco López and Fray Juan de Santa María. For their protection went Captain Francisco Sánchez Chamuscado with a dozen soldiers. Doubtless the soldiery had mines as well as martyrs in mind. By this time Spanish settlements had been pushed into the northern states of modern Mexico, where mines of silver and gold had greatly enriched the explorers. There was always hope of new and better diggings. Our greatest interest in this expedition is that it traced a new route. Taking off from a settlement in southern Chihuahua, Rodríguez and Chamuscado descended the Conchos River to one they called Guadalquivir, a new name for the Rio Grande, which they followed westward and through El Paso, the pass whose name has never been changed. From El Paso they traveled north into the country of the Piros Indians, and perhaps as far north as Tiguex. These friars, too, remained in La Tierra Nueva while Chamuscado returned to report no mines found. But he died on the way to Mexico City.

Then, in 1582, came Friar Bernardino Beltrán, accompanied by Don Antonio de Espejo, whom Hammond and Rey, in the introduction to their translation of *The Espejo Expedition into New Mexico*, describe as a gentleman under a cloud and eager to restore his good name by doughty deeds. Like Chamuscado, Espejo found no mines, though he journeyed well beyond the Hopi mesas on a false clue. But he made two notable contributions to our New Mexico.

Espejo, leaving Cicuyé, followed the Pecos River south until it met the Rio Grande and Chamuscado's trail. He had discovered the valley that was to produce such wealth in oil as Spain never dreamed of. And, in reporting on his travels, Espejo first used the words Nuevo Mexico, thus giving the state its historic name before the end of the sixteenth century.

For sixteenth-century Spaniards, New Mexico had produced only failure. What they sought was not there. But with Mexico and Peru still in his imagination, no viceroy would admit that rich mines would not be found in those arid northern lands. It only needed more expeditions with more daring or more persistent leaders. In any case the new lands must be colonized and held for Church and Crown.

XI

SPANISH SETTLERS

To HEAD the first colonizing expedition into New Mexico the Viceroy of New Spain chose Don Juan de Oñate, son of a rich mining man of Zacatecas. He was wealthy and had wealthy friends, and his wife, Doña Isabel, was a granddaughter of Hernán Cortés and of the lovely, mysterious Marina, or Malinche. In the New World there was no prouder heritage.

On Oñate's muster roll of 1595 appears the name of Gaspar Pérez de Villagrá, gentleman of Puebla, graduate of the University of Salamanca, and poet. At forty-three he was described as of medium stature and gray-haired—aging in that era when life did not begin at forty. Villagrá's *Historia de la Nueva Mexico,* published in Madrid in 1610, makes New Mexico the first state with a written history. Written with Homeric magnificence, replete with classical allusions, and fulsomely addressed to King Philip II, the *Historia* is not very good poetry, but it is useful as a first-hand account of stirring times. Gilberto Espinosa, recognizing its values, has made a readable translation in prose.

It took General Oñate two years to assemble and supply forces, and by then his commission had expired and his money was running low. His friends presented his case to the Viceroy, raised additional funds, and went on his bond for the rest. Finally, on January 26, 1598, Oñate, heavy and magnificent in his armor, could with spur and rein make his stallion curvet, order the bugle to call the advance, and see his splendid train begin to move. Doña Isabel had chosen to remain behind, but in the forefront rode their twelve-year-old son, Don Cristóbal, quite as elegantly got up as any hidalgo and as good a man on a horse.

It was a "colony" of 400 men, 130 with wives and children, and Indians to bear the burdens and to serve as interpreters when they could. There were also "eight seraphic, apostolic, preaching priests," as Benavides described them, with two lay brothers and friars, including Friar Alonzo Martínez as *comisario*. A large herd of animals was driven along to provide meat, and oxen pulled the eighty-three carts loaded with necessities and with the general's indispensable wardrobe of satin, velvet, and fine English cloth, his plumed hats and extra suits of armor. He had, of course, a tent to be set up each night with its bedsteads and *prie-dieu*.

Seen in a museum today, a *carreta* looks too frail to go ten miles; it is only a basket of saplings mounted on solid wooden wheels of cottonwood sections and put together with wooden pins and leather thongs. A *carreta* could not carry much of a load, and it was forever getting stuck in sand or mired in mud and having to be unloaded and freed. At worst the cause of its nerve-shattering creaking ignited the wheels and the whole cargo went up in smoke. But it took some load off human backs.

When an advance guard reached the Rio Grande at a point twenty-five miles below El Paso, they had suffered four fatiguing days without water. Horses plunged into the stream and drank until they burst. Men, too, drank until they lay waterlogged, "more like toads than men." The waters teemed with fish, which they caught and cooked and feasted upon, sitting in the shade of cottonwoods on the damp sand. But the slow-moving colony was still struggling through dry sand, and the sky remained a cloudless, hard, unrelenting blue. So they prayed. And it rained. This was known thereafter as "the Day of the Miraculous Shower."

The first colony entered New Mexico with austere religious rites, a miracle, and a play. At the pass, near modern El Paso, its members observed Holy Thursday. Villagrá writes: "Don Juan ordered a large chapel built. . . . That night was one of prayer and penance for all. The women and children came barefoot to pray. . . . The soldiers, with cruel scourges, beat their [own] backs unmercifully until the camp ran crimson with their blood. The humble Franciscan friars, barefoot and clothed in cruel thorny girdles, devoutly chanted their doleful hymns. . . . Don Juan, unknown to anyone except me, went to a secluded spot where he cruelly scourged himself, mingling bitter tears with the blood which flowed from his many wounds." These are the rites of the Penitentes, still practiced in New Mexico in Holy Week.

At El Paso, Oñate met friendly Indians and ordered the building of a leafy chapel where Mass was said and Friar Martínez preached. There, with the army "in their most gala attire with splendid accoutrements and glistening arms," the general took possession of the new land "and all contiguous territory." The day ended with a fiesta and a play written by Captain Marcos Farfán. This first drama, meant to edify the Indians, showed the natives welcoming the first priests joyfully and begging for baptism.

So Spain set her mark on New Mexico in a religion of blood and tears, a miracle bringing rain, and a play with a moral purpose.

Following the Rio Grande's brown stream and its shady *bosques* was pleasant enough, but cliffs closed in a few miles above modern Rincon and the route led up onto the hills. This was that waterless ninety miles of the Jornada del Muerto. Oñate made it without a death, but the carretas were so slowed down by the heavy sand that he left them in charge of his nephew and lieutenant, Vicente de Zaldívar

Mendoza, and pushed on with the troops. Now they would have to live on the country.

Oñate sighted his first pueblo at a spot that has since been drowned out by Elephant Butte Lake, his second near Socorro. The Indians were timid and fled at the sight of armored men on horseback, but trinkets lured them back, and the strangers were invited into the kiva. Villagrá's description of this visit is a prime example of how preconceptions color first impressions. He reports that the people greeted them in "a most hospitable manner . . . acting most friendly toward us and showing great reverence for the crucifix." But when they presented blankets he assumed that "they were hoping to entice with them the Castilian women whom they . . . coveted." And he repeated the old untruth that the natives held their women in common before marriage and that a man was allowed as many wives as he could support.

Villagrá was horrified at paintings he saw in the kiva; kachinas looked to him like demons with fierce and terrible features. And in a Tiguex pueblo he reported a more hideously shocking fresco: "Pictured upon the wall we saw the details of the martyrdom of those saintly men, Fray Agustín, Fray Juan, and Fray Francisco. The paintings showed us exactly how they had met their death, stoned and beaten by the savage Indians." These murals have never been found. The Governor decided to take no note of those martyrdoms then. So in the dead of night the Spaniards slipped out and went on.

They visited San Felipe and Santo Domingo. Neither was quite where the modern pueblo stands, but Oñate probably followed the damp sand road we know along the river under the black lava buttes. At Santo Domingo, on July 7, Oñate summoned a meeting of seven leaders from other pueblos and offered them the usual Spanish alternatives: peace and love as tribute-paying vassals of His Most Catholic Majesty, Philip II of Spain; or hellfire forever. The caciques chose Philip II.

Like his predecessors, Oñate followed the Rio Grande north, swinging eastward to miss White Rock Canyon. Thus he by-passed the site of Santa Fe and chose for his capital the pueblo of San Juan, where the fertile valley is wide and the views most splendid, with the Taos Mountains to the north, lava cliffs crowned by the Jemez range to the west, and to the south the Sangre de Cristo, looking more massive than peaked from this point. Oñate named his capital San Juan de los Caballeros, perhaps to honor both his officers and the saint on whose day he took it.

From there Oñate went or sent his lieutenants to look over his new domain. They went east to Picurís in the pretty Santa Barbara valley and over the divide to Taos. They went southeast past San Marcos and Galisteo to Pecos. They saw the nearby Tewa villages. So they were well traveled and could boast to the laggards when Zaldívar came in with the carts at the end of July. He had abandoned two thirds of them as the provisions were used up, but it had been an agonizingly slow trek for a young man, and Don Vicente was ready for something sprightlier.

In September a fiesta was celebrated. Friar Martínez had laid out a chapel, and it had been run up so fast that it was ready for dedication after two weeks of work. On September 8 "the Governor ordered a holiday to celebrate the occasion. The horsemen, gathered for a sham battle . . . skillfully clashed in combat, showing great dexterity in the handling of their arms." This drama, unlike Captain Farfán's lost play, is still performed in many places, usually on San Juan's day, June 24. It presents the defeat of the Moors at Granada in 1492, and is known as *Los Moros y los Cristianos*.

The chapel at San Juan, New Mexico's first church, is quite lost. But from that center the Franciscans began their task of civilizing the Pueblos. They visited all the Tewa villages and built a *convento* in one they called San Ildefonso. They reported "indoctrinating" the Keres and established a mission at Santo Domingo; perhaps they made a few converts among the Rio Grande Tiwa at Isleta and Sandia. On this basis they claimed sixty thousand converts, three times the number of the estimated total Indian population. George Kubler, whose *Religious Architecture in New Mexico* is based on the latest research, avers that not one church built before 1600 endures. So New Mexico's claim to sixteenth-century missions, the boast of earlier writers, disintegrates in the light of modern scholarship.

The seventeenth century was to be the century of missions. But Oñate was more interested in mines than in missions. As a mining man from rich Zacatecas, he doubtless hoped to find a silver lode over every hill. But he did not go over the right hills. Nor did his lieutenants, though they reported many adventures.

Young Vicente de Zaldívar was sent eastward, unhampered this time by *carretas*. With sixty mounted men he quickly reached the Pecos River and stopped to fish, as everybody still does. He pushed on across the rolling land that would have been all silver and gold in September, with grass taller than we know now, and a fine larder of leaping jackrabbits and antelope and of doves and quail on the wing. He saw Indians dressed and tented in finely tanned skins. But the big excitement was those woolly cattle, "so amusing . . . that there is not an individual so melancholy who, if he were to see them a hundred times a day, would not laugh heartily as many times. All agreed that one need only corral them to have a domestic herd that would be an unending source of wealth in meat, hides, and wool."

Juan de Montoya, writing to the king, relates that Zaldívar's men spent three days building a corral where they expected to trap ten thousand buffalo; they thought they saw that many near their camp. As these clumsy animals, "when they run seem to jump as if they were crippled," they considered the prey very easy. But when driven gently toward the trap those stubborn beasts "stampeded in the direction of the people with such violence that they broke through everything . . . and there was no way of stopping them. . . . Of the most terrible tenacity and courage . . . they are so tricky that if the one who is rounding them up stops, they go slowly and stop and roll like mules, and with this rest they renew their running." Zaldívar then tried roping calves, hoping that sucking domestic cows would gentle them. But the pesky little things just died. Even the native wildlife of New Mexico refused to co-operate. Zaldívar was forced to settle for killing buffalo for meat, as his successors were to do until the breed was eradicated. Montoya found the meat good; and both hides and wool were to prove valuable as exports to the mines in Chihuahua.

Montoya was apparently a learned priest who undertook to bound New Mexico correctly once and for all. "New Mexico," he wrote, "extends from the north to the strait located between Nombre de Dios and Panama, turning west within sight of the continent of China, with a narrow strait of ocean . . . which the geographers . . . locate on the maps by guesswork for we do not know the true facts." So Montoya was cautious; but he had no doubt that New Mexico was a peninsula extending northward between Newfoundland and China.

Oñate had been having trouble at San Juan. Disgusted with this poverty-stricken land, forty-five captains and soldiers had planned to desert. Oñate was lenient this time but when a similar plot was revealed later, Villagrá and Márquez were sent after the malcontents. The young officers summarily hanged the two they caught, and so stored up serious charges against themselves and their general for later investigation. But Oñate judged things settled enough to permit more exploring. He set out for the west, where lay the sea full of pearls.

Acoma was the scene of the most dramatic episodes of New Mexico's settling, and Villagrá raised them to melodramatic heights. They were the highlights of his life too. His drama opens at San Juan with an Acoma spy, Zutacapan, listening in. If he had overheard one of Oñate's exhortations to the Tewas he might well have decided that Acomas never never should be slaves. The general's assurance that all he did was for love always wound up with the threat of hellfire forever if his words were not heeded. When the Spaniards reached Acoma the trap was set.

Oñate, seasoned soldier, scented trouble and politely declined a cordial invitation to enter the kiva. But both Spaniards and Acomas had been impressed. The Spaniards had seen nothing like that towering rock island, whose only approach was over a trail of toe- and hand-holes in a crevasse. It looked impregnable to assault, and it was too high to demolish with such cannon as the general had. After a display of horsemanship on the plain, with a great clashing of armor and firing of arquebuses, he thought it best to go on peaceably. It must have occurred to the Acomas that the armor and arquebuses would be hard to beat.

At Zuñi, luckily for Villagrá, a heavy snow fell and horses strayed away. No Spaniard ever lost a horse if he could help it, so the soldiers rode back toward Acoma, searching. There, on a lonely plain, they came upon the poet chronicler who, setting out alone to overtake the general, had become suspicious of Zutacapan at Acoma, and had continued on his way. But his horse fell into a brush-covered hole. Was it a man-trap set by the wily Zutacapan or just a standard deer-trap? Villagrá knew, of course, that it was Acoma perfidy. So he went on afoot with his boots on backward to confuse his pursuers. This might be difficult to do, but it has passed in Villagrá's account for all these years. So the soldiers found him. It seems likely that they supplied him at once with paper and quills. He had much to write: imagined, wordy interchanges between Zutacapan, urging war, and more peaceably inclined Acomas.

Oñate pushed on as far as the Hopi villages. Walpi at least was as unscalable as Acoma, but the people there received him well, and he could add them to his list of peaceful conquests. By then it was December, cold and snowy, and the South Sea far away. The expedition decided to return to San Juan for Christmas. This too was just as well. Before he reached Acoma the general was met by a captain and six men come to report that Juan de Zaldívar, brother of Vicente of the *carretas* and the buffalo, had been ambushed and killed at Acoma. It seems that the kindly disposed Acoma leaders had left the village and Zutacapan was in command.

Grief-stricken over the death of his nephew and worried over the loss of twelve men out of his limited force, Oñate by-passed treacherous Acoma and went sadly on to San Juan. Here his son Don Cristóbal appears briefly as the messenger sent on ahead to notify the capital of the Governor's approach. Oñate appealed to the clergy and received their assurance that the punishment of Acoma would be a justified act of war. He named Vicente de Zaldívar to command the force sent to avenge his brother's murder.

Villagrá is at his best in describing this violent and bloody battle for Acoma. Beginning with the Indians howling derisively from the summit and the Spaniards confessing and being absolved below, it mounts through three days of vicious hand-to-hand fighting. The Spaniards, feinting on the north, had found another trail on the south. They gained the top and dropped a beam across a crevasse, only to be checked by a batch of yelling savages. But Villagrá, old as he was, leaped the gap and replaced the beam. The Spaniards had entered the pueblo.

Fighting on from about where the church now stands, they won the pueblo street by street, house by house, man by man. It was a mighty battle, up there under the clear January sky. At its height the Spaniards' battle cry was heeded. Even as they shouted *"Dios y Santiago!"* fighting Indians saw among them an apparition of Santiago mounted on a white horse and wielding a terrible swift sword. Villagrá's estimate that six hundred Indians were killed has been allowed to stand by serious historians. Steel and the saint had won again. Acoma, the impregnable, was altogether destroyed.

In that January of 1599, Oñate needed reinforcements badly. So he begged them of the Viceroy, reporting that great wealth lay just over the hill. Meanwhile Indians and colonists were starving, and dissatisfaction was mounting. The clergy ruled that, though Indians might be dying of starvation, Spaniards had to live. More and more Spaniards were talking more and more openly about deserting and heading south. Oñate was later accused of conniving at the killing of malcontents. He left loyal men in charge and set out for Quivira, reaching the Arkansas River. Near modern Wichita he had a brush with the Kaw Indians, but he found no wealth and he came home to find his colony in open rebellion.

During the general's absence, citizens of San Juan had again plotted to desert; the clergy permitted the dissidents to meet in the church. George P. Hammond, whose *Don Juan de Oñate* is authoritative, states: "It is clear that both the religious and military authorities were responsible for the flight of the colony." Each, of course, accused the other of pusillanimity in the inevitable trial years later. But they left in October 1601, and Oñate, back from that disappointing Kansas, found only a rump colony. He sent the ever faithful Vicente de Zaldívar to present his claims to the Viceroy and prepared to hold on.

It took months to get to Mexico City, months to return. By the time a ruling got back circumstances had changed. But the basic problem remained unaltered and was earnestly and responsibly debated: what to do with the Christianized Indians if the colony were abandoned? Would it be better to leave them to revert to heathenism or to remove them by force and save their souls?

Meanwhile Oñate was struggling to hold his colony together and to keep the Indians under control. He put down one revolt among the Jumanos, and the friars built a few churches. Then the general, a stubborn man, decided to make one more try for treasure. New Mexico was sterile and the Kansas plains were empty. But there might still be pearls in California. Late in 1604 he set out to see. Beyond the end of his former journey he followed the Colorado River to the Gulf of California. Friar Alonzo de Benavides, in his *Memorial on New Mexico*, pictures it: "Fully dressed and armed with a shield on his arm and sword in hand, he gallantly waded into water up to his waist, slashing the water with his sword and declaring: 'I take possession of this sea and harbor in the name of the King of Spain our lord.'" Oñate had found no pearls, but he had restated Spain's claim to the continent from gulf to gulf if not from sea to sea.

On his way back to San Juan, Oñate opened New Mexico's great stone autograph album. Midway between Zuñi and Acoma rises a stupendous mesa sheared off in a flat face of pale sandstone. The Spanish saw its steep walls and towering cliffs as a castle and called it El Morro. Because of its uses it is now commonly called Inscription Rock. On top are the ruins of an aboriginal village and at its foot there are fresh springs and plenty of firewood. That broad smooth sheet of stone is an invitation to carve; no boy of any age or any people could resist scratching there his name, his boast, or a picture. Most of the earliest inscriptions are undated, stone-hacked petroglyphs. Oñate's is the earliest carved in letters and dated. Its first phrase, repeated by all later Spaniards, has added a picturesque figure of speech to New Mexico's bilingual language: *"Pasó por aquí"* (there passed by here); it goes on: "Don Juan de Oñate from the discovery of the South Sea in 1605." There are many other Spanish names, incised with dagger points; the carefully blocked names and dates of U.S. Army engineers; and a scattering of less well-known names. The Park Service guards it now: New Mexico's autograph album is closed.

We do not know that Don Cristóbal accompanied his father on this successful effort to reach the South Sea; perhaps if he had he would have left his name on El Morro too. He was twenty-two now, and in 1608 the colony's *Cabildo,* dissatisfied with an officer sent to replace Don Juan de Oñate, named Don Cristóbal governor. But the Viceroy overruled the appointment. Oñate's son was too young and inexperienced, and "they say he scarcely knows how to read and write." New Mexico might make a good soldier out of a man, but it was no place to get an academic education.

As was customary, Oñate underwent a rigorous investigation. He was found guilty on various counts and was exiled from both New Mexico and New Spain. Several of his officers were tried with him, among them Villagrá and Zaldívar. Villagrá, was accused of, among other crimes, writing "beautiful but untrue accounts" of New Mexico. By chance, good or bad, this activity is no longer considered criminally actionable.

To inaugurate the new program, the Viceroy appointed as governor Don Pedro de Peralta, adjuring him to protect and support the missions and to move the capital to a better place. One of Don Pedro's first acts was to transport the seat of government and the colonists to the pleasant valley of the little Santa Fe River. This was in 1610, the established and certain date of our capital's founding. With Peralta, as *custodio* of the eight friars who accompanied him, went Friar Isidro Ordóñez. These two, Peralta and Ordóñez, were to make a deal of history in New Mexico and to set its tone for a century or so.

� ✿ �

XII

CHURCH AND STATE

❧ After Oñate's fiasco it had been decided that New Mexico, so disappointing as a producer of wealth, should be continued as a missionary province. The Crown granted the Franciscan Order an annuity of sixty thousand pesos to support the missions and, with its genius for organization, clearly defined the Order's ecclesiastical and military powers. The missionaries were to have control of their Indian converts; military and civil officials would serve primarily for their protection: it was so stated in every governor's instructions. Certainly the hope of finding mines, if not gold already minted, was never lost. So the two groups had divergent aims. The friars sought to Christianize the Indians; the governors probably always sought both gold and glory. Both brought to this distant frontier echoes of the ceaseless warring between Church and State which was disrupting seventeenth-century Europe. The century of missions was far from peaceful in New Mexico.

Establishing missions was of first importance. The friars set out at once to revive the Indians' fading Christianity, to rebuild the churches, and to found new missions. Men of faith and courage, they were often sent alone among savages who were outright hostile or who had been aroused against all white men by some one man's cupidity or lust. They learned enough Indian words to expound simple doctrine and explain the sacraments. They attended the dying; often they knew enough medicine to aid the ill. If one of them died a martyr, there were always others to take his place.

It was slow work and hard. These early missionaries often suffered cold and hunger, for they depended upon what their converts gave them until a regular mission supply service began in 1631. Meanwhile occasional caravans brought to each mission ten axes, three adzes, three spades, ten hoes, one medium-sized saw, one chisel, two augers, and one plane; a large latch for the church door and some smaller ones; and two small locks, a dozen hinges, and six thousand nails. Anything else the friar needed, such as pulleys or hoists, he was left to fabricate on the spot.

Building was perforce of the simplest. The friar just marked a cruciform outline on the ground, tucked up his skirts, rolled up his sleeves, and led his neophytes in building. Adobe was commonly used, and the bricklayers were Indian women and children who also plastered the walls and floors with mud and whitened the sanctuary inside with yeso or tinted it with colored earth. Men scorned this labor, but they cut, hauled, and worked logs. Walls three or four feet thick upheld pine logs overlaid with split cedar or aspen branches and a heavy dirt roof. With all this the Indians were familiar. The friars introduced such European ideas as high windows to light the altar like a clerestory and taught the best carpenters to carve designs remembered from New Spain or Spain across the sea and to prick out the patterns in color. As final touches of beauty and ceremonial necessity, the friars often taught some primitive artist to trace European scrolls in colored earth on walls or altars, to carve statues of the saints in wood, or to paint their pictures on wooden slabs or buffalo hides. Often, as in the churches at Laguna and Acoma, the painter's aboriginal ideas come charmingly through.

It was crude work at best, but often the floor plan the friar stepped off, the ceiling's height, and the placement of windows, altar, choir loft, and pulpit made a balanced perfection more beautiful than any modern church in New

Mexico can show. And the adzed surfaces, carved corbels, spiral pulpits, and simple frescoes are finer in their poverty than anything bought since factory-made articles have become available.

Each mission included workshops and barns, tilled fields, vegetable gardens and orchards. Many Franciscans were learned men, but their practical knowledge, ingenuity, and plain horse-sense were surely more useful than all their erudition. They were not only preaching Christianity; they were also trying to eradicate the old customs and to replace them with European folkways. So the friars taught the care and breeding of domestic animals and the uses of new crops. They introduced European vegetables, including such unlikely ones as artichokes and cucumbers. Peach and apricot trees began to flush the spring along the ditches, and one friar introduced wine grapes. Among the amenities were the *rosas de Castilla* that still throw their fragrant golden blankets of bloom over walls and fences.

Early seventeenth-century mission architecture may be studied in its purity only in ruins, but they are noble ruins. Every traveler between Las Vegas and Santa Fe may see the earth-colored bulk of the Pecos mission church, built before 1635. Also of that era is the mission church of San Diego on the Jemez River. Built with massive stone bastions and a belfry that served as a watchtower too, it is a marvel of symmetry and dignity standing among the junipers above the shaded stream.

On a day's drive out of Albuquerque one may visit the missions of the Tiwas of the Manzano Mountains, the Piros farther south, and the Jumanos of the saline plains. Ruins now, they retain a dreamlike quality that was first described by Charles Fletcher Lummis in his *Land of Poco Tiempo*. He wrote of these pueblos as the "Cities that Were Forgotten," and sharply scolded the American traveler for visiting castles on the Rhine instead of in New Mexico's mountains. These cities were not only forgotten, but also deserted when Apache raids had reduced their life to sheer horror and dread. A later writer, Paul A. F. Walter, has named them *The Cities that Died of Fear*, as in truth they did. That fear is reflected in a crumbling stone and adobe watchtower that stands near an ancient apple orchard. One gnarled antiquated tree was, according to tradition, planted by the friars who named the range Manzano, which means apple tree. The tree has never been cut to date it by counting its rings. Farther south is Cuarai on a giant spring known as Punto de Agua (Point of Water).

This spring is a joyous thing in an arid land. Its wide basin collects the spring-fresh and filtered water from the whole southeastern slope of the Manzanos. And it is so clear that watercress seems to drag its silver roots in air. Its fragrance is of wild mint, and for much of the summer wild verbena runs all over the place in a violet carpet. Alders, sycamores, and willows help to make bright green this sheltered cup on the edge of the pine forest.

Lummis, fresh from the verdant East, saw the rolling saline plain as ashen desolation, ghastly, weird. The Salt Lakes struck him as accursed, though he knew that they had always given freely of their salt and baking soda. And the ruined mission church at Los Jumanos he described as "a wraith in pallid stone . . . above dead grass . . . a spectral city." Perhaps only a New Mexican's eye can catch the subtle gradations of metal colors and gem colors in this scene: the gold and silver of grasses, the copper of certain shrubs, and the soft tones of amethyst, sapphire, and watery beryl where the plain dips into shadow. The walls do rise palely; the stones are gray, gray-blue, and yellow-gray.

Nobody remembers by what curious quirk the name Gran Quivira was applied to Los Jumanos pueblo, protected now as the Gran Quivira National Monument. Protection is necessary because the legend of treasure is still linked to the name. The Park Service ranger, who is developing a little museum, is often asked for permits to dig. Somebody has found a new map; has heard an old tale. No treasure has been found to date.

The last of these dreamlike mission ruins is that of Abó in a southern canyon of the Manzanos. The way to it may be traced from the highway by the homes and corrals built of heavy squared stones and timber plundered from the church. After the Apache raids had ceased, simple people came back to where there were good water and ready wood and stone to build with.

Other seventeenth-century missions were destroyed in the Indian uprising of 1680 and later rebuilt in a different place or so "restored" that little of the original remains. Thus Isleta's sturdy San Agustín was rebuilt with its magnificent buttresses in the eighteenth century. It took nineteenth-century taste to top it with silly steeples that mar its dignity as a tipsy hat would mar a noble face. Zia had a convent early in the century and probably a chapel. The present exquisite adobe structure dates from the early eighteenth century, but embodies seventeenth-century features in its beautifully balanced façade with a bell hung in the center and a balcony over the door.

Our most sympathetic picture of seventeenth-century missionarying in New Mexico comes from Friar Alonzo de Benavides, who came north in 1625 as *custodio* and first *comisario* of the Holy Office. He remained four years, traveled widely, and wrote a report so remarkable that he was sent to Spain to present it personally to the King, and perhaps to get more money for missions. He did both.

In his *Memorial*, Benavides could name fifty churches served by twenty-six friars. Among them was Santa Fe's first church for non-Indians, on the site of the present cathedral. Altogether Benavides's work did much to warm and enliven the fervor of the missionaries. It also led to great improvement in the caravans due every two years. Benevides complained that "five and six years are wont to pass without royal officials bethinking themselves about us—and God knows what it costs to remind them." Dr. France Scholes, in *New Mexico Mission Supply Service*, shows that dependable regularity was not established until Friar Tomas Manso took over in 1631.

This friar, whom Dr. Scholes considers one of New Mexico's greatest men, organized an overland service longer than, and quite as hazardous as, the later Santa Fe Trail; it too crossed deserts and mountains and was menaced by hostile Indians. For twenty-five years, Manso directed the caravans as efficiently as a modern railroader handles trains, and maintained his schedules. His trains consisted of thirty-two wagons hauled by mules or oxen, and the necessary muleteers, herdsmen, servants, and military escort.

Dr. Scholes has printed full cargo lists containing such items as sacramental wine, prepared candlewax, altar cloths and rugs, choir robes of Chinese damask, paintings and images of holy figures, a silver chalice, and copper and brass vessels for holy water. More mundane were hats for the friars, woolen stockings, sackcloth, linen, sheets, and blankets. For the infirmaries came medicines, soap, pins, syringe, lancet, barber's scissors, copper cupping instruments, and a grindstone. To spice and sweeten the diet came honey in jugs, conserves, raisins and almonds, pepper, cinnamon, and saffron. Even now lucky people dig up ancient copper, brass, and iron pots and basins that came in the caravans. There were, besides, food for the journey and as much luggage as enterprising civilians could get aboard.

Benavides found New Mexico large, and both too cold and too hot. "At a latitude of 40 degrees, north winds always predominate, and snow remains on the ground most of the year . . . rivers freeze; iron-bound wagons cannot cross. To prevent sacred wine from freezing in the chalice, the padres keep braziers burning." In summer, on the other hand, "tallow candles and salt pork melt," and he found a total lack of breeze. But this dreadful land abounded in myriads of souls to save, and the friars had found hordes of them clamoring for baptism.

This marvelous aboriginal eagerness for conversion was owing to a miracle. Missionaries newly come from Spain brought word of a Franciscan nun, María de Jesús de la Concepción, who had been appearing to the Indians in New Mexico. Although Sister María had never been to the New World, her knowledge of New Mexico's Indians seemed great. Several padres told Benavides that Jumanos Indians had come in for four summers begging baptism and saying that a lady in blue had been visiting them. Shown a portrait of the Spanish nun, they recognized it, though they said that she was young and not old like the painting. Missionaries sent to the Jumano country met a procession of people bearing a flower-decked cross they said the nun had directed them to make.

When Benavides went to Spain to report to the King, he sought out the nun in her convent. She confirmed all the tales, adding that she had often appeared to Indians three or four times in twenty-four hours. She had flown fifteen or twenty thousand miles on her errands of conversion. Benavides wrote: "She has a beautiful face, very white although rosy, with large black eyes. . . . Her habit is the same as our habit, coarse gray sackcloth . . . and the cord of St. Francis." Later he mentioned that her cloak was blue; the Indians had always described her as garbed in blue. In writing to his "paternities in New Mexico," the friar ended by saying that he had obtained the very habit in which she made her flights and that "the veil radiates such a fragrance that it is a comfort to the spirit."

Benavides's report glowed not only with miracles, but also with good tidings of all sorts. He found the Indians wearing clothes and shoes. They were excellent farmers. Houses were of stone, strong and beautiful, and the work of the friars was beyond compare. At Picurís he praised a school "of all the arts"; at Taos, "a marvelous choir of wonderful boy musicians"; Friar Cristóbal de Quiros at San Felipe "has taught and trained these Indians well, not only in the things pertaining to our Holy Catholic faith, but in the ways of civilization, such as reading, writing, and singing, as well as playing all kinds of musical instruments." At Pecos he found all baptized and well instructed; the friars had brought in craftsmen to teach the Indians carpentry. Even in recalcitrant Zuñi some boys had been taught to chant. But those Indians kept their sacred fire glowing; Benavides thought they worshipped it. The Church had hard going in Zuñi.

Benavides also found troublous matters. In Taos an old woman inspired by the Devil urged women to live in concubinage. She was killed by a bolt of lightning on a clear day and everybody got married. The friars constantly complained of concubinage; perhaps they meant marriages not blessed by the Church. Monogamy was the rule among the Pueblos, though one sober historian notes that it was "a rather brittle monogamy."

The Jemez, like the Zunis, were hard to keep "reduced." Benavides found them "indomitable and belligerent; above all, great idolators." But they were "gay by nature, always talking of dances and games." More than once they burned out a padre and retired to the mountains, but finally Friar Martín Arvide got them to sow and garner crops, to learn crafts, to attend school. Even the cacique, who had proudly worn a necklace of Christian ears, turned docile. This was the same Friar Martín who had been almost killed at Picurís because he scolded an old Indian for resisting the baptizing of his son.

In 1612 Friar Isidro Ordóñez arrived as *comisario*; Dr.

Scholes believes his commission was forged. At once he entered upon a struggle with Governor Peralta which was to mar the century of missions with unworthy wrangling between Church and State.

Governor Peralta had set about building his new capital, La Villa Real de San Francisco de Santa Fe. He had laid it out with the Casa Real, known now as the Palace of the Governors, facing the plaza where the whipping-post and gibbet stood. It is noteworthy that a separate chapel was built *analco*, across the river, to serve the Tlaxcala Indians who had come from Mexico. This was San Miguel, later ambitiously labeled the oldest church in the United States. It is not even the oldest in New Mexico, and it has been often destroyed and rebuilt. But it has its charms, including the lay brother who recites all the baseless legends about it.

The first open break between Peralta and Ordóñez came when Ordóñez announced that any colonists who wished might return to New Spain. A clear infringement on the Governor's prerogatives, this act was also dangerous, as many desertions would weaken the colony. Some settlers did go.

The second break came when Ordóñez intercepted troops on the road to Taos and ordered them back to Santa Fe to celebrate the Pentecost. When the Governor countermanded the order, Ordóñez excommunicated him, demanding a fine and sentencing the Governor to appear before the church, barefooted and bearing a lighted candle, to receive absolution. Ordóñez declared himself an agent of the Holy Office and threatened to excommunicate anybody who even spoke to the Governor. What a day for the gossips, whispering indoors! Friar Tirado, the gentle guardian of Santa Fe, urged the Governor to comply and suggested a nice quiet absolution before dawn with only a few friends at hand. But the Governor demanded written orders before he would submit, and Ordóñez evidently preferred not to put himself on paper.

Dr. Scholes, whose *Church and State in New Mexico* is the authority for this long-drawn conflict, finds Ordóñez wrong in this case. Dr. Scholes's scholarly account, based on research in government and Holy Office records in Mexico, has given us a series of lively portraits of seventeenth-century men and women. As each accused was reported upon by himself, his friends, his bitterest enemies, and his official investigator, the amount of unsavory gossip and amusing incident brought into open court is amazing.

We know, for instance, that when Ordóñez demanded an escort for a journey to New Spain to report in person, Governor Peralta—one can almost see the sardonic gleam in his eye—offered to go himself, "that your fathership may be the better protected and served." This was not just what his fathership desired, and while he was in a rage he had the Governor's chair removed from its honored place near the altar and set outside. Peralta seated himself among the Indians. From that lowly station he heard Fray Ordóñez declaim: "Let no one persuade you that I do not have the same power and authority that the Pope in Rome has. . . . I can punish any person who is not obedient to the commandments of the Church and mine."

The Governor then set out for distant Mexico City to plead his own cause. But the implacable Ordóñez pursued and captured him more than once and jailed him in various pueblos, notably Santo Domingo, which had been declared the Franciscan center and ecclesiastical capital of New Mexico.

Dr. Scholes warns us that our only authority for this case is Friar Francisco Pérez Guerta, who was strongly pro-Peralta. But uncontroverted evidence shows Ordóñez as a man with an overweening will to power and extraordinary daring. He was not, as he claimed, an agent of the Holy Office. In due course he was tried by the Provincial of his Order; he was even sent to Rome. No record of his trial is known. Likewise the *residencia* of Peralta by his successor has been lost. So final judgment of these two powerful antagonists awaits some novelist or dramatist with a Freudian slant. We know only that they set the tone for another fifty years of bitter bickering.

The underlying disagreement never changed, but there was superficial variety aplenty. Governor Eulate was accused of approving the Pueblos' ancient ceremonies, but also of treating cruelly Indians who worked for him. This case resulted in the Viceroy's ruling that no outsiders should attend the Pueblos' elections; that feast days should be celebrated in the pueblos, so that the Indians would not have to travel to Santa Fe; that only a limited number of Indians should be called to leave their own fields to work for either governor or mission; that Indian women should work in Spanish homes "only with their husbands, and voluntarily"; and that no Indian's hair should be cut as punishment for a slight offense. Spain kept trying to enforce decent treatment of Indians.

Dr. Scholes's book is replete with rich human material that loses neither drama nor humor in his restrained, scholarly treatment. The tale that best reflects the century's mediæval style is that of Governor Bernardo López de Mendizábal and his high-born lady, Doña Teresa. They arrived in the state we like to associate with our Spanish governors, bringing a carriage, a bed with velvet hangings, a gilded desk, silver plate, expensive clothes, and boots of finest Cordovan leather. Many of these luxuries the Governor bartered for slaves, herds, and other goods to ship out. Governors were forbidden to enter trade, but Dr. Scholes finds that they commonly did.

The new Governor also brought books; among them a

copy of Ariosto's *Orlando Furioso* belonging to Doña Teresa, who had lived in Italy with her father, a Spanish diplomat. She had a few familiar belongings to offset the forlornness of that adobe Casa Real, with its dirt floors and leaky dirt roofs. There was not much mitigation for her outside her home: her husband was constantly embroiled in quarrels that surrounded her with enemies and brought spying eyes even into her bedroom.

Against López de Mendizábal all the usual accusations were brought, and some most unusual ones. It was reported that when the Cabildo asked for better quarters, the Governor replied that he rated those elected councilmen on a par with his Negress and his mule and that their meeting place was good enough. More serious were the charges of heresy brought against both the Governor and his wife. Prying servants testified that they had been seen at night in their bedroom performing acts that were sure proof of Judaism. Both had been observed, so deponents swore, bathing and washing their hair on Friday nights. Obviously only Jews could so violate the proper Christian rite of the Saturday night bath. The Governor's defense was that he did not bathe on Fridays and sometimes did not wash his hair for weeks on end.

Doña Teresa was charged by servants with reading a book in a foreign tongue, even with laughing as she read. So the lady's one solace in her loneliness was cited as proof of heresy. Both were cleared of these charges, but López de Mendizábal had died poor in the Holy Office prison before the verdict. One may hope that Doña Teresa was able to return to Spain. So disappears from history New Mexico's first woman with a book.

Throughout the century, governors' charges against the clergy were equally harsh. A friar was accused of beating a Hopi shaman into a bloody mass and burning him with turpentine. One in Taos was charged by women and boys with immoral practices. These were flagrantly unusual cases, and the offenders were brought to trial. Lesser charges were that the friars used Indian lands to raise their crops and pasture their herds, as laymen were not allowed to do; that they employed Indians without pay while laymen had to pay wages; that they imported too many luxuries. The religious countered by stating that their bulging granaries fed all the people in times of famine; that they were teaching proper farming and herding; that they needed fine churches and rich furnishings to impress their Indian neophytes. They were always jealous of their immunity from civil law and their right to govern all Indians except those living in Santa Fe.

What the Indians made of this ceaseless quarreling is not hard to imagine. It could not be hidden from them; often they were involved in it. The wonder is not that the Pueblos revolted in 1680, but that they had not revolted long before.

The decade preceding 1680 was full of horror. In 1670 a drought reduced the people to eating hides boiled with herbs and roots. Epidemic followed. The Apaches rose up and their hordes rolled over the exposed pueblos. In 1672 the missions in the Manzano Mountains and on the plains were abandoned; the cities died of fear. The friars might have held the Pueblos, many of whom had fully accepted Catholicism, if they had had food to give. But the missions, too, were famine-stricken. Friar Francisco de Ayeta arrived with the mission caravan in 1674, but what he brought was too little and too late.

In 1675, in the midst of the Indians' distress, Governor Treviño decided to suppress all "superstitious practices" for good. Forty-seven medicine men were tried for sorcery and three were hanged. Among those released was a man of the sort best treated fairly or killed. This was Popé, a powerful shaman of San Juan. Affronted by the trial and by a close watch kept on him at home, Popé moved to Taos, where

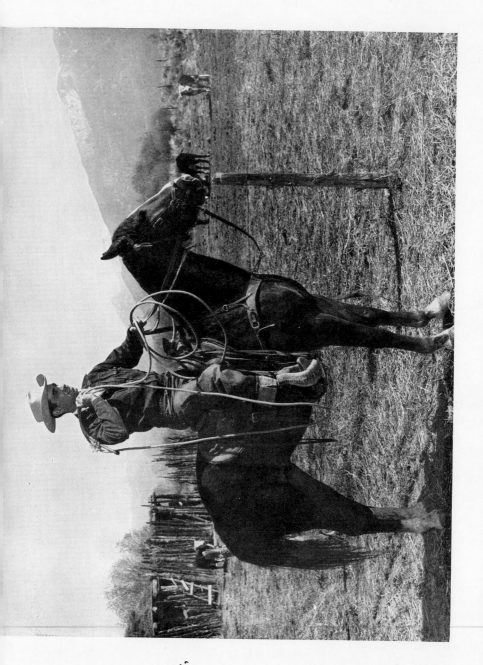

11 *Ernest Gutierrez, Taos County Agricultural Agent.*

VERNE SACKETT, TAOS

12   *A Navajo who remembers the exile to Fort Sumner in 1864.*

he was revered as having supernatural powers. He named his ghostly guides, but his best allies were the Pueblos' utter disillusionment with the Spaniards and their religion, and the deep underlying faith in the kachinas. The new gods had not saved them; perhaps the old gods could.

Popé proved himself a great leader, astute, far-seeing, and ruthless at need. In a Taos kiva he met a few leaders and worked out a plan. Messengers were sent to all the pueblos, even as far as Hopiland. Few knew what was going on; it was New Mexico's best-kept secret until the making of the atomic bomb. Leaders in every pueblo received a knotted cord, one knot to be untied each day. When all the knots were undone it would be the time to kill every Spaniard: friars, women and children—everybody. The date set was August 11, 1680.

Then something went wrong. On August 9 several Indians reported to Governor Otermín in Santa Fe. Governors from Tanos pueblos corroborated the rumor, adding that only two knots were still untied. The Governor acted, but not quickly enough. Charles Wilson Hackett, in his authoritative *Revolt of the Pueblo Indians*, says that Otermín did not realize the seriousness of the uprising. He sent word to the nearby villages to be on the alert "in order that the churches might not be profaned and that a force of men might be put under arms upon the shortest possible notice."

Popé moved much faster. At once he sent runners speeding over the ancient trails, light in moccasins and G-strings, doubtless winged with feathers. Hackett does not mention horses; men go faster anyhow. So the date was changed, and before sunset on August 10 all the Pueblos knew. All had begun to kill. It was a hideous day of slaughter, with priests killed at the altars; women and children massacred; men cut down with their own stolen weapons.

One of Popé's cleverest moves was to assure the Governor in Santa Fe that the colonists in Rio Abajo, down river, had all been killed, and the Rio Abajo people that the Governor and all residents of the Villa were gone. As a matter of fact, both groups were carrying on pluckily.

Otermín, slow to believe the truth, delayed until the thirteenth, when he ordered the inhabitants of La Cañada and Los Cerrillos into the Villa Real. There he crowded into barricaded patios about a thousand refugees and their animals. Only about a hundred men were able and armed. Indians swarmed in from all sides. One leader, Juan from Galisteo, wrapped in red taffeta plundered from the church, offered a choice: all Spaniards to leave peacefully, or war. Otermín chose to fight. Sallying out, he drove off the Tanos, who destroyed San Miguel as they went. But Pueblo reinforcements were coming from the north, and Otermín was forced back to the Casa Real, which he held until the Indians cut off the water supply. Finally, in a council of officers, the Spaniards agreed to abandon the Villa Real and retire to Isleta, where they hoped to find any Rio Abajo survivors.

Meanwhile the Lieutenant Governor of the Rio Abajo, Alonso García, had gathered in the fleeing, horror-stricken people from as far west as Jemez, from the mountain settlements to the east and Santo Domingo to the north, and had brought them to Isleta. That pueblo had not revolted; it was the Spaniards' refuge. About fifteen hundred of them huddled there, believing that all the Rio Arriba folk had been killed. García's letters to Otermín were not answered. Finally he decided to go south to meet Friar Ayeta with the mission caravan. But he had found time to fill thirteen folio pages with notarized statements from his officers and the religious. No Spanish officer ever forgot that future and inevitable investigation.

So García was ready for Otermín, who arrived in a fury at what he took to be his lieutenant's dereliction. Together they went south. The religious were reverently bearing what they had been able to save from the churches. The people had very little. But Ayeta met them in time to save them from starvation.

This retreat was the abandonment of Spain's northernmost colony; the worst setback that powerful empire had ever known. The desolate survivors, established at El Paso, were so disheartened that when volunteers were called for a reconquest, only six former colonists stepped up. But others, mostly very young and raw recruits from villages farther south, responded. By November 5, 1681, the indomitable Otermín was armed, provisioned, and at the head of 130 soldiers ready to ride north.

This effort at reconquest was a sad and confused failure. Otermín bivouacked with his main troop at Isleta, sending Juan Domínguez de Mendoza ahead to learn how many Indian apostates were ready to surrender. Amnesty was offered; the friars stood by to hear confessions and to absolve all penitents. Many Indians, beginning with Isleta, abjured their error and wept as they begged absolution. Weeping, the friars granted it, and, weeping, the soldiery looked on. But this was a gigantic ruse.

The Indians' leader, one Luis Tupatú of Picurís, was scheming to trap the Spanish at Cochití; he had even baited the trap with pretty maidens bathed for the occasion. But, as always, there was a leak. This time one Alonso Catití warned his Spanish half-brother. Mendoza retreated to Isleta, where Otermín called a council of war. It had been a snowy December, the Manzanos were powdered down onto the skirts of the mesa, the dry grass was scanty, the horses were weakening. Afoot, the Spanish would be at the mercy of the Indians, who were counting on that. They decided to get out while they still could. The friars' great concern was to save the faithful Isletas; they took with them 385, who were settled at El Paso.

New Mexico was Indian again, but many man-made

beauties had been destroyed. After Otermín's retreat, the Pueblos had set about cleansing their homes of every reminder of their serfdom and oppression. All along his march Otermín found the pueblos deserted; the people had joined their Apache allies in the mountains. The churches had been demolished, the altars desecrated in ways too vile to name, and in the plazas were piled the charred remnants of burned crosses, crucifixes, sacred statues, and paintings. Everywhere they found kachinas, those "heathen idols," prayer sticks, sacred meal, and dance regalia. The friars reverently burned the holy articles that had been profaned; the soldiery made an orgy of destroying every pueblo as they retreated. So New Mexico suffered two destructive orgies.

In 1682 the Pueblos seemed to have won. Spain had lost her colony. But the Spanish Empire was still the greatest in the world, and the Church, in spite of Protestantism marching on in Europe and beginning to invade the New World, was still the most potent force in Christendom. Neither Empire nor Church could admit final defeat in New Mexico. So a strong man was chosen, and in 1692 the reconquest began.

XIII

RECONQUERED PROVINCE

⊏⊐ To RECONQUER that lost province, the Viceroy of New Spain chose Don Diego de Vargas Zapata y Luján Ponce de León y Contreras, more handily known as De Vargas. Born in Madrid of illustrious lineage, Don Diego was a soldier, a proved administrator, a deeply religious man, and a man rich enough to reconquer the lost province "at his own expense." The only authentic portrait of him, which hangs in Madrid, shows the true Spanish aristocrat, slender to narrowness, with long head, aquiline nose, and sallow face framed in long black hair. He wore a hairline mustache and a minute goatee.

Appointed Governor General of New Mexico in 1691, De Vargas was delayed in getting started, but once past El Paso, he made a swift and easy march up the Rio del Norte, finding the pueblos deserted. From hills and mesas bright black eyes doubtless watched that armored advance led by flags and the cross. But the people stayed hidden. On the night of September 12, 1692, De Vargas camped within sight of the Villa Real, which was occupied by Tanos Indians. The army spent the night in prayer, the priests giving absolution to all, and at dawn advanced, crossing the Santa Fe River at Agua Fria and approaching the town from the northwest.

The Indians were howling imprecations from the housetops, but making no sally. The Spaniards cut off the water, as the Indians had done before. De Vargas then sent in his trumpeter offering peace and pardon to all who would surrender. Pueblo allies were coming in, but the Spanish easily made them prisoners without violence. One among them, Domingo, became convinced of De Vargas's fair intentions and, after long parley, persuaded the Tanos to yield. Always cunning bargainers, the besieged demanded that De Vargas enter the walled enclosure accompanied only by the *custodio* and six soldiers, all without sidearms. The General then proved his courage by walking unarmed through a gangway between high walls and into a fortified place. "Who," he said, "will not risk himself to secure perpetual glory and an illustrious name?" Those he did indeed secure.

The Indians recanted, begging absolution of the priests and forgiveness of the General. In the plaza, the soldiers erected a leafy arbor where Mass was said. It looked like a peaceful occupation rather than a conquest. De Vargas then set out for the northern pueblos.

At San Juan, Luis Tapatú, he who had tried to trap Otermín's lieutenant at Cochití, stood upon his dignity, refusing to surrender unless given a welcome suitable to his rank as ruler of all the pueblos. De Vargas agreed and the Indian approached, dressed in skins and crowned with a heart-shaped shell. De Vargas greeted him with the formal embrace and the two exchanged gifts—animal pelts from the Indian, a horse from the white man.

Tapatú, having bowed the knee, begged for help against the Apaches, who had been a constant nuisance. Tapatú, the potentate, shrank considerably on closer view. De Vargas rode on, offering peace, forgiveness, and protection. With promises he won all the pueblos, from Taos, Pecos, and Jemez, to Zuni and distant Hopiland, known then and for many years thereafter as Moqui, a Zuni word applied to them in derogation.

On his return from the west, De Vargas left his sprawling inscription on El Morro. It reads: "Here was General Don Diego de Vargas who conquered for our Holy Faith and the royal crown all New Mexico at his own expense in the year 1692."

Then he returned to Mexico to report the peaceful occupation of the lost province. This conquest was so salving to Spanish pride—the loss of New Mexico had been the Empire's greatest setback—that a special leaflet was issued in De Vargas's honor: *El Mercurio Volante* (the Flying Mercury), which Irving Leonard has translated into such easy English that it reads like today's newspaper. De Vargas was extolled as *El Reconquistador*, who had restored the lost province once and for all. But the appearance of finality was false.

After months of rest and recruiting, De Vargas started north again with eight hundred colonists, women and children in *carretas*, domestic animals in dusty droves, dogs underfoot. This was a colonizing expedition. Danger was past. De Vargas, finding the Indians friendly all along the way, soon left his slow-moving caravan and pushed on to prepare the Royal City.

On December 16, a cold, bright day, the Governor General rode into Santa Fe, still occupied by the Tanos. Almost at once the Spaniards called upon the Indians for corn. The shivering friars asked permission to move into the Casa Real. The Cabildo, too, wished to occupy its old quarters. De Vargas had promised the Indians that nothing would be taken from them, but the old pattern was coming through. Indians must feed and house their betters. The Tanos, refusing to go into the snowy mountains to cut timbers to rebuild the chapel, offered a kiva as a good place for worship. When they were ordered to move back to their ancient pueblo of Galisteo, leaving Santa Fe to the intruders, a war was on.

This time there was little talk; hundreds of colonists were demanding shelter. De Vargas moved quickly to the assault, with Santiago on a banner and his name on every soldier's lips. By nightfall the Tanos had surrendered. De Vargas ordered seventy of them executed. Four hundred others, including women and children, were given to the Spaniards as "servants." Enslaved. It was the end of the Tano group. Only a few families in Santo Domingo still recognize their descent from the Tano.

This time it would be *conquista*. Civilized man, with fire and sword, would "reduce" the savage to Christianity. The ensuing months were filled with hideous, blood-soaked warfare. The histories and the legends relate dramatic tales of fights at the Black Mesa above San Ildefonso, at the old pueblo of Jemez, and at Acoma. The true conquest was not done until 1696. De Vargas, like governors before him, was tried, imprisoned, and dishonored; but he was cleared. He served a second term as Governor General and died in Bernalillo in 1704. His remains were later removed to the parish church in Santa Fe, which was rebuilt into the Cathedral, where they still lie. But De Vargas's most venerated monument is the chapel of El Rosario.

It was long believed that De Vargas carried on his horse a statue of the Virgin, and that before the battle for Santa Fe he prayed to her for victory, promising to erect a chapel in her honor. But Fra Angelico Chavez, Franciscan, poet, painter, World War II veteran, and historian, has uncovered new evidence. In *La Conquistadora, Our Lady of the Conquest*, loving in tone and sound in scholarship, he states that the statue was in Santa Fe long before De Vargas's day. It may have been brought by Benavides in 1625; its title may refer to the original conquest. It was not mentioned in church or civil records because it was owned by a *cofradía* (lay fraternity) to which De Vargas belonged. In any case he built the chapel of El Rosario where his camp stood by the river, and every June the faithful of the ancient villa carry La Conquistadora from the cathedral to the chapel one Sunday and back again the next. The processions are most impressive, with hundreds of marchers and the elegant little image, richly garbed in brocades and jewels, borne on the shoulders of four reverently proud young girls. The statue had suffered during the ages, but in 1933 Gustave Baumann's delicate artist's hands brought back its original grace and beauty; and modern taste has decreed a style of wardrobe that must be followed by donors of its adornment.

De Vargas was succeeded by a century of governors whose chronicles are monotonous in the similarity of their problems: to hold what had been retaken, rebuild what had been destroyed, expand Spain's reach, and make new converts. Only a few left names or deeds memorable today.

In 1706 Governor Cuervo ordered settlers to move south from Bernalillo to a shady ford on the Rio del Norte. The town they built he named in honor of the Viceroy, el Duque de Alburquerque. Later and lazier spellers have dropped an r from this name, but the town's unique name is still a publicity asset.

In 1716, the Governor, the Marqués de Peñuela, decreed a fiesta in Santa Fe to honor De Vargas and his Reconquistadores. If this annual September observance does not come to us with quite unbroken continuity, it was certainly inaugurated by Governor Peñuela nearly two hundred and fifty years ago.

Peñuela's successor, Don Juan Ignacio Flores Mogollón, gave his name to a mountain range that might better have honored the Apaches who held it so long against so many. The Spanish were forever unable to conquer the Apaches, but the desert tribes were more amenable. The Austrian Jesuit, Padre Eusebio Francisco Kino, converted the gentle Pimas and Papagos, traveling on foot or burro-back across the deserts as far as the Colorado River. This was to be the western boundary of New Mexico until 1863, when Arizona was cut off as a separate territory.

To the north neither Padre Kino nor his successors succeeded with the Hopis. Even today's motorist, driving comfortably from Tucson or from the Rio Grande, must gain a deep respect for the devout friars who toiled on foot over that sand and rock to carry their faith to people whose land promised the invader nothing.

But one feels an equal respect for the Hopis on those gray and craggy mesas where sturdy, industrious, and weatherwise men with stone-age tools managed to raise crops and live. They had also developed fine weaving, basketry, pottery, and a religion that infused all life. Yearly they welcomed kachinas with dance; at intervals they performed rites to keep the life forces active and beneficent. This was the deep conviction that made the friars' efforts forever futile.

Both Jesuits and Franciscans tried to convert the Hopis; four military expeditions were sent against them. When missionaries came, the Hopis talked; they even built churches. When the military showed fight, they fought. Like diplomats of the first rank, the aborigines yielded many points, but held to their main proviso: that they be left free to worship in their own way. This stipulation was of course unthinkable to the seventeenth-century Spanish Catholic.

Friars thought that the people desired conversion; they even persuaded a few of them to move into settlements on the Rio Grande. But their shamans, whom the Franciscans called *caciques demoniados*, held out to the bitter end. And it was bitter. Even when drought and starvation had more than decimated the tribe, they remained obdurate. So they saved for a more tolerant age some of the most exquisite ceremonial dances in the world. And they left also an amazing example of slow martyrdom for the principle of religious freedom.

Eastward, the problem was that the plains Indians simply

did not stay converted. Henry W. Kelly, in *Franciscan Missions of New Mexico,* reports that the Navajos told Fray Miguel Menchero that they "were grown up and could not become Christians because they had been raised like the deer." They were willing to "give some of the children to have water thrown upon them" . . . but the elders would not become Christians. They had, they coolly stated, submitted to the water because the missionaries rewarded them with picks and hoes. No presents, no baptism.

One point on which Indians and Spaniards agreed was the importance of business. Indians liked to swap tanned hides for manufactured articles, especially weapons and ammunition. Both sides had captives to trade. The Spanish settled recaptured whites and Christian Indians in certain villages—a plaza of Belén, the hamlets of Abiquiu and Tomé. Captives taken in war were bought and sold in open market, especially at the huge annual fair at Taos, which brought together Pueblo and Plains Indians and every Spaniard who was not in jail or sick in bed. In good years all went well. In bad years fighting might result, or Indians returning home might detour to raid a settlement. Governors never had enough soldiers to defend the people assailed by Utes from the north, Comanches and Navajos from the east, Apaches from north and west. Bancroft describes New Mexico at that time as a habitable island surrounded by impenetrable wilderness. The vast empty terra incognita to the north could be disregarded. But east and west, Spain's precarious hold was threatened.

The eighteenth century was a century of world wars centering in Europe, some faint repercussion of which was always felt in far New Mexico. As other countries continued to expand, Spain had to look to her empire's remotest boundaries. She claimed vastly more than she could possibly patrol. In North America her explorers had covered the lands from Florida to California, and as far north as the

sixtieth parallel. She had even made some effort to connect
these far-flung settlements. As early as 1650, Spanish expeditions had pushed north from Mexico into the land of the
Tejas Indians, which seemed too remote to be worth settling. But before the end of the century France was threat-
ening Spain there, thanks to a highly picturesque traitor.

This was Don Diego de Peñalosa, a Spaniard who had
thrilled the court of Louis XIV with tales of rich lands beyond the River Michipi. Peñalosa certainly had wrongs to
avenge. He had been governor of New Mexico from 1661
to 1665, after which he had been tried by the Holy Office,
stripped of his wealth, and humiliated beyond bearing. But
his pride was not broken. For his penitential walk through
the streets of Mexico City bearing the green candle he appeared arrayed in velvet and lace. He then tried to reach
Spain to present his defense, but was denied permission to
enter that country. When he tried to sell out to the English,
the Spanish ambassador in London blocked him. But at the
French court Peñalosa aroused a lively interest, especially in
the ambitious mind of young Robert Cavalier, Sieur de La
Salle. In 1684 La Salle landed at Matagorda Bay on the
Texas coast of the Gulf of Mexico.

When that news reached Mexico it threw that viceregal
city into a ferment. After that there was no doubt that
Spain would hold the lands along the Gulf, distant as they
were. Several presidios were established and abandoned,
missions were begun and deserted. The first one to take root
was built on the San Antonio River in 1718; this was to become famous as the Alamo.

With the establishment of the California missions about
the middle of the century, Spain had some show of settlement from ocean to ocean. But the tiny hamlets and lonely
missions were so far apart that their administration was a
growing problem. In 1776, as part of a general reorganization of Spain's colonial administration, the wide empty

spaces that were to become Texas, New Mexico, Arizona, and the northern states of Mexico were united as Las Provincias Internas. But paper changes made government no easier.

In that same fateful year of 1776, on the fourth of July, two friars, Silvestre Vélez de Escalante and Francisco Atanacio Domínguez, left Santa Fe to try to find a route beyond the land of the Moquis to the settlements on San Francisco Bay. They reached only some spot in southern Utah or northern Arizona—a ford on the turbulent Colorado is named the Padres' Ford—but they had covered eighteen hundred miles of what was to become the famous Spanish Trail from New Mexico to California.

Spain was struggling to hold the vastest empire the world had ever seen, but it was a losing fight. Other vigorous peoples were exploring all the continents. Above all, what had happened on the Atlantic seaboard in that fateful year of 1776 was going to determine New Mexico's political fate. But these world-shaking events were little noted by the simple people who were the ancestors of modern New Mexicans.

XIV

SPANISH COLONIAL LIFE

☞ COLONIAL New Mexico has been pictured as the scene of a luxurious life among the *ricos*, with a happy peasantry dancing, singing, and fiestaing—and all of pure Spanish blood. But none of these notions holds up upon investigation. Even the myth of pure Spanish blood evaporates before facts, as all pure-blood myths do. As we have seen, every expedition drew from the whole Spanish empire and was accompanied by hundreds of Mexican Indians to do the heavy work; even an occasional Negro is cited: Father Chavez found that De Vargas's drummer was a Negro.

From Oñate's time on, there was also an embryo middle class of farmers and artisans who peddled their produce and worked for wages. On the whole they were steady folk, but among them were such drifters as infest any frontier—offscourings of the mines in northern Mexico, and even fugitives from justice. Good people and bad were ignorant, superstitious, largely illiterate. In 1681 only three out of 147 recruits for the reconquest of New Mexico could sign the muster roll. Of New Mexico women appearing before the Inquisition in Mexico, none could write her name.

This middle class, as always, produced men of force and talent who rose to power. There were not enough hidalgos, who owned the best lands, to fill all the offices. The entire non-Indian population seldom exceeded one thousand, of whom eighty per cent were of mixed blood, as church records prove. Father Chavez, studying the church archives, found that even some haughty families have forgotten a lovely Pocahontas or Malinche of an ancestress. He also found that tracing any family tree beyond 1700 involves guesswork, all records having been destroyed in 1680. But from the reconquest on, the record is clear. No yearner for membership in something-or-other can show a better documented lineage than can any New Mexico villager.

The life these people lived was grim, what with the hazards of weather, the menace of Indian attack, isolation, and utter neglect by a weakening government. By happy chance, we have an excellent account of the colony by a hidalgo of the early nineteenth century. *La Exposición sucinta y sencilla de la provincia del Nuevo Mexico*, a succinct and simple report published in Cadiz in 1812, was the work of New Mexico's only delegate to the Spanish *cortés*.

This delegate, elected by the mayors and prominent men, was Don Pedro Pino, a wealthy and distinguished descendant of one of De Vargas's captains. His report is available in an excellent translation by Carroll and Haggard in a volume that also contains notes made in 1832 by Don Antonio Barreiro, a lawyer representing the Republic of Mexico. This gives a fascinating picture of the last days of the Spanish colony, with sidelights from the Mexican era.

Don Pedro left Santa Fe in October 1811. The inspired priest, Hidalgo, had already cried out against Spanish oppression in his *grito de Dolores*, thus setting off the revolution that was to establish Mexico as an independent republic. Don Pedro knew nothing of this as he journeyed nine hundred leagues from Santa Fe to Vera Cruz. No wonder Don Pedro reached Spain too late to sit in the *cortés*. Out of this disappointment came a couplet, meaner than the facts warrant:

> *Don Pedro fué*
> *Don Pedro vino.*

New Mexico's representative did more than go and come —if not for king and *cortés*, certainly for posterity. His report gives us a detailed picture of a life that had probably changed little in over one hundred years.

The function of any representative, then as now, is to extol his district, blame its backwardness on governmental neglect, and, of course, to ask for money. In performing these duties Don Pedro was pre-eminent. In praise he wrote: "In 118 years, New Mexico has maintained a state of warfare with thirty-three wild tribes and . . . has not lost one span within its old boundaries." This he thinks proves loyalty to Spain and the desire to continue as "part of the Crown of Castile." The people, Don Pedro wrote, were "poor and harmless with no defense whatever, with no soldiers, with no formal treasury, with no constitution, and with no laws to protect the settlements, agriculture, or industry." Settlers who volunteered to fight against the Indians provided their own arms—rifles, pistols, bows, arrows, and shields. "Likewise they must pay for their own ammunition and supplies." Many men, he adds, were ruined by a single campaign and were forced to sell their children into peonage to supply their own needs. Don Pedro did not mention that rich men often paid or supplied the men who served under them; he himself did so.

Don Pedro found his Indian neighbors "hardly different from us." His description of the Pueblos suggests that the friars had done their work well. "Many Indians can read and write . . . all speak Spanish . . . have good reasoning power, keen judgment, and a natural persuasive eloquence. They are slow to deliberate; they act in everything in common accord; and in their dealings they are extremely honest and truthful. . . . They rarely suffer from hunger because their foresight leads them to act with caution."

Don Pedro foresaw the Indians' early end. "Ancient Americans, now you belong to history alone and your remains will shortly perish!" He was, perhaps, the first of a long line of mourners who still grieve at the passing of the Indian, who will probably outlast us all.

Don Pedro recommended the establishment of five presidios at strategic points and a military academy to train officers. The Santa Fe presidio he thought useless, and he advised selling its adobe wall and moving the troops. Doubtless Don Pedro aroused some citizens to indignant protest against tearing down the fine old wall in the name of progress, as similar proposals still arouse Santa Feans. Anyhow, this recommendation was disregarded as were his others. When *Licenciado* Barreiro knew Santa Fe twenty years later, a crumbling remnant of the old wall still stood.

Otherwise Santa Fe had changed little. Barreiro found El Palacio "substantial, but in the worst condition imaginable." It was faced by the Castrense, the military chapel, of which no trace remains. On the west side of the plaza stood "a clean and beautiful oratorio" that the finest ladies of the city delighted in cleaning and adorning. The rest of the plaza was enclosed by private dwellings and it had "frame porticos all around." In the center stood a sundial, the only timepiece in town, with the maxim: *Vita fugit sicut umbra* (Life flees like a shadow). Barreiro found the rest of Santa Fe disordered and disagreeable. Only the private homes "although constructed of adobe and very low, are quite comfortable and very clean." He, a Mexican from a chimneyless land, was much impressed by fireplaces. He also found several clothing stores and a brisk commerce.

Santa Fe's population, according to the ubiquitous Baron Humboldt, was about five thousand in Don Pedro's day. Besides being capital of the province, Santa Fe was the administrative center of settlements from El Bado de San Miguel, near Las Vegas, to Jemez. Albuquerque headed the Rio Abajo—six towns including Socorro and Laguna. The largest district, taking in all the northern settlements, was Santa Cruz de la Cañada.

Santa Cruz with its handsome church seems the gateway to a dreamlike vision of old New Mexico. Now as then, people graze their flocks on the pale gold hills and farm along the bosky Santa Cruz stream. In Chimayó, weavers still make striped blankets on their ancestors' heavy wooden looms. The Santuario still attracts pilgrims to pray or to carry off the miraculously healing sand. Farther up the mountain, in Cundiyó and Córdova, woodcarvers carry on the family tradition. And at the apex, where tiny Truchas sits just under the blue-green peaks, one gets a daily pageant of light and shadow across hundreds of miles of valley and plain and the yearly modulations from golden yellow of aspen in the fall through the silvery snows of winter to spring's tender green and summer's lushness.

Don Pedro Pino, Spanish colonial, showed himself amazingly modern at times. He noted that as the Pueblos had enough land to make a living, "they do not have [the] vagrants or beggars that swarm like lice in . . . Mexico." He commended "the good discipline and cleanliness which contribute so much to public health." And he warned: "Let the nation be fully informed: the means of establishing peace in New Spain lies in giving every one an interest in the property of the territory as is being done in my province." If Spain had heeded, if Mexico had heeded, these wise words from New Mexico in 1812, how many revolutions might have been avoided!

Don Pedro also warned his sovereign against the United States. Its citizens, he wrote, "knowing that by possessing this province, they would be masters from the North Sea to the South Sea . . . have tried with . . . lucrative commerce and promises of . . . protective laws to unite this territory to Louisiana." Even in 1812, Don Pedro could see destiny marching westward.

But Don Pedro, the hidalgo, could not see an evil that was to make the United States occupation easier. This was peonage; it marked New Mexico deeply until yesterday, if not today. The *patrón* had more lands and grazed more sheep than his poor village neighbors, and commanded the work of many others held in debt. He considered himself, of course, the protector of them all. How it really was is best presented by later arrivals. John Ayers, in *A Soldier's Experiences in New Mexico*, called emancipation "a greater boon to these enslaved Mexicans than even to the Negroes. . . . By their laws, peons could be brought back if they ran away. They could punish them in any way; it was worse than slavery, for slaves had a mercantile value while if a peon died his place was filled with no loss but the small debt he was working out." At best, when the *patrón* was kind and looked after his people in old age or illness, the peon's attitude of dependence and subservience was going to prove a poor basis for American citizenship. And for both villager and peon there was no way out.

There were few schools, and Barreiro found those deplorable owing to "neglect, carelessness, the ignorance of teachers, and the lack of interest of the authorities." There were, of course, no college, no lawyers, no physician. The one surgeon was paid by the soldiers. A few hidalgos were taught by the priests, but there was no educated class. Like English county squires of the same period, hidalgos held themselves high and maintained strict standards of morals and manners; their very derelictions were according to rule. A gentleman fought at need, entertained lavishly, guarded his women and kept them ignorant, and had no truck with books or thought. Few books are among the treasures of our old Spanish families. Thought was taboo throughout the Spanish empire, a ban heartily endorsed by the Church. Even Republican Mexico, in 1823, limited its guarantee to protect "the life, liberty, property, and civil rights" of foreigners to those "who profess the Roman Catholic Apostolic Religion."

Barreiro, the Mexican lawyer, reported that crime was never punished because "no one knows how to conduct an examining trial, to prepare a defense, or to prosecute a case." Jails, he wrote, were "only a few filthy rooms in the capital." But Don Pedro Pino found that prisoners were "rewarded rather than punished . . . since they spend their time in noisy revelry . . . and at night they escape and go to dances."

Life's monotony was broken by the annual buffalo-hunt on the plains and by the winter caravan to Chihuahua. At La Joya, south of Socorro, as many as five hundred merchants might gather with their loaded *carretas* and their retainers. A captain would be elected and sentries assigned to guard the van and rear; there was always danger of Apache attack.

Hidalgos were such a vision as no movie could better. Riding small wiry horses descended from Arabians, they sat hand-tooled and silver-studded saddles, handled ornate bridles with vicious bits, and with huge roweled spurs roused their steeds to spectacular curvetings. Their sombreros were flat-topped, black, and held on by a chin strap. Woolen pantaloons with leather jackets and leggings were eminently practical, and the finely woven serape was warm and rainproof. But it also lent color and swank. The peon, also mounted, emulated as well as he could his *patrón*'s elegance, but he wore high moccasins instead of hand-made boots, and settled for silverless saddle and bridle. But the wide hat and the swinging serape were his, and he rode with as much skill and dash as any aristocrat.

Often *trobadores* rode with the caravan to sing in camp at night and to enter contests in Mexico. Rubén Cobos found that one singer, Martín Chicoria, was claimed a hundred years later by a score of hamlets. According to legend, Chicoria had been forced to go to stand up for New Mexico against a famed singer of Chihuahua. There the *trobador*

Gracia poked fun at the New Mexicans as buffalo hunters and unfit to sing among gentlemen. Chicoria was held to have won with a neat pun on Gracia's name, which means grace. Such verses translate poorly, but many old people still remember the skill and wit of those impromptu singers.

New Mexico's trade went east and west as well as south. Eastward, Mexican citizens first traced the route that would be known as the Santa Fe Trail. Tempted by the "lucrative commerce" that Don Pedro mentioned, they went even beyond the plains, where they captured slaves, and as far as the Missouri settlements.

Antonio Armijo, in 1829, followed the trail of Escalante and Domínguez even beyond their ford, and extended the Old Spanish Trail to the Pacific. LeRoy Hafen, who has made the most exhaustive study of Armijo's journey, believes that he followed Jedediah Smith's route from the Great Salt Lake to California. But Armijo was the first to make it through from Santa Fe to San Diego. He also visited El Pueblo de los Angeles, known for many years only as El Pueblo. Armijo reported that his party was hospitably received by Californians, "who were very surprised to see them arrive from a direction that until then was unknown; and they traded the products they brought with them for mules, horses, and stock." Mexicans often thereafter traded mules to Missourians. Enter the Missouri mule, via Santa Fe!

Armijo apologized that "the empresarios, although . . . courageous, rugged, and eager to discover new lands, are lacking in instruction and literature . . . to note the various products of the territory the Mexican Republic possessed in this region; and they are able only to say that there exist suitable locations for establishing new villages and that in the hills there appear variously colored rocks or veins. . . ."

Armijo had opened a trade route that was to see twenty years of heavy use before the U.S. Army broke new trails.

He did not mention its most hideous activity, the running down of desert Indian children to be sold as slaves. This was an evil not only of Mexican trade expeditions, but also of many of the earlier expeditions from the States.

Colonial life in New Mexico was narrow and hard, seemingly without a future. But even in the 1820's strong, rough, tough men were already on their way. They would demolish much that was pleasant, but they would in time give the people a chance to make their own future. The old ways persisted in spite of superficial changes, and life in New Mexico is still much modified by the life of the Spanish colony.

OUR SPANISH HERITAGE

⊂⊋ LIFE in modern New Mexico is deeply marked by
the life Don Pedro Pino knew, perhaps most deeply by
what was so familiar to him that he did not mention it:
things like houses and clothing, food, and ways of thought.
Above all, who would ever have thought that the Spanish
language would greatly modify the talk of those incoming
heretics, or that spoken Spanish would be corrupted by a
new vocabulary?

The speediest and most thoughtless tourist must perforce
learn some Spanish words. How else will he be warned
when an *arroyo* is up, follow a ditch when an *acequia* is
mentioned, know when he is told to turn at a tank in the
desert that the word is a mispronunciation of the Spanish *es-
tanque* (watering pool)? In town how will he find the *plaza;*
know that a *portal* is not a gate but a porch; that a *patio*,
like a *placita*, is inside a house; that a *cantina* is the place to
seek liquid refreshment; and that food may be looked for in
la cocina (the kitchen)? Faced with a menu he may not
recognize *tortillas* and *sopaipillas* as breadstuffs, and he may
learn only with tears that *chile* is far from chilly. Spanish
place names dot our map even where they are most hei-
nously mispronounced by people least appreciative of our
Spanish heritage.

This patrimony of ours is not an unmixed blessing. In so
far as we enjoy the benefits of a second tongue and an outlook on two cultures, it is enriching and good. Much of
New Mexico's charm and grace of living are owing to our

Spanish background, as appears in many a remote hamlet where life is closer to the Spanish colony than to the modern state.

An old gentleman sits on a backless chair on the sunny side of the house. The dooryard is damp and hard from watering and sweeping. His garden of beans, chile, squash, and corn is moist from the ditch gurgling against a wooden gate. A dog suns himself. A chicken pecks around. A visitor is welcomed with an ease suggestive of a castle, not a mud hut. The señora, emerging for a greeting, may be wiping wet hands on an apron, and her hair may be tied in a towel, but she offers no apology as she sets another chair. Poverty is evident, but the dignity of people comfortable with themselves is dominant.

Life in such a village is hard. If water fails, there may not be enough to eat. Every summer men go off to work on ranches, the beet fields of Colorado, or the sheep camps of Wyoming, leaving a village of widows. But it is a village firmly centered in the Church, in family, and in neighborliness. The priest has immense influence. Simple faith is expressed in regular attendance at Mass, in the care of the old carved *santos* or in modern plaster images, and in processions on the saint's day.

Many of the old people do not speak English, though they may understand more than they pretend. Younger people can speak it, but prefer not to. Children are called upon to act as interpreters. They speak English at school, Spanish everywhere else. If the old people become confiding they will protest that the old ways were better. The Church is losing its power. Young people go off to town where they learn nothing good. Women vote. The government is taking our land away to sell to rich gringos. The word *gringo* and the tone of its use reveal resentment against people still regarded as interlopers. These villagers are an unadjusted people—citizens, but outside the current of the state's life, and easily dominated politically. Hatred of the gringo is the undercurrent of many a politician's campaign; bossism, certainly no New Mexico invention, is easily founded on the traditional respect for the old Spanish *patrón*. Today he may be a descendant of the old hidalgo or a son of the sheep-herder or small farmer. He may even be a gringo. In any case the step from *patrón* to political boss was no step at all. And freedom from the *patrón*-boss is clearly related to a knowledge of English.

In so far, then, as half our population has been handicapped by lack of English, our Spanish patrimony—misused—has made New Mexico a backward state by any national standards. In literacy, individual income, and health we lag. After one hundred years as citizens of the United States, many New Mexicans do not speak English and are therefore unable to appreciate the best of our country or to protect themselves from its worst elements. This backwardness is not the fault of the Spanish-speaking villager. The really backward elements have always been, and still are, the powerful in politics, government, and even education.

Thoughtful educators admit that we have the teachers, the skills, and the will to learn that could give every New Mexican citizen a mastery of English within one school generation, twelve years. Yet this question is never brought before the legislature or mentioned in a political campaign. Most amazingly, it gets little attention from teachers, whose powerful lobby is most concerned with teachers' welfare. So education in New Mexico, where half the population is rural, Spanish-speaking, and Catholic, follows lines laid down long ago in New England. The child gets little that bears on his life at home. And the parent, too realistic to share the Nordic's blind faith in book learning, judges by results. Nina Otero, in *Old Spain in Our Southwest*, tells a charming tale of a boatman who was shamed by an educated traveler for not being schooled. Next day—as is the way of tales—the boat upset and the educated traveler, who could not swim, was sinking fast when the ignorant boatman rescued him.

Parents who, like the boatman, distrust schooling keep children out of school to work, to attend a fiesta or a funeral, or because the children do not want to go. The child's indifference is often due to sheer boredom. In many schools one teacher handles six or even eight grades. She may have half an hour a day, then, in which to give the pre-firsts a little English. For long hours they sit squirming under the assault of strange and incomprehensible words. No wonder they quit. As many as five thousand a year fall out before the third grade, the language of their country forever an unknown tongue. Of those who stay, many fall behind one grade, two grades, three grades. Then they are older than other children in their class. Frustrated, they leave school, still with no workable English, or they enter the ranks of pachucos—juvenile knife-fighters.

Equally short-sighted is our failure to teach Spanish in the lower grades, where the Spanish-speaking child should learn to read and write his parent's tongue and gain a respect for it. The English-speaking child might gain even more—a breadth of thought and appreciation sadly lacking now. So we throw away our state's truest distinction—that it is the only state in the union truly bilingual and bicultural—and make instead a state with a split personality and many unnecessary problems. This is our heritage not from the Spanish, but from the ignorant invaders from the States. Ralph Emerson Twitchell, in his *Leading Facts of New Mexico History*, tells us that Missouri troops tossed out of the government buildings official papers that they could not have read even in English. William A. Pile, Governor from 1869 to 1870, had his servants haul off old papers that offended his Protestantism by reference to "His Most Catholic Majesty." This tale is suggestive, though it may be apochryphal. But irreplaceable papers blew about Santa Fe's dusty streets or were used to wrap meat or chewing tobacco. Later Governors pleaded with Congress for as little as $15,000 to translate documents that were piled in dusty heaps or sinking into sodden masses under leaky roofs, and were refused. Don Donaciano Vigil, custodian of land records, managed to salvage enough to make property records fairly complete. And W. H. H. Davis, first U.S. Attorney, and later acting Governor, saved what he could. He later produced one of New Mexico's classics, *El Gringo*. But such educated and appreciative men were rare on our frontier.

Yet thanks to a few people of good taste, largely writers and artists, many features of the old Spanish life have been brought back to enrich our lives. In architecture, decoration, and dress, as well as in speech and food, the modern state is the colony's heir. This is especially true of building.

Transients may overlook really luxurious homes on the hills outside Taos, Santa Fe, or Albuquerque because they sit close to earth instead of looming grandly above it. These copy the houses that had to be fortresses as well as homes. This long, low adobe structure, simple to the point of poverty, but in line with the current taste for the functional and unadorned, promises to become a stereotype as unalterable as the mid-Victorian house.

Stern necessity determined this architecture. Adobe was the only material at hand, and Indians knew how to make sun-dried bricks with straw and lay them up with mud. For protection, they made walls too thick for an arrow to pierce, and inner courtyards where women could work in safety and animals could be loaded. This patio was entered through a *zaguan* wide enough for *carretas* and carriages, but well protected by a ten-foot gate of thick boards held together by iron bars. Windows, even after glass came in, were closed by solid barred shutters. Before the railroad came there was little glass: small sheets of mica let some light through. Floors were of adobe; Spaniards learned from the Pueblos how to harden them with oxblood. Indian, too, was the corner fireplace, made to take upright sticks, and perfect on the draw.

The gentleman's house differed from the peasant's only in size and decoration. The peon's hut, like the Indian's, was only as wide as the length of the piñon or cedar beams growing near by, but the rich hidalgo could send his peons to the mountains for tall trees to roof rooms fifteen or twenty feet wide. Often they were adorned with carving on exposed beams and corbels, and painted with the earth colors so hard to reproduce with modern paint. Such houses graciously adjust to different ways. Walls too thick for arrows are now pierced by French doors and picture windows that seem suitable enough; the *zaguan* is now a heated entrance-hall, floored with hardwood, waxed tile, or brick; and the patio is still completely right for a climate of strong sun and stiff winds.

Set among the modern furnishings are a few wobbly, hand-hewn cupboards and benches, and Navajo rugs or Chimayo blankets bought in curio shops, looted from old houses and churches, or copied by enterprising merchants. All reflect the dire poverty of the Spanish frontier, but also the people's overmastering desire to retain the amenities of a life known elsewhere.

The *rico* brought from Mexico as much as he could load on a burro or a *carreta*. That amounted to a few painted chests, pictures of the saints which could be rolled, sacred statues, and mirrors. Imagine the excitement when the family saw these treasures unwrapped from blankets and skins! For the ladies came lace mantillas, the Chinese embroidered shawls that we call "Spanish," delicate embroideries from Manila, jewels—gold filigree from Mexican craftsmen and whatever had come from Paris, London, or Madrid—and clothes.

In Santa Fe, a week or two before the annual Fiesta, descendants of those ladies parade in elegant costumes brought a century and more ago from Europe capitals. Nothing of lady's, gentleman's, or child's wardrobe failed to reach New Mexico. If its style was a year or two late, that mattered to nobody.

On the whole life was austere, and most of its appurtenances home-made. Lewis Garrard, who wrote *Wah-to-Yah* at the age of nineteen, described the Taos home of Ceran St. Vrain, who, as a rich merchant on the Santa Fe Trail, probably had more than most. "A handsomely furnished room with a fireplace in one corner and walls hung with portraits of holy characters and crosses. . . . At supper I sat at table and ate potatoes for the first time in several months. . . . A mattress was unrolled from the wall where in daytime it served as a seat, and I turned in between sheets. Yes, sheets! A house, a table, vegetables, and sheets!" But there was no bedstead and probably no chair. Chests, benches, and stools would have served. They serve now as coffee tables or occasionals.

Women working in the patio made sheets of home-grown cotton and stuffed mattresses with wool kept fresh and fluffy by many washings and sunnings. Weaving was man's work, but women did the long-stitch wool embroidery we call *colcha* because it was used on bedspreads. Illiterate women with quick eyes for color and form copied Chinese or East Indian designs on chests, and their skilled fingers turned out pieces of true artistry.

Other specialists made clothes. Women wore the full, short cotton skirts that New Mexico scorned until they were imported from Mexico and sold in shops to Eastern women. They were topped by the low-necked blouse that shocked newcomers. Both Garrard and W. H. H. Davis protested that more concealment would be more seductive. But the dark cotton rebozo provided concealment as desired, as well as shade, some warmth, and coquetry ad lib. This was the peasant woman's dress. The lady, who may have dressed so at home, went abroad wrapped in a *tápalo*, a fine black cashmere shawl with heavy knotted silk fringe. The *tápalo* has disappeared only within the last generation. Even now one may see an old lady so muffled slipping into a church. For feast days the *patrona* wore her imported finery, as she does now.

Smoking was another feminine grace. Ladies carried their tobacco, *punche*, and cornhusk wrappings in tiny silver bottles and boxes, and rolled their own. The puritanical Davis was shocked, but young Garrard found that "smoking certainly does enhance the charms of the Mexican señoritas who, with neatly rolled up shucks between their coral lips, perpetrate winning smiles." Newcomers were staggered too by the general habit of protecting the complexion by smearing it with red clay. Mr. Davis found this "no less than disgusting." But before the *baile* the red was washed off and replaced by a heavy white powder made of ground bones.

Men's serapes and trousers were home-made, as were the white drawers emerging from the plantaloons' side split. Leatherworkers on the ranches made high boots that served as chaps. They even made saddles, though the hidalgo's finest boots and saddles came from Mexico, as did his flat Spanish hat with chin strap. Resident silversmiths made buttons for the hidalgo's clothes and heavy ornaments for the horse's trappings, as well as household ware.

Table service consisted of bowls, plates, and platters; cups, goblets, and ewers; spoons, forks, and ladles. Knives did not appear; food was served in pieces that could be managed with fork and spoon. Much of this fine silverware has been lost, traded for china when the Yankee came in, melted

down, or abandoned as worthless. One of the finest bowls
known was found outdoors with chickens drinking from it.
But the silver gleam caught Mrs. Field's eye through the
blackened filth, and she bought it. This was Mary Lester
Field, who in 1886 brought from her Tennessee home an un-
erring eye for the beautiful and, as a young matron in Albuquerque, began a collection that has few equals. She
found goblets that had long served in kitchens, spoons and
forks rubbed sideways by scraping on iron pots, cups
marked by babies' teeth, and beakers that had been banged
on heavy tables. When it became known that she was buying, many pieces were smuggled to her under heavy *tápalos*
at night by impoverished old ladies.

This fine collection now belongs to the University of
New Mexico, where visitors may see it. While hallmarks
are hard to read, some appear to be Spanish; others are easily
identified as Mexican because Mexican work was severely
plain and quite unlike the ornate Spanish styles of the time.

The meals served in rich homes on silver pieced out by
pottery, and in poor homes on pottery without silver, were
the original of today's "Mexican food." It was better then
because it was made more slowly. Corn softened in lye,
hand-ground, and patted into tortillas to serve fresh from
the hot stone has a richer taste than mill-ground meal. Beans
simmered all day and all night in a pot set deep in hot ashes
have a savor worthy of the spicy sauce. Meat dressed with
many lesser herbs as well as the ubiquitous chile, and cooked
until all is well blended has flavor no electric stove can im-
part. And wheaten loaves baked in outdoor ovens come out
with a thick crust you can still crunch in a pueblo where
Indian women prefer to bake that way.

This was the diet: mutton, beef, poultry, varied by game;
corn, and beans. A little wheat was raised and some rice was
shipped in. Vegetables were mostly used as flavoring, but
fruits appeared fresh in season and dried the rest of the year.

Although the diet was limited, provision was lavish; families were large and hospitality was boundless. Any passerby was welcomed as an honored guest. The beautiful Spanish phrase "this is your house" was certainly true as long as a guest stayed in it. Such a home was the hacienda of Colonel Manuel Chaves at San Mateo. Frances Douglas de Kalb, who visited there in the 1890's with her husband, Charles Fletcher Lummis, remembered "spaciousness, vast acreage, and a great house, always immaculate and with many guests there. The kitchen was filled with happy and willing servants." One was called La Cautiva (the captive) because she had been taken in a raid on Indians and had become loved as a member of the family. "The mother Doña Vicenta was as fine a woman as I ever met. She was deeply religious, prayers in the house were frequent." Like all such ladies, Doña Vicenta was supreme in her home. Her children stood until given permission to sit, kissed her hand at greeting and parting, never smoked in her presence. As *patrona* she commanded all the serving women and men about the house. Keys hung at her belt, and she unlocked storerooms and cupboards.

Lummis, himself, was struck by less housewifely matters. In letters to the *Chillicothe* (Ohio) *Leader* in 1885, he described the house as having a wide central hallway. The influence of the States was shown, too, in flowered wallpaper on adobe walls, Brussels carpets, lace curtains at long windows, paintings, mirrors, and heavy walnut furniture. This was the typical rich home after trade with the States was safe. Young Lummis grew most lyrical over the charms of the Chaves daughters "with orbs of jet . . . wherein a little devil lurked" and their skill at the piano and in song. With evenings and firelight, songs in English and Spanish, gay games and dances, crisp cakes and wine, no wonder the youth thought he could have stayed a lifetime.

Such scenes marked the end of the old, the beginning of.

13 *The Billy
the Kid Mu-
seum in Old
Mesilla.*

NEW MEXICO
STATE TOURIST
BUREAU

14 *Sadie Orchard of Hillsboro in the 1880's.*

the new. But much of the old was to linger long. The two
sons of this family, Amado and Ireneo, law graduates of
George Washington University and quite of the modern
world, were still stately Spanish gentlemen whose backs
never relaxed even in old age. The daughters, educated in
feminine arts by mother and nuns, stayed in the traditional
life.

That life was gay enough. Even in Don Pedro Pino's day,
heavy coaches lumbered over wheel-cut tracks, carrying
ladies from hacienda to hacienda. Marriages arranged in
family council led to extensive entertaining. Festivals in celebration of Christmas, Mardi Gras, Easter, and saints' days
often lasted for weeks. Fiestas illustrated the democracy-
with-aristocracy that is Spain's great gift to civilized living.
However autocratic the *patrón*, however meekly the peon
kissed his hand and took his orders, there was an easy ca-
maraderie between them. The Don and Doña attended the
village church or invited the villagers to their private chapel.
They all danced at the *bailes*, and the singers, caroling impromptu verses, freely poked fun at the greatest and
grandest.

The *bailes*, or fandangoes, are by no means gone, just
changed. Hardwood floors have replaced hard earth or
boards rubbed with tallow; electric lights, the tallow dips;
and name-orchestras, the old *música*: fiddler, guitarist, and
accordionist. But the smooth, swift grace of the dancers is
unchanged. And many of the old dances are college favorites now, not only in New Mexico, but as far away as
Massachusetts, where a couple of Harvard students from
Santa Fe made them popular. Prime favorite is *La Var-
soviana*, a coquettish sort of schottische said to have been
taken from Warsaw to Spain by Napoleon's troops, and so
to Mexico. But college students quickly learn others too,
and many are popular.

Among the losses we deplore is the *trobador*. The im-

promptu singer is rare nowadays, but *corridos*, ballads, are
a natural folk-expression still. A crime, an accidental killing,
the virtues of a political candidate, especially the fate of
soldiers, are occasions for a song. One *corrido* popular near
Albuquerque recites in sixteen verses the tale of Lieutenant
Eloy Baca, who was killed in Germany. Another rather
sadly reflects the need of the Spanish-speaking citizen to
prove himself.

> *Me voy de soldado razo*
> *Y cuando me halle en compañia*
> *Muy lejos ya de mi tierra*
> *Les probaré que mi raza*
> *Sabe morir donde quiera.*

> I go as a soldier of my race
> And when I find myself with others
> Far from my homeland
> I shall prove to them that my race
> Knows how to die anywhere.

Still unnoticed by our English-speaking population, these
folksongs attract students to a wealth of music and verse,
sometimes related to mediæval European songs, but a truly
indigenous art too. They are secular, religious, ribald, sentimental, and occasional.

Equally unappreciated are the old morality plays, written
long ago by missionaries to instruct their Indian converts.
Los Moros y Los Cristianos, which opened in San Juan in
1598, still runs in many places, but most dramatically in San
Juan. A swashbuckling version of the defeat of the Moors in
Spain, it is often played on horseback with Moors in miters
and floating ribbons, Spaniards in helmets and armor, all
bearing lances and equally proficient in handling their quick
ponies. A fresco of this spirited encounter, painted by

Dorothy Stewart, suitably adorns Albuquerque's Little Theatre.

Many villages present favorite plays annually. *Adán y Eva* is performed during Lent in Atrisco near Albuquerque. *El Niño Perdido*, about the Christ Child disputing with the elders, has kept many a bright boy out of school in Cañón de Taos to learn the long actionless role of the Child.

The play of plays widely performed at Christmas time is *Los Pastores*, a simple tale of the shepherds following the star to Bethlehem. As Mary sings a tender lullaby, gifts are brought not by kings bearing frankincense and myrrh, but by ragged shepherds offering the new baby blankets and other warm things for his comfort. New Mexico villagers understand a poor mother and child in a stable. But they can also burlesque human indolence in Bartolo, a shepherd just too sleepy to go see the miraculous Child.

From such poor but reverent people comes New Mexico's beautiful custom of holiday lights. Long ago flat roofs glowed on Christmas Eve with rows of rosy lanterns, paper sacks holding candles set in sand. Before the people had paper sacks, they built tiny fires on the roofs or in front of the houses, as the Indians still do in Taos, to light the Christ Child on his way. These were the *luminarias*. Purists prefer to call the lighted sacks *faroles* (lanterns). But so many people have learned to say *luminarias* that the word has become part of our common speech. The custom has been generally adopted not only for Christmas, but for other holidays as well.

A curious survival not yet fully understood is the dance drama *Los Matachines*. Given in both Spanish villages and Indian pueblos, it seems to reflect the struggle between good, in the person of a white veiled child, and evil, amusingly portrayed by a man with horns and a tail. Features of its costuming suggest Morocco; it may be related to the morris dancing of old England. *Los Matachines* is widely known throughout the Spanish world; it is danced in the Philippines, from where laborers have brought it to Hawaii. Perhaps in time it will return to the mainland on its long trail back to its source in Spain.

Los Matachines is danced every year in the Sandia Mountain village of San Antonio in fulfillment of a vow. Once, the villagers say, in an Apache raid the savages came in such hordes that not all the men in the village seemed able to stop them. Then suddenly San Antonio appeared among them as a child dressed in blue, and with his miraculous aid they drove off the attackers. After that the villagers built a chapel just were the saint had appeared, and promised to honor him with *Los Matachines* every year. Once, so village tradition tells, they neglected the dance, and the spring dried up. They have never neglected it since.

Modern life is not destroying this lovely legend. During World War II a San Antonio mother vowed that if her sons came home safely they would dance *Los Matachines*. In time they both returned from the European theater, safe and well. The pious mother had not lived to see the fulfillment of her vow, though the dutiful sons did, of course, take part in the dance on the next San Antonio day.

Persistent old superstitions are less gracious relics of Spain in New Mexico. As to witches and omens, it is hard to tell how much of our Spanish heritage is Indian. The two groups interchanged their phobias and their herb remedies as they mingled their habits and their bloodstreams. *Brujo* (witch) and *curandero* (curer) are common words in pueblo and town. An Albuquerque woman, blaming her pains on the bad offices of her sister-in-law, called on a *curandero* from Santo Domingo. An old *curandero* in Los Lunas makes a good living with herbs and spells; many of his patients are Isleta Indians. Owls are considered bad omens by both whites and Indians, and all tell tales of people malevolently turned into animals or birds. Fear of the evil eye is widespread: even a kindly gaze, too long or too intent, may cause a woman to cover her child's head and turn away.

This dark tide of fear rises even into educated classes and comes into courts of law. In the 1930's a man was tried for the murder of his wife. His defense was that only by killing her body could he save her soul from dark spells put upon her. Another man, a highly competent technician, paid a quack fifty dollars to prove that his bride's illness was caused by witchcraft, and another fifty to point out the witch. This the *curandero* did by showing the old woman's face in a broken egg. The man swore he saw it! They caught the witch by beating a black dog that ran along just ahead of the wagon. When they reached home, sure enough, the suspect was badly bruised! Knowledge of the evil's origin, as in our best psychiatric clinics, brought relief.

Strangers are often struck by the New Mexican's preference for suffering and horror, especially in his religion. It is as though a hard life in a harsh land had made violence natural. Old saints carved in wood, the *bultos*, or painted, the *santos*, realistically portray agonies and are plentifully bedecked with blood. This preoccupation, whatever its source, reaches its maximum in the observances of the Penitentes, properly called Los Hermanos de Luz (The Brothers of Light), which has been important in New Mexico since Oñate's day. Their self-flagellations are personal penance, but also penance offered as remission for the sins of the world. Such an Order naturally gained power when priests were few and their visits rare, and the *Hermano Mayor* read prayers from little notebooks that are still cherished. Naturally too, such an Order extended its influence into politics and the courts. It is still a common claim that no Penitente can be convicted of a crime where the Order is strong.

Approved by the Church for centuries, the Penitentes lost their clerical support in 1828, when most of the Franciscans, as loyal Spaniards, left the Mexican Republic.

Bishop Saipointe, successor to Archbishop Lamy, prohibited their appearances in the churches; later clerics condemned them altogether. But the Penitentes kept right on with their observances. Finally, in 1948, Archbishop Edwin V. Byrne extended to them the blessing and protection of the Catholic Church, provided the order "proceeds with moderation" under the Church's supervision.

In "the Penitente counties," the minor wailing of their flute, the *pito*, may be heard at intervals throughout the year. On visits to sick or dying brothers, the members shuffle along chanting to the *pito*'s plaint, one of the saddest, lonesomest sounds imaginable. During Lent men go often to the *morada*, set always away from the village.

This two-roomed adobe chapel may be recognized by its lack of windows and by heavy crosses leaning near. Hidden ceremonies within culminate in Holy Week, when the Brothers re-enact the Passion. Accompanied by the *pito*, flagellants move in slow procession, their heads hidden in black sacks, their bare backs bleeding under the yucca lash and redly soaking their white cotton drawers. Bare feet are tortured on stones and thorns. No man cries out. One bears the heavy cross, falling as Jesus did, and often taking lashes from his fellows. Within memory, the *Cristo* was tied to the cross and left hanging there for minutes. Our grandfathers remembered seeing men nailed to the cross. There are reports of deaths and the tradition that a man's shoes, left on his doorstep, were the family's notice that he had died in holy penance.

Penitentes are religious men, performing rites full of meaning for them. Much has been written about them. The best account, factual and sympathetic at once, is *Brothers of Light* by Alice Corbin Henderson. Her husband, William Penhallow Henderson, enhanced the text with drawings that convey well the poignance of simple men in a stern land, seeking. A recurrent phrase in one of their chants is

"*Dénos, Señor, buena muerte*" (Give us, Lord, a good death), as though only death could compensate for a life so hard. But the final note is one of joyous hope. After a midnight ceremony of black terror, noise of chains and rattles, groans, and the slapping of wet whips, there comes suddenly a knocking on the door. "Who knocks?" On the answer "*Jesu Cristo!*" the door is opened, candles are lit, and the hours and days of torment yield to the glory of holy Saturday and the promise of Easter.

These ceremonies may be seen. Visitors who come with reverence and good manners are not turned away. Real friends may be invited in; prayers are offered for them.

So our Spanish heritage offers enrichment to those who have eyes to see, wit to use. Even those who have no Spanish blood nor any claim to conquering ancestors may enjoy the widening view of another language popularly spoken and the culture that made it. Much beauty comes to us from our Spanish heritage, not only in material things we can use and in mediæval folkways we can enjoy, but also in manners we could adopt with profit. New Mexico is, too, the sensitive point at which the two American cultures meet, overlap, and amalgamate. But often the effort at amalgamation is rough and ugly. Human beings are not yet civilized enough to let this union develop as beautifully as it should. Too often we have let our Spanish heritage hamper rather than help us.

XVI

THE NEW NEW MEXICAN

New Mexico's most pressing problem is that faced by our citizens whose mother tongue is Spanish. In a sense it is a problem of Americanization, but in this case the foreign of language and custom were here first and in large majority, a lead they retained for a century; it is estimated that in 1950 the Spanish-speaking citizens formed about forty per cent of the population. A century ago, when the United States took New Mexico over from Mexico, it honorably declared all the inhabitants citizens with the right to vote, to freedom of religion, and to property. No provision was made to teach English to the new citizens, and English was the basic need—the tool for building a new life, the weapon and shield against dishonorable men who followed the honorable government. The only excuse is that it was fifty years too soon. At the end of the century, Puerto Rico and the Philippines were given opportunities that would have put New Mexico fifty years ahead of where it is now.

In the twentieth century the Spanish-speaking people are themselves beginning to solve their own problem of adjusting to new ways of life and thought and of realizing themselves as American citizens without either humility or arrogance. The touchiness of the matter—and of some people —is indicated by New Mexico's nervousness about names and hyphens. Only here nobody rests quite securely as an "American." If you are not a Spanish-American or "Hispano," you are an Anglo-American or "Anglo." This latter group includes Irish, Italians, Germans, Eastern Europeans,

Scandinavians, Asiatics, and, most aptly after all, Negroes.
A Negro bootblack, asked what was being paid for votes
this year, answered: "I dunno, boss, they ain't got round to
us Anglos yet."

The word *Mexican*, so proudly borne by a great people,
is taboo in New Mexico. Only a young man, highly educated, rich, and related to distinguished families in Mexico,
can say: "Don't call me Spanish-American. I'm American,
and I'm Mexican, and proud of both!" The word *Mexican*
is commonly held to imply the disrespect or condescension
accorded to inferiors. It was countered by the derogatory
word *gringo*. Originally probably it meant only "foreigner"; the manner of its expression could make it a fighting word. But nowadays the unfitness of Anglo is so apparent that gringo is used quite easily.

When the Americans first came into New Mexico—and a
heterogeneous lot they were—there was no doubt what they
were, nor any doubt that the people they found here, even
while New Mexico was still a Spanish colony, were Mexicans. No problem of nomenclature arose—unless some New
Mexicans, understanding Mexico's revolt from Spain, dis-
liked being called Spanish, as Mexicans, Cubans, and many
other Americans still do. In 1898 the uninformed wondered
if people of Spanish heritage would fight against Spain.
They were eager to, volunteered in numbers, and made a
fine record as Rough Riders. Teddy Roosevelt delighted to
honor them, often visited New Mexico, appointed Miguel
Antonio Otero governor of the state, and stood sponsor for
Theodore Roosevelt Armijo.

So far Mexican was a name no man need be ashamed of.
Old newspaper files contain the most adulatory obituaries
of Mexican gentlemen. But by 1918 the whole country was
hyphenized. German-American was not desirable; many
weaklings changed their German names. French-American,
on the other hand, was fine. And Spanish-American was in-

vented when Four Minute Men, lauding the readiness of Mexican boys to go off to fight, were reminded that they were not Mexican nationals, but Americans like anybody else. So the Four Minute Men agreed and the newspapers concurred that Spanish-American it should be. And so it is.

This naming is awkward; it becomes paradoxical when it is applied to Mexican nationals coming into New Mexico. How depressing for a Mexican citizen to be assured that his former nation is unworthy, that he must refuse to be called by its name.

Other problems are more pressing as young people learn English and take on new ways. The old dependence upon the *patrón* and the old fatalism are weakening. The phrase *"Dios lo quiere,"* God wills it, is being superseded by "I'll not let that happen again," as up-and-coming young people are developing by their own efforts into citizens any state could be proud of.

This new New Mexican may be the son of an hidalgo, but he is more apt to be the son of a villager. Often related to the big-house family, he was more like the European small farmer than like the mediæval serf. But the enterprising youngster may well be the grandson of the peon or even the slave. If so, he may suffer from New Mexico's brand of snobbery. A lady tickles her ego by referring to people of her surname but of humble origin as *"esos indios"* (those Indians). One politician describes his hearers as descendants of Spanish grandees and himself as son of a sheep-herder who made good. Thus he bows at once to Spanish pride and the log-cabin tradition.

Some politicians take advantage of the old reverence for the *patrón*, and are not above winning votes by arousing resentment against gringos. Though slavery ended with the Fourteenth Amendment and peonage was abolished—on paper—by suitable New Mexico legislation, the old ways clung. Ignorant people, confused by the new laws and given no chance to learn English, continued to work for the *patrón*, to do as he said, to borrow from him. Debt peonage persisted. It may still persist. It is common practice to prepay sheep-herders and other workers. It is not uncommon for a powerful politician rancher to jail workmen who have taken the advance but have failed to show up on the job. But the most un-American hangover was the persistence of the *patrón* as the political boss.

Recently a rancher who employed some sixty workers was invited to a meeting: they must know how the *patrón* wished them to vote. The rancher, innocent of our Spanish heritage, seized the opportunity to make what he thought an effective speech on the importance of the vote and the voter's independence. The men listened respectfully, but after the gringo had walked away one followed him. "Señor," he said, "you are right. That was a fine speech. But who pays us our dollar?"

It is a rare aspirant for office who refuses to take advantage of such a situation. In fact, New Mexico's political habits, so folksy and so funny, are due to the use of this handy political weapon by both parties. Nor is this a proper complaint against the gringo. He merely followed the lead and learned the techniques of the old Spanish families in dealing with their people. The Spanish word for people, *gente*, has a special connotation in New Mexico. The don's *gente* do as he says.

With the U.S. occupation, the rich dons—many of whom had already been educated in the States—easily overcame the language difficulty, intermarried with the newcomers, and merged so completely with them that strangers studying New Mexico often do not recognize them as Spanish. Such men went into politics and were clever at it. The don could deliver the county or precinct vote unfailingly, and was rewarded with a fair share of offices. But it is notable that the Spanish-speaking counties were not favored in the distribution of political plums, in spite of the fact that Spanish-speaking voters were in the majority until the middle 1930's. Perhaps the political *patrón* was not clever enough; more likely he was closer to the thinking of the aristocratic Spanish hidalgo than to the American faith in an enlightened citizenry. Even bosses from the poorer groups, as they delivered the vote and gained power, married the pretty daughter or sister of the real don and became *patrones* themselves. Such men did nothing to inculcate democratic ideas in their less fortunate neighbors and little to protect them from political or financial exploitation.

Nor did the Church, preoccupied with spiritual matters and distressed to see the Protestant churches making converts, make any unified effort to teach English. Bishop Lamy opened a school for boys in 1850, and a few others followed, but only those who could pay attended these schools. A few bright youngsters learned good English in Protestant mission schools, where it was emphasized. But both Protestant ministers and Catholic priests preached in Spanish. Many still do, though in some cases they have been forced to turn to English by young members of their congregations. So the mass of the population was left trapped in a foreign language and ideology. New Mexico's public school system dates from 1891, but for many years teachers were often political appointees who spoke English poorly or not at all. Before World War I many counties had no high schools. Consequently few students reached college, and few educated leaders with democratic ideas appeared to offset the old domination by the *patrón*.

As new *patrones* rose to power, many young dons who could not adjust to the American pattern slipped into a less favored position. Rich young men, knowing that if a storm wiped out ten thousand sheep there would be more sheep, used to finding plenty of money in the strongbox, and believing that work was degrading and close trading unworthy of a gentleman, were at a sad disadvantage against frontier lawyers with a tradition of hard work, canny trading, and long saving. So the young hidalgo (literally, son of somebody)—when his horse failed to win, or gambling debts piled up—could easily find some son of nobody from "the States" ready to make a loan or at least to talk business. Such talks usually concerned the family grant.

Gringos on the make found the land-grant situation most interesting—and profitable. The United States had guaranteed to recognize all existing valid land claims. In case of a Spanish or Mexican grant, an act of Congress was necessary, but Congress was generally lenient and most claims were allowed. But lands had been poorly surveyed or not surveyed at all; often boundaries were described by such perishable landmarks as trees, ditches, and adobe walls; not infrequently ownership had devolved, through the years, upon dozens—even hundreds—of heirs. Many cases were in the courts for years, especially after 1890, when Congress wearied of grant cases and set up the Court of Private Land Claims. Many lawyers now became specialists in land-grant cases. Often the attorney worked for a contingent fee, accepting part of the grant for his services. It was not unknown—if terms were not too well defined at the start or if a case took many years—for the lawyer to end as owner of the whole grant. Some lawyers actually ended their lives land-poor.

Cases of community grants were the most complicated. Here ignorance of the new laws was often decisive, especially ignorance of American tax procedure. Owners of grants could sign a "petition for partition," which permitted selling the grant and paying off the owners in cash. Getting such petitions became almost a profession. Spanish-speaking men, often briefless lawyers, would reach every heir—those in the penitentiary and the insane asylum, as well as university professors and men doing well in the East. Then a sale was held. The instigator of the affair might be the only bidder on the courthouse steps. One more grant would go into gringo hands, and more landowners would become seekers for day labor at low wages.

This is not ancient history; it is a recurring scene. As late as 1950 grants were still bought for 35 cents an acre when assessed valuation was $1.04 an acre for grazing land, as high as $6.00 an acre for cultivated plots. The biggest upset of recent years came through the Middle Rio Grande Conservancy District, which bonded landowners for an elaborate program of draining ditches and flood control. Many owners could not meet the payments, and their farms are now owned by gringos who work in Albuquerque.

Now and again village people have held onto their grant. Chilili in the Manzano Mountains, far in arrears on taxes, was advised by the county agricultural agent to take legal advice, and its lawyer negotiated a Farm Security Loan. Chilili then paid up its back taxes and the people owned their own grant; they then began to market the yield of their forest lands through a co-operative. Thus the United States, one hundred years late, is at long last helping its New Mexico citizens to keep their lands and help themselves.

But there are few Chililis and thousands of displaced villagers. In town they try valiantly to Americanize themselves without such aid as eastern cities offer the immigrant. An overgrown boy, guyed on the playground for his accent, turns ugly and ends in juvenile court. A girl, resentful of her old-fashioned family, evades their control, runs the streets, and comes eventually to the Welfare Home. Most parents try to help; many struggle hard to speak English at home, hoping their children will have no accent.

One mother, believing in progress but in parental control too, required her children—sons as well as daughters—to turn all their wages over to her. She administered the family budget cannily, bought plain food, and worked hard: she acquired oilcloth for the kitchen, scatter rugs and standing lamps for the living-room, better dishes, and mechanical aids —all bought on the installment plan. She could not explain her policy in English, but what she said was: "I want my children to have the best, and when they have payments to meet they do not waste their money."

Many such families, trying to get ahead, meet discrimination in getting jobs. New Mexico has a better record of fair dealing than many states, but a native daughter must admit —with shame—that even here good people are often hurt and hampered by prejudice. This is most true in counties settled by people from the southern states and those in which the evangelical churches are strongest. New Mexico is fighting a battle for decency. The question is: will the old easy tolerance of our grandfathers be blotted out by hordes of newcomers, or will there be among the newcomers enough people of good feeling to offset the prejudice of those who know no better?

Despite manifold handicaps the young Spanish-speaking citizen is forging ahead, becoming a new New Mexican. And he is doing it in the best American style, by individual initiative, courage, and brains. This is nothing new: always, in New Mexico as elsewhere, the class that seemed doomed to be forever poor and ignorant has produced a few individuals who could force themselves up and out. First they thought the only way to get ahead was through politics, so they played politics, demanding certain offices for men with Spanish names. Young lawyers, fearing they would never get the fat fees, sought political appointment. Some left the state to practice in eastern states. Few stuck it out at home, weathering the lean years as any young lawyer must expect to weather them. Business was easier. Many enterprising men, owning a village store and handling sheep as a sideline, made a comfortable living and sent their children to eastern schools. But New Mexico still had no strong middle class of Spanish heritage.

World War I made some change. Youths who had been no farther from home than Ranchos or Arroyo Hondo saw foreign lands and great cities. Many brought home medals or citations for bravery; most importantly, they brought home the realization that they were American citizens. But the burden of ignorance was still heavy. Few could speak fluent English. The real advance was to come through tragedy.

A professor of sociology said: "I'm a Republican, but I must admit that the Republican party consistently played the old *patrón* game. Their machines won elections by subsidizing local leaders to bring in the vote. But when the depression struck and people were desperate for jobs and food, the old system broke down and federal agencies took over. For the first time simple people found help in their government. Of course it made the state Democratic at one stroke; but best of all it broke the power of the bosses and developed young local leaders."

Here, at long last, was government helping the poor man, not—as one old villager said—"helping the rich to rob the poor of their meagerness." Scrawny, sullen boys grew sturdy and busy in CCC camps. Older men, shy and hesitant before a teacher, were won by a matter-of-fact approach, and enrolled in literacy classes to the number of 1,474. Fortunately the work was directed by Mrs. Adelina Otero Warren, herself a balanced product of two cultures, and she based the courses on actual vocabulary needs and taught teachers to meet their classes with old-fashioned dignity. As one result, many older men subscribed for newspapers, and five hundred unschooled youngsters were able to sign up for the draft as literates.

PWA projects provided work, reduced hazards on highways, and built many needed public buildings, as well as some buildings of a highly private nature. One privy bore the legend "PWA Project." But the WPA contributed even more to Americanization than the PWA. The WPA music project, directed by Mrs. Helen Chandler Ryan, published a *New Mexico Song and Game Book* that carried our customs far. Many choruses and orchestras earned small fame at home, and one singer of old songs became a night-club success in New York. But the most important result of the WPA program was that New Mexicans got, for the first time, the true American idea that poverty was no insurmountable handicap and no disgrace; that a man needed no *patrón*; that if presidents have come from log cabins and captains of industry from work gangs, so could presidents come from adobe huts and tycoons from sheep camps. New Mexico was beginning to develop its own valid and solid middle class.

One young man, son of a family that had lost its land grant and of a father who believed in education, found the going hard. "In high school I began to run with a gang. We all felt queer because of our accent, we wanted obscurely to get even. I might have gone bad if things hadn't got so tight at home; there really wasn't much to eat. So my brother and I stood in line and signed up for the CCC. It was a fine experience. And when they moved me out to make room for others, I got a WPA job and then a wife. . . . A Spanish wife! My mother had warned us never to marry a *gringa*; she said gringas only wanted what they could get out of a man, but a true Spanish wife would help him to get ahead. Mine certainly did. She kept her job and insisted I finish at the University. Then the war came and I worked in Relocation Centers and finally in Japan. I'm not allowed to say much about that." This veteran graduated and became a teacher. Working nights, he took an advanced degree in philosophy. He needs philosophy when ignorant and prejudiced parents protest having their children taught by him because he is an Hispano. He says he has no trouble with children, but only with parents. But even parents can learn.

One parent who protested at his son's riding in a bus driven by a Spanish-speaking man and filled with Spanish-speaking children, was referred to the school principal, our friend with the degree in philosophy. Although he looked altogether gringo, his Spanish name gave pause to the father, who demanded to see the county superintendent. But when he heard there the same Spanish name and found the superintendent a suave and amused American gentleman proud of his long Spanish ancestry, the gringo decided to accept the queer ways of this new state.

Such a superintendent has his difficulties with old style politicos too; they demand teaching posts for "our people," regardless of qualifications. One superintendent met this by outlining the qualifications of two applicants; one well-trained, the other not. "Which would you choose to teach your children?" So the one from Ohio got the job over the school board president's niece. But the pressure is great. Another superintendent offended Spanish parents when he proposed pre-school classes to teach their children English. Discrimination was the cry. But he won, to the children's great advantage. Children love to learn English. One tiny tot who had been too shy to play with English-speaking children—whose parents hoped he would swap languages with them—was their first visitor when they came home after months away. Bounding into their house with eyes shining, the little fellow cried: "How do you do, Mrs. B? How do you do, Mr. B? Welcome home! Now I can speak English."

Shyness and a proud desire to avoid discrimination often act as bars quite as effective as the occasional discrimination that undeniably exists. Some employers refuse to hire men with Spanish names; certain labor unions have barred them openly or connived to keep them overlong as apprentices. During World War II a PX at an army camp in New Mex-

ico advertised for clerks, stating: "Only Anglos need apply."
The Governor of New Mexico, showered with protests, referred them to the Commanding Officer of the military district, who had it corrected at once. But private
groups cannot be so easily controlled. On occasion, even
church groups have made Spanish converts so uncomforta-
ble that they have ceased to attend services. Apprehensive
of such slights, members of a Spanish Protestant church declined to attend a party given by an English-speaking congregation of the same faith. These are the difficulties—personal as well as social—which the new New Mexican meets.
But his problems are not as important as are the gallantry,
determination, and humor with which he is solving them.

Some New Mexicans, aided if not abetted by sentimental
sympathizers and designing politicians, make rather a profession of their woes. Too many would-be leaders, even if
they take off with "*nuestro glorioso pasado*," pass quickly
on from "our glorious past" to a dreary present in which
our "poor people" are forever put upon. Their followers
naturally demand certain political jobs as their right, expect to pass easily through schools as some politico's appointees, and lay every failure not to their own fault but
to nasty discrimination. They are least concerned with improving their fitness.

This group is more than offset by the new New Mexican
who has no time for repining and whose pride is in himself,
not in his ancestors. So we had forebears on horseback?
Fine! So we had others that were hard put to it to eat? Not
so good, but true. But we refuse to bask in a warm nostalgic
glow over past glories or to melt into tears over our poverty,
past or present. Such young men and women squirm at being considered pitiful and helpless. They repudiate such
books as George Sanchez's *Forgotten People*, dealing with
the seamier side of life in Taos County. "Don't you believe
a word of it!" cries one of them.

These spunkier New Mexicans find several solutions. Some of them get up and get out. It may be no farther than to the nearest town, a vocational training school, or wherever they can obtain whatever it takes to qualify as a good workman. They are found in factories, stores, business, and the professions from coast to coast, in universities in this country and other countries, and with business firms or government service in foreign lands, where their Spanish and natural suavity are great assets. These often brilliant men and women have certainly deprived New Mexico and their own villages of leadership. Others may be just as lost by staying at home to play the old-fashioned political game. Those who portend the best for the state's future are making a career of working at home. They include the best educators, and workers in public health, agriculture, and home economics. Their policy is well expressed by a few of them.

Ernesto Gutierrez, agricultural graduate and county agent, says: "Our job is to live at home, plant recommended seeds, control pests, spray and fertilize, practice rotation. Save our land, improve it, use it!" Slim and hard, in tight blue jeans, field boots, and a tall hat, he drives his own car because the county does not provide one, visits every farm, and helps everywhere. He grows enthusiastic over every evidence of sound farming; but, as the county has no demonstration agent, he is just as proud of a cellarful of canned food as of a good job of contour plowing or ditch grading. Here is a smart and snappy young American who believes in production, improvements, and self-help. He considers it his job to reduce the number of poor people by helping every one to dig his own acres and make them produce to capacity. His enthusiasm is a refreshing sight.

Such young people work hard with Parent-Teacher Associations, 4-H Clubs, co-operatives, and Soil Conservation districts, and promote rural electrification. Their protégés often win state and even national prizes. They do not favor

Spanish-speaking children, but who would not be proud when a village girl in Rio Arriba County spells down the state and goes to Washington, or a Doña Ana County girl sees her Spanish name lead for state president of the 4-H Clubs?

Many such youngsters go on to vocational schools or to college. Those who cannot, have learned the priceless lesson of self-confidence and the value of old-fashioned ways that prevailed in the villages long ago: hard work, thrift, and dependability. Like their grandfathers, they pay their bills. If they go to town they are likely to become good workmen rather than whiners.

Gilbert Lopez worked up to be foreman in a foundry and is slowly building his own home. It took three years to floor the living-room, and his wife decided on steel casement windows before a bathroom. Now she has both. They had rented out an extra room during those three years, and had saved the money for these improvements. "If I can do it," he says, "anybody can."

Joe Rivera, who ran away from home to go to school and worked his way from the age of fourteen, became an organizer in the sawmill workers' union and was elected state president of the American Federation of Labor.

The young people who get to college are most articulate about their handicaps and how they are overcoming them. As county high schools were established, more and more young people from poor families enrolled in state universities. There they met many difficulties because they spoke English with a Spanish accent and because they were poor. Few were invited to join fraternities and sororities, though young people of Spanish families of wealth and social glamor became "Greeks." The discrimination is social and snobbish. In any case, these adolescent standards have had little effect on returning GI's seeking an education.

One veteran, studying law and planning to run for county sheriff after graduation, said: "Fraternities don't bother me. I've got all the friends I need. Besides, I've got a wife and two kids and a political machine to build."

Girl students show more sensitiveness than the men. One Spanish-speaking girl, working her way through college, said: "Something that happened in high school made me realize that I might be considered not acceptable. So I didn't accept any sorority invitations. I think many Spanish girls do that." This girl, pretty, dainty, exquisitely turned out, is most successful in an exacting departmental job. Others like her take honors in class, go on to graduate work, but hold apart in quiet dignity.

Men students are preparing for the professions—education, law, pharmacy, medicine. If they contemplate business it is as a means to an end. One told a success story the equal of any. "I was born," he said, "in a tiny mountain hamlet where I never heard English. My father took us to town for school, but in high school I still had to translate every question into Spanish in my mind, think of the answer in Spanish and translate that into English. By that time some smart gringo had put up his hand and the teacher put me down as a stupid Mex. But I wasn't. I learned and I graduated tops. I was in China for four years and I tried out dozens of American and British accents before I found the one I liked best." He spoke easily with an accent more cultivated than that of most Americans.

Another veteran broke a national record as a salesman and refused a post as manager of a branch in Mexico. "I think I'll finish my law first. Then I'll take that job and make enough to live on while I build up my practice. . . . Last summer I made $3,500. That's enough."

Another, studying government, is going into politics. "My county is one of the dirtiest in the state. I think I'll

clean it up. Of course, I'll have to buck some pretty ugly
gringo bosses. But it'd be fun to see a Mex cleaning out the
dirty gringos—now wouldn't it?"

Another, more realistic, perhaps with less humor, plans
to play the game with the bosses. "It's the only way; get in
and play it the way they do. . . . But I'll never play the
racial game. I've already told one native I'd never vote for
him; all he ever does is wave the bloody shirt. . . . Sure
there's discrimination. It's harder to get ahead if you're
Spanish. It's not enough to be good; you've got to be super.
O.K., I'll be super."

"The racial game" is becoming more discredited with
every campaign, even against the increasing flood of people
from states where only certain names and heritages are considered correct. One defeated candidate stated it well. "I was
getting along all right, even in that gringo precinct, when
that paper came out with its blast, daring people to vote
against me because of my Spanish name. That cooked my
goose. Lots of people who were going to vote for me
changed their minds. I don't blame 'em. We've got to take
our chances like anybody."

Another candidate, campaigning in a county where prejudice is rife, related his experience with a grin. "When I
walked into that meeting in the church I felt antagonism
like a wave. I was Spanish; they talked about making New
Mexico 'a white man's country'—even in the churches they
talked like that! But I said to myself: 'Now brother, keep
your shirt on. If they feel like that it is because they are
ignorant. It's up to you to teach them; teach them by what
you do.' So I was very quiet, but when I had a chance I
matched a joke with a joke, I talked with a group of men
during supper; and when they asked me to speak I told them
what I hoped for New Mexico. They listened respectfully.
Afterward the preacher came up and said: 'I've never voted

for an Hispano, but I'm going to vote for you!' I thought if I'd won a preacher I wasn't doing so badly."

New Mexico is not out of the woods yet, that darkling forest where good people have been held back by lack of a chance to learn. But quietly and often unnoticed, we are developing leaders who, while holding to the best Spanish traditions, have accepted the best United States tradition and are coming ahead under their own power, using every advantage that a free land offers, relying on themselves, and making good. These are the new New Mexicans who will finally bring our state to its full maturity as the heir of two fine cultures.

PART THREE

Gringo

XVII

GRINGO DISCOVERERS

◆ MEXICO lost her northern provinces to a new country, whose explorers came neither for God nor glory, but for gain. They came as individuals seeking, first, furs and then trade with Mexico. That astute patriots back in Washington saw far beyond them to a frontier on the Pacific was proved by what followed. Even the first official explorer of the unknown land between Mexico and the United States appears to have been quite innocent of what his adventure might lead to. This was Zebulon Montgomery Pike, and his orders were to find the headwaters of the Arkansas, which flowed into the Mississippi in U.S. territory, and to return to Natchitoches by way of the Red River, also presumed to rise in the Rockies. This was an error of several hundred miles, but it gave Pike a chance to see a lot of Spanish territory.

Pike's expedition, in 1805–6, revealed basic differences between the homespun republic and the resplendent empire. Pike was no general, but a lieutenant who was promoted to captainship on the way. He came not in plumed helmet and glittering mail with an armored army, but with a handful of soldiers and a civilian doctor. Nobody carried the cross. Pike's detail was supplied with whisky, corn meal, pork, gunpowder, salt, and tobacco for its use, and with calico and knives for the Indian trade. The men had a few tents and blankets, and their clothes were too light. Like many later travelers, they thought they were going into warm country.

Pike saw, even rounded, the peak that bears his name, though he neither climbed nor named it. As usual with U.S. discoveries in the Southwest, the Spaniards had been there earlier. The Americans had a bitter-cold and trying January as they crossed the divide and came upon a clear rushing stream they took to be the Red River. They were actually in the Rio Grande watershed, and when Pike built a fort and raised the stars and stripes he was in Spanish territory. There he was taken into pleasant captivity by Lieutenant Don Facundo Melgares, who met him with a troop of militia mounted on white horses in stunning contrast with its officers' black steeds. In view of New Mexico's dire poverty, this was clearly an effort to impress. Pike and his captor became good friends, and the young gringo certainly saw more as a prisoner than as an explorer. Pike's own story, *The Expedition of Zebulon Montgomery Pike*, is the first of many officers' books on the new land, and, like them all, very readable and amusing for its upstage Protestantism and U.S. indignation at having to conform to Spanish law. Pike reports courteous treatment all the way.

Even before Pike, a few lone drifters from the States had appeared in Santa Fe: Baptiste Laland and James Pursley were there in 1806. But the real westward movement began after Pike's book was published. Trappers came first; then traders.

Trapping, especially for beaver for men's hats, began on the streams Lewis and Clark had followed. It produced one of our national heroes, idol of men who yearn for a hardy, womanless world—or think they do. The trapper went alone, needing only salt and gunpowder, knife, gun, and traps. He killed his food, made his clothes, got along well with Indians on the live-and-let-live principle, and wed an

Indian girl. When he had a good stack of furs he put into this or that "hole" to sell his pelts, swap tales, replenish supplies, and find the needed release of liquor, women, and the gambling that reduced him again to gun, knife, and traps. In the northern mountains trappers worked for large companies, rugged individuals enriching men of wealth sitting comfortably in officers back in St. Louis. Farther south they worked as "free trappers," men on their own. They drifted into New Mexico by way of the Colorado Rockies and worked on through the Mogollons to the Gila and Colorado rivers. Among these men were Mexican trappers, a fact that our writers have overlooked. We are likely to see things from our own point of view, and in this case we lack records. Mexican trappers left no written record, and their names do not appear on the tax rolls: only gringos had to pay for permission to trap.

Taos was the rendezvous of trappers and mountain men. Major Jacob Fowler of Kentucky, who put in there in 1821, described his visit. "A collection of men and ladys of the Spanyerds Had a fandango . . . wheare they appeered to injoy them Selves With the Prest at their head." Major Fowler, a surveyor and described as an educated man by his granddaughter, who wrote the introduction to his *Journal of Jacob Fowler*, encountered so many difficulties in his travels that he ended by misspelling "difficulties" twelve ways.

The mountain men were the real discoverers of the West. From Canada to Mexico, they trapped beaver on every creek, followed every river, crossed every divide, learned to avoid every precipice and to shelter in every cave. They knew the Rockies intimately and in detail; the maps they carried in their heads had no blank spaces. As guides, the trappers led the traders who followed soon, and as scouts they showed old moccasin-worn trails to such "pathfinders" as Frémont and Kearny. Then, as soldiers, even as officers, they proved invaluable to the country they had never considered changing for another. Perhaps the archetype of such men was New Mexico's Kit Carson, the illiterate boy who ran away from an apprenticeship in Missouri and became a legend in his lifetime.

Like the early Spanish explorers, these gringos were agog to tell their adventures, and apparently every one who could write and many who could not spell wrote books. Unfortunately, we have no account of how this invasion looked to the Mexicans. How enriched our history would be if we had such diaries and private letters as vitalize our pre-Revolutionary and pre-Civil war periods! After Don Pedro Pino's report to the King in 1812 we have no first-hand account of the natural fears and forebodings of Mexican citizens as they watched the relentless advance of the United States bringing the end of the world they knew. We need, too, their detailed picture of the interlopers. We know only from old gossip and family tradition that they were considered ignorant, boorish heretics, with only an occasional man among them with whom a gentleman could be at ease. If the *ricos* wrote anything, their confidences have disappeared into coffers in Mexico or were prudently burned when the new government took over. We have only one comment, quoted by Twitchell. Don Mariano Chaves, sending his son to a St. Louis school, said: "These heretics are going to overrun all this country. Go learn their language and come back prepared to defend your people." That lad was José Francisco Chaves, who became one of the most distinguished citizens of the territory of New Mexico and its representative in the United States Congress from 1865 to 1871.

Before the United States took over, Mexico had revolted from Spain, and New Mexico was part of the Mexican Republic. We have an amusing account of those days in General Thomas James's *Three Years Among the Mexicans and Indians*. He found Santa Fe all freshly whitewashed and the churches adorned with fine altar vessels and hangings for the celebration. Governor Melgares, who had been a friend to Pike, told General James that his Spanish passport would no longer serve, but he would be welcomed and no duties would be assessed. The general was the last trader with no complaint about duties.

As a citizen of a country experienced in celebrating independence, James was consulted. He recommended a liberty pole, a flag, and a salute to each province of the new republic. He suggested an eagle as an emblem, but the Mexicans decided on clasped hands to typify the unity of all nations.

James writes: "I informed the governor that all was ready for the raising of the flag, which honor belonged to him. 'Oh, do it yourself,' he said, 'you understand such things.' So I raised the first flag in the free and independent state of New Mexico."

Santa Fe, however, understood fiesta. A local painter had decorated a stage, on which little girls posed as Independence, Religion, and Union, and where eloquent gentlemen made stirring speeches. The general thought the handsomest people were the San Felipe Indians in their hand-woven cotton garments and coral and turquoise jewelry. "They danced with admirable harmony," he wrote. Altogether he found that the Indians acted with "more moderation and restraint than the Spaniards," who, he complained, "abandoned themselves to the most reckless dissipation and profligacy." He had never seen such gambling. Even ladies gambled away their money, then their jewels, and finally their gold-fringed shawls, leaving the tables only to find more riches to risk.

Even as the fiesta ended, word came that Navajos had attacked settlements in the Rio Abajo. James watched Melgares review his troops: "a gang of tatterdemalions . . . of all colors, some bare-headed, others bare-backed. . . . Most were armed with bows and arrows, a few had guns that looked as if they had been imported by Cortés, while others had iron hooks fastened to the end of poles which passed for lances." By the time the militia got going, the Navajos had killed all the people in several villages, destroyed what they could not take, driven off all the cattle, and swept north along the Rio Grande to raid Taos and be on their way.

This is what New Mexico's citizens faced when fourteen men of good families gathered in Santa Fe in 1851 to organize a legislature. Two of them were disqualified because they could neither read nor write. They were all inexperienced. Yet Twitchell makes a plea for proper recognition of these men in place and street names. They were our first legislators; they were earnest and generous, serving without pay; and they had good intentions. They even discussed establishing schools. But the province had no money; it would be some years before trade with the States would begin to bring in duties.

Trade was the great hope. It was profitable even when the only transportation was long trains of mules, each loaded with two hundred pounds of goods. But in 1824 Captain William Becknell daringly brought to Santa Fe 25 wagons, 81 men, 150 horses and mules. On his return he took back $180,000 in gold packed in rawhide sacks, and $10,000 worth of furs.

But the enterprising men were not all in Missouri. In 1828, just a year after Antonio Armijo's successful trek to California, twenty-six Mexicans made it to Independence and came home rich. Trade on the Santa Fe Trail was well

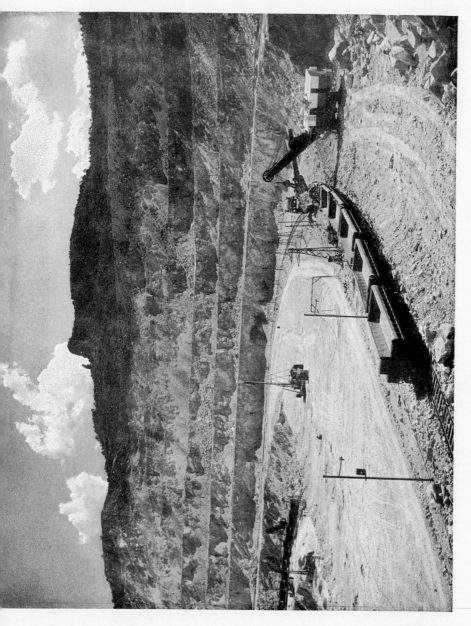

15   The open-pit copper mine at Santa Rita and the rock that was named for the Saint.

CAPLIN AND THOMPSON, OLD ALBUQUERQUE

16　The Bell
Ranch near
Tucumcari uses
the old-time
chuck wagon.

CAPLIN AND
THOMPSON, OLD
ALBUQUERQUE

established by 1860, when it employed ten thousand men and was estimated as worth four or five million dollars annually to the traders.

In those days, once a year a dusty caravan stopped just over the hills from Santa Fe so that the men could trim their beards and wash, don new shirts, tie new crackers to their whips, and roll into town with as much dash as could be got out of footsore beasts. *"La caravana! La caravana!"* To New Mexicans this trade meant better goods at lower prices and the excitement of dealing with gringos with their harsh speech and free ways. Conservative families held back; especially they tried to hold their daughters back. Lesser folk, including the daughters, took the newcomers to their hearts. Even the most rigid families' ramparts were breached by some diplomatic merchant from Kentucky like James Magoffin, some physician from Maryland like Henry Connelly, some engaging rascal like Richens Lacy Wootton, who ran away from one of Virginia's first families rather than go to school.

In 1824 the Bent brothers from Virginia built a trading-post on the Arkansas near where the Purgatoire (Picket Wire) River came in. This was Bent's Fort; its walls were four feet thick; at its corners were watchtowers; its courtyards could contain a small army; its storerooms could supply the whole Southwest; and its living quarters housed every traveler on the trail. William Bent, who stayed with the fort, married an Arapaho. His brother Charles settled in Taos, where he married Maria Ignacia of the rich Jaramillo family. Her sister, Josefa, became Mrs. Kit Carson. So these two men were committed to New Mexico. They made much of its history—Charles Bent as governor and Kit Carson as guide, scout, officer, and Indian agent. Perhaps their most important contribution was keeping the trust and friendship of their wives' people while remaining patriotic citizens of the United States. Kit Carson even held the admiration of Indians he defeated. He was an honorable, square-dealing gentleman, and modest withal.

When twenty-two-year-old Franz Huning took his first look at Santa Fe in 1849, he found "the branch of industry . . . most flourishing and lucrative was monte and faro. The government spent much money in those days in this territory . . . and . . . gambling places were crowded every night. . . . Every time I went to those places I saw there, and bucking, a small thin, bow-legged man of about forty." Kit Carson! Young Huning had read a book about the famous scout illustrated with a picture of a tall man with flowing beard, "clad all over in ornamental buckskins, mounted on a powerful charger. He was in the act of killing two Indians . . . one with a pistol, the other with a large Bowie knife. . . . In later years when he was a colonel . . . and was stationed with his regiment in Albuquerque . . . one day I showed him the picture. 'Why,' he exclaimed with his thin voice, 'is that me?' "

We know Santa Fe Trail days better than most eras because so many men and women, who rode those swaying wagons or prodded those heavy oxen across the rutted plains wrote about it. The classic of the trail is *The Commerce of the Prairies* by Josiah Gregg, who first crossed the plains in 1844. One hundred wagons was the usual train made up by several merchants. Oxen were to prove better draft animals than the more temperamental mules, and those slow beasts set the day's journey at ten or twelve miles. Among the wagons were a few Dearborn carriages for the ladies, many animals for replacements, and mounted men to serve as guides and hunters. The first leg of the journey was easy enough, as the trail crossed long-grass country with frequent streams and shady groves. But at Council Grove experienced men rode cautiously, alert for signs that Indians were near, and discipline was tightened. At night wagons were swung into a circle with wheels interlocked, sentinels were posted, and men rode around the grazing animals, crooning softly to calm them.

At the ford of the Arkansas there was a choice of routes, each with its special hazards: steep mountain grades on the northern trail, long waterless stretches on the southern. To-day's traveler may see for himself how difficult this terrain was for wagon trains, even as he sits comfortably in a Pullman on the Santa Fe Railroad, whose tracks follow both old trails.

In a rainy season or when the grass was good, the shorter southern route was preferred. At Cimarron Crossing on the Arkansas, barrels were filled with water, animals made to drink all they would, and late in the day the train set out to cross the Staked Plains, whose flatness had so impressed Coronado's men. Here the men from the States met the Mexican *ciboleros*, buffalo hunters often more deadly with a lance than the best shot with a musket. Traders relieved the long day's drag by running buffalo or dashing after antelope or deer.

Within New Mexico's modern boundary the trail crosses a rolling prairie where grass runs forever before the wind and cloud shadows smudge its creamy bowl like smoke-stains on the creaminess of pottery. The land lies in bowls marked off by straight dark lines that are narrow canyons where cottonwoods and willows find footing and cattle always find water. For here the mountains are not far away and streams converge to form the Mora, the Red, and finally the Canadian. The motorist, speeding at seventy miles per hour over good roads, comes at times upon shallow grass-grown ruts that were cut more than a century ago by loaded wagons. Flyers see them clearly from the air. The New Mexico Historical Society has erected markers: Josiah Gregg's Route. But best of all we can follow the same landmarks the traders knew. Nobody could miss the island of dark basalt, whose outline is so like straining beasts pulling a prairie schooner, that is Wagon Mound. Here the two trails joined.

The northern route followed the Arkansas River toward the Rockies. And every wagon train stopped at Bent's Fort, where one hundred men worked as carpenters, smiths, butchers, wranglers, storekeepers, and clerks. Mountain men came in with their hides to be pressed and stored and Indians stopped to barter and to visit their close friends and relatives, the Bents. There were billiard tables, a telescope, and often a doctor. Every novelist of the Trail has made Bent's Fort the scene of a birth or a death, a seduction or an eye-gouging fight.

Bent's Fort was so closely linked with our history that New Mexico seems to have begun there. But beyond it there remained a long crawl up over the foothills of the Rockies to the pass that was the true gateway to New Mexico. The Spanish Peaks lifted ever closer to the blue, as animals labored more and more heavily in the thinning air to reach Raton Pass.

Two miles a day was good time crossing the Pass. Beasts strained and men pushed, sweated, and swore on the way up. On the other side they lashed wheels together and held back just as hard going down. Axles broke on stones, hot-boxes developed, animals died, delicate ladies like Susan Magoffin trembled with fright.

Here, at a spot that the modern tourist-catcher would consider a realized dream, Richens Lacy Wootton made a road that was an engineering feat, and set up a tollgate. Doubtless his welcome was worth the fee he charged. His stone-and-adobe house was warm from a big fireplace before which the weary traveler could sit to hear tales of how the big game heads on the wall had been taken, of scouting with Kit Carson, and of trading trips with the Bents and St. Vrain. In time the tollman became "Uncle Dick Wootton" and his home a stage stop. Then the Santa Fe Railroad took over his road and left of Uncle Dick only a name on a watertower.

Beyond Raton Pass there was another choice of mountain trail or grassy track across the plains. Taos tempted some loaded wagons and many animal trains to cross the Sangre de Cristo range into that rich wheat-growing valley. The road traversed, as it still does, fertile uplands and canyons alive with game and veined with coal and precious metals, to the high Moreno valley, beyond which it dropped down into Taos. On the eastern slope lay the 1,700,000 acres of highly productive land that was to be best known as the Maxwell Land Grant. Granted by the Republic of Mexico to Charles Beaubien and Guadalupe Miranda, it came to Lucian B. Maxwell of Illinois when he married Luz Beaubien. When Maxwell failed, British capitalists and then Hollanders owned that vast empire which came finally into the hands of an Oklahoma oil magnate, who gave it to the Boy Scouts of America. There at Philmont young Americans, properly directed, may now play at pioneering and learn emasculated tales of the true pioneers. The Maxwell Land Grant has attracted many fiction writers. Its true story would reveal the actual history of New Mexico.

The trail for Santa Fe avoided the mountains and led south past Wagon Mound and toward Hermit's Peak. There lived one of New Mexico's first escapists: Juan María Augustine Anna, an Italian nobleman who came west with Don Manuel Romero in 1863. Seeking solitude, the count was too kind not to heed a call for help, and when a child he had treated was cured of smallpox his fame as a healer was set. The Italian made no claim as a healer, but sufferers came to beg his touch. The Penitentes built a shelter for him and every year placed there another cross to mark their penitential procession. Less credulous friends worried about the lonely man. Mr. Watrous at La Junta, where the Mora River and Coyote Creek join, watched nightly for a fire on Hermit's Peak. If he did not see it he would go or send aid. La Junta is called Watrous now; from there the traveler can see how clearly that flame would have shown against the sky above the peak.

The hermit, wearied at last by his fame as a healer, moved to Las Cruces and found haven in a cave in the Organ Mountains. There Sheriff Mariano Barela made with him another pact about a nightly fire. One sad night, when the fire failed, the sheriff went with assistance and found the old Italian's body thrust through by an Apache lance.

In the Santa Fe Trail days there was a settlement at the Gallinas River where Las Vegas stands, but more important was El Bado de San Miguel on the Pecos. It is off the highway now, and nobody has marked the ford where so many thousands of wagons splashed across the river on the way to Santa Fe. But beyond San Miguel, modern roads and the railroad follow the old ruts closely, especially where the old Indian trails wound through Glorieta Pass and Apache Canyon.

Franz Huning wrote that where teamsters began to dress up for arrival in the capital, final bets were laid as to whether Santa Fe was in New Mexico or New Mexico in Santa Fe, "a question that had been much in dispute all the way from Independence." So the tenderfoot might wonder. But the men of the trail, like the mountain men before them, knew well the country they traversed. After they had learned the way across the mountains, the Army had only to follow.

XVIII

THE GRINGO OCCUPATION

⊂⊒   NEW MEXICO was occupied by the United States as
an incident of the war with Mexico. Texas had achieved its
independence of Mexico in 1836; within ten years boundary disputes had given expansionists in Congress cause for
war with the neighboring republic. Manifest Destiny was the
watchword; the Pacific was the goal. New Mexico was little known, but there it was, sprawling from wherever Texas
ended to wherever California began. It would have to be
taken on the way to California. This was construed by the
invaders as "freeing New Mexicans from oppression and
making them citizens of the best of all nations." An army
was recruited, mostly in the border states, and Stephen
Watts Kearny was put in command.

Kearny was a veteran of the War of 1812, and he knew
the West from the Yellowstone to Bent's Fort, which he
had visited as colonel of the First Dragoons stationed at
Leavenworth, Kansas. Kearny was no tenderfoot in 1845
when he was named brigadier general and commander of
the 1,658 men who composed the Army of the West.

This was a volunteer army, the very essence of democracy, and reading about it arouses sympathy for the hardest-
boiled sergeant. Among its store clerks, farmers, trappers,
and ox drivers came a few lawyers and doctors who were
elected officers because of prowess in court or on the political stump. The men wore no uniforms. Their long hair and
beards were upkempt, and their home-made hats were
adorned with souvenirs or thongs and fishhooks that might

come in handy. But they could handle their guns and Bowie knives, and when they reached the settlements they proved adept at raiding orchards and cornfields. They had only scorn for the regular army, and shook off discipline as lightly as fleas; they had to be urged to get up in the morning, to wear coats, to salute. Regular Army officers doubted that such a crew could ever be made into soldiers, and their reports are peppered with doubt and scorn. But the way had been prepared for this undisciplined command by the gentleman who, perhaps, did the real job of taking New Mexico away from Mexico.

This was the Kentuckian, James Magoffin, who had traded along the trail to Chihuahua, where he had served as United States consul, married Señorita María Gertrudes Valdez, and become widely popular as Don Santiago. A smooth-talking Irishman with a well-stocked mind, a genial host with a well-stocked cellar, and a sound patriot, Don Santiago was better than any invading army. Thomas H. Benton, the westward-looking senator from Missouri, had introduced James Magoffin to President Polk and to Secretary of War Marcy, and they had decided to send Mr. Magoffin west with the Army. What else was agreed history does not relate. Nor do we know what Don Santiago said to Governor Armijo in Santa Fe, or how he spent his money there. He soon went on to Chihuahua; he may have had a mission there, too. His many friends in that city seemed to think so. General Wool, who had gone into Mexico with General Zachary Taylor, was advancing on Chihuahua from the east. Even as they exchanged champagne suppers with their old friend Don Santiago, wary Mexican officials were keeping an eye on James Magoffin, whom they knew as a loyal United States citizen and an astute trader.

Then one day the Mexican judge advocate of Chihuahua handed his friend Magoffin an unopened letter addressed to

him; it had been found among the papers of Dr. Henry
Connelly, just captured near El Paso. On opening it,
Magoffin found that it contained a letter from General
Kearny commending James Magoffin for facilitating the
capture of New Mexico. If the Mexican judge had read
those words he would have had to arrest his good friend
Don Santiago as a spy. But the Mexican gentleman bowed
formally to his friend with twinkling eyes and without mentioning the letter, which Magoffin burned. He thus also destroyed proof that the United States owed him some fifty
thousand dollars for service rendered and expenses incurred.
Years later the Congress awarded his family thirty thousand
dollars.

Manuel Armijo, Governor of the Department of New
Mexico, has long figured as the villain of the piece. But it
is well to remember that we know him only through the
reports of his enemies, many of which lose force on further research. Most writers follow Twitchell in describing
Armijo as an ignorant sheep-herder who founded his fortune on stolen sheep. But he came of the *rico* Armijo
family, and his mother was one of the even richer Chavez's.
Manuel was born about 1800 at Los Poblanos, still a fine
hacienda near Albuquerque, and he was well enough educated to write a decent letter, as may be seen in the New
Mexico archive. He was a trader on the Santa Fe Trail in
partnership with Adolph Speyer. Armijo had been Governor in 1828, but he came to real power in 1837 when he
put down a revolt of malcontents at Santa Cruz de la
Cañada. He was then a dictator, a loyal imitator of his idol,
the Mexican general and president, Antonio López de
Santa Ana.

As Governor, Armijo was vigorous and stern. He faced
disloyalty at home, Indians on the borders, a threatened
gringo invasion, and an empty treasury. He sought money

from rich men, to whom he granted vast lands; he taxed mines; and he placed an impost of five hundred dollars on every wagonload from the States, regardless of its weight. Traders countered by reloading at Pecos Pueblo to reduce the number of wagons. Richard L. Wilson, in *Short Ravelings from a Tall Yarn*, explains that they resented the duty "especially as it was . . . for the sole use and benefit of his obesity, the Governor." Doubtless, Armijo got a rake-off; it was the custom of his country. But he managed to collect a fat tariff without discouraging the traders, who were worth some million pesos per year to New Mexico. Armijo is notable as a governor of New Mexico because he never asked the central government for money.

In 1840 Armijo had warned the Mexican government against gringo encroachment, naming such outposts as Bent's Fort as "the protection of robbers, either foreigners or Mexicans." In 1846 his apprehensions were justified. From Bent's Fort, General Kearny addressed a proclamation to Governor Armijo: "I come by orders of my government to take possession of the country over part of which you are now presiding as governor." He then crossed the Arkansas River into Mexican territory. The invasion had begun.

Kearny's march into New Mexico was uneventful; it was even disappointing to a group of young soldiers who rode sixty miles in one night to catch up because they heard there was going to be a battle. There was no battle. At Las Vegas the general mounted the roof of a house on the plaza and read his proclamation. He came as a friend to bring the blessings of self-government to the people. He absolved them from allegiance to the Mexican government and Governor Armijo; he promised that "not a pepper, not an onion shall be disturbed or taken"; but he also promised dire and quick consequences to anyone who promised to be quiet and was not. "I am not a Catholic myself . . . but at least one-third of my army are Catholics, and I respect a good Catholic as much as a good Protestant."

This army had much to say about the new land and said it well. Officers' books reflect character and opinion, and many include accurate comments on geology and geography, flora and fauna, people and their ways. These books are well printed and illustrated with fine, sensitive drawings and maps of an engineer's precision. Above all, they vibrate with the joy of youth riding into an unknown country where discomforts and dangers only spiced the adventure. Among them, those gringos saw everything and they had a lot of fun.

Lieutenant J. W. Abert of the Topographical Engineers heard mockingbirds in the osage hedges, the meadow lark's liquid call, and the whirr of partridges rising. There on the prairies, grass topped the boot of a mounted man and the streams ran pebbly and clear. In the short-grass country he met long-eared jackrabbits that seemed larger than the bounding balls that were antelope. The air was fresh and clear and ever headier as he neared the mountains. They killed buffalo and saw Indians; once young Abert lay awake all night with his rifle at hand because they had seen Pawnees that day. In camp they feasted on buffalo tongue and venison, quail and doves, and now and then fish.

It was not all paradise. There were days and nights of rain, and there were dust storms. Mules proved recalcitrant, and horses got away. Men sickened from drinking puddle water. Young Abert himself was taken with a fever and had to stay at Bent's Fort while General Kearny went on. There he talked with a voyageur who knew all the mountains, saw Magoffin, met Ceran St. Vrain and "Karson." Not everybody could spell the famous scout's name, but every young man saw him. Abert wrote with awe of the mountains' grandeur and of the toughness of Raton Pass.

When the soldiers reached the settlements, their interest shifted to the people, all strange in dress and manner. Now and then they met a well-dressed and well-mounted hidalgo. Usually they saw country folk on burros: men sitting on the animals' rumps, guiding them with kicks in the ribs or whacks on the neck and "*Arre, burro!*" Sometimes a couple rode the same beast. Sometimes both walked beside four little mouse-gray legs bearing a huge circle of piñon wood or of hay trailing in the dust. Always such people spoke with heads down and eyes averted from the gringos they had been warned against.

Beyond Las Vegas there was still hope of a battle. So the troops rode on confidently, spurs jangling, guidons unfurled, guns at the ready. But there was no battle, and the brisk advance settled into a dull jog. Some captured Mexicans reported that Armijo awaited them at a defile that would prove a regular Thermopylæ; others said that he had fled. So the troops crossed the Pecos and came to the ruins of Cicuyé. West Point had rather muffed history and archæology: the young officers described the old mission as an Aztec castle or a temple where maidens were sacrificed in a perpetual fire.

Near there a fat Mexican on a burro told Kearny that General Armijo had indeed absconded. So the volunteers, deprived of a battle, rode unopposed through Apache Canyon. As any traveler can see, a handful of determined men there could have held an army larger than Kearny's. But Armijo had decamped—he turned up later in Socorro—and his army had melted away. The way to Sante Fe was open.

This defection of Armijo's and what Mexico made of it remain mysteries. Had Magoffin bought him off? Was he an arrant coward? No record of a court martial has come to light, so maybe Mexico did not consider him gravely at fault. The Mexican historian, José María Roa Barcena,

quotes a letter of August 26, 1846, stating that Armijo's officers had pulled out with the auxiliaries, leaving the Governor nothing to do but retire. In any case there was no defense, and this gringo invasion has been called Occupation
and not Conquest.

On August 18, 1846, General Kearny read another proclamation from the roof of the Palace of the Governors, then
under its third flag, as Mexico's red, white, and green with
its eagle, snake, and cactus sank before the red, white, and
blue. Even that proud emblem was to be hauled down by a
conqueror before the stars and stripes would fly over New
Mexico forever.

General Kearny named Charles Bent Governor of New
Mexico, and His Excellency entertained the officers at dinner with fine wines and appointments as correct as any in
the States. The young officers mooned over dark eyes under
lace mantillas and swooned at the smooth grace of the
dancers.

Less formally, the young dragoons, officers and men,
were making themselves at home in Santa Fe. In the market they bought fruits, cheese, bread, wine, and the fiery
distillation known as Taos Lightning; they had all learned
enough Spanish for that. The biggest money changed hands
at Tules's place, where Palace Avenue still meets Burro
Alley. Tules Barcela, formerly Governor Armijo's *querida*,
had become wholeheartedly *gringa*. Once she even lent an
embarrassed colonel enough money to pay off his men,
asking only that he escort her to the regimental ball—which
he did, to the scandalization of the ladies of the town.

General Kearny had done well. Without firing a shot, he
had taken over a vast territory. By a couple of proclama-
tions, spoken in English to people who did not understand
it, several oaths of allegiance parroted by men speaking
from the heart or through clenched teeth, New Mexico was
declared part of the United States and all who opposed the

idea traitors to it. Then the general rode on. Like so many to follow, he could not wait to get to California. But he left officers and troops behind to keep the peace and to explore the new possession. In charge of the military government in Santa Fe he left Colonel Sterling Price, a Virginian who had come along with the Missouri Volunteers. The main body of the Missourians, under Colonel Alexander W. Doniphan, was ordered to join General Wool in Chihuahua. If James Magoffin had done as well there as he had in New Mexico, all should go well.

Kearny started west by the shortest route: down the Rio del Norte to below Socorro, westward through the mountains to the Gila, and down the Colorado to California, where he would join General Frémont. But because emigrants were anticipated even then and a wagon road would be needed, Captain Cooke was detached from the command to swing south and find a level passage.

This West Pointer's trigger-quick temper found explosive material on every hand. In Santa Fe he had been put in command of a battalion from Colorado and Utah, Mormons who had brought their families. Among the 448 people were 25 women, uncountable children, 20 laundresses, and 60 men so ill they had to be accommodated in wagons. By stern purges, Cooke reduced his command to those who could walk, though he complained to Kearny: "The numerous guides and hirelings you sent me . . . had been idle for weeks; and I found I was to venture with my wagons into a region unknown to any of them." Cooke's professional contempt for this chuckleheaded amateur war-making salts even his military reports.

Cooke's command struggled across the Jornada del Muerto and, skirting the Mimbres range, came into the Apache country, where the Indians made the friendly proposal that they should invade Mexico together: "You want the land and we want the plunder." As usual, Indians had no use for fighting people one day and protecting them the next.

It was tough going. Often Cooke had to send scouts ahead to find water holes or puddles; sometimes they had to hack their way through mesquite thickets. Rations ran low, men grew ill, wayworn, and exhausted. As they ate up the food they abandoned wagons—the first of the dry wood and rusty iron that would mark this trail to California. Once the colonel wrote his general that he had decided "to send my useless guides to give you information." When he reached the Colorado, the resourceful Cooke tried boating on it with wagon-bed pontoons "with flattering success." Thus he pioneered a waterway that was to take many travelers into those western reaches of New Mexico.

At San Diego, Cooke, characteristically, wrote Kearny: "Thus, General, whilst fortune was conducting you to battles and victories, I was fated to devote my best energies to more humble labors." But Philip St. George Cooke had crossed New Mexico from Raton Pass to California and had laid out the wagon road that was to serve many years before it became a motor highway.

The troops left behind in Santa Fe were seeing New Mexico. Abert, on reconnaissance south of Santa Fe, was surprised "by the many men and children who both read and write, but they have no books. I can only recollect to have seen a Roman Catholic catechism at Padillas." Of the *ricos*, he wrote: "We saw several who had been to Union College, St. Louis. They speak French and English and understand their own language grammatically." At Manzano he heard Don Pedro Baca, who had been to New Orleans, telling his untraveled neighbors about big steamboats on water and little steamboats running on iron roads on land. At Albuquerque the priest quizzed his guests. Did they know the square, the circle, the triangle? Satisfied, the padre then turned to "a very handsome lady who graced the establishment," and declared the officers astronomers and mathematicians. Doubtless this was the easiest examination a West Pointer ever faced!

Abert was appalled at the condition of the poor, who, he wrote, "live not one whit better than the Negroes on a plantation; and the rico, like the planter, possesses everything." Captain A. R. Johnston of the dragoons reported the poor man's distrust of the rich. Of buying horses, he wrote: "Their people have so seldom been dealt with honorably that they cannot believe anyone is dealing fairly with them."

It is only fair to set against such comment Barcena's words: "North American historians draw a somber picture of the state of barbarism to which the tyranny of Armijo and the *ricos* . . . had reduced the population, and in the next line assert . . . that Santa Fe abounded in gambling houses and saloons established by their *regeneradores* [reformers] and that the licentious conduct of the soldiers promptly aroused . . . a vicious hatred of the Americans. To this had come the new Eden that Kearny's proclamation had promised."

Kearny had proclaimed that all who wished might go to Mexico, but that those who swore loyalty to the United States and then conspired against it would be considered traitors. So the Mexican of honor faced a dilemma. If he did not like the newcomers—as many did not; or considered them heretics—as many did; if he was loath to give up his ancient privileges—and this must have been the general, however unconscious, reaction—he would prefer Mexico. But it would be hard to leave lands owned by his family for generations. He might choose to fight for his home and the life and faith he believed in.

Some brave and honorable men who chose to fight met in the dark of night in Santa Fe and planned a general uprising. They were men of the best families; among them

were priests; they fully understood what they risked. Their
plot was discovered. It is said that Gertrudes Barcelo, having put her money on the new regime, learned what was
afoot from a lover and betrayed him to Don Donaciano
Vigil, Lieutenant Governor. There is no written proof of
who the conspirators were. It is told that an agreement
signed by all of them was hidden between a board ceiling
and an adobe roof. This has never come to light, nor have
any other papers. As late as January 20, 1847, the unreconciled Mexican Inspector of Arms, Don Antonio María
Trujillo, issued orders to all officers in New Mexico to call
out the inhabitants "in defense of our abandoned country."
The unfortunate Don Antonio was tried as a traitor and
hanged.

Most of the other conspirators got away to Mexico, but
were later pardoned and allowed to return. Only Colonel
Manuel Chaves, who did not run away, was tried. His defense, pleaded by Captain W. Z. Angney, was that he was
not a United States citizen, and that therefore his act was
not treason, but patriotism toward Mexico. He was ac-
quitted and, like the other conspirators, lived out an honorable life as a useful citizen and a gallant officer of the
United States.

The fullest account of this conspiracy, in Twitchell's
Military Occupation of New Mexico, is based on old men's
tales. Here again we meet the major difficulty in writing
the early history of New Mexico—the lack of private papers. Did the hidalgos or their families destroy correspondence with Mexico and with each other? In contrast with
the South's glorification of its Confederate forebears, it is
noteworthy that no New Mexico family boasts of an ancestor's loyalty to Mexico.

The discovery of the Santa Fe plot did not end the revolt.
In Taos and in Mora it went on. Governor Bent, knowing
of the discontent but trusting his friends and neighbors,

went to Taos for Christmas with his family. On January 19, Indians from the pueblo and Mexicans still loyal to Mexico attacked his house and mortally wounded the Governor in the sight of his children. While he lay dying and terrified citizens took refuge in Padre Martínez's house, the insurgents started south.

Colonel Price was advancing from Santa Fe with a force that included Captain St. Vrain, whose young son had been murdered in Taos, and Manuel Chaves, who had declined a commission and was marching sturdily as a private in the ranks of the country he had chosen at last. Price defeated one insurgent band at La Cañada, another at Embudo, and advanced on Taos. On February 3 he was bombarding that pueblo, where the last stand was made. It took all day, cost the lives of fifteen men, and demolished the church, whose gaunt and empty shell still stands. But it was a victory.

The revolt at Mora was similarly and summarily suppressed at Colonel Price's order. A few sporadic outbreaks followed, but within weeks New Mexico was finally and firmly United States territory.

We have a boy's excited account of the subsequent trial in Garrard's *Wah-to-Yah*. It struck him as "a great assumption of the Americans to conquer a country and then arraign the revolting inhabitants for treason." He found the prisoners "ill-favored, half-scared, sullen fellows." Five men were found guilty of murder, one of treason. In Garrard's judgment, the sentences for murder were correct, but of the other he writes: "Treason, indeed! What did the poor fellow know about his new allegiance? I left the room sick at heart."

The unsolved puzzle of the Taos revolt is: Did Padre Martínez direct it or not? Carson and St. Vrain thought he did. Charles Bent, before he became Governor, had expressed hatred and distrust of Padre Martínez in letters to Manuel Alvarez, United States consul in Santa Fe. "The priest will spare no means to injure me, but if he will attack me fairly, publicly, and above board, I am certain he will not accomplish his end. . . . But here [in Taos] the priest can prove anything." When the Alvarez papers, in the New Mexico archive, are fully studied we may understand what really happened in Taos.

Padre Martínez is New Mexico's most brilliant and controversial figure. Born in 1793 of a *rico* family of Rio Arriba, he lost wife and child in early youth and then went to Durango to study for the priesthood. On his return to New Mexico in 1822 he was given the church at Taos, where he proved energetic, domineering, and full of ideas. He bought the press that *Licenciado* Barreiro had shipped into Santa Fe and printed church rituals, textbooks, and the newspaper, *El Crepúsculo* (The Dawn), which still appears regularly in Taos. At his own expense the padre conducted a school for girls as well as for boys. And he protested to the bishop of Durango against tithes that were impoverishing the people, and against church fees so high that many babies were left unbaptized and many couples could not afford to marry. Padre Martínez was New Mexico's first liberal and first modern. Was he also the last unreconciled Mexican?

Pedro Sánchez, in a wholly uncritical little book, quotes him: "The American government resembles a burro; but on this burro lawyers will ride, not priests." Such a man, such a priest, might well have preferred to institute reforms as a Mexican and a Catholic. Sánchez tells us that Padre Martínez, aroused by frightened people after Bent's killing, quickly dressed and took command. He assembled all the peaceful inhabitants, including Americans, posted armed men on the flat roof, sent a courier to Santa Fe, and kept everybody reassured, fed, quiet until the arrival of Price's troop.

Taos gossip prefers the other version, as Taos chuckles to

recall that Padre Martínez's vigor was not limited to good works. More than one Taos County Martínez, in these lax days, boasts of descent from the padre and one of the lovely ladies who graced his home. They also remember that he hated heretics and was outspoken in his dislike of gringos. It is hard to believe that a man so intelligent, confessor and confidant of his people, could have been ignorant of a widespread conspiracy. But the priest kept his own secret and was never openly accused. Later he served in the New Mexico territorial legislature and was its presiding officer. His people never lost confidence in him. Even when the puritanical Bishop Lamy unfrocked him in 1856 for his irregularities, Padre Martínez continued to say Mass in a private chapel, serving his parishioners until he died in 1867.

The Army of the West had thus subdued the Mexicans within a few months, but the Indians still remained. The nomadic tribes were continuing their raids on settlements and crops, though the Pueblos, after the Taos revolt, had fully accepted the new allegiance, hoping for protection and often serving with the U.S. troops.

Lieutenant Simpson, riding against recalcitrant Navajos with Colonel Washington in 1850, wrote of Pueblo soldiers with admiration and respect. Of a pass in the Tunecha Mountains he related: "Here, if anywhere, the enemy would dispute our advance. . . . Forty Pueblos . . . (Captain Dodge voluntarily offering to lead them) were pushed forward in advance. . . . I had noticed with my glass several of the enemy upon the heights . . . and it was not at all improbable that they were strongly posted on the still more commanding heights." So the U.S. officer, far enough away to need a glass, watched the Pueblos advance into what he considered certain danger. He commended them. "The Pueblo Indians having gallantly gained the heights . . . the infantry was then ordered to move forward." In those days the Pueblos were the expendables.

Despite Pueblo prowess, this Indian business was going to take longer than anticipated, and forts were established: in 1851 Fort Sumner was built on the Pecos and Fort Burgwin on the Canadian to keep an eye on the Comanches, Fort Defiance in the very center of the unsubdued Navajos. Fort Sheldon, on the Rio Grande at the edge of Apacheria, was erected in 1869 as a tribute to the growing power of the Apache chief Geronimo. The most important was Fort Union, built in 1851 on the Mora, where the old trails met and where the forage was good. As the distributing center for the whole Southwest, Fort Union was splendidly constructed of stone and adobe. It consisted of nine sets of officers' quarters, two barracks, hospital, storehouse, smokehouse, workshops, icehouse, laundry, and jail. Its ample parade ground saw many a dashing review for some of the country's most prominent officials, and the forays it sent out trained many a young lieutenant who made history later. This famous fort is now gone. The government, abandoning Fort Union in 1894, after forty years of service, left it to vandals. A few years ago one could find bits of carved wood or hand-wrought iron, but only foundations remain now. Even the military cemetery has had no care—its headstones are toppled, their names erased.

In 1851 a territorial government was set up in New Mexico and officials appointed—the Governor, district judges who sat together as the supreme court, and United States district attorneys. Self-government was lodged in the legislative assembly of two chambers, whose members were elected by the districts. Its acts could be, and on occasion were, voided by the Congress of the United States. Naturally, most members of the assembly were new to United States citizenship. They were proud and eager to be worthy, but quite unaccustomed to the democratic process and without a word of English. The interpreter became an essential part of New Mexico's legislature, as well as of its courts and political meetings. The terrifying, but often laughable confusions, frustrations, and corruptions that resulted have been well presented by three lawyers. W. W. H. Davis, a gentleman of extreme correctness, expressed his consternation well in *El Gringo*. A later period, after newcomers from the States had learned how to deal with hidalgos and maneuver land laws, is set forth in *Fabulous Frontier* by William A. Keleher. *Black Robed Justice*, by Arey Poldervaart, fills interstices in the tale.

These books show how the United States botched its first opportunity to teach self-government to people alien in language and custom. New Mexico's advance, during her century as part of the United States, from an unkempt, poverty-stricken, and neglected frontier province to a dignified state has been the work of her people without such aid in teaching the new language and customs as the United States gave other non-English-speaking peoples who entered the Union at the end of the century.

XIX

TEXANS KEEP COMING

⧉ TEXAS has always looked toward New Mexico covetously, yearning to own it as a nation, a state, or individually. For more than a century Texans have kept coming in various guises and with various projects to occupy New Mexico. Beginning in early June, traffic flows all summer in an unbroken stream from Texas to New Mexico. This flood brings dollars, free spenders, many investors, and some fine and desirable people. Unfortunately it also brings prejudices capable of lessening New Mexico's extraordinary opportunity to make of its diverse heritages a richly patterned and truly democratic community. So far, New Mexico's record of fair dealing between peoples is better than that of its neighbors. But as Texans come in, and where they dominate, bad feeling grows and discrimination is practiced.

It is true that many broad-minded people come from Texas, that many narrow, bigoted, and stupidly intolerant folk come from other states or have grown up right in New Mexico. But so many Texans come bringing that state's inability to forget the war with Mexico that New Mexico applies the term *tejanos* to all prejudiced newcomers. Back of the dislike this expresses lie history and apprehension for the future.

In 1841, the Honorable Mirabeau Bonaparte Lamar, President of the Republic of Texas, conceived the idea of sending an expedition to Santa Fe. The five-year-old republic was broke, and it might be possible to divert some lucrative trade from the Santa Fe Trail to Texas. A military force was sent along for protection and—as President Lamar worded it—"for the occupation of New Mexico in case the people desired to become members of the Texas republic." President Lamar and his more imaginative advisors expected all New Mexicans to jump at the chance.

This venture was based on Texas's claim to all land east of the Rio Grande. The treaty of 1836, recognizing Texas's independence of Mexico, established the Rio Grande as the boundary between them. Texas construed that to mean the river's entire length up through New Mexico to its headwaters in Colorado—an assumption that blandly disregarded New Mexico's more than two hundred and fifty years as a political entity. New Mexico's eastern boundary had never been determined, but it had extended well over into what is now Texas. There are two distinct histories of this claim and its fate, one taught in Texas, the other of general acceptance.

Proceeding from this untenable premise, the Texas Expedition erred in its method of approach. Its three hundred soldiers, recruited by fiery reminders of the war with Mexico, and commanded by twenty-seven-year-old Brigadier General Hugh McLeod, were too warlike and too many to pass as a guard for artless merchants seeking trade, and too few to give a good account of themselves in a fight. Moreover, they lacked experience and knowledgeable guides. This whole junket may well rank as the first appearance of the feckless tenderfoot.

The prize tenderfoot was George Wilkins Kendall, editor of the *New Orleans Picayune*, who went along to share and report a triumphant adventure. If Mr. Kendall was not the first war correspondent, he was surely the most innocent. Starting from Austin, where the command was hailed oratorically as the "Texian Invincibles," Kendall's *Narrative of the Texas-Santa Fe Expedition* shows the Texans committing every blunder that makes the dude a figure of comedy.

While still in country teeming with fish and game, the Texans butchered their animals and so faced starvation when the going got tougher. They forced needless fights with Indians; lost goods, equipment, and even lives in stampedes; and because they could not take care of themselves, were often ill. Kendall makes it plain that the Invincibles were pretty well defeated before they ever reached New Mexico.

Mexico's excellent spy system had kept the authorities informed, and Governor Armijo was waiting and watching. In September he sent out Captain Dámaso Salazar, who met the expedition, pretty hungry by now and dragging, near the pink stone town of Anton Chico on the Pecos. Captain Salazar picked up three men as spies. Of these, one was killed trying to escape, another was executed. To Kendall, believer in the trade excursion theory, this seemed infamous murder. Hubert Howe Bancroft, dean of historians of the Southwest, considers it an accepted act of war, a judgment in which other disinterested historians concur.

Later the entire command of what Bancroft calls "the filibusters" surrendered in two lots, one of them betrayed by a traitor named Lewis. Kendall maintains that they were tricked by the wily and dishonorable Mexicans into giving up their arms. Manuel Alvarez, United States consul in Santa Fe, wrote that if the Texans had shown fight they would have won: "all the most respectable people had determined not to resist."

Kendall's account is a classic of vituperation and hatred, especially of Salazar, whom he charged with starving the prisoners and either letting the weak die or shooting them and cutting off their ears as proof that they had not escaped. Bancroft offers no defense of such atrocities, but interjects the note "if they were true." He sums it up: "The Texan adventurers were, at best, engaged in a risky invasion of an enemy's territory; fortune was against them, and disaster resulted, for which they deserve but little sympathy. Armijo and his men, on the contrary, had the most wonderful good luck in defending their country, and merit but little of the obloquy that has been heaped upon them."

General Houston, then President of Texas, appealed to the world, urging all friendly powers to mediate in behalf of the Texan prisoners in Mexico. Houston could only insist that even if they had been outlaws before, the terms of their capitulation had brought them within the pale of civilized warfare. It was agreed that after the reprehensible Salazar had taken them to El Paso they were committed to the care of a well-bred hidalgo, Don Elias Gonzales, who had had them treated well. In time the survivors were returned to Texas.

Texas was not ready to give up. The expedition of 1841 had been a failure, but in 1843 Colonel Warfield, with a detachment of vengeful Texans, raided the little town of Mora on its mountain stream. The invaders were thrown out, leaving a crop of hates. In that same year one hundred and eighty Texans, under Colonel Jacob Snively, attacked the Trail caravan on the Arkansas. Captain Cooke, still the correct West Pointer among savages, turned them back. By this time Texan vindictiveness had passed beyond all control, and a gang attacked a small wagon-train, property of Don José Antonio Chaves, whose family Kendall had named as friendly and helpful to the limping captives of '41. The name Chaves Creek still marks the spot where Don José and his servants were killed. A deep scar of hatred still throbs in New Mexico at mention of that name. By lucky chance the Captain McDaniel who led that attack had killed Chaves on United States soil. McDaniel and his associates were tried in a United States court, convicted, and hanged for murder.

Official Texas was moving along more legal channels. After Kearny's occupation, Texas assumed that the United

States would acknowledge her claim to all land east of the Rio Grande. Several gentlemen in high places seemed to admit it. President Polk was quoted as referring to "the right . . . justly asserted by Texas to the whole territory east of the Rio Grande." So Texas, in 1848, appointed Spruce M. Baird as Judge of Santa Fe County, one of four New Mexico counties that Texas had laid out on paper. One of these extended well down into Chihuahua; another ran in a long panhandle up into Wyoming.

The new judge, even faced with a job of such proportions, began by exuding hope. His letters, long unknown, have been released by his family and published in *New Spain and the West*. Baird wrote; "General Armijo espouses our cause with some zeal and is decidedly the first man in that region. I bought him out lock, stock, and barrel." But Mr. Baird may not have bought as much as he thought. Before long he was reporting "the New Mexican population openly hostile," though he, an office-holder, considered them misled by Americans animated "solely by a desire to figure as public functionaries themselves." Such men, he found, had put "frightful stories in circulation among the Mexicans . . . that we would destroy their religion, confiscate their property, hang and enslave their people for former acts of rebellion."

The prevailing attitude was probably expressed by the editor of the *Santa Fe Republican*. "We would now inform our Texas friends that it is not necessary to send us a judge . . . for there is not a citizen, either American or Mexican, that will ever acknowledge themselves as citizens of Texas until it comes from a higher authority. . . . Texas should show a little sense and not have it publicly announced that Texas' smartest men were tarred and feathered."

New Mexico was still under military rule, though two parties were trying to set up civil government. One hoped for admission to the Union as a state; the other would settle for territorial status. This kept affairs in such a turmoil that nobody had time for Mr. Baird. Colonel Washington evaded him all summer, reducing the would-be judge to a state of frustration that would demand a psychiatrist today. Mr. Baird decided to retire.

Feeling easier in Independence, Missouri, Mr. Baird prepared for his government some statesmanlike thoughts. The people of New Mexico, he explained, were one fourth Pueblo Indians. Of the rest, three quarters were peons "without shirts, shoes, or hats, and not worthy to be trusted in any way. The remainder, to say the least of them, are Mexicans." Such people, "even if they desired unanimously to be incorporated with us," would be troublesome. And as "all the interest Texas has is in the territory unappropriated, the mines, etc. . . . Perhaps it would be good policy to consent to their having a territorial government, reserving to Texas the proceeds of the public lands, mines, etc. . . . We would lose nothing and get rid of a troublesome and worthless set of customers." On a rough diagram appended to his report, Mr. Baird wrote: "It is important to make our boundary above El Paso to command the trade of Chihuahua for Texas. Texas should retain the Pecos valley for it will afford one of the finest settlements in the world. The country north of Santa Fe is not worth much."

Texas's failure in 1841, hard as it was on the Texans concerned, has been good for New Mexicans. For despite fair promises of citizenship and equal rights, Texas as a state and many Texans as individuals have, during the century since then, been notably unfair to their own Spanish-speaking citizens. It was good for the United States because hatred of *tejanos* helped keep New Mexico loyal to the Union when Texas again tried invasion in 1861. Even Texas profited by the effort, if not the failure, of 1841 because its congressman prevailed upon Congress in 1850 to settle "the boundary question" by paying Texas ten million dollars as compensation.

New Mexico was naturally a prize in the national struggle between free and slave states. Mr. Baird thought that the men he did not like "would dismember our state and turn the abolitionists against us." To New Mexicans, *tejanos* advocated slavery.

Negro slavery was no question in New Mexico: in 1853 there were only seventeen Negroes in the territory, mostly "body servants" of Southern officers. But many hidalgos feared legislation that would affect their Indian slaves and peons. At the time of the Emancipation Proclamation there were some six hundred Indian slaves in the territory. The territorial legislature was not thinking only of Negroes when, in 1859, it passed an act "for the protection of slave property in the territory." And the *ricos'* real concern was manifested in an act "providing for the arrest of fugitive servants who were bound to their masters under contract." Courts were prohibited from interfering with the masters' discipline "unless such correction was in a cruel manner with clubs or stripes." To protect the time-honored and comfortable institution of peonage, many educated Spanish gentlemen were ready to throw their lots in with the Confederacy.

In an interesting study, *New Mexico and the Sectional Controversy*, Loomis Morton Ganaway relates that Texas, disregarding Spanish and Mexican land grants, had awarded veterans of its wars good acres in the Rio Grande valley above El Paso, "not specific as to location." So all during the 1850's Texans came drifting into New Mexico—long men with long rifles and long memories of the Alamo and the expedition of 1841. With ease they dispossessed simple people whose ownership went back to De Vargas, and thus added to the hates that would grow and spread.

Part of the difficulty lay in a faulty boundary. When Mexico and the United States signed the Treaty of Guadalupe Hidalgo in 1848 they used an inaccurate map. In time an international boundary commission awarded the disputed area to Mexico, thus enraging the Texans who had dispossessed the Mexicans. When protests to Santa Fe and Washington did not bring action, Texas began to show signs of starting a private war, and Uncle Sam paid off. The United States now bought from Mexico 45,000 square miles of desert and mountainous country, Apache-infested but otherwise empty. This was the Gadsden Purchase of 1853, which gave us such a straight international line. Congress added all the new territory to New Mexico, and the New Mexico legislature extended Doña Ana County to the California line.

In the fifties the scattered inhabitants of Doña Ana County were as isolated as any lost tribes of history. They had uncharted wilderness to the north of them, Mexico to the south of them, Apaches forever raiding them, and their capital at Santa Fe, far beyond the waterless Jornada del Muerto. So they petitioned Congress for a separate territory with the parallel 33° 40' as its northern boundary. In 1860 the active leaders, meeting in Tucson, elected Lewis S. Owings of Mesilla Governor of Arizona Territory.

Arizona's first appearance as a political entity ended abruptly in February 1861, when Texas seceded from the Union and sent Philip T. Herbert up from El Paso to claim Mesilla for the Confederacy. Flags, still cherished in the little Mesilla Museum, were going up and down at a great rate.

James Magoffin, from his rambling old adobe house at Magoffinsville (now a part of El Paso), supported Mr. Herbert, as did Simeon Hart, a miller who had made a fortune supplying United States troops, but who was reported to have offered the Confederacy $300,000 for its war coffers. Sylvester Mowry, editor of the Tubac *Arizonian* and mine owner, was as active in the Tucson area. These gentlemen were not credited with wholehearted Southern sympathies, but just with a sane eye to business. A detachment of troops marching eastward from California to join the Confederacy was welcomed in Tucson and in Mesilla, the only towns the new territory could boast.

A newspaper reports a meeting in Mesilla on March 4, 1861, at which speeches rose to bombastic heights. "The hell of abolitionism glooms to the north—the Eden of liberty, equality, and right smiles upon you from the south. Choose between them." They chose the Confederacy, but with the far-sighted proviso that "Arizona become a part of the Confederacy, and not a part of any state that has seceded."

Ganaway writes: "In contrast with the participation of the natives in territorial affairs at Santa Fe . . . no such support was solicited from them at Mesilla." He quotes *The Mesilla Times:* "One good company of Texas cavalry can do more to insure their [Mexicans'] loyalty to the Confederacy than all the offices in the territory." Wiser observers suggested that this point of view would pay off for the Union. It did.

Federal officials in Santa Fe had been slow to realize what was going on. But they awoke with a jolt when Fort Bliss went over to the Confederacy in July and Lieutenant Colonel John R. Baylor occupied Mesilla. Then Governor Connelly, he who had written that incriminating letter to Magoffin, called for volunteers. His best line was that the Confederates were *tejanos* coming to seek vengeance.

Baylor easily overcame a feeble defense at Fort Fillmore. The Confederate Territory of Arizona was now a going concern, and Confederate officials set out for their remote posts among the Apaches. But time moved faster than traffic in those days. Few appointees had reached their bases when all was over.

17 *Marking
sheep.*

CAPLIN AND
THOMPSON, OLD
ALBUQUERQUE

18 White-
faced Here-
fords have
replaced the
Longhorns.

CAPLIN AND
THOMPSON, OLD
ALBUQUERQUE

In December, Brigadier General Henry L. Sibley set out from Fort Bliss to take over all New Mexico for the Confederacy. Sibley was well known in Albuquerque as a major in the United States Army. Old inhabitants recollected that he had sent many sturdy mules and horses south, replacing them with scrub stock. Sibley had won a few residents of the Rio Abajo to the Confederate cause; there were a few trials for treason later. But most New Mexicans remained loyal to the United States.

The first battle was near Fort Craig at Val Verde, a leafy ford on the Rio Grande. Regulars manning the fort surrendered, and Sibley's Confederates swept on north, leaving many folktales of chapels used as stables, wine casks broken, and women raped or threatened by drunken soldiers. Perhaps few of these tales could be substantiated; invaders are always so accused. But these family legends, passed down through the generations, have edged New Mexico tongues with the tone still heard in the word *tejano*.

At Albuquerque, Sibley found that the Union troops had decamped after burying three cannon in the plaza, where they were found years later. Sibley raised the stars and bars over the plaza, raided stores, took over a well-known house as headquarters, mounted his cannon where Laguna Boulevard now crosses Central Avenue, and fought a brisk engagement with the bluecoats in the sandhills. Again the Union troops retreated, leaving the way to Santa Fe undefended.

Governor Connelly and the territorial officials had left the ancient capital and were headed for Fort Union. New Mexico's few regulars and volunteers were not enough to hold the territory. The only hope was that volunteers from Colorado and California would come to stem this graycoated tide. Sibley took Santa Fe without firing a shot, and the fourth flag floated over the old adobe Palace of the Governors. But not for long.

California, purged of its Southern sympathizers when its Confederates marched east to join the Texans, had recruited the California Column. This now came marching along Cooke's route and found Tucson abandoned; Americans had gone east, Mexicans had retired below the border. Mesilla, too, was empty, and the Californians raised the stars and stripes there again.

At the same time volunteers from Colorado, the Pikes Peakers, were marching south. Governor Connelly had had some difficulty with his recruiting, but there was a detachment of New Mexico volunteers too. With this force Colonel J. M. Chivington of the regular Army met General Sibley in Glorieta Pass, near where General Armijo had failed to stand against Kearny. Colonel Manuel Chaves, who had risen since he marched as a private with Colonel Price, proposed a plan. Knowing his men and the mountain trails, he led them over the hills at night. At dawn of March 27 he fell with a crash on the unready Confederates. This surprise led to the rout of the Confederates, who retired down the Rio Grande and back to Texas. The Daughters of the American Revolution have marked the spot where the Confederates set up a dressing station for their wounded.

Although little noted among the greater battles being fought far to the east, this skirmish was a decisive one. If the Confederacy had held New Mexico, its way would have been open to California and sorely needed gold. Instead Sibley left Santa Fe on April 8 and retreated down the valley, where he was given a final trouncing at Peralta near Albuquerque by Major Jose D. Sena with a New Mexico volunteer company. New Mexicans of Spanish blood had proved their loyalty and their worth in battle, and had saved themselves from such indignities as their cousins have suffered in Texas.

After the Civil War, Texans kept coming, but as individuals seeking to better themselves. The war left many of them with only a ragged uniform and a gun. They had courage, enterprise, and the spirit of adventure. They also had, or knew how to get, cattle. So they invaded New Mexico, seeking better range for their stock and a life untrammeled by laws. Beyond the Texas settlements stretched an enormous emptiness in which no marker indicated the New Mexico border and there was no real water until one reached the Pecos. Eastern and southern New Mexico filled up with Texans, in a manner of speaking; there must have been at least two or three to the square mile. Along with them came many Missourians: the Southern and border states were sending their young men west. Few Northerners came into southern and eastern New Mexico, and the mores and way of thinking were—and still are—strongly Southern.

Only in Little Texas, as this area is called, could a candidate for high office be refused service in a barbershop. One politician, advised by a seasoned politician to avoid *tejano* places, insisted: "Nobody is going to discriminate against me. I'm an American citizen seeking votes; they'll treat me all right." The Anglo adviser said: "When that dirty *tejano* told him to go on down the street, it just broke his heart."

This ugly un-Americanism, so at variance with all New Mexico's tradition, can be understood only by knowing the people who brought it and who maintain it. Most of them were ignorant. The sprinkling of educated Southern gentlemen was not enough to mark the mentality of the region. Nor did the cowboy's easy tolerance long prevail. The typical cowboy was unschooled. Often he had to sign with a cross, but he was essentially a decent fellow, able to work with anybody and judge him by what he did. This appears at once in old-timers' talk. They speak with the Texas drawl, but their words reflect the friendliness that "folks is folks." Their words are gentle, their judgments broad.

The cruel prejudice in which the Ku Klux Klan could be

planted came later with women and preachers bringing the crude fundamentalist cults of the Southern frontier. They had the ignoramus's distrust of strange customs and a language they could not understand. They brought the South's phobia against the Negro and the *tejano's* hatred of Mexicans. To them God was a Protestant Nordic and only their ways were His. Too often the preaching they heard only confirmed their dull provincialism. Eastern New Mexico saw a curious mingling of the fringes of two diverse but equally rich and complex civilizations. Both groups, with few exceptions, were quite unaware of the splendors of the other's past, or even of their own. And these newcomers, living far from the current of New Mexico's life, had little chance to learn better.

People coming into the Rio Grande valley, from both North and South, dealt with hidalgos quite the equal of their best in wit, education, and political acumen. *Tejanos* saw few of these people; when they went to Santa Fe as office-seekers or officials they often were not invited into the hidalgos' homes. So the gulf remained wide and deep. People of the eastern counties, instead of becoming better New Mexicans, have too often become more Texan. They have sent their children to school in Texas or farther into the South. Only lately has the University of Texas begun work in race relations, as have the most thoughtful Southerners. But this new spirit has been slow to infuse New Mexico's Little Texas. The old spirit still shows itself in ways that are puzzling and amusing or tragic and enraging.

In these *tejano* counties the phrase "a good church member" is the accolade of respectability. Yet the churches practice discrimination. A young Catholic converted to the Baptist faith was treated so rudely that he returned to the faith of his fathers. A lady, all white-gloved for Easter service, asked: "Why does Peter Hurd want to live over there amongst all those Mexicans?" Pete Hurd, besides being an artist and a polo player in cowboy boots, is a complete New Mexican who recognizes no difference between Hispano, Anglo, Jew, Negro, Nisei—or even *tejano*—until they give themselves away. Even at their best, these churches and their ministers make no concerted efforts to lead their followers to practice the Christian brotherhood they preach.

The most odious manifestation of intolerance, the Ku Klux Klan, took root in 1928 in Little Texas, with Roswell as its center. Negroes were not the main target; the American Protestant Association was pumping up hatred against Catholics and Jews. As Spanish-speaking citizens were generally Catholics, two prejudices dovetailed neatly. And a new invasion from the Southern states, described by an eyewitness as "a lot of scum," made recruiting easy. Thoughtful, educated, and generally decent Roswell people held aloof, taking too little note, though the Masons and the Elks refused the Klan a meeting-place. Within the year a thousand men had masked and sheeted themselves, six hundred women were Kamelias, a youth organization was started, and organizers were turning to the rest of the state.

Outside Roswell the Klan had scant success in New Mexico. Even in nearby Artesia and Carlsbad the klans were puny and soon died. In Clovis the leading politicians—mostly Southern Methodists and Baptists—saw to it that organizers were not welcomed. Efforts to establish the Klan in Tucumcari and Clayton aborted. Las Cruces and Socorro would have none of it.

The Klan could not cross the mountains. At an altitude it met the prevailing climate of New Mexico—Catholic—and the unargumentative, quiet tolerance of the frontier. It tried burning crosses in Albuquerque, where membership was reported at from three hundred to three thousand. But reporters, covering sheeted meetings out on the mesa, made more of the curious gapers than of what the maskers were up to. Sheriff Tony Ortiz, with a couple of deputies, rode in and ordered them to unmask. Father Mandalari, a wise old Jesuit, directed his people to do nothing that would stir up "useless dissension." And M. L. Fox, editor of the *Albuquerque Morning Journal*, advised his readers throughout the state not to be suckers.

Even in Roswell sensible men had kept control of state and town offices. Few whippings were reported. Before 1930 the Kleagle had become involved in a scandal and members had begun to fall away and to claim that they had never been members. So the Klan passed, but the fanaticism it highlighted did not. In every political campaign somebody makes a loose remark about "keeping this a white man's state," meaning a state of prejudice. So far the spreaders of prejudice have succeeded only in the peripheral counties. The amusing and the tragic appear where petty personal prejudice can operate.

It was tragic that a Roswell hotel in 1949 refused to serve a banquet to a high school graduating class because it came from a Catholic school and families that spoke Spanish. It is more deeply tragic that even the Catholic Church, proud of its tolerance, maintains two parishes in Roswell—one for Anglos, one for Hispanos. A priest, asked what the clergy were doing to fuse those two congregations, said: "Why, nothing. I never thought of it." *Tejano* mores seem stronger than the Catholic Church.

It is funny that an old lady worried when her son went to teach in a Spanish-speaking community. He had been a football star and had come home from World War II with a few wounds and a decoration. Yet she trembled lest her darling be put upon by "those dreadful Mexicans!" It is amusing that a bride of impeccable Anglo ancestry was cold-shouldered when she went to her husband's town in Little Texas because she was a brunette and had been a teacher of Spanish. Happily she could laugh until they learned the truth and then try to teach them a few basic facts of life, history, democracy, Christianity, and related topics.

Texans keep coming, Texans from many states, but *tejanos* all. Lyle Saunders, in an unpublished paper, remarks that newcomers do not arrive as babes who will mature in the New Mexico tradition; they come as adults with all their folk-beliefs intact. And they are spreading.

These newcomers, with their notions, have not been contained in the southern and eastern parts of New Mexico. Since the opening of lands to homesteading early in this century, they have spread. With the development of industry in the oil fields and at Los Alamos and Albuquerque, the center of the state is increasingly infected. Industry timidly panders to wrong feelings. Employers state that employees would refuse to work alongside whoever is under discussion. If they ask the employees or try it out, it appears —nine times out of ten—that there is no objection. A few labor unions are also at fault, though by keeping certain groups unprotected they are building up a body of scab labor. Too often unions that discriminate turn out to be dominated by Texans.

In education, where, above all, New Mexico's old-time friendly equality should prevail, *tejano* influence grows as teachers who think like *tejanos* swarm in to take advantage of New Mexico's good salaries and retirement benefits.

Efforts to educate *tejanos* are many and various; they are largely personal, but often take on a mass effect. A wise school-principal—who happened to be part Indian—noting that every fall brought on an epidemic of Anglo-Hispano fights, announced that football practice would begin a week before school opened. This brought out all the well-muscled youths, who got to be such good friends before registration day that they forgot about being Anglo or Hispano and settled down to make the team.

Even where Negroes are concerned—always a more difficult case—New Mexico is making progress. An advanced Negro student, who had brought his wife to the University summer school, was amazed to find that he was matter-of-factly assigned space in a dormitory reserved for married students. Students boycotted a barbecue stand that refused service to Negroes, and brought about a change. A football coach, recently arrived from Texas, referred a Negro who had come out for practice to the President. That New Mexican asked: "Are you a student of the University? Then go get your suit." When the New Mexico Military Institute at Roswell announced that its team would not meet one from Phoenix that included a Negro, an influential alumnus put in a long distance call. The Arizona team was received.

Like every fight for decency, New Mexico's fight is slow, often discouraging. The question is always there: will these ignorant newcomers overwhelm us before we can teach them to appreciate New Mexico's fine tradition of tolerance? As prejudice is always founded on ignorance, and as ignorance can be cured, New Mexico may succeed in eradicating the *tejano* mores and in developing along its own traditional lines.

XX

FRONTIER PEOPLE

⊂⋲ THE MOVIES and the westerns have given us an idea
of the frontier as distorted as Russia's picture of the United
States as a land of gangsters and lynchings. The separate
facts may be right, but the emphasis is wrong. On the frontier there were wild men and wilder women, but they
formed a noisy, noisome excrescence on the workaday life
of ordinary people. Pioneers were of all kinds. Some were
spectacular—adventurous, dull, highly educated, rich, saintly,
or evil. Most were mediocre—hard pressed by poverty, ill
educated or not educated at all, and generally decent. Coming first in ones or twos and then in dribbles, the emigrants
began to come in waves as word of free lands and big opportunities got back to the States and over to Europe.

These people brought a mélange of standards and beliefs
which might have proved too incendiary to make fusion
possible. But all pioneers met conditions so hard and so
identical that they developed a tolerance readily recognizable as that of the frontier. It accepts others' beliefs, not
with studied broad-mindedness, but with a humorous admission that everybody has a right to his notions, however
silly or strange.

This attitude prevailed even in New Mexico, where pioneering was complicated by the Spanish frontier it met and
by the fact that settlers came from both North and South,
bringing their sectional hates. The people who came along
the Santa Fe Trail were best fitted to adjust to New Mexico's unique pattern because many of them were Europeans

who spoke at least two languages and readily learned another. Among them were Frenchmen from Louisiana, Germans leaving a fatherland already too militarized, and a sprinkling of Jews whose contribution to New Mexico's sanity has never been adequately celebrated. Both Germans and Jews were strong Unionists and hence Republicans, but they took little part in the violent political squabbles that became hotly sectional after the Civil War. To learn what really happened in a tense time in a New Mexico town, talk with the fiery Irish or the resentful Spanish citizen, the unreconciled Confederate or the stern Yankee. He will give you the color. Then drop in on the German or Jewish merchant, hotelkeeper, or editor. He will chuckle: "Oh, yes, I remember how mad they got. It was like this." His version is as objective as good reporting.

Englishmen came along the Trail seeking adventure if that was their bent, refuge if they were scapegraces whose remittance depended upon their not going home, or investment if they were rich. In the first class was George Frederick August Ruxton, who was a true mountain man, a keen observer, and an upstage British officer who never lost his attitude of condescension. In *In the Old West* he described Doniphan's Missourians as proof that "Americans never will make soldiers." The remittance men were sometimes vague and bleary from drink, but always courteous and correct of speech—gentlemen among savages.

Several of the investors wrote their own stories, notably Captain William French, Irish by birth but stiffly British officer to the backbone. His *Recollections* recall wild days in the territory's southwestern corner. He made his home, or, more properly, established his estate, on the San Francisco River, where only a few ruined walls remain to mark his bunkhouse; the mansion is gone, but legends are numerous. Mrs. Franklin Wheaton-Smith, who lives now on the Mimbres, remembers well the old English Christmas parties when she was a child at Mogollon.

Mrs. Wheaton-Smith's father was Ernest Craig, an English mining engineer who was employed in Colorado by James McKay, a Pittsburgh millionaire. There McKay's daughter Anne attracted the young engineer's notice by putting a match to a stick of dynamite in the belief that it was a candle. Young Craig grabbed the dynamite and, as his daughter puts it, "decided he'd better marry her to make sure she didn't blow them all up."

Later, Mr. Craig found his Last Chance Mine at Mogollon, a mining camp reached even now by a steep hairpin road that clings to the mountain's eyebrow, testing not only a driver's nerve, but also his ability to keep his eye on the road instead of on the lovely valley spreading out below like green plush brocaded with silver. At every turn the road makes a suicidal run out onto beetling cliffs, but whirls away just before it plunges over among the feathery firs and candle-like blue spruce. Mogollon is a ghost town now, where gaunt gray houses follow the stream's noisy course, and only Mr. Holland in the store recalls how it was. He remembers the Craig family well and how the lady posted when she rode, but the children were soundly Western. Mr. Craig, he said, "went back to England and went into politics. He got into the House of Lords, and that's the best-paying job in England."

Their daughter was educated in England but returned to New Mexico after losing her husband in World War II. Relatives in England protested, but Mrs. Wheaton-Smith, who bought the Mimbres Hot Springs near the Gila, is making on her broad New Mexico acres a life more like the life her ancestors knew than anything in present-day England. She is, besides, a convinced and loyal New Mexican.

Another Englishman who came to stay was Montague Stevens, who brought his cultivated English bride to a ranch near the San Augustine Plains. Stevens left a reputation for unvarying success; he succeeded, so they say, in failing at everything he undertook. He also is remembered as a square-shooter, a man to trust, and a mighty hunter, who bred a pack of bear dogs and made legends with his hunts. He has told his own tale well in *Meet Mr. Grizzly*, but Agnes Morley Cleaveland, in *No Life for a Lady*, gives a more amusing picture of the Stevens's home as seen by a New Mexico ranch girl. Riding seventy miles one day to call, she found the new Mrs. Stevens washing clothes: "She wore an apple-green taffeta petticoat, a rose boudoir jacket, and a huge flower-trimmed leghorn hat." The English aristocrat was proving equal to the occasion. Naturally she won the friendly respect of her caller, who offered some helpful hints.

Kearny's army had brought, from many states, a sampling of citizens of every sort. Not a few coming to conquer were conquered by the country and stayed. Among them were young men of enterprise and education who were to become leaders in business and politics and to build the territory into the state. New Mexico had a longer period of tutelage than most; it was not admitted to statehood until 1910. During the territorial days, these young lawyers and go-getters were appointed governors and judges or elected delegates to Congress. Some men, appointed in the East, came west feeling and acting like proconsuls. Even in the middle of the twentieth century, recent arrivals from the East, seeking political office in New Mexico, campaign as devoted sons of her soil. Some Easterners have represented New Mexico in Congress while retaining their Eastern interests. Such men generally move "back east" when their political careers in New Mexico come to an end. Others have stayed on to found families who still contribute richly to the state's life. Perhaps none has so long a history as the Waldo family.

A James Waldo was on the Trail in 1828, and his son or nephew, Dr. David Waldo, was a captain in Doniphan's regiment, a trader and physician in Taos. His younger brother, Lawrence, was killed at Mora in the revolt that followed the murder of Governor Bent at Taos. Lawrence's son Henry became a prominent citizen of Las Vegas, an attorney for the Santa Fe Railroad with enormous political influence, and a justice of New Mexico's supreme court. And his grandson, Waldo Rogers, ascended the district bench in Albuquerque in 1951.

William McGuinness, who was in the battle for Albuquerque when Sibley took the town, rescued a little girl's doll from the terrible *tejanos* as he helped her family to escape. In due time he married her and established the town's first newspaper. His son, an attorney, likes to recall that his father refused several acres of sandhills in payment of an overdue bill for advertising. Those sandhills now are Albuquerque's most valuable property.

The Army also left teamsters and sutlers, who turned from supplying the Army to storekeeping, and ended as merchants with whole counties in their debt. Every county has a powerful family so founded.

To such a family belonged the Sergeant brothers, who, coming west soon after the Civil War, settled on remote but rich farming and grazing lands on the Chama, where one of their sisters joined them. Among her sons was Tom Burns, charming Irishman who married Señorita Josefina Gallegos of Abiquiu. He was, as Irishmen typically were, a Democrat, and Rio Arriba County was having its one brief period of Democratic domination. But young Tom Burns ran afoul of the Democratic boss, Antonio Joseph, son of a Portuguese nobleman who had been forced to flee his country and change his name. When Burns saw voters who asked for Republican ballots tossed bodily down the courthouse steps, he became a Republican, as the Burns-

Sergeant families have been ever since. The second Tom Burns attended Notre Dame as a small boy, but at sixteen was judged competent to stay at home and run the store. Later he met and married Señorita María Luisa Ortiz Tirado, of a distinguished family of Mexico. Their son, after a period in the diplomatic service, has returned to ranching in Rio Arriba County.

Irish names dot our map, and Irishmen have had much to do with making our history. James Thomas Cassidy ran away from Ireland with peddlers, made his way across the United States, and in 1855 built a store and home in Mora, where they still stand. When he needed help he sent back to Ireland for brothers and cousins. So John Doherty came to work in Tom Cassidy's store. When he was shot at by a political rival, he moved with his wife and thirteen children to Union County, where he achieved his ambition of owning as much land as was included in the Irish Free State. His neighbors say that at his death, John Doherty left each of his thirteen children one thousand head of cattle and one million dollars.

The aftermath of the Civil War colored New Mexico politics for years with lurid lights uglier than the nostalgic blue and gray. Doña Ana County, where the new town of Las Cruces had grown up to rival Confederate Mesilla, was torn between two powerful leaders: Colonel Albert J. Fountain, a Northerner who had entered New Mexico with the California Column, and Albert Bacon Fall, whose father had ridden with Morgan's Raiders in Missouri. Fountain was a Republican and Fall a Democrat, though he later became a Republican and was best known as a member of President Harding's cabinet.

In 1894 Colonel Fountain, as attorney for the newly created New Mexico Stock Association, had secured indictments against seventeen men accused of crimes—mostly cattle-stealing—against members of the Association. At that time Lincoln Plaza, now known as Old Lincoln, was the county seat, and Colonel Fountain had a drive of one hundred and sixty miles to his home in Las Cruces. He drove a buckboard with two horses, and his nine-year-old son Henry was with him. Somewhere between La Luz and the Organ Mountains they disappeared. The buckboard was found, but no trace of either man or boy, dead or alive, has ever been located. Four years later, three men were tried for the murder of the boy. Colonel Fountain was not mentioned. Albert Bacon Fall was one of the attorneys for the defense, so the trial reflected the old political and personal rivalry of Fountain and Fall. In a brilliant defense, the three accused ranchers were cleared, but popular opinion does not yet consider the case closed. Its mention is still good for a verbal row between adherents of the two old enemies.

Less well known and even more tragic is the story of the Rascón-Beckwith-Johnson families, which involves not only North and South, but our two frontiers. The story began between 1810 and 1820 when a wealthy citizen of Chihuahua named Rascón moved to Texas with his Spanish-German wife and their two lovely daughters. Of the two girls the most beguiling was Refugio, who caught the eye of a young Virginian and ex-Confederate named Beckwith, who had forgotten nothing. In no time he and the lovely Refugio were married, and their daughters grew up to carry on the family tradition of lovely girls.

At Seven Rivers Mr. Beckwith made his home in true Virginia tradition. His large adobe house, with pitched roof extending over verandas all around, was the epitome of comfort, with plenty of servants, cottonwood shade against the sun, and fireplaces to mitigate the winter's chill. Hospitality was boundless; every passerby was welcome. So it was natural that young William Charles Johnson should be brought there by his pals after he had been wounded in a brush with Indians, probably about 1873, though William

Johnson, who tells the story, does not like to date his birth very accurately.

Young Johnson, after his discharge from the 4th Ohio, had heard from Texas: "Grass is belly deep. Come on." So he was accepted in the Beckwith home as a Texas cowboy driving cattle to Fort Bayard. But he was fated never to reach Fort Bayard. During a pleasant convalescence, the Yankee wooed and won Carmelita, widely known as the star of the Beckwith beauties. Their romance was to have a tragic ending.

The Johnsons had one son, William, and Carmelita was again "expecting" when old Beckwith, sitting on a wagon's tongue as his son-in-law rode up with a bunch of cowboys, heard in casual conversation that Johnson was an ex-Union soldier. Without hesitation the old Confederate, retired but still bellicose, drew a bead and killed the "damned Yankee." So honor was satisfied, his daughter widowed, his grandson orphaned, and he had to become a fugitive in Texas. But not before a hot-headed cowboy named Wallace Ollinger had shot at him, demolishing a handsome nose.

The widowed Carmelita Beckwith Johnson then went to live with the family of her mother's cousin, Don Nicolás Pino, a descendant of Don Pedro Pino. Don Nicolás, as William Johnson said, "owned all the sheep in the Estancia Valley" and was politically prominent, so the Johnson family lived both on the ranch at Galisteo and in the Governor's Palace in Santa Fe. But the widow had not gone alone with her children. A faithful cowboy had ridden along to guard and to serve her: the Wallace Ollinger who had ruined Beckwith's aristocratic nose, and whose brother was to come to fame by being killed by Billy the Kid. In time the widow married the cowboy and had a son who became a prominent Standard Oil man in Mexico.

Young William Johnson stayed in the West. After freighting in Colorado and punching cattle in New Mexico, he served as a Rough Rider in Cuba, did a stretch in the Philippines, and put in a restful interlude in Hawaii, where he married a New England teacher. They came finally to live in the ghost town of Kingston, where Mr. Johnson—exceedingly tall, slow-spoken, but most verbose—has won the title of "Windy" Johnson. Mrs. Johnson is bedridden; her lovely face is luminous with soul, her words are spiced with humorous understanding, her reading is Jane Austen.

Among the workers and builders of the state was a crew known as Rawhiders. Often border mountaineers who had escaped service in both Union and Confederate armies, they were known for the rawhide they used to make shoes or chaps or to splice a broken axle or spoke. The men rode scrawny horses, scorned all work, and seldom killed their own poor cattle, finding stolen meat tastier. Their women were slatterns and skilled at putting forth their ragged youngsters to appeal to ranch women's generous hearts. Rawhiders of all ages chewed tobacco. When the supply ran low, they mounted the smartest little John Wesley or Thomas Jefferson on the fastest horse and sent him to town for more.

This picture comes from James A. McKenna's *Black Range Tales*. McKenna, a Catholic, said the Rawhiders had no religion. Probably they had that debasement of the faiths of John Wesley and Roger Williams common to Southern mountaineers. In heritage they were—much as some of us hate to admit it—the true Anglos. It is pleasanter to remember that in New Mexico's clear air, and especially through intermarriage with non-Anglo elements, the descendants of those do-nothings and slatterns have produced worthy citizens.

The word "marriage," at some points in our history, was only a manner of speaking. McKenna, true frontiersman, writes of matings like those of birds in the spring. As the Catholic Church frowned upon unions with heretics, and as often there was no church at all, these easy habits were inevitable, and many a union established without legal sanction or clerical blessing resulted in families well founded in affection and responsibility.

Under the influence of men trained in the law and of women demanding respectability, the territorial legislature in 1882 passed a law providing that a man living unlawfully with more than one woman would be ineligible for public office and liable to a $500 fine and five years' imprisonment. Naturally, there ensued an amazing amount of scurrying around to find somebody qualified to perform a marriage service. Anybody. Any marriage service.

Dr. P. T. Martin of Taos told a tale that he called the first marriage in E-town (as Elizabethtown was popularly called). Once, during the 1880's, when gold production in the Moreno valley between Cimarron and Taos was at its height, a Virginia colonel, living in E-town, got himself appointed justice of the peace and announced that decency had arrived. Dr. Martin described the colonel: "He wore his pants in his boots, a plug hat, and he liked stud poker and liquor. And he could sling words!"

Dr. Martin related that one Saturday night a miner from the Mystic Mine, in town to celebrate, singled out a lady. But she was not, as usual, acquiescent. "It is different now," she said. "The only way is for you to marry me." "And how do we do that?" he asked. The lady explained about the colonel, and the miner readily agreed. So the wedding procession started, stopping at every saloon and finally reaching the one where the Justice sat, his plug hat on the back of his head, his boots on a table. Pleased with the effect of his moral crusade, the colonel righted himself at once and called for silence. But what ceremony to use? E-town had neither law book nor prayer book, nor could the officer of the law recall any suitable words. But he was dashed only momentarily. Clearing his throat, he ordered the couple to stand before him, stayed his swaying against the bar, and intoned in full Virginia accents:

"Underneath this roof in stormy weathah
This buck and squaw now come togethah
Let none but Him who rules the thundah
Set this buck and squaw asundah.

Now you're married, by God, and let's all have a drink."

So frontier New Mexico had its dismal and its comic aspects. But the people who built the state and stamped its character were the sort that figures little in the movies— families who came in covered wagons with a few head of stock, took up land, and stayed. Most of them came poor. A few made fortunes, but usually they made only good reputations and established families who continue active in the state's life.

Squire L. Barker—that was his name, not a title—drifted westward and finally settled on Sapello Creek above its junction with the Mora River. Where the valley was wide enough Squire Barker and his sons farmed; on the hills they cut timber to build stout houses and barns; on the uplands they ran cattle and bred good horses. Hard work was the daily rule. Fun consisted in riding all day to dance all night with neighbors from fifty miles away, or in hunting. The boys knew every inch of mountain and canyon from Hermit's Peak to Wheeler's. One of them, Elliott, in *The Dogs Bark Treed*, writes of that trackless wilderness as intimately as a lady describing her garden, and of his horses and dogs as personal friends.

Elliott's brother, S. Omar Barker, is one of New Mexico's best interpreters as poet, raconteur, and writer of westerns with the flavor and rhythm of absolute truth. With his writer-wife he inhabits a hideaway at the top of Sapello Canyon, where the air smells of wild mint, wild clematis, and wild raspberries in season and pine needles all the time.

All the members of that family are useful citizens carrying on in their several ways the zeal for righteousness which made their father leave his plough or his branding to preach a funeral or lead a prayer-meeting.

Such families depended largely upon the mother, and not only in sentimental ways either. The typical woman of the frontier was sturdy, hard-working, lacking perhaps the learning of books, but knowledgeable about childbirth, nursing, and simple remedies. A true helpmeet, she did her share of cattle-driving and bull-whacking, as well as of her specialties of childbearing and cooking. But however crude the life women lived, they brought amenities. Lace tidies appeared in brothels, silverware graced tables set under lean-tos, churches were set going as soon as possible. The "chippies" at Hillsboro subscribed most of the money that opened the first church in Kingston. Women opened the Deming Ladies Hospital with no money; each woman put in hours a week cleaning, cooking and scrubbing, as well as nursing.

Before there were hospitals or even doctors, women shouldered those jobs; in some places they still do so. A good type was Ma'am Jones, wife of Heiskell Jones, who had left West Virginia with his family about 1880. The nine Jones youngsters were born in various places, including New Mexico's Lincoln County, where they finally settled. On Hondo Creek they had good farmland, but mostly Pa and the boys rode the range, hiring out as hands and dealing in whatever offered. The line between law and outlawry was tenuous and wavering.

Ma'am Jones never wavered in anything. Virginia-born, she taught her children good English and proper manners. The boys rose when a lady entered the room, offered chairs, removed their hats, never swore in a lady's presence. Her eldest and probably her favorite was John. He was his mother's constant aid, even seeing her through childbirth once when the neighbor woman failed to come. He was a gentle-seeming boy, never loud or coarse, never pugnacious. Yet somehow John killed fourteen men before he was himself killed at twenty-six somewhere in Texas.

Ma'am Jones could cope with anything. She never raised her voice, but her quietest word was heeded. And she was beautiful, close to six feet tall, with the broad, deep-bosomed figure of the childbearing woman. Her black hair grew down to her feet and was always brushed to shining, braided smoothly, and wound round and round her queenly head. She had clear, warm skin and a friendly smile, but her eyes were sharp rather than limpid, and they reflected both spirit and a shrewd mind. Ma'am was a judge of men, and men knew it. Her house, wherever it was, whether or not it had walls or a roof, was immaculate, shining with cleanliness. "Soap and water," she used to say, "will cure most anything." The heavy hand-woven bed and table linen, brought from Virginia, was boiled and sunned to snowy whiteness; most of it was used up making bandages, for Ma'am Jones served as midwife, nurse, and doctor. She knew the herbs; her natural cleanliness doubtless forestalled many an infection, for she boiled everything she used, and her cool competence contributed that valuable therapeutic agent, confidence.

Once when the whole neighboring Casey family came down with smallpox, and Heiskell was not at home, Ma'am took what she thought would be needed, caught her easiest mare, adjured the older children to be good until Pa got home, mounted sidesaddle, and with the baby on a pillow rode off fifty miles to help. Pa followed with the other children in the wagon as soon as he got home. Living in a tent, Pa and Ma'am Jones labored day and night. They buried three Caseys, but saved the parents and the other two children. None of the Joneses caught the disease; perhaps Ma'am's constant boiling helped.

Different, but as useful in her way, was Sadie Orchard

of Hillsboro. She was a tiny, high-bosomed woman with short feet in shorter shoes, tight spitcurls, and a wicked chuckle to punctuate her obscenities and profanities. Coming from a questionable past, Sadie had achieved respectability by marriage with Harry Orchard. Together they operated a resort of many purposes in Lake Valley on the railroad and ran a stage up through Hillsboro to Kingston in the boom days of the 1880's. Later Sadie opened a hotel in Hillsboro, known to all New Mexico's lawyers for cleanliness and good food. There they stayed during court terms; her terse, unquotable comments on them were doubtless just. Forty years later, during World War I, Sadie Orchard was discovered doubling for whatever Sierra County lacked: doctor, nurse, hospital, and undertaker. She fed the family of a man serving his term in the penitentiary, shopped "for them chippies up on the hill," cut the hair of "old Tom the Chinaman," who dreaded shears. During the flu epidemic she nursed many a family until all had recovered or died, washing, cleaning, cooking, laying out the bodies, lining the board coffin, and coming home to cut the geraniums and bleeding hearts grown in her dining-room window for just such occasions. For a bad woman, Sadie was of the best.

At the other end of the social scale was Mrs. Ada McPherson Morley, whose daughter, Agnes Morley Cleaveland, has written her story too well for another to touch it. Mrs. Morley came from Iowa with her husband, William Raymond Morley, the competent engineer who surveyed the Santa Fe Railroad's route over Raton Pass. Mrs. Morley, widowed young, left an even finer monument in the family she managed to raise and educate at Princeton and Stanford while she ran cattle on the San Augustine Plains. Mrs. Morley's standards were rigid: the Presbyterian Church; the Republican Party; the WCTU, which she helped to found in New Mexico; good English. She succeeded in giving her children a sense of superiority that demanded superior standards without snobbery.

Other women whose husbands were able to protect them gave an unexpected cachet to frontier life. They were the ladies whose grand pianos are still every town's boast, who lived in large houses with servants, whose clothes came from such style centers as St. Louis and Kansas City, and who brought true sophistication as well as mannerisms and evening dinner. They, too, were found in every county, but the most revealing types were perhaps those in the lower Pecos valley.

The southeastern corner of New Mexico—all Lincoln County in its heyday—was a land that made men rich. John Chisum, who came to New Mexico in 1864, was the best-known and the most aggressive; he held more water holes, dominated more land, and hired more men than most. But there were others who conducted continuous undercover warfare for power.

Cattle rustling was not criminal, much as the victim disapproved of it. Jesse Evans, who put in a stretch with Billy the Kid, rustled for some of the best citizens. The entire Lincoln County War of 1880 began with the killing of a wealthy Englishman and involved a cultivated churchman from Philadelphia and an Irishman keeping store with a retired German officer. It was a fight between factions in which Governor Lew Wallace, representing law and order, was only a helpless bystander. Many of these men had been trained in tough border-fighting before, during, and after the Civil War. Captain J. C. Lea, whose grandson Tom was to become famous as painter and novelist, had served as a Confederate soldier in Missouri. The Coes rode with Billy the Kid's gang. Marion Turner and Heiskell Jones were proud of having run out the Mormons. Colonel Maurice Garland Fulton, deepest student of this period, sums it up: "They were men of their times; they were no archangels."

These men made money, and their wives contributed the amenities. Captain Lea's wife promoted and saw established in 1895 the New Mexico Military Institute, one of the best in the country. But the tone of Pecos valley society was set by men and women of the great world. In the Carlsbad Museum a gentle lady, who seemed to be a resident of the town, pointed to the exhibits—old photographs of stately gentlemen and ladies in bustles, pieces of good glass and china such as might be found in Eastern museums. "This town," she said proudly, "is not New Mexico of Mexicans and Indians. Our town was settled by gentlemen. They brought water from the mountains and planted trees along our streets, and they were able to invest in developing the country."

Two men had most to do, in the last decade of the nineteenth century, with the metamorphosis of the Pecos valley from cattle range to farmland. James John Hagerman was a Canadian who had prospered in Michigan and in Colorado before he became fired with the possibilities of the Pecos valley. His partner was a New Yorker, Charles B. Eddy; the county still bears his name, though the town was renamed Carlsbad when the discovery of mineral waters roused the hope that it would rival the German spa. These two men opened the valley with a railroad and pushed irrigation. At the Hagerman home on the Old Chisum ranch, Mrs. Hagerman presided over elegant silver and cultivated conversation, and Mr. Hagerman made a valuable collection of eighteenth-century books. Their son Herbert was one of New Mexico's territorial governors.

Charles DeBremond, a Swiss officer, chose the Pecos valley after searching the whole West for the most desirable spot for colonization. Using Italian workmen, who had come as immigrants to the United States and eventually to the Pecos valley, he built a stone house at Carlsbad and planted a vineyard and orchards. Later he experimented with Karakul sheep. He also found time to drill a unit of the New Mexico guard, which served in Mexico in 1914 and won distinction in World War I as Battery A, New Mexico Unit. The colonel, a dashing officer with full military mustache, dressed habitually in riding breeches and boots, carried a crop, and rode thoroughbred horses.

Quite as military and even more spectacular was Major Etienne de Peyster Bujac, Huguenot from Baltimore, who was tall and dark with brilliant eyes. The major wore Norfolk jackets, an enormous velour hat, and a turquoise-studded belt. His boots were made by a Frenchman who had followed him west.

Mrs. DeBremond, a rigid Presbyterian, was accustomed to invite a priest to her home in Carlsbad to stay overnight and say Mass for her Catholic maid. Mrs. Bujac made her home a center of a hunting group. These homes were built in the current mid-Victorian style, surrounded by gardens and orchards, and served by trained people. There was no thought of "going Western." Their effort was to maintain the standards they had brought from home. Happily those standards made for a smooth adjustment with the best ways of the frontier people and of the old Spanish families. Out of this curious mixture of types have come New Mexico's comfortable lack of snobbery and its ability to get along with all sorts of people.

XXI

THE MINING MAN

THE OLDEST mine in the United States is in Los Cerrillos, the little hills twenty miles south of Santa Fe, where Indians dug out turquoise at Mount Chalchihuitl. This name, the Aztec word for Mexican jade, might well have been applied to New Mexico's sky-stone by the discoverers. Martin W. Pollock, a mining engineer working near Madrid, estimates that about one hundred thousand tons of rock had been removed from the pit that is still traceable under a growth of piñon and cedar. Indian miners knew the trick of splitting rock by heating it and then throwing water on it. Broken rubble was then carried away on human backs and so thoroughly picked over that not the tiniest bits of turquoise have been found on the dumps. Even the site worked in the eighties as the Tiffany Mine has been long abandoned. The romantic like to believe that Santo Domingo and San Felipe Indians go there at night to dig out their best stones, but mining men consider this unlikely.

The Spanish did little about the turquoise, though legend has it that a cave-in at Chalchihuitl was one cause of the Revolt of 1680. Spain was interested in gold and silver, and every explorer—not believing his predecessor's assurance that there was none—tried again. Often the lode reported just over the hill remains the shimmering lure that leads today's seeker on. The first of these was La Sierra Azul, a mountain somewhere north of Moquiland that was blue with copper and silver and perhaps with quicksilver, too.

For years explorers crawled all over those mountains and reported traces of copper, lead, alum, and sulphur, as well as silver. But the rich vein never materialized.

Coronado's men mined sulphur in the Jemez Mountains and made gunpowder at Bernalillo, giving New Mexico its first manufacturing enterprise. And lowly salt from lakes between Quemado and Zuñi, in the lower Estancia valley and near El Paso, proved worth hauling on burros to the mines in Chihuahua. Such things would not enrich a kingdom; Spain turned to missionarying. So New Mexico first played its trick of withholding the treasure sought and coming through with something else: not gold, but souls to save; not water, but oil; not oil, but potash—or nothing at all except a good yarn. The mining man never gives up, and thereby hang all the tales of picturesque failures and lucky strikes.

The earliest mine of lasting value is near Silver City. In 1800 an Apache chief showed traces of copper to his friend, Lieutenant Colonel José Manuel Carrasco, who named the place Santa Rita del Cobre. A rock standing above the site has the outlines of a kneeling woman, and a local legend has it that the colonel thought it resembled his favorite saint, Santa Rita, and therefore gave her name to the mine. In 1804 Carrasco sold out to Don Manuel Elguea, a Chihuahua banker, who began to ship long burro-trains of copper to Mexico on its way to the royal mint in Spain. Zebulon Pike reported in 1806 that those open pits were yielding twenty thousand mule loads a year. Elguea, secure in his government contract, erected rough smelting works protected by a triangular adobe fort. One of its watchtowers still stands, lost among modern mining buildings. In 1822 James Pattie and his son leased the mines for one thousand dollars a year and worked them for five years. The Patties were unique in including the Apaches in their contract, and they had no Indian troubles in the very center of Apacheria. Pattie lost out only when he entrusted thirty thousand dollars to a friend who robbed him, leaving him cleaned out. The Apaches said: "Never trust a white man."

All the other Apache tales are of hideous attacks on wagon trains and lonely ranch-houses, with men killed fighting for their women, who saw their children dashed to death and were themselves carried off into trackless mountains. J. Frank Dobie, who has the storyteller's best gift of believing what he hears, relates, in *Apache Gold and Yaqui Silver*, many an enthralling yarn of how Apaches scared off or even killed prospectors who came near their hidden mines, and how the Apaches brought in gold dust to exchange for guns and powder. "The Lost Adams Diggings" were lost, according to Adams, a prospector who reported a fabulous gold strike in 1864, because the Apaches had "made him forget" the clearly marked trail. Only Santa Rita was an Apache's gift to a white man he could trust.

Santa Rita caught New Mexico history as it passed. Kit Carson worked there as a teamster for Robert McKnight, one of Kearny's army, who made a fortune out of the mines before the Apaches cut off his supplies by stealing an eighty-mule pack train. In 1862 Confederate General Sibley made headquarters at Santa Rita before he was turned back by the California Column.

In 1873 the first U.S. patent to the Santa Rita mining property was issued after its purchase from the heirs of Elguea, who were found scattered throughout Mexico and Europe. The purchaser was a Colorado company, which then worked the mine, erected a small smelter, and shipped high-grade ore and black copper to the nearest railroad, in Colorado. Mules were still the mode of transportation, but the mine's fame was traveling faster than its copper. During the next twenty years the mine changed hands several times. One of its owners was William Randolph Hearst, who sold it in 1899 to the Santa Rita Company.

Silver City, by the turn of the century, contained all the elements of New Mexico's frontier in highest concentration: miners from Wales, southeastern Europe, Mexico, and the States; squatters on the big cattle ranches still held by cattlemen who did not hesitate to shoot; a "Chink" washee-washee conducting a brisk smuggling in opium and compatriots; merchants trying to do business and stay out of trouble; and a lurid and luxurious red-light district across the arroyo, which, in a cloudburst, rose to a roaring flood but never cut the town off from the ladies for very long. And to top the pile was a group of sophisticated Main Liners from Philadelphia, brought by mining interests or by tuberculosis to Dr. Bullock's fine Cottage Sanatorium. Such men and women gave the town a sophisticated tone during the first decades of the century, and this has marked its life ever since. Bachelors from Princeton entertained elegantly and organized theatricals. George McCreary, each day, drove his ailing wife behind a smartly caparisoned mule to the Chinese restaurant for tea. Out on the Gila, Tom Lyons, known locally as "the Lion," built a splendid hunting-lodge not long before the First World War, and furnished it with fine furniture, even a grand piano taken apart and shipped out into the mountains on pack mules. John M. Sully, graduate of the Massachusetts Institute of Technology, suspected a vast copper deposit from the lumps of pure copper he picked up on the dumps, and spent fifty thousand dollars to prove it. He then went east to interest big capital.

In 1909 the Chino Copper Company was organized, and the Santa Fe soon thereafter built west from Rincon to Silver City, and Grant County had become important in the territory. John M. Sully, manager of the Chino Copper Company, Percy Wilson, its attorney, and Tom Lyon, representing the cattle "barons," attended every session of the legislature with other interested gentlemen, who made laws without the necessity of running for office—or the danger of being retired by democratic processes. Their highest accolade is: "They kept taxes down!"

By a series of purchases lasting over several years, the Chino Copper Company was absorbed, early in the twentieth century, by the Kennecott Copper Corporation. As the Chico Mines Division, the old Santa Rita operation ranks fourth among the country's open-pit mines, with a production valued at some twenty-two million dollars annually. The region also produces considerable quantities of lead and zinc.

The Chino Mines Division manager is proud of its housing, its clubs, and its efforts to overcome certain employees' prejudices. The earlier policy of housing Mexican nationals in a separate section is breaking down as the miners maintain better homes and gardens. The kneeling figure of Santa Rita still presides over the hilly town and the vast amphitheater of the open pit, with its lovely striations of green and turquoise, yellow and rose, all under a shimmering and sunny sky.

Although California was the land of the great gold rush in 1849, the first gold strike west of the Mississippi was made in New Mexico, twenty years before the California Gold Rush and all but forgotten in that stampede. In 1828 a sheep-herder on the Juan Ortiz Grant, south of Mount Chalchihuitl, picked up a stone that resembled the gold-bearing nuggets of his native Sonora. This was the Old Placer; in 1839 the New Placer was discovered in the San Pedro Mountains. Both were dry; lack of water has always hampered mining in this area. The Mexicans once tried hauling their ore to water, but generally they panned by shaking it in hand-hewn wooden *bateas*. Even with such crude implements, Josiah Gregg estimated that they extracted between sixty and eighty thousand dollars a year. The grim and hideous life at those mines is well described by Ruth Laughlin in *The Wind Leaves No Shadow*. She imagines a forlorn youth here for her heroine, who was to become the fabulous Tules of Santa Fe.

In 1861 a group of men from the States patented the Ortiz Grant, which, perhaps by Yankee ingenuity, had been expanded from the hundred acres of Juan Ortiz's modest holding to some 69,458 acres. The new company had grandiose plans, even proposing to bring water from the Pecos River with enough force to sluice out the rock with hydraulic jets. This was never done, but the company cleared a couple of million dollars by dry washing. The placers are still dry, but the latest owner, George W. Potter, continues to explore and to confer with local inhabitants, who offer to lead him to hidden lodes—even to tons of bullion buried at low levels during the revolt of 1680. Mining men say most such dreamers are honest. The range is streaked with "stringers," thin veins of gold not worth developing without water. Among present dreams of solving that problem is a proposal to tap the subsurface waters of the dry Galisteo Creek.

The most famous effort to mine without water was made by Thomas Alva Edison, who set up an experimental works at Dolores to develop an electrostatic process for separating gold from sand. His operation, carried on in strictest secrecy, seemed to succeed, but finally it failed. The Wizard lost two million dollars in New Mexico without getting gold. He even ran true to form in missing what lay underfoot. Mr. Edison was, at that time, seeking a substance to make a heat-resistant filament for his electric globe. Doubtless he was not looking for it in New Mexico. But in 1950 Martin Pollock, idly panning along a cut Edison had dug, noticed a sluggish movement among the light and dark particles in his pan. He took the particles of ore to town for testing; he put ultraviolet rays on them. Sure enough, he had found scheelite, from which tungsten is derived. Tungsten was what Mr. Edison had needed.

The Palace Hotel, known now as the Old Rock House, was built soon after the Civil War, when Richard Rodney Green brought from Kentucky five hundred head of cattle, a string of pure-bred horses, wagons loaded with fine furniture, and a large family. At Cerrillos, he paid Cochiti Indians $1,600 to build his three-story stone mansion, and Mrs. Green made a garden whose traces still remain in fine trees, a grape arbor, and a Virginia creeper against the walls. Cerrillos, during the mining boom, was as lurid as any Western town and its roster of distinguished visitors is longer than most.

Mr. Green's store sold miners' supplies for gold dust; his stage ran full from Santa Fe; and his hotel was a center of lavish entertaining and reckless gambling. One poker game there is said to have run four days and nights. Dr. Palmer lived there, and was at hand to sew up the fight victims. Governor Lew Wallace stayed awhile with his wife during the 1880's, when he was working on *Ben-Hur*. Another Governor, less discreet, maintained a love-nest in the upstairs suite with the bay window. The Kentucky Greens politely entertained two Union generals: General Phil Sheridan, who stopped in passing, and ex-President Grant, who was losing money in a mine at Golden in the San Pedros. Sarah Bernhardt stopped at the Palace while she played at the Cerrillos Opera House. And Theodore Roosevelt was so "dee-lighted" with Calvin Green's ambidexterity with six-shooters that he took the boy along as a Rough Rider.

These tales and many more are told by Mrs. Anna Vergolio, whose husband bought the house in 1913, when Cerrillos was still expecting to become a large city. Mrs. Nellie Trigg, a later owner, is most interested in gathering stories about Mrs. Green's mystical powers and her influence with the Indians. Harold Trigg, who runs Brahma cattle, says that Indians still reverence Mrs. Green so much

19 *Visitors must show passes at the main gate to Los Alamos.*

ATOMIC ENERGY
COMMISSION

20   ABOVE: *Arroyo at Mexican Springs before planting, March 17, 193*

BELOW: *Arroyo at Mexican Springs, May 30, 1940.*

UNITED STATES SOIL CONSERVATION SERVIC

that they show him good springs long overgrown and lost. To a cattleman a spring is worth more than much fine gold.

With gold discoveries came the prospector, symbol of hope invincible. Staked by men in the towns, he would load his burro with a keg of water, a sack of beans, bacon and salt, his pick and pan, and his blanket or sheepskin. Months later he would show up again with evidence of a real strike, or more likely with just enough trace of gold to extract another stake from his backer. The prospector has not disappeared. Even in prosaic Albuquerque some two hundred prospectors and treasure-seekers hole up between sorties to study their ancient maps and raise money for another try. In their minds New Mexico is underlaid not only with gleaming gold, shining silver, and green copper, but with untold wealth buried by some conqueror, missionary, or *hacendado* in iron-bound chests often topped by the bones of the peons who buried it. Treasure seekers include a priest who can decipher mediæval Latin charts, sober attorneys, and widows with maps left by deceased finders of treasure now lost.

New Mexico never became a large gold producer, but during the seventies and eighties mining was the territory's leading industry, and many a newcomer made a tidy fortune by grub-staking prospectors. The precious metal occurs in many parts of the state in lodes and placers, but too often in veins that soon pinch out or where lack of water or too much water—New Mexico's twin evils—have taken the profit out of mining.

The Old Abe Gold Mine at White Oaks, in the Jicarilla Mountains, produced several million dollars before it was flooded out. The story of White Oaks has been told charmingly in *Land of Heart's Desire* by Emerson Hough, who lived there in the 1880's with a group of young bachelors who were to serve the state and nation later as a senator, a governor, a congressman, and a Secretary of the Interior.

The Aztec and Mystic mines produced much gold for the owners of the Maxwell Land Grant during the last years of the nineteenth century, when Elizabethtown, in the Moreno valley, was a roaring mining camp. During those years, bitter charges and countercharges of high-grading or stealing ore led to a series of murders, culminating in the decapitation of Arthur Manby in Taos in 1929. On July 4 of that year, Manby's body was found in his own house, fully clothed but headless, and a skull, gnawed clean, was found in the next room with Manby's police dog, maddened by lack of water. The case seemed to have a connection with older murders and disappearances at E-town. A woman named Teresa Ferguson was the daughter of one of the miners who had charged the owners of the Aztec Mine with high-grading. She was also Manby's heiress, and he had acted as her representative in a long series of litigations. As the case of Manby's death has never come to trial, it remains one of New Mexico's unsolved mysteries, an unending topic of conversation and speculation.

Bland, in the Jemez above Cochiti, lasted longer as a ghost town. Recently one could enter the hotel, see the bell marked "Ring for night clerk," and find glasses—but, alas, no bottles—still on the shelves. The Washington Mine, too, produced well until water flooded the workings. In many such cases, mining men believe that gold remains in the mines, but in quantities too small to repay the expensive operations required to keep the workings free of water. Gold is now mined only as a secondary product in New Mexico.

Silver also failed to put New Mexico among the first producers, but it, too, had its strikes and made its towns. Socorro was a wild town when the Santa Fe Railroad ended there and stages took off for White Oaks, Lincoln, and Roswell, and for the mines in the Magdalenas. Miners, track workers, gamblers, and desperadoes added their personal quarrels to the racial and religious rows already present, and so produced a hell's broth that led to a vigilante organization. In time the vigilantes became equally lawless and were, with difficulty, reduced to law and order. But Socorro was getting rich.

Silver was booming in the Magdalenas, and a mine had been discovered on the edge of Socorro. A smelter was established; hauling was big business. But the Santa Fe, which has often given and taken away, built on down to El Paso in 1882, killing Socorro at one blow. A revival began in World War I, when the Sherwin-Williams Paint Company began to work lead and zinc mines in the Magdalenas. During the second World War more life was brought to the town by the working of volcanic products to make building-blocks.

Sierra County is full of tales. Negroes continue to show up with maps of the location of the Lost Nigger Diggings, reported by Negro troops chasing Geronimo, but never found again. Its biggest thrill was in 1880 when two prospectors, following a ten-inch stringer, burst suddenly into a chamber "as big as a house," whose silver-studded walls flashed in the lantern's beam. This was the Bridal Chamber, which produced fifteen million dollars before it shrank to a stringer again.

In that same year, Jack Sheddon was run out of Lake Valley—not a puritanical place—because of his addiction to "dizzy dames and John Barleycorn." Kenny relates that Sheddon drifted up the North Percha Creek, where he fell asleep and woke to find his head pillowed on a rock that assayed almost pure silver. This was the Solitaire Mine. By Christmas, Kingston was a town of 1,800; within three years its population was six thousand and it had twenty-two saloons and three newspapers. But Kingston long remained a tent town. There was no time to build. Even the store was a tent. Only the big saloon on the gulch was a frame building. There gamblers gathered in the silver the miners dug for, and "gay ladies" made life pleasanter for all. McKenna tells that when smallpox hit the camp those Shady Lane girls offered to nurse the patients if the doctor would agree to stay sober.

The teacher was a young Irishman, with smiling blue eyes in a ruddy face, whom everybody liked. His name was Edward Doheny. Once when Doheny's beloved wife Carrie was sick, Johnny Moffet, who had just struck it rich, lent him the money to take her to El Paso. When Moffet was old and broke in California and Ed Doheny was one of the richest men in the country, he remembered and cared for his old friend. Another friend of Doheny's, then and later, was Albert Bacon Fall, who was beginning a varied career "pounding a drill up in Kingston," as Sadie Orchard said.

A useful though unglamorous mineral product is coal. Both anthracite and bituminous coal are found near Cerrillos at Madrid, one of the few places in the world where the two types occur together. Anthracite is shipped from Madrid to zinc smelters in Amarillo, Texas, and to the Kaiser steel mills in California. Bituminous is mined near Gallup and near Raton; mining men believe there are extensive coal fields not yet worked.

The first large coal development was on the Maxwell Land Grant. The Phelps-Dodge Company in 1906 purchased the mines at Dawson and, under Dr. James Douglas, made them models of safety. Influenced by Dr. Douglas, who was deeply aware of the discomforts and hazards of a miner's life underground, the Phelps-Dodge Company became one of the first to try to make that life not only safe, but also pleasant. Dawson lasted fifty-five years, and then closed down, becoming a modern ghost town in 1950.

Gallup, which advertises Navajos, is a center of large coal fields operated by the American Coal Company, whose miners are a polyglot sampling of immigrants from Europe and Asia. The town's history has been turbulent with labor troubles, Communist charges, and some latter-day vigilante violence that New Mexico has offset by decent court procedures.

Mining in New Mexico has by no means settled into routine. Mining engineers may speak lightly of the old-time prospector, but they all keep on prospecting, though with many differences. Modern prospectors—both week-enders and professionals—travel in station wagons, carry Geiger counters, belong to the New Mexico Miners and Prospectors Association, and consult its magazine's list of "critical and strategic minerals" wanted by the General Services Administration. The January 1951 list included fifty-two items, running from aluminum and antimony through cobalt, fluorspar, mica, and nickel to tin and zinc. Some of these minerals are already in profitable production in New Mexico.

Tin offers one of the most seductive and disputable of prospectors' dreams. Essential to our country in both peace and war, tin now comes from British Malaya, the Belgian Congo, and Bolivia. The U.S. Bureau of Mines and the Geological Survey have reported that reserves of tin in the United States, including Alaska, amount to no more than seven thousand short tons. This statement is met by loud disclaim in the Black range, where Robert H. Hartson says he can see more tin than that in one canyon. Mrs. Madelyn Caraway, "the tin lady," knows that New Mexico's tin is the purest in the world and in sufficient supply to free our country from foreign dependence. Therein, "the tin lady" believes, lies the difficulty: international cartels have prevented government financing of an invaluable resource lying there on top of the ground ready to be washed out by the simplest placer methods.

Bauxite was found in 1907 in the hills in Grant County, and the site was acquired by the Mellon interests, but has never been put into active production. Molybdenum has been worked for a quarter of a century in one mine east of Questa, and beryllium has been discovered near Embudo. On the Navajo reservation, near the Four Corners, helium was discovered in 1942 in quantities to justify the erection of two large plants that were later closed down.

Naturally, the greatest hope of our "atomic state" is that uranium and perhaps pitchblende may be found in quantities sufficient to relieve our country from dependence on the Belgian Congo. Even Paddy Martinez, a Navajo sheepherder, knew that canary-colored rocks might be uranium. One day he reported that he had seen some in the broken hills north of Grants. Geiger counters proved him right. Mining men offered ten-per-cent royalties for digging privileges, and the Santa Fe Railroad, which had been selling off land thereabouts, began quietly buying it back again and generously outfitted Paddy's whole family for the winter.

The area where Paddy Martinez made his find has attracted prospectors from the whole West, as well as serious investors. The Anaconda Copper Company soon began buying up land and leasing claims throughout the district.

Since Paddy Martinez made his uranium find, New Mexico has become the largest producer of uranium ore in the United States. The increase in production has amounted to as much as 61 per cent annually; and the daily milling capacity, since four new processing plants were placed in operation in 1958, has risen to about 12,000 tons. The AEC estimates the reserve of uranium ore at 54.9 million tons, and it has guaranteed the purchase of uranium oxide in concentrates from domestic ores produced and delivered from April 1, 1962, through December 31, 1966, at the price of $8.00 per pound. Exploration and development of these resources continues at an increased pace each year.

None of New Mexico's paradoxes is more amusing than the emergence into usefulness of volcanic waste. Pumice, always of some value as an abrasive, has been utilized to make building-blocks. Scoria, lava blown shaggy when it was a hot liquid, makes an even stronger block. Albuquerque supports several factories that bid fair to make our typical house volcanic instead of earthy. Perlite, a volcanic rock that pops like popcorn when heated, is being crushed and screened in a plant in Socorro and shipped for finishing into light-weight plaster and insulation. In Mora, mica, disregarded ever since glass supplanted it in windows, is being mined and shipped off to roofing factories. These developments are of great value to New Mexico, though they have not yet industrialized the state, which remains primarily a producer of raw materials. Among the few minerals that are finished in New Mexico are abrasive pumice, which is processed at a plant in Grants established in 1939; fluorspar, which occurs widely throughout the state and is shipped to steel mills and chemical plants from a factory established at Los Lunas in 1941; and barite. Barite is the latest comer, and has been produced in finished form only since 1950 at a plant near San Antonio, eleven miles south of Socorro.

Oil is also cited as a "home industry," though less than ten per cent of the state's output is processed in New Mexico. Pipelines owned by the oil compaines carry most of it to the Gulf coast and even to California. New Mexico congressmen are forever fighting for a fair division of this resource.

Oil was first discovered on the Navajo reservation, to the disgust of the Indians, who had hoped for water. Exploration then shifted to the state's southeastern corner, but the first producer was in San Juan County, after the Navajos had been persuaded that money for leases and royalties paid into the tribal coffers might prove as valuable as the water they had hoped to find. Oil wells on the reservation at Ute Dome, Hogback, and Rattlesnake, were all producing before 1924, when three drillers brought in a gusher near Artesia. All this was of minor importance if compared with the fabulous oil fields elsewhere, but in 1926 the Hobbs pool came in with a gush that brought all the biggest companies to New Mexico and shifted the state's population and its tax structure.

Oil men complain that the twenty million dollars a year they pay in royalties, lease rentals, and assorted taxes practically support the state. They fail to mention that they lease most of their land from the state at five to fifty dollars an acre while paying private owners as much as three thousand dollars. Nor do they recall that they are removing one of the state's irreplaceable resources at great profit to themselves.

Oil has brought a new invasion of Texans zooming in high-powered cars along roads that have cut the high grasslands. Raw scars mark the pipelines; tall skeletal doodlebugs have replaced windmills; and the cowboy is yielding to the doodler, that highly paid specialist who knows oil fields from Venezuela to Saudi Arabia. Haberdashers in Hobbs tempt these men with the most expensive clothes; jewelers display gemmed fraternal charms and cufflinks. There are expensive stores for women too, but Hobbs is a man's town whose men are technicians. The chamber of commerce boasts a great number of Phi Beta Kappa keys. But Hobbs, with its twenty thousand population, has no book store; a few books are hidden behind expensive office furniture and vaguely pointed out by a young woman: "There may be a best seller here somewhere."

Lea County's rapid growth has intensified the *tejano* atmosphere of eastern New Mexico. Drillers ordinarily own no property; they buy in Texas, read Texas papers. Despite state laws, Lea County maintains separate schools for Negroes. One powerful oil man offered to send to Santa Fe "the best damned state senator that money can buy." It is a recurrence, despite motors and Phi Beta Kappa keys, of the lawless days of a century ago.

A sideline of the oil business is the production of gas, which began in 1929 when the El Paso Natural Gas Company put in its first pipeline from the Hobbs field to the city of El Paso. It was buying, processing, and selling flare gas—the escaping gas that was formerly burned as waste—and giving Hobbs a weirdly hellish look. In twenty years, the El Paso Natural Gas Company has built 5,700 miles of pipelines, through which it serves large areas of New Mexico, Arizona, Texas, and California. Its longest pipeline, from Jal near Hobbs to San Francisco, is 1,200 miles. By 1950 the company had completed a pipeline from New Mexico's San Juan basin across Arizona to the California border, where it delivers gas to the Pacific Gas and Electric Company. Two hundred and eighteen miles of this line's four-hundred and fifty miles lie within the Navajo reservation. The Navajo Council, in entering into an agreement with the Company, insisted that Navajos should be employed for all work they are competent to do, and the Company finds them good workers.

New Mexico's most de luxe mining is potash, suitably located in the gentleman's town of Carlsbad. During World War I lack of potash threatened United States agriculture with disaster, as most of our supply came from Germany. Potash had been discovered near Amarillo, but as Texas had no federal lands the U.S. Bureau of Mines explored the Permian Basin farther west near Carlsbad, where a driller for oil had found potash as early as 1912. By 1929 private capital had been interested and two companies were soon in operation.

The industry has achieved the major miracle of turning Carlsbad into a mining town without destroying its gentlemanly aspect. The companies have erected pleasant houses of light-colored plaster, where miners water lawns and tend flower gardens after work.

The mines themselves are an eye-opener to one who has

seen the dark and dusty inferno of a coal mine or felt the airlessness of almost any underground operation. One enters the potash mine in a large elevator manned by men in mushrooom-shaped hats that are reminiscent of the Army's tin hats, but are made of plastic. At a depth of a thousand feet the vast, light chambers suggest the Carlsbad Caverns rather than any mine. Fresh air is pumped in, miners travel on trolleys along wide tunnels lighted by electricity and separated by heavy columns of ore left standing. There are no unsightly timbers. There is nothing unsightly. Everything is beautiful, for potash is a sparkling, rosy crystal. Chemically it is a salt, potassium and chlorine, and tastes like salt; it was laid down by the sea eons ago.

The operation consists of drilling holes into the walls of solid potash. Nobody will say how much potash may underlie New Mexico; guesses go as high as three hundred million tons. The electric drill, jiggling in a man's gloved hand, seems the only part of the whole business that a woman could not do if she could drive a car. But ramming in the explosive would be no difficulty, and from there on everything is done by levers or pushbuttons. Great machines cut out enormous chunks of soft ore that are than lifted and dropped into shuttle buggies and finally dumped into trains that carry tons of ore to the elevators. Trains above ground haul the loads to the crushers and brine tanks, where the potash is finished. Most of New Mexico's potash is shipped to the southeastern seaboard.

New Mexico's mining man has come a long way from the sheep-herder who picked up a nugget, the miner with his crude *batea*, the prospector, or even the promoter who gave no thought to the miner as a man. But he is still prospecting and still finding what he was not looking for.

XXII

THE STOCKMAN

TIME was when a man was a cattleman or a sheepman. The two were enemies because cattlemen believed that
sheep destroyed the range for cattle. The emergence in one
person of the stockman who runs both sheep and cattle indicates how indisputable facts can be disproved within a
generation. During the same time the animals have changed.
Long-legged, lightly fleeced sheep able to walk across several states to market have evolved into ovine balls of heavy
wool and tender lamb-chops that are gently transported by
rail or motor. And the thundering herds of longhorns,
swimming rivers, stampeding, outrun or soothed by hard-
riding, singing cowboys, have disappeared into hornless,
unsexed makers of meat.

The sheepman is no longer the don in softest deerskin
and wide hat with silver braid, nor is the cattleman that hero
astride a pinto. The stockman is a businessman in a business
suit, driving a fluid-drive car, calculating pounds of meat
instead of heads of animals, and supporting several organizations for the advancement of his business and political interests. The enemy most fulminated against nowadays is the
federal government.

The stockman has always used federal domain, but he
never ceases to kick like a bay steer against any regulation
of it, though, at bottom, he and the federal man seek the
same thing: more and better meat from less land.

In New Mexico the sheep business came first. Every
Spanish expedition brought cattle, pigs, and goats, as well

as sheep. Sheep found themselves most at home. Mutton
became the habitual diet; Navajos learned to weave; everybody wore wool; and blankets were a popular article of
trade with New Spain long before the conquest was complete. In the nineteenth century, flocks were driven to markets in California and then "the States." *Ricos* became rich,
and life in New Mexico was based on the flocks.

Some *ricos* owned thousands of acres of land granted
them by the King of Spain and even more generously by
the Mexican governors. Under old Spanish law, grazing
lands were free to all. The *rico* came to control them much
as the later stockman did, by simply owning more animals.
This resulted in the *partido* system of running on shares.
The poor man entered into a contract to care for a rich
man's sheep and to return at the end of the year a specified
number of rams, wethers, ewes, and lambs. Such *ricos* as the
Chavezes and Oteros of Valencia County and Don José
Leandro Perea of Bernalillo owned hundreds of thousands
of sheep out on *partido*. Some *partidarios* became owners of
considerable flocks of their own. But most of them remained dependent on the *patrón* and developed into the
type of easily led voter whose psychology has so deeply
marked New Mexico's political scene.

Mexicans were sheepmen, and remained so after they became American citizens. The gold rush to California opened
a new market for meat; wool was for years an inconsider-
able side line. Taking mutton on the hoof to California was
a profitable business and a large part of life. In 1849 Don
Antonio José Luna drove 10,000 wethers to California over
a trail not far from the modern highway. Thereafter he, his
sons, and his associates, the Oteros, made the journey regularly.

Once when Don Antonio José's son found himself pressed
for money in California, he sent a message to his father. Don
Antonio José called on his old friend, Marcelino Abeyta, an

Isleta Indian, who readily dug up the needed ten thousand dollars. It was literal digging; bankers said that Indians always brought in gold coins that smelled of the earth.

Another son, Don Solomon, became the archetype of the sheepman-*patrón-politico*. Invariably elected treasurer of Valencia County, he saw to it that its considerable taxes from the Santa Fe Railroad were scrupulously managed. Other offices did not interest him, but Solomon Luna's heavy figure, dark Romanesque features, and quiet force were felt in Republican councils when the state was smoothly operated by a junta of lawyers representing mines, railroads, and livestock.

After United States troops had subdued the Plains Indians, sheep lands were extended and little plazas grew up in eastern New Mexico, southern Colorado, and the Texas Panhandle. Long trains of wool wagons now crawled across the plains to Kansas City. Don Silvestre Mirabal of San Rafael made a fortune in the eighties. Wool had then supplanted meat as the trade article: gringos refused mutton—the Army never succeeded in feeding it to soldiers. Sheepgrowers in the 1930's taxed themselves for a national advertising campaign based on the slogan "Eat More Lamb." But the consumption of mutton remains low, and seventy per cent of our country's finished lamb goes to eastern markets, where English taste prevails.

The names Otero and Mirabal are still potent in the sheep business, as are Ortiz y Pino of Galisteo and various others. But nowadays New Mexico's livestock interests are dominated by gringos and by Spanish families who have disappeared under English names.

The Hubbells, whose progenitor, James L. Hubbell, came to New Mexico from Connecticut in 1848 and married a Chaves Gutierrez, still own large ranches near the Arizona border, where two brothers and the sons of one of them live. A third brother in Albuquerque manages the office with its unchanging sign: *Ocupamos hombres para las bor-regas* (We hire men for the sheep). And Tom Burns of Tierra Amarilla, also third generation New Mexican, has broken his family's record for marrying Spanish by bringing home a bride from Minneapolis.

The Burns and Sergeant families typify the gringos who entered the sheep business as storekeepers. Sheep being the only collateral and no banks being available, the storekeeper carried sheepmen on his books until wool was sheared or lambs were shipped. Now and again he had to take over; he was then a sheepman. Such men are found in every county. Arriving poor, but young and vigorous, they grew rich and established families still powerful. George and Frank Bond of Quebec and their friend Archibald Mac-Arthur established stores in many towns, and finally became wool merchants as well as ranchers. Stewart Mac-Arthur has kept both store and ranches near Wagon Mound. Germans came too. Louis Huning established a mercantile and stock business in Valencia County. Charles Ilfeld established himself in Las Vegas, and his family carries on there and in Albuquerque.

In most such families, where sons and grandsons have "stayed with the sheep," methods have not changed much. They employ men whose fathers and grandfathers worked for their fathers; the relationship between bossman and worker is a combination of humorous respect on both sides and a common devotion to the sheep. At all crises the owner is with the sheep. Wives say: "He's out lambing— or shearing—or shipping." If drought or storm menaces the herds, he may be on the job for weeks. Such work has made a type.

Ruddy of face, sturdy of body, slow of speech, and quick of eye, he covers miles of territory. Now he goes in a jeep or car, but he still sees every poisonous weed, broken wire, or droopy lamb. He stops at every sheep camp where the iron stove stands outside the tent along with the skillet and coffeepot, the water keg, and the drowsy dog. Attentively he hears and makes notes of the sheep-herder's report of encroaching pingue, which is poisonous to sheep, lowering water holes, coyotes' howls heard at night, and what is needed.

Sheep are the dumbest and most dependent of creatures, and must be fussed over every minute. They are herded along in bands of from 1,500 to 2,500 by a herder and his assistant, the *campero* who cooks, moves camp, and fetches burroloads of beans, coffee, lard, and flour for the men, of feed and salt for the sheep. Often he brings water. Both these men are overseen by the *caporal*, a mounted man often old and always dignified. He rides the rounds, sees that bands are moved as the grass dictates, and tallies sheep strayed, diseased, or attacked by wolves or coyotes. The sheep-herder never leaves his sheep.

In New Mexico the word "sheep-herder" has become one of scorn. "Just a sheep-herder," they say in derogation. But Captain Clark M. Carr, who had hired hundreds of them, said: "Where else can you entrust twenty thousand dollars of perishable property to an illiterate and be sure that he will care for it with intelligence and devotion?" Captain Carr had in mind the happy days when sheep-herders were paid thirty dollars a month, a wage that has risen with the general rise in the cost of living to one hundred dollars a month for the sheep-herder and ninety dollars for his helper. In New Mexico it is customary to employ two men for each band of sheep, but in some states one man does the entire job and is paid correspondingly. Even at the higher wage, it is difficult to find sheep-herders, as young Americans do not care for that lonely life among the bleating flocks. Consequently many ranchers have recourse to "wetbacks," Mexicans who have crossed the Rio Grande illegally. They will work for less and, above all, they have the feeling for sheep. Fred Huning said: "Not everybody can herd sheep; not one in a hundred will stay with it."

This transformation of the old peon sheep-herder into the modern New Mexican has hastened changes that were probably coming anyway as Texas stockmen bought land in New Mexico and introduced modern methods. In the eastern counties, where twelve to fourteen inches of annual rainfall make deep sod and sheep do not have to be moved from winter to summer range, ranchers began—as early as 1915—to fence their pastures with woven wire, fortified against wolves and coyotes with barbed wire underground. Here herders have been replaced by fence riders, who often ride in jeeps. But sheep are still sheep, and their needs condition the year's rhythm.

Ewes are bred in the fall, and lambing occurs from early spring to early summer, depending upon climate and altitude. Expectant mothers are gently herded to a spot chosen for good feed and water, sometimes with a man-made shelter. On the A. D. Jones ranch in Lea County the lambing sheds are only less comfortable than a hospital maternity ward.

After twenty days baby lambs can survive on tender grass, and the herders begin to move their charges to summer range in the mountains. If winter snows have been heavy, grass will be good and water holes not too far apart. Then many pounds of wool and meat are assured. Long drought may bring tragedy. Then owners scour the state, and even other states, to rent "grass"; often they load their animals on trucks or boxcars for a long haul to grass before they are too weakened to be moved. Such a year may result in heavy loss. Lambs are ready to be earmarked, as breeding stock or as animals to be shipped to market, before the fly season begins.

Sheep are shorn when the fleeces are heaviest. Expert hand shearers who formerly traveled in bands through many states are being replaced by mechanical clippers. Many New Mexico owners now employ professional shearers with mechanical equipment. In these cases, the shearers tour the ranches and, with the assistance of the local sheepherders, push the blatting animals into corrals where they are caught, run rapidly over by the whirring knives, and let go, peeled to the yellow skin, often flecked with blood and bleating piteously. The wool is tramped down in a sack by a man muffled against the dust in a red kerchief.

The wool market is in Boston, and wool became a dependable crop when Boston buyers began to come to New Mexico in the eighties. Las Vegas was then one of the world's most important wool centers. Joe Taichert, still a wool merchant there, remembers when loaded wool wagons would back up four or five miles waiting to reach the crowded plaza, where bidding was conducted by the lifting of a finger. Because wool was hauled up the Pecos from the southeastern counties, where shearing began in April, and from northern New Mexico, where it ended late in July, Las Vegas had a long busy season. At the turn of the century big dealers like Gross Blackwell and Charles Ilfeld were weighing in one hundred wagons a day.

This steady demand for wool led to improved stock. The old *churros*, descendants of the Spanish *merinos*, were good foragers and able to defend themselves with their large horns, but they gave only two or three pounds of wool. When they were bred up with Rambouillet rams from Utah, Idaho, and Montana, the clip increased, until the average weight is now seven or eight pounds. When the Bond-MacArthur Company began about 1900 to weigh lambs they averaged forty pounds; thirty years later the average was sixty-five. This Rambouillet sheep is New Mexico's preferred strain for both wool and mutton, but a new strain has been developed.

Amos Dee Jones, ranching on the caprock near Roswell,

crossed Rambouillet, with their dense heavy wool, with the DeLaine, whose wool is longer and finer. It took him thirty years but he stabilized and registered a *Debouillet*, a strain whose rams sell all over New Mexico and are moving into other states. After Mr. Jones's death the business was carried on by Mrs. Jones, the old foreman, Dick Miller, and the Jones's sons.

Met at luncheon in Roswell, Mrs. Jones seemed the typical small-town lady in flowered hat and dainty frock. Even on her ranch, seventy-five miles southeast of Roswell, Mrs. Jones was not the newcomer's idea of how a ranchwoman should look. She did not affect fringed buckskin or cowboy boots, though her suit was practical, her shoes stout, and her hat designed for protection from the weather. At the ranch-house, with its tree-shaded pool by the pump, she got lunch: steak, fried potatoes, tomatoes, hot biscuits, jellies and pickles, pies and cakes, and a tall pot of coffee. She let the men talk. Driving over the range she deferred to her twenty-year-old son. But her gentile questions went deep.

"I see José hasn't mended that fence yet. . . . What's the matter with that ewe's hind leg? . . . Are you going to move that band soon?" She was proud of the animals' broad chests, indicating strong hearts, and the five-inch wool. A fleece, parted, shows dusty gray on top, then white, and then yellow grease above the pink skin. The guest room was piled with fleeces ready for exhibition, and the mantel was loaded with trophy cups. Mrs. Jones proposed taking her son to Australia to study methods there.

New Mexico's sheepmen are a conservative lot, but a few have ventured into exotic schemes. Colonel DeBremond's daughter and her husband, Laurie Hagerman, for example, produced Karakul lambs, whose pelts were shipped to the New York fur market as Persian lamb. Goats figure more largely than Karakul lambs in the state's economy, especially Angora goats, whose strong silky hair makes mohair and plush. Any goat, even the long-haired Angora, can climb over rocky country inaccessible to sheep, and will eat grasses sheep do not find palatable. Several ranchers in the southeastern counties have gone in for Angoras, but the romantic story is that of Mrs. Armer & Sons, a firm of Sierra County.

When Mrs. Reid was left a widow with six children in 1892, her only asset was a herd of native goats. So she fed goat milk to the children and sold what they did not need. When she married Leven Edward Armer in 1894, Mrs. Armer went in for Angoras, recently introduced into New Mexico. In 1900 she amazed the industry by paying $1,050 for a champion buck. Now her son, Robert Reid, who heads the business, has a house filled with silver cups and blue ribbons.

The Reid ranch near Hillsboro is shaded by black walnuts, and the air is warmly spiced with creosote bush. The white stucco house, with its fenced flower-garden, is completely modern and furnished throughout with mohair: upholstery and curtains, bedspreads and table covers, rugs, and a banner woven with the Eastern Star emblem presented to Mrs. Reid when she was a Worthy Matron. In pens outside, animals being groomed for the state fair were wrapped in gunny sacks to protect their long hair, for all the world like ladies in a beauty shop. In the production of mohair New Mexico is second only to Texas.

New Mexico's cattle business began when the great herds were driven north from Texas over the famous Chisum Trail and others less known. John Chisum, finding the grass deep and sweet along the Pecos, settled there. Others followed, pre-empted the water holes, and spread out. So they encountered sheep whose smell they did not like, whose meat they would not eat, and whose owners and herders were of the hated breed of Mexican.

The fallacious belief that sheep ruined the range by crop-
ping close was due to the overgrazing that had exhausted
many of the best grasses. Grama, curly mesquite, the sedges,
and needle grasses had almost disappeared. Moreover, cattle
refused to drink where sheep had watered, offended by the
ovine smell. So the trigger-happy *tejano*, finding lowly
sheep-herders on the range, made nothing of shooting.
Every old sheepman can relate his father's experience, if not
his own, of sheep camps destroyed and bands scattered and
killed, of sheep-herders beaten or even murdered. The last
range row occurred just before World War I, when Ray
Morley tried to introduce Karakul on his cattle ranches in
the San Augustine Plains. Both cattle and sheepmen resented it. But Morley was no man to monkey with, and he
prevailed long enough to abandon Karakuls on his own
volition.

With cattle came the cowboy, a national hero who had
pretty well disappeared by 1900, but who has been forever
embalmed in writing and resurrected in the movies. He belonged to the era of the longhorns, who made legend, but
whose meat was tough and stringy. John Chisum had
prophesied that beef would some day be sold by the pound
instead of the head, but as late as 1906 Ray Morley was still
running longhorns on the San Augustine Plains. But the
broad, quiet, rosy Herefords, with their bland white faces,
had already appeared; they would produce the meat and the
fifty-thousand-dollar bulls. Black Angus were brought from
England about 1890, but they remain the fancy of a few
men and do not threaten to replace Herefords.

Cattle-growing is an important part of New Mexico's
economy, and the cattleman is still an impressive figure. The
New Mexico Cattle Growers Association, with over two
thousand members, brings together handsome gentlemen in
soft beige cords, fancy-topped boots with sloping heels, and
pale hats wide enough to satisfy any Hopalong Cassidy fan.

Their talk is of improvement in range management, better grass, water, weather, and production. Always production. These men are primarily producers of beef, pounds of beef, and more beef from fewer beasts. One sold six hundred head of cattle in 1950 for more than two thousand had brought him in 1900. A calf increase of fifty per cent was then considered good; a man who does not now get calves from seventy-five per cent of the cows bred is held of no account.

At home on the range the cattleman is a charming gentleman, with the accent on gentle. Handling beasts seems to develop a quiet demeanor, unemphatic speech, and measured movement.

Such a man is Ben Floersheim, whose Las Jaritas Ranch (The Willows) in Mora County was founded by his father, a merchant gone into sheep. Ben prefers cattle: "Sheep," he says, "are too little." He owns sixty-three thousand acres of land and runs cattle on thirty-nine thousand acres of additional state land. This is the favored northwest corner of the state, where the finest grasses grow—black and blue grama, galleta, and buffalo grass. Its normal rainfall is sixteen inches, and the land's long slope from the Sangre de Cristo to the plain is cut by the Mora, the Red, and lesser streams. Driving across that rolling prairie, the motorist would never suspect the hidden canyons with wooded sides and the clear streams that spread into pools where youngsters fish and swim.

Las Jaritas headquarters, three miles from the gate, lies in a land dimple beside the willow-shaded pool that gave the place its name. Battleship order prevails in barns, stables, and tool sheds, where everything is in its place and shining. No rubbish litters the graveled courts; men driving their rounds stop for every misplaced plank, bit of wire, or blowing paper. Never did pickups so justify their name. Ben Floersheim loves his land and his animals, and he cares for both with the combination of an agricultural college training and a faith reminiscent of his Old Testament ancestors.

The Floersheim home, surrounded by a walled garden and as well equipped as a city apartment, is like many a ranch home, as Mrs. Floersheim is like the up-to-date ranchwoman. Efficient in the house, these women can pinch-hit outdoors and they find time for the League of Women Voters, the PTA, or a bridge club in town. One of them, poking her kerchiefed head into a beauty shop in Clayton, called: "I'm going to put my clothes through the laundromat and leave my list at the grocers; then I'll be back for my permanent."

Las Jaritas is not considered a large ranch in New Mexico, though the state's oversized ranches are disappearing. The last to be reduced was the Bell Ranch in San Miguel and Guadalupe counties, where the Canadian cuts through broken land as richly colored as the Navajo reservation. That ranch, named La Campana for a rocky upthrust that resembles a bell, was the Pablo Montoya Grant. In the 1850's it went into gringo hands. It then included several small ranches and two hamlets that have recently been drowned in Concha Lake. At its greatest the Bell Ranch covered two million acres, and its owners and managers led baronial lives. In 1949 it was cut into four parts and one was bought by Mrs. Thomas B. Hoover to add to her T4 Ranch.

Like Mrs. Jones of Roswell, Mrs. Hoover is accepted by stockmen as a sound businesswoman and cattle-grower. In her modern home near Tucumcari she is a gracious hostess and a solicitous grandmother, but on the range she rides like a man, directs like a man, is respected like a man. She went into business when her first husband, Harold Krohn, died, leaving her with a big ranch and a small daughter. She smiles to recall a couple of managers who picked her as easy. "But," she smiles, "I was a trained bookkeeper and I always handled my own accounts."

The headquarters ranch was bought by a Texas corporation that does business as the Bell Ranch, Inc., and continues to use the bell-shaped brand. Its manager, George Ellis, lives in the rambling old adobe house that has known its Indian fights. A day on the ranch now is probably not unlike any day within the last fifty years. Cowboys ride in to the chuck wagon for dinner; and if the chuck wagon is now a pickup truck, it is driven by the same old "hooligan," who also fetches wood and water, peels potatoes, and polices camp. His opposite, the horse-wrangler, has not been mechanized; as of old he brings up the remounts and holds them in a rope corral.

The "hands," jogging in, could qualify for the movies, but only as background, so unpretentious are their tight chaps, worn hats, and colorless clothes. Only George Ellis, Jr., sporting fine chaps of pinto horsehair, looks as though he had seen a movie.

Mrs. Ellis said that most of these young men had served in the Navy. "Cowboys are afraid that in the Army they might have to walk." They ate quietly, then each man neatly scraped his leaving into a hole half-filled with cans and potato peelings and dropped his plate and utensils into a tub. Proceeding to the rope corral, he shouted for the mount he wanted: Buster, Chigger, Runt, Badger. He then transferred his saddle from the morning's mount, swung aboard, and was ready.

The day's job was regular fall work: to brand and alter any calves missed in the spring roundup and separate those to be shipped or held for breeding. Any cow showing up without a calf had her horns tipped with huge shears that crunched like a heavy tree falling. "If she shows up again without a calf she's earned a ticket to Kansas City," Mrs. Ellis said.

Like the sheepman, the cattleman has vastly increased the production of meat. The goal is a four-hundred-pound weaner calf and a seventy-five per cent calf crop. This emphasis on meat has led to gentle handling that would have outraged the old-timer. Unnecessary roping, dragging, and bull-dogging are frowned upon. Many ranchers now keep their stock on fenced and irrigated pastures, often planted with special grasses.

In the Estancia valley, the Valley Irrigation Company began, in 1948, to pump what they hope is an inexhaustible supply of seepage from the Ortiz and Sandia mountains onto arid acres where generations of dry farmers have made only a precarious living. Walter Mayer, the enthusiastic ranch-manager, says that the 1,800 acres of planted and irrigated pastures produce 150 times as much beef per acre as does range land. The fenced acres are beautiful to see, with the soft greening of winter wheat or oats, summer alfalfa, and a varied diet of grasses. They are protected from wind by a planting of juniper, elm, Chinese elm, Russian olive, and hackthorn, which make a pyramidal wall almost as impervious as stone. Of five thousand trees planted, not one was lost. This experiment may be another step toward removing New Mexico from the position of producing only raw materials for processing in other states. These pastures are raising the grain that is needed to ready steers for the slaughter. Sheep need no supplemental feeding. In 1950 lambs one hundred days old were sold directly to the Safeway Stores, Inc., at weight eighty pounds, thus eliminating several middlemen.

The extreme of such nursing is to be seen on Winfield Morten's Rancho de Abiquiu just under the escarpment where old Abiquiu sits. On the ranch, irrigated pastures make a bucolic foreground, with fat kine knee-deep in grass and calves gamboling in the bosky. The ranch-house is as luxurious as a Hollywood set, with shaded patios and tiled verandas. Only frescoes suggest the wild days and the wild ways of raising cattle. Mr. Morten made a fortune erecting prefabricated houses at White Rock, a town on the Pajarito Plateau built for construction workers employed at the near-by city of Los Alamos, where the atomic bomb was made. Mr. Morten later went into raising blooded bulls to improve New Mexico's stock. He calls himself "a cattleman's cattleman."

Gentleman's ranching has taken in horse-raising too. Some racers from New Mexico have done well on California tracks, and the state fair in Albuquerque is maintained by the ponies. Popular as both racers and show ponies are the palominos, so named by the Spanish for the gold or creamy coat that suggests a stain. Their best breeder, Warren Shoemaker of Watrous, has won silver cups and blue ribbons, and has suffered many a disappointment. For the palomino is a biological sport; in one season Shoemaker's best mares may produce only bay, sorrel, and one white colt, and not one golden beauty with white mane and tail.

Such developments seem normal. The earth-shaking change was the union of cattle and sheep on one ranch. Captain Burton Mossman, an Arizona Ranger and courageous, tried it about 1930 on the Diamond A Ranch east of the Pecos. Others in that area followed suit. Floyd Lee, operating the old Fernandez Ranch at San Mateo as a cattle ranch, stocked part of his lands with sheep, thus reverting to the original character of the ranch when the Chavez family operated it as a sheep ranch. The Second World War, with its high prices for beef, encouraged many sheepmen to try cattle. As they did, the superstitions disappeared and the old phobias were forgotten.

Garfield Paltenghe, who lives in the New England house his grandfather built on his ranch near Wagon Mound, is convinced that sheep and cattle improve the range for each other. Sheep eat small forage that cattle scorn; cattle relish the coarser grasses that sheep will not touch. The only difficulty remaining is that cattle do not like the sheep smell and will not drink where sheep have been. On the Magdalena Stock Drive, that three-mile-wide fenced promenade through which stock walk one hundred miles to the railhead, tanks are reserved for fastidious cows; water is carried for sheep.

So the cattleman and the sheepman have become one. They maintain separate associations because many of their technical problems differ, but they meet in the New Mexico Stock Growers Association, where they air the same troubles: bad weather, noxious weeds, a market gone sour just as there is a big increase in the flocks or herds. Always some department of the federal government is attacked by one or more speakers, though the stockman, of all citizens, gets most aid from the nation.

He has always used government land. In an arid country, owning a few scattered water holes gave a man control of thousands of acres of public grazing land. When the government opened the public domain to homesteading in 1862, the stockman's rage knew no bounds. He was right in stating that in the arid West a man could not support a family on the 160 acres first allowed, nor on the 320 acres of later legislation; even the 640 acres of the stock-raising act of 1916 were too few in New Mexico, where it takes an average of about 70 acres to feed one cow, 15 acres to graze one sheep. Stockmen managed well enough by acquiring the water holes and watching the forlorn hordes who tried dry farming starve into destitution and pull out. Meanwhile the conflict between homesteaders and stockmen had precipitated a range war even more bitter than that between cattlemen and sheepmen.

Dozens of thrillers have been written about these battles between strong men who proposed to protect their own, with guns if necessary, and the misguided nesters or squatters. Perhaps Conrad Richter's *Sea of Grass* is best balanced between sympathy for the pitiful little man and appreciation for the rancher's love of his wind-blown grass. In this case, too, the stockmen came round; most of them are now irrigating and farming the range. The difference, they aver, is that they use both land and water sensibly.

The stockman's land problem has been partly solved by the Taylor Grazing Act of 1934, which leased the public domain to men already in possession of it. This act favored the stockman already entrenched; the only way to acquire range lands now is by purchasing land that has grazing rights.

Stock-growers admit that their business has been saved from financial disaster by a series of congressional acts beginning with the Farm Credit Administration and leading to the long-term, low-interest government loans they count on now. They also enjoy price supports, and they may (and often do) call on federal agencies for technical advice. What they cannot abide is supervision. Stockmen in national convention and through their powerful congressional lobby have proposed that the federal lands they use should be sold to them without competitive bidding and at their price. In New Mexico, where stockmen are a political power, they prefer state control. As New Mexico lands are leased for the benefit of schools, the state land office is concerned with revenue rather than with land management. In all these matters sheepmen and cattlemen are in happy harmony. Perhaps we are witnessing here the last stand of the old frontiersman, who resented any restraint and did his own policing and shooting. Perhaps he is too new in business to share the eastern businessman's respect for the expert.

In spite of his grousing, the stockman is primarily a producer; nobody is more important in the nation's economy. In New Mexico his endeavors bring in over one hundred million dollars annually; the state ranks high in the production of meat, and constantly improved methods may, in time, give it a higher rating.

All this shows in the stockman. Often heavy-set, always with face burned and eyes crinkled by the sun, he has neither ulcers nor a sour disposition. His humor is often sardonic, but he sees the joke on himself. He has laughed over the ending of the cattle and sheep wars in the union of sheep and cattle on the same range. He has gone in for the farming for which he damned the squatter. Perhaps we shall live to see an end to his hatred of his active partner, the federal man.

ᙩ ᙰ ᙩ

XXIII

THE FEDERAL MAN

⃝ Recently a banker in Silver City said, plain-
tively: "I remember when the only federal employee I knew
was the postmaster!" He was doubtless wrong; he knew
Army officers, men in the Land Office and on Border Patrol,
and immigration officers. But he knew nothing like the number of men and women now on the federal payroll in New
Mexico. Nor the rate at which their numbers increase.

The government employee appears most spectacularly
and expensively in the armed forces and the Atomic Energy
Commission. Largely because of New Mexico's climate,
three of the nation's most important air bases are here: Kirt-
land Air Force Base at Albuquerque, a research and development center, Hollomon Air Force Base near Alamogordo,
and a less important one at Roswell, Walker Air Force Base.
The AEC, in addition to Los Alamos, where the atomic
bomb was first made, maintains Sandia Base at Albuquerque,
the top Special Weapons Project; the White Sands Proving
Ground, where the first atomic bomb was tested; and other
hush-hush installations.

The Army, accustomed to requisitioning what it needs,
proposed in 1948 to extend the White Sands Proving
Ground by taking in some one thousand square miles of
range land, thus dispossessing about fifty ranch families.
"Fair compensation" was offered, but what can be fair
compensation for the loss of a man's inherited home, the
only way of livelihood he knows? New Mexicans protested,
and the military agreed to a less extensive bombing range.
But at Los Alamos the Army won.

Los Alamos (the Cottonwoods) rests on the Pajarito

Plateau where Indians lived well and where the Ramon Vigil Grant later supported large flocks and herds. In time the grant came into the hands of a Michigander, Ashley Pond, who had become a first-rate New Mexican. On a pine-grown upland above leafy canyons, he founded the Los Alamos School for Boys on a basis of outdoor living, horses, and a respect for country as well as people. As director he chose Albert Connell, a cultivated New Yorker, who had been a Forest Ranger and a Boy Scoutmaster. The school was a Boy Scout troop mounted: it maintained a fire lookout during the fire season, and its summer session consisted of camping trips into the virgin forests of the Jemez range. Its masters, from eastern universities, consistently sent well-qualified students to the country's best colleges.

Then one day in 1942 Army officers dropped in for lunch. Mr. Connell was used to guests for lunch, and paid little heed. But he attended all right when word came that the United States was buying him out. His "not for sale" was brushed aside. Uncle Sam would pay well, would buy everything down to the kitchen brushes, the inkwells, and the guest towels. Immediate possession was demanded. So said, so done. Within a few months boys and masters were gone and the very name Los Alamos disappeared from consciousness. When J. Robert Oppenheimer's daughter was born there the birth certificate read: "Rural area, Sandoval County, New Mexico."

J. Robert Oppenheimer is the adopted New Mexican and nuclear physicist who directed the Manhattan Project at Los Alamos. Tall, gangling, with big feet, out-thrust head, and dark hair cropped to a scrub brush, he has a gentle, almost timid manner that expresses the same courtesy with the janitor, the San Ildefonso Indian, or the top scientist. Only the combination of one of the best brains of all time with compassionate human understanding could mold a face of such rare beauty. From childhood "Oppie" had spent vacations in New Mexico in a mountain cabin or astride a horse. Few men have known our mountains as he knows them. There he rested from his studies in England and Germany, and from his work as professor of physics at the University of California and the California Institute of Technology. When he was called to head the work at Los Alamos, nobody doubted that the best scientist had been chosen. Surprisingly, he proved to be also a first-rate administrator and "able to explain anything to a Congressman."

No secret was ever better kept than that of Los Alamos. The schoolboys had it that they were moving out for the Ethiopian Ski Corps or the Scandinavian Camel Artillery. Santa Feans saw lights against the Jemez peaks, but knew nothing. Guesses included a submarine base, with underground channel to the Pacific, and a home for pregnant WAC's. When the Truman Committee sent a scout to Santa Fe, he was referred to the President and retired in good order. One officer who made an indiscreet remark was relieved the next morning. Only the veteran reporter, Brian Boru Dunne, dared write in the *Santa Fe New Mexican* that "buses were coming in loaded with Indians, people jabbering Spanish, and Nobel Prize winners." Robert Oppenheimer now and again rode over the divide to his cabin on the Pecos; he was attended by an armed and very saddlesore protector. And Captain William S. Parsons's sister in Albuquerque complained that his visits were spoiled by his military guard. Captain Parsons, later Rear Admiral, was the New Mexican who "armed the bomb"—gave it, just before reaching Hiroshima, the final touch to activate it.

What life on "the hill" was like has gradually come out. Only a small core of scientists knew what was going on. Others signed up for the duration-and-six-months for specific jobs as clerks, plumbers, firemen—everything required for a town of 3,500 that rapidly expanded to 7,600. The gates were not locked, and people went into Santa Fe as necessary. They accepted no social engagements, but were known in stores and restaurants. A scientist's wife said: "We must have been as marked as though we wore a scarlet A." She signed a number, not a name for her automobile license.

GI's from the entire country, offered "special assignment," volunteered in the hope of overseas pay and adventure. Arrived at Lamy, they had no idea where they were, and when they emerged from covered vans to find themselves on a New Mexico mountain most of them were indignant. Later, of course, their pride knew no bounds. A couple of soldiers stationed at Sandia Base were assigned to drive heavy trucks from Los Alamos to a place near Alamogordo. They went always at night at a fast clip, and they were supplied with passes signed by the Governor and directing state police to let them go. Such stories came out later.

At Los Alamos tension mounted steadily all through 1943, 1944, and 1945. During the spring months of 1945 it became terrific. Eddie Brooks, Fire Chief at Los Alamos, said: "You could feel the tension like a physical thing." Wives knew only that everything depended upon saying nothing and asking no questions.

In that tense mid-July, Eddie Brooks was ordered to send to Alamogordo a fire truck driven by a dependable man, ordered late at night to start at dawn. By July 15 a hundred or so men had left for Alamogordo: technicians, truckers, guards, and cooks. A full camp operation was needed at a place called "Trinity." Scientists, headed by Oppenheimer, went. Those left at Los Alamos hied themselves to lookouts on mountain peaks. Nobody knew whether the bomb would explode or not. On paper they knew, but this was to be the proof. Then, at the lowest hour before dawn, the skies were lit up by such a flare as had never been seen be-

21 *Elephant Butte Lake.*

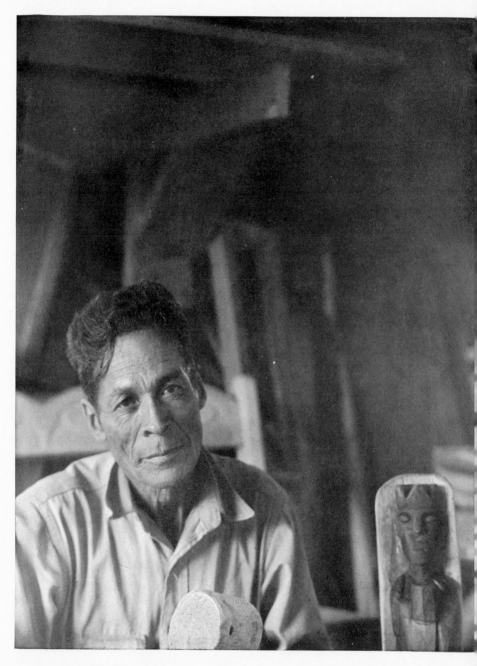

22 *Patrocino Barela of Taos; his wood sculptures have been shown widely.*

fore. It aroused people in various parts of the state. Gallup people heard an explosion, and the *Gallup Independent* queried the Commanding Officer at Alamogordo. "Yes," he replied, "there has been an explosion. Nobody hurt. Nothing serious." A blind girl in Albuquerque saw a flash of light. Ranchers near Alamogordo thought they had seen the end of the world. But curiosity soon petered out.

The scientists who came back to Los Alamos were more than ever wordless. Haggard, bewhiskered, distraught, and weary to exhaustion, they spoke only of going to the South Pacific. Some took shots and tests for the tropics. Captain Parsons made a last visit to his sister in Albuquerque.

Then came August 6, 1945—Hiroshima. Los Alamos people got the news over the public address system. "The President announces . . ." Eddie Brooks, who had gone to Denver for a few days "to get free of strain and catch up on my sleep," heard it over the radio. The atomic bomb had all but ended the war with Japan.

Los Alamos suffered the postwar slump with the rest of the country; it was a deeper slump only because it followed a tighter wind-up. GI's wanted only to get out. "Just let me out of this and I never want to see New Mexico again." Of 1,500 released from Los Alamos, 700 came back to stay.

Scientists yearned to return to their laboratories and classrooms—above all they wanted nothing to do with politics; they hoped to evade the consequences of what they had released. Eddie Brooks said: "It was hard to hold level."

In time it was decided to maintain the laboratories at Los Alamos, but to surround them with a civilian town. In 1946, the Atomic Energy Commission succeeded the Army, and a private concern, the Zia Company, built a town north of the "restricted area" in which silvery wire mesh fences in the huge silvery laboratories that reflect the sun's rays like mirrors.

The AEC's first job was to repair the havoc that the

Army had wrought by chopping down the pines that had sheltered the school's pleasant log and stone buildings, bull-dozing the land into dusty desolation, and erecting hideous barracks. The only bit of beauty left was a golf links for officers, with greens kept verdant by sprays of New Mexico's precious water. The AEC laid out pleasant streets among the trees left standing, built attractive double houses with small gardens and wide windows on magnificent views. There is a community center with stores, but only one of each category, and no liquor store. The only place to buy bottled cheer is at White Rock, a town built for construction workers, but almost empty because many workers—a mobile lot—prefer to live in trailers. Los Alamos is a model town, but far from typical. It has a higher than average IQ owing to its scientific and technical population, and a lower than average age. There are more children in primary than in high school. Theoretically self-governing, it has a city council that is often overruled by the AEC director, a civilian who has, so far, been a retired military man. It is easier to doff a uniform than a state of mind.

The citizens of Los Alamos are a high-grade cross-section of the nation. As newcomers to New Mexico they were uninformed but interested. They soon spread out among the Indians, seeing dances and buying blankets and pottery for their homes. They were cordial, if a bit curious about their Spanish-speaking associates, and notably without prejudice. When a rabbi asked the personnel officer for a list of Jews, that official knew nobody as a Jew. An announcement on the bulletin board brought together enough to found a synagogue. And when barbers refused to serve the one Negro resident, the barbers were replaced.

Los Alamos was part of Sandoval County, which had always been completely dominated by one family. When the state switched from Republican to Democratic control, the family changed, but not the method of political control. The few politically uncontrolled masters up at remote Los Alamos made no difference—even if their votes were counted. Now, with the appearance of thousands of gringo voters who would not take orders, disaster threatened. New Mexico first met the threat by denying them the vote as residents of a federal reservation and subject only to federal jurisdiction. Some Los Alamos people, quick to understand New Mexico's phobias, threatened to petition Texas for admission. But before Texas could come again, Los Alamos was made a county with land taken from Santa Fe, Rio Arriba, and Sandoval counties. The Governor appointed county commissioners, who chose a sheriff. His deputies were put into horizon-blue uniforms and set to man the gate, where every visitor must show a pass and declare his intentions, although in time the necessity of passes was dropped and people could come and go as they wished. The state legislature had only overlooked giving Los Alamos County representation in the legislature—an oversight easily rectified. Otherwise, the Civil Service Commission has ruled that AEC employees are subject to the Hatch Act and may hold state and local offices only if that does not involve becoming a candidate representing a political party. Only employees of the construction company may play the political game in the new county.

All this military and atomic development has changed New Mexico more in a decade than everything in the previous centuries changed it. Near Los Alamos workers earn such wages as New Mexicans cannot match; the domestic servant, the "chile picker," and the sheep-herder have all but disappeared. In 1950, the Albuquerque Chamber of Commerce gloated over an annual payroll of forty-two-million dollars, to say nothing of its related building boom and other money-makers. But politically these new citizens have upset all the dopesters. Intelligently interested, they join leagues and associations, invite speakers to address them, listen to campaigners, and have a disturbing tendency to cut across party lines. Altogether these new citizens will probably be bothersome to the politicians, but very salutary for the state.

Advantageous as this addition to the electorate is, destruction brought them here. So it is good to turn to another federal man, one who is not spraying our water away but conserving it; who asks no man to give up his ranch but only so to operate it that it will produce more bountifully; who demolishes no trees to make dusty towns, but who tries to preserve our forests forever. He knows that our national resources can be managed to improve forest and range while halting the hideous erosion that makes dust bowls and causes floods of incalculable cost in misery as well as money. If he has failed conspicuously in any regard it has been in making the public understand this.

As an individual, the conservationist is typical of our largest and most useful body of citizens. He makes the headlines neither for fabulous fortunes nor for hideous crimes. He just does his job, lives on a small income, educates his children as well as he can, and takes part, as does his wife, in community efforts. He appears ageless. Never very young, he grows old imperceptibly, and by then he has reached retirement age. Quiet and unemotional, he seldom spills over about his work, but he genuinely loves the good earth, and is dedicated to preserving it. Often he has chosen this work in preference to a more remunerative job; a few such men live useful lives in the Southwest who would be semi-invalids in a damp climate. These men believe in the ends they serve, beliefs more and more confirmed by experience. So they work steadily with conviction and meet their vicissitudes with humor. It takes humor to bear unfair criticism from men you are trying to serve and to make no boast when they finally adopt your recommendations as their own ideas.

The idea of conservation appeared during President Theodore Roosevelt's administration. Gifford Pinchot, son of a rich and cultivated Pennsylvanian, observed that bad lumbering practices were destroying our forests, and resolved to devote his life to saving them. He went abroad to study forestry because there was no school in this country. His friend Roosevelt, who knew and understood the West, shared his enthusiasms, and under the President's influence the Congress, in 1905, created the Forest Service as part of the Department of Agriculture. The Bureau of Reclamation had already been established, but that bureau's primary function was irrigation. The Forest Service was the first federal agency devoted to the intelligent use of land and water for the general good.

The Forest Service brought into the West a kind of man sure to infuriate the rancher. He was college-bred; Pinchot had seen to it that a school of forestry was established at Yale. Few ranchers had been to college then. Scientific in mind and training, the Forester was a conserver as opposed to the ruthless exploiter and gambler who was still the national idol. Moreover he succeeded the Land Office, whose primary purpose had been to get the public domain into private ownership, really to give the land away.

The Forest Service, with no control over private lands, wished to bring all public forest and watershed lands into the National Forests so that they could be properly managed. Its first concern was to lessen the destruction of our forests by fire, blight, or misuse. People who are old enough remember that our mountains used to smoke for weeks in the dry season: sheep-herders or woodcutters had let their campfires get out of hand. Forest Service regulation and education have reduced such carelessness, and the forest lookout's quick spotting of a fire and the Service's mobilization to fight it often save many thousands of acres a year in New Mexico.

On federal lands leased to private companies the Forest Service marks timber to be cut, saving immature trees for the future. On state lands overcutting is often permitted; there one company may grow rich while the forest deteriorates.

The Forest Service is mindful of watersheds as well as of timber stands. This accounts for the signs, so mirth-provoking to the visitor: "Entering such-and-such a forest," where not a tree is in sight. It also accounts for the Jornada Experiment Station between Las Cruces and the Organ Mountains.

These plains had suffered unduly from overgrazing. In the old days the only way a man could hold his land was by keeping it fully stocked. Too often that meant the overgrazing that so weakens plants that they cannot recover from drought. This happened in the bad drought year of 1912, when losses ran as high as fifty and sixty per cent of the herds. Cattlemen then petitioned the government for aid, and under President Taft two hundred thousand acres were withdrawn from use for study. The area is still administered by the Forest Service, but is leased to two cattlemen who must comply with government rulings. In spite of the "bureaucratic restrictions" decried by critics, it is noteworthy that there is a long list of applicants ready to take up the lease if the present lessees should ever relinquish it.

It is government policy to operate the Jornada Experiment Station so economically that any stockman could apply its methods; there is no extravagant use of government money. The range's remarkable productivity is owing, according to Fred Ares, the Range Conservationist, to simple, sensible methods. During the summer, cattle are kept on tobosa grass, which is palatable until the rains begin. This leaves the black grama to ripen slowly; it cures as it stands, is good all winter, and will produce twice as much beef as inferior grasses. Often redistribution of stock will help as much as reduction of herds. Cottonseed meal, used as supplemental feed, and salt are set far from water holes to make the cows graze widely. Altogether this station has provided the whole arid West with guidance while its lessees are producing over four hundred thousand pounds of beef a year.

An even more impressive demonstration of restoring misused land to usefulness was made by the Soil Conservation Service on the Ojo del Espiritu Santo Grant in Sandoval County. Here the infamous Rio Puerco had dug a canyon so deep that irrigation had become impossible, and farms and towns were left high and dry in dusty ruin. Rest and care are actually bringing that desolated land back into productivity as though it had really been touched by a Spring of the Holy Spirit.

The grant by that poetic name was awarded to one Cabeza de Baca in 1743. In time it became part of the vast holdings of Don José Leandro Perea of Bernalillo, who ran eighty thousand sheep there, to its destruction. Finally the grant came, as a contingent fee, into the possession of Thomas Benton Catron, archetype of the clever lawyer who dealt in land and politics. He served as United States senator and died land-poor. Catron, like Perea, permitted the abuse that made the area a perfect field for a before-and-after demonstration. This became possible in 1935, when the government bought several land grants both to save land and to help small ranchers and farmers. The Ojo del Espiritu Santo Grant, enlarged to 124,000 acres, posed the most difficult problem. Only men confident of their methods would have tackled it. But Hugh Calkins and Eastburn Smith of the Soil Erosion Service, later the Soil Conservation Service, jumped at the chance. One said: "There was no book to throw at them, so we just tried out all our ideas." Most of them worked.

If the methods were untried the men were not; they knew soils and grasses and were experienced with this type of land. Luck played a part: the project was given two hundred CCC workers for two years. Rehabilitation of youth was to go along with rebuilding land. What was done there for both men and land makes one believe in universal training of youth to conserve, not to kill. (Although in the stern days of 1942 good soldiers came out of the CCC.) In 1935 drastic measures were indicated. The entire grant was heavily overgrazed. One Wyoming outfit was running thirteen thousand head; the Forest Service had set four thousand as the outside limit for safety. And the range was overrun by stock trespassing without payment.

Drive over the grant now with federal men. Roads are what they take off from; the truck, under a strong twist on the wheel, leaps the bank and goes bounding off from hillock to hillock as the men point out salient features. Often the whole party is ordered out to observe on hands and knees just how bad grasses are yielding to good. On parts of this range even poor grasses are a step in the right direction. Eastburn Smith said: "When we took over the grass wouldn't hide a prairie dog." Now there are no prairie dogs, but there is grass.

Ring grass is just better than no grass at all. As feed it is of no value, but any growth tends to nail down soil in which better grass can grow. Salt sacaton and snake weed come next; still poor, they make way for various gramas, wheat grass or blue stem, the best for stock, and even wild rice, which the Indians are glad to see come back. Happily nature, given a chance, moves from bad to better to good. Grazing was cut to a minimum; only a few permits were issued to Jemez and Zia Indians and some Spanish ranchers who had long depended on this range. Trespass stock was got rid of. Then more positive measures were undertaken.

Land had suffered deeply from flash floods; once started, arroyos grow at both ends at an alarming rate. So trenches were dug across any cut where it began, and check dams were built to spread the water before it had force enough to slash the land. All this was done economically, using only native materials, and to prove what could be done anywhere, given knowledge and labor. Borrow pits were seeded with fifteen or sixteen types of good grasses. Many of them took hold; one can see how a gash in land heals like a wound in flesh.

So much is routine and can be done wherever land has not yet been reduced to desert sands. But more could be done with CCC labor. A pipeline from the mountains filled a large pool for watering stock, and there the boys planted trees. The gray-green of Russian olive and the willow's reddish wands are massed against verdant cottonwood; and the water reflects reeds and rushes besides offering bass, blue gill, and sun perch. On the hills, cottonwoods and Chinese elms were planted, but without much hope. There they stand, however, looking incongruous, but giving full-leaved shade. Maybe the whole Southwest could be so shaded.

This project has attracted students from foreign countries in which mismanagement has reduced the good valleys of antiquity to present deserts. Few parts of the United States have gone so far; there is still time for intelligent men to save their own lands. To this end the Soil Conservation Service has worked out a democratic procedure.

Under state laws—New Mexico's dates from 1937— twenty-five landowners in any given area may petition the state for permission to organize a Soil Conservation District. Two thirds of their number may complete the organization, whose purpose is to "nail down rainfall," halt erosion, and improve and conserve both range and farm. District members go in for spreader dams and diversion of arroyos. They practice crop rotation, terracing and contour plowing, and the fall plowing called chiseling, which leaves clods too heavy to blow away as dust. Such a program depends upon the intelligent co-operation of every farmer; no one's land is safe unless his neighbor's is. "How much does it blow?"

is the question nowadays. The farmer who lets his land blow away rates rather like the old horse-thief.

The Service is often active at the start, and it always stands ready with technical advice. At the beginning the SCS lent the Districts such equipment as bulldozers and trucks and land planes. The District charged its members for the maintenance and operation. As that equipment has worn out, the Districts have bought their own.

New Mexico is well organized; all sorts of landowners are active, though most members are small operators. Some wealthy ranchers held back, even opposed the organization, but in time most of them have joined their District.

In the lower Pecos valley cotton farmers were the leaders. On the Ruidoso, Pete Hurd, who farms and raises quarter horses when he is not painting, took time out to organize his neighborhood. His small ranch is a model. Grama grass is coming back on the hills, his polo ponies graze in the apple orchard, and when a devastating hailstorm made the arroyo rage madly, his dams protected his home. Pete had had his artist and writer friends digging there for years.

In the Cuba area John Young, a Republican scornful of anything New Dealish, was convinced and took the lead even against prominent landowners. He tells a couple of stories.

As the District's treasurer he is responsible for advancing credit for equipment. He tells of one farmer who needed help to build stock tanks; his debt was one thousand dollars. His land and stock were then valued at under four thousand dollars. Two years after his tanks were in operation he refused ten thousand dollars for his land.

Jacobo Herrera, a small operator, needed a dirt storage tank. He requested a bulldozer; the cost would be $350. Jacobo had only fifty dollars; he offered his note for three hundred dollars, agreeing to pay off in a year. John Young, always cagey, was dubious. "If you pay out in five years you'll be doing well. Don't promise more than you can do. How do I know you won't quit and go to work for the lumber company?" But he knew his man; this was pure front. Jacobo paid off his loan not in five years or even in one, but within three months, when he had sold his first crop of one hundred sacks of wheat.

This is democracy at its intelligent best. This is the federal man serving as technical adviser, at hand when called upon, never intrusive, never autocratic. Observing the conservationist at work, it is hard to understand the rancor that some ranchers register against him. Many complaints—especially those of autocratic behavior—boil down to an elderly stockman's dislike of some individual youngster "all full of theories"; often the trouble is caused by the enthusiast's wrong approach. The most diplomatic federal men have learned never to mention how many head of stock are on the range, but only to say how more beef can be produced.

A complaint that concerns the average citizen is that our many conservation services are divided between the Departments of Interior and of Agriculture, and this makes for bad feeling among them, especially in Washington, where endless rows are the rule. The Hoover Commission of 1948 recommended a reorganization to bring all agencies for the administration of public lands under one head. This could be a great money-saver as well as a breeder of harmony.

One consolidation has paid off brilliantly. The General Land Office and the Grazing Service have been united as the Bureau of Land Management, which administers about one fifth of New Mexico's land area, some fourteen million acres. This bureau has the distinction of being the only government agency that takes in more than it spends. In New

Mexico it realizes some six million dollars annually from oil and gas leases and grazing fees. Perhaps this portends the ideal solution of the problem of the federal man, that he should so educate the public to sound conservation that his job will consist only of leasing the public lands at a good fee.

XXIV

WATER

WATER is what New Mexico never has enough of—except where and when it has too much. It is drought or gully-washer. Rainfall is called "spotty": a feeble word for a range of from fifty to two hundred per cent of normal. The state's average of only fifteen inches annually is not enough to raise crops, though it serves to maintain gazing for a limited number of livestock. How to stretch this sparse supply enough to permit farming has been the preoccupation of New Mexico's peoples since records began. How they succeeded or failed is our history.

Indians lived where there was water, they danced their prayers for plenty of it, they moved when the supply failed. All this they still do.

The Spanish, knowing similar semi-arid lands, settled along the streams, plotted ditches, based their laws on the distribution of water and the sensible use of land. They, too, prayed when water failed, carrying their holy images out into thirsty fields to invoke saintly aid. They, too, still do this.

These peoples worked with nature, using carefully what God vouchsafed, certain that only supernatural powers could increase the amount. It took the gringo, traditional nonconformist, without the humility of acceptance, to try to dominate nature and produce water where there was none.

New Mexico's last hundred years have been largely a struggle to turn its range land into farms. Advertisers encourage immigration by promising irrigated farms, even while water tables sink and towns go dry every summer. The simple proposition that the population already here—or here several years ago—would be infinitely better off if no newcomers arrived is rank heresy, and its promulgator will doubtless be tried for subversive ideas.

The Spanish had dug wells for home use, but it was the United States government that offered a bonus for water in the midst of the Jornada del Muerto. A man named Martin accepted the challenge. But after months of digging, his last spadeful of sand was as dry as the first. Then one morning his eyes were dazzled by a silver flash at the bottom of his well. A living spring was there; it has flowed ever since.

Wells now became commonplace, and with the arrival of the windmill salesman in the seventies water was produced by New Mexico's one unfailing resource. Whatever may be exhausted—minerals, water, oil, sound sense, or good men—there is no indication that wind will ever fail us. So windmills came to spin mistily atop their long-legged towers and to fill the tanks where cattle drink. The windmill was only the first machine. The battle was now joined. The gringo, with all his ingenuity, defied nature's implacable, imminent resistance. Up to the mid-twentieth century odds seem about even. Nature has upset every one of man's efforts; man has thought up a new attack every time. There are battles in every drainage basin, but the war began in the Pecos.

The Pecos, rising up under the Truchas Peaks east of Santa Fe, cold as ice and clear as air, gathers itself together in a boggy place where mariposa lilies, lady's-slippers, and columbine abound, and dashes off down the canyon as a sparkling stream. The upper Pecos canyon is the perfect recreation area. Tall pines and blue spruce rise with the slopes, and alders and willows shade pools where rainbow and mountain trout defy the fisherman. Deer and even elk peer through aspen thickets, and a clumsy bear may waddle slowly up from the Forest Service road. The Pecos gains other streams good also for fishing and mountain cabins, and emerges from its canyon near ancient Cicuyé.

The Gallinas, rising on the other side of the divide, separates Old and New Las Vegas and carries its silt into the Pecos, which goes on past the old stage stops. Tecolotito is strung along the river in bright green fields separated by red sandstone houses with fresh white trim—homes commodious enough for comfortable, partriarchal living. Many old families have lost their lands or prefer life in town. The mill site is marked only by a ruined storehouse and the canal, where the wheel swished dripping to grind the wheat. At Anton Chico many old houses are empty, but one store still serves a large area mostly settled by newcomers.

Up to this point the river has proved amenable. But where country flattens out and is treeless, the Pecos seems to lose heart. Near Las Colonias, where Coronado is reputed to have forded the Pecos, the stream ducks underground. But within ten miles it bobs up again in a series of brackish springs and goes on past Santa Rosa, the largest town in Guadalupe County, which depends on cattle and the railroad to keep it busy. Puerto de Luna, said to have been called "Gate of the Moon" by Coronado's men, seems sleepily ancient in spite of a filling station and a modern school. The Pecos is slow-moving here, probably flowing more underground than above. Near Santa Rosa the Blue Hole flashes color back to the sky, but has never revealed its depth; and ranchers report stumbling on bottomless wells harboring queer antediluvian reptiles.

Below Santa Rosa the Pecos flows gently down its wide valley. It knew the cattle drives; its first towns were cow towns. But the Pecos, famous for having "no law west of," resents man's control and has found devious ways to give him his come-uppance.

The first effort to bridle the Pecos came about because Pat Garrett, between his killing of Billy the Kid in 1881 and his second notable role in the Fountain case in 1895, found his farm too high above the Hondo for irrigating. But Berrendo Creek might, he thought, be flumed across the Hondo. Then why not dam them both and irrigate many acres even as far away as Roswell? Capital would be needed, but capital was within the imagination and reach of Charles Eddy, cattleman turning capitalist. So the new pattern emerged. Big irrigation projects, financed by "foreign" capital, began to turn grazing lands into farms.

The Pecos Irrigation and Investment Company, founded by Eddy, but taken over by James John Hagerman in 1889, began to irrigate old John Chisum's range. Eddy and Hagerman were to fall out, but before they did they had built five canals and three dams on the Pecos, had tempted a railroad to build into the valley in 1890, and had seen a rush of settlers under the Homestead and Desert Entry acts of Congress.

The panic of 1893 almost wiped out the small farmers, who were saved when Hagerman dug deep into his own reserves. But the flood of 1904 wrought havoc that even his devoted faith could not surmount. The company then petitioned the government for help, and President Theodore Roosevelt, under the Reclamation Act of 1902, took over. The gringo had now enlisted his best ally against nature, government funds.

Meanwhile the Pecos valley had been granted a lavish gift of the gods. In 1891 Nathan Jaffa, digging a well, was rewarded with a rush of artesian water. For eons of time water seeping down from the Sacramentos and the caprock had sunk into the porous limestone below the topsoil. Uncapped now, it gushed up through artesian wells in seemingly exhaustless supply. Used first to beautify lawns and gardens, it was inevitably turned into irrigation ditches. Six-inch pipes poured out from 500 to 1,500 gallons per minute. Hagerman planted 600 acres in an apple orchard and by 1905, 485 wells irrigating apple trees had turned the valley into a fairylike scene scented by blossoms in spring and ripe apples in fall.

One W. T. Hamilton of Ohio offered farms on Berrendo Creek with the promise that a forty-acre orchard would be worth at least forty-thousand dollars in six years. He advertised apple country better than anything in Oregon because New Mexico was two thousand miles nearer eastern markets and its shorter haul would be an easy downhill slide with no Rockies to cross. The soil was touted as richer than that of the Nile delta. A wide range of fruit crops was as sure as sun-up. Special trains from Chicago and Ohio cities brought hordes of eager buyers. Dr. George W. Crile came —only one of many physicians and surgeons; also listed were dentists, merchants, teachers, farmers, and capitalists. Capitalists were going to be needed.

Five out of the first six Februaries produced balmy days, and streams running full of melting mountain snows brought out the blossoms in fragrant clouds of pink-touched white. But in New Mexico it often happens that if spring comes winter is not far behind. In the sixth year came frost to turn the delicate blossoms black and ugly. Even smudge-pots could not save the trees often enough to make apples a paying crop. By 1920 apple trees past maturity were being cut out and replaced by cotton.

Meanwhile nature had been quietly demonstrating that when you use up water stored through millennia there isn't any more. In 1915 the artesian wells began to dry up; by 1925 the area of flowing wells had shrunk from 663 square miles to 425. Farms were sold for seventy-five dollars with all improvements, or offered for sale with no takers. The artesian boom had burst.

Irrigation remains New Mexico's main dependence. The dams grow larger and more complicated as misuse of land and the vagaries of the rivers produce new evils that necessitate new measures of control. It was soon apparent that larger, stouter dams could do more than divert water into irrigation ditches; they could also impound run-off water for later beneficial use. This is the water that comes in summer cloudbursts to tear loose and sweep away the earth in dense brown rivulets and swirl them into arroyos that block the highways: flash floods, gone in a few hours. But soil is gone too, fields have been inundated and houses washed away, and wealth incalculable has been dumped into the river. What could be sounder practice than to catch the run-off behind dams and release it as needed?

The first big project was an effort to tame the Rio Grande. A dam at the Elephant Butte, near the Valverde Ford, was the dream of a couple of Las Cruces lawyers, who saw that the new Bureau of Reclamation might make the Mesilla valley more fabulously productive than the Pecos. By 1914 the Bureau had finished its most ambitious project up to that time: a cement dam 235 feet high had made a lake 40 miles long and 3 miles wide at its greatest extension; it would hold enough water to irrigate 145 miles of river bottom in New Mexico, Texas, and Mexico. This meant 363 miles of canals to be maintained by tax assessments against the irrigated acreage. All seemed well. Land prices rose, settlers swarmed, experienced farmers began leveling the old hummocky fields with machines; land that had become overgrown with useless salt grass was reclaimed.

Then the river took measures. Underground seepage may have been foreseen by the Reclamation engineers, but they had not provided for it. Drainage ditches were required; this meant additional mortgaging. Some small farmers not apt at learning new ways sold out. But there were few foreclosures, largely because the Federal Land Banks, established in 1916, stabilized the district. Loans were made on land, not on perishable livestock, and each borrower was required to take five per cent of his loan in bank stock. So the farmer came out owning not only his land but his stock in the bank. Most farmers were able to repay their original loans within a few years.

This development has been a success. Protected from the east winds by the rugged blue spires of the Organ Mountains, the irrigated fields make a bright green strip two miles wide along a river now well disciplined. One hundred and twenty-six miles of dikes, built by the International Boundary and Water Commission, allow a bit of meandering, but no destructive outbreak. In normal times the channel between dikes makes a pretty green pasture; in flash floods the dikes hold. The river itself is about 150 feet wide and 2 feet deep.

The largest crop is cotton, which has produced its inevitable by-product, migrant labor. Mesilla valley farmers employ Mexican nationals brought in by the U.S. Farm Bureau under contract with the Mexican government and leased to farmers. This arrangement is criticized by labor unions, but it suits both the farmers, who get labor when they want it, and the Mexicans, who work a few months and then go home with fat wages, hoping to return another year.

The Mesilla valley's early fame for the production of fine wines and brandies remains one of New Mexico's unrealized dreams. Pass wine and Pass brandy appear only in old books, and the priest who delighted Europeans with the product of his winery at Mesilla has no successors. Grapes are raised only for local use, though their flavor is exquisite. Cantaloupes, ripening later than the Arizona crop and that of Colorado, have been abandoned because of shipping and marketing uncertainties. But experiments continue. D. F. Stahmann, a Minnesotan, has put in three thousand acres of pecan trees and a plant for shelling nuts on the place. When the trees are small he raises alfalfa as a "downstairs crop" under the trees of his orchard. He gins his own cotton and runs some 1,300 sheep on his foothills. In 1949 he employed 280 Mexican laborers, housed well near a civic center with store, barbershop, and offices. For his family Mr. Stahmann has built a thirty-thousand-dollar home decorated by a Mexican artist. His neighbor Apodaca has an equally work-manlike establishment that centers in a stately mansion in-herited from his uncle, a priest. According to the law, lands held under Reclamation projects are limited to 160 acres. But many large holdings were bought before the project began.

So the Rio Grande in southern New Mexico serves man well. But above Elephant Butte Dam it remains the Rio Bravo. The middle valley, centering in Albuquerque, is perennially petitioning Congress for funds to save it from the river. In seventy-five years sixteen floods have ruined farms, demolished villages, and threatened Albuquerque, which still faces a possible major catastrophe whenever the river rises a few inches. This condition was long in the mak-ing. Irrigation had waterlogged the land, and silting had aggraded the river bed until it was four feet higher than the town's busiest corner; and the valley had become a long narrow marsh where cat-tails grew, mosquitoes bred in swarms, and migrating water-fowl fed well. People were losing their farms and might lose their town. More than irrigation, the middle valley needed drainage and flood control.

Public-spirited men, failing to enlist the Bureau of Rec-lamation, finally incorporated under the state laws as the Middle Rio Grande Conservancy District, and set out to sell bonds. By the time their surveys were completed in 1929 they faced a depressed bond market. But the river, the ruthless, implacable river, kept right on increasing its threat. The bonds were sold, valley folk were assessed, many small owners were forced out, and politicians made capital out of big owners selling small ones down the river. But the valley was drained.

Three hundred and sixty-three miles of canals, at a cost of ten million dollars, saved 120,000 acres for farming. The original planners, alive to the danger of silting, had included a dam up on the Chama, whose muddy flood first chokes the clear Rio Grande near Española. El Vado Dam makes a lake that is kept stocked for fishing and releases water for irrigation as needed. But the river at Albuquerque continues to build up its silty bed; no company will insure Albuquerque property against flood damage.

New Mexico's third major dam is on the South Canadian, a stream that rises in the Sangre de Cristos above Raton, picks up the Mora near Las Vegas, and flows east. Approaching the plains, the South Canadian has dug deep canyons between colored mesas looking like aspiring mountains that have been sliced off. Here cattle slither down to water as did the thirsty animals on the shorter Santa Fe Trail. Always a silt-bearer, the river grew unruly in the Texas Panhandle, where farms were in constant danger of flash floods. Texas, which had done very well in the Rio Grande Compact, hoped for a generous share of the Canadian's waters. New Mexico's Senator Dennis Chavez held out until he got what he called "the first compact which fully protects New Mexico's present and future on an interstate stream."

Primarily for flood control, the Conchas Dam project was extended to water some forty-two thousand acres whose owners obligated themselves to repay the cost of some sixteen million dollars over a period of forty years. Holdings were limited to 16 acres, and except for some large family farms, most of the land still belongs to modest farmers who raise forage crops, small grains, cotton, and sugar beets.

Dams reduce flood danger and hold water for irrigation. Their evil is that they also hold silt, which masses up behind the dam to its ultimate ruination. Elephant Butte Dam still holds enough water to irrigate the district through three years of drought, but if sedimentation continues it may not do so much longer. Less ambitious projects are less subject to silt danger. A diversion dam on the Pecos River above Fort Sumner turns six thousand acres of open range into farms of alfalfa, sweet potatoes, fruits, and melons. Several dams below the Elephant Butte bring under cultivation thousands of acres in New Mexico, Texas, and Chihuahua. There are, besides, many small dams utilizing waters that would otherwise be a menace or a waste.

Waste of our scanty supply of water is overwhelming. More than ninety per cent is lost through evaporation and transpiration. In the *bosques* above Elephant Butte Dam useless salt grass, willows, cottonwoods, and tamarisks evaporate enough water—so an engineer computed—to supply ten cities the size of Albuquerque, its size at latest quotation. Careless farmers further reduce our precious life-stream by allowing their ditches to leak over the roads; Albuquerque, faced with a water shortage every summer, squanders its water by letting its park sprays turn hilly streets into streams.

New Mexico's only substantial source of additional water is in its least known river, the San Juan, which embraces nearly ten thousand square miles of New Mexico before it sweeps on toward the west. In San Juan County industrious Mormons have built small community canals that bring some thirty thousand acres under cultivation. Farmington, Fruitland, Bloomfield, Water Flow, and Flora Vista are trade centers for farmers raising small grains, forage crops, and orchards too far north to blossom unseasonably. Navajos have used the San Juan too, but not up to capacity, and their badly eroded reservation dumps into the river much of the silt that is rapidly filling up Lake Mead above Hoover Dam. New Mexico's San Juan thus becomes a menace to Los Angeles.

The San Juan brought New Mexico into the long and acrimonious dispute over the waters of the vast Colorado River drainage which affects seven of the United States and two states in Mexico. While Arizona and California continue to bicker, New Mexico has accepted as her share 11.25 per cent of the water originating above Lee's Ferry; the rest must be allowed to go on to the other states. But New Mexico still has to agree on the best use to make of its share.

According to Spanish law and usage, water belongs to him who puts it to beneficial use; first user in time is first in right. The United States made this sensible ruling the law throughout the West. New Mexico, then, must find ways to put the San Juan to beneficial use or eventually see some other state get its water. This affects the residents of San Juan County (including the Navajo Indians) immediately, and other citizens of the state more remotely.

The Indian Service, trying to help seventy thousand Navajos to make a decent living, hopes to increase their irrigated lands. Dams on the San Juan at Fruitland and Hog Back irrigate some ten thousand acres on the reservation. Others proposed at Shiprock and Monument Rocks might add seventy thousand and from thirty to forty thousand acres respectively. White citizens in San Juan County believe their arable lands might be increased also.

Eager go-getters in other parts of the state are convinced that New Mexico's share of the San Juan is some three hundred thousand acre feet a year more than can be put to economical use on the San Juan. They propose to dam that river high up in Colorado, where it is a swift mountain stream, and so divert its waters through tunnels, canals, and a series of reservoirs into the Chama River above El Vado Dam. The cost is estimated at 250 million dollars. These waterworks could irrigate some one hundred thousand additional acres in the Rio Grande drainage, develop hydroelectric power, and help scour sediment out of the stream beds. All this might save Albuquerque from the catastrophic flood that is admittedly inevitable unless presently worsening conditions are corrected.

Saving Albuquerque has become a matter of national importance since the Air Force and the Atomic Energy Commission have found it an advantageous site for vast undertakings. In 1950 the Army Corps of Engineers inaugurated the Jemez Canyon Dam to check the silt brought in by the Jemez's frequent flash floods. An earth dam, protected from upstream pressure by a stone riprap, will slow down the flow and hold the sediment. Cleared water will then be released into the Rio Grande in amounts that will not cause damage. Army engineers propose a similar settling basin on the Chama and a dredging of the Rio Grande for twenty miles above Elephant Butte. All this should straighten the main channel and help the stream to cleanse itself.

Thus engineers think of controlling an entire river system in order to save the valley. They hope they have provided for most likely disasters, but they readily admit that complete success will depend upon arresting the destruction of the upper watershed, which has steadily increased ever since man-made erosion began to upset nature's balance. "Engineers," said one of them, "can only hope to buy time by setting up a framework for future and long-range plans. And that depends finally upon what the people will do."

What the people should do is to halt erosion where it would be easiest to control, on the upper levels—a solution that the American mind shies away from. Popular discussions of reclamation and flood control picture the lake above the dam where resort owners can advertise water sports. But public interest is best caught by plans for more and larger dams, involving federal funds, fat contracts, and large payrolls. The gringo is still trying to outwit nature with ever more ingenuity and concrete, or to bypass nature's processes by pretending that they do not exist.

It is easiest to disregard nature when unseen water is in question. Pump irrigation has pointed up the struggle between advocates of conservation of natural resources for a distant future and of unthinking people who would heedlessly exhaust them to satisfy present greed. Grandsons of men whose windmills watered a few head of stock observed that motor pumps would bring up water in artesianlike flow. Why not tap "underground lakes and streams" and go into farming? The answer is that subterranean water does not always stand in vast pools or flow in dark rivers; it often inches slowly along through beds of gravel; ultimately it depends upon rainfall for renewal. And New Mexico's rainfall still averages only fifteen inches annually. Water, even hidden water, is not an inexhaustible resource. Engineers not hired by exploiting companies or chambers of commerce agree on this, and their judgment is confirmed by what has happened and is happening daily.

The lower Pecos valley first exhausted its surface water; then by reckless use of its artesian waters dried up that resource. The water level has dropped thirty-two feet in twenty-five years. In places it actually dropped two hundred feet. Farmers then turned to pump irrigation; turbine pumps could reach deeper sources of water, and in the 1920's dessicated artesian wells were brought back.

Always in New Mexico's lush times there have been voices crying of the wilderness to come. So as Pecos valley farmers set about pumping up another debacle for themselves, some far-sighted men warned that pumping the deep water would surely deplete the supply faster than rainfall could replace it, especially as erosion on the slopes of the

Sacramentos was upsetting nature's method of holding water for slow seepage.

Through the efforts of such men the New Mexico legislature passed a law to control ground water as surface water had long been controlled—by allocating it on the basis of what a certain basin can produce. This, the first ground water code in the nation, has become the model. It had to be tested in the courts because of the claim that a landowner owned "all above and below the surface" of his property. In 1930 the State Supreme Court ruled that underground waters are public waters and that later comers who infringe on former rights err just as though they emptied a ditch without regard to downstream neighbors.

Authority was vested in the state, but the law provides for the organization of water-users to work with the State Engineer. The Pecos valley farmers, having known a couple of scares, have organized successfully and formed a salutary public opinion. No man there could look his neighbor in the eye if his misuse of water were endangering the general supply.

Lands more lately irrigated still produce water-users who believe in inexhaustible supplies. The town of Portales was named for a porchlike rock that overhung a wide, clear spring known to cattle-drivers as a permanent watering place. It is dry now. But, owing partly to rural electrification, seven hundred pumps in Roosevelt County irrigate some thirty thousand acres that produce peanuts and sweet potatoes and sustain enough milch cows and chickens to make the county the state's leader in dairy produce. Portales citizens insist that their falling water table will surely come back: "Just give it time!" They blandly disregard the fact that Roosevelt County pump farmers are refused loans by the Federal Reserve Bank, which evidently does not agree that the falling water table will rise again.

Luna County, where judicious use of the underground

Mimbres River has turned the sandiest stretches of old Doña Ana County into profitable farms, has increased its irrigated area from thirteen to twenty thousand acres without danger to its water table. The Estancia valley's pale chiaroscuro plain is delighting former dry farmers with fields of wheat irrigated by pump. This, too, promises to be a sound development. These water tables are closely watched by the State Engineer and the U.S. Geological Survey.

Lea County, latest to develop, is New Mexico's richest county, with good grazing and plenty of oil at Hobbs. But war prices, sustained by government subsidy, tempted ranchers to go in for agriculture too, and during the war controls were lax. So hundreds of pumps are sucking out waters stored in Pleistocene times in the vast gravelly saucer of the High Plains. During the ages the Pecos and the Canadian, digging their canyons, have cut off the plains from the slope of the Rockies, and their only source of water now is the clouds. Rainfall is woefully inadequate to maintain the water level, which engineers say is fast sinking below the economic pumping level.

At Los Alamos, New Mexico's newest and most scientific citizens at first showed an amazing innocence of where water comes from. That atomic city certainly needed drinking- and bathing-water; it also demanded lawns and gardens, an eighteen-hole golf course, and swimming pools. As it grew larger, its engineers soon were depleting the Pajarito Plateau's surface water. It was once proposed to pipe water through the range from the Valle Grande. The director said: "There we won't be taking water from anybody." Nobody, older New Mexicans knew, except all the prior users of the western Jemez watershed, including four pueblos. The newest had met the oldest New Mexicans. So Los Alamos settled for pumps that bring water from depths as great as two thousand feet on the Rio Grande side. AEC engineers boast that they have got a permanent supply;

other engineers are not so sure. But all seems to go well, and Los Alamos is purifying its sewage water to sprinkle its golf course.

The battle for the waters never ends. Conservationists would appraise our resources and build on them. No more unpopular program could be devised. The "practical man" vastly prefers big doings, and in his dreaming nothing is too fantastic. A Lea County farmer, warned that he was pumping the High Plains dry, said: "Well when we've used it up, we'll go back to pumping stock water and raise cattle again." A Roosevelt County businessman says: "Oh, yes, we'll pump the land dry, but by that time they'll invent something to produce synthetic water." A rancher, sensible and successful, has a dreamy young scientist working on producing water from rocks, not like Moses, but like a chemist—by reducing rocks to their component parts and recombining said parts into H_2O.

Then came rainmaking. Professional rainmakers promised to produce rain by seeding the clouds, and ranchers organized to hire them. Rain fell, though not always in sufficient quantities or where it was wanted. In 1950 a flood on the Ruidoso may have been caused by rainmaking at Socorro, and a drought on the Rio Grande may have been caused by emptying the clouds over Colorado. When the Mesilla valley farmers ordered snow to fill Elephant Butte Lake, farmers in the middle valley protested that a double dose of snow—if nature should contribute her quota later—might well wash out Albuquerque. Navajos, urged to contribute to rainmaking in their district, suggested that their rain be tinted pink so they could be sure the white man was not getting all the benefit. Possibilities of litigation seemed endless. Senator Clinton P. Anderson introduced a bill in Congress to establish federal control of rainmaking. Meanwhile scientists who are conducting basic research into the matter are reserved in their claims.

Dr. E. J. Workman, president of New Mexico's School of Mines and one of the inaugurators of sound study and controlled experimentation, makes few claims. "It may prove possible to supply some of the missing ingredients necessary for rain and snow making, but one cannot get water out of the air unless the air contains water at near-saturation conditions." New Mexico's old bugaboo arises in a new form. You cannot get water unless there is water. Dr. Workman explains that even when there is water in the upper air most of it may evaporate as it falls through dry air near the surface. Every native recalls magnificent thunderstorms seen in the upper atmosphere which seemed to be caught by lower layers of clouds without letting one raindrop reach the ground. Dr. Workman concludes with the old unpopular warning: "If we expect to maintain a normal increase in the standards of people already here, we shall have to get more water or conserve our water better." New Mexico remains an arid state, above as well as below. And the ingenious gringo has not yet devised a more certain method of bringing water either from the earth or the clouds than the tried ways of the Indian dance and the Catholic procession.

꧁ ꧂

XXV

ARTIST DISCOVERERS

Of all New Mexico's discoverers the men and women of artistic perception have found the treasure most enriching to the life and spirit of the state. Being sensitive and observant people, these newcomers saw beauty in landscape that had often seemed repellent. Because they knew other cultures, they realized what a storehouse of primitive arts they had come upon. By their work they spread the news far and wide and gradually even taught New Mexicans to value what they had. This revelation came not only from painters, but also from students of the ancient peoples and their arts, and from collectors who saved many examples of the best work for the inspiration of later workers.

The first students were archæologists such as Adolph Bandelier, ethnologists such as Washington Matthews. The first propagandist to trumpet the news abroad was Charles F. Lummis. A few people had valued and collected the fine old things before the artists' arrival. Governor and Mrs. Prince had filled their home on Santa Fe's Sena Plaza with excellent blankets, baskets, and pottery. Mrs. Mary Lester Field of Albuquerque had collected embroideries and *santos*, as well as silver. James Seligman's collection finally so overflowed his house that he set up a notable shop near the Cathedral in Santa Fe. There were others, but these writers and collectors merely heralded a spring they did not make. The freshet began when painters discovered the new landscape and began to record it.

In 1897 Ernest L. Blumenschein was commissioned by

McClure's Magazine to illustrate a story about Indians. A Santa Fe ticket agent, asked where to find Indians, advised Fort Wingate. So "Blumie," whose story called for Papagos, was set down in the middle of the Navajo country in a blinding snowstorm. By good luck an Army wagon gave him a lift to the fort several miles away, and the violin he always carried made him friends. In time he learned that his Indians were hundreds of miles farther on, and he went to Phoenix. But "Blumie's" nostrils had caught the whiff of New Mexico, and the next summer he was back with his friend Bert Phillips. From Denver they drove to Taos on their way to Mexico. One sight of that pueblo's terraced mass and sheeted Indians was enough: the Taos art colony was born.

Its development was to be along highly individualistic lines. As it was almost inaccessible over difficult mountain roads or the narrow-guage Denver and Rio Grande Western Railroad (known as Dangerous and Rapidly Growing Worse), and with no comforts whatever, only an intrepid seeker would reach it and stay on. Yet Taos was to put New Mexico on the country's art map and give it such advertising as could not possibly be bought.

In 1914 six men organized the Taos Society of Artists and offered anybody anywhere group exhibitions at no charge except transportation and insurance. At a time when there were practically no art galleries west of the Mississippi, and nobody in the art world had heard of New Mexico, these men sent forth pictures that immediately attracted wide attention. Blumenschein, Walter Ufer, and Victor Higgins won coveted prizes, and their work was bought by the best galleries. They had even booked shows for Honolulu and Shanghai, but the United States's entry into World War I caused them to be canceled.

No show was now complete without an Indian in a white sheet reflecting the fire's glow or the flicker of sunlight through yellow aspens. Every artist was overwhelmed by the glory of the clear light, the magnificence of mountains, the paintability of strong Indian faces. Such things became the hallmark of New Mexico's school, if it could be called a school; the similarity was always in subject matter, never in method. Each painter used the technique he had learned in eastern or European schools, but the best of them soon outgrew the obviously picturesque and discovered subtler beauties. Blumenschein, Higgins, and Ufer turned to experiments with light on mountains and clouds. Kenneth Adams lovingly depicted the wisdom of wrinkled old women in both paintings and lithographs, and found truth in the Indian's frank approach to our angular landscape. Oscar Berninghaus and Ward Lockwood caught humor as well as beauty in Indian and Spanish life. More cautious painters continue to produce the ever salable yellow aspens, posed Indians, and chile strings against adobe walls.

Taste for these themes was trained by the Santa Fe Railroad, whose publicity man, William Haskell Simpson, was a poet who loved pictures, but who had an eye for business. Why not use paintings to advertise the country and attract tourists? Artists were given passes to come west and paint; their pictures were bought and hung in ticket offices; every year's Santa Fe calendar carried a Taos painting by Irving Couse. The Santa Fe's affiliated Harvey System was developing the taste for good crafts. Business had discovered New Mexico.

Santa Fe's art colony was of later growth and broader base. From the beginning it was linked with archæology. Edgar L. Hewitt's work at Puyé and at the Rito de los Frijoles had led the Archæological Institute of America to establish its first school in this hemisphere: the School of American Research in Santa Fe. Dr. Hewitt was blessed with the support of Frank Springer of Cimarron, an Iowa lawyer who had made a fortune on the Maxwell Land

23 *La Madera ski run near Albuquerque.*

24 *Mountain trails are endless.*

CAPLIN AND
THOMPSON, OLD
ALBUQUERQUE

Grant, and who was politically powerful. In 1907 the territorial legislature established the Museum of New Mexico in the Palace of the Governors. Ten years later the state built the Art Museum, modeled on old mission churches, and Mr. Springer engaged Donald Beauregard to decorate its St. Francis Auditorium with paintings of the work of the Franciscans from Yucatan to New Mexico. Other artists followed when war in Europe forced them to desert the Left Bank and seek quaintness nearer home. Santa Fe thought itself ready to lead the world in both art and archæology.

The old capital now became infused with a new and heady spirit. A new world had been discovered, a ferment was in the air. Everybody was young, eager to learn, ready to try anything. Seeing an Indian dance was not a matter of a couple of pleasant afternoon hours. Devotees like Witter Bynner stayed in a pueblo for days to witness the preliminary rites. He entertained Indian friends in his adobe house, where he had mingled Chinese and Indian art; he made of himself a walking showcase of Navajo jewelry; he reproduced Indian cadences in his poetry. Alice Corbin Henderson, from her bed at Sunmount Sanatorium, inspired younger poets and tuned her own delicate ear to the rhythms of old *alabados* and *corridos*. Jane Henderson, before she married Gus Baumann, lived for months in Santa Clara learning to sing in true Indian style.

These people were seeing what most New Mexicans had never seen before—the true art of Indian handiwork, the pageantry of Indian dances, the dignity and suitability of adobe houses, the grace of Spanish crafts. They took it all in great gulps. They bought crumbling adobe houses for a few dollars and did their own remodeling or hired neighbors to lay adobes and raise beams; furnished dirt-floored rooms with old furniture; used pottery for dishes; took to a diet of chile and beans. Willie Henderson turned from painting to making furniture with adze and wooden pins. The Cinco

Pintores made their street, El Camino del Monte Sol, an art center. Most of them were poor; living was simple, but thinking was high, wide, and handsome.

Inspired by Jane Baumann, the "colony" organized the Santa Fe Players and produced old melodramas and modern shockers. They gave his first hearings to Lynn Riggs, who was living in Sarah McComb's chicken house while he wrote *Green Grow the Lilacs*, which reached Broadway twice, the second time as *Oklahoma!* They shook up the moribund fiesta by setting up an Indian market in the old Palace's portal and by reviving old Spanish plays and dances. With the brashest humor they burlesqued the sanctified historical pageant with a "hysterical pageant" that pulled no punches. Will Shuster built a hideous monstrosity to be burned as Zozobra, Old Man Gloom, and so established a tradition that calls him away from his easel every year.

New Mexico was now the place every artist had to visit. Many distinguished names adorn the list of exhibitors. Robert Henri stayed a while. Marsden Hartley painted the high mountains. B. J. O. Nordfeldt and Russell Cowles produced in New Mexico work that enhanced well-established reputations. These men were mature and finished painters, who in turn reflected all the movements of European and American art, but who developed no new technique here. John Sloan, known in Philadelphia and New York as one of the thoroughly American "ashcan school," made a summer home on Delgado Street. But he found no ashcans in New Mexico. His paintings of pueblos, of Indian and Spanish types, are full of shimmering light and sunshine. Perhaps his greatest contribution to New Mexico life was his wife Dolly, a sixty-inch dynamo, a veteran of suffrage parades and less successful movements in New York. She now threw herself into the effort to defeat the Bursum Bill and save the Pueblos' lands; she lined up so many New York writers in a cause they had never heard of that New Mexico's Indians became front page stuff and the *Santa Fe New Mexican* was displayed on New York newsstands. Its editor, Dana Johnson, was a most effective mouthpiece; serious in his beliefs and believing always in preserving the state's beauty and distinction, he wrote with humor, versified with pungent wit, poked up the stodgy, and restored balance to the intense.

A loftier tone was contributed by Mary Austin, who had brought from California her mystical preoccupation with "Amerindian culture" and Spanish arts. Whether she was a woman of genius or an uneven performer with flashes of good writing, Mrs. Austin was certainly practical. Crowned with queenly braids, wrapped in a Spanish shawl, and enthroned on the bootblack's stand in the Chamber of Commerce, she pushed for action. Her followers laughed at her, but they loved her—and she led them. She stirred young men to physical labor on the Acoma church, making it leakproof while saving it from the tin roof that was tempting the padre. She raised money to purchase and restore the Sanctuario above Chimayo, which was then presented to the Catholic Church. She gave her blessing to the Indian Tribal Arts Association, which, headed by the Sloans and the Misses Elizabeth and Martha White, undertook to hold Indian craftsmen to their highest standards and to educate the public to appreciate the best. Defeat of the Bursum Bill led to the New Mexico Association on Indian Affairs, which enlisted the time and political skill of people of leisure who had chosen New Mexico. Led by Mrs. Margretta Dietrich, this organization has befriended Indians as individuals and as tribes, and has become a congressional lobby to be reckoned with. Its eastern associate is the Association on American Indian Affairs, whose president, Oliver La Farge, combines ability as a writer with organizational skill and knowledge of Indian problems.

Indians for the first time met respectful comprehension.

After centuries of the white man's scorn, smug superiority, or condescension, their dances were witnessed by quietly attentive people who recognized their artistry and religious content. Their handiwork was judged with artistic discrimination. Naturally Indians responded eagerly to strangers who advocated the revival of old pottery forms, old dyes in weaving, old techniques in basketry, and ancient and significant designs. Frank Applegate lived among the Hopis, found pottery clay banks that had been forgotten, revived the potters' old skills.

Indians had long been painters. Kenneth Chapman, an authority on Indian design, believes that the tradition of kiva mural painting had never been lost. In 1902 he found a Navajo drawing good landscapes on boxtops in a trading-post. When John DeHuff and Dorothy Dunn encouraged children in the Indian School at Santa Fe, they eagerly made pictures of what they knew. When the Museum was established, Indians were given space to work, and Maria Martinez's pottery soon appeared in Fifth Avenue shops. Julian and Crescencio, who painted the designs on her pottery, were given paper and watercolors and began to make paintings for sale. The Indian's precise line, balanced design, impeccable color sense, and specialized knowledge produced pictures of dances, animals, and Indian life which won plaudits from the most critical. Indian painting went into museums and collections, and was reproduced in the most expensive form. Fred Kabotie the Hopi, Velino Shije of Zia, Alfonso Roybal of San Ildefonso, and others were recognized artists.

Perhaps an even greater gift was the artists' recognition of the value of the dying Spanish culture. Shy old men, who had hidden the old plays, now had auditors who recognized a medieval folk-art. Old women, who had been ashamed of their wool embroideries, saw their *colchas* respectfully handled by artists who recognized the old patterns. *Santeros,* whose holy figures had been repudiated by the devout in favor of plaster saints from religious supply houses, found their carvings in cottonwood and their paintings with earth colors in demand by collectors. Families of woodcarvers revived their art, especially in the secluded village of Cordova.

Jose Dolores Lopez became famous for his unpainted woodcarvings; one was bought by the Museum of Modern Art. After his death in 1937, his son George carried on the family tradition. In Taos, Patricino Barela, given a start by Vernon Hunter under the WPA Art Project, has become famous for his simple, imaginative work. After his child's serious illness he made a figure of a frightened father in the hands of an all-powerful doctor.

Altogether the artists' greatest gift to New Mexico was respectful appreciation. Out of this grew the effort to save the old arts and to aid their further development. But artists were to kill the thing they loved. Even as the Philistines they deplored, artists felt the great American urge and went into business. A group of them opened the Spanish and Indian Shop in Santa Fe, and artists were now to be met in the pueblos talking a weak-willed Indian into selling ceremonial objects, or in Spanish villages tempting a family's neediest member into giving up the chest that had traveled the Chihuahua Trail. This started the craze for native crafts in household decoration, and a general buying spree ensued.

Competition grew keen. "I got all the doors in that village. I don't know what I'll do with them, but at least nobody else will get them." Such handmade bits were built into remodeled houses at Santa Fe and Taos. A village's entire economy could be upset by these new neighbors, and the farmer's water supply was often reduced to the danger point as the new residents diverted the stream not only for crop irrigation, but much more for unproductive gardens. Tragic tales are often told as funny.

"I wanted that orchard so nobody would ever cut off my

view. Jose held out; said he was the family trustee and had to keep that land for his unmarried sisters. But one day when he was drunk he signed up. He had power of attorney, you see. . . . You should have seen him next day. Battered is the word. It seems his brothers had beaten him up when they found out he'd sold out the old maid sisters. Jose wanted to revoke the sale. One sister, he said, had planted a tree when her lover died and didn't want to lose it. But I had the paper."

As roads and plumbing reached Taos, the camp followers of the artistic shock troops moved in. Bankers co-operated in the foreclosing of mortgages, and whole villages were made over. Mabel Dodge came west with Maurice Stern, whose New Mexico paintings created a furor in New York. Mabel's extensive adobe mansion swarmed with the *cognoscenti*. John Marin and Max Weber visited. Robinson Jeffers's poetry and D. H. Lawrence's prose gave a new dimension to the literature beginning to burgeon in New Mexico. Mabel herself wrote several books marked by sensitive observation, especially after her marriage with Tony Luhan gave her an in-law's view of Indian life. Willa Cather was a Taos visitor, though she wrote more of *Death Comes for the Archbishop* in Mary Austin's Casa Querida in Santa Fe, where Don Amado Chaves told her the stories that lend such verisimilitude to her novel.

In Taos, Bert and Elizabeth Harwood remodeled Cap Simpson's old home. Later Elizabeth opened there a gallery where every artist and craftsman could show. At her death she left the place to the University, which maintains it as the Harwood Foundation. Artists were now coming in on John Dunne's stage from Taos Junction; in good weather the road was open from Raton over the divide from Cimarron. Taos was an art center equal to Provincetown or Woodstock.

Andrew Dasburg moved up from Santa Fe, bringing his

almost religious love for the land. "I felt as though I had come upon the Garden of Eden; everything was pristine." His paintings of landscape, figures, still-life, all reflect this awe; his superb technique and understanding criticism have influenced many younger painters.

Among the discoverers were photographers. Ansel Adams, Edward Weston, and Ernie Knee made studies of land and people which had both artistic and documentary value. Laura Gilpin, beginning with posed Indians, developed a more revealing manner that culminated in a magnificent book, *Rio Grande, River of Destiny*. Paul Strand sought the delicate designs hidden in old adobe or in the weathered timbers of the ghost town of E-town.

With Paul Strand came his wife Becky and Georgia O'Keeffe. The two women provided sharp accents to the kaleidoscope of pueblos on dance days by appearing in long black capes and flat black hats. O'Keeffe was quite unaware of comment. She had found her land, and was soon painting white skulls in the hard desert light. Her New Mexico canvases, shown in New York by Alfred Stieglitz, won highest critical approval and established O'Keeffe as one of the greatest living women painters. Her home in Abiquiu, with its large empty adobe rooms, is a fitting workshop for O'Keeffe's paintings, so imaginatively conceived and so definitely stated with clarity of line and color.

In the late twenties, business took over. The Santa Fe Railroad pushed its advertising, and the Harvey System began hauling tourists around under the guidance of girl couriers; both tried to uphold standards of taste while commercializing the Indian arts and crafts. Bert Staples, out near Gallup, set Navajos to making flat silver, cigarette boxes, and ash trays as fine as the best New England work. The Kirk brothers at Manuelito soon joined in; others caught the fever. Navajo blankets were now sold as Navajo rugs, Chimayo weavers supported entrepreneurs in Santa Fe, woodcarvers and leatherworkers were trained. New Mexico's oldest styles of architecture became the only thing. It seemed a triumph of good taste. But the triumph was too complete.

Slowest to catch on to the money value of New Mexico's arts and its scenery was its own business community. Businessmen had consistently disregarded artists as queer ducks; they had never understood the value of the unpaid publicity artists give the state. Belatedly they woke up. Chambers of commerce began to inquire what there was in the neighborhood that tourists might like to see, and to issue lurid advertising. In 1935 the state established its Tourist Bureau and began to advertise in national magazines. Out of this flurry have come small shops, a few small factories, a considerable debasement of standards, and a blind destruction of precisely what attracts visitors. Old plazas are neon-lighted; old houses are remodeled out of all grace and charm; fine trees that sheltered caravans or armies and that could still offer shady relief are cut down. Saddest of all, standards in the arts have been prostituted by tasteless middlemen and by the Indian's ingrained adaptability. Good potters began to slap out lopsided jars and to paint them with garish colors. Such atrocities are actually sold in the portal of the Museum, where the artists had set up a market dedicated to fine work.

Indian painters, while retaining their accuracy and precision, have let their themes grow stereotyped. One of them said: "All they'll buy are deer and buffalo dancers or hunters. So I make what they want." This conviction was established when the WPA used Indians to decorate government buildings, and confirmed when ticket offices and drive-in theaters ordered more of the same. More than one hundred Indians are turning out their two-dimensional figures in high colors and lively motion. Gay pictures on the wall, but an impasse for the artists.

Art teachers hope to free the Indian from this thrall, to "help him to free himself." But what white artist, himself the product of European schools, can enter into the Indian's tradition enough to do more than impose his own values? A few Indians, like Gerald Nailer and Francisco Abeyta, have experimented with contemporary styles. Both are Navajos, always successful borrowers. But the true development of an Indian art must await the Indian genius who will grow from his own deep indigenous root and not from a graft.

A promising development is Fred Kabotie's Hopi silver. Some critics disdain his exquisite jewelry and table silver as "not Indian." But Kabotie is Indian, his work is beautiful, it is giving his people a new craft. He is perhaps the first Indian artist to defy white mentors.

Art schools and art talk have naturally produced swarms of home-grown aspirants. Some are promising, some are doomed to enjoy their endeavors in private. Few Spanish names appear on any national list, though several who show in New Mexico promise well. David Gonzales sold his first painting to Cady Wells—a spirited typhoon done in deck paint on a strip of canvas while he was in the Navy. Juan Candelaria has shown his photographs widely. Two gringos figure in national magazines and galleries: Sam Smith and Peter Hurd. Tom Lea is a native of Roswell, but he lives and works in El Paso, and Texas claims him.

Sam Smith, born in Texas, was transplanted early, and is a New Mexican. He paints experimentally as a young man trying to find himself, but strongly as to color and design with a profound feeling for cloud and tree shadows and gentle villages, but for tortured Penitentes, too. His experience as an Army combat artist painting Negroes of the Gold Coast, Chinese villages, and oriental bazaars has certainly deepened his understanding of New Mexico.

New Mexico-born Peter Hurd, having studied with N. C. Wyeth and married his daughter, returned to the place he loved most—the Ruidoso Canyon, where *paisano* and cowboy meet and the landscape is dominated by sunshine. Hurd has developed his own style of painting in tempera on yeso, a technique related to his work as a muralist. Nobody catches New Mexico's light quite as Hurd does, and when he paints a water hole in the desert it is clearly an answer to prayer.

Hurd's native Roswell is generating some of the fervor of Santa Fe's most effervescent period. The Roswell Museum, under the genial leadership of Paul Horgan, is making a permanent Hurd collection. Its early director, Thomas Messer, began cleverly with a showing of Bob Crosby's rodeo trophies, followed with frontier dress, and when he offered Mestrovic's drawings ranch people came readily and enjoyed the show. Horgan helped arrange museum concerts, and Horgan has broadened his field from sympathetic and perceptive novels and stories to a study of the Rio Grande from its Colorado spring to the Texas delta.

Most artists continue to follow the old, well-worn trails to Santa Fe and Taos, and to Albuquerque whose reputation is of later growth. A few are so ungracious as to scoff at the men who made the trails they follow. Some are drifters; many stay. New Mexico has more resident artists per capita than any other state in the land. A tourist guide lists seventy "people in the arts" in Santa Fe. These include dancers, makers of ceramics and jewelry, photographers, and sculptors. Taos has not so many, but quite as wide a range, and more galleries that sell. The 1940 Fiesta Show at Santa Fe listed 269 painters; nobody is refused. A critic rated the offering as "ranging from mediocre to lousy." But it included work of many men welcomed in New York's best galleries. A show in Albuquerque listed seventy-one painters with their addresses: even the state's commercial center has its artists, though they lack a colony's cohesiveness.

New Mexico has still developed no school of painting,

though its color, light, and angular land-forms, as well as the Indian's way of simplifying them into symbols, have affected all its artists in some degree. New Mexico might have invented cubism, but did not; and the Indian influence is not comparable with that of African sculpture on Picasso and on others of the French school.

Gustave Baumann, still the discoverer after thirty years, has reproduced pictographs and used them. His wood-block prints and gay puppet figures have caught much native humor. And only Gus could have seen fat dullards, haughty dames, and querulous snoopers in gourds and, with a few lines and a deft twist in the mounting, made them into delightful figures of fun.

Agnes Sims, who studied pictographs from the Galisteo Basin, has used the lively skinny figures in painting and has incorporated Indian symbols for water, snakes, rain, and horizon into her paintings depicting Indian life.

Experimenting goes on. Pansy Stockton has named "sun paintings" the pictures she makes by pasting on boards bits of bark, leaves, moss, pine needles, and milkweed floss. For the New Mexico sky only the bluebird's feather will do, but by its clever use she makes a mere flash of blue suggest a wide empyrean.

Dorothy Stewart gathered together her arts and interests in her Galeria Mejico, where a pink entrance with iron grille leads into a high-walled studio. There she presented musicians, speakers, and pictures too esoteric for the general public. There she printed her *Hamlet*, a series of wood-block prints to illustrate a masterly selection of quotations. This was set and printed by hand in old type on an old press; its type was distributed after one hundred impressions had been sold for twenty-five dollars a copy.

Sculpture, despite statuesque models with bronze skins, has proved too costly to develop far. Bruce Saville, who lived in Santa Fe for a few years, made an excellent series of Indian dance figures. Allan Clark and George Blodgett figured in eastern shows. Eugenie Shonnard, using techniques learned from Rodin, used native cedar and sandstone to carve figures at once solid and poetic.

All the arts lag behind painting. Collections of native music remain largely untouched. Aaron Copland's ballet score, *Billy the Kid*, used frontier and cowboy songs. J. Donald Robb, Dean of Fine Arts at the University, was the first to use Spanish songs. His opera *Little Joe*, based on Robert Bright's novel *The Life and Death of Little Joe*, used twenty-five Spanish themes. It opens with a crashing dissonance that suggests the land's harshness—a theme repeated in the scenery designed by Lloyd Goff and painted by Ted Schuyler; simple village life unfolds in song and dance. Its high point is in a Penitente scene, with its underlying fear and suffering. As a first work, it lacks dramatic force, but *Little Joe* may well be a significant first in New Mexico music.

Much as New Mexico has been written about, its writers are few compared with its painters, and its best books have been the work of outsiders. Willa Cather and Conrad Richter have won widest renown with our history, Oliver La Farge and Frank Waters with the Indian. Even writers of the Westerns truest to detail and talk are often newcomers who saw cowboys at firsthand. Of the natives, Ruth Laughlin turned to her birthplace when she wrote of Doña Tules, the gambler of Santa Fe, and Harvey Fergusson has been preoccupied with the times of his pioneering grandfather. Bill Mauldin, who became one of the best-loved cartoonists of World War II, tells in *A Sort of a Saga* of his boyhood in La Luz—a sort of a Tom Sawyer. Only Fergusson has essayed the modern scene with clear-eyed realism, but even he has presented Spanish life as a dying phenomenon, typifying it in an unsuccessful hero. Sensitive people are sure to see it so. We await the novelist whose hero may start as a pitiful "Little Joe," but end as head of a department in a great university, an authority on Inter-American affairs, a successful Wall Street operator, as actor, musician, congressman, or as a success in smaller but important fields.

Painting still dominates New Mexico's art scene. Practitioners of the latest schools, like their predecessors, are excited by new beauties of light and form and moved by the Indian's symbolism. Raymond Jonson, beginning with complicated and beautiful "earth rhythms," has developed a nonrepresentational style that has deeply influenced his students at the University. Cady Wells's landscapes, often mystical and involved, reflect his deep awareness of our rectangular land masses. Only Howard Schleeter shows a direct inspiration from Indian work, especially from Mimbres pottery designs. His gemlike color and rich texture are the result of early training, but his design seems truly New Mexican. Hilaire Hiler, whose reputation was well established before he saw New Mexico, makes a point of seeking nothing here; he likes the climate. A unique contribution to the artistic presentation of New Mexico is that of Theodore Van Soelen. His first work was typical of the newcomer who saw the striking features of landscape and painted fine studies of aspens and cottonwoods, adobes and warmly glowing earth tones. Later work, both paintings and lithographs, reflects Van Soelen's wide knowledge and sensitive appreciation of the New Mexico scene. In addition, he has become one of New Mexico's best-known portraitists. Artists continue to come to New Mexico, but the days of discovery are past. However revealing the modern artist's experience may be to the individual, he is not the herald of a new scene. He lives in New Mexico, writes or paints, but he is no molder of opinion, no fighter for causes. The causes his predecessors fought for have been taken over by ladies of competence backed by maturity and wealth, and the wonders they presented to the world have become commonplace in tourist advertising.

XXVI

LAND OF ENCHANTMENT

☖ NEW MEXICO advertises itself as "the land of enchantment," and it has indeed something to appeal to every taste from the crudest to the most cultivated. The discriminating visitor must find his own way to what he will find rewarding. He can lift his eyes above the garish signboards to the reddish sandstone cliffs with purple shadows. Perhaps he can even smile at the signboard's blatant untruths that offer fake wonders without shame in a land whose authentic wonders have attracted students for a century. Cliff dwellings made to order, historic wells unknown to historians, fairly recent brick houses plastered over to pass as "old haciendas."

"Forty-eight-foot rattlesnake. Alive! Man-eating Mountain Lion! Tarantulas! Wild animals!" Westbound the note is one of warning. "Desert ahead! Last chance for water!" This sells desert water-bags, though filling stations are seldom more than twenty miles apart all the way to California.

Most travelers drive quickly on, intent on reaching Colorado in the summer, Arizona or California in the winter, or home again at every season's end. The average length of the tourist's stay in New Mexico is four and a half days, though even the speeders spend enough to make the tourist business the state's largest revenue-producer, topping even oil. The State Tourist Bureau estimated in 1950 that an average of $135 million a year is left by out-of-state cars, including buses; oil brings in a mere $120 million. Chambers of commerce, awake at last, try to hold motorists for one more day, but their efforts are not very inspired.

People like to see things, to know what they are seeing, to feel that it is unique. There are no Carlsbad Caverns back home; thousands of visitors a day thrill to that underground wonderland. Those caverns are New Mexico's only national park, but its eight national monuments are likewise manned by Park Service rangers who are well-informed and courteous as well as efficient guardians against vandalism. There are, besides, five state parks and nine state monuments with small collections that people peer at in earnest attempts to understand prehistoric life.

Otherwise the vast human pageant that has moved across these uplands and valleys remains hidden from the eastern visitor, who thinks our history began in Virginia. There are no museums except the state institutions in Santa Fe and a few small ones of local interest. Even Albuquerque, crossroads of the highways and the state's largest city, is so absorbed in its desire to become a second Chicago or Los Angeles that it makes no official effort to detain the daily stream of visitors. "What is there to see here? . . . Oh, well, let's go on to Santa Fe."

From the middle of May to the middle of September the automobiles spin along the highways as though the singing tires were held to the asphalt. But even among these speeders are a few people with ears to hear of a Pueblo Corn Dance just a mile down the arroyo or over the hill; with eyes to see the beauty of the tall standard fluttering above the flat adobe roofs massed with people brightly colored, and to feel the deep meaning behind the throbbing drums, the deep-toned chant, and the precisely changing figures of the dance.

These are the visitors who stay over a day or two or try a different route on the return journey. Once felt, the New Mexico magic has great drawing power; it pulls obliquely away from the tried and dully safe. It could make the motorist leave the Will Rogers Highway in Arizona to angle across the Mogollon Mountains, where parklike pine forests are carpeted with grass and starred with white desert poppies, scarlet pentstemon, and purple bee balm. He may come upon an archæologist digging for a missing link or casting for a trout. He may sit rocking with a lion-hunter or a prospector, whose verbiage is as unforgettable as it is unreproducible. If he listens he will come back to stay.

Likewise the visitor to the Carlsbad Caverns, letting his eye be caught by the waxy bloom of yucca on the desert, may be lured northward to Lincoln Plaza, the Ruidoso, and the Mescalero reservation. The lovely, noisy Ruidoso has been throttled by tourist camps and the sort of gambling resorts that are invisible to state or county police. But apple orchards offer crisp and tangy fruit, and there are hidden canyons where one can relive the Lincoln County War and try to get an Apache to tell where his tribal gold mine is.

The motorist who stays on the Butterfield stage route will dip into Texas and may cross into Mexico at El Paso before continuing along Cooke's road to the sea. But there is much to linger for in Doña County. Las Cruces is marked by three crosses on a hill. There is a legend to the effect that the crosses were erected in memory of Spanish colonists who were massacred there during the early nineteenth century, though no historical date is given. When the town was laid out in 1849, it was naturally known as Las Cruces (The Crosses). In time it became a wealthy town; the Hotel Amador is still replete with the elegance of pre-gringo days. Its splendid mahogany furniture was hauled from New Orleans by the first Amador, who presumably placed over the bedroom doors those delicately lettered names of girls: Anita, Luisa, Rosa. Its wide central hall is filled with relics of Maximilian's Mexico: lace fans, old guns, letters, papers, and paintings. A wax matador in full regalia stands by the stairs, and a wax Numidian proffers a card tray to the guest on his way into the modern bar with chromium trim or to the dining patio.

Mesilla, capital of the Confederate State of Arizona, is three miles off the highway, where it drowses pleasantly under its cottonwoods. A starkly modern church dominates the plaza, but low adobe buildings surround it and its most aggressive business house is the Billy the Kid Cantina. No New Mexico character, except Kit Carson, slept in more places than the redoubtable Kid, who was once caught and convicted in Mesilla.

La Posta, where the stages drew up dusty or muddy, sometimes battle-scarred, serves excellent Mexican meals and displays Henry Griggs's uncatalogued collection of good, bad, and indifferent articles. La Posta belongs to the family of Albert Fountain, who still hope to establish the truth of the colonel's disappearance in the White Sands. The Fountain homes and others are opened to visitors on a Sunday in May. None of Mesilla's homes is very old, but they are reminiscent of the easy living before either the Union or the Confederacy took over.

An older fiesta of deeper meaning occurs on December 12, day of the Indian Virgin of Guadalupe. Celebrated throughout the Southwest, this fiesta is most Mexican in Las Tortugas, a misnomer for the villages of San Juan and Guadalupe near Las Cruces. Scores of people come from Mexico, the prevailing language is Spanish, and venders squat on the ground beside their piles of pottery or braziers of savory foods, just as they do in the neighboring republic.

The fiesta begins early on December 11, when worshippers start the long, dusty, stony climb to the Virgin's shrine on a near-by hill. In sterner days many of the devout went on their knees and all fasted. Now they walk, carrying lunch boxes or thermos bottles. But the pilgrimage remains an act of devotion or of gratitude for favors granted, and villagers tell of many miracles the Guadalupana has wrought.

At dusk of a quiet December 11, the two villages sparkled with *faroles* on the roofs, and *luminarias* of dry cactus wood flared redly toward a skyful of stars. The only sound came from the violins and drums of dancers near the church. Three groups were dancing: Los Matachines, not very expert; Los Aztecas, said to be recent arrivals from Mexico —among their costumes was one feathered headdress reminiscent of the *Danza de las Plumas* of Oaxaca; the third group, accompanied by the chanting of old men of strongly marked Indian features, consisted of women, whose black cotton dresses were cut like those of Pueblo women.

No authoritative study of these dances has been made. Las Cruces people think the Indians are Piros, refugees from the Manzano "cities that died of fear." But the Pueblo dance group is called Los Tiwas, and a woman from Isleta, where they speak Tiwa, said she could understand the old men's chant. They are altogether a curious survival of Mexican and Pueblo rites; degenerate, unexplained. Perhaps for most participants the fiesta's true significance is Catholic, not Indian, though it centers in a long adobe house called El Pueblo.

When dark had fully come, a ruby diadem suddenly gleamed on the hilltop, where the pilgrims had lit their cruciform bonfire. Then three luminous streams began to flow down the slope as the worshippers descended, each one carrying a torch or, more likely, a flashlight. It would be hours before they arrived; the dancers went to supper. At El Pueblo a few men waited and when the time was right they lit *faroles* there. People began to gather quietly, coming on foot or in cars.

As the procession came nearer it seemed to move under a white blur. Each pilgrim was carrying a sotol wand tipped with an ivory-white flower fashioned of a yucca leaf and

tied with aromatic creosote leaves. This is very Mexican—
to make a beautiful thing of wild plants artfully put together.

At El Pueblo's closed door, the pilgrims begged admit-
tance. A voice within denied them. "You are bad people,
robbers." "No, we are the devout, come to venerate Our
Lady." "Enter then," and the doors were flung open, light
streamed forth, harsh against the warm glow of the moon
laced with silver starlight. This was the fiesta's culmination,
though there was more dancing on the Guadalupe's "very
day."

Few New Mexico fiestas are so unaffected by efforts to
appeal to the tourist. Most of them, even saint's day observances, have been dressed up for tourists with a historical parade, an elected queen, a rodeo, and a noisy carnival.

San Geronimo Day at Taos has grown into a three-day
program that lists vespers in the pueblo and the sundown
dance among a score of events including a livestock show,
square dancing, a Kangaroo Kourt for those not suitably
dressed, and a costume ball. Even tourists for whom this is
done complain that "our dear old Taos is being ruined by
tourists."

Santa Fe's fiesta opens with a candlelit and very reverent
procession from the Cathedral to the Cross of the Martyrs.
Hundreds of worshippers walk slowly to the Latin chanting
of young Mexican seminarists, and the archbishop presides
over a ceremony honoring the martyred missionaries to the
Indians. The Indians take part quite calmly.

Of the artists who rescued this fiesta from its tawdry middle period, only Will Shuster still does his stint of building
Zozobra for burning, and Dorothy Stewart mobilizes a
group to paint quaint banners for the plaza. Two little
theaters offer fiesta plays. But the fiesta is most marked by
its changes.

It is fashionable now for Santa Fe residents to leave town

during fiesta or to by-pass the town as they drive from one cocktail party to another. Tourists skirt the plaza on their way from hotel bar to Museum art show or to buy the bad Indian pottery displayed in the Museum's portal. This leaves the plaza free for old people, who sit chatting in Spanish or minding babies while older youngsters ride the merry-go-round—still best known as Tio Vivo (Lively Uncle). Country people circulate among the booths, eating, shooting, hailing each other; at night they dance in the streets. Santa Fe's fiesta has come back to the people again.

Other towns feature rodeos. Las Vegas's Cowboys Reunion on the Fourth of July is the outgrowth of the first Rough Riders Reunion held there in 1899, with Colonel Teddy Roosevelt as the honored guest. Aging Rough Riders are invited to lead the parade in hacks, and every male citizen is required to raise whiskers. Whiskers are demanded at every frontier show, but other features vary. At Cimarron, where they raise fine horses, races are important. At Grants, where Navajo cowboys often win the prizes, other Navajos dance by firelight. But always the rodeo is the thing.

This most western of sports has at last received academic recognition, and riders, ropers, and bull-doggers now vie with quarterbacks for campus hero worship. New Mexico's University and Agricultural College have joined institutions in nine other states to organize the National Intercollegiate Rodeo Association, which holds meets and promulgates rigid rules. New Mexico's Aggies, right off the range, have brought home prizes. Cattlemen are delighted to help finance a sport that demands horses, cattle, trailers, and feedlots as well as expensive equipment.

Most of New Mexico's staged festivals occur in summer, when tourists abound. The most splendid spectacle is Gallup's Inter-tribal Indian Ceremonial in August. It has expanded, in thirty years, from a get-together of a few Navajos and Zunis to a concourse of seven thousand Indians from thirty-one tribes.

The audience faces a backdrop of tepees and covered wagons, where the Indians camp, and masses of Indians in dance regalia await their turn to perform. The smooth efficiency of the management and the Indians' perfect stage-presence combine to produce a magnificent production, especially at night, when tall bonfires almost outshine the spotlights. No dance is given in its entirety: Indians wish it so, and most visitors would be bored by the complete dances. But the sampling is good. As dancers grow more professional year after year, they develop the mannerisms of stars and tend to substitute the white man's Indian love lyrics for their own strong rhythms. But the whole retains a genuine Indian flavor, and the hall of exhibits demands high standards in the Indian crafts it shows.

The people who choose to stay in New Mexico generally have tastes that make them feel at home with the country or its people, as though a strong land would welcome only its own. The true dude ranch that handles dudes along with cattle is not here. Nor is the movie star's elaborately expensive resort. Back in the nineties the railroads built a few enormous hotels, but only Cloudcroft Lodge in the Sacramentos still keeps afloat, with week-enders from military posts at El Paso and Alamogordo. At nine thousand feet there is not much one can do. Tennis, golf, even dancing are too strenuous. Guests stay indoors at card tables or huddle behind plate glass windshields on the verandas. But the drive up is magnificent; it follows the railroad's many switchbacks, revealing wide views of the pastel Tularosa Basin with a long low-lying cloud far away that turns out to be the White Sands.

New Mexico has many hot springs of tested therapeutic value: Faywood, Ojo Caliente, Truth or Consequences, and others less advertised—but they remain simple places for simple people with arthritis. No elegant spas have been developed.

The favorite resorts are in the mountains, near art colonies or pueblos, or far out on the Navajo reservation, where traders have added guest rooms or fixed up hogans with windows and running water. Many serious students who had summered happily in New Mexico studying primitive cultures were called upon for advice during World War II, when our government suddenly faced the need to deal with alien peoples.

Other visitors, not serious at all, love to poke about among ruins. The Gallina Bench Ranch advertises that it has no modern conveniences and only one mail a week, but it can show hundreds of ruined towers on Dead Man's Mesa where prehistoric men lived. The ranch is reached by a dirt road that curls around cliffs under the northern escarpment of the Jemez range, with its familiar striations of sulphur yellow, bone white, and terra cotta. Below the cliffs the Chama River prances companionably along until the road bumps into it on a damp and sandy beach. There the visitor hails the ranch and somebody comes to man the rowboat and ferry the guest across. Surely this is the only dude ranch reached by boat?

The Ghost Ranch, set against the Chama valley's northern wall, uses a cow's skull as its insigne; its ghosts were those of cattle-thieves hanged to its tall cottonwoods. There a sheep-herder was scared out of his wits by a monster that moved. Paleontologists later identified the specter as the skeleton of a phytosaur, which accommodatingly moved enough in the breeze to justify the sheep-herder's scare.

Diagonally across the state the amateur archæologist may stop at the Gila Hot Springs Ranch and visit ruins that may connect the Mogollon with the Pueblo culture. "Doc" Campbell and his wife, a granddaughter of Tom Lyons the "cattle baron," offer luxury in the famous hunting-lodge;

and riding, fishing, and hunting in a hidden paradise, accessible only on horseback.

Most guest ranches are easy to reach by motor, and they offer the softest possible "roughing it," with good beds and plumbing in log cabins, good horses and guides, and the certainty that there will be ham for dinner in case the trout fail to rise. Such places are as small and friendly as private homes, and their guests come back year after year.

Corkin's Lodge on the Brazos is so sure of its regular professors and judges that it does not advertise, but just looks for early arrivals when the Brazos Falls begin to twist over the cliffs in their two thousand feet of spray. They dry up when the snow waters have run off Brazos Mesa, but the guests stay on to fish all summer, and even into the fall for hunting.

Los Pinos, on the upper Pecos, "where the road ends and the trails begin," allows favored guests to ride to Lake Katherine—named for the ranch owner who discovered it.

Evergreen Valley, at the top of Gallinas Creek above Las Vegas, is a lush green meadow ringed with stately conifers and guarded by tall cliffs of red and blue granite. Housekeeping cabins are tucked away, almost unseen, among the spruce and fir trees.

Such places attract people who need rest, love remoteness, and can be endlessly entertained riding new trails through pine and aspen forests where shy lady's-slippers hide or one can gather armfuls of columbine or mariposa lilies. Most of them close in September, but a few stay open for the fall's hunting.

Trout fishing is New Mexico's summer sport; lakes and streams are kept stocked with brook and rainbow trout and guarded against violation. The best trout water is in the eight-hundred-foot gorge of the Rio Grande, whose swiftness over a rocky bed makes it "a tackle buster." All its tributaries, like all New Mexico's mountain streams, are trout streams. They come tumbling clear and cold from the peaks to delight true fishermen in hip boots, who whip the water with limber rods all day, and at evening fry the catch over a fire in camp. More sedentary sportsmen may prefer fishing from a boat on Eagle Nest Lake in the Moreno valley, where anybody should be able to pull in a trout of from one to three pounds, and where seven-pounders are taken now and then.

Warm-water fishing is a by-product of irrigation and flood control; every artificial lake above a dam is kept stocked with bass, crappie, and catfish. This accounts for automobiles on the highways with boats lashed on top, and for regattas on Elephant Butte and Conchas lakes.

New Mexicans are sportsmen; most fishing and hunting licenses are sold to residents of the state. The Game Protective Association of some eight thousand members includes men from the professions, from business, and from labor, who work together to see that the law protects the game and is obeyed. They train their sons to be self-reliant, to make a camp, to pack a horse, to ride, and to be wise and wary with a gun. Here persists the frontier in the easy democracy of men who judge each other by what they are and can do.

Most migratory ducks and geese feed in the valleys, where hunters in heavy coats sit in blinds to await the opalescent dawn and the whirr of the birds rising. This they still do, though draining marshes for flood control lessens the feeding grounds. Nothing has disturbed the blue quail in the foothills, and pheasants, introduced and protected as a pleasant exotic, have made very free with chickens' feed in the barnyard. The prairie chicken, so important a food on the Santa Fe Trail, was almost lost during the dust bowl era, but is coming back.

New Mexico's toughest sport is offered by the mountain lion and the bear, both of which must be run with dogs.

The grizzly has disappeared, but the smaller black bear can test any hunter's skill and endurance. The mountain lion—known also as cougar or panther—"painter" in frontier lingo—is never a man-eater as advertised. But he can give a man and his dogs a good long run and at times a dangerous clawing when, as Elliott Barker wrote, "The Dogs Bark 'Treed.'"

Six of the New Mexico life zones, as defined by C. Hart Merriam, are found in New Mexico's rise from plain to peak. On the hottest deserts of the subtropical zone, the road runner flashes through mesquite thickets and the gopher tortoise suns himself under the cactus. Up above timberline, in the subarctic zone, one may hear the whistling marmot, which sounds like a strayed member of one's party, or the pika's note, like that of a hermit thrush. Mule deer and elk are found in all brushy, timbered country, but the Virginia white tail appears only in some protected areas, and the fantail is limited to the Gila and Apache national forests.

Care is bringing back some animals the mountain man knew but that had been lost by indiscriminate killing. No open season is permitted on javelina, squirrels, or mountain sheep. This lordly animal with the heavy horns was once reduced to a few individuals, but now is found in the Guadalupe Mountains near Carlsbad and in the Sandias, where he can peer down on Albuquerque. The beaver may be taken only under special permit; his dams are considered valuable to hold water for fishing pools and as an aid to erosion control. Antelope have been hunted for several seasons; those dainty beasts had almost vanished from their native plains, but by a special technique developed by New Mexico's Game Department they have been trapped and moved to suitable range.

Autumn brings many out-of-state hunters, on the whole a self-reliant lot who know what they want and how to find it. Winter likewise brings people of special knowledge and interests. They come to see the finest of the Indian dances: the Shalako at Zuñi, one of the most elaborate masked, ancient kachina ceremonies; and Christmas dances in the pueblo mission churches which offer a dramatic union of kachina and Catholic image—"the Jesus kachina." On Twelfth Night the pueblos dance to honor the newly elected governors, and not many weeks pass without a stylized hunting dance in some pueblo. Always the Navajos are dancing when winter has made "the thunder sleep." The winter's pageantry ends only with the Holy Week observances of the Penitentes and Easter dances in the pueblos. Winter is, for many, the best time for catching echoes of our long past.

In winter, as always, most travelers drive quickly through New Mexico. The roads are black and smooth; they lead to places beyond. Such travelers see only a treeless land with funny flat-topped houses, and they hurry eagerly on to something more familiar.

Those who will find something for them in New Mexico come soon to a promontory on which to stop and breathe deeply. They look far across immense, silent emptiness, shadowed by dark rocks or river courses marked by trees, and their eyes rise to mountains massed against the overpowering sky. Looking, they feel the long thin procession of human beings which has moved slowly across this land, working and worshipping, and in passing leaving many traces of the ways they found good.

꩜ ꩜ ꩜

BOOKS RECOMMENDED FOR
FURTHER READING

NEW MEXICO's story has been written in several languages, especially in Spanish and English. Anthropologists have reconstructed the record of its prehistoric, pre-literate Indians from ruins and legends and have published their findings in government reports and scientific journals and books. Spanish reports covering three hundred years of history remain, to a large extent, in still unstudied archives in Spain and Mexico. A few Spanish documents have been translated into English; many have been used as bases for historical studies. Historians continue assiduously to delve into these musty archives, often discovering documents that modify previously held opinions. New Mexico's last hundred years have been recorded by travelers and traders, Army officers, government employees, and a few sober historians. The entire pageant of the three peoples has been presented in whole or in part by an endless and growing number of writers of all sorts.

A complete list of books on New Mexico would be a manifest absurdity here. Lyle Saunders's bibliography, *A Guide to Materials Bearing on Cultural Relations in New Mexico*, includes five thousand titles, of which he estimates that well over one thousand are books. The present list includes books consulted and some books readily accessible to a reader who might wish to widen or deepen his knowledge of New Mexico.

I. FIRST DISCOVERERS

Blackwelder, Eliot: *The Great Basin*
Calvin, Ross: *River of the Sun*

Hibben, Frank C.: *The Lost Americans*
Long, Haniel: *Interlinear to Cabeza de Vaca*

II. First Settlers

Lummis, Charles F: *The Cities that were Forgotten*
Walter, Paul A. F.: *The Cities that Died of Fear*
Wissler, Clark: *The American Indian; an introduction to the anthropology of the new world.*
Wormington, H. M.: *Prehistoric Indians of the Southwest*

III. The Way of the Kachinas

Bandelier, Adolph F. A.: *The Delight Makers*
Parsons, Elsie Clews: *Pueblo Indian Religion* (2 Vols.)

IV. Changing Pueblo Life

Adair, John: *Silversmiths of the Southwest*
La Farge, Oliver (ed.): *The Changing Indian*
Lummis, Charles F.: *Mesa, Canyon, and Pueblo*
Guthe, Carl E.: *Pueblo Pottery-making; a study at the village of San Ildefonso*
Parsons, Elsie Clews: *The Pueblo of Jemez*
Waters, Frank: *The Man Who Killed the Deer*

V. The Modern Pueblo

Bynner, Witter: *Indian Earth*
Grant, Blanche C.: *Taos Indians*
Henderson, Alice Corbin: *Red Earth*
Larkin, Margaret: *El Cristo* (a play)
Lawrence, D. H.: *The Woman Who Rode Away*
Marriott, Alice: *María: The Potter of San Ildefonso*
Sedgewick, Mary K.: *Acoma, the Sky City*
Underhill, Ruth M.: *First Penthouse Dwellers of America*

VI. The Traditional Navajo

Amsden, Charles A.: *Navajo Weaving; its technic and history*

Coolidge, Dane and Mary: *The Navajo Indians*

Coolidge, Mary R.: *The Rainmakers, Indians of Arizona and New Mexico*

Gillmor, Frances: *Traders to the Navajo*

Haile, Berard (for the Franciscan Fathers): *An Ethnologic Vocabulary of the Navaho Language*

Haile, Berard: *Origin legend of the Navaho Enemy Way*

Kelly, Henry W.: *Franciscan Missions of New Mexico, 1740–60*

Kluckhohn, Clyde: *Beyond the Rainbow*

La Farge, Oliver: *Enemy Gods*

Matthews, Washington: *The Mountain Chant, a Navajo Ceremony*

——: *The Night Chant, a Navajo Ceremony*

Newcomb, Franc J.: *Navajo Omens and Taboos*

——: *The Navajo Shooting Chant*

——: *The Mountain Chant*

Reichard, Gladys A.: *Spider Woman; a story of Navajo weavers and chanters*

——: *Dezba, Woman of the Desert*

——: *Compulsive Prayer*

Schevill, Margaret Erwin: *Beautiful on the Earth*

Wheelwright, Mary Cabot: *Navajo Creation Myth*

VII. The Modern Navajo

Corle, Edwin: *People on the Earth*

Faunce, Hilda: *Desert Wife*

Gillmor, Frances: *Windsinger*

Haile, Berard: *The Padres Present the Navaho War Dance (Squaw Dance)*

La Farge, Oliver: *Laughing Boy*

Leighton, Alexander and Dorothea: *The Navaho Door*
Leighton, Dorothea and Kluckhohn, Clyde: *Children of the People*
Sanchez, George I.: *The People, a Study of the Navajos*
Simpson, J. H.: *Journal of a Military Reconnaissance from Santa Fe, New Mexico to the Navajo country*

VIII. THE WARLIKE APACHE

Bourke, John Gregory: *The Medicine Man of the Apaches*
Bartlett, John Russell: *Personal Narrative of Explorations*
Clum, Woodworth: *Apache Agent, the story of John P. Clum*
Davis, Britton: *The Truth about Geronimo*
Benton, Colonel C. B.: *Sgt. Neil Erickson and the Apaches, with a description of Fort Craig, N. M.* (*The Westerners Brand Book*)
Opler, Morris Edward: *An Apache Life-way*

IX. THE MODERN APACHE

Barrett, S. M. (ed.): *Geronimo's Story of His Life*

X. SPANISH DISCOVERERS

Bolton, Herbert E.: *Coronado and the Turquoise Trail*
Castañeda, Pedro de Nagera: *Relación de la Jornada de Cíbola*
Hallenbeck, Cleve: *The Journey of Fray Marcus de Niza*
Hammond, George P. and Rey, Agapito (trans. and eds.): *Expedition into New Mexico by Antonio de Espejo, 1582–83*
———: *Obregón's History of 16th Century Exploration in Western America entitled Chronicle*

XI. SPANISH SETTLERS

Espinosa, Gilberto (trans.): *Historia de la Nueva Mexico, by Gaspar Pérez de Villagrá*

Hammond, George P.: *Don Juan de Oñate and the founding of New Mexico*

Horgan, Paul: *Habit of Empire*

Kubler, George: *Religious Architecture in New Mexico*

XII. CHURCH AND STATE

Ayer, Mrs. Edward E. (trans.): *Memorial of Fray Alonso de Benavides*

Hackett, Charles Wilson: *Revolt of the Pueblo Indians of New Mexico in 1680*

Lummis, Charles F.: *The Land of Poco Tiempo*

Scholes, France V.: *The Supply Service of the New Mexico Missions in the 17th Century*

——: *Church and State in New Mexico, 1610–1650*

——: *Problems in the Early Ecclesiastical History of New Mexico*

XIII. RECONQUERED PROVINCE

Chapman, Charles Edward: *Colonial Hispanic America*

Chavez, Angelico: *La Conquistadora, Our Lady of the Conquest*

Kelly, Henry W.: *Franciscan Missions of New Mexico*

Kidder, Alfred Vincent: *An Introduction to Southwestern Archæology*

Leonard, Irving A. (trans.): *The Flying Mercury (El Mercurio Volante by Don Carlos de Siguenza y Góngora)*

Thomas, Alfred B.: *Forgotten Frontiers; a study of the Spanish Indian policy of Don Juan Bautista de Anza, governor of New Mexico, 1777–87*

XIV. SPANISH COLONIAL LIFE

Barker, Ruth Laughlin: *Caballeros*

Binkley, William C.: *Early Expansionist Movements in Texas*

Bustamente, Carlos: *Expedición de los Tejanos reducida a las fuerzas del General Armijo, en 1841*

Carroll, H. Bailey and Haggard, J. Villasana (trans.): *Three New Mexico Chronicles, which includes Don Pedro Pino's La Exposición sucinta y sencilla de la provincia del Nuevo Mexico*

Fergusson, Erna: *Mexican Cookbook*

Hafen, LeRoy (intro. and notes): *Antonio Armijo's Journal of 1829–30*

Jaramillo, Cleofas M.: *Shadows of the Past*

Waters, Frank: *People of the Valley*

XV.   Our Spanish Heritage

Dickey, Roland F. and Goff, Lloyd Lózes: *New Mexico Village Arts*

Foreman, Grant (ed.): *A Pathfinder in the Southwest; the itinerary of Lieutenant A. W. Whipple*

Garrard, Lewis: *Wah-to-Yah and the Taos Trail*

Henderson, Alice Corbin: *Brothers of Light*

Hollen, W. Eugene: *The Lost Pathfinder; Zebulon M. Pike*

Horgan, Paul: *From a Royal City*

Lummis, Charles F.: *New Mexico David and other stories and sketches of the Southwest*

Otero-Warren, Nina: *Old Spain in Our Southwest*

Otis, Raymond: *Miguel of the Bright Mountain*

Robb, J. Donald: *Little Joe* (an opera)

Twitchell, Ralph Emerson: *Leading Facts of New Mexico History*

XVI.   The New New Mexican

Calvin, Ross and Walter, Paul, Jr.: *The Population of New Mexico*

Sanchez, George I.: *Forgotten People: a study of New Mexico*

Works Progress Administration; Ryan, Helen Chandler
(ed.): *The Spanish American Song and Game Book*

XVII. GRINGO DISCOVERERS

Domenech, Abbé Em.: *Seven Years' Residence in the Great
Deserts of North America* (2 Vols.)
Fowler, Jacob (ed. by Elliott Coues): *The Journal of Jacob
Fowler*
Gregg, Josiah: *Commerce of the Prairies; the journal of a
Santa Fe trader*
Pike, Zebulon Montgomery (ed. by M. M. Quaife): *South-
western Expedition of Zebulon M. Pike*
Rister, Carl Coke: *Southwestern Frontier, 1865–81*
Vestal, Stanley: *Old Santa Fe Trail*
Webb, James Josiah: *Journal of a Santa Fe Trader*
Wislizenus, A.: *Memoir of a Tour to Northern Mexico*

XVIII. THE GRINGO OCCUPATION

Abert, Lieutenant J. W.: *Report of Lieutenant J. W. Abert
of his examination of New Mexico in the years 1846–47*
Anderson, Maxwell: *Night over Taos* (a play)
Barcena, José María Roa: *Recuedos de la Invasión Norte-
americana*
Benton, Thomas H.: *Thirty Years' View*
Calvin, Ross (ed.): *Lieutenant Emory Reports*
Connelley, William Elsey: *Doniphan's Expedition and the
Conquest of New Mexico and California*
Cooke, Philip St. George: *The Conquest of New Mexico
and California*
Davis, William Watts Hart: *El Gringo, or New Mexico
and her people*
Donnelly, Thomas C.: *The Government of New Mexico*
Grant, Blanche C. (ed.): *Kit Carson's Own Story*
Hughes, John T.: *Doniphan's Expedition*
Keleher, W. A.: *The Maxwell Land Grant*

Laughlin, Ruth: *The Wind Leaves No Shadow*
Magoffin, Susan: *Down the Santa Fe Trail and into Mexico*
Robinson, Jacob S.: *A Journal of the Santa Fe Expedition under Colonel Doniphan*
Sabin, Edwin Legrand: *Kit Carson Days, 1809–1868*
Sánchez, Pedro: *Memorias del Padre José Martínez*
Thomlinson, M. H.: *The Garrison of Fort Bliss*
Twitchell, Ralph Emerson: *The history of the Military Occupation of the Territory of New Mexico from 1846 to 1851 by the Government of the United States*
Vestal, Stanley: *Kit Carson*
Wilson, Richard L.: *Short Ravelings from a Tall Yarn*

XIX. TEXANS KEEP COMING

Crichton, Kyle: *Law and Order, Ltd.*
Ganaway, Loomis Morton: *New Mexico and the Sectional Controversy*
Kendall, George Wilkins: *Narratives of the Texan-Santa Fe Expedition*
Binkley, William Campbell (ed.): *New Spain and the West (including Spruce M. Baird's letters)*

XX. FRONTIER PEOPLE

Cleaveland, Agnes Morley: *No Life for a Lady*
Church, Peggy Pond: *Foretaste*
——: *Family Journey*
Fergusson, Erna: *Murder and Mystery in New Mexico*
——: *Albuquerque*
Fergusson, Harvey: *Home in the West*
——: *Grant of Kingdom*
——: *Blood of the Conquerors*
French, William: *Some Recollections of a Western Ranchman, New Mexico 1883–99*
Horgan, Paul: *Figures in a Landscape*
——: *Return of the Weed*

Keleher, W. A.: *Fabulous Frontier*
McKenna, James A.: *Black Range Tales*
Otero, Miguel: *My Life on the Frontier*
Poldervaart, Arie: *Black Robed Justice*
Ruxton, George F. A.: *Wild Life in the Rocky Mountains*
——: *In the Old West*

XXI. THE MINING MAN

Dobie, J. Frank: *Apache Gold and Yaqui Silver*
——: *Coronado's Children; tales of lost mines and buried treasures of the Southwest*
Hough, Emerson: *Land of Heart's Desire*
Jones, Fayette Alexander: *The Mineral Resources of New Mexico (Bulletin 1, Mineral Resources Survey of New Mexico; New Mexico School of Mines)*
Northrop, Stuart A.: *Minerals of New Mexico (University of New Mexico bulletin)*
Wroth, James S.: *Commercial Possibilities of the Texas-New Mexico Potash Deposits (Bureau of Mines publication)*

XXII. THE STOCKMAN

Adams, Andy: *The Log of the Cowboy*
Dearing, Frank (ed.) and Dobie, J. Frank (intro.): *The Best Novels and Stories of Eugene Manlove Rhodes*
Hough, Emerson: *Story of the Cowboy*
Larkin, Margaret (collected and ed.): *Singing Cowboy*
Richter, Conrad: *Sea of Grass*
Taylor, T. U.: *The Chisholm Trail and Other Routes*
Wentworth, Edward N.: *America's Sheep Trails*
——: *Shepherd's Empire*

XXIII. THE FEDERAL MAN

Moles, Hunter Stephen: *Ranger District Number Five*
Pinchot, Gifford: *Training of a Forester*

XXIV. Water

XXV. Artist Discoverers

GLOSSARY

acequia	an irrigation ditch
alabado	a hymn
baile	a dance or ball
batea	a large shallow pan used for washing sand to recover gold or other valuable minerals
bayeta	a kind of baize
bay steer	a reddish-brown steer. Cowmen think the Hereford steer of that color is especially vicious
Blessing Chant	a Navajo ceremony
bolson	a flat-floored desert valley
borrow pits	a bank or pit from which earth is taken for use in filling or embanking
bosque	woods
bull-roarer	a slat of wood tied to the end of a thong: used in religious rites
cabildo	a town council
cacique	a chief
campero	the man who maintains the sheep camp
caporal	an overseer on a sheep ranch
cap rock	a top layer of consolidated rock holding a steep cliff by protecting it from erosion
carreta	a cart
chile	pepper
cibolero	a buffalo hunter
colcha	coverlet
comisario	delegate
convento	monastery or nunnery

corrido	a ballad dealing usually with current events
cortés	legislature
custodio	the Director of the Franciscan missionaries in a given area, such as New Mexico was
Devil Dance	a dance of the Apaches, more properly called Crown Dance
Diné	Navajo word meaning people
doodlebug	any scientific device by which it is claimed that minerals, including petroleum, water, etc., may be located
farol	a lantern
fetich	a material object supposed to possess magical powers
gringo	among Spanish-Americans, a foreigner
gully-washer	a rain heavy enough to wash gullies into the land
hacendado	the proprietor of a hacienda
high-grading	stealing rich ore from a mine
hogan	a Navajo house
Hoop Dance	a dance done with hoops
jerky	jerked beef; a mispronunciation of the Spanish word *charqui*
kachina	a supernatural in the Pueblo mythology; the word is also applied to dolls made in the image of the supernaturals
kiva	in Pueblo architecture, a ceremonial chamber
Koshare	a clown or fun-maker in Pueblo Indian dances
Licenciado	lawyer
lightning-frame	a jointed frame, like lazy tongs or fold-

	ing lattice, used in Navajo dances to simulate the lightning
luminarias	festival lights
malpais	country underlain by dark lava, especially basalt
mano	a hand stone for grinding maize
manta	a shawl; also cotton cloth
mescal	a small cactus
metate	a stone used for grinding cereal seeds
olla	a jar
paisano	countryman, peasant
partidario	share-cropper or lessee of sheep
partido	the share of a herd of sheep turned over to a partidario on shares
patrón(a)	proprietor, boss
quarter horse	a type of horse developed on the ranges of the United States; so called from its high speed for a short distance (a quarter of a mile)
querido(a)	dear, a term of endearment
rebozo	a scarf of cotton or silk
residencia	a court held to examine into the conduct of a retiring official
riprap	loose rocks placed at the ends of a dam to prevent its eroding away
santero	a maker of religious images, especially saints
Santo	holy; a saint
shaman	a medicine man, a tribal worker of magic
sopaipilla	a sort of fritter made of tortilla dough fried in deep fat
sotol	any yucca-like plant of the southwestern United States and adjacent Mexico

spreader dam	an earth dam, thrown up on the surface of the land to spread surface water and prevent its cutting a gully
stick-kick race	a race in which runners kick sticks
tablita	a headdress worn by Pueblo Indian women in dances
talus	rock debris at the base of a cliff or slope
tápalo	a cloth worn as a scarf
tejano	Texan
tiswin	a fermented beverage made by the Apache Indians
tortilla	a thin, flat, unleavened cake, as of maize, baked on a heated iron or stone
travois	a primitive vehicle, formerly used by the Plains Indians of North America, consisting of two trailing poles serving as shafts for a dog or horse and bearing a platform or net for the load
trobador	troubadour, versifier, poet
tufa	a porous rock formed as a deposit from springs or streams
wickiup	the hut used by the nomadic Indian tribes of the western and southwestern United States
yeso	gypsum, used as plaster
Yeibechai	supernaturals in Navajo mythology. The word is also applied to a dance in which masked dancers represent the supernaturals
zaguan	a gate or entrance way into a patio

Index

ii   Index

Index

A Note on the Type

This book was set on the Linotype in Janson, a recutting made direct from type cast in matrices made by Anton Janson some time between 1660 and 1687. This type is an excellent example of the influential and singularly sturdy Dutch types that prevailed in England prior to Caslon. It was from the Dutch types that Caslon developed his own incomparable designs.

The book was composed by the Plimpton Press, Norwood, Mass. Printed and bound by the Haddon Craftsmen, Inc., Scranton, Pa. Typography and binding designs are by W. A. Dwiggins.